UTHACALTHING

Uthacalthing's driver held the door of his wheel-car for him, but he stretched his arms and inhaled deeply. "I am thinking that it might be a nice idea to go for a walk," he told her. "The embassy is only a short distance from here. Why don't you take a few hours off, Corporal, and spend some time with your family and friends?"

"B-but sir . . ."

"I will be all right," he said firmly. He bowed, and felt her rush of innocent joy at the simple courtesy. She bowed deeply in return.

Delightful creatures, Uthacalthing thought as he watched the car drive off. *I have met many neo-chimpanzees who seem to have the glimmerings of a true sense of humor.*

I hope they survive.

THE UPLIFT WAR

David Brin

BANTAM BOOKS
TORONTO · NEW YORK · LONDON · SYDNEY · AUCKLAND

THE UPLIFT WAR

A Bantam Spectra Book / July 1987

ISBN 0-553-25121-X

Published simultaneously in the United States and Canada

*To Jane Goodall, Sarah Hrdy,
and all the others who are
helping us at last to learn to understand.*

*And to Dian Fossey, who died fighting
so that beauty and potential might live.*

Glossary
and
Cast of Characters

Anglic—The language most commonly used by the Terragens—people descended from Earth humans, chimpanzees, and dolphins.

Athaclena—Daughter of the Tymbrimi ambassador, Uthacalthing. Leader of the Irregular Army of Garth.

Fiben Bolger—A neo-chimpanzee ecologist and lieutenant in the colonial militia.

Bururalli—The last prior race to be allowed to lease Garth; a newly uplifted race which reverted and nearly ruined the planet.

"Chen"—Anglic term for a male neo-chimpanzee.

"Chim"—Anglic term for a member of the neo-chimpanzee client race (male or female).

"Chimmie"—Anglic term for a female neo-chimpanzee.

"Fem"—Anglic term referring to a female human.

Galactics—Senior starfaring species which lead the community of the Five Galaxies. Many have become "patron" races, participating in the ancient tradition of Uplift.

Garthling—A rumored native creature of Garth—a large animal survivor of the Bururalli Holocaust.

Gubru—A pseudo-avian Galactic race hostile to Earthlings.

Ifni—"Infinity" or Lady Luck.

Gailet Jones—Chimmie expert on Galactic Sociology. Holder of an unlimited birthright ("white card"). Leader of the urban uprising.

Kault—Thennanin ambassador to Garth.

Library—An ancient storehouse of cross-referenced knowledge. One of the major foundations of the society of the Five Galaxies.

"Man"—Anglic term referring to both male and female human beings.

Mathicluanna—Athaclena's deceased mother.

Lydia McCue—An officer in the Terragens Marines.

"Mel"—Anglic term referring specifically to a male human.

Nahalli—A race that was patron to the Bururalli and paid a great penalty for the crimes of their clients.

Megan Oneagle—Planetary Coordinator for the Terran leasehold colony world on Garth.

Robert Oneagle—Captain in the Garth Colonial Militia Forces and son of the Planetary Coordinator.

Pan argonostes—Species name of the Uplifted client race of neo-chimpanzees.

Major Prathachulthorn—A Terragens Marine officer.

"Ser"—A term of respect used toward a senior Terran of either gender.

Soro—A senior Galactic race hostile toward Earth.

Streaker—A dolphin-crewed starship that has made a critical discovery far across the galaxy from Garth. The repercussions of this discovery have led to the present crisis.

Suzerain—One of three commanders of the Gubru invasion force, each in charge of a different area: Propriety, Bureaucracy, and the Military. Overall policy is decided by consensus of the three. A Suzerain is also a candidate for Gubru royalty and full sexuality.

Sylvie—A "green-card" female neo-chimpanzee.

Synthians—One of the few Galactic species openly friendly toward Earth.

Tandu—A Galactic starfaring race of frightening rapacity and hostility toward Earth.

Thennanin—One of the fanatic Galactic races involved in the present crisis. Humorless, but known for a sense of honor.

"Tingers and tumb"—The small and large toes of a neo-chimpanzee, which retain some grasping ability.

Tursiops amicus—The species name of Uplifted neo-dolphins.

Tymbrimi—Galactics renowned for their adaptability and biting sense of humor. Friends and allies of Earth.

Uplift—The ancient process by which older starfaring races bring new species into Galactic culture, through breeding and genetic engineering. The resulting "client" species serves its "patron" for a period of indenture in order to pay off this debt. The status of a Galactic race is partly determined by its genealogy of patrons, and by its list of clients Uplifted.

Uthacalthing—Tymbrimi ambassador to the colony world of Garth.

Wolflings—Members of a race which achieved starfaring status without the help of a patron.

Tymbrimi
Words and Glyphs

fornell—Glyph of uncertainty.

fsu'usturatu—Glyph of sympathetic hilarity.

gheer transformation—The surge of hormones and enzymes which allows Tymbrimi to alter their physiologies quickly, at some cost.

k'chu-non—Tymbrimi word for patronless wolflings.

k'chu-non krann—An army of wolflings.

kenning—Sensing glyphs and empathy waves.

kiniwullun—Glyph of recognition of "what boys do."

kuhunnagarra—Glyph of indeterminacy postponed.

la'thsthoon—Intimacy in pairs.

lurrunanu—A penetration glyph, for enticing another to become suspicious.

l'yuth'tsaka—Glyph expressing contempt for the universe.

nahakieri—A deep level of empathy on which a Tymbrimi can sometimes sense loved ones.

nuturunow—Glyph that helps stave off gheer reaction.

palanq—A shrug.

rittitees—Glyph of compassion for children.

sh'cha'kuon—A mirror to show others how they appear outside.

s'ustru'thoon—A child seizing what she needs of her parent.

syrtunu—A sigh of frustration.

syulff-kuonn—Anticipation of a nasty practical joke.

syullf-tha—Joy of a puzzle being solved.

teev'nus—The futility of communication.

totanoo—Fear-induced withdrawal from reality.

tu'fluk—A joke unappreciated.

tutsunucann—Glyph of dreadful expectation.

usunltlan—Web of protection while in close contact with another.

zunour-thzun—Glyph remarking on how much there is left to experience.

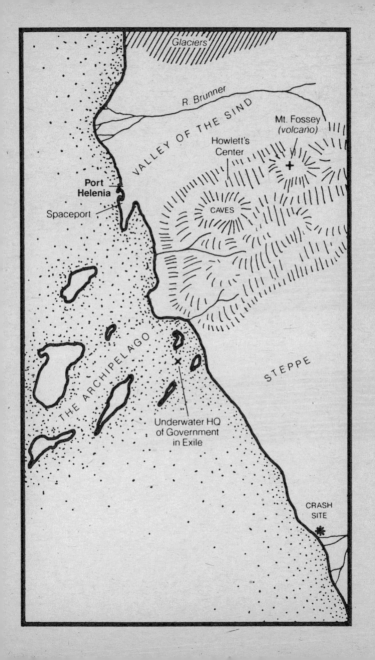

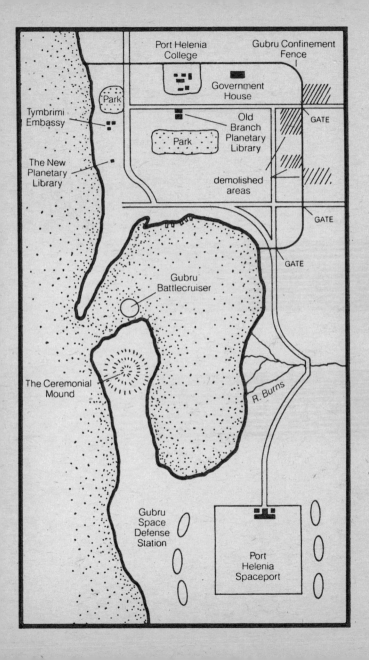

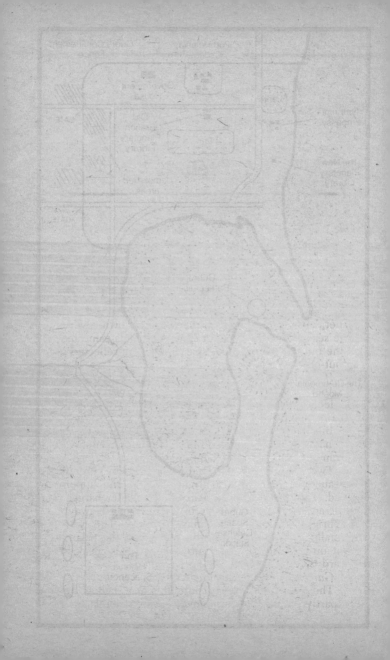

Prelude

How strange, that such an insignificant little world should come to matter so much.

Traffic roared amid the towers of Capital City, just beyond the sealed crystal dome of the official palanquin. But no sound penetrated to disturb the bureaucrat of Cost and Caution, who concentrated only on the holo-image of a small planet, turning slowly within reach of one down-covered arm. Blue seas and a jewel-bright spray of islands came into view as the bureaucrat watched, sparkling in the reflected glow of an out-of-view star.

If I were one of the gods spoken of in wolfling legends . . . the bureaucrat imagined. Its pinions flexed. There was the feeling one had only to reach out with a talon and seize . . .

But no. The absurd idea demonstrated that the bureaucrat had spent too much time studying the enemy. Crazy Terran concepts were infecting its mind.

Two downy aides fluttered quietly nearby, preening the bureaucrat's feathers and bright torc for the appointment ahead. They were ignored. Aircars and floater barges darted aside and regimented lanes of traffic melted away before the bright beacon of the official vehicle. This was status normally accorded only royalty, but within the palanquin all went on unnoticed as the bureaucrat's heavy beak lowered toward the holo-image.

Garth. So many times the victim.

The outlines of brown continents and shallow blue seas lay partly smeared under pinwheel stormclouds, as decep-

1

tively white and soft to the eye as a Gubru's plumage. Along just one chain of islands—and at a single point at the edge of the largest continent—shone the lights of a few small cities. Everywhere else the world appeared untouched, perturbed only by occasional flickering strokes of stormbrewed lightning.

Strings of code symbols told a darker truth. Garth was a poor place, a bad risk. Why else had the wolfling humans and their clients been granted a colony leasehold there? The place had been written off by the Galactic Institutes long ago.

And now, unhappy little world, you have been chosen as a site for war.

For practice, the bureaucrat of Cost and Caution thought in Anglic, the beastly, unsanctioned language of the Earthling creatures. Most Gubru considered the study of alien things an unwholesome pastime, but now the bureaucrat's obsession seemed about to pay off at last.

At last. Today.

The palanquin had threaded past the great towers of Capital City, and a mammoth edifice of opalescent stone now seemed to rise just ahead. The Conclave Arena, seat of government of all the Gubru race and clan.

Nervous, anticipatory shivers flowed down the bureaucrat's head-crest all the way to its vestigial flight feathers, bringing forth chirps of complaint from the two Kwackoo aides. How could they finish preening the bureaucrat's fine white feathers, they asked, or buff its long, hooked beak, if it didn't sit still?

"I comprehend, understand, will comply," the bureaucrat answered indulgently in Standard Galactic Language Number Three. These Kwackoo were loyal creatures, to be allowed some minor impertinences. For distraction, the bureaucrat returned to thoughts of the small planet, Garth.

It is the most defenseless Earthling outpost . . . the one most easily taken hostage. That is why the military pushed for this operation, even while we are hard-pressed elsewhere in space. This will strike deeply at the wolflings, and we may thereby coerce them to yield what we want.

After the armed forces, the priesthood had been next to agree to the plan. Recently the Guardians of Propriety had ruled that an invasion could be undertaken without any loss of honor.

That left the Civil Service—the third leg of the Perch of Command. And there consensus had broken. The bureaucrat's superiors in the Department of Cost and Caution had demurred. The plan was too risky, they declared. Too expensive.

A perch cannot stand long on two legs. There must be consensus. There must be compromise.

There are times when a nest cannot avoid taking risks.

The mountainous Conclave Arena became a cliff of dressed stone, covering half the sky. A cavernous opening loomed, then swallowed the palanquin. With a quiet murmur the small vessel's gravitics shut down and the canopy lifted. A crowd of Gubru in the normal white plumage of adult neuters already waited at the foot of the landing apron.

They know, the bureaucrat thought, regarding them with its right eye. *They know I am already no longer one of them.*

In its other eye the bureaucrat caught a last glimpse of the white-swaddled blue globe. Garth.

Soon, the bureaucrat thought in Anglic. *We shall meet soon.*

The Conclave Arena was a riot of color. And such colors! Feathers shimmered everywhere in the royal hues, crimson, amber, and arsene blue.

Two four-footed Kwackoo servants opened a ceremonial portal for the bureaucrat of Cost and Caution, who momentarily had to stop and hiss in awe at the grandeur of the Arena. Hundreds of perches lined the terraced walls, crafted in delicate, ornate beauty out of costly woods imported from a hundred worlds. And all around, in regal splendor, stood the Roost Masters of the Gubru race.

No matter how well it had prepared for today, the bureaucrat could not help feeling deeply moved. Never had it seen so many queens and princes at one time!

To an alien, there might seem little to distinguish the bureaucrat from its lords. All were tall, slender descendants of flightless birds. To the eye, only the Roost Masters' striking colored plumage set them apart from the majority of the race. More important differences lay underneath, however. These, after all, were queens and princes, possessed of gender and the proven right to command.

Nearby Roost Masters turned their sharp beaks aside in order to watch with one eye as the bureaucrat of Cost and Caution hurried through a quick, mincing dance of ritual abasement.

Such colors! Love rose within the bureaucrat's downy breast, a hormonal surge triggered by those royal hues. It was an ancient, instinctive response, and no Gubru had ever proposed changing it. Not even after they had learned the art of gene-altering and become starfarers. Those of the race who achieved the ultimate—color and gender—had to be worshipped and obeyed by those who were still white and neuter.

It was the very heart of what it meant to be Gubru.

It was good. It was the way.

The bureaucrat noticed that two other white-plumed Gubru had also entered the Arena through neighboring doors. They joined the bureaucrat upon the central platform. Together the three of them took low perches facing the assembled Roost Masters.

The one on the right was draped in a silvery robe and bore around its narrow white throat the striped torc of priesthood.

The candidate on the left wore the sidearm and steel talon guards of a military officer. The tips of its crest feathers were dyed to show the rank of stoop-colonel.

Aloof, the other two white-plumed Gubru did not turn to acknowledge the bureaucrat. Nor did the bureaucrat offer any sign of recognizing them. Nevertheless, it felt a thrill. *We are three!*

The President of the Conclave—an aged queen whose once fiery plumage had now faded to a pale pinkish wash—fluffed her feathers and opened her beak. The Arena's acoustics automatically amplified her voice as she chirped for attention. On all sides the other queens and princes fell silent.

The Conclave President raised one slender, down-covered arm. Then she began to croon and sway. One by one, the other Roost Masters joined in, and soon the crowd of blue, amber, and crimson forms was rocking with her. From the royal assemblage there rose a low, atonal moaning.

"Zooooon . . ."

"Since time immemorial," the President chirped in formal Galactic Three. "Since before our glory, since before our patronhood, since before even our Uplift into sentience, it has been our way to seek balance."

The assembly chanted in counter rhythm.

> *"Balance on the ground's brown seams,*
> *Balance in the rough air streams,*
> *Balance in our greatest schemes."*

"Back when our ancestors were still pre-sentient beasts, back before our Gooksyu patrons found us and uplifted us to knowledge, back before we even spoke or knew tools, we had already learned this wisdom, this way of coming to decision, this way of coming to consensus, this way of making love."

"Zoooon . . ."

"As half-animals, our ancestors still knew that we must . . . must choose . . . must choose three."

> *"One to hunt and strike with daring,*
> *for glory and for territory!*
> *One to seek the righteous bearing,*
> *for purity and propriety!*
> *One to warn of danger looming,*
> *for our eggs' security!"*

The bureaucrat of Cost and Caution sensed the other two candidates on either side and knew they were just as electrically aware, just as caught up in tense expectation. There was no greater honor than to be chosen as the three of them had been.

Of course all young Gubru were taught that this way was best, for what other species so beautifully combined politics and philosophy with lovemaking and reproduction? The system had served their race and clan well for ages. It had brought them to the heights of power in Galactic society.

And now it may have brought us to the brink of ruin.

Perhaps it was sacrilegious even to imagine it, but the bureaucrat of Cost and Caution could not help wondering if one of the other methods it had studied might not be better after all. It had read of so many styles of government used by other races and clans—autarchies and aristocracies, technocracies and democracies, syndicates and meritocracies. Might not one of those actually be a better way of judging the right path in a dangerous universe?

The idea might be irreverent, but such unconventional thinking was the reason certain Roost Masters had singled

out the bureaucrat for a role of destiny. Over the days and
months ahead, someone among the three would have to be
the *doubting* one. That was ever the role of Cost and Caution.

"In this way, we strike a balance. In this way, we seek
consensus. In this way, we resolve conflict."

"*Zooon!*" agreed the gathered queens and princes.

Much negotiation had gone into selecting each of the
candidates, one from the military, one from the priestly orders, and one from the Civil Service. If all worked out well, a
new queen and two new princes would emerge from the
molting ahead. And along with a vital new line of eggs for the
race would also come a new *policy*, one arising out of the
merging of their views.

That was how it was supposed to end. The *beginning*,
however, was another matter. Fated eventually to be lovers,
the three would from the start also be competitors. Adversaries.

For there could be only one queen.

"We send forth this trio on a vital mission. A mission of
conquest. A mission of coercion.

"We send them also in search of unity . . . in search of
agreement . . . in search of consensus, to unite us in these
troubled times."

"*Zooooon!*"

In the eager chorus could be felt the Conclave's desperate wish for resolution, for an end to bitter disagreements.
The three candidates were to lead just one of many battle
forces sent forth by the clan of the Gooksyu-Gubru. But
clearly the Roost Masters had special hopes for this triumvirate.

Kwackoo servitors offered shining goblets to each candidate. The bureaucrat of Cost and Caution lifted one and
drank deeply. The fluid felt like golden fire going down.

First taste of the Royal Liquor . . .

As expected, it had a flavor like nothing else imaginable.
Already, the three candidates' white plumage seemed to glis-
ten with a shimmering *promise* of color to come.

*We shall struggle together, and eventually one of us shall
molt amber. One shall molt blue.*

And one, presumably the strongest, the one with the best policy, would win the ultimate prize.

A prize fated to be mine. For it was said to have all been arranged in advance. Caution *had* to win the upcoming consensus. Careful analysis had shown that the alternatives would be unbearable.

"You shall go forth, then," the Conclave President sang. "You three new Suzerains of our race and of our clan. You shall go forth and win conquest. You shall go forth and humble the wolfling heretics."

"Zooooon!" the assembly cheered.

The President's beak lowered toward her breast, as if she were suddenly exhausted. Then, the new Suzerain of Cost and Caution faintly heard her add,

"You shall go forth and try your best to save us. . . ."

PART ONE

Invasion

Let them uplift us, shoulder high. Then we will see over their heads to the several promised lands, from which we have come, and to which we trust to go.

W. B. YEATS

1

Fiben

There had never been such traffic at Port Helenia's sleepy landing field—not in all the years Fiben Bolger had lived here. The mesa overlooking Aspinal Bay reverberated with the numbing, infrasonic growl of engines. Dust plumes obscured the launching pits, but that did not prevent spectators from gathering along the peripheral fence to watch all the excitement. Those with a touch of psi talent could tell whenever a starship was about to lift off. Waves of muzzy uncertainty, caused by leaky gravitics, made a few onlookers blink quickly moments before another great-strutted spacecraft rose above the haze and lumbered off into the cloud-dappled sky.

The noise and stinging dust frayed tempers. It was even worse for those standing out on the tarmac, and especially bad for those forced to be there against their will.

Fiben certainly would much rather have been just about anywhere else, preferably in a pub applying pints of liquid anesthetic. But that was not to be.

He observed the frenetic activity cynically. *We're a sinking ship*, he thought. *And all th' rats are saying a'dieu*.

Everything able to space and warp was departing Garth in indecent haste. Soon, the landing field would be all but empty.

Until the enemy arrives . . . whoever it turns out to be.

"Pssst, Fiben. Quit fidgeting!"

Fiben glanced to his right. The chim standing next to him in formation looked nearly as uncomfortable as Fiben felt. Simon Levin's dress uniform cap was turning dark just above his bony eye ridges, where damp brown fur curled under the rim. With his eyes, Simon mutely urged Fiben to straighten up and look forward.

Fiben sighed. He knew he should try to stand at attention. The ceremony for the departing dignitary was nearly over, and a member of the Planetary Honor Guard wasn't supposed to slouch.

But his gaze kept drifting over toward the southern end of the mesa, far from the commercial terminal and the departing freighters. Over there, uncamouflaged, lay an uneven row of drab, black cigar shapes with the blocky look of fighting craft. Several of the small scoutboats shimmered as technicians crawled over them, tuning their detectors and shields for the coming battle.

Fiben wondered if Command had already decided which craft he was to fly. Perhaps they would let the half-trained Colonial Militia pilots draw lots to see who would get the most decrepit of the ancient war machines, recently purchased cut-rate off a passing Xatinni scrap dealer.

With his left hand Fiben tugged at the stiff collar of his uniform and scratched the thick hair below his collarbone. *Old ain't necessarily bad*, he reminded himself. *Go into battle aboard a thousand-year-old tub, and at least you know it can take punishment.*

Most of those battered scoutboats had seen action out on the starlanes before human beings ever heard of Galactic civilization . . . before they had even begun playing with gunpowder rockets, singeing their fingers and scaring the birds back on homeworld Earth.

The image made Fiben smile briefly. It wasn't the most respectful thing to think about one's patron race. But then, humans hadn't exactly brought his people up to be reverent.

Jeez, this monkey suit itches! Naked apes like humans may be able to take this, but we hairy types just aren't built to wear this much clothing!

At least the ceremony for the departing Synthian Consul seemed to be nearing completion. Swoio Shochuhun—that pompous ball of fur and whiskers—was finishing her speech of farewell to the tenants of Garth Planet, the humans and chims she was leaving to their fate. Fiben scratched his chin again, wishing the little windbag would just climb into her launch and get the hell out of here, if she was in such a hurry to be going.

An elbow jabbed him in the ribs. Simon muttered urgently. "Straighten up, Fiben. Her Nibs is looking this way!"

Over among the dignitaries Megan Oneagle, the grayhaired Planetary Coordinator, pursed her lips and gave Fiben a quick shake of her head.

Aw, hell, he thought.

Megan's son, Robert, had been a classmate of Fiben's at Garth's small university. Fiben arched an eyebrow as if to say to the human administrator that *he* hadn't asked to serve on this dubious honor guard. And anyway, if humans had wanted clients who didn't scratch themselves, they never should have uplifted chimpanzees.

He fixed his collar though, and tried to straighten his posture. Form was nearly everything to these Galactics, and Fiben knew that even a lowly neo-chimp had to play his part, or the clan of Earth might lose face.

On either side of Coordinator Oneagle stood the other dignitaries who had come to see Swoio Shochuhun off. To Megan's left was Kault, the hulking Thennanin envoy, leathery and resplendent in his brilliant cape and towering ridge crest. The breathing slits in his throat opened and closed like louvered blinds each time the big-jawed creature inhaled.

To Megan's right stood a much more humanoid figure, slender and long-limbed, who slouched slightly, almost insouciantly in the afternoon sunshine.

Uthacalthing's amused by something. Fiben could tell. *So what else is new?*

Of course Ambassador Uthacalthing thought *everything* was funny. In his posture, in the gently waving silvery tendrils that floated above his small ears, and in the glint in his golden, wide-cast eyes, the pale Tymbrimi envoy seemed to say what could not be spoken aloud—something just short of insulting to the departing Synthian diplomat.

Swoio Shochuhun sleeked back her whiskers before stepping forward to say farewell to each of her colleagues in turn. Watching her make ornate formal paw motions in front of Kault, Fiben was struck by how much she resembled a large, rotund raccoon, dressed up like some ancient, oriental courtier.

Kault, the huge Thennanin, puffed up his crest as he bowed in response. The two uneven-sized Galactics exchanged pleasantries in fluting, highly inflected Galactic Six. Fiben knew that there was little love to be lost between them.

"Well, you can't choose your friends, can you?" Simon whispered.

"Damn right," Fiben agreed.

It was ironic. The furry, canny Synthians were among Earth's few "allies" in the political and military quagmire of the Five Galaxies. But they were also fantastically self-centered and famous cowards. Swoio's departure as much as guaranteed there would be no armadas of fat, furry warriors coming to Garth's aid in her hour of need.

Just like there won't be any help from Earth, nor Tymbrim, them having enough problems of their own right now.

Fiben understood GalSix well enough to follow some of what the big Thennanin said to Swoio. Kault apparently did not think much of ambassadors who skip out on their posts.

Give the Thennanin that much, Fiben thought. Kault's folk might be fanatics. Certainly they were listed among Earth's present official enemies. Nevertheless, they were known everywhere for their courage and severe sense of honor.

No, you can't always choose your friends, or your enemies.

Swoio stepped over to face Megan Oneagle. The Synthian's bow was marginally shallower than the one she had given Kault. After all, humans ranked pretty low among the patron races of the galaxy.

And you know what that makes you, Fiben reminded himself.

Megan bowed in return. "I am sorry to see you go," she told Swoio in thickly accented GalSix. "Please pass on to your people our gratitude for their good wishes."

"Right," Fiben muttered. "Tell all th' other raccoons thanks a whole bunch." He wore a blank expression, though, when Colonel Maiven, the human commander of the Honor Guard, looked sharply his way.

Swoio's reply was filled with platitudes.

Be patient, she urged. The Five Galaxies are in turmoil right now. The fanatics among the great powers are causing so much trouble because they think the Millennium, the end of a great era, is at hand. They are the first to act.

Meanwhile, the moderates and the Galactic Institutes must move slower, more judiciously. But act they would, she assured. In due time. Little Garth would not be forgotten.

Sure, Fiben thought sarcastically. *Why, help might be no more'n a century or two away!*

The other chims in the Honor Guard glanced at one other and rolled their eyes in disgust. The human officers were more reserved, but Fiben saw that one was rotating his tongue firmly in his cheek.

Swoio stopped at last before the senior member of the diplomatic corps, Uthacalthing Man-Friend, the consul-ambassador from the Tymbrimi.

The tall E.T. wore a loose black robe that offset his pale skin. Uthacalthing's mouth was small, and the unearthly separation between his shadowed eyes seemed very wide. Nevertheless, the humanoid impression was quite strong. It always seemed to Fiben as if the representative of Earth's greatest ally was always on the verge of laughing at some joke, great or small. Uthacalthing—with his narrow scalp-ruff of soft, brown fur bordered by waving, delicate tendrils—with his long, delicate hands and ready humor—was the solitary being on this mesa who seemed untouched by the tension of the day. The Tymbrimi's ironic smile affected Fiben, momentarily lifting his spirits.

Finally! Fiben sighed in relief. Swoio appeared to be finished at last. She turned and strode up the ramp toward her waiting launch. With a sharp command Colonel Maiven brought the Guard to attention. Fiben started mentally counting the number of steps to shade and a cool drink.

But it was too soon to relax. Fiben wasn't the only one to groan low as the Synthian turned at the top of the ramp to address the onlookers one more time.

Just what occurred then—and in exactly what order—would perplex Fiben for a long time afterward. But it appeared that, just as the first fluting tones of GalSix left Swoio's mouth, something bizarre happened across the landing field. Fiben felt a scratchiness at the back of his eyeballs and glanced to the left, just in time to see a lambency shimmer around one of the scoutboats. Then the tiny craft seemed to *explode*.

He did not recall diving to the tarmac, but that's where he found himself next, trying to burrow into the tough, rubbery surface. *What is it? An enemy attack so soon?*

He heard Simon snort violently. Then a chorus of sneezes followed. Blinking away dust, Fiben peered and saw that the little scoutcraft still existed. It hadn't blown up, after all!

But its *fields* were out of control. They coruscated in a

deafening, blinding display of light and sound. Shield-suited engineers scurried to shut down the boat's malfunctioning probability generator, but not before the noisome display had run everyone nearby through all the senses they had, from touch and taste all the way to smell and psi.

"Whooee!" the chimmie to Fiben's left whistled, holding her nose uselessly. "Who set off a stinkbomb!"

In a flash Fiben knew, with uncanny certainty, that she had called it right. He rolled over quickly, in time to see the Synthian Ambassador, her nose wrinkled in disgust and whiskers curled in shame, scamper into her ship, abandoning all dignity. The hatch clanged shut.

Someone found the right switch at last and cut off the horrible overload, leaving only a fierce aftertaste and a ringing in his ears. The members of the Honor Guard stood up, dusting themselves and muttering irritably. Some humans and chims still quivered, blinking and yawning vigorously. Only the stolid, oblivious Thennanin Ambassador seemed unaffected. In fact, Kault appeared perplexed over this unusual Earthling behavior.

A stinkbomb. Fiben nodded. *It was somebody's idea of a practical joke.*

And I think I know whose.

Fiben looked closely at Uthacalthing. He stared at the being who had been named Man-Friend and recalled how the slender Tymbrimi had smiled as Swoio, the pompous little Synthian, launched into her final speech. Yes, Fiben would be willing to swear on a copy of Darwin that at that very moment, just *before* the scoutboat malfunctioned, Uthacalthing's crown of silvery tendrils had lifted and the ambassador had smiled as if in delicious *anticipation*.

Fiben shook his head. For all of their renowned psychic senses, no Tymbrimi could have caused such an accident by sheer force of will.

Not unless it had been arranged in advance, that is.

The Synthian launch rose upward on a blast of air and skimmed out across the field to a safe distance. Then, in a high whine of gravitics, the glittering craft swept upward to meet the clouds.

At Colonel Maiven's command, the Honor Guard snapped to attention one last time. The Planetary Coordinator and her two remaining envoys passed in review.

It might have been his imagination, but Fiben felt sure

that for an instant Uthacalthing slowed right in front of him. Fiben was certain one of those wide, silver-rimmed eyes looked directly at him.

And the other one winked.

Fiben sighed. *Very funny,* he thought, hoping the Tymbrimi emissary would pick up the sarcasm in his mind. *We all may be smokin' dead meat in a week's time, and you're making with practical jokes.*

Very funny, Uthacalthing.

2

Athaclena

Tendrils wafted alongside her head, ungentle in their agitation. Athaclena let her frustration and anger fizz like static electricity at the tips of the silvery strands. Their ends waved as if of their own accord, like slender fingers, shaping her almost palpable resentment into *something* . . .

Nearby, one of the humans awaiting an audience with the Planetary Coordinator sniffed the air and looked around, puzzled. He moved away from Athaclena, without quite knowing why he felt uncomfortable all of a sudden. He was probably a natural, if primitive, empath. Some men and women were able vaguely to *kenn* Tymbrimi empathy-glyphs, though few ever had the training to interpret anything more than vague emotions.

Someone else also noticed what Athaclena was doing. Across the public room, standing amid a small crowd of humans, her father lifted his head suddenly. His own corona of tendrils remained smooth and undisturbed, but Uthacalthing cocked his head and turned slightly to regard her, his expression both quizzical and slightly amused.

It might have been similar if a human parent had caught his daughter in the act of kicking the sofa, or muttering to herself sullenly. The frustration at the core was very nearly the same, except that Athaclena expressed it through her Tymbrimi aura rather than an outward tantrum. At her father's glance she hurriedly drew back her waving tendrils and wiped away the ugly sense-glyph she had been crafting overhead.

That did not erase her resentment, however. In this crowd of Earthlings it was hard to forget. *Caricatures,* was Athaclena's contemptuous thought, knowing full well it was both unkind and unfair. Of course Earthlings couldn't help being what they were—one of the strangest tribes to come upon the Galactic scene in aeons. But that did not mean she had to like them!

It might have helped if they were *more* alien . . . less like hulking, narrow-eyed, awkward versions of Tymbrimi. Wildly varied in color and hairiness, eerily *off* in their body proportions, and so often dour and moody, they frequently left Athaclena feeling depressed after too long a time spent in their company.

Another thought unbecoming the daughter of a diplomat. She chided herself and tried to redirect her mind. After all, the humans could not be blamed for radiating their fear right now, with a war they hadn't chosen about to fall crushingly upon them.

She watched her father laugh at something said by one of the Earthling officers and wondered how he did it. How he bore it so well.

I'll never learn that easy, confident manner.
I'll never be able to make him proud of me.

Athaclena wished Uthacalthing would finish up with these Terrans so she could speak to him alone. In a few minutes Robert Oneagle would arrive to pick her up, and she wanted to have one more try at persuading her father not to send her away with the young human.

I can be useful. I know I can! I don't have to be coddled off into the mountains for safety, like some child!

Quickly she clamped down before another glyph-of-resentment could form above her head. She needed distraction, something to keep her mind occupied while she waited. Restraining her emotions, Athaclena stepped quietly toward two human officers standing nearby, heads lowered in earnest conversation. They were speaking Anglic, the most commonly used Earth-tongue.

"Look," the first one said. "All we really know is that one of Earth's survey ships stumbled onto something weird and totally unexpected, out in one of those ancient star clusters on the galactic fringe."

"But what *was* it?" the other militiaman asked. "What did they find? You're in alien studies, Alice. Don't you have any idea what those poor dolphins uncovered that could stir up such a ruckus?"

The female Earthman shrugged. "Search me. But it didn't take anything more than the hints in the *Streaker's* first beamed report to set the most fanatic clans in the Five Galaxies fighting each other at a level that hasn't been seen in megayears. The latest dispatches say some of the skirmishes have gotten pretty damn rough. You saw how scared that Synthian looked a week ago, before she decided to pull out."

The other man nodded gloomily. Neither human spoke for a long moment. Their tension was a thing which arched the space between them. Athaclena *kenned* it as a simple but dark glyph of uncertain dread.

"It's something big," the first officer said at last, in a low voice. "This may really be it."

Athaclena moved away when she sensed the humans begin to take notice of her. Since arriving here in Garth she had been altering her normal body form, changing her figure and features to resemble more closely those of a human girl. Nevertheless, there were limits to what such manipulations could accomplish, even using Tymbrimi body-imagery methods. There was no way really to disguise who she was. If she had stayed, inevitably, the humans would have asked her a Tymbrimi's opinion of the current crisis, and she was loathe to tell Earthlings that she really knew no more than they did.

Athaclena found the situation bitterly ironic. Once again, the races of Earth were in the spotlight, as they had been ever since the notorious "Sundiver" affair, two centuries ago. This time an interstellar crisis had been sparked by the first starship ever put under command of *neo-dolphins*.

Mankind's second client race was no more than two centuries old—younger even than the neo-chimpanzees. How the cetacean spacers would ever find a way out of the mess they had inadvertently created was anyone's guess. But the repercussions were already spreading halfway across the

Central Galaxy, all the way to isolated colony worlds such
as Garth.

"Athaclena—"

She whirled. Uthacalthing stood at her elbow, looking
down at her with an air of benign concern. "Are you all right,
daughter?"

She felt so small in Uthacalthing's presence. Athaclena
couldn't help being intimidated, however gentle he always
was. His art and discipline were so great that she hadn't even
sensed his approach until he touched the sleeve of her robe!
Even now, all that could be *kenned* from his complex aura
was the whirling empathy-glyph called *caridouo* . . . a father's love.

"Yes, Father. I . . . I am fine."

"Good. Are you all packed and ready for your expedition
then?"

His words were in Anglic. She answered in Tymbrim-
dialect Galactic Seven.

"Father, I do not wish to go into the mountains with
Robert Oneagle."

Uthacalthing frowned. "I had thought that you and Robert were friends."

Athaclena's nostrils flared in frustration. Why was
Uthacalthing purposely misunderstanding her? He had to
know that the son of the Planetary Coordinator was unobjec-
tionable as a companion. Robert was as close to a friend as
she had among the young humans of Port Helenia.

"It is partly for *Robert's* sake that I urge you to recon-
sider," she told her father. "He is shamed at being ordered to
'nursemaid' me, as they say, while his comrades and classmates are all in the militia preparing for war. And I certainly
cannot blame him for his resentment."

When Uthacalthing started to speak she hurried on.
"Also, I do not wish to leave you, Father. I reiterate my
earlier arguments-of-logic, when I explained how I might be
useful to you in the weeks ahead. And now I add to them this
offering, as well."

With great care she concentrated on crafting the glyph
she had composed earlier in the day. She had named it
ke'ipathye . . . a plea, out of love, to be allowed to face
danger at love's side. Her tendrils trembled above her ears,
and the construct quavered slightly over her head as it began
to rotate. Finally though, it stabilized. She sent it drifting

over toward her father's aura. At that moment, Athaclena did
not even care that they were in a room crowded with hulking, smooth-browed humans and their furry little chim clients.
All that mattered in the world was the two of them, and the
bridge she so longed to build across this void.

Ke'ipathye fell into Uthacalthing's waiting tendrils and
spun there, brightening in his appreciation. Briefly, Athaclena
gasped at its sudden beauty, which she knew had now grown
far beyond her own simple art.

Then the glyph fell, like a gentle fog of morning dew, to
coat and shine along her father's corona.

"Such a fine gift." His voice was soft, and she knew he
had been moved.

But . . . She knew, all at once, that his resolve was
unshifted.

"I offer you a *kenning* of my own," he said to her. And
from his sleeve he withdrew a small gilt box with a silver
clasp. "Your mother, Mathicluanna, wished for you to have
this when you were ready to declare yourself of age. Although we had not yet spoken of a date, I judge that now is
the time for you to have it."

Athaclena blinked, suddenly lost in a whirl of confused
emotions. How often had she longed to know what her dead
mother had left in her legacy? And yet, right now the small
locket might have been a poison-beetle for all the will she
had to pick it up.

Uthacalthing would not be doing this if he thought it
likely they would meet again.

She hissed in realization. "You're planning to fight!"

Uthacalthing actually *shrugged* . . . that human gesture
of momentary indifference. "The enemies of the humans are
mine as well, daughter. The Earthlings are bold, but they are
only wolflings after all. They will need my help."

There was finality in his voice, and Athaclena knew that
any further word of protest would accomplish nothing but to
make her look foolish in his eyes. Their hands met around the
locket, long fingers intertwining, and they walked silently out
of the room together. It seemed, for a short span, as if they
were not two but three, for the locket carried something of
Mathicluanna. The moment was both sweet and painful.

Neo-chimp militia guards snapped to attention and opened
the doors for them as they stepped out of the Ministry
Building and into the clear, early spring sunshine. Uthacalthing

accompanied Athaclena down to the curbside, where her backpack awaited her. Their hands parted, and Athaclena was left grasping her mother's locket.

"Here comes Robert, right on time," Uthacalthing said, shading his eyes. "His mother calls him unpunctual. But I have never known him to be late for anything that mattered."

A battered floater wagon approached along the long gravel driveway, rolling past limousines and militia staff cars. Uthacalthing turned back to his daughter. "Do try to enjoy the Mountains of Mulun. I have seen them. They are quite beautiful. Look at this as an opportunity, Athaclena."

She nodded. "I shall do as you asked, Father. I'll spend the time improving my grasp of Anglic and of wolfling emotional patterns."

"Good. And keep your eyes open for any signs or traces of the legendary Garthlings."

Athaclena frowned. Her father's late interest in odd wolfling folk tales had lately begun to resemble a fixation. And yet, one could never tell when Uthacalthing was being serious or simply setting up a complicated jest.

"I'll watch out for signs, though the creatures are certainly mythical."

Uthacalthing smiled. "I must go now. My love will travel with you. It will be a bird, hovering"—he motioned with his hands— "just over your shoulder."

His tendrils touched hers briefly, and then he was gone, striding back up the steps to rejoin the worried colonials. Athaclena was left standing there, wondering why, in parting, Uthacalthing had used such a bizarre human metaphor.

How can love be a bird?

Sometimes Uthacalthing was so strange it frightened even her.

There was a crunching of gravel as the floater car settled down at the curb nearby. Robert Oneagle, the dark-haired young human who was to be her partner-in-exile, grinned and waved from behind the machine's tiller, but it was easy to tell that his cheery demeanor was superficial, put on for her benefit. Deep down, Robert was nearly as unhappy about this trip as she was. Fate—and the imperious rule of adults— had thrown the two of them together in a direction neither of them would have chosen.

The crude glyph Athaclena formed—invisible to Robert—

was little more than a sigh of resignation and defeat. But she kept up appearances with a carefully arranged Earthling-type smile of her own.

"Hello, Robert," she said, and picked up her pack.

3

Galactics

The Suzerain of Propriety fluffed its feathery down, displaying at the roots of its still-white plumage the shimmering glow that foretold royalty. Proudly, the Suzerain of Propriety hopped up onto the Perch of Pronouncement and chirped for attention.

The battleships of the Expeditionary Force were still in interspace, between the levels of the world. Battle was not imminent for some time yet. Because of this, the Suzerain of Propriety was still dominant and could interrupt the activities of the flagship's crew.

Across the bridge, the Suzerain of Beam and Talon looked up from its own Perch of Command. The admiral shared with the Suzerain of Propriety the bright plumage of dominance. Nevertheless, there was no question of interfering when a religious pronouncement was about to be made. The admiral at once interrupted the stream of orders it had been chirping to subordinates and shifted into a stance of attentive reverence.

All through the bridge the noisy clamor of Gubru engineers and spacers quieted to a low chittering. Their four-footed Kwackoo clients ceased their cooing as well and settled down to listen.

Still the Suzerain of Propriety waited. It would not be proper to begin until all Three were present.

A hatchway dilated. In stepped the last of the masters of

the expedition, the third member of the triarchy. As appropriate, the Suzerain of Cost and Caution wore the black torc of suspicion and doubt as it entered and found a comfortable perch, followed by a small covey of its accountants and bureaucrats.

For a moment their eyes met across the bridge. The tension among the Three had already begun, and it would grow in the weeks and months ahead, until the day when consensus was finally achieved—when they molted and a new queen emerged.

It was thrilling, sexual, exhilarating. None of them knew how it would end. Beam and Talon started with an advantage, of course, since this expedition would begin in battle. But that dominance did not have to last.

This moment, for instance, was clearly one for the priesthood.

All breaks turned as the Suzerain of Propriety lifted and flexed one leg, then the other, and prepared to pronounce. Soon a low crooning began to rise from the assembled avians.

—*zzooon*.

"We embark on a mission, holy mission," the Suzerain fluted.
—*Zzooon*—
"Embarking on this mission, we must persevere"
—*Zzooon*—
"Persevere to accomplish four great tasks"
—*Zzooon*—
"Tasks which include *Conquest* for the glory of our Clan, zzooon"
—*ZZooon*
"Conquest and *Coercion*, so we may gain the Secret,
    the Secret that the animal Earthlings clutch talon-tight,
        clutch to keep from us, zzooon"
—*ZZooon*—
"Conquest, Coercion, and *Counting Coup* upon our
    enemies winning honor and submitting our foes to shame,
        avoiding shame ourselves, zzooon"
—*ZZooon*—
"Avoiding shame, as well as Conquest and Coercion, and last, and last to prove our worthiness,

our worthiness before our ancestrals,
our worthiness before the Progenitors whose time of Return
has surely come
    Our worthiness of Mastery, zzzoooon"

    The refrain was enthusiastic.
—*ZZzooon!*—

    The two other Suzerains bowed respectfully to the priest,
and the ceremony was officially at an end. The Talon Soldiers
and Spacers returned to work at once. But as the bureaucrats
and civil servants retreated toward their own sheltered of-
fices, they could be heard clearly but softly crooning.

    "All . . . all . . . all of that. But one thing, one thing
more. . . .

    "First of all . . . survival of the nest. . . ."

    The priest looked up sharply and saw a glint in the eye of
the Suzerain of Cost and Caution. And in that instant it knew
that its rival had won a subtle but important point. There was
triumph in the other's eye as it bowed again and hummed
lowly.

"*Zooon.*"

4

Robert

    Dappled sunlight found gaps in the rain forest canopy,
illuminating streaks of brilliant color in the dim, vine-laced
avenue between. The fierce gales of mid-winter had ebbed
some weeks back, but a stiff breeze served as a reminder of
those days, causing boughs to dip and sway, and shaking loose

moisture from the prior night's rain. Droplets made fat,
plinking sounds as they landed in little shaded pools.

It was quiet in the mountains overlooking the Vale of
Sind. Perhaps more silent than a forest ought to be. The
woods were lush, and yet their superficial beauty masked a
sickness, a malaise arising from ancient wounds. Though the
air carried a wealth of fecund odors, one of the strongest was
a subtle hint of decay. It did not take an empath to know that
this was a sad place. A melancholy world.

Indirectly, that sadness was what had brought Earthlings
here. History had not yet written the final chapter on Garth,
but the planet was already on a list. A list of dying worlds.

One shaft of daylight spotlighted a fan of multicolored
vines, dangling in apparent disorder from the branches of a
giant tree. Robert Oneagle pointed in that direction. "You
might want to examine those, Athaclena," he said. "They can
be trained, you know."

The young Tymbrimi looked up from an orchidlike bloom
she had been inspecting. She followed his gesture, peering
past the bright, slanting columns of light. She spoke carefully
in accented but clearly enunciated Anglic.

"What can be trained, Robert? All I see there are vines."

Robert grinned. "Those very forest vines, Athaclena.
They're amazing things."

Athaclena's frown looked very human, in spite of the
wide set of her oval eyes and the alien gold-flecked green of
their large irises. Her slightly curved, delicate jaw and angled
brow made the expression appear faintly ironic.

Of course, as the daughter of a diplomat Athaclena might
have been taught to assume carefully tutored expressions at
certain times when in the company of humans. Still, Robert
was certain her frown conveyed genuine puzzlement. When
she spoke, a lilt in her voice seemed to imply that Anglic was
somehow limiting.

"Robert, you surely don't mean that those hanging tendril-
plants are *pre-sentient*, do you? There are a few autotrophic
sophont races, of course, but this vegetation shows none of
the signs. Anyway . . ." The frown intensified as she concentrated. From a fringe just above her ears her Tymbrimi ruff
quivered as silvery tendrils waved in quest. ". . . Anyway, I
can sense no emotional emissions from them at all."

Robert grinned. "No, of course you can't. I didn't mean

to imply they have any Uplift Potential, or even nervous systems per se. They're just rain forest plants. But they do have a secret. Come on. I'll show you."

Athaclena nodded, another human gesture that might or might not be naturally Tymbrimi as well. She carefully replaced the flower she had been examining and stood up in a fluid, graceful movement.

The alien girl's frame was slender, the proportions of her arms and legs different from the human norm—longer calves and less length in the thighs, for instance. Her slim, articulated pelvis flared from an even narrower waist. To Robert, she seemed to *prowl* in a faintly catlike manner that had fascinated him ever since she arrived on Garth, half a year ago.

That the Tymbrimi were lactating mammals he could tell by the outline of her upper breasts, provocatively evident even under her soft trail suit. He knew from his studies that Athaclena had two more pair, and a marsupial-like pouch as well. But those were not evident at present. Right now she seemed more human—or perhaps elfin—than alien.

"All right, Robert. I promised my father I would make the best of this enforced exile. Show me more of the wonders of this little planet."

The tone in her voice was so heavy, so resigned, that Robert decided she had to be exaggerating for effect. The theatrical touch made her seem oddly more like a human teenager, and that in itself was a bit unnerving. He led her toward the cluster of vines. "It's over here, where they converge down at the forest floor."

Athaclena's ruff—the helm of brown fur that began in a narrow stroke of down on her spine and rose up the back of her neck to end, caplike, in a widow's peak above the bridge of her strong nose—was now puffed and riffled at the edges. Over her smooth, softly rounded ears the cilia of her Tymbrimi corona waved as if she were trying to pick out any trace of consciousness other than theirs in the narrow glade.

Robert reminded himself not to overrate Tymbrimi mental powers as humans so often did. The slender Galactics did have impressive abilities in detecting strong emotions and were supposed to have a talent for crafting a form of *art* out of empathy itself. Nevertheless, true telepathy was no more common among Tymbrimi than among Earthlings.

Robert had to wonder what she was thinking. Could she

know how, since they had left Port Helenia together, his
fascination with her had grown? He hoped not. The feeling
was one he wasn't sure he even wanted to admit to himself
yet.

The vines were thick, fibrous strands with knotty protru-
sions every half-meter or so. They converged from many
different directions upon this shallow forest clearing. Robert
shoved a cluster of the multicolored cables aside to show
Athaclena that all of them terminated in a single small pool of
umber-colored water.

He explained. "These ponds are found all over this continent, each connected to the others by this vast network of
vines. They play a vital role in the rain forest ecosystem. No
other shrubs grow near these catchments where the vines do
their work."

Athaclena knelt to get a better view. Her corona still
waved and she seemed interested.

"Why is the pool colored so? Is there an impurity in the
water?"

"Yes, that's right. If we had an analysis kit I could take
you from pond to pond and demonstrate that each little puddle
has a slight overabundance of a different trace element or
chemical. "The vines seem to form a network among the giant
trees, carrying nutrients abundant in one area to other places
where they're lacking."

"A trade compact!" Athaclena's ruff expanded in one of
the few purely Tymbrimi expressions Robert was certain he
understood. For the first time since they had left the city
together he saw her clearly excited by something.

He wondered if she was at that moment crafting an
"empathy-glyph," that weird art form that some humans swore
they could sense, and even learn to understand a little.
Robert knew the feathery tendrils of the Tymbrimi corona
were involved in the process, somehow. Once, while accompanying his mother to a diplomatic reception, he'd noticed
something that *had* to have been a glyph—floating, it seemed,
above the ruff of the Tymbrimi Ambassador, Uthacalthing.

It had been a strange, fleeting sensation—as if he had
caught something which could only be looked at with the
blind spot of his eye, which fled out of view whenever he
tried to focus on it. Then, as quickly as he had become aware
of it, the glimpse vanished. In the end, he was left unsure it
had been anything but his imagination after all.

"The relationship is symbiotic, of course," Athaclena pronounced. Robert blinked. She was talking about the vines, of course.

"Uh, right again. The vines take nourishment from the great trees, and in exchange they transport nutrients the trees' roots can't draw out of the poor soil. They also flush out toxins and dispose of them at great distances. Pools like this one serve as banks where the vines come together to stockpile and trade important chemicals."

"Incredible." Athaclena examined the rootlets. "It mimics the self-interest trade patterns of sentient beings. And I suppose it is logical that plants would evolve this technique sometime, somewhere. I believe the Kanten might have begun in such a way, before the Linten gardeners uplifted them and made them starfarers."

She looked up at Robert. "Is this phenomenon catalogued? The Z'Tang were supposed to have surveyed Garth for the Institutes before the planet was passed over to you humans. I'm surprised I never heard of this."

Robert allowed himself a trace of a smile. "Sure, the Z'Tang report to the Great Library mentions the vines' chemical transfer properties. Part of the tragedy of Garth was that the network seemed on the verge of total collapse before Earth was granted a leasehold here. And if that actually happens half this continent will turn into desert.

"But the Z'Tang missed something crucial. They never seem to have noticed that the vines *move* about the forest, very slowly, seeking new minerals for their host trees. The forest, as an active trading community, *adapts*. It changes. There's actual hope that, with the right helpful nudge here and there, the network might become a centerpiece in the recovery of the planet's ecosphere. If so, we may be able to make a tidy profit selling the technique to certain parties elsewhere."

He had expected her to be pleased, but when Athaclena let the rootlets fall back into the umber water she turned to him with a cool tone. "You sound *proud* to have caught so careful and intellectual an elder race as the Z'Tang in a mistake, Robert. As one of your teledramas might put it, 'The Eatees and their Library are caught with egg on their faces once again.' Is that it?"

"Now wait a minute. I—"

"Tell me, do you humans plan to hoard this information,

gloating over your cleverness each time you dole out portions? Or will you flaunt it, crying far and wide what any race with sense already knows—that the Great Library is not and never has been perfect?"

Robert winced. The stereotypical Tymbrimi, as pictured by most Earthlings, was adaptable, wise, and often mischievous. But right now Athaclena sounded more like any irritable, opinionated young fem with a chip on her shoulder.

True, some Earthlings went too far in criticizing Galactic civilization. As the first known "wolfling" race in over fifty megayears, humans sometimes boasted too loudly that they were the only species now living who had bootstrapped themselves into space without anybody's help. What need had they to take for granted everything found in the Great Library of the Five Galaxies? Terran popular media tended to encourage an attitude of contempt for aliens who would rather look things up than find out for themselves.

There was a reason for encouraging this stance. The alternative, according to Terragens psychological scientists, would be a crushing racial inferiority complex. Pride was a vital thing for the only "backward" clan in the known universe. It stood between humanity and despair.

Unfortunately, the attitude had also alienated some species who might otherwise have been friendly to Mankind.

But on that count, were Athaclena's people all that innocent? The Tymbrimi, also, were famed for finding loopholes in tradition and for not being satisfied with what was inherited from the past.

"When will you humans learn that the universe is *dangerous*, that there are many ancient and powerful clans who have no love of upstarts, especially newcomers who brashly set off changes without understanding the likely consequences!"

Now Robert knew what Athaclena was referring to, what the real source of this outburst was. He rose from the poolside and dusted his hands. "Look, neither of us really knows what's going on out there in the galaxy right now. But it's hardly *our* fault that a dolphin-crewed starship—"

"The *Streaker*."

"—that the *Streaker* happened to discover something bizarre, something overlooked all these aeons. Anyone could have stumbled onto it! Hell, Athaclena. We don't even know what it was that those poor neo-dolphins found! Last anyone heard, their ship was being chased from the Morgran transfer point to Ifni-knows-where by twenty different fleets—all fighting over the right to capture her."

Robert discovered his pulse was beating hard. Clenched hands indicated just how much of his own tension was rooted in this topic. After all, it is frustrating enough whenever your universe threatens to topple in on you, but all the more so when the events that set it all off took place kiloparsecs away, amid dim red stars too distant even to be seen from home.

Athaclena's dark-lidded eyes met his, and for the first time he felt he could sense a touch of understanding in them. Her long-fingered left hand performed a fluttering half turn.

"I hear what you are saying, Robert. And I know that sometimes I am too quick to cast judgments. It is a fault my father constantly urges me to overcome.

"But you ought to remember that we Tymbrimi have been Earth's protectors and allies ever since your great, lumbering slowships stumbled into our part of space, eighty-nine paktaars ago. It grows wearying at times, and you must forgive if, on occasion, it shows."

"What grows wearying?" Robert was confused.

"Well, for one thing, ever since Contact we have had to learn and endure this assemblage of wolfling clicks and growls you have the effrontery to call a language."

Athaclena's expression was even, but now Robert believed he could actually sense a faint *something* emanating from those waving tendrils. It seemed to convey what a human girl might communicate with a subtle facial expression. Clearly she was teasing him.

"Ha ha. Very funny." He looked down at the ground.

"Seriously though, Robert, have we not, in the seven generations since Contact, constantly urged that you humans and your clients go slow? The *Streaker* simply should not have been prying into places where she did not belong—not while your small clan of races is still so young and helpless.

"You cannot keep on poking at the rules to see which are rigid and which are soft!"

Robert shrugged. "It's paid off a few times."

"Yes, but now your—what is the proper, beastly idiom? —your cows have come home to roost?"

"Robert, the fanatics won't let go now that their passions are aroused. They will chase the dolphin ship until she is captured. And if they cannot acquire her information that

way, powerful clans such as the Jophur and the Soro will seek
other means to achieve their ends."

Dust motes sparkled gently in and out of the narrow
shafts of sunlight. Scattered pools of rainwater glinted where
the beams touched them. In the quiet Robert scuffed at the
soft humus, knowing all too well what Athaclena was driving
at.

The Jophur, the Soro, the Gubru, the Tandu—those
powerful Galactic patron races which had time and again
demonstrated their hostility to Mankind—if they failed to
capture *Streaker*, their next step would be obvious. Sooner
or later some clan would turn its attention to Garth, or Atlast,
or Calafia—Earth's most distant and unprotected outposts—
seeking hostages in an effort to pry loose the dolphins' mysterious secret. The tactic was even *permissible*, under the loose
strictures established by the ancient Galactic Institute for
Civilized Warfare.

Some civilization, Robert thought bitterly. The irony was
that the dolphins weren't even likely to behave as any of the
stodgy Galactics expected them to.

By tradition a client race owed allegiance and fealty to its
patrons, the starfaring species that had "uplifted" it to full
sentience. This had been done for *Pan* chimpanzees and
Tursiops dolphins by humans even before Contact with
starfaring aliens. In doing so, Mankind had unknowingly mimicked a pattern that had ruled the Five Galaxies for perhaps
three billion years.

By tradition, client species served their patrons for a
thousand centuries or more, until release from indenture freed them to seek clients of their own. Few Galactic
clans believed or understood how much freedom had been
given dolphins and chims by the humans of Earth. It was
hard to say exactly what the neo-dolphins on the *Streaker*'s
crew would do if humans were taken hostage. But that,
apparently, wouldn't stop the Eatees from trying. Distant
listening posts had already confirmed the worst. Battle fleets
were coming, approaching Garth even as he and Athaclena
stood here talking.

"Which is worth more, Robert," Athaclena asked softly,
"that collection of ancient space-hulks the dolphins are supposed to have found . . . derelicts that have no meaning at all
to a clan as young as yours? Or your *worlds*, with their farms
and parks and orbit-cities? I cannot understand the logic of

your Terragens Council, ordering *Streaker* to guard her secret, when you and your clients are so vulnerable!"

Robert looked down at the ground again. He had no answer for her. It did sound illogical, when looked at in that way. He thought about his classmates and friends, gathering now to go to war without him, to fight over issues none of them understood. It was hard.

For Athaclena it would be as bad, of course, banished from her father's side, trapped on a foreign world by a quarrel that had little or nothing to do with her. Robert decided to let her have the last word. She had seen more of the universe than he anyway and had the advantage of coming from an older, higher-status clan.

"Maybe you're right," he said. "Maybe you're right."

Perhaps, though, he reminded himself as he helped her lift her backpack and then hoisted his own for the next stage of their trek, *perhaps a young Tymbrimi can be just as ignorant and opinionated as any human youth, a little frightened and far away from home.*

5

Fiben

"*TAASF scoutship* Bonobo *calling scoutship* Proconsul. . . . *Fiben, you're out of alignment again. Come on, old chim, try to straighten her out, will you?*"

Fiben wrestled with the controls of his ancient, alien-built spacecraft. Only the open mike kept him from expressing his frustration in rich profanity. Finally, in desperation, he kicked the makeshift control panel the technicians had installed back on Garth.

That did it! A red light went out as the antigravity verniers suddenly unfroze. Fiben sighed. *At last!*

Of course, in all the exertion his faceplate had steamed up. "You'd think they'd come up with a decent ape-suit after all this time," he grumbled as he turned up the defogger. It was more than a minute before the stars reappeared.

"What was that, Fiben? What'd you say?"

"I said I'll have this old crate lined up in time!" he snapped. "The Eatees won't be disappointed."

The popular slang term for alien Galactics had its roots in an acronym for "Extraterrestrials." But it also made Fiben think about food. He had been living on ship paste for days. What he wouldn't give for a fresh chicken and palm leaf sandwich, right now!

Nutritionists were always after chims to curb their appetite for meat. Said too much was bad for the blood pressure. Fiben sniffed.

Heck, I'd settle for a jar of mustard and the latest edition of the Port Helenia Times, he thought.

"Say, Fiben, you're always up on the latest scuttlebutt. Has anyone figured out yet who's invading us?"

"Well, I know a chimmie in the Coordinator's office who told me she had a friend on the Intelligence Staff who thought the bastards were Soro, or maybe Tandu."

"Tandu! You're kidding I hope." Simon sounded aghast, and Fiben had to agree. Some thoughts just weren't to be contemplated.

"Ah well, my guess is it's probably just a bunch of Linten gardeners dropping by to make sure we're treating the plants all right."

Simon laughed and Fiben felt glad. Having a cheerful wingman was worth more than a reserve officer's half pay.

He got his tiny space skiff back onto its assigned trajectory. The scoutboat—purchased only a few months back from a passing Xatinni scrap hauler—was actually quite a bit older than his own sapient race. While his ancestors were still harassing baboons beneath African trees, this fighter had seen action under distant suns—controlled by the hands, claws, tentacles of *other* poor creatures similarly doomed to skirmish and die in pointless interstellar struggles.

Fiben had only been allowed two weeks to study schematics and remember enough Galactiscript to read the instruments. Fortunately, designs changed slowly in the aeons-old Galactic culture, and there were basics most spacecraft shared in common.

One thing was certain, Galactic technology was impressive. Humanity's best ships were still bought, not Earthmade. And although this old tub was creaky and cranky, it would probably outlive him, this day.

All around Fiben bright fields of stars glittered, except where the inky blackness of the Spoon Nebula blotted out the thick band of the galactic disk. That was the direction where Earth lay, the homeworld Fiben had never seen, and now probably never would.

Garth, on the other hand, was a bright green spark only three million kilometers behind him. Her tiny fleet was too small to cover the distant hyperspacial transfer points, or even the inner system. Their ragged array of scouts, meteoroid miners, and converted freighters—plus three modern corvettes—was hardly adequate to cover the planet itself.

Fortunately, Fiben wasn't in command, so he did not have to keep his mind on the forlorn state of their prospects. He had only to do his duty and wait. Contemplating annihilation was not how he planned to spend the time.

He tried to divert himself by thinking about the Throop family, the small sharing-clan on Quintana Island that had recently invited him to join in their group marriage. For a modern chim it was a serious decision, like when two or three human beings decided to marry and raise a family. He had been pondering the choice for weeks.

The Throop Clan did have a nice, rambling house, good grooming habits, and respectable professions. The adults were attractive and interesting chims, all with green genetic clearances. Socially, it would be a very good move.

But there were disadvantages, as well. For one thing, he would have to move from 'Port Helenia back out to the islands, where most of the chim and human settlers still lived. Fiben wasn't sure he was ready to do that. He liked the open spaces of the mainland, the freedom of mountains and wild Garth countryside.

And there was another important consideration. Fiben had to wonder whether the Throops wanted him because they really liked him, or because the Neo-Chimpanzee Uplift Board had granted him a blue card—an open breeding clearance.

Only a white card was higher. Blue status meant he could join any marriage group and father children with only minimal genetic counseling. It couldn't help but have influenced the Throop Clan's decision.

"Oh, quit kiddin' yourself," he muttered at last. The matter was moot, anyway. Right now he wouldn't take long odds on his chances of ever even seeing home again alive.

"Fiben? You still there, kid?"

"Yeah, Simon. What'cha got?"

There was a pause.

"I just got a call from Major Forthness. He said he has an uneasy feeling about that gap in the fourth dodecant."

Fiben yawned. "Humans are always gettin' uneasy feelings. Alla time worryin'. That's what it's like being big-time patron types."

His partner laughed. On Garth it was fashionable even for well-educated chims to "talk grunt" at times. Most of the better humans took the ribbing with good humor; and those who didn't could go chase themselves.

"Tell you what," he told Simon. "I'll drift over to the ol' fourth dodecant and give it a lookover for the Major."

"We aren't supposed to split up," the voice in his headphones protested weakly. Still, they both knew having a wingman would hardly make any difference in the kind of fight they were about to face.

"I'll be back in a jiffy," Fiben assured his friend. "Save me some of the bananas."

He engaged the stasis and gravity fields gradually, treating the ancient machine like a virgin chimmie on her first pink. Smoothly, the scout built up acceleration.

Their defense plan had been carefully worked out bearing in mind normally conservative Galactic psychology. The Earthlings' forces were laid out in a mesh with the larger ships held in reserve. The scheme relied on scouts like him reporting the enemy's approach in time for the others to coordinate a timed response.

Problem was that there were too few scouts to maintain anywhere near complete coverage.

Fiben felt the powerful thrum of engines through his seat. Soon he was hurtling across the star-field. *Got to give the Galactics their due,* he thought. Their culture was stodgy and intolerant—sometimes almost fascistic—but they did build well.

Fiben itched inside his suit. Not for the first time, he wished some human pilots had been small enough to qualify for duty in these tiny Xatinni scouts. It would serve them right to have to smell themselves after three days in space.

Often, in his more pensive moods, Fiben wondered if it had really been such a good idea for humans to meddle so, making engineers and poets and part-time starfighters out of apes who might have been just as happy to stay in the forest. Where would he be now, it they refrained? He'd have been dirty perhaps, and ignorant. But at least he'd be free to scratch an itch whenever he damn well pleased!

He missed his local Grooming Club. Ah, for the glory of being curried and brushed by a truly sensitive chen or chimmie, lazing in the shade and gossiping about nothing at all. . . .

A pink light appeared in his detection tank. He reached forward and slapped the display, but the reading would not go away. In fact, as he approached his destination it grew, then split, and divided again.

Fiben felt cold. "Ifni's incontinence . . ." He swore, and grabbed for the code-broadcast switch. "Scoutship *Proconsul* to all units. They're behind us! Three . . . no, *four* battlecruiser squadrons, emerging from B-level hyperspace in the fourth dodecant!"

He blinked as a fifth flotilla appeared as if out of nowhere, the blips shimmering as starships emerged into real-time and leaked excess hyperprobability into the real-space vacuum. Even at this distance he could tell that the cruisers were *large*.

His headphones brought a static of consternation.

"*My Uncle Hairy's twice-bent manhood! How did they know there was a hole in our line there?*"

". . . *Fiben, are you sure? Why did they pick that particular . . .*"

". . . *Who th' hell are they? Can you . . . ?*"

The chatter shut down at once as Major Forthness broke in on the command channel.

"*Message received*. Proconsul. *We're on our way. Please switch on your repeater, Fiben.*"

Fiben slapped his helmet. It had been years since his militia training, and a guy tended to forget things. He switched over to telemetry so the others could share everything his instruments picked up.

Of course broadcasting all that data made him an easy target, but that hardly mattered. Clearly their foe had known where the defenders were, perhaps down to the last ship. Already he detected seeker missiles streaking toward him.

So much for stealth and surprise as the advantages of the weak. As he sped toward the enemy—whoever the devils were—Fiben noticed that the emerging invasion armada stood almost directly between him and the bright green sparkle of Garth.

"Great," he snorted. "At least when they blast me I'll be headed for home. Maybe a few hanks of fur will even get there ahead of the Eatees.

"If anyone wishes on a shooting star, tomorrow night, I hope they get whatever th'fuk they ask for."

He increased the ancient scout's acceleration and felt a rearward push even through the straining stasis fields. The moan of engines rose in pitch. And as the little ship leaped forward it seemed to Fiben that it sang a song of battle that sounded almost joyful.

6

Uthacalthing

Four human officers stepped across the brick parquet floor of the conservatory, their polished brown boots clicking rhythmically in step. Three stopped a respectful distance from the large window where the ambassador and the Planetary Coordinator stood waiting. But the fourth continued forward and saluted crisply.

"Madam Coordinator, it has begun." The graying militia commander pulled a document from his dispatch pouch and held it out.

Uthacalthing admired Megan Oneagle's poise as she took the proffered flimsy. Her expression betrayed none of the dismay she must be feeling as their worst fears were confirmed.

"Thank you, Colonel Maiven," she said.

Uthacalthing couldn't help noticing how the tense junior officers kept glancing his way, obviously wondering how the Tymbrimi Ambassador was taking the news. He remained outwardly impassive, as befitted a member of the diplomatic corps. But the tips of his corona trembled involuntarily at the froth of tension that had accompanied the messengers into the humid greenhouse.

From here a long bank of windows offered a glorious view of the Valley of the Sind, pleasantly arrayed with farms and groves of both native and imported Terran trees. It was a lovely, peaceful scene. Great Infinity alone knew how much longer that serenity would last. And Ifni was not confiding her plans in Uthacalthing, at present.

Planetary Coordinator Oneagle scanned the report briefly. "Do you have any idea yet who the enemy is?"

Colonel Maiven shook his head. "Not really, ma'am. The fleets are closing now, though. We expect identification shortly."

In spite of the seriousness of the moment, Uthacalthing found himself once again intrigued by the quaintly archaic dialect humans used here on Garth. At every other Terran colony he had visited, Anglic had taken in a potpourri of words borrowed from Galactic languages Seven, Two, and Ten. Here, though, common speech was not appreciably different from what it had been when Garth was licensed to the humans and their clients, more than two generations ago.

Delightful, surprising creatures, he thought. Only here, for instance, would one hear such a pure, ancient form— addressing a female leader as "ma'am." On other Terran-occupied worlds, functionaries addressed their supervisors by the neutral "ser," whatever their gender.

There were other unusual things about Garth as well. In the months since his arrival here, Uthacalthing had made a private pastime of listening to every odd story, every strange tale brought in from the wild lands by farmers, trappers, and members of the Ecological Recovery Service. There had been rumors. Rumors of strange things going on up in the mountains.

Of course they were silly stories, mostly. Exaggerations and tall tales. Just the sort of thing you would expect from wolflings living at the edge of a wilderness. And yet they had given him the beginnings of an idea.

Uthacalthing listened quietly as each of the staff officers

reported in turn. At last, though, there came a long pause—
the silence of brave people sharing a common sense of doom.
Only then did he venture to speak, quietly. "Colonel Maiven,
are you certain the enemy is being so thorough in isolating
Garth?"

The Defense Councilor bowed to Uthacalthing. "Mr.
Ambassador, we know that hyperspace is being mined by
enemy cruisers as close in as six million pseudometers, on at
least four of the main levels."

"Including D-level?"

"Yes, ser. Of course it means we dare not send any of our
lightly armed ships out on any of the few hyperpaths available, even if we could have spared any from the battle. It also
means anyone trying to get *into* Garth system would have to
be mighty determined."

Uthacalthing was impressed. *They have mined D-level.
I would not have expected them to bother. They certainly* don't
want anybody interfering in this operation!

This spoke of substantial effort and cost. Someone was
sparing little expense in this operation.

"The point is moot," the Planetary Coordinator said.
Megan was looking out over the rolling meadows of the Sind,
with its farmsteads and environmental research stations. Just
below the window a chim gardener on a tractor tended the
broad lawn of Earth-breed grass surrounding Government
House.

She turned back to the others. "The last courier ship
brought orders from the Terragens Council. We are to defend ourselves as best we can, for honor's sake and for the
record. But beyond that all we can hope to do is maintain
some sort of underground resistance until help arrives from
the outside."

Uthacalthing's deepself almost laughed out loud, for at
that moment each human in the room tried hard *not* to look
at him! Colonel Maiven cleared his throat and examined his
report. His officers pondered the brilliant, flowering plants.
Still, it was obvious what they were thinking.

Of the few Galactic clans that Earth could count as
friends, only the Tymbrimi had the military strength to be of
much assistance in this crisis. Men had faith that Tymbrim
would not let humans and their clients down.

And that *was* true enough. Uthacalthing knew the allies
would face this crisis together.

But it was also clear that little Garth was a long way out on the fringe of things. And these days the homeworlds had to take first priority.

No matter, Uthacalthing thought. *The best means to an end are not always those that appear most direct.*

Uthacalthing did not laugh out loud, much as he wanted to. For it might only discomfit these poor, grief-stricken people. In the course of his career he had met some Earthlings who possessed a natural gift for high-quality pranksterism—a few even on a par with the best Tymbrimi. Still, so many of them were such terribly dour, sober folk! Most tried so desperately hard to be serious at the very moments when humor could most help them through their troubles.

Uthacalthing wondered.

As a diplomat I have taught myself to watch every word, lest our clan's penchant for japes cause costly incidents. But has this been wise? My own daughter has picked up this habit from me . . . this shroud of seriousness. Perhaps that is why she has grown into such a strange, earnest little creature.

Thinking of Athaclena made him wish all the more he could openly make light of the situation. Otherwise, he might do the human thing and consider the danger she was in. He knew that Megan worried about her own son. *She underrates Robert*, Uthacalthing thought. *She should better know the lad's potential.*

"Dear ladies and gentlemen," he said, savoring the archaisms. His eyes separated only slightly in amusement. "We can expect the fanatics to arrive within days. You have made conventional plans to offer what resistance your meager resources will allow. Those plans will serve their function."

"However?" It was Megan Oneagle who posed the question. One eyebrow arched above those brown irises—big and set almost far enough apart to look attractive in the classic Tymbrimi sense. There was no mistaking the look.

She knows as well as I that more is called for. Ah, if Robert has half his mother's brains, I'll not fear for Athaclena, wandering in the dark forests of this sad, barren world.

Uthacalthing's corona trembled. "*However*," he echoed, "it does occur to me that now might be a good time to consult the Branch Library."

Uthacalthing picked up some of their disappointment. Astonishing creatures! Tymbrimi skepticism toward modern

Galactic culture never went so far as the outright contempt so many humans felt for the Great Library!

Wolflings. Uthacalthing sighed to himself. In the space above his head he crafted the glyph called *syullf-tha*, anticipation of a puzzle *almost* too ornate to solve. The specter revolved in expectancy, invisible to the humans—although for a moment Megan's attention seemed to flutter, as if she were just on the edge of noticing something.

Poor Wolflings. For all of its faults, the Library is where everything begins and ends. Always, somewhere in its treasure trove of knowledge, can be found some gem of wisdom and solution. Until you learn that, my friends, little inconveniences like ravening enemy battle fleets will go on ruining perfectly good spring mornings like this one!

7

Athaclena

Robert led the way a few feet ahead of her, using a machete to lop off the occasional branch encroaching on the narrow trail. The bright sunshine of the sun, Gimelhai, filtered softly through the forest canopy, and the spring air was warm.

Athaclena felt glad of the easy pace. With her weight redistributed from its accustomed pattern, walking was something of an adventure in itself. She wondered how human women managed to go through most of their lives with such a wide-hipped stance. Perhaps it was a sacrifice they paid for having big-headed babies, instead of giving birth early and then sensibly slipping the child into a postpartum pouch.

This experiment—subtly changing her body shape to make it seem more humanlike—was one of the more fascinating aspects of her visit to an Earth colony. She certainly could not have moved among local crowds as inconspicuously on a world of the reptiloid Soro, or the sap-ring-creatures of Jophur. And in the process she had learned a lot more about physiological control than the instructors had taught her back in school.

Still, the inconveniences were substantial, and she was considering putting an end to the experiment.

Oh, Ifni. A glyph of frustration danced at her tendril tips. *Changing back at this point might be more effort than it's worth.*

There were limits to what even the ever-adaptable Tymbrimi physiology could be expected to do. Attempting too many alterations in a short time ran the risk of triggering enzyme exhaustion.

Anyway, it was a little flattering to *kenn* the conflicts taking shape in Robert's mind. Athaclena wondered. *Is he actually attracted to me?* A year ago the very idea would have shocked her. Even Tymbrimi boys made her nervous, and Robert was an alien!

Now though, for some reason, she felt more curiosity than revulsion.

There was something almost hypnotic about the steady rocking of the pack on her back, the rhythm of soft boots on the rough trail, and the warming of leg muscles too long leashed by city streets. Here in the middle altitudes the air was warm and moist. It carried a thousand rich scents, oxygen, decaying humus, and the musty smell of human perspiration.

As Athaclena trudged, following her guide along the steep-sided ridgeline, a low rumbling could soon be heard coming from the distance ahead of them. It sounded like a rumor of great engines, or perhaps an industrial plant. The murmur faded and then returned with every switchback, just a little more forceful each time they drew near its mysterious source. Apparently Robert was relishing a surprise, so Athaclena bit back her curiosity and asked no questions.

At last, though, Robert stopped and waited at a bend in the trail. He closed his eyes, concentrating, and Athaclena thought she caught, just for a moment, the flickering traces of primitive emotion-glyph. Instead of true *kenning,* it brought to mind a *visual* image—a high, roaring fountain painted in garish, uninhibited blues and greens.

He really is getting much better, Athaclena thought. Then she joined him at the bend and gasped in surprise.

Droplets, trillions of tiny liquid lenses, sparkled in the shafts of sunlight that cut sharply through the cloud forest. The low rumble that had drawn them onward for an hour was suddenly an earthshaking growl that rattled tree limbs left and right, reverberating through the rocks and into their bones. Straight ahead a great cataract spilled over glass-smooth boulders, dashing into spume and spray in a canyon carved over persistent ages.

The falling river was an extravagance of nature, pouring forth more exuberantly than the most shameless human entertainer, prouder then any sentient poet.

It was too much to be taken in with ears and eyes alone. Athaclena's tendrils waved, seeking, *kenning*, one of those moments Tymbrimi glyphcrafters sometimes spoke of—when a *world* seemed to join into the mesh of empathy usually reserved for living things. In a time-stretched instant, she realized that ancient Garth, wounded and crippled, could still sing.

Robert grinned. Athaclena met his gaze and smiled as well. Their hands met and joined. For a long, wordless time they stood together and watched the shimmering, ever-changing rainbows arch over nature's percussive flood.

Strangely, the epiphany only made Athaclena feel sad, and even more regretful she had ever come to this world. She had not wanted to discover beauty here. It only made the little world's fate seem more tragic.

How many times had she wished Uthacalthing had never accepted this assignment? But wishing seldom made things so.

As much as she loved him, Athaclena had always found her father inscrutable. His reasoning was often too convoluted for her to fathom, his actions too unpredictable. Such as taking this posting when he could have had a more prestigious one simply by asking.

And sending her into these mountains with Robert . . . it hadn't been just "for her safety," she could tell that much. Was she actually supposed to chase those ridiculous rumors of exotic mountain creatures? Unlikely. Probably Uthacalthing only suggested the idea in order to distract her from her worries.

Then she thought of another possible motive.

Could her father actually imagine that she might enter into a self-other bond . . . with a *human?* Her nostrils flared to twice their normal size at the thought. Gently, suppressing her corona in order to keep her feelings hidden, she relaxed her grip on Robert's hand, and felt relieved when he did not hold on.

Athaclena crossed her arms and shivered.

Back home she had taken part in only a few, tentative practice bondings with boys, and those mostly as class assignments. Before her mother's death this had been a cause of quite a few family arguments. Mathicluanna had almost despaired of her oddly reserved and private daughter. But Athaclena's father, at least, had not pestered her to do more than she was ready for.

Until now, maybe?

Robert was certainly charming and likable. With his high cheekbones and eyes pleasantly set apart, he was about as handsome as a human might hope to get. And yet, the very fact that she might think in such terms shocked Athaclena.

Her tendrils twitched. She shook her head and wiped out a nascent glyph before she could even realize what it would have been. This was a topic she had no wish to consider right now, even less than the prospect of war.

"The waterfall is beautiful, Robert," she enunciated carefully in Anglic. "But if we stay here much longer, we shall soon be quite damp."

He seemed to return from a distant contemplation. "Oh. Yeah, Clennie. Let's go." With a brief smile he turned and led the way, his human empathy waves vague and far away.

The rain forest persisted in long fingers between the hills, becoming wetter and more robust as they gained altitude. Little Garthian creatures, timid and scarce at the lower levels, now made frequent skittering rustles behind the lush vegetation, occasionally even challenging them with impudent squeaks.

Soon they reached the summit of a foothill ridge, where a chain of spine-stones jutted up, bare and gray, like the bony plates along the back of one of those ancient reptiles Uthacalthing had shown her, in a lesson book on Earth history. As they removed their packs for a rest, Robert told her that no one could explain the formations, which topped many of the hills below the Mountains of Mulun.

"Even the Branch Library on Earth has no reference,"

he said as he brushed a hand along one of the jagged monoliths. "We've submitted a low-priority inquiry to the district branch at Tanith. Maybe in a century or so the Library Institute's computers will dig up a report from some long-extinct race that once lived here, and then we'll know the answer."

"Yet you hope they do not," she suggested.

Robert shrugged. "I guess I'd rather it were left a mystery. Maybe we could be the first to figure it out." He looked pensively at the stones.

A lot of Tymbrimi felt the same way, preferring a good puzzle to any written fact. Not Athaclena, however. This attitude—this resentment of the Great Library—was something she found absurd.

Without the Library and the other Galactic Institutes, oxygen-breathing culture, dominant in the Five Galaxies, would long ago have fallen into total disarray—probably ending in savage, total war.

True, most starfaring clans relied far too much on the Library. And the Institutes only *moderated* the bickering of the most petty and vituperative senior patron lines. The present crisis was only the latest in a series that stretched back long before any now living race had come into existence.

Still, this planet was an example of what could happen when the restraint of Tradition broke down. Athaclena listened to the sounds of the forest. Shading her eyes, she watched a swarm of small, furry creatures glide from branch to branch in the direction of the afternoon sun.

"Superficially, one might not even know this was a holocaust world," she said softly.

Robert had set their packs in the shade of a towering spine-stone and began cutting slices of soyastick salami and bread for their luncheon. "It's been fifty thousand years since the Bururalli made a mess of Garth, Athaclena. That's enough time for lots of surviving animal species to radiate and fill some of the emptied niches. Right now I guess you'd probably have to be a zoologist to notice the sparse species list."

Athaclena's corona was at full extension, *kenning* faint traceries of emotion from the surrounding forest. "*I* notice, Robert," she said. "I can feel it. This watershed lives, but it is lonely. It has none of the life-complexity a wildwood should know. And there is no trace of Potential at all."

Robert nodded seriously. But she sensed his distance

from it all. The Bururalli Holocaust happened a long time ago, from an Earthling's point of view.

The Bururalli had also been new, back then, just released from indenture to the Nahalli, the patron race that uplifted them to sentience. It was a special time for the Bururalli, for only when its knot of obligations was loosened at last could a client species establish unsupervised colonies of its own. When their time came the Galactic Institute of Migration had just declared the fallow world Garth ready again for limited occupation. As always, the Institute expected that local lifeforms—especially those which might some day develop Uplift Potential—would be protected at all cost by the new tenants.

The Nahalli boasted that they had found the Bururalli a quarrelsome clan of pre-sentient carnivores and uplifted them to become perfect Galactic citizens, responsible and reliable, worthy of such a trust.

The Nahalli were proven horribly wrong.

"Well, what do you expect when an entire race goes completely crazy and starts annihilating everything in sight?" Robert asked. "Something went wrong and suddenly the Bururalli turned into berserkers, tearing apart a world they were supposed to take care of.

"It's no wonder you don't detect any Potential in a Garth forest, Clennie. Only those tiny creatures who could burrow and hide escaped the Bururalli's madness. The bigger, brighter animals are all one with yesterday's snows."

Athaclena blinked. Just when she thought she had a grasp of Anglic Robert did this to her again, using that strange human penchant for *metaphors*. Unlike similes, which *compared* two objects, metaphors seemed to declare, against all logic, that unlike things were the same! No Galactic language allowed such nonsense.

Generally she was able to handle those odd linguistic juxtapositions, but this one had her baffled. Above her waving corona the small-glyph *teev'nus* formed briefly—standing for the elusiveness of perfect communication.

"I have only heard brief accounts of that era. What happened to the murderous Bururalli themselves?"

Robert shrugged. "Oh, officials from the Institutes of Uplift and Migration finally dropped by, about a century or so after the holocaust began. The inspectors were horrified, of course.

"They found the Bururalli warped almost beyond recognition, roaming the planet, hunting to death anything they could catch. By then they'd abandoned the horrible technological weapons they'd started with and nearly reverted to tooth and claw. I suppose that's why some small animals did survive.

"Ecological disasters aren't as uncommon as the Institutes would have it seem, but this one was a major scandal. There was galaxy-wide revulsion. Battle fleets were sent by many of the major clans and put under unified command. Soon the Bururalli were no more."

Athaclena nodded. "I assume their patrons, the Nahalli, were punished as well."

"Right. They lost status and are somebody's clients now, the price of negligence. We're taught the story in school. Several times."

When Robert offered the salami again, Athaclena shook her head. Her appetite had vanished. "So you humans inherited another reclamation world."

Robert put away their lunch. "Yeah. Since we're two-client patrons, we had to be allowed colonies, but the Institutes have mostly handed us the leavings of other peoples' disasters. We have to work hard helping this world's ecosystem straighten itself out, but actually, Garth is really nice compared with some of the others. You ought to see Deemi and Horst, out in the Canaan Cluster."

"I have heard of them." Athaclena shuddered. "I do not think I ever want to see—"

She stopped mid-sentence. "I do not . . ." Her eyelids fluttered as she looked around, suddenly confused. *"Thu'un dun!"* Her ruff puffed outward. Athaclena stood quickly and walked—half in a trance—to where the towering spine-stones overlooked the misty tops of the cloud forest.

Robert approached from behind. "What is it?"

She spoke softly. "I sense something."

"Hmmph. That doesn't surprise me, with that Tymbrimi nervous system of yours, especially the way you've been altering your body form just to please me. It's no wonder you're picking up static."

Athaclena shook her head impatiently. "I have *not* been doing it just to please you, you arrogant human male! And I've asked you before kindly to be more careful with your horrible metaphors. A Tymbrimi corona is not a radio!" She gestured with her hand. "Now please be quiet for a moment."

Robert fell silent. Athaclena concentrated, trying to *kenn* again. . . .

A corona might not pick up static like a radio, but it could suffer interference. She sought after the faint aura she had felt so very briefly, but it was impossible. Robert's clumsy, eager empathy flux crowded it out completely.

"What was it, Clennie?" he asked softly.

"I do not know. Something not very far away, off toward the southeast. It felt like people—men and neo-chimpanzees mostly—but there was something else as well."

Robert frowned. "Well, I guess it might have been one of the ecological management stations. Also, there are isolated freeholds all through this area, mostly higher up, where the seisin grows."

She turned swiftly. "Robert, I felt Potential! For the briefest moment of clarity, I touched the emotions of a pre-sentient being!"

Robert's feelings were suddenly cloudy and turbulent, his face impassive. "What do you mean?"

"My father told me about something, before you and I left for the mountains. At the time I paid little attention. It seemed impossible, like those fairy tales your human authors create to give us Tymbrimi strange dreams."

"Your people buy them by the shipload," Robert interjected. "Novels, old movies, threevee, poems . . ."

Athaclena ignored his aside. "Uthacalthing mentioned stories of a creature of this planet, a native being of high Potential . . . one who is supposed to have actually survived the Bururalli Holocaust." Athaclena's corona foamed forth a glyph rare to her . . . *syullf-tha*, the joy of a puzzle to be solved. "I wonder. Could the legends possibly be true?"

Did Robert's mood flicker with a note of relief? Athaclena felt his crude but effective emotional guard go opaque.

"Hmmm. Well, there *is* a legend," he said. "A simple story told by wolflings. It could hardly be of interest to a sophisticated Galactic, I suppose."

Athaclena eyed him carefully and touched his arm, stroking it gently. "Are you going to make me wait while you draw out this mystery with dramatic pauses? Or will you save yourself bruises and tell me what you know at once?"

Robert laughed. "Well, since you're so persuasive. You just *might* have picked up the empathy output of a Garthling."

Athaclena's broad, gold-flecked eyes blinked. "That is the name my father used!"

"Ah. Then Uthacalthing has been listening to old seisin hunters' tales. . . . Imagine having such after only a hundred Earth years here. . . . Anyway, it's said that one large animal did manage to escape the Bururalli, through cunning, ferocity, and a whole lot of Potential. The mountain men and chims tell of sampling traps robbed, laundry stolen from clotheslines, and strange markings scratched on unclimbable cliff faces.

"Oh, it's probably all a lot of eyewash." Robert smiled. "But I did recall those legends when Mother told me I was to come up here. So I figured, so that it wouldn't be a total loss, I might as well take a Tymbrimi along to see if she could flush out a Garthling with her empathy net."

Some metaphors Athaclena understood quite readily. Her fingernails pressed into Robert's arm. "So?" she asked with a questing lilt. "That is the entire reason I am in this wilderness? I am to be a sniffer-out of smoke and legends for you?"

"Sure," Robert teased. "Why else would I come out here, all alone in the mountains with an alien from outer space?"

Athaclena hissed through her teeth. But within she could not help but feel pleased. This human sardonicism wasn't unlike reverse-talk among her own people. And when Robert laughed aloud, she found she had to join him. For the moment all worry of war and danger was banished. It was a welcome release for both of them.

"If such a creature exists, we must find it, you and I," she said at last.

"Yeah, Clennie. We'll find it together."

8

Fiben

TAASF Scoutship *Proconsul* hadn't outlived its pilot after all. It had seen its last mission—the ancient boat was dead in space—but within its bubble canopy life still remained.

Enough life, at least, to inhale the pungent stench of a six days unwashed ape—and to exhale an apparently unceasing string of imaginative curses.

Fiben finally ran down when he found he was repeating himself. He had long ago covered every permutation, combination, and juxtaposition of bodily, spiritual, and hereditary attributes—real and imaginary—the enemy could possibly possess. That exercise had carried him all the way through his own brief part in the space battle, while he fired his popgun weaponry and evaded counterblows like a gnat ducking sledgehammers, through the concussions of near-misses and the shriek of tortured metal, and into an aftermath of dazed, confused bemusement that he did not seem to be dead after all. Not yet at least.

When he was sure the life capsule was still working and not about to sputter out along with the rest of the scoutboat, Fiben finally wriggled out of his suit and sighed at his first opportunity to scratch in days. He dug in with a will, using not only his hands but the tingers and tumb of his left foot, as well. Finally he sagged back, aching from the pounding he had been through.

His main job had been to pass close enough to collect good data for the rest of the defense force. Fiben guessed that zooming straight down the middle of the invading fleet probably qualified. Heckling the enemy he had thrown in for free.

It seemed the interlopers failed to appreciate his running commentary as *Proconsul* plunged through their midst. He'd lost count of how many times close calls came near to cooking him. By the time he had passed behind and beyond the onrushing armada, *Proconsul's* entire aft end had been turned into a glazed-over hunk of slag.

The main propulsion system was gone, of course. There was no way to return and help his comrades in the desperate, futile struggle that followed soon after. Drifting farther and farther from the one-sided battle, Fiben could only listen helplessly.

It wasn't even a contest. The fighting lasted little more than a day.

He remembered the last charge of the corvette, *Darwin*, accompanied by two converted freighters and a small swarm of surviving scoutboats. They streaked down, blasting their way into the flank of the invading host, turning it, throwing one wing of battlecruisers into confusion under clouds of smoke and waves of noisome probability waves.

Not a single Terran craft came out of that maelstrom. Fiben knew then that TAASF *Bonobo*, and his friend Simon, were gone.

Right now, the enemy seemed to be pursuing a few fugitives off toward Ifni knew where. They were taking their time, cleaning up thoroughly before proceeding to supine Garth.

Now Fiben resumed his cursing along a new tack. All in a spirit of constructive criticism, of course, he dissected the character faults of the species his own race was unfortunate enough to have as patrons.

Why? he asked the universe. *Why did humans—those hapless, hairless, wolfling wretches—have the incredibly bad taste to have uplifted neo-chimpanzees into a galaxy so obviously run by idiots?*

Eventually, he slept.

His dreams were fitful. Fiben kept imagining that he was trying to speak, but his voice would not shape the sentences, a nightmare possibility to one whose great-grandfather spoke only crudely, with the aid of devices, and whose slightly more distant ancestors faced the world without words at all.

Fiben sweated. No shame was greater than this. In his

dream he sought speech as if it were an object, a thing that might be *misplaced,* somehow.

On looking down he saw a glittering gem lying on the ground. Perhaps *this* was the gift of words, Fiben thought, and he bent over to take it. But he was too clumsy! His thumb refused to work with his forefinger, and he wasn't able to pluck the bauble out of the dust. In fact, all of his efforts seemed only to push it in deeper.

Despairing finally, he was forced to crouch down and pick it up with his lips.

It *burned*! In his dream he cried out as a terrible searing poured down his throat like liquid fire.

And yet, he recognized that this was one of those strange nightmares—the kind in which one could be both objective *and* terrified at the same time. As one dreamself writhed in agony, another part of Fiben witnessed it in a state of interested detachment.

All at once the scene shifted. Fiben found himself standing in the midst of a gathering of bearded men in black coats and floppy hats. They were mostly elderly, and they leafed through dusty texts as they argued with each other. *An oldtime Talmudic conclave*, he recognized suddenly, like those he had read about in comparative religions class, back at the University. The rabbis sat in a circle, discussing symbolism and biblical interpretation. One lifted an aged hand to point at Fiben.

"He that lappeth like an animal, Gideon, he shall thou not take . . ."

"Is that what it means?" Fiben asked. The pain was gone. Now he was more bemused than fearful. His pal, Simon, had been Jewish. No doubt that explained part of this crazy symbolism. What was going on here was obvious. These learned men, these wise human scholars, were trying to illuminate that frightening first part of his dream for him.

"No, no," a second sage countered. *"The symbols relate to the trial of the infant Moses! An angel, you'll recall, guided his hand to the glowing coals, rather than the shining jewels, and his mouth was burned . . ."*

"But I don't see what that *tells* me!" Fiben protested.

The oldest rabbi raised his hand, and the others all went silent.

"The dream stands for none of those things. The symbolism should be obvious," he said.

"It comes from the oldest book . . ."

The sage's bushy eyebrows knotted with concern.

". . . And Adam, too, ate from the fruit of the Tree of Knowledge . . ."

"Uh," Fiben groaned aloud, awakening in a sweat. The gritty, smelly capsule was all around him again, and yet the vividness of the dream lingered, making him wonder for a moment which was real after all. Finally he shrugged it off. "Old *Proconsul* must have drifted through the wake of some Eatee probability mine while I slept. Yeah. That must be it. I'll never doubt the stories they tell in a spacer's bar again."

When he checked his battered instruments Fiben found that the battle had moved on around the sun. His own derelict, meanwhile, was on a nearly perfect intersect orbit with a planet.

"Hmmmph," he grunted as he worked the computer. What it told him was ironic. *It really is Garth.*

He still had a little maneuvering power in the gravity systems. Perhaps enough, just maybe, to get him within escape pod range.

And wonder of wonders, if his ephemerides were right, he might even be able to reach the Western Sea area . . . a bit east of Port Helenia. Fiben whistled tunelessly for a few minutes. He wondered what the chances were that this should happen. A million to one? Probably more like a trillion.

Or was the universe just suckering him with a bit of hope before the *next* whammy?

Either way, he decided, there was some solace in thinking that, under all these stars, someone out there was still thinking of him personally.

He got out his tool kit and set to work making the necessary repairs.

9

Uthacalthing

Uthacalthing knew it was unwise to wait much longer. Still he remained with the Librarians, watching them try to coax forth one more valuable detail before it was time at last to go.

He regarded the human and neo-chimpanzee technicians as they hurried about under the high-domed ceiling of the Planetary Branch Library. They all had jobs to do and concentrated on them intently, efficiently. And yet one could sense a ferment just below the surface, one of barely suppressed fear.

Unbidden, *rittitees* formed in the low sparking of his corona. The glyph was one commonly used by Tymbrimi parents to calm frightened children.

They can't detect you, Uthacalthing told *rittitees*. And yet it obstinately hovered, trying to soothe young ones in distress.

Anyway, these people aren't children. Humans have only known of the Great Library for two Earth centuries. But they had thousands of years of their own history before that. They may still lack Galactic polish and sophistication, but that deficit has sometimes been an advantage to them.

Rarely. Rittitees was dubious.

Uthacalthing ended the argument by drawing the uncertain glyph back where it belonged, into his own well of being.

Under the vaulted stone ceiling towered a five-meter gray monolith, embossed with a rayed spiral sigil—symbol of the Great Library for three billion years. Nearby, data loggers filled crystalline memory cubes. Printers hummed and spat bound reports which were quickly annotated and carted away.

This Library station, a class K outlet, was a small one indeed. It contained only the equivalent of one thousand times all the books humans had written before Contact, a pittance compared with the full Branch Library on Earth, or sector general on Tanith.

Still, when Garth was taken this room, too, would fall to the invader.

Traditionally, that should make no difference. The Library was supposed to remain open to all, even parties fighting over the territory it stood upon. In times like these, however, it was unwise to count on such niceties. The colonial resistance forces planned to carry off what they could in hopes of using the information somehow, later.

A pittance of a pittance. Of course it had been his suggestion that they do this, but Uthacalthing was frankly amazed that the humans had gone along with the idea so vigorously. After all, why bother? What could such a small smattering of information accomplish?

This raid on the Planetary Library served his purposes, but it also reinforced his opinion of Earth people. They just never gave up. It was yet another reason he found the creatures delightful.

The hidden reason for this chaos—his own private jest— had called for the dumping and misplacing of a few specific megafiles, easily overlooked in all of this confusion. In fact, nobody appeared to have noticed when he briefly attached his own input-output cube to the massive Library, waited a few seconds, then pocketed the little sabotage device again.

Done. Now there was little to do but watch the wolflings while he waited for his car.

Off in the distance a wailing tone began to rise and fall. It was the keening of the spaceport siren, across the bay, as another crippled refugee from the rout in space came in for an emergency landing. They had heard that sound all too infrequently. Everyone already knew that there had been few survivors.

Mostly the traffic consisted of departing aircraft. Many mainlanders had already taken flight to the chain of islands in the Western Sea where the vast majority of the Earthling population still made its home. The Government was preparing its own evacuation.

When the sirens moaned, every man and chim looked up briefly. Momentarily, the workers broadcast a complex fugue of anxiety that Uthacalthing could almost taste with his corona.

Almost taste?

Oh, what lovely, surprising things, these metaphors, Uthacalthing thought. *Can one taste with one's corona? Or touch with one's eyes? Anglic is so silly, yet so delightfully thought provoking.*

And do not dolphins actually see with their ears?

Zunour'thzun formed above his waving tendrils, resonating with the fear of the men and chims.

Yes, we all hope to live, for we have so very much left to do or taste or see or kenn. . . .

Uthacalthing wished diplomacy did not require that Tymbrimi choose their dullest types as envoys. He had been selected as an ambassador because, among other qualities, he was *boring*, at least from the point of view of those back home.

And poor Athaclena seemed to be even worse off, so sober and serious.

He freely admitted that it was partly his own fault. That was one reason he had brought along his own father's large collection of pre-Contact Earthling comic recordings. The Three Stooges, especially, inspired him. Alas, as yet Athaclena seemed unable to understand the subtle, ironic brilliance of those ancient Terran comedic geniuses.

Through *Sylth*—that courier of the dead-but-remembered—his long-dead wife still chided him, reaching out from beyond life to say that their daughter should be home, where her lively peers might yet draw her out from her isolation.

Perhaps, he thought. *But Mathicluanna had had her try.* Uthacalthing believed in his own prescription for their odd daughter.

A small, uniformed neo-chimpanzee female—a chimmie—stepped in front of Uthacalthing and bowed, her hands folded respectfully in front of her.

"Yes, miss?" Uthacalthing spoke first, as protocol demanded. Although he was a patron speaking to a client, he generously included the polite, archaic honorific.

"Y-your excellency." The chimmie's scratchy voice trembled slightly. Probably, this was the first time she had ever spoken to a non-Terran. "Your excellency, Planetary Coordinator Oneagle has sent word that the preparations have been completed. The fires are about to be set.

"She asks if you would like to witness your . . . er, program, unleashed."

As Uthacalthing's eyes separated wider in amusement, the wrinkled fur between his brows flattening momentarily. His "program" hardly deserved the name. It might better be called a devious practical joke on the invaders. A long shot, at best.

Not even Megan Oneagle knew what he was really up to. That necessity was a pity, of course. For even if it failed—as was likely—it would still be worthy of a chuckle or two. A laugh might help his friend through the dark times ahead of her.

"Thank you, corporal," he nodded. "Please lead the way."

As he followed the little client, Uthacalthing felt a faint sense of regret at leaving so much undone. A good joke required much preparation, and there was just not enough time.

If only I had a decent sense of humor!

Ah, well. Where subtlety fails us we must simply make do with cream pies.

Two hours later he was on his way back to town from Government House. The meeting had been brief, with battle fleets approaching orbit and landings expected soon. Megan Oneagle had already moved most of the government and her few remaining forces to safer ground.

Uthacalthing figured they actually had a little more time. There would be no landing until the invaders had broadcast their manifesto. The rules of the Institute for Civilized Warfare required it.

Of course, with the Five Galaxies in turmoil, many starfaring clans were playing fast and loose with tradition right now. But in this case observing the proprieties would cost the enemy nothing. They had already won. Now it was only a matter of occupying the territory.

Besides, the battle in space had showed one thing. It was clear now the enemy were *Gubru*.

The humans and chims of this planet were not in for a pleasant time. The Gubru Clan had been among the worst of Earth's tormentors since Contact. Nonetheless, the avian Galactics were sticklers for rules. By their own interpretation of them, at least.

Megan had been disappointed when he turned down her

offer of transportation to sanctuary. But Uthacalthing had his
own ship. Anyway, he still had business to take care of here
in town. He bid farewell to the Coordinator with a promise to
see her soon.

"Soon" was such a wonderfully ambiguous word. One of
many reasons he treasured Anglic was the wolfling tongue's
marvelous untidiness!

By moonlight Port Helenia felt even smaller and more
forlorn than the tiny, threatened village it was by day. Winter
might be mostly over, but a stiff breeze still blew from the
east, sending leaves tumbling across the nearly empty streets
as his driver took him back toward his chancery compound.
The wind carried a moist odor, and Uthacalthing imagined he
could smell the mountains where his daughter and Megan's
son had gone for refuge.

It was a decision that had not won the parents much
thanks.

His car had to pass by the Branch Library again on its
way to the Tymbrimi Embassy. The driver had to slow to go
around another vehicle. Because of this Uthacalthing was
treated to a rare sight—a high-caste Thennanin in full fury
under the streetlights.

"Please stop here," he said suddenly.

In front of the stone Library building a large floatercraft
hummed quietly. Light poured out of its raised cupola, creating a dark bouquet of shadows on the broad steps. Five
clearly were cast by neo-chimpanzees, their long arms exaggerated in the stretched silhouettes. Two even longer penum-
bral shadows swept away from slender figures standing close
to the floater. A pair of stoic, disciplined Ynnin—looking like
tall, armored kangaroos—stood unmoving as if molded out of
stone.

Their employer and patron, owner of the largest silhouette, towered above the little Terrans. Blocky and powerful,
the creature's wedgelike shoulders seemed to merge right
into its bullet-shaped head. The latter was topped by a high,
rippling crest, like that of a helmeted Greek warrior.

As Uthacalthing stepped out of his own car he heard a
loud voice rich in guttural sibilants.

"*Natha'kl ghoom'ph? Veraich'sch hooman'vlech! Nittaro
K'Anglee!*"

The chimpanzees shook their heads, confused and clearly
intimidated. Obviously none of them spoke Galactic Six. Still,

when the huge Thennanin started forward the little Earth-lings moved to interpose themselves, bowing low, but ada-mant in their refusal to let him pass.

This only served to make the speaker angrier. "*Idatess! Nittaril kollunta . . .*"

The large Galactic stopped abruptly on seeing Uthacalthing. His leathery, beaklike mouth remained closed as he switched to Galactic Seven, speaking through his breathing slits.

"Ah! Uthacalthing, ab-Caltmour ab-Brma abKrallnith ul-Tytlal! I see you!"

Uthacalthing would have recognized Kault in a city choked with Thennanin. The big, pompous, high-caste male knew that protocol did not require use of full species names in casual encounters. But now Uthacalthing had no choice. He had to reply in kind.

"Kault, ab-Wortl ab-Kosh ab-Rosh ab-Tothtoon ul-Paimin ul-Rammin ul-Ynnin ul-Olumimin, I see you as well."

Each "ab" in the lengthy patronymic told of one of the patron races from which the Thennanin clan was descended, back to the eldest still living. "Ul" preceded the name of each client species the Thennanin had themselves uplifted to starfaring sentience. Kault's people had been very busy, the last megayear or so. They bragged incessantly of their long species name.

The Thennanin were idiots.

"Uthacalthing! You are adept in that garbage tongue the Earthlings use. Please explain to these ignorant, half-uplifted creatures that I wish to pass! I have need to use the Branch Library, and if they do not stand aside I shall be forced to have their masters chastise them!"

Uthacalthing shrugged the standard gesture of regretful inability to comply. "They are only doing their jobs, Envoy Kault. When the Library is fully occupied with matters of planetary defense, it is briefly allowable to restrict access solely to the lease owners."

Kault stared unblinkingly at Uthacalthing. His breathing slits puffed. "*Babes,*" he muttered softly in an obscure dialect of Galactic Twelve—unaware perhaps that Uthacalthing understood. "*Infants, ruled by unruly children, tutored by juvenile delinquents!*"

Uthacalthing's eyes separated and his tendrils pulsed with irony. They crafted *fsu'usturatu*, which sympathizes, while laughing.

Damn good thing Thennanin have a rock's sensitivity to empathy. Uthacalthing thought in Anglic as he hurriedly erased the glyph. Of the Galactic clans involved in the current spate of fanaticism, the Thennanin were less repulsive than most. Some of them actually believed they were acting in the best interests of those they conquered.

It was apparent whom Kault meant when he spoke of "delinquents" leading the clan of Earth astray. Uthacalthing was far from offended.

"These *infants* fly starships, Kault," he answered in the same dialect, to the Thennanin's obvious surprise. "The neo-chimpanzees may be the finest clients to appear in half a megayear . . . with the possible exception of their cousins, the neo-dolphins. Shall we not respect their earnest desire to do their duty?"

Kault's crest went rigid at the mention of the other Earthling client race. "My Tymbrimi friend, did you mean to imply that you have heard more about the dolphin ship? Have they been found?"

Uthacalthing felt a little guilty for toying with Kault. All considered, he was not a bad sort. He came from a minority political faction among the Thennanin which had a few times even spoken for peace with the Tymbrimi. Nevertheless, Uthacalthing had reasons for wanting to pique his fellow diplomat's interest, and he had prepared for an encounter like this.

"Perhaps I have said more than I should. Please think nothing more of it. Now I am saddened to say that I really must be going. I am late for a meeting. I wish you good fortune and survival in the days ahead, Kault."

He bowed in the casual fashion of one patron to another and turned to go. But within, Uthacalthing was laughing. For he knew the real reason Kault was here at the Library. The Thennanin could only have come looking for him.

"Wait!" Kault called out in Anglic.

Uthacalthing looked back. "Yes, respected colleague?"

"I . . . ." Kault dropped back into GalSeven. "I must speak with you regarding the evacuation. You may have heard, my ship is in disrepair. I am at the moment bereft of transport."

The Thennanin's crest fluttered in discomfort. Protocol and diplomatic standing were one thing, but the fellow obviously would rather not be in town when the Gubru landed. "I

must ask therefore. Will there be some opportunity to discuss
the possibility of mutual aid?" The big creature said it in a
rush.

Uthacalthing pretended to ponder the idea seriously.
After all, his species and Kault's were officially at war right
now. He nodded at last. "Be at my compound about midnight
tomorrow night—no later than a mictaar thereafter, mind you.
And please bring only a minimum of baggage. My boat is
small. With that understood, I gladly offer you a ride to
sanctuary."

He turned to his neo-chimp driver. "That would only be
courteous and proper, would it not, corporal?"

The poor chimmie blinked up at Uthacalthing in confusion. She had been selected for this duty because she knew
GalSeven. But that was a far cry from penetrating the arcana
that were going on here.

"Y-yessir. It, it seems like the kind thing to do."

Uthacalthing nodded, and smiled at Kault. "There you
are, my dear colleague. Not merely correct, but *kind*. It is
well when we elders learn from such wise precociousness,
and add that quality to our own actions, is it not?"

For the first time, he saw the Thennanin blink. Turmoil
radiated from the creature. At last though, relief won out
over suspicion that he was being played for the fool. Kault
bowed to Uthacalthing. And then, because Uthacalthing had
included her in the conversation, he added a brief, shallow
nod to the little chimmie.

"For my clientsss and myssselfff, I thank you," he said
awkwardly in Anglic. Kault snapped his elbow spikes, and his
Ynnin clients followed him as he lumbered into the floater.
The closing cupola cut off the sharp dome light at last. The
chims from the Library looked at Uthacalthing gratefully.

The floater rose on its gravity cushion and moved off
rapidly. Uthacalthing's driver held the door of his own wheelcar
for him, but he stretched his arms and inhaled deeply. "I am
thinking that it might be a nice idea to go for a walk," he told
her. "The embassy is only a short distance from here. Why
don't you take a few hours off, corporal, and spend some time
with your family and friends?"

"B-but ser . . ."

"I will be all right," he said firmly. He bowed, and felt
her rush of innocent joy at the simple courtesy. She bowed
deeply in return.

Delightful creatures, Uthacalthing thought as he watched the car drive off. *I have met a few neo-chimpanzees who even seem to have the glimmerings of a true sense of humor.*

I do hope the species survives.

He started walking. Soon he had left the clamor of the Library behind him and passed into a residential neighborhood. The breeze had left the night air clear, and the city's soft lights did not drive away the flickering stars. At this time the Galactic rim was a ragged spill of diamonds across the sky. There were no traces to be seen of the battle in space; it had been too small a skirmish to leave much visible residue.

All around Uthacalthing were sounds that told of the difference of this evening. There were distant sirens and the growl of aircraft passing overhead. On nearly every block he heard someone crying . . . voices, human or chim, shouting or murmuring in frustration and fear. On the fluttering level of empathy, waves beat up against one another in a froth of emotion. His corona could not deflect the inhabitants' dread as they awaited morning.

Uthacalthing did not try to keep it out as he strolled up dimly lit streets lined with decorative trees. He dipped his tendrils into the churning emotional flux and drew forth above him a strange new glyph. It floated, nameless and terrible, Time's ageless threat made momentarily palpable.

Uthacalthing smiled an ancient, special kind of smile. And at that moment nobody, not even in the darkness, could possibly have mistaken him for a human being.

There are many paths, . . . he thought, again savoring the open, undisciplined nuances of Anglic.

He left the thing he had made to hang in the air, dissolving slowly behind him, as he walked under the slowly wheeling pattern of the stars.

10

Robert

Robert awoke two hours before dawn.

There was a period of disorientation as the strange feelings and images of sleep slowly dissipated. He rubbed his eyes, trying to clear his head of muzzy, clouded confusion.

He had been running, he recalled. Running as one does sometimes but only in dreams—in long, floating steps that reach for leagues and seem barely to touch down. Around him had shifted and drifted vague shapes, mysteries, and half-born images that slipped out of reach even as his waking mind tried to recall them.

Robert looked over at Athaclena, lying nearby in her own sleeping bag. Her brown Tymbrimi ruff—that tapered helm of soft brown fur—was puffed out. The silvery tendrils of her corona waved delicately, as if probing and grappling with something invisible in the space overhead.

She sighed and spoke very low—a few short phrases in the rapid, highly syllabic Tymbrimi dialect of Galactic Seven.

Perhaps that explained his own strange dreams, Robert realized. He must have been picking up traces of hers!

Watching the waving tendrils, he blinked. For just a moment it had seemed as if something *was* there, floating in the air just above the sleeping alien girl. It had been like . . . like . . .

Robert frowned, shaking his head. It hadn't been *like* anything at all. The very act of trying to compare it to something else seemed to drive the thing away even as he thought about it.

64

Athaclena sighed and turned over. Her corona settled down. There were no more half glimmers in the dimness.

Robert slid out of his bag and fumbled for his boots before standing. He felt his way around the towering spine-stone beneath which they had made camp. There was barely enough starlight to find a path among the strange monoliths.

He came to a promontory looking over toward the westward mountain chain, and the northern plains to his right. Below this ridgetop vantage point there lay a gently rippling sea of dark woods. The trees filled the air with a damp, heavy aroma.

Resting his back against a spine-stone, he sat down on the ground to try to think.

If only the adventure were all there was to this trip. An idyllic interlude in the Mountains of Mulun in the company of an alien beauty. But there was no forgetting, no escaping the guilty sureness that he should not be here. He really ought to be with his classmates—with his militia unit—facing the troubles alongside them.

That was not to be, however. Once again, his mother's career had interfered with his own life. It was not the first time Robert had wished he were not the son of a politician.

He watched the stars, sparkling in bright strokes that followed the meeting of two Galactic spiral arms.

Perhaps if I had known more adversity in my life, I might be better prepared for what's to come. Better able to accept disappointment.

It wasn't just that he was the son of the Planetary Coordinator, with all of the advantages that came with status. It went beyond that.

All through childhood he had noticed that where other boys had stumbled and suffered growing pains, he had always somehow had the knack of moving gracefully. Where most had groped their way in awkwardness and embarrassment toward adolescence and sexuality, he had slipped into pleasure and popularity with all the comfort and ease of putting on an old shoe.

His mother—and his starfarer father, whenever Sam Tennace sojourned on Garth—had always emphasized that he should *watch* the interactions of his peers, not simply let things happen and accept them as inevitable. And indeed, he began to see how, in every age group, there were a few like him—for whom growing up was *easier* somehow. They stepped.

lightly through the morass of adolescence while everyone else slogged, overjoyed to find an occasional patch of solid ground. And it seemed many of those lucky ones accepted their happy fate as if it were some sign of divine election. The same was true of the most popular girls. They had no empathy, no compassion for more normal kids.

In Robert's case, he had never sought a reputation as a playboy. But one had come, over time, almost against his will. In his heart a secret fear had started to grow: a superstitition that he had confided in nobody. Did the universe balance all things? Did it take away to compensate for whatever it gave? The Cult of Ifni was supposed to be a starfarer's joke. And yet sometimes things seemed so *contrived!*

It was silly to suppose that trials only hardened men, automatically making them wise. He knew many who were stupid, arrogant, and mean, in spite of having suffered.

Still . . .

Like many humans, he sometimes envied the handsome, flexible, self-sufficient Tymbrimi. A young race by Galactic standards, they were nevertheless old and galaxy-wise compared with Mankind. Humanity had discovered sanity, peace, and a science of mind only a generation before Contact. There were still plenty of kinks to be worked out of Terragens society. The Tymbrimi, in comparison, seemed to know themselves so well.

Is that the basic reason why I am attracted to Athaclena? Symbolically she is the elder, the more knowledgeable one. It gives me an opportunity to be awkward and stumble, and enjoy the role.

It was all so confusing, and Robert wasn't even certain of his own feelings. He was having fun up here in the mountains with Athaclena, and that made him ashamed. He resented his mother bitterly for sending him, and felt guilty about that as well.

Oh, if only I'd been allowed to fight! Combat, at least, was straightforward and easy to understand. It was ancient, honorable, simple.

Robert looked up quickly. There, among the stars, a pinpoint had flared up to momentary brilliance. As he watched, two more sudden brightnesses burst forth, then another. The sharp, glowing sparks lasted long enough for him to note their positions.

The pattern was too regular to be an accident . . . twenty

degree intervals above the equator, from the Sphinx all the way across to the Batman, where the red planet Tloona shone in the middle of the ancient hero's belt.

So, it has come. The destruction of the synchronous satellite network had been expected, but it was startling actually to witness it. Of course this meant actual landings would not be long delayed.

Robert felt a heaviness and hoped that not too many of his human and chim friends had died.

I never found out if I had what it takes when things really counted. Now maybe I never will.

He was resolved about one thing. He would do the job he had been assigned—escorting a noncombatant alien into the mountains and supposed safety. There was one duty he had to perform tonight, while Athaclena slept. As silently as he could, Robert returned to their backpacks. He pulled the radio set from his lower left pouch and began disassembling it in the dark.

He was halfway finished when another sudden brightening made him look up at the eastern sky. A bolide streaked flame across the glittering starfield, leaving glowing embers in its wake. Something was entering fast, burning as it penetrated the atmosphere.

The debris of war.

Robert stood up and watched the manmade meteor lay a fiery trail across the sky. It disappeared behind a range of hills not more than twenty kilometers away. Perhaps much closer.

"God keep you," he whispered to the warriors whose ship it must have been.

He had no fear of blessing his enemies, for it was clear which side needed help tonight, and would for a long time to come.

11

Galactics

The Suzerain of Propriety moved about the bridge of the flagship in short skips and hops, enjoying the pleasure of pacing while Gubru and Kwackoo soldiery ducked out of the way.

It might be a long time before the Gubru high priest would enjoy such freedom of movement again. After the occupation force landed, the Suzerain would not be able to set foot on the "ground" for many miktaars. Not until propriety was assured and consolidation complete could it touch the soil of the planet that lay just ahead of the advancing armada.

The other two leaders of the invasion force—the Suzerain of Beam and Talon and the Suzerain of Cost and Caution—did not have to operate under such restrictions. That was all right. The military and the bureaucracy had their own functions. But to the Suzerain of Propriety was given the task of overseeing Appropriateness of Behavior for the Gubru expedition. And to do that the priest would have to remain perched.

Far across the command bridge, the Suzerain of Cost and Caution could be heard complaining. There had been unexpected losses in the furious little fight the humans had put up. Every ship put out of commission hurt the Gubru cause in these dangerous times.

Foolish, short-sighted carping, the Suzerain of Propriety thought. The physical damage done by the humans' resistance had been far less significant than the ethical and legal harm. Because the brief fight had been so sharp and effec-

68

tive, it could not simply be ignored. It would have to be *credited*.

The Earth wolflings had recorded, in action, their opposition to the arrival of Gubru might. Unexpectedly, they had done it with meticulous attention to the Protocols of War.

> They may be more than mere clever beasts—
>> More than beasts—
> Perhaps they and their clients should be studied—
>> Studied—zzooon

. That gesture of resistance by the tiny Earthling flotilla meant that the Suzerain would have to remain perched for at least the initial part of the occupation. It would have to find an excuse, now, the sort of *casus belli* that would let the Gubru proclaim to the Five Galaxies that the Earthlings' lease on Garth was null and void.

Until that happened, the Rules of War applied, and in enforcing them, the Suzerain of Propriety knew there would be conflicts with the other two commanders. Its future lovers and competitors. Correct policy demanded tension among them, even if some of the laws the priest had to enforce struck it, deep down, as stupid.

> Oh for the time, may it be soon—
>> Soon, when we are released from rules—zzooon
> Soon, when Change rewards the virtuous—
>> When the Progenitors return—zzooon

The Suzerain fluttered its downy coat. It commanded one of its servitors, a fluffy, imperturbable Kwackoo, to bring a feather-blower and groomer.

> The Earthlings will stumble—
> They will give us justification—zzooon

12

Athaclena

That morning Athaclena could tell that something had happened the night before. But Robert said little in answer to her questions. His crude but effective empathy shield blocked her attempts at *kenning*.

Athaclena tried not to feel insulted. After all, her human friend had only just begun learning to use his modest talents. He could not know the many subtle ways an empath could use to show a desire for privacy. Robert only knew how to close the door completely.

Breakfast was quiet. When Robert spoke she answered in monosyllables. Logically, Athaclena could understand his guardedness, but then there was no rule that said *she* had to be outgoing, either.

Low clouds crested the ridgelines that morning, to be sliced by rows of serrated spine-stones. It made for an eerie, foreboding scene. They hiked through the tattered wisps of brumous fog in silence, gradually climbing higher in the foothills leading toward the Mountains of Mulun. The air was still and seemed to carry a vague tension Athaclena could not identify. It tugged at her mind, drawing forth unbeckoned memories.

She recalled a time when she had accompanied her mother into the northern mountains on Tymbrim—riding gurval-back up a trail only slightly wider than this one—to attend a Ceremony of Uplift for the Tytlal.

Uthacalthing had been away on a diplomatic mission, and nobody knew yet what type of transport her father would be able to use for his return trip. It was an all-important

70

question, for if he was able to come all the way via A-level
hyperspace and transfer points, he could return home in a
hundred days or less. If forced to travel by D-level—or
worse, normal space—Uthacalthing might be away for the
rest of their natural lives.

The Diplomatic Service tried to inform its officers' families as soon as these matters were clear, but on this occasion
they had taken far too long. Athaclena and her mother had
started to become public nuisances, throwing irksome anxiety
shimmers all over their neighborhood. At that point it had
been politely hinted that they ought to get out of the city for
a while. The Service offered them tickets to go watch the
representatives of the Tytlal undergo another rite of passage
on the long path of Uplift.

Robert's slick mind shield reminded her of Mathicluanna's
closely guarded pain during that slow ride into purple-frosted
hills. Mother and daughter hardly spoke to each other at all
as they passed through broad fallow parklands and at last
arrived at the grassy plain of an ancient volcano caldera.
There, near a solitary symmetrical hilltop, thousands of
Tymbrimi had gathered near a swarm of brightly colored
canopies to witness the Acceptance and Choice of the Tytlal.

Observers had come from many distinguished starfaring
clans—Synthians, Kanten, Mrgh'4luargi—and of course a
gaggle of cachinnatous humans. The Earthlings mixed with
their Tymbrimi allies down near the refreshment tables, making a boisterous high time of it. She remembered her attitude
then, upon seeing so many of the atrichic, bromopnean
creatures. *Was I really such a snob?* Athaclena wondered.

She had sniffed disdainfully at the noise the humans
made with their loud, low laughter. Their strange, applanate
stares were everywhere as they strutted about displaying
their bulging muscles. Even their females looked like caricatures of Tymbrimi weightlifters.

Of course, Athaclena had barely embarked on adolescence back on that day. Now, on reflection, she recalled that
her own people were just as enthusiastic and flamboyant as
the humans, waving their hands intricately and sparking the
air with brief, flashing glyphs. This was, after all, a great day.
For the Tytlal were to "choose" their patrons, and their new
Uplift Sponsors.

Various dignitaries rested under the bright canopies. Of
course the immediate patrons of the Tymbrimi, the Caltmour,

could not attend, being tragically extinct. But their colors and
sigil were in view, in honor of those who had given the
Tymbrimi the gift of sapience.

Those present were honored, however, by a delegation
of the chattering, stalk-legged Brma, who had uplifted the
Caltmour long, long ago.

Athaclena remembered gasping, her corona crackling in
surprise, when she saw that another shape curled under a
dark brown covering, high upon the ceremonial mount. It
was a Krallnith! The seniormost race in their patron-line had
sent a representative! The Krallnith were nearly torpid by
now, having given over most of their waning enthusiasm to
strange forms of meditation. It was commonly assumed they
would not be around many more epochs. It was an honor to
have one of them attend, and offer its blessing to the latest
members of their clan.

Of course, it was the Tytlal themselves who were the
center of attention. Wearing short silvery robes, they nonetheless looked much like those Earth creatures known as
otters. The Tytlal legatees fairly radiated pride as they prepared for their latest rite of Uplift.

"Look," Athaclena's mother had pointed. "The Tytlal
have elected their muse-poet, Sustruk, to represent them.
Do you recall meeting him, Athaclena?"

Naturally she remembered. It had been only the year
before, when Sustruk visited their home back in the city.
Uthacalthing had brought the Tytlal genius by to meet his
wife and daughter, shortly before he was to leave on his latest
mission.

"Sustruk's poetry is simpleminded doggerel," Athaclena
muttered.

Mathicluanna looked at her sharply. Then her corona
waved. The glyph she crafted was *sh'cha'kuon*, the dark
mirror only your own mother knew how to hold up before
you. Athaclena's resentment reflected back at her, easily seen
for what it was. She looked away, shamed.

It was, after all, unfair to blame the poor Tytlal for
reminding her of her absent father.

The ceremony was indeed beautiful. A glyph-choir of
Tymbrimi from the colony-world Juthtath performed "The
Apotheosis of Lerensini," and even the bare-pated humans
stared in slack-jawed awe, obviously *kenning* some of the
intricate, floating harmonies. Only the bluff, impenetrable

Thennanin ambassadors seemed untouched, and they did not seem to mind at all being left out.

After that the Brma singer Kuff-Kufft crooned an ancient, atonal paean to the Progenitors.

One bad moment for Athaclena came when the hushed audience listened to a composition specially created for the occasion by one of the twelve Great Dreamers of Earth, the whale named Five Bubble Spirals. While whales were not officially sentient beings, that fact did not keep them from being honored treasures. That they dwelled on Earth, under the care of "wolfling" humans, was one more cause for resentment by some of the more conservative Galactic clans.

Athaclena recalled sitting down and covering her ears while everyone else swayed happily to the eerie cetacean music. To her it was worse than the sound of houses falling. Mathicluanna's glance conveyed her worry. *My strange daughter, what are we to do with you?* At least Athaclena's mother did not chide aloud or in glyph, embarrassing her in public.

At last, to Athaclena's great relief, the entertainment ended. It was the turn of the Tytlal delegation, the time of Acceptance and Choice.

Led by Sustruk, their great poet, the delegation approached the supine Krallnith dignitary and bowed low. Then they made their allegiance to the Brma representatives, and afterward expressed polite submissiveness to the humans and other patron-class alien visitors.

The Tymbrimi Master of Uplift received obeisance last. Sustruk and his consort, a Tytlal scientist named Kihimik, stepped ahead of the rest of their delegation as the mated pair chosen above all others to be "race representatives." Alternately, they replied as the Master of Uplift read a list of formal questions and solemnly noted their answers.

Then the pair came under the scrutiny of the Critics from the Galactic Uplift Institute.

Thus far it had been a perfunctory version of the Fourth Stage Test of Sentience. But now there was one more chance for the Tytlal to fail. One of the Galactics focusing sophisticated instruments on Sustruk and Kihimik, was a *Soro* . . . no friend of Athaclena's clan. Possibly the Soro was looking for an excuse, *any* excuse, to embarrass the Tymbrimi by rejecting their clients.

Discreetly buried under the caldera was equipment that had cost Athaclena's race plenty. Right now the scrutiny of the Tytlal was being cast all through the Five Galaxies. There was much to be proud of today, but also some potential for humiliation.

Of course Sustruk and Kihimik passed easily. They bowed low to each of the alien examiners. If the Soro examiner was disappointed, she did not show it.

The delegation of furry, short-legged Tytlal ambled up to a cleared circle at the top of the hill. They began to sing, swaying together in that queer, loose-limbed manner so common among the creatures of their native planet, the fallow world where they had evolved into pre-sentience, where the Tymbrimi had found and adopted them for the long process of Uplift.

Technicians focused the amplifier which would display for all those assembled, and billions on other worlds, the choice the Tytlal had made. Underfoot, a deep rumbling told of powerful engines at work.

Theoretically, the creatures could even decide to reject their patrons and abandon Uplift altogether, though there were so many rules and qualifications that in practice it was almost never allowed. Anyway, nothing like that was expected on that day. The Tymbrimi had excellent relations with their clients.

Still, a dry, anxious rustling swept the crowd as the Rite of Acceptance approached completion. The swaying Tytlal moaned, and a low hum rose from the amplifier. Overhead a holographic image took shape, and the crowd roared with laughter and approval. It was the face of a Tymbrimi, of course, and one everyone recognized at once. Oshoyoythuna, Trickster of the City of Foyon, who had included several Tytlal as helpers in some of his most celebrated jests.

Of course the Tytlal had reaffirmed the Tymbrimi as their patrons, but choosing Oshoyoythuna as their symbol went far beyond that! It exclaimed the Tytlal's pride in what it really meant to be part of their clan.

After the cheering and laughter died down, there remained only one part of the ceremony to finish, the selection of the Stage Consort, the species who would speak for the Tytlal during the next phase of their Uplift. The humans, in their strange tongue, called it the Uplift Midwife.

The Stage Consort had to be of a race outside of the Tymbrimi's own clan. And while the position was mostly ceremonial, a Consort could legally intervene on the new client species' behalf, if the Uplift process appeared to be in trouble. Wrong choices in the past had created terrible problems.

No one had any idea what race the Tytlal had chosen. It was one of those rare decisions that even the most meddle-some patrons, such as the Soro, had to leave to their charges.

Sustruk and Kihimik crooned once more, and even from her position at the back of the crowd Athaclena could sense a growing feeling of anticipation rising from the furry little clients. The little devils had cooked up something, that was certain!

Again, the ground shuddered, the amplifier murmured once more, and holographic projectors formed a blue cloudi-ness over the crest of the hill. In it there seemed to float murky shapes, flicking back and forth as if through backlit water.

Her corona offered no clue, for the image was strictly visual. She resented the humans their sharper eyesight as a shout of surprise rose from the area where most of the Earthlings had congregated. All around her, Tymbrimi were standing up and staring. She blinked. Then Athaclena and her mother joined the rest in amazed disbelief.

One of the murky figures flicked up to the foreground and stopped, grinning out at the audience, displaying a long, narrow grin of white, needle-sharp teeth. There was a glitter-ing eye, and bubbles rose from its glistening gray brow.

The stunned silence lengthened. For in all of Ifni's starfield, nobody had expected the Tytlal to choose *dolphins*!

The visiting Galactics were stricken dumb. *Neo-dolphins* . . . why the second client race of Earth were the youngest acknowledged sapients in all five galaxies—much younger than the Tytlal themselves! This was unprecedented. It was astonishing.

It was . . .

It was hilarious! The Tymbrimi cheered. Their laughter rose, high and clear. As one, their coronae sparkled upward a single, coruscating glyph of approval so vivid that even the Thennanin Ambassador seemed to blink and take notice. Seeing that their allies weren't offended, the humans joined in, hooting and slapping their hands together with intimidat-ing energy.

Kihimik and most of the other assembled Tytlal bowed, accepting their patrons' accolade. Good clients, it seemed they had worked hard to come up with a fine jest for this important day. Only Sustruk himself stood rigid at the rear, still quivering from the strain.

All around Athaclena crested waves of approval and joy. She heard her mother's laughter, joining in with the others.

But Athaclena herself had backed away, edging out of the cheering crowd until there was room to turn and flee. In a full *gheer* flux, she ran and ran until she passed the caldera's rim and could drop down the trail out of sight or sound. There, overlooking the beautiful Valley of Lingering Shadows, she collapsed to the ground while the waves of enzyme reaction shook her.

That horrible dolphin . . .

Never since that day had she confided in anyone what she had seen in the eye of the imaged cetacean. Not to her mother, nor even her father, had she ever told the truth . . . that she had sensed deep within that projected hologram a *glyph*, one rising from Sustruk himself, the poet of the Tytlal.

Those present thought it was all a grand jest, a magnificent blague. They thought they knew why the Tytlal had chosen the youngest race of Earth as their Stage Consort . . . to honor the clan with a grand and harmless joke. By choosing dolphins, they seemed to be saying that they *needed* no protector, that they loved and honored their Tymbrimi patrons without reservation. And by selecting the humans' second clients, they also tweaked those stodgy old Galactic clans who so disapproved of the Tymbrimi's friendship with wolflings. It was a fine gesture. Delicious.

Had Athaclena been the only one, then, to see the deeper truth? Had she imagined it? Many years later on a distant planet, Athaclena shivered as she recalled that day.

Had she been the only one to pick up Sustruk's third harmonic of laughter and pain and confusion? The muse-poet died only days after that episode, and he took his secret with him to his grave.

Only Athaclena seemed to sense that the Ceremony had been no joke, after all, that Sustruk's image had not come from his thoughts but out of *Time*! The Tytlal had, indeed, chosen their protectors, and the choice was in desperate earnest.

Now, only a few years later, the Five Galaxies had been sent into turmoil over certain discoveries made by a certain obscure client race, the youngest of them all. Dolphins.

Oh, Earthlings, she thought as she followed Robert higher

into the Mountains of Mulun. *What have you done?*

No, that was not the right question.

What, oh what is it you are planning to become?

That afternoon the two wanderers encountered a steep field of plate ivy. A plain of glossy, wide-brimmed plants covered the southeastward slope of the ridge like green, overlapping scales on the flank of some great, slumbering beast. Their path to the mountains was blocked.

"I'll bet you're wondering how we'll get across all this to the other side," Robert asked.

"The slope looks treacherous," Athaclena ventured. "And it stretches far in both directions. I suppose we'll have to turn around."

There was something in the fringes of Robert's mind, though, that made that seem unlikely. "These are fascinating plants," he said, squatting next to one of the plates—a shieldlike inverted bowl almost two meters across. He grabbed its edge and yanked backward hard. The plate stretched away from the tightly bound field until Athaclena could see a tough, springy root attached to its center. She moved closer to help him pull, wondering what he had in mind.

"The colony buds a new generation of these caps every few weeks, each layer overlapping the prior one," Robert explained as he grunted and tugged the fibrous root taut.

"In late autumn the last layers of caps flower and become wafer thin. They break off and catch the strong winter winds, sailing into the sky, millions of 'em. It's quite a sight, believe me, all those rainbow-colored kites drifting under the clouds, even if it is a hazard to flyers."

"They are seeds, then?" Athaclena asked.

"Well, spore carriers, actually. And most of the pods that litter the Sind in early winter are sterile. Seems the plate ivy used to rely on some pollinating creature that went extinct during the Bururalli Holocaust. Just one more problem for the ecological recovery teams to deal with." Robert shrugged. "Right now, though, in the springtime, these early caps are rigid and strong. It'll take some doing to cut one free."

Robert drew his knife and reached under to slice away at the taut fibers holding the cap down. The strips parted suddenly, releasing the tension and throwing Athaclena back with the bulky plate on top of her.

"Oops! I'm sorry, Clennie." She felt Robert's effort to

suppress laughter as he helped her struggle out from under the heavy cap. *Just like a boy . . .* Athaclena thought.

"Are you okay?"

"I am fine," she answered stiffly, and dusted herself off. Tipped over, the plate's inner, concave side looked like a bowl with a thick, central stem of ragged, sticky strands.

"Good. Then why don't you help me carry it over to that sandy bank, near the dropoff."

The field of plate ivy stretched around the prominence of the ridge, surrounding it on three sides. Together they hefted the detached cap over to where the bumpy green slope began, laying it inner face up.

Robert set to work trimming the ragged interior of the plate. After a few minutes he stood back and examined his handiwork. "This should do." He nudged the plate with his foot. "Your father wanted me to show you everything I could about Garth. In my opinion your education'd be truly lacking if I never taught you to ride plate ivy."

Athaclena looked from the upended plate to the scree of slick caps. "Do you mean . . ." But Robert was already loading their gear into the upturned bowl. "You cannot be serious, Robert."

He shrugged, looking up at her sidelong. "We can backtrack a mile or two and find a way around all this, if you like."

"You *aren't* joking." Athacleana sighed. It was bad enough that her father and her friends back home thought her too timid. She could not refuse a dare offered by this *human*. "Very well, Robert, show me how it is done."

Robert stepped into the plate and checked its balance. Then he motioned for her to join him. She climbed into the rocking thing and sat where Robert indicated, in front of him with her knees on either side of the central stump.

It was then, with her corona waving in nervous agitation, that it happened again. Athaclena sensed something that made her convulsively clutch the rubbery sides of the plate, setting it rocking.

"Hey! Watch it, will you? You almost tipped us over!"

Athaclena grabbed his arm while she scanned the valley below. All around her face a haze of tiny tendrils fluttered. "I *kenn* it again. It's down there, Robert. Somewhere in the forest!"

"What? *What's* down there?"

"The entity I *kenned* earlier! The thing that was neither

man nor chimpanzee! It was a little like either, and yet different. And it reeks with Potential!"

Robert shaded his eyes. "Where? Can you point to it?"

Athaclena concentrated. She tried localizing the faint brush of emotions.

"It . . . it is gone," she sighed at last.

Robert radiated nervousness. "Are you sure it wasn't just a chim? There are lots of them up in these hills, seisin gatherers and conservation workers."

Athaclena cast a *palang* glyph. Then, recalling that Robert wasn't likely to notice the sparkling essence of frustration. She *shrugged* to indicate approximately the same nuance.

"No, Robert. I have met many neo-chimpanzees, remember? The being I sensed was different! I'd swear it wasn't fully sapient, for one thing. And, there was a feeling of *sadness*, of submerged power. . . ."

Athaclena turned to Robert, suddenly excited. "Can it have been a 'Garthling'? Oh, let's hurry! We might be able to get closer!" She settled in around the center post and looked up at Robert expectantly.

"The famed Tymbrimi adaptability," Robert sighed. "All of a sudden you're *anxious* to go! And here I'd been hoping to impress and arouse you with a white-knuckler ride."

Boys, she thought again, shaking her head vigorously. *How can they think such things, even in jest?*

"Stop joking and let's be off!" she urged.

He settled into the plate behind her. Athaclena held on tightly to his knees. Her tendrils waved about his face, but Robert did not complain. "All right, here we go."

His musty human aroma was close around her as he pushed off and the plate began to slip forward.

It all came back to Robert as their makeshift sled accelerated, skidding and bouncing over the slick, convex caps of plate ivy. Athaclena gripped his knees tightly, her laughter higher and more bell-like than a human girl's. Robert, too, laughed and shouted, holding Athaclena as he leaned one way and then the other to steer the madly hopping sled.

Must've been eleven years old when I did this last.

Every jounce and leap made his heart pound. Not even an amusement park gravity ride was like this! Athaclena let out a squeak of exhilaration as they sailed free and landed again with a rubbery rebound. Her corona was a storm of silvery threads that seemed to crackle with excitement.

I only hope I remember how to control this thing right.

Maybe it was his rustiness. Or it might have been Athaclena's presence, distracting him. But Robert was just a little late reacting when the near-oak stump—a remnant of the forest that had once grown on this slope—loomed suddenly in their path.

Athaclena laughed in delight as Robert leaned hard to the left, swerving their crude boat wildly. By the time she sensed his sudden change of mood their spin was already a tumble, out of control. Then their plate caught on something unseen. Impact swerved them savagely, sending the contents of the sled flying.

At that moment luck and Tymbrimi instincts were with Athaclena. Stress hormones surged and reflexes tucked her head down, rolling her into a ball. On impact her body made its own sled, bouncing and skidding atop the plates like a rubbery ball.

It all happened in a blur. Giants' fists struck her, tossed her about. A great roar filled her ears and her corona blazed as she spun and fell, again and again.

Finally Athaclena tumbled to a halt, still curled up tight, just short of the forest on the valley floor. At first she could only lie there as the *gheer* enzymes made her pay the price for her quick reflexes. Breath came in long, shuddering gasps; her high and low kidneys throbbed, struggling with the sudden overload.

And there was *pain*. Athaclena had trouble localizing it. She seemed only to have picked up a few bruises and scrapes. So where . . . ?

Realization came in a rush as she uncurled and opened her eyes. The pain was coming from Robert! Her Earthling guide was broadcasting blinding surges of agony!

She got up gingerly, still dizzy from reaction, and shaded her eyes to look around the bright hillside. The human wasn't in sight, so she sought him with her corona. The searing painflood led her stumbling awkwardly over the glossy plates to a point not far from the upended sled.

Robert's legs kicked weakly from under a layer of broad plate ivy caps. An effort to back out culminated in a low, muffled moan. A sparkling shower of hot *agones* seemed to home right in on Athaclena's corona.

She knelt beside him. "Robert! Are you caught on something? Can you breathe?"

What foolishness, she realized, asking multiple questions when she could tell the human was barely even conscious!

I must do something. Athaclena drew her jack-laser from her boot top and attacked the plate ivy, starting well away from Robert, slicing stems and grunting as she heaved aside the caps, one at a time.

Knotty, musky vines remained tangled around the human's head and arms, pinning him to the thicket. "Robert, I'm going to cut near your head. Don't move!"

Robert groaned something indecipherable. His right arm was badly twisted, and so much distilled ache fizzed around him that she had to withdraw her corona to keep from fainting from the overload. Aliens weren't supposed to commune this strongly with Tymbrimi! At least she had never believed it possible before this.

Robert gasped as she heaved the last shriveled cap away from his face. His eyes were closed, and his mouth moved as if he were silently talking to himself. *What is he doing now?*

She felt the overtones of some obviously human rite-of-discipline. It had something to do with numbers and counting. Perhaps it was that "self-hypnosis" technique all humans were taught in school. Though primitive, it seemed to be doing Robert some good.

"I'm going to cut away the roots binding your arm now," she told him.

He jerked his head in a nod. "Hurry, Clennie. I've . . . I've never had to block this much pain before. . . ." He let out a shivering sigh as the last rootlet parted. His arm sprang free, floppy and broken.

What now? Athaclena worried. It was always hazardous to interfere with an injured member of an alien race. Lack of training was only part of the problem. One's most basic succoring instincts might be entirely wrong for helping someone of another species.

Athaclena grabbed a handful of coronal tendrils and twisted them in indecision. *Some things have to be universal!*

Make sure the victim keeps breathing. That she had done automatically.

Try to stop leaks of bodily fluids. All she had to go on

were some old, pre-Contact "movies" she and her father had watched on the journey to Garth—dealing with ancient Earth creatures called cops and robbers. According to those films, Robert's wounds might be called "only scratches." But she suspected those ancient story-records weren't particularly strong on realism.

Oh, if only humans weren't so frail!

Athaclena rushed to Robert's backpack, seeking the radio in the lower side pouch. Aid could arrive from Port Helenia in less than an hour, and rescue officials could tell her what to do in the meantime.

The radio was simple, of Tymbrimi design, but nothing happened when she touched the power switch.

No. It has to work! She stabbed it again. But the indicator stayed blank.

Athaclena popped the back cover. The transmitter crystal had been removed. She blinked in consternation. How could this be?

They were cut off from help. She was completely on her own.

"Robert," she said as she knelt by him again. "You must guide me. I cannot help you unless you tell me what to do!"

The human still counted from one to ten, over and over. She had to repeat herself until, at last, his eyes came into focus. "I . . . I think my arm's b- busted, Clennie. . . ." He gasped. "Help get me out of the sun . . . then, use drugs. . . ."

His presence seemed to fade away, and his eyes rolled up as unconsciousness overcame him. Athaclena did not approve of a nervous system that overloaded with pain, leaving its owner unable to help himself. It wasn't Robert's fault. He was brave, but his brain had shorted out.

There was one advantage, of course. Fainting damped down his broadcast agony. That made it easier for her to drag him backward over the spongy, uneven field of plate ivy, attempting all the while not to shake his broken right arm unduly.

Big-boned, huge-thewed, overmuscled human! She cast a glyph of great pungency as she pulled his heavy body all the way to the shady edge of the forest.

Athaclena retrieved their backpacks and quickly found Robert's first aid kit. There was a tincture she had seen him use only two days before, when he had caught his finger on a wood sliver. This she slathered liberally over his lacerations.

Robert moaned and shifted a little. She could feel his
mind struggle upward against the pain. Soon, half automatically, he was mumbling numbers to himself once again.

Her lips moved as she read the Anglic instructions on a
container of "flesh foam," then she applied the sprayer onto
his cuts, sealing them under a medicinal layer.

That left the arm—and the agony. Robert had mentioned
drugs. But *which* drugs?

There were many little ampules, clearly labeled in both
Anglic and GalSeven. But directions were sparse. There was
no provision for a non-Terran having to treat a human without benefit of advice.

She used logic. Emergency medicines would be pack-
aged in gas ampules for easy, quick administration. Athaclena
pulled out three likely looking glassine cylinders. She bent
forward until the silvery strands of her corona fell around
Robert's face, bringing close his human aroma—musty and in
this case so very male. "Robert," she whispered carefully in
Anglic. "I know you can hear me. Rise within yourself! I need
your wisdom out in the here-and-now."

Apparently she was only distracting him from his rite-of-
discipline, for she sensed the pain increase. Robert grimaced
and counted out loud.

Tymbrimi do not curse as humans do. A purist would say
they make "stylistic statements of record" instead. But at
times like this few would be able to tell the difference.
Athaclena muttered caustically in her native tongue.

Clearly Robert was not an adept, even at this crude
"self-hypnosis" technique. His pain pummeled the fringes of
her mind, and Athaclena let out a small trill, like a sigh. She
was unaccustomed to having to keep out such an assault. The
fluttering of her eyelids blurred vision as would a human's
tears.

There was only one way, and it meant exposing herself
more than she was accustomed, even with her family. The
prospect was daunting, but there didn't seem to be any
choice. In order to get through to him at all, she had to get a
lot closer than this.

"I . . . I am here, Robert. Share it with me."

She opened up to the narrow flood of sharp, discrete
agones—so un-Tymbrimi, and yet so eerily familiar, almost as
if they were *recognizable* somehow. The quanta of agony

dripped to an uneven pump beat. They were little hot, searing balls—lumps of molten metal.

. . . lumps of metal . . . ?

The weirdness almost startled Athaclena out of contact. She had never before experienced a *metaphor* so vividly. It was more than just a comparison, stronger than saying that one thing was *like* another. For a moment, the agones had *been* glowing iron globs that burned to touch. . . .

To be human is strange indeed.

Athaclena tried to ignore the imagery. She moved toward the *agone* nexus until a barrier stopped her. *Another metaphor?* This time, it was a swiftly flowing stream of pain—a river that lay across her path.

What she needed was an *usunltlan*, a protection field to carry her up the flood to its source. But how did one shape the mind-stuff of a human!

Even as she wondered, drifting smoke-images seemed to fall together around her. Mist patterns flowed, solidified, became a shape. Athaclena suddenly found she could visualize herself standing in a small boat! And in her hands she held an oar.

Was this how *usunltlan* manifested in a human's mind? As a *metaphor?*

Amazed, she began to row upstream, into the stinging maelstrom.

Forms floated by, crowding and jostling in the fog surrounding her. Now one blur drifted past as a distorted face. Next, some bizarre animal figure snarled at her. Most of the grotesque things she glimpsed could never have existed in any real universe.

Unaccustomed to *visualizing* the networks of a mind, it took Athaclena some moments to realize that the shapes represented memories, conflicts, emotions.

So many emotions! Athaclena felt an urge to flee. One might go mad in this place!

It was Tymbrimi curiosity that made her stay. That and duty.

This is so strange, she thought as she rowed through the metaphorical swamp. Half blinded by drifting drops of pain, she stared in wonderment. Oh, to be a true telepath and *know*, instead of having to guess, what all these symbols meant.

There were easily as many drives as in a Tymbrimi

mind. Some of the strange images and sensations struck her
as familiar. Perhaps they harkened back to times before her
race or Robert's learned speech—her own people by Uplift
and humans doing it the hard way—back when two tribes of
clever animals lived very similar lives in the wild, on far
separated worlds.

It was most odd seeing with two pairs of eyes at once.
There was the set that looked in amazement about the metaphorical realm and her real pair which saw Robert's face
inches from her own, under the canopy of her corona.

The human blinked rapidly. He had stopped counting in
his confusion. She, at least, understood some of what was
happening. But Robert was feeling something truly bizarre. A
word came to her: *déjà vu* . . . quick half-rememberings of
things at once both new and old.

Athaclena concentrated and crafted a delicate glyph, a
fluttering beacon to beat in resonance with his deepest brain
harmonic. Robert gasped and she felt him reach out after it.

His metaphorical self took shape alongside her in the little
boat, holding another oar. It seemed to be the way of things,
at this level, that he did not even ask how he came to be there.

Together they cast off through the flood of pain, the
torrent from his broken arm. They had to row through a
swirling cloud of *agones*, which struck and bit at them like
swarms of vampire bugs. There were obstacles, snags, and
eddies where strange voices muttered sullenly out of dark
depths.

Finally they came to a pool, the center of the problem.
At its bottom lay the gestalt image of an iron grating set in a
stony floor. Horrible debris obstructed the drain.

Robert quailed back in alarm. Athaclena knew these had
to be emotion-laden memories—their fearsomeness given shape
in teeth and claws and bloated, awful faces. *How could humans let such clutter accumulate?* She was dazed and more
than a little frightened by the ugly, animate wreckage.

"*They're called neuroses,*" spoke Robert's inner voice.
He knew what they were "looking" at and was fighting a terror
far worse than hers. "*I'd forgotten so many of these things! I
had no idea they were still here.*"

Robert stared at his enemies below—and Athaclena saw
that many of the faces below were warped, angry versions of
his own.

"*This is my job now, Clennie. We learned long before*

*Contact that there is only one way to deal with a mess like
this. Truth is the only weapon that works:"*

The boat rocked as Robert's metaphoric self turned and
dove into the molten pool of pain.

Robert!

Froth rose. The tiny craft began to buck and heave,
forcing her to hold tightly to the rim of the strange *usunltlan.*
Bright, awful hurt sprayed on all sides. And down near the
grating a terrific struggle was taking place.

In the outer world, Robert's face ran streams of perspiration. Athaclena wondered how much more of this he could
take.

Hesitantly, she sent her image-hand down into the pool.
Direct contact *burned*, but she pushed on, reaching for the
grating.

Something grabbed her hand! She yanked back but the
grip held. An awful thing wearing a horrid version of Robert's
face leered up at her with an expression twisted almost out of
recognition by some warped lust. The thing pulled hard,
trying to drag her into the noisome pool. Athaclena screamed.

Another shape streaked in to grapple with her assailant.
The scaly hold on her arm released and she fell back into the
boat. Then the little craft started speeding away! All around
her the lake of pain flowed toward the drain. But her boat
moved rapidly the other way, upstream against the flow.

Robert is pushing me out, she realized. Contact narrowed, then broke. The metaphorical images ceased abruptly.
Athaclena blinked rapidly, in a daze. She knelt on the soft
ground. Robert held her hand, breathing through clenched
teeth.

"Had to stop you, Clennie. . . . That was dangerous for
you. . . ."

"But you are in such pain!"

He shook his head. "You showed me where the block
was. I . . . I can take care of that neurotic garbage now that I
know it's there . . . at least well enough for now. And . . .
and have I told you yet that a guy wouldn't have any trouble
at all falling in love with you?"

Athaclena sat up abruptly, amazed at the non sequitur.
She held up the three gas ampules. "Robert, you must tell
me which of these drugs will ease the pain, yet leave you
conscious enough to help me!"

He squinted. "The blue one. Snap it under my nose, but

don't breathe any yourself! No . . . no telling what para-
endorphins would do to you."

When Athaclena broke the ampule a small, dense cloud
of vapor spilled out. About half went in with Robert's next
breath. The rest quickly dispersed.

With a deep, shuddering sigh, Robert's body seemed to
uncoil. He looked up at her again with a new light in his
eyes. "I don't know if I could have maintained consciousness
much longer. But it was almost worth it . . . sharing my mind
with you."

In his aura it seemed that a simple but elegant version of
zunour'thzun danced. Athaclena was momentarily taken aback.

"You are a very strange creature, Robert. I . . ."

She paused. The *zunour'thzun* . . . it was gone now, but
she had not imagined *kenning* that glyph. How could Robert
have learned to make it?

Athaclena nodded and smiled. The human mannerisms
came easily, as if imprinted.

"I was just thinking the same thing, Robert. I . . . I, too,
found it worthwhile."

13

Fiben

Just above a cliff face, near the rim of a narrow mesa,
dust still rose in plumes where some recent crashing force
had torn a long, ugly furrow in the ground. A dagger-shaped
stretch of forest had been shattered in a few violent seconds
by a plunging thing that roared and skipped and struck again—
sending earth and vegetation spraying in all directions—before
finally coming to rest just short of the sheer precipice.

It had happened at night. Not far away, other pieces of

even hotter sky-debris had cracked stone and set fires, but here the impact had been only a glancing blow.

Long minutes after the explosive noise of collision ebbed there remained other disturbances. Landslides rattled down the nearby cliff, and trees near the tortured path creaked and swayed. At the end of the furrow, the dark object that had wreaked this havoc emitted crackling, snapping sounds as superheated metal met a cool fog sweeping up from the valley below.

At last things settled down and began returning to normal. Native animals nosed out into the open again. A few even approached, sniffed the hot thing in distaste, then moved on about the more serious business of living one more day.

It had been a bad landing. Within the escape pod, the pilot did not stir. That night and another day passed without any sign of motion.

At last, with a cough and a low groan, Fiben awoke. *"Where . . . ? What . . . ?"* he croaked.

His first organized thought was to notice that he had just spoken Anglic. *That's good,* he considered, numbly. *No brain damage, then.*

A neo-chimpanzee's ability to use language was his crucial possession, and far too easily lost. Speech aphasia was a good way to get reassessed—maybe even registered as a genetic probationer.

Of course samples of Fiben's plasm had already been sent to Earth and it was probably too late to recall them, so did it really matter if he were reassessed? He had never really cared what color his procreation card was, anyway.

Or, at least, he didn't care any more than the average chim did.

Oh, so we're getting philosophical, now? Delaying the inevitable? No dithering, Fiben old chim. Move! Open your eyes. Grope yourself. Make sure everything's still attached.

Wryly put, but less easily done. Fiben groaned as he tried to lift his head. He was so dehydrated that separating his eyelids felt like prying apart a set of rusty drawers.

At last he managed to squint. He saw that the clearshield of the pod was cracked and streaked with soot. Thick layers of dirt and seared vegetation had been speckled, sometime since the crash, by droplets of light rain.

Fiben discovered one of the reasons for his disorientation—

the capsule was canted more than fifty degrees. He fumbled with the seat's straps until they released, letting him slump against the armrest. He gathered a little strength, then pounded on the jammed hatch, muttering hoarse curses until the catch finally gave way in a rain of leaves and small pebbles.

Several minutes of dry sneezing ensued, finishing with him draped over the hatch rim, breathing hard.

Fiben gritted his teeth. "Come on," he muttered subvocally. "Let's get *outta* here!" He heaved himself up. Ignoring the uncomfortable warmth of the outer shell and the screaming of his own bruises, he squirmed desperately through the opening, turning and reaching for a foothold outside. He felt dirt, *blessed ground*. But when he let go of the hatch his left ankle refused to support him. He toppled over and landed with a painful thump.

"Ow!" Fiben said aloud. He reached underneath and pulled forth a sharp stick that had pierced his ship briefs. He glared at it before throwing it aside, then sagged back upon the mound of debris surrounding the pod.

Ahead of him, about twenty feet away, dawn's light showed the edge of a steep dropoff. The sound of rushing water rose from far below. *Uh*, he thought in bemused wonder at his near demise. *Another few meters and I wouldn't've been so thirsty right now*.

With the rising sun the mountainside across the valley became clearer, revealing smoky, scorched trails where larger pieces of space-junk had come down. *So much for old* Proconsul, Fiben thought. Seven thousand years of loyal service to half a hundred big-time Galactic races, only to be splattered all over a minor planet by one Fiben Bolger, client of wolflings, semi-skilled militia pilot. What an undignified end for a gallant old warrior.

But he had outlived the scoutboat after all. By a little while at least.

Someone once said that one measure of sentience was how much energy a sophont spent on matters other than survival. Fiben's body felt like a slab of half-broiled meat, yet he found the strength to grin. He had fallen a couple million miles and might yet live to someday tell some smart-aleck, two-generations-further-uplifted grandkids all about it.

He patted the scorched ground beside him and laughed in a voice dry with thirst.

"Beat *that*, Tarzan!"

14

Uthacalthing

". . . We are here as friends of Galactic Tradition, protectors of propriety and honor, enforcers of the will of the ancient ones who founded the Way of Things so long ago. . . ."

Uthacalthing was not very strong in Galactic Three, so he used his portable secretary to record the Gubru Invasion Manifesto for later study. He listened with only half an ear while going about completing the rest of his preparations.

. . . with only half an ear . . . His corona chirped a spark of amusement when he realized he had used the phrase in his thoughts. The human metaphor actually made his own ears itch!

The chims nearby had their receivers tuned to the Anglic translation, also being broadcast from the Gubru ships. It was an "unofficial" version of the manifesto, since Anglic was considered only a wolfling tongue, unsuitable for diplomacy.

Uthacalthing crafted *l'yuth'tsaka*, the approximate equivalent of a nose-thumb and raspberry, at the invaders. One of his neo-chimpanzee assistants looked up at him with a puzzled expression. The chim must have some latent psi ability, he realized. The other three hairy clients crouched under a nearby tree listening to the doctrine of the invading armada.

". . . in accordance with protocol and all of the Rules of War, a rescript has been delivered to Earth explaining our grievances and our demands for redress . . ."

Uthacalthing set one last seal into place over the hatch of the Diplomatic Cache. The pyramidal structure stood on a bluff overlooking the Sea of Cilmar, just southwest of the other buildings of the Tymbrimi Embassy. Out over the ocean all seemed fair and springlike. Even today small fishing boats cruised out on the placid waters, as if the sky held nothing unfriendlier than the dappled clouds.

In the other direction, though, past a small grove of Thula great-grass, transplanted from his homeworld, Uthacalthing's chancery and official quarters lay empty and abandoned.

Strictly speaking, he could have remained at his post. But Uthacalthing had no wish to trust the invaders' word that they were still following all of the Rules of War. The Gubru were renowned for interpreting tradition to suit themselves.

Anyway, he had made plans.

Uthacalthing finished the seal and stepped back from the Diplomatic Cache. Offset from the Embassy itself, sealed and warded, it was protected by millions of years of precedent. The chancery and other embassy buildings might be fair game, but the invader would be hard-pressed to come up with a satisfactory excuse for breaking into this sacrosanct depository.

Still, Uthacalthing smiled. He had confidence in the Gubru.

When he had backed away about ten meters he concentrated and crafted a simple glyph, then cast it toward the top of the pyramid where a small blue globe spun silently. The warder brightened at once and let out an audible hum. Uthacalthing then turned and approached the waiting chims.

"... *list as our first grievance that the Earthlings' client race, formally known as* Tursiops amicus, *or 'neo-dolphin,' has made a discovery which they do not share. It is said that this discovery portends major consequences to Galactic Society.*

The Clan of Gooksyu-Gubru, as a protector of tradition and the inheritance of the Progenitors, will not be excluded! It is our legitimate right to take hostages to force those half-formed water creatures and their wolfling masters to divulge their hoarded information ..."

A small corner of Uthacalthing's thoughts wondered just what the humans' other client race had discovered out there beyond the Galactic disk. He sighed wistfully. The way things worked in the Five Galaxies, he would have to take a long voyage through D-level hyperspace and emerge a million years from now to find out the entire story. By then, of course, it would be ancient history.

In fact, exactly what *Streaker* had done to trigger the

present crisis hardly mattered, really. The Tymbrimi Grand
Council had calculated that an explosion of some sort was due
within a few centuries anyway. The Earthlings had just managed to set it off a bit early. That was all.

Set it off early . . . Uthacalthing hunted for the right
metaphor. It was as if a child had escaped from a cradle,
crawled straight into a den of Vl'Korg beasts, and slapped the
queen right in the snout!

*". . . second grievance, and the precipitate cause for our
ennomic intervention here, is our strong suspicion that Uplift
irregularities are taking place on the planet Garth!*

*"In our possession is evidence that the semi-sentient client
species known as 'neo-chimpanzee' is being given improper
guidance, and is not being properly served by either its
human patrons or its Tymbrimi consorts. . . ."*

*The Tymbrimi? Improper consorts? Oh, you arrogant
avians shall pay for that insult,* Uthacalthing vowed.

The chims hurried to their feet and bowed low when he
approached. *Syulff-kuonn* glimmered briefly at the tips of his
corona as he returned the gesture.

"I wish to have certain messages delivered. Will you
serve me?"

They all nodded. The chims were obviously uncomfortable with each other, coming as they did from such different
social strata.

One was dressed proudly in the uniform of a militia
officer. Two others wore bright civilian clothes. The last and
most shabbily dressed chim bore a kind of breast panel-
display with an array of keys on both sides, which let the poor
creature perform a semblance of speech. This one stood a
little behind and apart from the others and barely lifted his
gaze from the ground.

"We are at your service," said the clean-cut young lieutenant, snapping to attention. He seemed completely aloof to
the sour glances the gaudily clad civilians cast his way.

"That is good, my young friend." Uthacalthing grasped
the chim's shoulder and held out a small black cube. "Please
deliver this to Planetary Coordinator Oneagle, with my compliments. Tell her that I had to delay my own departure to
Sanctuary, but I hope to see her soon."

I am not really lying, Uthacalthing reminded himself.
Bless Anglic and its lovely ambiguity!

The chim lieutenant took the cube and bowed again at

precisely the correct angle for showing bipedal respect to a senior patron ally. Without even looking at the others, he took off at a run toward his courier bike.

One of the civilians, apparently thinking Uthacalthing would not overhear, whispered to his brightly clad colleague. "I hope th' blue-card pom skids on a mud puddle an' gets his shiny uniform all wet."

Uthacalthing pretended not to notice. It sometimes paid to let others believe Tymbrimi hearing was as bad as their eyesight.

"These are for you," he told the two in the flashy clothes, and he tossed each of them a small bag. The money inside was GalCoin, untraceable and unquestionable through war and turmoil, for it was backed by the contents of the Great Library itself.

The two chims bowed to Uthacalthing, trying to imitate the officer's precision. He had to suppress a delighted laugh, for he sensed their *foci*—each chim's center of consciousness— had gathered in the hand holding the purse, excluding nearly all else from the world.

"Go then, and spend it as you will. I thank you for your past services."

The two members of Port Helenia's small criminal underworld spun about and dashed off through the grove. Borrowing another human metaphor, they had been "his eyes and ears" since he had arrived here. No doubt they considered their work completed now.

And thank you for what you are about to do, Uthacalthing thought after them. He knew this particular band of probationers well. They would spend his money well and gain an appetite for more. In a few days, there would be only one source of such coin.

They would have new employers soon, Uthacalthing was sure.

". . . have come as friends and protectors of pre-sentient peoples, to see that they are given proper guidance and membership in a dignified clan . . ."

Only one chim remained, trying to stand as straight as he could. But the poor creature could not help shifting his weight nervously, grinning anxiously.

"And what—" Uthacalthing stopped abruptly. His tendrils waved and he turned to look out over the sea.

A streak of light appeared from the headland across the

bay, spearing up and eastward into the sky. Uthacalthing
shaded his eyes, but he did not waste time envying Earthling
vision. The glowing ember climbed into the clouds, leaving a
kind of trail that only he could detect. It was a shimmering of
joyful departure that surged and then faded in a few brief
seconds, unraveling with the faint, white contrail.

Oth'thushutn, his aide, secretary, and friend, was flying
their ship out through the heart of the battle fleet surrounding Garth. And who could tell? Their Tymbrimi-made craft
was specially built. He even might get through.

That was not Oth'thushutn's job, of course. His task was
merely to make the attempt.

Uthacalthing reached forth in *kenning*. Yes, something
did ride down that burst of light. A sparkling legacy. He drew
in Oth'thushtn's final glyph and stored it in a cherished place,
should he ever make it home to tell the brave Tym's loved
ones.

Now there were only two Tymbrimi on Garth, and
Athaclena was as safe as could be provided for. It was time for
Uthacalthing to see to his own fate.

". . . *to rescue these innocent creatures from the warped
Uprearing they are receiving at the hands of wolflings and
criminals* . . ."

He turned back to the little chim, his last helper. "And
what about you, Jo-Jo? Do you want a task, as well?"

Jo-Jo fumbled with the keys of his panel display.

YES, PLEASE
HELP YOU IS ALL I ASK

Uthacalthing smiled. He had to hurry off and meet Kault.
By now the Thennanin Ambassador would be nearly frantic,
pacing beside Uthacalthing's pinnace. But the fellow could
just wait a few moments more.

"Yes," he told Jo-Jo. "I think there is something you can
do for me. Do you think you can keep a secret?"

The little genetic reject nodded vigorously, his soft brown
eyes filled with earnest devotion. Uthacalthing had spent a
lot of time with Jo-Jo, teaching him things the schools here
on Garth had never bothered to try—wilderness survival
skills and how to pilot a simple flitter, for instance. Jo-Jo was
not the pride of neo-chimp Uplift, but he had a great heart,

and more than enough of a certain type of cunning that
Uthacalthing appreciated.

"Do you see that blue light, atop the cairn, Jo-Jo?"

JO-JO REMEMBERS,

the chim keyed.

JO-JO REMEMBERS ALL YOU SAID.

"Good." Uthacalthing nodded. "I knew you would. I shall
count on you, my dear little friend." He smiled, and Jo-Jo
grinned back, eagerly.

Meanwhile, the computer-generated voice from space
droned on, completing the Manifesto of Invasion.

"*. . . and give them over for adoption by some appropriate elder clan—one that will not lead them into improper
behavior . . .*"

Wordy birds, Uthacalthing thought. Silly things, really.

"We'll show them some 'improper behavior,' won't we,
Jo-Jo?"

The little chim nodded nervously. He grinned, even
though he did not entirely understand.

15

Athaclena

That night their tiny campfire cast yellow and orange
flickerings against the trunks of the near-oaks.

"I was so hungry, even vac-pac stew tasted delicious,"
Robert sighed as he put aside his bowl and spoon. "I'd
planned to make us a meal of baked plate ivy roots, but I

don't guess either of us will have much appetite for that delicacy soon."

Athaclena felt she understood Robert's tendency to make irrelevant remarks like these. Tymbrimi and Terran both had ways of making light of disaster—part of the unusual pattern of similarity between the two species.

She had eaten sparingly herself. Her body had nearly purged the peptides left over from the *gheer* reaction, but she still felt a little sore after this afternoon's adventure.

Overhead a dark band of Galactic dust clouds spanned fully twenty percent of the sky, outlined by bright hydrogen nebulae. Athaclena watched the starry vault, her corona only slightly puffed out above her ears. From the forest she felt the tiny, anxious emotions of little native creatures.

"Robert?"

"Hmmm? Yes, Clennie?"

"Robert, why did you remove the crystals from our radio?"

After a pause, his voice was serious, subdued. "I'd hoped not to have to tell you for a few days, Athaclena. But last night I saw the communication satellites being destroyed. That could only mean the Galactics have arrived, as our parents expected.

"The radio's crystals can be picked up by shipborne resonance detectors, even when they aren't powered. I took ours out so there'd be no chance of being found that way. It's standard doctrine."

Athaclena felt a tremor at the tip of her ruff, just above her nose, that shivered over her scalp and down her back. *So, it has begun.*

Part of her longed to be with her father. It still hurt that he had sent her away rather than allow her to stay at his side where she could help him.

The silence stretched. She *kenned* Robert's nervousness. Twice, he seemed about to speak, then stopped, thinking better of it. Finally, she nodded. "I agree with your logic in removing the crystals, Robert. I even think I understand the protective impulse that made you refrain from telling me about it. You should not do that again, though. It was foolish."

Robert agreed, seriously. "I won't, Athaclena."

They lay in silence for a while, until Robert reached over with his good hand and touched hers. "Clennie, I . . . I want you to know I'm grateful. You saved my life—"

"Robert," she sighed tiredly.

"—but it goes beyond that. When you came into my mind you showed me things about myself . . . things I'd never known before. That's an important favor. You can read all about it in textbooks, if you want. Self-deception and neuroses are two particularly insidious human plagues."

"They are not unique to humans, Robert."

"No, I guess not. What you saw in my mind was probably nothing by pre-Contact standards. But given our history, well, even the sanest of us needs reminding from time to time."

Athaclena had no idea what to say, so she remained silent. To have lived in Humanity's awful dark ages must have been frightening indeed.

Robert cleared his throat. "What I'm trying to say is that I know how far you've gone to adapt yourself—learning human expressions, making little changes in your physiology . . ."

"An experiment." She shrugged, another human mannerism. She suddenly realized that her face felt warm. Capillaries were opening in that human reaction she had thought so quaint. She was blushing!

"Yeah, an experiment. But by rights it ought to go both ways, Clennie. Tymbrimi are renowned around the Five Galaxies for their adaptability. But we humans are capable of learning a thing or two, also."

She looked up. "What do you mean, Robert?"

"I mean that I'd like you to show me some more about Tymbrimi ways. Your customs. I want to know what your landsmen do that's equivalent to an amazed stare, or a nod, or a grin."

Again, there was a flicker. Athaclena's corona reached, but the delicate, simple, ghostly glyph he had formed vanished like smoke. Perhaps he was not even aware he had crafted it.

"Um," she said, blinking and shaking her head. "I cannot be sure, Robert. But I think perhaps you have already begun."

Robert was stiff and feverish when they struck camp the next morning. He could only take so much anesthetic for his fractured arm and remain able to walk.

Athaclena stashed most of his gear in the notch of a gum beech tree and cut slashes in the bark to mark the site.

Actually, she doubted anyone would ever be back to reclaim it. "We must get you to a physician," she said, feeling his brow. His raised temperature clearly was not a good sign.

Robert indicated a narrow slot between the mountains to the south. "Over that way, two days march, there's the Mendoza Freehold. Mrs. Mendoza was a nurse practitioner before she married Juan and took up farming."

Athaclena looked uncertainly at the pass. They would have to climb nearly a thousand meters to get over it.

"Robert, are you sure this is the best route? I'm certain I have intermittently sensed sophonts emoting from much nearer, over that line of hills to the east."

Robert leaned on his makeshift staff and began moving up the southward trail. "Come on, Clennie," he said over his shoulder. "I know you want to meet a Garthling, but now's hardly the time. We can go hunting for native pre-sentients after I've been patched up."

Athaclena stared after him, astonished by the illogic of his remark. She caught up with him. "Robert, that was a strange thing to say! How could I think of seeking out native creatures, no matter how mysterious, until you were tended! The sophonts I have felt to the east were clearly humans and chimps, although I admit there *was* a strange, added element, almost like . . ."

"Aha!" Robert smiled, as if she had made a confession. He walked on.

Amazed, Athaclena tried to probe his feelings, but the human's discipline and determination was incredible for a member of a wolfling race. All she could tell was that he was disturbed—and that it had something to do with her mention of sapient thoughts east of here.

Oh, to be a true telepath! Once more she wondered why the Tymbrimi Grand Council had not defied the rules of the Uplift Institute and gone ahead to develop the capability. She had sometimes envied humans the privacy they could build around their lives and resented the gossipy invasiveness of her own culture. But right now she wanted only to break *in* there and find out what he was hiding!

Her corona waved, and if there had been any Tymbrimi within half a mile they would have winced at her angry, pungent opinion of the way of things.

*   *   *

Robert was showing difficulty before they reached the crest of the first ridge, little more than an hour later. Athaclena knew by now that the glistening perspiration on his brow meant the same thing as a reddening and fluffing of a Tymbrimi's corona—overheating.

When she overheard him counting under his breath, she knew that they would have to rest. "No." He shook his head. His voice was ragged. "Let's just get past this ridge and into the next valley. From there on it's shaded all the way to the pass." Robert kept trudging.

"There is shade enough here," she insisted, and pulled him over to a rock jumble covered by creepers with umbrella-like leaves, all linked by the ubiquitous transfer-vines to the forest in the valley floor.

Robert sighed as she helped him sit back against a boulder in the shade. She wiped his forehead, then began unwrapping his splinted right arm. He hissed through his teeth.

A faint purpling discolored the skin near where the bone had broken. "Those are bad signs, aren't they, Robert?"

For a moment she felt him begin to dissemble. Then he reconsidered, shaking his head. "N-no. I think there's an infection. I'd better take some more Universal . . ."

He started to reach for her pack, where his aid kit was being carried, but his equilibrium failed and Athaclena had to catch him.

"Enough, Robert. You cannot walk to the Mendoza Freehold. I certainly cannot carry you, and I'll not leave you alone for two or three days!

"You seem to have some reason to wish to avoid the people who I sensed to the east of here. But whatever it is, it cannot match the importance of saving your life!"

Robert let her pop a pair of blue pills into his mouth and sipped from the canteen she held for him. "All right, Clennie," he sighed. "We'll turn eastward. Only promise you'll coronasing for me, will you? It's lovely, like you are, and it helps me understand you better . . . and now I think we'd better get started because I'm babbling. That's one sign that a human being is deteriorating. You should know that by now."

Athaclena's eyes spread apart and she smiled. "I was already aware of that, Robert. Now tell me, what is the name of this place where we are going?"

"It's called the Howletts Center. It's just past that second set of hills, over that way." He pointed east by southeast.

"They don't like surprise guests," he went on, "so we'll want to talk loudly as we approach."

Taking it by stages, they made it over the first ridge shortly before noon and rested in the shade by a small spring. There Robert fell into a troubled slumber.

Athaclena watched the human youth with a feeling of miserable helplessness. She found herself humming Thlufall-threela's famous "Dirge of Inevitability." The poignant piece for aura and voice was over four thousand years old, written during the time of sorrow when the Tymbrimi patron race, the Caltmour, were destroyed in a bloody interstellar war.

Inevitability was not a comfortable concept for her people, even less than for humans. But long ago the Tymbrimi had decided to try all things—to learn all philosophies. Resignation, too, had its place.

Not this time! she swore. Athaclena coaxed Robert into his sleeping bag and got him to swallow two more pills. She secured his arm as best she could and piled rocks alongside to keep him from rolling about.

A low palisade of brush around him would, she hoped, keep out any dangerous animals. Of course the Bururalli had cleared Garth's forests of any large creatures, but that did not keep her from worrying. Would an unconscious human be safe then, if she left him alone for a little while?

She placed her jack-laser within reach of his left hand and a canteen next to it. Bending down she touched his forehead with her sensitized, refashioned lips. Her corona unwound and fell about his face, caressing it with delicate strands so she could give him a parting benediction in the manner of her own folk, as well.

A deer might have run faster. A cougar might have slipped through the forest stillness more silently. But Athaclena had never heard of those creatures. And even if she had, a Tymbrimi did not fear comparisons. Their very race-name was adaptability.

Within the first kilometer automatic changes had already been set in motion. Glands rushed strength to her legs, and changes in her blood made better use of the air she breathed. Loosened connective tissue opened her nostrils wide to pass still more, while elsewhere her skin tautened to prevent her breasts from bouncing jarringly as she ran.

The slope steepened as she passed out of the second narrow valley and up a game path toward the last ridge before her goal. Her rapid footfalls on the thick loam were light and soft. Only an occasional snapping twig announced her coming, sending the forest creatures scurrying into the shadows. A chittering of little jeers followed her, both in sound and unsubtle emanations she picked up with her corona.

Their hostile calls made Athaclena want to smile, Tymbrimi style. Animals were so serious. Only a few, those nearly ready for Uplift, ever had anything resembling a sense of humor. And then, after they were adopted and began Uplift, all too often their patrons edited whimsy out of them as an "unstable trait."

After the next kilometer Athaclena eased back a bit. She would have to pace herself, if for no other reason than she was overheating. That was dangerous for a Tymbrimi.

She reached the crest of the ridge, with its chain of ubiquitous spine-stones, and slowed in order to negotiate the maze of jutting monoliths. There, she rested briefly. Leaning against one of the tall rocky outcrops, breathing heavily, she reached out with her corona. The tendrils waved, searching.

Yes! There were humans close by! And neo-chimpanzees, too. By now she knew both patterns well.

And . . . she concentrated. There was something else, also. Something tantalizing.

It had to be that enigmatic being she had sensed twice before! There was that queer quality that at one moment seemed Earthly and then seemed to partake strongly of this world. And it was *pre-sentient*, with a dark, serious nature of its own.

If only empathy were more of a directional sense! She moved forward, tracing a way toward the source through the maze of stones.

A shadow fell upon her. Instinctively, she leaped back and crouched—hormones rushing combat strength into her hands and arms. Athaclena sucked air, fighting down the *gheer* reaction. She had been expecting to encounter some small, feral survivor of the Bururalli Holocaust, not anything so large!

Calm down, she told herself. The silhouette standing on the stone overhead was a large biped, clearly a cousin to Man and no native of Garth. A chimpanzee could never pose a threat to her, of course.

"H-hello!" She managed Anglic over the trembling left by the receding *gheer*. Silently she cursed the instinctive reactions which made Tymbrimi dangerous beings to cross but which shortened their lives and often embarrassed them in polite company.

The figure overhead stared down at her. Standing on two legs, with a belt of tools around its waist, it was hard to discern against the glare. The bright, bluish light of Garth's sun was disconcerting. Even so, Athaclena could tell that this one was very large for a chimpanzee.

It did not react. In fact, the creature just stared down at her.

A client race as young as neo-chimpanzees could not be expected to be too bright. She made allowances, squinting up at the dark, furry figure, and enunciated slowly in Anglic.

"I have an emergency to report. There is a *human being*," she emphasized, "who is injured not far from here. He needs immediate attention. You must please take me to some humans, right now." She expected an immediate response, but the creature merely shifted its weight and continued to stare.

Athaclena was beginning to feel foolish. Could she have encountered a particularly stupid chim? Or perhaps a deviant or a sport? New client races produced a lot of variability, sometimes including dangerous throwbacks—witness what had happened to the Bururalli so recently here on Garth.

Athaclena extended her senses. Her corona reached out and then curled in surprise!

It was the pre-sentient! The superficial resemblance— the fur and long arms—had fooled her. This wasn't a chim at all! It was the alien creature she had sensed only minutes ago!

No wonder the beast hadn't responded. It had had no patron yet to teach it to talk! *Potential* quivered and throbbed. She could sense it just under the surface.

Athaclena wondered just what one said to a native pre-sophont. She looked more carefully. The creature's dark, furry coat was fringed by the sun's glare. Atop short, bowed legs it carried a massive body culminating in a great head with a narrow peak. In silhouette, its huge shoulders merged without any apparent neck.

Athaclena recalled Ma'chutallil's famed story about a spacegleaner who encountered, in forests far from a colony settlement, a child who had been brought up by wild limb-runners. After catching the fierce, snarling little thing in his nets, the hunter had aura-cast a simple version of *sh'cha'kuon*, the mirror of the soul.

Athaclena formed the empathy glyph as well as she could remember it.

SEE IN ME—AN IMAGE OF THE VERY YOU

The creature stood up. It reared back, snorting and sniffing at the air.

She thought, at first, it was reacting to her glyph. Then a noise, not far away, broke the fleeting connection. The pre-sentient chuffed—a deep, grunting sound—then spun about and leaped away, hopping from spine-stone to spine-stone until it was gone from sight.

Athaclena hurried after, but uselessly. In moments she had lost the trail. She sighed finally and turned back to the east, where Robert had said the Earthling "Howletts Center" lay. After all, finding help had to come first.

She started picking her way through the maze of spine-stones. They tapered off as the slope descended into the next valley. That was when she passed around a tall boulder and nearly collided with the search party.

"We're sorry we frightened you, ma'am," the leader of the group said gruffly. His voice was somewhere between a growl and the croaking of a pond full of bug-hoppers. He bowed again. "A seisin picker came in and told us of some sort of ship crash out this way, so we sent out a couple of search parties. You haven't seen anythin' like a spacecraft comin' down, have you?"

Athaclena still shivered from the Ifni-damned overreaction. She must have looked terrifying in those first few seconds, when surprise set off another furious change response. The poor creatures had been startled. Behind the leader, four more chims stared at her nervously.

"No, I haven't," Athaclena spoke slowly and carefully, in order not to tax the little clients. "But I do have a different sort of emergency to report. My comrade—a human being—was injured yesterday afternoon. He has a broken arm and a possible infection. I must speak to someone in authority about having him evacuated."

The leader of the chims stood a bit above average in

height, nearly a hundred and fifty centimeters tall. Like the others he wore a pair of shorts, a tool-bandoleer, and a light backpack. His grin featured an impressive array of uneven, somewhat yellowed teeth.

"I'm sufficiently in authority. My name is Benjamin, Mizz . . . Mizz . . ." His gruff voice ended in a questioning tone.

"Athaclena. My companion's name is Robert Oneagle. He is the son of the Planetary Coordinator."

Benjamin's eyes widened. "I see. Well, Mizz Athac- . . . well ma'am . . . you must have heard by now that Garth's been interdicted by a fleet of Eatee cruisers. Under th' emergency we aren't supposed to use aircars if we can avoid it. Still, my crew here is equipped to handle a human with th' sort of injuries you described. If you'll lead us to Mr. Oneagle, we'll see he's taken care of."

Athaclena's relief was mixed with a pang as she was reminded of larger matters. She had to ask. "Have they determined who the invaders are yet? Has there been a landing?"

The chimp Benjamin was behaving professionally and his diction was good, but he could not disguise his perplexity as he looked at her, tilting his head as if trying to see her from a new angle. The others frankly stared. Clearly they had never seen a person like her before.

"Uh, I'm sorry, ma'am, but the news hasn't been too specific. The Eatees . . . uh." The chim peered at her. "Uh, pardon me, ma'am, but you aren't human, are you?"

"Great Caltmour, no!" Athaclena bristled. "What ever gave you the . . ." Then she remembered all the little external alterations she had made as part of her experiment. She must look very close to human by now, especially with the sun behind her. No wonder the poor clients had been confused!

"No," she said again, more softly. "I am no human. I am Tymbrimi."

The chims sighed and looked quickly at one another. Benjamin bowed, arms crossed in front of him, for the first time offering the gesture of a client greeting a member of a patron-class race.

Athaclena's people, like humans, did not believe in flaunting their dominance over their clients. Still, the gesture helped mollify her hurt feelings. When he spoke again, Benjamin's diction was much better.

"Forgive me, ma'am. What I meant to say was that I'm not really sure who the invaders are. I wasn't near a receiver when their manifesto was broadcast, a couple of hours ago. Somebody told me it was the Gubru, but there's another rumor they're Thennanin."

Athaclena sighed. Thennanin or Gubru. Well, it could have been worse. The former were sanctimonious and narrow-minded. The latter were often vile, rigid, and cruel. But neither were as bad as the manipulative Soro, or the eerie, deadly Tandu.

Benjamin whispered to one of his companions. The smaller chimp turned and hurried down the trail the way they had come, toward the mysterious Howletts Center. Athaclena caught a tremor of anxiety. Once again she wondered what was going on in this valley that Robert had tried to steer her away from, even at risk to his own health.

"The courier will carry back word of Mr. Oneagle's condition and arrange transport," Benjamin told her. "Meanwhile, we'll hurry to give him first aid. If you would only lead the way . . ."

He motioned her ahead, and Athaclena had to put away her curiosity for now. Robert clearly came first. "All right," she said. "Let us go."

As they passed under the standing stone where she had had her encounter with the strange, pre-sentient alien, Athaclena looked up. Had it really been a "Garthling"? Perhaps the chims knew something about it. Before she could begin to ask, however, Athaclena stumbled, clutching at her temples. The chims stared at the sudden waving of her corona and the startled, narrow set of her eyes.

It was part sound—a keening that crested high, almost beyond hearing—and partly a sharp *itch* that crawled up her spine.

"Ma'am?" Benjamin looked up at her, concerned. "What is it?"

Athaclena shook her head. "It's . . . It is . . ."

She did not finish. For at that moment there was a flash of gray over the western horizon—something hurtling through the sky toward them—*too fast!* Before Athaclena could flinch it had grown from distant dot to behemoth size. Just that suddenly a giant ship appeared, stock-still, hovering directly over the valley.

Athaclena barely had enough time to cry out, "Cover

your ears!" Then thunder broke, a crash and roar that knocked all of them to the ground. The boom reverberated through the maze of stones and echoed off the surrounding hillsides. Trees swayed—some of them cracking and toppling over—and leaves were ripped away in sudden, fluttering cyclones.

Finally the pealing died away, diffracting and diminishing into the forest. Only after that, and blinking away tremors of shock, did they at last hear the low, loud growl of the ship itself. The gray monster cast shadows over the valley, a huge, gleaming cylinder. As they stared the great machine slowly settled lower until it dropped below the spine-stones and out of sight. The hum of its engines fell to a deep rumble, uncovering the sound of rockfalls on the nearby slopes.

The chims slowly stood up and held each others' hands nervously, whispering to each other in hoarse, low voices. Benjamin helped Athaclena to stand. The ship's gravity fields had struck her fully extended corona unprepared. She shook her head, trying to clear it.

"That was a warship, wasn't it?" Benjamin asked her. "These other chims here haven't ever been to space, but I went up to see the old *Vesarius* when it visited, a couple years back, and even she wasn't as big as that thing!"

Athaclena sighed. "It was, indeed, a warship. Of Soro design, I think. The Gubru are using that fashion now." She looked down at the Earthling. "I would say that Garth is no longer simply interdicted, Chim Benjamin. An invasion has begun."

Benjamin's hands came together. He pulled nervously at one opposable thumb, then the other. "They're hovering over the valley. I can hear 'em! What are they up to?"

"I don't know," she said. "Why don't we go look?"

Benjamin hesitated, then nodded. He led the group back to a point where the spine-stones opened up and they could gaze out over the valley.

The warship hovered about four kilometers east of their position and a few hundred meters above the ground, draping its immense shadow over a small cluster of off-white buildings on the valley floor. Athaclena shaded her eyes against the bright sunshine reflected from its gunmetal gray flanks.

The deep-throated groan of the giant cruiser was ominous. "It's just hoverin' there! What are they doing?" one of the chims asked nervously.

Athaclena shook her head in Anglic. "I do not know." She sensed fear from humans and neo-chimps in the settlement below. And there were other sources of emotion as well.

The invaders, she realized. Their psi shields were down, an arrogant dismissal of any possibility of defense. She caught a gestalt of thin-boned, feathered creatures, descendants of some flightless, pseudo-avian species. A rare real-view came to her briefly, vividly, as seen through the eyes of one of the cruiser's officers. Though contact only lasted milliseconds, her corona reeled back in revulsion.

Gubru, she realized numbly. Suddenly, it was made all too real.

Benjamin gasped. "Look!"

Brown fog spilled forth from vents in the ship's broad underbelly. Slowly, almost languidly, the dark, heavy vapor began to fall toward the valley floor.

The fear below shifted over to panic. Athaclena quailed back against one of the spine-stones and wrapped her arms over her head, trying to shut out the almost palpable aura of dread.

Too much! Athaclena tried to form a glyph of peace in the space before her, to hold back the pain and horror. But every pattern was blown away like spun snow before the hot wind of a flame.

"They're killing th' humans and 'rillas!" one of the chims on the hillside cried, running forward. Benjamin shouted after him. "Petrie! Come back here! Where do you think you're going?"

"I'm goin' to help!" the younger chim yelled back. "And you would too, if you cared! You can hear 'em screamin' down there!" Ignoring the winding path, he started scrambling down the scree slope itself—the most direct route toward the roiling fog and the dim sounds of despair.

The other two chims looked at Benjamin rebelliously, obviously sharing the same thought. "I'm goin' too," one said.

Athaclena's fear-narrowed eyes throbbed. What were these silly creatures doing now?

"I'm with you," the last one agreed. In spite of Benjamin's shouted curses, both of them started down the steep slope.

"Stop this, right now!"

They turned and stared at Athaclena. Even Petrie halted suddenly, hanging one-handed from a boulder, blinking up at her. She had used the Tone of Peremptory Command, for only the third time in her life.

"Stop this foolishness and come back here immediately!" she snapped. Athaclena's corona billowed out over her ears. Her carefully cultured human accent was gone. She enunciated Anglic in the Tymbrimi lilt the neo-chimpanzees must have heard on video countless times. She might *look* rather human, but no human voice could make exactly the same sounds.

The Terran clients blinked, open-mouthed.

"Return at once," she hissed.

The chims scrambled back up the slope to stand before her. One by one, glancing nervously at Benjamin and following his example, they bowed with arms crossed in front of them.

Athaclena fought down her own shaking in order to appear outwardly calm. "Do not make me raise my voice again," she said lowly. "We must work together, think coolly, and make appropriate plans."

Small wonder the chims shivered and looked up at her, wide-eyed. Humans seldom spoke to chims so peremptorily. The species might be indentured to man, but by Earth's own law neo-chimps were nearly equal citizens.

We Tymbrimi, though, are another matter. Duty, simple duty had drawn Athaclena out of her *totanoo*—her fear-induced withdrawal. Somebody had to take responsibility to save these creatures' lives.

The ugly brown fog had stopped spilling from the Gubru vessel. The vapor spread across the narrow valley like a dark, foamy lake, barely covering the buildings at the bottom.

Vents closed. The ship began to rise.

"Take cover," she told them, and led the chims around the nearest of the rock monoliths. The low hum of the Gubru ship climbed more than an octave. Soon they saw it rise over the spine-stones.

"Protect yourselves."

The chims huddled close, pressing their hands against their ears.

One moment the giant invader was there, a thousand meters over the valley floor. Then, quicker than the eye could follow, it was gone. Displaced air clapped inward like a giant's hand and thunder batted them again, returning in rolling waves that brought up dust and leaves from the forest below.

The stunned neo-chimps stared at each other for long moments as the echoes finally ebbed. Finally the eldest chim, Benjamin, shook himself. He dusted his hands and grabbed the young chen named Petrie by the back of his neck, marching the startled chim over to face Athaclena.

Petrie looked down shamefaced. "I . . . I'm sorry, ma'am," he muttered gruffly. "It's just that there are humans down there and . . . and my mates. . . ."

Athaclena nodded. One should try not to be too hard on a well-intended client. "Your motives were admirable. Now that we are calm though, and can plan, we'll go about helping your patrons and friends more effectively."

She offered her hand. It was a less patronizing gesture than the pat on the head he seemed to have expected from a Galactic. They shook, and he grinned shyly.

When they hurried around the stones to look out over the valley again, several of the Terrans gasped. The brown cloud had spread over the lowlands like a thick, filthy sea that flowed almost to the forest slopes at their feet. The heavy vapor seemed to have a sharply defined upper boundary barely licking at the roots of nearby trees.

They had no way of knowing what was going on below, or even if anybody still lived down there.

"We will split into two groups," Athaclena told them. "Robert Oneagle still requires attention. Someone must go to him."

The thought of Robert lying semi-conscious back there where she had left him was an unrelenting anxiety in her mind. She had to know he was being cared for. Anyway, she suspected most of these chims would be better off going to Robert's aid than hanging around this deadly valley. The creatures were too shaken and volatile up here in full view of the disaster. "Benjamin, can your companions find Robert by themselves, using the directions I have given?"

"You mean without leading them there yourself?" Benjamin frowned and shook his head. "Uh, I dunno, ma'am. I . . . I really think you ought to go along."

Athaclena had left Robert under a clear landmark, a

giant quail-nut tree close to the main trail. Any party sent
from here should have no trouble finding the injured human.

She could read the chim's emotions. Part of Benjamin
anxiously wished to have one of the renowned Tymbrimi here
to help, if possible, the people in the valley. And yet he had
chosen to try to send her away!

The oily smoke churned and rolled below. She could
distantly sense many minds down there, turbulent with fear.

"I will remain," she said firmly. "You have said these
others are a qualified rescue team. They can certainly find
Robert and help him. Someone must stay and see if anything
can be done for those below."

With a human there might have been argument. But the
chimps did not even consider contradicting a Galactic with a
made up mind. Client-class sophonts simply did not do such
things.

In Benjamin she sensed a partial relief . . . and a counterpoint of dread.

The three younger chims shouldered their packs. Solemnly they headed westward through the spine-stones, glancing back nervously until they passed out of sight.

Athaclena let herself feel relieved for Robert's sake. But
underneath it all remained a nagging fear for her father. The
enemy must certainly have struck Port Helenia first.

"Come, Benjamin. Let's see what can be done for those
poor people down there."

For all of their unusual and rapid successes in Uplift,
Terran geneticists still had a way to go with neo-dolphins and
neo-chimpanzees. Truly original thinkers were still rare in
both species. By Galactic standards they had made great
strides, but Earthmen wanted even more rapid progress. It
was almost as if they suspected their clients might have to
grow up very quickly, very soon.

When a good mind appeared in *Tursiops* or *Pongo* stock,
it was carefully nurtured. Athaclena could tell that Benjamin
was one of those superior specimens. No doubt this chim had
at least a blue card procreation right and had already sired
many children.

"Maybe I'd better scout ahead, ma'am," Benjamin suggested. "I can climb these trees and stay above the level of
the gas. I'll go in and find out how things lie, and then come
back for you."

Athaclena felt the chim's turmoil as they looked out on the lake of mysterious gas. Here it was about ankle deep, but farther into the valley it swirled several man-heights into the trees.

"No. We'll stay together," Athaclena said firmly. "I can climb trees too, you know."

Benjamin looked her up and down, apparently recalling stories of the fabled Tymbrimi adaptability. "Hmmm, your folk might have once been arboreal at that. No respect intended." He gave her a wry, unhinged grin. "All right then, miss, let's go."

He took a running start, leaped into the branches of a near-oak, scampered around the trunk and darted down another limb. Then Benjamin jumped across a narrow gap to the next tree. He held onto the bouncing branch and looked back at her with curious brown eyes.

Athaclena recognized a challenge. She breathed deeply several times, concentrating. Changes began with a tingling in her hardening fingertips, a loosening in her chest. She exhaled, crouched, and took off, launching herself into the near-oak. With some difficulty she imitated the chim, move by move.

Benjamin nodded in approval as she landed next to him. Then he was off again.

They made slow progress, leaping from tree to tree and creeping around vine-entangled trunks. Several times they were forced to backtrack around clearings choked with the slowly settling fumes. They tried not to breathe when stepping over thicker wisps of the heavy gas, but Athaclena could not help picking up a whiff of pungent, oily stuff. She told herself that her growing itch was probably psychosomatic.

Benjamin kept glancing at her surreptitiously. The chim certainly noticed some of the changes she underwent as the minutes passed—a limbering of the arms, a rolling of the shoulders and loosening and opening of the hands. He clearly had never expected to have a Galactic keep up with him this way, swinging through the trees.

He almost certainly did not know the price the *gheer* transformation was going to cost her. The hurt had already begun, and Athaclena knew this was only the beginning.

The forest was full of sounds. Small animals scurried past them, fleeing the alien smoke and stench. Athaclena picked up quick, hot pulses of their fear. As they reached the top of a knoll overlooking the settlement, they could hear faint cries—frightened Terrans groping about in a soot-dark forest.

Benjamins' brown eyes told her that those were his friends down there. "See how the stuff clings to the ground?" he said. "It hardly rises a few meters over the tops of our buildings. If only we'd built *one* tall structure!"

"They would have blasted that building first," Athaclena pointed out. "And *then* released their gas."

"Hmmph." Benjamin nodded. "Well, let's go see if any of my mates made it into the trees. Maybe they managed to help a few of the humans get high enough as well."

She did not question Benjamin about his hidden fear— the thing he could not bring himself to mention. But there was something added to his worry about the humans and chims below, as if that were not already enough.

The deeper they went into the valley, the higher among the branches they had to travel. More and more often they were forced to drop down, stirring the smoky, unraveling wisps with their feet as they hurried along their arboreal highway. Fortunately, the oily gas seemed to be dissipating at last, growing heavier and precipitating in a fine rain of gray dust.

Benjamin's pace quickened as they caught glimpses of the off-white buildings of the Center beyond the trees. Athaclena followed as well as she could, but it was getting harder and harder to keep up with the chim. Enzyme exhaustion took its toll, and her corona was ablaze as her body tried to eliminate heat buildup.

Concentrate, she thought as she crouched on one waving branch. Athaclena flexed her legs and tried to sight on the blur of dusty leaves and twigs opposite her.

Go.

She uncoiled, but by now the spring was gone from her leap. She barely made it across the two-meter gap. Athaclena hugged the bucking, swaying branch. Her corona pulsed like fire.

She clutched the alien wood, breathing open-mouthed, unable to move, the world a blur. *Maybe it's more than just gheer pain*, she thought. *Maybe the gas isn't just designed for Terrans. It could be killing me.*

It took a couple of moments for her eyes to focus again, and then she saw little more than a black-bottomed foot covered with brown fur . . . Benjamin, clutching the tree branch nimbly and standing over her.

His hand softly touched the waving, hot tendrils of her corona. "You just wait here and rest, miss. I'll scout ahead an' be right back."

The branch shuddered once more, and he was gone.

Athaclena lay still. She could do little else except listen to faint sounds coming from the direction of the Howletts Center. Nearly an hour after the departure of the Gubru cruiser she could still hear panicky chimp shrieks and strange, low cries from some animal she couldn't recognize.

The gas was dissipating but it still stank, even up here. Athaclena kept her nostrils closed, breathing through her mouth.

Pity the poor Earthlings, whose noses and ears must remain open all the time, for all the world to assault at will. The irony did not escape her. For at least the creatures did not have to listen with their *minds.*

As her corona cooled, Athaclena felt awash in a babble of emotions . . . human, chimpanzee, and that other variety that flickered in and out, the "stranger" that had by now become almost familiar. Minutes passed, and Athaclena felt a little better . . . enough to crawl along the limb to where branch met trunk. She sat back against the rough bark with a sigh, the flow of noise and emotion surrounding her.

Maybe I'm not dying after all, at least not right away.

Only after a little while longer did it dawn on her that something was happening quite nearby. She could sense that she was being *watched*—and from very close! She turned and drew her breath sharply. From the branches of a tree only six meters away, four sets of eyes stared back at her—three pairs deep brown and a fourth bright blue.

Barring perhaps a few of the sentient, semi-vegetable Kanten, the Tymbrimi were the Galactics who knew Earthlings best. Nevertheless, Athaclena blinked in surprise, uncertain just what it was she was seeing.

Closest to the trunk of that tree sat an adult female neo-chimpanzee—a "chimmie"—dressed only in shorts, holding a chim baby in her arms. The little mother's brown eyes were wide with fear.

Next to them was a small, smooth-skinned human child dressed in denim overalls. The little blond girl smiled back at Athaclena, shyly.

But it was the fourth and last being in the other tree that had Athaclena confused.

She recalled a neo-dolphin sound-sculpture her father had brought home to Tymbrim from his travels. This was just after that episode of the ceremony of Acceptance and Choice of the Tytlal, when she had behaved so strangely up in that extinct volcano caldera. Perhaps Uthacalthing had wanted to play the sound-sculpting for her to draw her out of her moodiness—to prove to her that the Earthly cetaceans were actually charming creatures, not to be feared. He had told her to close her eyes and just let the song wash over her.

Whatever his motive, it had had the opposite effect. For in listening to the wild, untamed patterns, she had suddenly found herself immersed in an *ocean*, hearing an angry sea squall gather. Even opening her eyes, seeing that she still sat in the family listening room, did not help. For the first time in her life, sound overwhelmed vision.

Athaclena had never listened to the cube again, nor known anything else quite so strange . . . until encountering the eerie metaphorical landscape within Robert Oneagle's mind, that is.

Now she felt that way again! For while the fourth creature across from her looked, at first, like a *very* large chimpanzee, her corona was telling quite another story.

It cannot be!

Calmly, placidly, the brown eyes looked back at her. The being obviously far outweighed all the others combined, yet it held the human child on its lap delicately, carefully. When the little girl squirmed, the big creature merely snorted and shifted slightly, neither letting go nor taking its gaze from Athaclena. Unlike normal chimpanzees, its face was very black.

Ignoring her aches, Athaclena edged forward slowly so as not to alarm them. "Hello," she said carefully in Anglic.

The human child smiled again and ducked her head shyly against her furry protector's massive chest. The neo-chimp mother cringed back in apparent fear.

The massive creature with the high, flattened face merely nodded twice and snorted again.

It fizzed with Potential!

Athaclena had only once before encountered a species living in that narrow zone between animal and accepted client-class sophont. It was a very rare state in the Five Galaxies, for any newly discovered pre-sentient species was soon registered and licensed to some starfaring clan for Uplift and indenture.

It dawned on Athaclena that this being was already far along toward sentience!

But the gap from animal to thinker was supposed to be impossible to cross alone! True, some humans still clung to quaint ideas from the ignorant days before Contact—theories proposing that true intelligence could be "evolved." But Galactic science assured that the threshold could only be passed with the aid of another race, one who had already crossed it.

So it had been all the way back to the fabled days of the first race—the Progenitors—billions of years ago.

But nobody had ever traced patrons for the humans. That was why they were called *k'chu-non* . . . wolflings. Might their old idea contain a germ of truth? If so, might this creature also . . . ?

Ah, no! Why did I not see it at once?

Athaclena suddenly knew this beast was not a natural find. It was not the fabled "Garthling" her father had asked her to seek. The family resemblance was simply too unmistakable.

She was looking at a gathering of *cousins*, sitting together on that branch high above the Gubru vapors. Human, neo-chimpanzees, and . . . what?

She tried to recall what her father had said about humanity's license to occupy their homeworld, the Earth. After Contact, the Institutes had granted recognition of mankind's de facto tenancy. Still, there were Fallow Rules and other restrictions, she was certain.

And a few special Earth species had been mentioned in particular.

The great beast radiated Potential like . . . A *metaphor* came to Athaclena, of a beacon burning in the tree across from her. Searching her memory Tymbrimi fashion, she at last drew forth the name she had been looking for.

"Pretty thing," she asked softly. "You are a *gorilla*, aren't you?"

16

The Howletts Center

The beast tossed its great head and snorted. Next to it, the mother chimp whimpered softly and regarded Athaclena with obvious dread.

But the little human girl clapped her hands, sensing a game. " 'Rilla! Jonny's a 'rilla! Like me!" The child's small fists thumped her chest. She threw back her head and crowed a high-pitched, ululating yell.

A gorilla. Athaclena looked at the giant, silent creature in wonderment, trying to remember what she had been told in passing so long ago.

Its dark nostrils flared as it sniffed in Athaclena's direction, and used its free hand to make quick, subtle hand signs to the human child.

"Jonny wants to know if you're going to be in charge, now," the little girl lisped. "I hope so. You sure looked tired when you stopped chasing Benjamin. Did he do something bad? He got away, you know."

Athaclena moved a little closer. "No," she said. "Benjamin didn't do anything bad. At least not since I met him—though I am beginning to suspect—"

Athaclena stopped. Neither the child nor the gorilla would understand what she now suspected. But the adult chim knew, clearly, and her eyes showed fear.

"I'm April," the small human told her. "An' that's Nita. Her baby's name is Cha-Cha. Sometimes chimmies give their babies easy names to start 'cause they don't talk so good at first," she confided.

116

Her eyes seemed to shine as she looked at Athaclena. "Are you *really* a Tym . . . bim . . . Tymmbimmie?"

Athaclena nodded. "I am Tymbrimi."

April clapped her hands. "Ooh. They're goodguys! Did you see the big spaceship? It came with a big boom, and Daddy made me go with Jonny, and then there was gas and Jonny put his hand over my mouth and I couldn't breathe!"

April made a scrunched up face, pantomiming suffocation.

"He let go when we were up in th' trees, though. We found Nita an' Cha-Cha." She glanced over at the chims. "I guess Nita's still too scared to talk much."

"Were you frightened too?" Athaclena asked.

April nodded seriously. "Yeth. But I had to stop being scared. I was th' only *man* here, and I hadda be in charge, and take care of ever'body.

"Can you be in charge now? You're a really pretty Tymbimmie."

The little girl's shyness returned. She partly buried herself against Jonny's massive chest, smiling out at Athaclena with only one eye showing.

Athaclena could not help staring. She had never until now realized this about human beings—of what they were capable. In spite of her people's alliance with the Terrans, she had picked up some of the common Galactic prejudice, imagining that the "wolflings" were still somehow feral, bestial. Many Galactics thought it questionable that humans were truly ready to be patrons. No doubt the Gubru had expressed that belief in their War Manifesto.

This child shattered that image altogether. By law and custom, little April *had* been in charge of her clients, no matter how young she was. And her understanding of that responsibility was clear.

Still, Athaclena now knew why both Robert and Benjamin had been anxious not to lead her here. She suppressed her initial surge of righteous anger. Later, she would have to find a way to get word to her father, after she had verified her suspicions.

She was almost beginning to feel Tymbrimi again as the *gheer* reaction gave way to a mere dull burning along her muscles and neural pathways. "Did any other humans make it into the trees?" she asked.

Jonny made a quick series of hand signs. April interpreted, although the little girl may not have clearly understood the implications. "He says a few tried. But they weren't fast enough. . . . Most of 'em just ran aroun' doin' 'Man-Things.' That's what 'rillas call the stuff humans do that 'rillas don't understand," she confided lowly.

At last the mother chim, Nita, spoke. "The g-gas . . ." She swallowed. "Th' gas m-made the humans weak." Her voice was barely audible. "Some of us chims felt it a little. . . . I don't think the 'rillas were bothered."

So. Perhaps Athaclena's original surmise about the gas was correct. She had suspected it was not intended to be immediately lethal. Mass slaughter of civilians was something generally frowned upon by the Institute for Civilized Warfare. Knowing the Gubru, the intent was probably much more insidious than that.

There was a cracking sound to her right. The large male chim, Benjamin, dropped onto a branch two trees away. He called out to Athaclena.

"It's okay now, miss! I found Dr. Taka and Dr. Schultz. They're anxious to talk to you!"

Athaclena motioned for him to approach. "Please come here first, Benjamin."

With typical *Pongo* exaggeration, Benjamin let out a long-suffering sigh. He leaped branch to branch until he came into view of the three apes and the human girl. Then his jaw dropped and his balancing grip almost slipped. Frustration wrote across his face. He turned to Athaclena, licking his lips, and cleared his throat.

"Don't bother," she told him. "I know you have spent the last twenty minutes trying, in the midst of all this turmoil, to arrange to have the truth hidden. But it was to no avail. I know what has been going on here."

Benjamin's mouth clapped shut. Then he shrugged. "So?" he sighed.

To the four on the branch Athaclena asked, "Do you accept my authority?"

"Yeth," April said. Nita glanced from Athaclena to the human child, then nodded.

"All right, then. Stay where you are until somebody comes for you. Do you understand?"

"Yes'm." Nita nodded again. Jonny and Cha-Cha merely looked back at her.

Athaclena stood up, finding her balance on the branch, and turned to Benjamin. "Now let us talk to these Uplift specialists of yours. If the gas has not completely incapacitated them, I'll be interested to hear why they have chosen to violate Galactic Law."

Benjamin looked defeated. He nodded resignedly.

"Also," Athaclena told him as she landed on the branch next to him. "You had better catch up with the chims and gorillas you sent away—in order that I would not see them. They should be called back.

"We may need their help."

17

Fiben

Fiben had managed to fashion a crutch out of shattered tree limbs lying near the furrow torn up by his escape pod. Cushioned by tatters of his ship-suit, the crutch jarred his shoulder only *partially* out of joint each time he leaned on it.

Hummph, he thought. *If the humans hadn't straightened our spines and shortened our arms I could've knuckle-walked back to civilization.*

Dazed, bruised, hungry . . . actually, Fiben was in a pretty good mood as he picked his way through obstacles on his way northward. *Hell, I'm alive. I can't really complain.*

He had spent quite a lot of time in the Mountains of Mulun, doing ecological studies for the Restoration Project, so he could tell that he had to be in the right watershed, not too far from known lands. The varieties of vegetation were all quite recognizable, mostly native plants but also some that had been imported and released into the ecosystem to fill gaps left by the Bururalli Holocaust.

Fiben felt optimistic. To have survived this far, even up to crash-landing in familiar territory . . . it made him certain that Ifni had further plans for him. She had to be saving him for something special. Probably a fate that would be particularly annoying and much more painful than mere starvation in the wilderness.

Fiben's ears perked and he looked up. Could he have imagined that sound?

No! Those were voices! He stumbled down the game path, alternately skipping and pole-vaulting on his makeshift crutch, until he came to a sloped clearing overlooking a steep canyon.

Minutes passed as he peered. The rain forest was so damn dense!

There! On the other side, about halfway downslope, six chims wearing backpacks could be seen moving rapidly through the forest, heading toward some of the still smoldering wreckage of TAASF *Proconsul*. Right now they were quiet. It was just a lucky break they had spoken as they passed below his position.

"Hey! Dummies! Over here!" He hopped on his right foot and waved his arms, shouting. The search party stopped. The chims looked about, blinking as the echoes bounced around the narrow defile. Fiben's teeth bared and he couldn't help growling low in frustration. They were looking everywhere *but* in his direction!

Finally, he picked up the crutch, whirled it above his head, and threw it out over the canyon.

One of the chims exclaimed, grabbing another. They watched the tumbling branch crash into the forest. *That's right*, Fiben urged. *Now think. Retrace the arc backwards.*

Two of the searchers pointed up his way and saw him waving. They shrieked in excitement, capering in circles.

Forgetting momentarily his own little regression, Fiben muttered under his breath. "Just my luck to be rescued by a bunch of grunts. Come on, guys. Let's not make a thunder dance out of it."

Still, he grinned when they neared his hillside clearing. And in all the subsequent hugging and backslapping he forgot himself and let out a few glad hoots of his own.

18

Uthacalthing

His little pinnace was the last craft to take off from the Port Helenia space-field. Already detection screens showed battle cruisers descending into the lower atmosphere.

Back at the port, a small force of militiamen and Terragens Marines prepared to make a futile last stand. Their defiance was broadcast on all channels.

"*. . . We deny the invader's rights to land here. We claim the protection of Galactic Civilization against their aggression. We refuse the Gubru permission to set down on our legal lease-hold.*

"*In earnest of this, a small, armed, Formal Resistance Detachment awaits the invaders at the capital spaceport. Our challenge . . .*"

Uthacalthing guided his pinnace with nonchalant nudges on the wrist and thumb controllers. The tiny ship raced southward along the coast of the Sea of Cilmar, faster than sound. Bright sunshine reflected off the broad waters to his right.

. . . should they dare to face us being to being, not cowering in their battleships . . .

Uthacalthing nodded. "Tell them, Earthlings," he said softly in Anglic. The detachment commander had sought his advice in phrasing the ritual challenge. He hoped he had been of help.

The broadcast went on to list the numbers and types of weapons awaiting the descending armada at the spaceport, so the enemy would have no justification for using overpowering force. Under circumstances such as these, the Gubru would

121

have no choice but to assail the defenders with ground troops. And they would have to take casualties.

If the Codes still hold, Uthacalthing reminded himself. *The enemy may not care about the Rules of War any longer.* It was hard to imagine such a situation. But there had been rumors from across the far starlanes . . .

A row of display screens rimmed his cockpit. One showed cruisers coming into view of Port Helenia's public news cameras. Others showed fast fighters tearing up the sky right over the spaceport.

Behind him Uthacalthing heard a low keening as two stilt-like Ynnin commiserated with each other. Those creatures, at least, had been able to fit into Tymbrimi-type seats. But their hulking master had to stand.

Kault did not just stand, he paced the narrow cabin, his crest inflating until it bumped the low ceiling, again and again. The Thennanin was not in a good mood.

"*Why*, Uthacalthing?" he muttered for what was not the first time. "Why did you delay for so long? We were the very last to get out of there!"

Kault's breathing vents puffed. "You told me we would leave night before last! I hurried to gather a few possessions and be ready and you did not come! I waited. I missed opportunities to hire other transport while you sent message after message urging patience. And then, when you came at last after dawn, we departed as blithely as if we were on a holiday ride to the Progenitors' Arch!"

Uthacalthing let his colleague grumble on. He had already made formal apologies and paid diplomatic gild in compensation. No more was required of him.

Besides, things were going just the way he had planned them to.

A yellow light flashed on the control board, and a tone began to hum.

"What is that?" Kault shuffled forward in agitation. "Have they detected our engines?"

"No." And Kault sighed in relief.

Uthacalthing went on. "It isn't the engines. That light means we've just been scanned by a probability beam."

"*What?*" Kault nearly screamed. "Isn't this vessel shielded? You aren't even using gravitics! What anomalous probability could they have picked up?"

Uthacalthing shrugged, as if the human gesture had been

born to him. "Perhaps the unlikelihood is intrinsic," he suggested. "Perhaps it is something about us, about our own fate, that is glowing along the worldlines. That may be what they detect."

Out of his right eye he saw Kault shiver. The Thennanin race seemed to have an almost superstitious dread of anything having to do with the art/science of reality-shaping. Uthacalthing allowed *looth'troo*—apology to one's enemy—to form gently within his tendrils, and reminded himself that his people and Kault's were officially at war. It was within his rights to tease his enemy-and-friend, as it had been ethically acceptable earlier, when he had arranged for Kault's own ship to be sabotaged.

"I shouldn't worry about it," he suggested. "We've got a good head start."

Before the Thennanin could reply, Uthacalthing bent forward and spoke rapidly in GalSeven, causing one of the screens to expand its image.

"*Thwill'kou-chlliou!*" he cursed. "Look at what they are doing!"

Kault turned and stared. The holo-display showed giant cruisers hovering over the capital city, pouring brown vapor over the buildings and parks. Though the volume was turned down, they could hear panic in the voice of the news announcer as he described the darkening skies, as if anyone in Port Helenia needed his interpretation.

"This is not well." Kault's crest bumped the ceiling more rapidly. "The Gubru are being more severe than the situation or their war rights here merit."

Uthacalthing nodded. But before he could speak another yellow light winked on.

"What is it now?" Kault sighed.

Uthacalthing's eyes were at their widest separation. "It means we are being chased by pursuit craft," he replied. "We may be in for a fight. Can you work a class fifty-seven weapons console, Kault?"

"No, but I believe one of my Ynnin—"

His reply was interrupted as Uthacalthing shouted, "Hold on!" and turned on the pinnace's gravitics. The ground screamed past under them. "I am beginning evasive maneuvers," he called out.

"Good," Kault whispered through his neck vents.

Oh, bless the Thennanin thick skull, Uthacalthing thought.

He kept control over his facial expression, though he knew his colleague had the empathy sensitivity of a stone and could not pick up his joy.

As the pursuing ships started firing on them, his corona began to sing.

19

Athaclena

Green fingers of forest merged with the lawns and leafy-colored buildings of the Center, as if the establishment were intended to be inconspicuous from the air. Although a wind from the west had finally driven away the last visible shreds of the invader's aerosol, a thin film of gritty powder covered everything below a height of five meters, giving off a tangy, unpleasant odor.

Athaclena's corona no longer shrank under an overriding roar of panic. The mood had changed amid the buildings. There was a thread of resignation now . . . and intelligent anger.

She followed Benjamin toward the first clearing, where she caught sight of small groups of neo-chimps running pigeon-toed within the inner compound. One pair hurried by carrying a muffled burden on a stretcher.

"Maybe you shouldn't go down there after all, miss," Benjamin rasped. "I mean it's obvious the gas was designed to affect humans, but even us chims feel a bit woozy from it. You're pretty important . . ."

"I am Tymbrimi," Athaclena answered coolly. "I cannot sit here while I am needed by clients and by my peers."

Benjamin bowed in acquiescence. He led her down a stairlike series of branches until she set foot with some relief

on the ground. The pungent odor was thicker here. Athaclena
tried to ignore it, but her pulse pounded from nervousness.

They passed what had to have been facilities for housing
and training gorillas. There were fenced enclosures, play-
grounds, testing areas. Clearly an intense if small-scale effort
had gone on here. Had Benjamin really imagined that he
could fool her simply by sending the pre-sentient apes into
the jungle to hide?

She hoped none of them had been hurt by the gas, or in
the panicky aftermath. She remembered from her brief History of Earthmen class that gorillas, although strong, were
also notoriously sensitive—even fragile—creatures.

Chims dressed in shorts, sandals, and the ubiquitous
tool-bandoleers hurried to and fro on serious errands. A few
stared at Athaclena as she approached, but they did not stop
to speak. In fact, she heard very few words at all.

Stepping lightly through the dark dust, they arrived at
the center of the encampment. There, at last, she and her
guide encountered humans. They lay on couches on the steps
of the main building, a mel and a fem. The male human's
head was entirely hairless, and his eyes bore traces of epicanthic
folding. He looked barely conscious.

The other "man" was a tall, dark-haired female. Her skin
was very black—a deep, rich shade Athaclena had never
encountered before. Probably she was one of those rare "pure
breed" humans who retained the characteristics of their ancient "races." In contrast, the skin color of the chims standing
next to her was almost pale pink, under their patchy covering
of brown hair.

With the help of two older-looking chims, the black
woman managed to prop herself up on one elbow as Athaclena
approached. Benjamin stepped forward to make the intro-
ductions.

"Dr. Taka, Dr. Schultz, Dr. M'Bzwelli, Chim Frederick,
all of the Terran Wolfling Clan, I present you to the respected
Athaclena, a Tymbrimi ab-Caltmour ab-Brma ab-Krallnith
ul-Tytlal."

Athaclena glanced at Benjamin, surprised he was able to
recite her species honorific from memory.

"Dr. Schultz," Athaclena said, nodding to the chim on the
left. To the woman she bowed slightly lower. "Dr. Taka."
With one last head incline she took in the other human and
chim. "Dr. M'Bzwelli and Chim Frederick. Please accept my

condolences over the cruelty visited on your settlement and your world."

The chims bowed low. The woman tried to, as well, but she failed in her weakness.

"Thank you for your sentiments," she replied, laboriously. "We Earthlings will muddle through, I'm sure. . . . I do admit I'm a little surprised to see the daughter of the Tymbrimi ambassador pop out of nowhere right now."

I'll just bet you are, Athaclena thought in Anglic, enjoying, this once, the flavor of human-style sarcasm. *My presence is nearly as much a disaster to your plans as the Gubru and their gas!*

"I have an injured friend," she said aloud. "Three of your neo-chimpanzees went after him, some time ago. Have you heard anything from them?"

The woman nodded. "Yes, yes. We just had a pulse from the search party. Robert Oneagle is conscious and stable. Another group we had sent to seek out a downed flyer will be joining them shortly, with full medical equipment."

Athaclena felt a tense worry unwrap in the corner of her mind where she had put it. "Good. Very good. Then I will turn to other matters."

Her corona blossomed out as she formed *kuouwassooe,* the glyph of presentiment—though she knew these folk would barely catch its fringes, if at all.

"First, as a member of a race that has been in alliance with yours ever since you wolflings burst so loudly upon the Five Galaxies, I offer my assistance during this emergency. What I can do as a fellow patron, I shall do, requiring in return only whatever help you can give me in getting in touch with my father."

"Done." Dr. Taka nodded. "Done and with our thanks."

Athaclena took a step forward. "Second—I must exclaim my dismay on discovering the function of this Center. I find you are engaged in unsanctioned Uplift activities on . . . on a *fallow* species!"

The four directors looked at each other. By now Athaclena could read human expressions well enough to know their chagrined resignation. "Furthermore," she went on, "I note that you had the poor taste to commit this crime on the planet Garth, a tragic victim of past ecological abuse—"

"Now just a minute!" Chim Frederick protested. "How

can you compare what we're doing with the holocaust of the
Burur—"

"Fred, be quiet!" Dr. Schultz, the other chim, cut in
urgently.

Frederick blinked. Realizing it was too late to take back
the interruption, he muttered on. ". . . th' only planets
Earthclan's been allowed to settle have been other Eatees'
messes. . . ."

The second human, Dr. M'Bzwelli, started coughing.
Frederick shut up and turned away.

The human male looked up at Athaclena. "You have us
against the wall, miss." He sighed. "Can we ask you to let us
explain before you press charges? We're . . . we're not representatives of our government, you understand. We are . . .
private criminals."

Athaclena felt a funny sort of relief. Old pre-Contact
Earthling flat movies—especially those copsandrobbers thrillers so popular among the Tymbrimi—often seemed to re-
volve around some ancient lawbreaker attempting to "silence
the witness." A part of her had wondered just how atavistic
these people actually were.

She exhaled deeply and nodded. "Very well, then. The
question can be put aside during the present emergency.
Please tell me the situation here. What is the enemy trying to
accomplish with this gas?"

"It weakens any human who breathes it," Dr. Taka answered. "There was a broadcast an hour ago. The invader
announced that affected humans must receive the antidote
within one week, or die.

"Of course they are offering the antidote only in urban
areas."

"Hostage gas!" Athaclena whispered. "They want all the
planet's humans as pawns."

"Exactly. We must ingather or drop dead in six days."

Athaclena's corona sparked anger. Hostage gas was an
irresponsible weapon, even if it was legal under certain limited types of war.

"What will happen to your clients?" Neo-chimps were
only a few centuries old and should not be left unwatched in
the wilderness.

Dr. Taka grimaced, obviously worried as well. "Most
chims seem unaffected by the gas. But they have so few
natural leaders, such as Benjamin or Dr. Schultz here."

Schultz's brown, simian eyes looked down at his human friend. "Not to worry, Susan. We will, as you say, muddle through." He turned back to Athaclena. "We're evacuating the humans in stages, starting with the children and old folks tonight. Meanwhile, we'll start destroying this compound and all traces of what's happened here."

Seeing that Athaclena was about to object, the elderly neo-chimp raised his hand. "Yes, miss. We will provide you with cameras and assistants, so you may collect your evidence, first. Will that do? We would not dream of thwarting you in your duty."

Athaclena sensed the chim geneticist's bitterness. But she had no sympathy for him, imagining how her father would feel when he learned of this. Uthacalthing liked Earthlings. This irresponsible criminality would wound him deeply.

"No sense in handing the Gubru a justification for their aggression," Dr. Taka added. "The matter of the gorillas can go to the Tymbrimi Grand Council, if you wish. Our allies may then decide where to go from there, whether to press formal charges or leave our punishment to our own government."

Athaclena saw the logic in it. After a moment she nodded. "That will do, then. Bring me your cameras and I shall record this burning."

20

Galactics

To the fleet admiral—the Suzerain of Beam and Talon—the argument sounded silly. But of course that was always the way of it among civilians. Priests and bureaucrats always argued. It was the fighters who believed in action!

Still, the admiral had to admit that it was thrilling to take part in their first real policy debate as a threesome. This was the way Truth was traditionally attained among the Gubru, through stress and disagreement, persuasion and dance, until finally a new consensus was reached.

And eventually . . .

The Suzerain of Beam and Talon shook aside the thought. It was much too soon to begin contemplating the Molt. There would be many more arguments, much jostling and maneuvering for the highest perch, before that day arrived.

As for this first debate, the admiral was pleased to find itself in the position of arbiter between its two bickering peers. This was a good way to begin.

The Terrans at the small spaceport had issued a well-written formal challenge. The Suzerain of Propriety insisted that Talon Soldiers must be sent to overcome the defenders in close combat. The Suzerain of Cost and Caution did not agree. For some time they circled each other on the dais of the flagship's bridge, eyeing each other and squawking pronouncements of argument.

"Expenses must be kept low!
      Low enough that we need not,
           Need not burden other fronts!"

The Suzerain of Cost and Caution thus insisted that this expedition was only one of many engagements currently sapping the strength of the clan of Gooksyu-Gubru. In fact, it was rather a side-battle. Matters were tense across the Galactic spiral. In such times, it was the job of the Suzerain of Cost and Caution to protect the clan from overextending itself.

The Suzerain of Propriety huffed its feathers indignantly in response.

"What shall expense matter,
                  mean,
          signify,
      stand for, if we fall,
                  topple,
          drop,
      plummet from grace
      in the eyes of our Ancestrals?"

We must do what is right! *Zoooon!*"

Observing from its own perch of command, the Suzerain of Beam and Talon watched the struggle to see if any clear patterns of dominance were about to manifest themselves. It was thrilling to hear and see the excellent argument-dances performed by those who had been chosen to be the admiral's mates. All three of them represented the finest products of "hot-egg" engineering, designed to bring out the best qualities of the race.

Soon, it was obvious that its peers had reached a stalemate. It would be up to Suzerain of Beam and Talon to decide.

It certainly would be less costly if the expeditionary force could simply ignore the insolent wolflings below until the hostage gas forced them to surrender. Or, with a simple order, their redoubt could be reduced to slag. But the Suzerain of Propriety refused to accept either option. Such actions would be catastrophic, the priest insisted.

The bureaucrat was just as adamant not to waste good soldiers on what would be essentially a gesture.

Deadlocked, the two other commanders eyed the Suzerain of Beam and Talon as they circled and squawked, fluffing their glowing white down. Finally, the admiral ruffled its own plumage and stepped onto the dais to join them.

> "To engage in ground combat would cost,
> would mean expense.
> But it would be honorable,
> admirable.
>
> "A third factor decides,
> swings the final vote.
> That is the training need of
> Talon Soldiers.
> Training against wolfling troops.
>
> "Ground forces shall attack them, beam to beam, hand to talon."

The issue was decided. A stoop-colonel of the Talon Soldiers saluted and hurried off with the order.

Of course with this resolution Propriety's perch position

would rise a little. Caution's descended. But the quest for dominance had only just begun.

So it had been for their distant ancestors, before the Gooksyu turned the primitive proto-Gubru into starfarers. Wisely, their patrons had taken the ancient patterns and shaped and expanded them into a useful, logical form of government for a sapient people.

Still, part of the older function remained. The Suzerain of Beam and Talon shivered as the tension of argument was released. And although all three of them were still quite neuter, the admiral felt a momentary thrill that was deeply, thoroughly sexual.

21

Fiben and Robert

The two rescue parties encountered each other more than a mile into the high pass. It was a somber gathering. The three who had started out that morning with Benjamin were too tired to do more than nod to the subdued group returning from the crash site.

But the battered pair who had been rescued exclaimed on seeing each other.

"Robert! Robert Oneagle! When did they let you out of study hall? Does your mommy know where you are?"

The injured chim leaned on a makeshift crutch and wore the singed remains of a tattered TAASF ship-suit. Robert looked up at him from the stretcher and grinned through an anesthetic haze.

"Fiben! In Goodall's name, was that *you* I saw smokin' out of the sky? Figures. What'd you do, fry ten megacredits' worth of scoutboat?"

Fiben rolled his eyes. "More like five megs. She was an old tub, even if she did all right by me."

Robert felt a strange envy. "So? I guess we got whomped."

"You could say that. One on one we fought well. Would've been all right if there'd been enough of us."

Robert knew what his friend meant. "You mean there's no limit to what could've been accomplished with—"

"With an infinite number of monkeys?" Fiben cut in. His snort was a little less than a laugh but more than an ironic grin.

The other chims blinked in consternation. This level of banter was a bit over their heads, but what was more disturbing was how blithely this chen interrupted the human son of the Planetary Coordinator!

"I wish I could've been there with you," Robert said seriously.

Fiben shrugged. "Yeah, Robert. I know. But we all had orders." For a long moment they were silent. Fiben knew Megan Oneagle well enough, and he sympathized with Robert.

"Well I guess we're both due for a stint in the mountains, assigned to holdin' down beds and harassing nurses." Fiben sighed, gazing toward the south. "If we can stand the fresh air, that is." He looked down to Robert. "These chims told me about the raid on the Center. Scary stuff."

"Clennie'll help 'em straighten things out," Robert answered. His attention had started to drift. They obviously had him doped to a dolphin's blowhole. "She knows a lot . . . a lot more'n she thinks she does."

Fiben had heard about the daughter of the Tymbrimi ambassador. "Sure," he said softly, as the others lifted the stretcher once again. "An Eatee'll straighten things out. More likely'n not, that girl friend of yours will have everybody thrown in the clink, invasion or no invasion!"

But Robert was now far away. And Fiben had a sudden strange impression. It was as if the human mel's visage was not entirely Terran any longer. His dreamy smile was distant and touched with something . . . unearthly.

22

Athaclena

A large number of chims returned to the Center, drifting in from the forest where they had been sent to hide. Frederick and Benjamin set them to work dismantling and burning the buildings and their contents. Athaclena and her two assistants hurried from site to site, carefully recording everything before it was put to the torch.

It was hard work. Never in her life as a diplomat's daughter had Athaclena felt so exhausted. And yet she dared not let any scrap of evidence go undocumented. It was a matter of duty.

About an hour before dusk a contingent of gorillas trooped into the encampment, larger, darker, more crouched and feral-looking than their chim guardians. Under careful direction they took up simple tasks, helping to demolish the only home they had ever known.

The confused creatures watched as their Training and Testing Center and the Clients' Quarters melted into slag. A few even tried to halt the destruction, stepping in front of the smaller, soot-covered chims and waving vigorous hand signs—trying to tell them that this was a bad thing.

Athaclena could see how, by their lights, it wasn't logical. But then, the affairs of patron-class beings often did seem foolish.

Finally, the big pre-clients were left standing amid eddies of smoke with small piles of personal possessions—toys, mementos, and simple tools—piled at their feet. They stared blankly at the wreckage, not knowing what to do.

By dusk Athaclena had been nearly worn down by the

133

emotions that fluxed through the compound. She sat on a tree stump, upwind of the burning clients' quarters, listening to the great apes' low, chuffing moans. Her aides slumped nearby with their cameras and bags of samples, staring at the destruction, the whites of their eyes reflecting the flickering flames.

Athaclena withdrew her corona until all she could *kenn* was the Unity Glyph—the coalescence to which all the beings within the forest valley contributed. And even that under-image wavered, flickered. She saw it *metaphorically*—weepy, drooping, like a sad flag of many colors.

There was honor here, she admitted reluctantly. These scientists had been violating a treaty, but they couldn't be accused of doing anything truly unnatural.

By any real measure, gorillas were as ready for Uplift as chimpanzees had been, a hundred Earth years before Contact. Humans had been forced to make compromises, back when Contact brought them into the domain of Galactic society. Officially, the tenancy treaty which sanctioned their rights to their homeworld was intended to see to it that Earth's fallow species list was maintained, so its stock of Potential for sentience would not be used up too quickly.

But everyone knew that, in spite of primitive man's legendary penchant for genocide, the Earth was still a shining example of genetic diversity, rare in the range of types and forms that had been left untouched by Galactic civilization.

Anyway . . . when a pre-sentient race was ready for Uplift, it was ready!

No, clearly the treaty had been forced on humans while they were weak. They were allowed to claim neo-dolphins and neo-chimps—species already well on the road to sapiency before Contact. But the senior clans weren't about to let *Homo sapiens* go uplifting more clients than anybody else around!

Why, that would have given wolflings the status of senior patrons!

Athaclena sighed.

It wasn't fair, certainly. But that did not matter. Galactic society depended on oaths kept. A treaty was a solemn vow, species to species. Violations could not go unreported.

Athaclena wished her father were here. Uthacalthing would know what to make of the things she had witnessed here—the well-intended work of this illegal center, and the vile but perhaps legal actions of the Gubru.

Uthacalthing was far away, though, too far even to touch within the Empathy Net. All she could tell was that his special rhythm still vibrated faintly on the *nahakieri* level. And while it was comforting to close her eyes and inner ears and gently *kenn* it, that faint reminder of him told her little. *Nahakieri* essences could linger longer after a person left this life, as they had for her dead mother, Mathicluanna. They floated like the songs of Earth-whales, at the edges of what might be known by creatures who lived by hands and fire.

"Excuse me, ma'am." A voice that was hardly more than a raspy growl broke harshly over the faint under-glyph, dispersing it. Athaclena shook her head. She opened her eyes to see a neo-chimp with soot-covered fur and shoulders stooped from exhaustion.

"Ma'am? You all right?"

"Yes. I am fine. What is it?" Anglic felt harsh in her throat, already irritated from smoke and fatigue.

"Directors wanna see you, ma'am."

A spendthrift with words, this one. Athaclena slid down from the stump. Her aides groaned, chim-theatrically, as they gathered their tapes and samples and followed behind.

Several lift-lorries stood at the loading dock. Chims and gorillas carried stretchers onto flyers, which then lifted off into the gathering night on softly humming gravitics. Their lights faded away into the direction of Port Helenia.

"I thought all the children and elderly were already evacuated. Why are you still loading humans in such a hurry?"

The messenger shrugged. The stresses of the day had robbed many of the chims of much of their accustomed spark. Athaclena was sure that it was only the presence of the gorillas—who had to be set an example—that prevented a mass attack of stress-atavism. In so young a client race it was surprising the chims had done so well.

Orderlies hurried to and from the hospital facility, but they seldom bothered the two human directors directly. The neo-chimp scientist, Dr. Schultz, stood in front of them and seemed to be handling most matters himself. At his side, Chim Frederick had been replaced by Athaclena's old traveling companion, Benjamin.

On the stage nearby lay a small pile of documents and

record cubes containing the genealogy and genetic record of every gorilla who had ever lived here.

"Ah, respected Tymbrimi Athaclena." Schultz spoke with hardly a trace of the usual chim growl. He bowed, then shook her hand in the manner preferred by his people—a full clasp which emphasized the opposable thumb.

"Please excuse our poor hospitality," he pleaded. "We had intended to serve a special supper from the main kitchen . . . sort of a grand farewell. But we'll have to make do with canned rations instead, I'm afraid."

A small chimmie approached carrying a platter stacked with an array of containers.

"Dr. Elayne Soo is our nutritionist," Schultz continued. "She tells me you might find these delicacies palatable."

Athaclena stared at the cans. Kóothra! Here, five hundred parsecs from home, to find an instant pastry made in her own hometown! Unable to help it, she laughed aloud.

"We have placed a full load of these, plus other supplies, aboard a flitter for you. We recommend you abandon the craft soon after leaving here, of course. It won't be long before the Gubru have their own satellite network in place, and thereafter air traffic will be impractical."

"It won't be dangerous to fly *toward* Port Helenia," Athaclena pointed out. "The Gubru will expect an influx for many days, as people seek antidote treatments." She motioned at the frantic pace of activity. "So why the near-panic I sense here? Why are you evacuating the humans so quickly? Who . . . ?"

Looking as if he feared to interrupt her, Schultz nevertheless cleared his throat and shook his head meaningfully. Benjamin gave Athaclena a pleading look.

"Please, ser," Schultz implored with a low voice. "Please speak softly. Most of our chims haven't really guessed . . ." He let the sentence hang.

Athaclena felt a cold thrill along her ruff. For the first time she looked closely at the two human directors, Taka and M'Bzwelli. They had remained silent all along, nodding as if understanding and approving everything being said.

The black woman, Dr. Taka, smiled at her, unblinkingly. Athaclena's corona reached out, then curled back in revulsion.

She whirled on Schultz. "You are killing her!"

Schultz nodded miserably. "Please, ser. Softly. You are right, of course. I have drugged my dear friends, so they can put up a good front until my few good chim administrators can finish here and get our people away without a panic. It was at their own insistence. Dr. Taka and Dr. M'Bzwelli felt they were slipping away too quickly from effects of the gas." He added sadly, weakly.

"You did not have to obey them! This is murder!"

Benjamin looked stricken. Schultz nodded. "It was not easy. Chim Frederick was unable to bear the shame even this long and has sought his own peace. I, too, would probably take my life soon, were my death not already as inevitable as my human colleagues'."

"What do you mean?"

"I mean that the Gubru do not appear to be very good chemists!" The elderly neo-chimp laughed bitterly, finishing with a cough. "Their gas is killing some of the humans. It acts faster than they said it would. Also, it seems to be affecting a few of us chims."

Athaclena sucked in her breath. "I see." She wished she did not.

"There is another matter we thought you should know about," Schultz said. "A news report from the invaders. Unfortunately, it was in Galactic Three; the Gubru spurn Anglic and our translation program is primitive. But we know it regarded your father."

Athaclena felt removed, as if she were hovering above it all. In this state her numbed senses gathered in random details. She could *kenn* the simple forest ecosystem—little native animals creeping back into the valley, wrinkling their noses at the pungent dust, avoiding the area near the Center for the fires that still flickered there.

"Yes." She nodded, a borrowed gesture that all at once felt alien again. "Tell me."

Schultz cleared his throat. "Well, it seems your father's star cruiser was sighted leaving the planet. It was chased by warships. The Gubru say that it did not reach the Transfer Point.

"Of course one cannot trust what they say. . . ."

Athaclena's hips rocked slightly out of joint as she swayed from side to side. Tentative mourning—like a trembling of the lips as a human girl might begin to sense desolation.

No. I will not contemplate this now. Later. I will decide later what to feel.

"Of course you may have whatever aid we can offer,"

Chim Schultz continued quietly. "Your flitter has weapons, as well as food. You may fly to where your friend, Robert Oneagle, has been taken, if you wish.

"We hope, however, that you will choose to remain with the evacuation for a time, at least until the gorillas are safely hidden in the mountains, under the care of some qualified humans who might have escaped."

Schultz looked up at her earnestly, his brown eyes harrowed with sadness.

"I know it is a lot to ask, honored Tymbrimi Athaclena, but will you take our children under your care for a time, as they go into exile in the wilderness?"

23

Exile

The gently humming gravitic craft hovered over an uneven row of dark, rocky ridge-spines. Noon-shortened shadows had begun to grow again as Gimelhai passed its zenith and the flyer settled into the dimness between the stone spines. Its engines grumbled into silence.

A messenger awaited its passengers at the agreed rendezvous. The chim courier handed Athaclena a note as she stepped out of the machine, while Benjamin hurried to spread radar-fouling camouflage over the little flitter.

In the letter Juan Mendoza, a freeholder above Lorne Pass, reported the safe arrival of Robert Oneagle and little April Wu. Robert was recuperating well, the message said. He might be up and about in a week or so.

Athaclena felt relieved. She wanted very much to see Robert—and not only because she needed advice on how to handle a ragged band of refugee gorillas and neo-chimpanzees.

Some of the Howletts Center chims—those affected by the Gubran gas—had gone to the city with the humans, hoping antidote would be given as promised . . . and that it would work. She had left only a handful of really responsible chim technicians to assist her.

Perhaps more chims would show up, Athaclena told herself—and maybe even some human officials who had escaped gassing by the Gubru. She hoped that somebody in authority might appear and take over soon.

Another message from the Mendoza household was written by a chim survivor of the battle in space. The militiaman requested help getting in touch with the Resistance Forces.

Athaclena did not know how to reply. In the late hours last night, as great ships descended upon Port Helenia and the towns on the Archipelago, there had been frantic telephone and radio calls to and from sites all over the planet. There were reports of ground fighting at the spaceport. Some said that it was even hand to hand for a time. Then there was silence, and the Gubru armada consolidated without further incident.

It seemed that in half a day the resistance so carefully planned by the Planetary Council had fallen completely apart. All traces of a chain of command had dissolved; for nobody had foreseen the use of hostage gas. How could anything be done when nearly every human on the planet was taken so simply out of action?

A scattering of chims were trying to organize here and there, mostly by telephone. But few had thought out any but the most nebulous plans.

Athaclena put away the slips of paper and thanked the messenger. Over the hours since the evacuation she had begun to feel a change within herself. What had yesterday been confusion and grief had evolved into an obstinate sense of determination.

I will persevere. Uthacalthing would require it of me and I will not let him down.

Wherever I am, the enemy will not thrive near me.

She would also preserve the evidence she had gathered, of course. Someday the opportunity might come to present it to Tymbrimi authorities. It could give her people an opportunity to teach the humans a badly needed lesson on how to behave as a Galactic patron race must, before it was too late.

If it was not too late already.

Benjamin joined her at the sloping edge of the ridge top. "There!" He pointed into the valley below. "There they are, right on time."

Athaclena shaded her eyes. Her corona reached forth and touched the network around her. *Yes. And now I see them, as well.*

A long column of figures moved through the forest below, some small ones—brown in color—escorting a more numerous file of larger, darker shapes. Each of the big creatures carried a bulging backpack. A few had dropped to the knuckles of one hand as they shuffled along. Gorilla children ran amidst the adults, waving their arms for balance.

The escorting chims kept alert watch with beam rifles clutched close. Their attention was directed not on the column or the forest but at the sky.

The heavy equipment had already made it by circuitous routes to limestone caves in the mountains. But the exodus would not be safe until all the refugees were there at last, in those underground redoubts.

Athaclena wondered what was going on now in Port Helenia, or on the Earth-settled islands. The escape attempt of the Tymbrimi courier ship had been mentioned twice more by the invaders, then never again.

If nothing else, she would have to find out if her father was still on Garth, and if he still lived.

She touched the locket hanging from the thin chain around her neck, the tiny case containing her mother's legacy—a single thread from Mathicluanna's corona. It was cold solace, but she did not even have that much from Uthacalthing.

Oh, Father. How could you leave me without even a strand of yours to guide me?

The column of dark shapes approached rapidly. A low, growling sort of semi-music rose from the valley as they passed by, like nothing she had ever heard before. *Strength* these creatures had always owned, and Uplift had also removed some of their well-known frailty. As yet their destiny was unclear, but these were, indeed, powerful entities.

Athaclena had no intention of remaining inactive, simply a nursemaid for a gang of pre-sentients and hairy clients. One more thing Tymbrimi shared with humans was understanding of the need to *act* when wrong was being done. The letter from the wounded space-chim had started her thinking.

She turned to her aide.

"I am less than completely fluent in the languages of Earth, Benjamin. I need a word. One that describes an unusual type of military force.

"I am thinking of any army that moves by night and in the shadow of the land. One that strikes quickly and silently, using surprise to make up for small numbers and poor weapons. I remember reading that such forces were common in the pre-Contact history of Earth. They used the conventions of so-called civilized legions when it suited them, and innovation when they liked.

"It would be a *k'chu-non krann*, a wolfling army, unlike anything now known. Do you understand what I am talking about, Benjamin? Is there a word for this thing I have in mind?"

"Do you mean . . . ?" Benjamin looked quickly down at the column of partly uplifted apes lumbering through the forest below, rumbling their low, strange marching song.

He shook his head, obviously trying to restrain himself, but his face reddened and finally the guffaws burst out, uncontainable. Benjamin hooted and fell against a spine-stone, then over onto his back. He rolled in the dust of Garth and kicked at the sky, laughing.

Athaclena sighed. First back on Tymbrim, then among humans, and now here, with the newest, roughest clients known—everywhere she found *jokers*.

She watched the chimpanzee patiently, waiting for the silly little thing to catch its breath and finally let her in on what it found so funny.

PART TWO

Patriots

Evelyn, a modified dog,
Viewed the quivering fringe
of a special doily,
Draped across the piano, with some surprise—

In the darkened room,
Where the chairs dismayed
And the horrible curtains
Muffled the rain,
She could hardly believe her eyes—

A curious breeze, a garlic breath
Which sounded like a snore,
Somewhere near the Steinway
(or even from within)
Had caused the doily fringe to waft
And tremble in the gloom—

Evelyn, a dog, having undergone
Further modification
Pondered the significance of
Short Person Behavior
In pedal-depressed panchromatic resonance
And other highly ambient domains . . .

"Arf!" she said.

FRANK ZAPPA

24

Fiben

Tall, gangling, storklike figures watched the road from atop the roof of a dark, low-slung bunker. Their silhouettes, outlined against the late afternoon sun, were in constant motion, shifting from one spindly leg to another in nervous energy as if the slightest sound would be enough to set them into flight.

Serious creatures, those birds. And dangerous as hell.

Not birds, Fiben reminded himself as he approached the checkpoint. Not in the Earthly sense, at least.

But the analogy would do. Their bodies were covered with fine down. Sharp, bright yellow beaks jutted from sleek, swept-back faces.

And although their ancient wings were now no more than slender, feathered arms, they could fly. Black, glistening gravitic backpacks more than compensated for what their avian ancestors had long ago lost.

Talon Soldiers. Fiben wiped his hands on his shorts, but his palms still felt damp. He kicked a pebble with one bare foot and patted his draft horse on the flank. The placid animal had begun to crop a patch of blue native grass by the side of the road.

"Come on, Tycho," Fiben said, tugging on the reins. "We can't hang back or they'll get suspicious. Anyway, you know that stuff gives you gas."

Tycho shook his massive gray head and farted loudly.

"I *told* you so." Fiben waved at the air.

A cargo wagon floated just behind the horse. The dented, half-rusted bin of the farm truck was filled with rough burlap

sacks of grain. Obviously the antigrav stator still worked, but
the propulsion engine was kaput.

"Come on. Let's get on with it." Fiben tugged again.

Tycho gamely nodded, as if the workhorse actually understood. The traces tightened, and the hover truck bobbed
along after them as they approached the checkpoint.

Soon, however, a keening sound on the road ahead
warned of oncoming traffic. Fiben hurriedly guided horse and
wagon to one side. With a high-pitched whine and a rush of
air, an armored hovercraft swept by. Vehicles like it had been
cruising eastward intermittently, in ones and twos, all day.

He looked carefully to make sure nothing else was coming before leading Tycho back onto the road. Fiben's shoulders hunched nervously. Tycho snorted at the growing,
unfamiliar scent of the invaders.

"Halt!"

Fiben jumped involuntarily. The amplified voice was
mechanical, toneless, and adamant. "Move, move to this side
. . . this side for inspection!"

Fiben's heart pounded. He was glad his role was to act
frightened. It wouldn't be hard.

"Hasten! Make haste and present yourself!"

Fiben led Tycho toward the inspection stand, ten meters
to the right of the highway. He tied the horse's tether to a
railed post and hurried around to where a pair of Talon
Soldiers waited.

Fiben's nostrils flared at the aliens' dusty, lavender aroma.
I wonder what they'd taste like, he thought somewhat savagely. It would have made no difference at all to his great-to-
the-tenth-grandfather that these were sentient beings. To his
ancestors, a bird was a bird was a bird.

He bowed low, hands crossed in front of him, and got his
first close look at the invaders.

They did not seem all that impressive up close. True,
the sharp yellow beak and razorlike talons looked formidable.
But the stick-legged creatures were hardly much taller than
Fiben, and their bones looked hollow and thin.

No matter. These were starfarers—senior patrons-class
beings whose Library-derived culture and technology were
all but omnipotent long, long before humans rose up out of
Africa's savannah, blinking with the dawnlight of fearful curiosity. By the time man's lumbering slowships stumbled upon
Galactic civilization, the Gubru and their clients had wrested

a position of some eminence among the powerful interstellar clans. Fierce conservatism and facile use of the Great Library had taken them far since their own patrons had found them on the Gubru homeworld and given them the gift of completed minds.

Fiben remembered huge, bellipotent battle cruisers, dark and invincible under their shimmering allochroous shields, with the lambent edge of the galaxy shining behind them. . . .

Tycho nickered and shied aside as one of the Talon Soldiers—its saber-rifle loosely slung—stepped past him to approach the tethered truck. The alien climbed onto the floating farm-hover to inspect it. The other guard twittered into a microphone. Half buried in the soft down around the creature's narrow, sharp breastbone, a silvery medallion emitted clipped Anglic words.

"State . . . state identity . . . identity and purpose!"

Fiben crouched down and shivered, pantomiming fear. He was sure not many Gubru knew much about neo-chimps. In the few centuries since Contact, little information would have yet passed through the massive bureaucracy of the Library Institute and found its way into local branches. And of course, the Galactics relied on the Library for nearly everything.

Still, verisimilitude was important. Fiben's ancestors had understood one answer to a threat when a counter-bluff was ruled out—submission. Fiben knew how to fake it. He crouched lower and moaned.

The Gubru whistled in apparent frustration, probably having gone through this before. It chirped again, more slowly this time.

"Do not be alarmed, you are safe," the vodor medallion translated at a lower volume than before. "You are safe . . . safe. . . . We are Gubru . . . Galactic patrons of high clan and family. . . . You are safe. . . . Young half-sentients are safe when they are cooperative. . . . You are safe. . . ."

Half-sentients . . . Fiben rubbed his nose to cover a sniff of indignation. Of course that was what the Gubru were bound to think. And in truth, few four-hundred-year-old client races could be called fully uplifted.

Still, Fiben noted yet another score to settle.

He was able to pick out meaning here and there in the invader's chirpings before the vodor translated them. But one

short course in Galactic Three, back in school, was not much
to go on, and the Gubru had their own accent and dialect.

". . . You are safe . . ." the vodor soothed. "The humans
do not deserve such fine clients. . . . You are safe. . . ."

Gradually, Fiben backed away and looked up, still
trembling. *Don't overact*, he reminded himself. He gave the
gangling avian creature an approximation of a correct bow of
respect from a bipedal junior client to a senior patron. The
alien would surely miss the slight embellishment—an extension of the middle fingers—that flavored the gesture.

"Now," the vodor barked, perhaps with a note of relief.
"State name and purposes."

"Uh, I'm F-Fiben . . . uh, s-s-ser." His hands fluttered
in front of him. It was a bit of theater, but the Gubru might
know that neo-chimpanzees under stress still spoke using
parts of the brain originally devoted to hand control.

It certainly looked as if the Talon Soldier was frustrated.
Its feathers ruffled, and it hopped a little dance. ". . . purpose . . . purpose . . . state your purpose in approaching the
urban area!"

Fiben bowed again, quickly.

"Uh . . . th' hover won't work no more. Th' humans are
all gone . . . nobody to tell us what to do at th' farm . . ."

He scratched his head. "I figured, well, they must need
food in town . . . and maybe some- somebody can fix th' cart
in trade for grain . . . ?" His voice rose hopefully.

The second Gubru returned and chirped briefly to the
one in charge. Fiben could follow its GalThree well enough
to get the gist.

The hover was a real farm tool. It would not take a genius
to tell that the rotors just needed to be unfrozen for it to run
again. Only a helpless drudge would haul an antigravity truck
all the way to town behind a beast of burden, unable to make
such a simple repair on his own.

The first guard kept one taloned, splay-fingered hand
over the vodor, but Fiben gathered their opinion of chims
had started low and was rapidly dropping. The invaders hadn't
even bothered to issue identity cards to the neo-chimpanzee
population.

For centuries Earthlings—humans, dolphins, and chims—
had known the galaxies were a dangerous place where it was
often better to have more cleverness than one was credited
for. Even before the invasion, word had gone out among the

chim population of Garth that it might be necessary to put on the old "Yes, massa!" routine.

Yeah, Fiben reminded himself. *But nobody ever counted on all the humans being taken away!* Fiben felt a knot in his stomach when he imagined the humans—mels, fems, and children—huddled behind barbed wire in crowded camps.

Oh yeah. The invaders would pay.

The Talon Soldiers consulted a map. The first Gubru uncovered its vodor and twittered again at Fiben.

"You may go," the vodor barked. "Proceed to the Eastside Garage Complex. . . . You may go . . . Eastside Garage. . . . Do you know the Eastside Garage?"

Fiben nodded hurriedly. "Y-yessir."

"Good . . . good creature . . . take your grain to the town storage area, then proceed to the garage . . . to the garage . . . good creature. . . . Do you understand?"

"Y-yes!"

Fiben bowed as he backed away and then scuttled with an exaggeratedly bowlegged gait over to the post where Tycho's reins were tied. He averted his gaze as he led the animal back onto the dirt embankment beside the road. The soldiers idly watched him pass, chirping contemptuous remarks they were certain he could not understand.

Stupid damned birds, he thought, while his disguised belt camera panned the fortification, the soldiers, a hover-tank that whined by a few minutes later, its crew sprawled upon its flat upper deck, taking in the late afternoon sun.

Fiben waved as they swept by, staring back at him.

I'll bet you'd taste just fine in a nice orange glaze, he thought after the feathered creatures.

Fiben tugged the horse's reins. "C'mon, Tycho," he urged. "We gotta make Port Helenia by nightfall."

Farms were still operating in the Valley of the Sind.

Traditionally, whenever a starfaring race was licensed to colonize a new world, the continents were left as much as possible in their natural state. On Garth as well, the major Earthling settlements had been established on an archipelago in the shallow Western Sea. Only those islands had been converted completely to suit Earth-type animals and vegetation.

But Garth was a special case. The Bururalli had left a mess, and something had to be done quickly to help stabilize the planet's rocky ecosystem. New forms had to be introduced from the outside to prevent a complete biosphere collapse. That meant tampering with the continents.

A narrow watershed had been converted in the shadow of the Mountains of Mulun. Terran plants and animals that thrived here were allowed to diffuse into the foothills under careful observation, slowly filling some of the ecological niches left empty by the Bururalli Holocaust. It was a delicate experiment in practical planetary ecology, but one considered worthwhile. On Garth and on other catastrophe worlds the three races of the Terragens were building reputations as biosphere wizards. Even Mankind's worst critics would have to approve of work such as this.

And yet, something was jarringly wrong here. Fiben had passed three abandoned ecological management stations on his way, sampling traps and tracer 'bots stacked in disarray.

It was a sign of how bad the crisis must be. Holding the humans hostage was one thing—a marginally acceptable tactic by modern rules of war. But for the Gubru to be willing to disturb the resurrection of Garth, the uproar in the galaxy must be profound.

It didn't bode well for the rebellion. What if the War Codes really had broken down? Would the Gubru be willing to use planet busters?

That's the General's problem, Fiben decided. *I'm just a spy. She's the Eatee expert.*

At least the farms were working, after a fashion. Fiben passed one field cultivated with zygowheat and another with carrots. The robo-tillers went their rounds, weeding and irrigating. Here and there he saw a dispirited chim riding a spiderlike controller unit, supervising the machinery.

Sometimes they waved to him. More often they did not.

Once, he passed a pair of armed Gubru standing in a furrowed field beside their landed flitter. As he came closer, Fiben saw they were scolding a chim farmworker. The avians fluttered and hopped as they gestured at the drooping crop. The foreman nodded unhappily, wiping her palms on her faded dungarees. She glanced at Fiben as he passed by along the road, but the aliens went on with their rebuke, oblivious.

Apparently the Gubru were anxious for the crops to come in. Fiben hoped it meant they wanted it for their hostages. But maybe they had arrived with thin supplies and needed the food for themselves.

He was making good time when he drew Tycho off the

road into a small grove of fruit trees. The animal rested, browsing on the Earth-stock grass while Fiben sauntered over behind a tree to relieve himself.

The orchard had not been sprayed or pest-balanced in some time, he observed. A type of stingless wasp was still swarming over the ping-oranges, although the secondary flowering had finished weeks before and they were no longer needed for pollination.

The air was filled with a fruity, almost-ripe pungency. The wasps climbed over the thin rinds, seeking access to the sweetness within.

Abruptly, without thinking, Fiben reached out and snatched a few of the insects. It was easy. He hesitated, then popped them into his mouth.

They were juicy and crunchy, a lot like termites. "Just doing my part to keep the pest population down," he rationalized, and his brown hands darted out to grab more. The taste of the crunching wasps reminded him of how long it had been since he had last eaten.

"I'll need sustenance if I'm to do good work in town tonight," he thought half aloud. Fiben looked around. The horse grazed peacefully, and no one else was in sight.

He dropped his tool belt and took a step back. Then, favoring his still tender left ankle, he leaped onto the trunk and shimmied up to one of the fruit-heavy limbs. *Ah*, he thought as he plucked an almost ripe reddish globe. He ate it like an apple, skin and all. The taste was tart and astringent, unlike the bland human-style food so many chims claimed to like these days.

He grabbed two more oranges and popped a few leaves into his mouth for good measure. Then he stretched back and closed his eyes.

Up here, with only the buzz of the wasps for company, Fiben could almost pretend he didn't have a care, in this world or any other. He could put out of his mind wars and all the other silly preoccupations of sapient beings.

Fiben pouted, his expressive lips drooping low. He scratched himself under his arm.

"Ook, ook."

He snorted—almost silent laughter—and imagined he was back in an Africa even his great-grandfathers had never seen, in forested hills never touched by his people's too-smooth, big-nosed cousins.

What would the universe have been like without men? Without Eatees? Without anyone at all but chimps?

Sooner or later we *would've invented starships, and the universe might have been ours.*

The clouds rolled by and Fiben lay back on the branch with narrowed eyes, enjoying his fantasy. The wasps buzzed in futile indignation over his presence. He forgave them their insolence as he plucked a few from the air as added morsels.

Try as he might, though, he could not maintain the illusion of solitude. For there arrived another sound, an added drone from high above. And try as he might, he couldn't pretend he did not hear alien transports cruising uninvited across the sky.

A glistening fence more than three meters high undulated over the rolling ground surrounding Port Helenia. It was an imposing barrier, put up quickly by special robot machines right after the invasion. There were several gates, through which the city's chim population seemed to come and go without much notice or impediment. But they could not help being intimidated by the sudden new wall. Perhaps that was its basic purpose.

Fiben wondered how the Gubru would have managed the trick if the capital had been a real city and not just a small town on a rustic colony world.

He wondered where the humans were being kept.

It was dusk as he passed a wide belt of knee-high tree stumps, a hundred meters before the alien fence. The area had been planned as a park, but now only splintered fragments lay on the ground all the way to the dark watchtower and open gate.

Fiben steeled himself to go through the same scrutiny as earlier at the checkpoint, but to his surprise no one challenged him. A narrow pool of light spilled onto the highway from a pair of pillar spots. Beyond, he saw dark, angular buildings, the dimly lit streets apparently deserted.

The silence was spooky. Fiben's shoulders hunched as he spoke softly. "Come on, Tycho. Quietly." The horse blew and pulled the floating wagon slowly past the steel-gray bunker.

Fiben chanced a quick glance inside the structure as he passed. A pair of guards stood within, each perched on one knotted, stick-thin leg, its sharp, avian bill buried in the soft down under its left arm. Two saber-rifles lay on the counter beside them, near a stack of standard Galactic faxboards.

The two Talon Soldiers appeared to be fast asleep!

Fiben sniffed, his flat nose wrinkling once more at the over-sweet alien aroma. This was not the first time he had seen signs of weaknesses in the reputedly invincible grip of the Gubru fanatics. They had had it easy until now—too easy. With the humans nearly all gathered and neutralized, the invaders apparently thought the only possible threat was from space. That, undoubtedly, was why all the fortifications he had seen had faced upward, with little or no provision against attack from the ground.

Fiben stroked his sheathed belt knife. He was tempted to creep into the guard post, slipping under the obvious alarm beams, and teach the Gubru a lesson for their complacency.

The urge passed and he shook his head. *Later,* he thought. *When it will hurt them more.*

Patting Tycho's neck, he led the horse through the lighted area by the guard post and beyond the gate into the industrial part of town. The streets between the warehouses and factories were quiet—a few chims here and there hurrying about on errands beneath the scrutiny of the occasional passing Gubru patrol skimmer.

Taking pains not to be observed, Fiben slipped into a side alley and found a windowless storage building not far from the colony's sole iron foundry. Under his whispered urging, Tycho pulled the floating hover over to the shadows by the back door of the warehouse. A layer of dust showed that the padlock had not been touched in weeks. He examined it closely. "Hmmm."

Fiben took a rag from his belt apron and wrapped it around the hasp. Taking it firmly in both hands, he closed his eyes and counted to three before yanking down hard.

The lock was strong, but, as he'd suspected, the ring bolt in the door was corroded. It snapped with a muffled "crack!" Quickly, Fiben slipped the sheaf and pushed the door along its tracks. Tycho placidly followed him into the gloomy interior, the truck trailing behind. Fiben looked around to memorize the layout of hulking presses and metalworking machinery before hurrying back to close the door again.

"You'll be all right," he said softly as he unhitched the animal. He hauled a sack of oats out of the hover and split it open on the ground. Then he filled a tub with water from a nearby tap. "I'll be back if I can," he added. "If not, you just enjoy the oats for a couple of days, then whinny. I'm sure someone will be by."

Tycho switched his tail and looked up from the grain. He gave Fiben a baleful look in the dim light and let out another smelly, gassy commentary.

"Hmph." Fiben nodded, waving away the smell, "You're probably right, old friend. Still, I'll wager *your* descendants will worry too much too, if and when somebody ever gives them the dubious gift of so-called intelligence."

He patted the horse in farewell and loped over to the door to peer outside. It looked clear out there. Quieter than even the gene-poor forests of Garth. The navigation beacon atop the Terragens Building still flashed—no doubt used now to guide the invaders in their night operations. Somewhere in the distance a faint electric hum could be heard.

It wasn't far from here to the place where he was supposed to meet his contact. This would be the riskiest part of his foray into town.

Many frantic ideas had been proposed during the two days between the initial Gubru gas attacks and the invaders' complete seizure of all forms of communication. Hurried, frenzied telephone calls and radio messages had surged from Port Helenia to the Archipelago and to the continental outlands. During that time the human population had been thoroughly distracted and what remained of government communications were coded. So it was mainly chims, acting privately, who filled the airwaves with panicked conjectures and wild schemes—most of them horrifically dumb.

Fiben figured that was just as well, for no doubt the enemy had been listening in even then. Their opinion of neo-chimps must have been reinforced by the hysteria.

Still, here and there had been voices that sounded rational. *Wheat hidden amid the chaff.* Before she died, the human anthropologist Dr. Taka had identified one message as having come from one of her former postdoctoral students—one Gailet Jones, a resident of Port Helenia. It was this chim the General had decided to send Fiben to contact.

Unfortunately, there had been so much confusion. No one but Dr. Taka could say what this Jones person looked like, and by the time someone thought to ask her, Dr. Taka was dead.

Fiben's confidence in the rendezvous site and password was slim, at best. *Prob'ly we haven't even got the night right,* he grumbled to himself.

He slipped outside and closed the door again, replacing the shattered bolt so the lock hung back in place. The ring tilted at a slight angle. But it could fool someone who wasn't looking very carefully.

The larger moon would be up in an hour or so. He had to move if he was going to make his appointment in time.

Closer to the center of Port Helenia, but still on the "wrong" side of town, he stopped in a small plaza to watch light pour from the narrow basement window of a working chim's bar. Bass-heavy music caused the panes to shake in their wooden frames. Fiben could feel the vibration all the way across the street, through the soles of his feet. It was the only sign of life for blocks in all directions, if one did not count quiet apartments where dim lights shone dimly through tightly drawn curtains.

He faded back into the shadows as a whirring patroller robot cruised by, floating a meter above the roadway. The squat machine's turret swiveled to fix on his position as it passed. Its sensors must have picked him out, an infrared glow in the misty trees. But the machine went on, probably having identified him as a mere neo-chimpanzee.

Fiben had seen other dark-furred forms like himself hurrying hunch-shouldered through the streets. Apparently, the curfew was more psychological than martial. The occupation forces weren't being strict because there didn't seem to be any need.

Many of those not in their homes had been heading for places like this—the Ape's Grape. Fiben forced himself to stop scratching a persistent itch under his chin. This was the sort of establishment favored by grunt laborers and probationers, chims whose reproductive privileges were restricted by the Edicts of Uplift.

There were laws requiring even humans to seek genetic counseling when they bred. But for their clients, neo-dolphins and neo-chimpanzees, the codes were far more severe. In this one area normally liberal Terran law adhered closely to Galactic standards. It was that or lose chims and 'fins forever to some more senior clan. Earth was far too weak to defy the most honored of Galactic traditions.

About a third of the chim population carried green reproduction cards, allowing them to control their own fertility,
subject only to guidance from the Uplift Board and possible
penalties if they weren't careful. Those chims with gray or
yellow cards were more restricted. They could apply, after
they joined a marriage group, to reclaim and use the sperm
or ova they stored with the Board during adolescence, before
routine sterilization. Permission might be granted if they
achieved meritorious accomplishments in life. More often, a
yellow-card chimmie would carry to term and adopt an em-
bryo engineered with the next generation of "improvements"
inserted by the Board's technicians.

Those with red cards weren't even allowed *near* chim
children.

By pre-Contact standards, the system might have sounded
cruel. But Fiben had lived with it all his life. On the fast
track of Uplift a client race's gene pool was always being
meddled with. At least chims were consulted as part of the
process. Not many client species were so lucky.

The social upshot, though, was that there were classes
among chims. And "blue-carders" like Fiben weren't exactly
welcome in places like the Ape's Grape.

Still, this was the site chosen by his contact. There had
been no further messages, so he had no choice but to see if
the rendezvous would be kept. Taking a deep breath, he
stepped into the street and walked toward the growling,
crashing music.

As his hand touched the door handle a voice whispered
from the shadows to his left.

"*Pink?*"

At first he thought he had imagined it. But the words
repeated, a little louder.

"*Pink?* Looking for a *party?*"

Fiben stared. The light from the window had spoiled his
night vision, but he caught a glimpse of a small simian face,
somewhat childlike. There was a flash of white as the chim
smiled.

"Pink Party?"

He let go of the handle, hardly able to believe his ears.
"I beg your pardon?"

Fiben took a step forward. But at that moment the door
opened, spilling light and noise out into the street. Several

dark shapes, hooting with laughter and stinking of beer-soaked fur, pushed him aside as they stumbled past. By the time the revelers were gone and the door had closed again, the blurry, dark alley was empty once more. The small, shadowy figure had slipped away.

Fiben felt tempted to follow, if only to verify that he had been offered what he thought he had. And why was the proposition, once tendered, so suddenly withdrawn?

Obviously, things had changed in Port Helenia. True, he hadn't been to a place like the Ape's Grape since his college days. But pimps pandering out of dark alleys were not common even in this part of town. On Earth maybe, or in old threevee films, but here on Garth?

He shook his head in mystification and pulled open the door to go inside.

Fiben's nostrils flared at the thick aromas of beer and sniff-hi and wet fur. The descent into the club was made unnerving by the sharp, sudden glare of a strobe light, flashing starkly and intermittently over the dance floor. There, several dark shapes cavorted, waving what looked like small saplings over their heads. A heavy, sole-penetrating beat pounded from amplifiers set over a group of squatting musicians.

Customers lay on reed mats and cushions, smoking, drinking from paper bottles, and muttering coarse observations on the dancers' performances.

Fiben wended his way between the close-packed, low wicker tables toward the smoke-shrouded bar, where he ordered a pint of bitters. Fortunately, colonial currency still seemed to be good. He lounged against the rail and began a slow scan of the clientele, wishing the message from their contact had been less vague.

Fiben was looking for someone dressed as a fisherman, even though this place was halfway across town from the docks on Aspinal Bay. Of course the radio operator who had taken down the message from Dr. Taka's former student might have gotten it all wrong on that awful evening while the Howletts Center burned and ambulances whined overhead. The chen had thought he recalled Gailet Jones saying something about "a fisherman with a bad complexion."

"Great," Fiben had muttered when given his instructions. "Real spy stuff. Magnificent." Deep down he was positive the clerk had simply copied the entire thing down wrong.

It wasn't exactly an auspicious way to start an insurrection. But that was no surprise, really. Except to a few chims who had undergone Terragens Service training, secret codes, disguises, and passwords were the contents of oldtime thrillers.

Presumably, those militia officers were all dead or interned now. *Except for me. And my specialty wasn't intelligence or subterfuge. Hell, I could barely jockey poor old TAASF* Proconsul.

The Resistance would have to learn as it went now, stumbling in the dark.

At least the beer tasted good, especially after that long trek on the dusty road. Fiben sipped from his paper bottle and tried to relax. He nodded with the thunder music and grinned at the antics of the dancers.

They were all males, of course, out there capering under the flashing strobes. Among the grunts and probationers, feeling about this was so strong that it might even be called religious. The humans, who tended to frown over most types of sexual discrimination, did not interfere in this case. Client races had the right to develop their own traditions, so long as they didn't interfere with their duties or Uplift.

And according to this generation at least, Chimmies had no place in the thunder dance, and that was that.

Fiben watched one big, naked male leap to the top of a jumbled pile of carpeted "rocks" brandishing a shaker twig. The dancer—by day perhaps a mechanic or a factory laborer—waved the noisemaker over his head while drums pealed and strobes lanced artificial lightning overhead, turning him momentarily half stark white and half pitch black.

The shaker twig rattled and boomed as he huffed and hopped to the music, hooting as if to defy the gods of the sky.

Fiben had often wondered how much of the popularity of the thunder dance came from innate, inherited feelings of brontophilia and how much from the well-known fact that fallow, unmodified chimps in the jungles of Earth were observed to "dance" in some crude fashion during lightning storms. He suspected that a lot of neo-chimpanzee "tradition" came from elaborating on the publicized behavior of their unmodified cousins.

Like many college-trained chims, Fiben liked to think he was too sophisticated for such simple-minded ancestor worship. And generally he did prefer Bach or whale songs to simulated thunder.

And yet there were times, alone in his apartment, when he would pull a tape by the Fulminates out of a drawer, put on the headphones, and try to see how much pounding his skull could take without splitting open. Here, under the driving amplifiers, he couldn't help feeling a thrill run up his spine as "lightning" bolted across the room and the beating drums rocked patrons, furniture, and fixtures alike.

Another naked dancer climbed the mound, shaking his own branch and chuffing loudly in challenge. He crouched on one knuckle as he ascended, a stylish touch frowned upon by orthopedists but meeting with approval from the cheering audience. The fellow might pay for the verisimilitude with a morning backache, but what was that next to the glory of the dance?

The ape at the top of the hill hooted at his challenger. He leapt and whirled in a finely timed maneuver, shaking his branch just as another bolt of strobe lightning whitened the room. It was a savage and powerful image, a reminder that no more than four centuries ago his wild ancestors had challenged storms in a like fashion from forest hilltops—needing neither man nor his tutling scalpels to tell them that Heaven's fury required a reply.

The chims at the tables shouted and applauded as the king of the hill jumped from the summit, grinning. He tumbled down the mound, giving his challenger a solid whack as he passed.

This was another reason females seldom joined the thunder dance. A full-grown male neo-chim had most of the strength of his natural cousins on Earth. Chimmies who wanted to participate generally played in the band.

Fiben had always found it curious that it was so different among humans. Their *males* seemed more often obsessed with the sound making and the females with dance, rather than vice versa. Of course humans were strange in other ways as well, such as in their odd sexual practices.

He scanned the club. Males usually outnumbered females in bars like this one, but tonight the number of chimmies seemed particularly small. They mostly sat in large groups of friends, with big males at the periphery. Of course there were the barmaids, circulating among the low tables carrying drinks and smokes, dressed in simulated leopard skins.

Fiben was beginning to worry. How was his contact to

know him in this blaring, flashing madhouse? He didn't see anyone who looked like a scar-faced fisherman.

A balcony lined the three walls facing the dance mound. Patrons leaned over, banging on the slats and encouraging the dancers. Fiben turned and backed up to get a better look . . . and almost stumbled over a low wicker table as he blinked in amazement.

There—in an area set aside by rope barrier, guarded by four floating battle-robots—sat one of the invaders. There was the narrow, white mass of feathers, the sharp breastbone, and that curved beak . . . but this Gubru wore what looked like a woolen cap over the top of its head, where its comblike hearing organ lay. A set of dark goggles covered its eyes.

Fiben made himself look away. It wouldn't do to seem too surprised. Apparently the customers here had had the last few weeks to get used to an alien in their midst. Now, though, Fiben did notice occasional glances nervously cast up toward the box above the bar. Perhaps the added tension helped explain the frantic mood of the revelers, for the Grape seemed unusually rowdy, even for a working chim's bar.

Sipping his pint bottle casually, Fiben glanced up again. The Gubru doubtless wore the caplike muff and goggles as protection from the noise and lights. The guard-bots had only sealed off a square area near the alien, but that entire wing of the balcony was almost unpopulated.

Almost. Two chims, in fact, sat within the protected area, near the sharp-beaked Gubru.

Quislings? Fiben wondered. *Are there traitors among us already?*

He shook his head in mystification. Why was the Gubru here? What could one of the invaders possibly find of worth to notice?

Fiben reclaimed his place at the bar.

Obviously, they're interested in chims, and for reasons other than our value as hostages.

But what were those reasons? Why should Galactics care about a bunch of hairy clients that some hardly credited with being intelligent at all?

The thunder dance climaxed in an abrupt crescendo and one final crash, its last rumblings diminishing as if into a cloudy, stormy distance. The echoes took seconds longer to die away inside Fiben's head.

Dancers tumbled back to their tables grinning and sweating, wrapping loose robes around their nakedness. The laughter sounded hearty—perhaps too much so.

Now that Fiben understood the tension in this place he wondered why anyone came at all. Boycotting an establishment patronized by the invader would seem such a simple, obvious form of *ahisma*, of passive resistance. Surely the average chim on the street resented these enemies of all Terragens!

What drew such crowds here on a weeknight?

Fiben ordered another beer for appearances, though already he was thinking about leaving. The Gubru made him nervous. If his contact wasn't going to show, he had better get out of here and begin his own investigations. Somehow, he had to find out what was going on here in Port Helenia and discover a way to make contact with those willing to organize.

Across the room a crowd of recumbent revelers began pounding the floor and chanting. Soon the shout spread through the hall.

"Sylvie! Sylvie!"

The musicians climbed back onto their platform and the audience applauded as they started up again, this time to a much gentler beat. A pair of chimmies crooned seductively on saxophones as the house lights dimmed.

A spotlight speared down to illuminate the pinnacle of the dancers' mound, and a new figure swept out of a beaded curtain to stand under the dazzling beam. Fiben blinked in surprise. What was a chimmie doing up there?

The upper half of her face was covered by a beaked mask crested with white feathers. The fem-chim's bare nipples were flecked with sparkles to stand out in the light. Her skirt of silvery strips began to sway with the slow rhythm.

The pelvises of female neo-chimpanzees were wider than their ancestors', in order to pass bigger-brained progeny. Nevertheless, swinging hips had never become an ingrained erotic stimulus—a male turn-on—as it was among humans.

And yet Fiben's heart beat faster as he watched her allicient movements. In spite of the mask his first impression had been of a young girl, but soon he realized that the dancer was a mature female, with faint marks of having nursed. It made her look all the more alluring.

As she moved the swaying strips of her skirt flapped

slightly and Fiben soon saw that the fabric was silvery only on the outside. On the inner face each stripe of fabric tinted gradually upward toward a bright, rosy color.

He flushed and turned away. The thunder dance was one thing—he had participated in a few himself. But this was altogether different! First the little panderer in the alley, and now this? Had the chims of Port Helenia gone sex-crazed?

An abrupt, meaty pressure came down upon his shoulder. Fiben looked to see a large, fur-backed hand resting there, leading up a hairy arm to one of the biggest chims he had ever seen. He was nearly as tall as a small man, and obviously much stronger. The male neo-chimp wore faded blue work dungarees, and his upper lip curled back to expose substantial, almost atavistic canines.

"S'matter? You don't like Sylvie?" the giant asked.

Although the dance was still in its languid opening phase, the mostly male audience was already hooting encouragement. Fiben realized he must have been wearing his disapproval on his face, like an idiot. A true spy would have feigned enjoyment in order to fit in.

"Headache." He pointed to his right temple. "Rough day. I guess I'd better go."

The big neo-chimp grinned, his huge paw not leaving Fiben's shoulder. "Headache? Or maybe it's too bold for ya? Maybe you ain't had your first sharin' yet, hm?"

Out of the corner of his eye Fiben saw a swaying, teasing display, still demure but growing more sensual by the moment. He could feel the seething sexual tension beginning to fill the room and couldn't guess where it might lead. There were important reasons why this sort of display was illegal . . . one of the few activities humans proscribed their clients.

"Of course I've been in sharings!" he snapped back. "It's just that here, in public, it—it could cause a riot."

The big stranger laughed and poked him amiably. "When!"

"I beg your par- . . . uh, what d'you mean?"

"I mean *when* did you first share, hm? From the way you talk, I'll bet it was one of those college parties. Right? Am I right, Mr. Bluecard?"

Fiben glanced quickly right and left. First impressions notwithstanding, the big fellow seemed more curious and drunk than hostile. But Fiben wished he'd go away. His size was intimidating, and they might be attracting attention.

"Yeah," he muttered, uncomfortable with the recollection. "It was a fraternity initiation—"

The chimmie students back at college might be good friends with the chens in their classes, but they were never invited to *sharings*. It was just too dangerous to think of green-card females sexually. And anyway, they tended to be paranoid about pregnancy before marriage and genetic counseling. The possible costs were just too great.

So when chens at the University threw a party, they tended to invite girl chims from the far side of the tracks, yellow- and gray-card chimmies whose flame-colored estrus was only an exciting sham.

It was a mistake to judge such behavior by human standards. *We have fundamentally different patterns*, Fiben had reminded himself back then, and many times since. Still, he had never found those sharings very satisfying or joyful. Maybe someday, when he found the right marriage group . . .

"Sure, my sis used to go to those college parties. Sounded like fun." The scarred chim turned to the bartender and slapped the polished surface. "Two pints! One for me an' one for my college chum!" Fiben winced at the loud voice. Several others nearby had turned to look their way.

"So tell me," his unwelcome acquaintance said, thrusting a paper bottle into Fiben's hand. "Ya have any kids yet? Maybe some that are registered, but you never met?" He did not sound unfriendly, rather envious.

Fiben took a long swallow of the warm, bitter brew. He shook his head, keeping his voice low. "It doesn't really work that way. An open birthright isn't the same as an unlimited—a white card. If the planners have used any of my plasm I wouldn't know it."

"Well why the hell not! I mean its bad enough for you bluesies, having to screw test tubes on orders from the Uplift Board, but to not even *know* if they've used the gunk . . . Hell, my senior group-wife had a planned kid a year ago . . . you might even be my son's gene-dad!" The big chim laughed and clapped Fiben again heavily on the shoulder.

This would never do. More heads were turning his way. All this talk about blue cards was not going to win him friends here. Anyway, he did *not* want to attract attention with a Gubru sitting less than thirty feet away. "I really have to be going," he said, and started to edge backward. "Thanks for the beer. . . ."

Somebody blocked his way. "Excuse me," Fiben said. He turned and came face to face with four chims clothed in bright zipsuits, all staring at him with arms crossed. One, a little taller than the others, pushed Fiben back toward the bar.

"Of course this one's got _offspring!_" the newcomer growled. He had trimmed his facial hair, and the remaining mustache was waxed and pointed.

"Just look at those paws of his. I'll bet he's never done a day of honest chim's work. Probably he's a tech, or a _scientist._" He made it sound as if the very idea of a neo-chimp wearing such a title was like a privileged child being allowed to play a complicated game of pretend.

The irony of it was that while Fiben's hands might be less callused than many here, under his shirt were burn-scars from crash landing on a hillside at Mach five. But it wouldn't do to speak of that here.

"Look, fellas, why don't I buy a round. . . ."

His money flew across the bar as the tallest zipsuiter slapped his hand. "Worthless crap. They'll be collectin' it soon, like they'll be collecting you ape aristocrats."

"_Shut up!_" somebody yelled from the crowd, a brown mass of hunched shoulders. Fiben glimpsed Sylvie, rocking up on the mound. The separate strips of her skirt rippled, and Fiben caught a glimpse that made him start with amazement. She really _was_ pink . . . her briefly exposed genitals in full estrus.

The zipsuiter prodded Fiben again. "Well, Mr. Collegeman? What good is your blue card gonna do you when the Gubru start collecting and sterilizing all you freebreeders? Hah?"

One of the newcomers, a slope-shouldered chim with a barbelate, receding forehead, had a hand in a pocket of his bright garment, gripping a pointed object. His sharp eyes seemed carnivorously intent, and he left the talking to his mustachioed friend.

Fiben had just come to realize that these guys had nothing to do with the big chim in the dungarees. In fact, that fellow had already edged away into the shadows. "I—I don't know what you're talking about."

"You don't? They've been goin' through the colonial records, bub, and picking up a lot of _college chims_ like you for questioning. So far they've just been taking samples, but

I've got friends who say they're planning a full-tilt purge.
Now what d'you think of that?"

"*Shut th' f'kup!*" someone yelled. This time several faces
turned. Fiben saw glazed eyes, flecks of saliva, and bared
fangs.

He felt torn. He wanted desperately to get out of here,
but what if there were some truth in what the zipsuits were
saying? If so, this was important information.

Fiben decided to listen a little while longer. "That's
pretty surprising," he said, putting an elbow on the bar. "The
Gubru are fanatical conservatives. Whatever they do to other
patron-level races, I'd bet they'd never interfere with the
process of Uplift. It's against their own religion."

Mustache only smiled. "Is that what your college education tells you, blue boy? Well it's what the *Galactics* are
saying that counts now."

They were crowding Fiben, this bunch who seemed
more interested in him than in Sylvie's provocative gyrations.
The crowd was hooting louder, the music beating harder.
Fiben's head felt as if it might crack under the noise.

". . . too cool to enjoy a working man's show. Never
done any real labor. But snap his fingers, an' our own chimmies
come running!"

Fiben could tell something was false here. The one with
the mustache was overly calm, his barratrous taunts too deliberate. In an environment like this, with all the noise and
sexual tension—a true grunt shouldn't be able to focus so well.

Probationers! he realized suddenly. Now he saw the
signs. Two of the zipsuited chims' faces bore the stigmata of
failed genetic meddling—mottled, cacophrenic features or
the blinking, forever-puzzled look of a cross-wired brain—
embarrassing reminders that Uplift was an awkward process,
not without its price.

He had read in a local magazine, not long before the
invasion, how the trendy crowd in the Probie community had
taken to wearing garishly colored zipsuits. Fiben knew, suddenly, that he had attracted the very worst kind of attention.
Without humans around, or any sign of normal civil authority, there was no telling what these red-cards were up to.

Obviously, he had to get out of here. But how? The
zipsuits were crowding him closer every moment.

"Look, fellas, I just came here to see what's happenin'.
Thanks for your opinion. Now I really gotta go."

"I got a better idea," the leader sneered. "How about we introduce you to a Gubru who'll tell you for himself what's goin' on? And what they're plannin' to do with college chims. Hah?"

Fiben blinked. Could these chens actually be cooperating with the invader?

He had studied Old Earth History—the long, dark centuries before Contract, when lonely and ignorant humanity had experimented horribly in everything from mysticism to tyranny and war. He had seen and read countless portrayals of those ancient times—especially tales of solitary men and women who had taken brave, often hopeless stands against evil. Fiben had joined the colonial militia partly in a romantic wish to emulate the brave fighters of the Maquis, the Palmach, and the Power Satellite League.

But history told of traitors, also: those who sought advantage wherever it could be found, even over the backs of their comrades.

"Come on, college chum. There's a bird I want you to meet."

The grip on his arm was like a tightening vice. Fiben's look of pained surprise made the mustachioed chim grin. "They put some extra strength genes into my mix," he sneered. "That part of their meddling worked, but not some of the others. They call me Irongrip, and *I* got no blue card, or even a yellow.

"Now let's go. We'll ask Bright Talon Squadron Lieutenant to explain what the Gubru's plans are for chim bright boys."

In spite of the painful pressure on his arm, Fiben affected nonchalance. "Sure. Why not? Are you willing to put a wager on it, though?" His upper lip curled back in disdain. "If I remember my sophomore xenology right, the Gubru are pretty sharply clocked into a diurnal cycle. I'll bet behind those dark goggles of his you'll find that bloody bird is fast *asleep*. Think he'll like being awakened just to discuss the niceties of Uplift with the likes of you?"

For all his bravado, Irongrip was obviously sensitive about his level of education. Fiben's put-on assurance momentarily set him back, and he blinked at the suggestion that anyone could possibly sleep through all the cacophony around them.

Finally he growled angrily. "We'll just see about that. Come on."

The other zipsuits crowded close. Fiben knew he wouldn't stand a chance taking on all six of them. And there would be no calling on the law for help, either. Authority wore feathers these days.

His escorts prodded him through the maze of low tables. Lounging customers chuffed in irritation as Irongrip nudged them aside, but their eyes, glazed in barely restrained passion, were all on Sylvie's dance as the tempo of the music built.

A glance over his shoulder at the performer's contortions made Fiben's face feel hot. He backed away without looking and stumbled into a soft mass of fur and muscle.

"Ow!" a seated customer howled, spilling his drink.

"Sorry," Fiben muttered, stepping away quickly. His sandals crunched upon another brown hand, producing yet another shout. The complaint turned into an outraged scream as Fiben ground the knuckle down then twisted away to apologize once again.

"Siddown!" a voice shouted from the back of the club. Another squeaked, "Yeah! Beat it! Yer inna way!"

Irongrip glared suspiciously at Fiben and tugged on his arm. Fiben resisted briefly, then released, coming forward suddenly and shoving his captor back into one of the wicker tables. Drinks and sniff stands toppled, sending the seated chims scrambling to their feet, huffing indignantly.

"Hey!"

"Watch it, ye bastid Probie!"

Their eyes, already aflame from both intoxicants and Sylvie's dance, appeared to contain little reason anymore.

Irongrip's shaven face was pale with anger. His grasp tightened, and he began to motion to his comrades, but Fiben only smiled conspiratorially and nudged him with his elbow. In feigned drunken confidence, he spoke loudly.

"See what you did? I *told* you not to bump these guys on purpose, just to see if they're too stoned to talk. . . ."

From the nearby chims there came a hiss of intaken breath, audible even over the music.

"Who *says* I can't talk!" one of the drinkers slurred, barely able to form the words. The tipsy Borachio advanced a step, trying to focus on the source of this insult. "Was it *you?*"

Fiben's captor eyed him threateningly and yanked him closer, tightening the vicelike grip. Still, Fiben managed to maintain his stage grin, and winked.

"Maybe they *can* talk, sorta. But you're right about them bein' a bunch o' knuckle-walkers. . . ."

"*What!*"

The nearest chim roared and grabbed at Irongrip. The sneering mutant adroitly stepped aside and chopped with the edge of his free hand. The drunk howled, doubled up, and collided with Fiben.

But then the inebriate's friends dove in, shrieking. The hold on Fiben's arm tore loose as they were all swamped under a tide of angry brown fur.

Fiben ducked as a snarling ape in a leather work harness swung on him. The fist sailed past and connected with the jaw of one of the zipsuited toughs. Fiben kicked another Probie in the knee as the chim grabbed for him, eliciting a satisfactory howl, but then all was a chaos of flying wickerwork and dark bodies. Cheap straw tables blew apart as they crashed down upon heads. The air filled with flying beer and hair.

The band increased its tempo, but it was barely to be heard over shrieks of outrage or combative glee. There was a wild moment as Fiben felt himself lifted bodily by strong simian arms. They weren't gentle.

"*Whoa-aoh!*"

He sailed over the riot and landed in a crash amidst a group of previously uninvolved revelers. The customers stared at him in momentarily stunned puzzlement. Before they could react, Fiben picked himself up from the rubble, groaning. He rolled out into the aisle, stumbling as a sharp pain seemed to lance through his still-tender left ankle.

The fight was spreading, and two of the bright zipsuits were headed his way, canines gleaming. To make matters worse, the customers whose party he had so rudely interrupted were on their feet now, chuffing in anger. Hands reached for him.

"Some other time, perhaps," Fiben said politely. He hopped out of the debris away from his pursuers, hurriedly threading between the low tables. When there was no other way forward, he didn't hesitate, but stepped up onto a pair of broad, hunched shoulders and launched off, leaving his erstwhile springboard grunting in yet another pile of splintered wicker.

Fiben somersaulted over a last row of customers and tumbled to one knee in a broad, open area—the dance floor. Only a few meters away towered the thunder mound, where the alluring Sylvie was bearing down for her final grind, apparently oblivious to the growing commotion below.

Fiben moved quickly across the floor, intending to dash past the bar and out one of the exits beyond. But the moment he stepped out into the open area a sudden blaze of light lanced down from above, dazzling him! From all sides there erupted a tremendous cheer.

Something had obviously pleased the crowd. But what? Peering up against the glare, Fiben couldn't see that the ecdysiast had done anything new and spectacular—at least no more so than before. Then he realized that Sylvie was looking straight at him! Behind the birdlike mask he could see her eyes watching him in amusement.

He whirled. So were most of those not yet enveloped by the spreading brawl. The audience was cheering *him*. Even the Gubru in the balcony appeared to be tilting its goggle-shielded head his way.

There wasn't time to sort out the meaning of this. Fiben saw that several more of his tormentors had broken free of the melee. They were distinctive in their bright clothes as they gestured to each other, moving to cut him off from the exits.

Fiben quashed a sense of panic. They had him cornered. *There* has *to be another way out*, he thought furiously.

And then he realized where it would be. The *performer's door*, above and behind the padded dance mound! The beaded portal through which Sylvie had made her entrance. A quick scramble and he'd be up and past her—and gone!

He ran across the dance floor and leaped onto the mound, landing upon one of the carpeted ledges.

The crowd roared again! Fiben froze in his crouch. The glaring spotlights had followed him.

He blinked up at Sylvie. The dancer licked her lips and rocked her pelvis at him.

Fiben felt simultaneously repelled and powerfully drawn. He wanted to clamber up and grab her. He wanted to find some dark niche in a tree branch, somewhere, and hide.

Down below the fight was still going strong, but had

stopped spreading. With only paper bottles and wicker furniture to use, the combatants seemed to have settled down to an amiable tumult of mutual mayhem, the original cause quite forgotten.

But on the edges of the dance floor stood four chims in bright zipsuits, watching him as they fingered objects in their pockets. There still looked to be only one way. Fiben clambered up onto another carpeted, "rocky" cleft. Again, the crowd cheered in intensifying excitement. The noise, smells, confusion . . . Fiben blinked at the sea of fervent faces, all staring up at him in expectation. What was happening?

A flash of motion caught Fiben's attention. From the balcony over the bar, someone was waving at him. It was a small chim dressed in a dark, hooded cloak, standing out in this frenzied crowd, more than anything else, by a facial expression that was calm, icy sharp.

Fiben suddenly recognized the little *pimp*, the one who had accosted him briefly by the door to the Ape's Grape. The chim's voice didn't carry over the cacophony, but somehow Fiben picked out the mouthed words.

"Hey, dummy, look up!"

The boyish face grimaced. The panderer pointed overhead.

Fiben glanced upward . . . just in time to see a sparkling mesh start to fall from the rafters overhead! He leaped aside purely on instinct, fetching hard against another "rock" as the fringe of the falling net grazed his left foot. Electric agony stroked his leg.

"Baboon shit! What in Goodall's name . . . ?" He cursed soundly. It took a moment for him to realize that part of the roaring in his ears was more applause. This turned into shouted cheers as he rolled over holding his leg, and thereby happened to escape yet another snare. A dozen loops of sticky mesh flopped out of a simulated rock to tauten over the area he had just occupied.

Fiben kept as still as possible while he rubbed his foot and glared about angrily, suspiciously. Twice he had almost been noosed like some dumb animal. To the crowd it might all be great fun, but he personally had no desire to be trussed up on some bizarre, lunatic obstacle course.

Below on the dance floor he saw bright zipsuits, left, right, and center. The Gubru on the balcony seemed interested, but showed no sign of intervening.

Fiben sighed. His predicament was still the same. The only direction he could go was up.

Looking carefully, he scrambled over another padded ridge. The snares appeared to be intended to be humiliating and incapacitating—and painful—but not deadly. Except in his case, of course. If *he* were caught, his unwanted enemies would be on him in a trice.

He stepped up onto the next "boulder," cautiously. Fiben felt a tickling falseness under his right foot and pulled back just as a trap door popped open. The crowd gasped as he teetered on the edge of the revealed pit. Fiben's arms windmilled as he fought for balance. From an uncertain crouch he leaped, and barely caught a grip on the next higher terrace.

His feet hung over nothingness. Fiben's breath came in heavy gasps. Desperately he wished humans hadn't edited some of his ancestors' "unnecessary" instinctive climbing skills just to make room for trivialities such as speech and reason.

He grunted and slowly scrambled up out of the pit. The audience clamored for more.

As he panted on the edge of the next level, trying to see in all directions at once, Fiben slowly became aware that a public address system was muttering over the noise of the crowd, repeating over and over again, in clipped, mechanical tones.

. . . more enlightened approach to Uplift . . . appropriate to the background of the client race . . . offering opportunity to all . . . unbiased by warped human standards . . .

Up in its box, the invader chirped into a small microphone. Its machine-translated words boomed out over the music and the excited jabber of the crowd. Fiben doubted one in ten of the chims below were even aware of the E.T.'s monologue in the state they were in. But that probably didn't matter.

They were being conditioned!

No wonder he had never heard of Sylvie's dance-mound striptease before, nor this crazy obstacle course. It was an innovation of the invaders!

But what was its *purpose*?

They couldn't have managed all this without help, Fiben thought angrily. Sure enough, the two well-dressed chims sitting near the invader whispered to each other and scribbled on clipboards. They were obviously recording the crowd's reactions for their new master.

Fiben scanned the balcony and noted that the little pimp in the cowled robe stood not far outside the Gubru's ring of robot guards. He spared a whole second to memorize the chim's boyish features. Traitor!

Sylvie was only a few terraces above him now. The dancer twitched her pink bottom at him, grinning as sweat beaded on his face. Human males had their own "instant" visual triggers: rounded female breasts and pelvises and smooth fem skin. None of them could compare with the electric shiver a little color in the right place could send through a male chim.

Fiben shook his head vigorously. "Out. Not in. You want out!"

Concentrating on keeping his balance, favoring his tender left ankle, he scrambled edgewise until he was around the pit, then crawled forward on his hands and knees.

Sylvie leaned over him, two levels up. Her scent carried even over the pungent aromas of the hall, making Fiben's nostrils flare.

He shook his head suddenly. There was *another* sharp odor, a cloying stink that seemed to be quite local.

With the little finger of his left hand he probed the terrace he had been about to climb upon. Four inches in he encountered a burning stickiness. He cried out and pulled back hard, leaving behind a small patch of skin.

Alas for instinct! His seared finger automatically popped into his mouth. Fiben almost gagged on the nastiness.

This was a fine fix. If he tried to move up or forward the sticky stuff would get him. If he retreated he would more than likely wind up in the pit!

This maze of traps did explain one thing that he had puzzled about, earlier. No wonder the chens below hadn't gone nuts and simply charged the hill the moment Sylvie showed pink! They knew only the cocky or foolhardy would dare attempt the climb. The others were content to observe and fantasize. Sylvie's dance was only the first half of the show.

And if some lucky bastard made it? Well, then, everybody would have the added treat of watching that, too!

The idea repelled Fiben. Private sharings were natural, of course. But this public lewdness was disgusting!

At the same time, he noted that he had already made it most of the way. He felt an old quickening in his blood. Sylvie swayed down a little toward him, and he imagined he could already touch her. The musicians increased their tempo, and strobes began flickering again, approaching like lightning. Artificial thunder echoed. Fiben felt a few stinging droplets, like the beginnings of a rainstorm.

Sylvie danced under the spots, inciting the crowd. He licked his lips and felt himself drawn.

Then, in the flicker of a single lightning flash, Fiben saw something equally enticing, more than attractive enough to pull him out of Sylvie's hypnotic sway. It was a small, green-lit sign, prim and legalistic, that shone beyond Sylvie's shoulder.

"EXIT," it read.

Suddenly the pain and exhaustion and tension caused something to release inside Fiben. He felt somehow lifted above the noise and tumult and recalled with instant clarity something that Athaclena said to him shortly before he left the encampment in the mountains to begin his trek to town. The silvery threads of her Tymbrimi corona had waved gently as if in a breeze of pure thought.

"There is a telling which my father once gave me, Fiben. It's a 'haiku poem,' in an Earthling dialect called Japanese. I want you to take it with you."

"Japanese," he had protested. *"It's spoken on Earth and on Calafia, but there aren't a hundred chims or men on Garth who know it!"*

But Athaclena only shook her head. *"Neither do I. But I shall pass the telling on to you, the way it was given to me."*

What came when she opened her mouth then was less sound than a crystallization, a brief substrate of meaning which left an imprint even as it faded.

> *Certain moments qualify,*
> *In winter's darkest storm,*
> *When stars call, and you fly!*

Fiben blinked and the sudden relived moment passed. The letters still glowed,

EXIT

shining like a green haven.

It all swept back, the noise, the odors, the sharp stinging of the tiny rainlike droplets. But Fiben now felt as if his chest had expanded twofold. Lightness spread down his arms and into his legs. They seemed to weigh next to nothing.

With a deep flexing of his knees he gathered himself and then launched off from his precarious perch to land on the edge of the next terrace, toes grasping inches from the burning, camouflaged glue. The crowd roared and Sylvie stepped back, clapping her hands.

Fiben laughed. He slapped his chest rapidly, as he had seen the gorillas do, beating countertime to the rolling thunder. The audience loved it.

Grinning, he stepped along the edge of the sticky patch, tracing its outline more by instinct than the faint difference in coloration. Arms spread wide for balance, he made it look harder than it actually felt.

The ledge ended where a tall "tree"—simulated out of fiberglass and green, plastic tassels—towered out of the slope of the mound.

Of course the thing was boobytrapped. Fiben wasted no time inspecting it. He leapt up to tap the nearest branch lightly and teetered precariously as he landed, drawing gasps from those below.

The branch reacted a delayed instant after he touched it . . . just time enough for him to have gotten a solid grip on it, had he tried. The entire tree seemed to writhe. Twigs turned into curling ropes which would have shared an arm, if he were still holding on.

With a yip of exhilaration, Fiben leaped again, this time grabbing a dangling rope as the branch swayed down again. He rode it up like a pole vaulter, sailing over the last two terraces—and the surprised dancer—and flew on into the junglelike mass of girders and wiring overhead.

Fiben let go at the last moment and managed to land in a crouch upon a catwalk. For a moment he had to fight for balance on the tricky footing. A maze of spotlights and unsprung traps lay all around him. Laughing, he hopped about tripping releases, sending wires, nets, and tangle-ropes spilling over onto the mound. There were tubs of some hot, oatmeallike substance which he kicked over. Splatters on the orchestra sent the musicians diving for cover.

Now Fiben could easily see the outlines of the obstacle

course. Clearly there was no real solution to the puzzle except the one he had used, bypassing the last few terraces altogether.

In other words, one had to cheat.

The mound was not a fair test, then. A chen couldn't hope to win by being more clever, only by letting others take the risks first, suffering pain and humiliation in the traps and deadfalls. The lesson the Gubru were teaching here was insidiously simple.

"Those bastards," he muttered.

The exalted feeling was beginning to fade, and with it some of Fiben's temporary sense of borrowed invulnerability. Obviously Athaclena had given him a parting gift, a post-hypnotic charm of sorts, to help him if he found himself in a jam. Whatever it was, he knew it wouldn't do to push his luck.

It's time to get out of here, he thought.

The music had died when the musicians fled the sticky oatmeal stuff. But now the the public address system was squawking again, issuing clipped exhortations that were beginning to sound a bit frantic.

. . . unacceptable behavior for proper clients . . . Cease expressions of approval for one who has broken rules . . . One who must be chastised . . .

The Gubru's pompous urgings fell flat, for the crowd seemed to have gone completely ape. When Fiben hopped over to the mammoth speakers and yanked out wires, the alien's tirade cut off and there rose a roar of hilarity and approval from the audience below.

Fiben leaned into one of the spotlights, swiveling it so that it swept across the hall. When the beam passed over them chims picked up their wicker tables and tore them apart over their heads. Then the spot struck the E.T. in the balcony box, still shaking its microphone in apparent outrage. The birdlike creature wailed and cringed under the sharp glare.

The two chimps sharing the VIP box dove for cover as the battle-robots rotated and fired at once. Fiben leaped from the rafters just before the spotlight exploded in a shower of metal and glass.

He landed in a roll and came to his feet at the peak of the dance mound . . . King of the Mountain. He concealed his limp as he waved to the crowd. The hall shook with their cheers.

They abruptly quieted as he turned and took a step toward Sylvie.

This was the payoff. Natural male chimpanzees in the wild weren't shy about mating in front of others, and even uplifted neo-chimps "shared" when the time and place was right. They had few of the jealousy or privacy taboos which made male humans so strange.

The evening's climax had come much sooner than the Gubru planned, and in a fashion it probably did not like, but the basic lesson could still be the same. Those below were looking for a vicarious sharing, with all the lessons psychologically tailored.

Sylvie's bird-mask was part of the conditioning. Her bared teeth shone as she wriggled her bottom at him. The many-slitted skirt whirled in a rippling flash of provocative color. Even the zipsuiters were staring now, licking their lips in anticipation, their quarrel with him forgotten. At that moment he was their hero, he was each of them.

Fiben quashed a wave of shame. *We're not so bad . . . not when you figure we're only three hundred years old. The Gubru want us to feel we're barely more than animals, so we'll be harmless. But I hear even humans used to sometimes revert like this, back in the olden days.*

Sylvie chuffed at him as he approached. Fiben felt a powerful tightening in his loins as she crouched to await him. He reached for her. He gripped her shoulder.

Then Fiben swung her about to face him. He exerted strength to make her stand up straight.

The cheering crowd fell into confused muttering. Sylvie blinked up at him in hormone-drenched surprise. It was apparent to Fiben that she must have taken some sort of drug to get into this condition.

"F-frontwards?" she asked, struggling with the words. "But Big-Beak s-said he wanted it to look natural. . . ."

Fiben took her face in his hands. The mask had a complex set of buckles, so he bent around the jutting beak to kiss her once, gently, without removing it.

"Go home to your mates," he told her. "Don't let our enemies shame you."

Sylvie rocked back as if he had struck her a blow.

Fiben faced the crowd and raised his arms. "Upspring of

the wolflings of Terra!" he shouted. "All of you. Go home to your mates! Together with our patrons we'll guide our *own* Uplift. We don't need Eatee outsiders to tell us how to do it!"

From the crowd there came a low rumbling of consternation. Fiben saw that the alien in the balcony was chirping into a small box, probably calling for assistance, he realized.

"Go home!" he repeated. "And don't let outsiders make spectacles of us again!"

The muttering below intensified. Here and there Fiben saw faces wearing sudden frowns—chims looking about the room in what he hoped was dawning embarrassment. Brows wrinkled with uncomfortable thoughts.

But then, out of the babble below, someone shouted up at him.

"Whassamatta? Can't ya' get it up?"

About half of the crowd laughed uproariously. There were follow-up jeers and whistles, especially from the front rows.

Fiben really had to get going. The Gubru probably didn't dare shoot him down outright, not in front of the crowd. But the avian had doubtless sent for reinforcements.

Still, Fiben couldn't pass up a good straight line. He stepped to the edge of the plateau and glanced back at Sylvie. He dropped his pants.

The jeers stopped abruptly, then the brief silence was broken by whistles and wild applause.

Cretins, Fiben thought. But he did grin and wave before rebuttoning his fly.

By now the Gubru was flapping its arms and squawking, pushing at the well-dressed neo-chimps who shared its box. They, in turn, leaned over to shout at the bartenders. There were faint noises that sounded like sirens in the distance.

Fiben grabbed Sylvie for one more kiss. She answered this time, swaying as he released her. He paused for one last gesture up at the alien, making the crowd roar with laughter. Then he turned and ran for the exit.

Inside his head a little voice was cursing him for an extroverted idiot. *This wasn't what the General sent you to town to do, fool!*

He swept through the beaded curtain but then stopped abruptly, face to face with a frowning neo-chimp in a cowled robe. Fiben recognized the small chim he had briefly seen twice this evening—first outside the door to the Ape's Grape and later standing just outside the Gubru's balcony box.

"You!" he accused.

"Yeah, me." the panderer answered. "Sorry I can't make the same offer as before. But I guess you've had other things on your mind tonight."

Fiben frowned. "Get out of my way." He moved to push the other aside.

"Max!" the smaller chim called. A large form emerged from the shadows. It was the huge, scar-faced fellow he had met at the bar, just before the zipsuited probationers showed up, the one so interested in his blue card. There was a stun gun in his meaty grasp. He smiled apologetically. "Sorry, chum."

Fiben tensed, but it was already too late. A rolling tingle washed over his body, and all he managed to do was stumble and fall into the smaller chim's arms.

He encountered softness and an unexpected aroma. *By Ifni,* he thought in a stunned instant.

"Help me, Max," the nearby voice said. "We've got to move fast."

Strong arms lifted him, and Fiben almost welcomed the collapse of consciousness after this last surprise—that the young-faced little "pimp" was actually a chimmie, a girl!

25

Galactics

The Suzerain of Cost and Caution left the Command Conclave in a state of agitation. Dealing with its fellow Suzerains was always physically exhausting. Three adversaries, dancing and circling, forming temporary alliances, separating and then reforming again, shaping an ever-changing synthesis. So it would have to be as long as the situation in the outer world was indeterminate, in a state of flux.

Eventually, of course, matters here on Garth would stabilize. One of the three leaders would prove to have been most correct, the best leader. Much rested upon that outcome, not least what color each of them would wear at the end, and what gender.

But there was no hurry to begin the Molt. Not yet. There would be many more conclaves before that day arrived, and much plumage to be shed.

Caution's first debate had been with the Suzerain of Propriety over using Talon Soldiers to subdue the Terragens Marines at the planetary spaceport. In fact, that initial argument had been little more than a minor squabble, and when the Suzerain of Beam and Talon finally tipped the scales, intervening in favor of Propriety, Caution surrendered with good grace. The subsequent ground battle had been expensive in good soldiery. But other purposes were served by the exercise.

The Suzerain of Cost and Caution had known that the vote would go that way. Actually, it had had no intention of winning their first argument. It knew how much better it was to begin the race in last place, with the priest and the admiral in temporary contention. As a result both of them would tend to ignore the Civil Service for a while. Setting up a proper bureaucracy of occupation and administration would take a lot of effort, and the Suzerain of Cost and Caution did not want to waste energy on preliminary squabbles.

Such as this most recent one. As the chief bureaucrat stepped away from the meeting pavilion and was joined by its aides and escorts, the other two expedition leaders could still be heard crooning at each other in the background. The conclave was over, yet they were still arguing over what had already been decided.

For the time being the military would continue the gas attacks, seeking out any humans who might have escaped the initial dosings. The order had been issued minutes ago.

The high priest—the Suzerain of Propriety—was worried that too many human civilians had been injured or killed by the gas. A few neo-chimpanzees had also suffered. This wasn't catastrophic from a legal or religious point of view, but it would complicate matters eventually. Compensation might have to be paid, and it could weaken the Gubru case if the matter ever came before interstellar adjudication.

The Suzerain of Beam and Talon had argued that adjudication was very unlikely. After all, with the Five Galaxies in an uproar, who was going to care about a few mistakes made on a tiny backwater dirtspeck such as this?

"We care!" the Suzerain of Propriety had declared. And it made its feelings clear by continuing to refuse to step off its perch onto the soil of Garth. To do so prematurely would make the invasion official, it stated. And that would have to wait. The small but fierce space battle, and the defiance of the spaceport, had seen to that. By resisting effectively, however briefly, the legal leaseholders had made it necessary to put off making any formal seizures for a while. Any further mistakes could not only harm Gubru claims here but prove terribly expensive as well.

The priest had fluttered its allochroous plumage after making that point, smugly certain of victory. After all, expense was an issue that would certainly win it an ally. Propriety felt it would surely be joined by Cost and Caution here!

How foolish, to think that the Molt will be decided by early bickerings such as these, the Suzerain of Cost and Caution had thought, and proceeded to side with the soldiery.

"Let the gassings go on, continue and seek out all those still in hiding," it had said to the priest's dismay and the admiral's crowing delight.

The space battle and landings *had* proved extraordinarily costly. But not as expensive as it all would likely have been without the Coercion Program. The gas attacks had achieved the objective of concentrating nearly the entire human population onto a few islands where they might be simply controlled. It was easy to understand why the Suzerain of Beam and Talon wanted it that way. The bureaucrat, also, had experience dealing with wolflings. It, too, would feel much more comfortable with all of the dangerous humans gathered where it could see them.

Soon, of course, something would have to be done to curtail the high costs of this expedition. Already the Roost Masters had recalled elements of the fleet. Matters were critical on other fronts. It was vital to keep a tight perch-grip on expenses here. That was a matter for another conclave, however.

Today, the military suzerain was riding high. Tomorrow? Well, the alliances would shift and shift again, until at last a new policy emerged. And a queen.

The Suzerain of Cost and Caution turned and spoke to one of its Kwackoo aides.

"Have me driven, taken, conveyed to my headquarters."

The official hover-barge lifted off and headed toward the buildings the Civil Service had appropriated, on headlands overlooking the nearby sea. As the vehicle hissed through the small Earthling town, guarded by a swarm of battle robots, it was watched by small crowds of the dark, hairy beasts the human wolflings prized as their eldest clients.

The Suzerain spoke again to its aide. "When we arrive at the chancery, gather the staff together. We shall consider, contemplate, evaluate the new proposal the high priest sent over this morning concerning how to manage these creatures, these neo-chimpanzees."

Some of the ideas suggested by the Propriety Department were daring to an extreme. There were brilliant features that made the bureaucrat feel proud of its future mate. *What a Threesome we shall make.*

There were other aspects, of course, that would have to be altered if the plan was not to lead to disaster. Only one of the Triumvirate had the sureness of grasp to see such a scheme to its final, victorious conclusion. That had been known in advance when the Roost Masters chose their Three.

The Suzerain of Cost and Caution let out a treble sigh and contemplated how it would have to manipulate the next leadership conclave. Tomorrow, the next day, in a week. That forthcoming squabble was not far off. Each debate would grow more urgent, more important as both consensus and Molt approached.

The prospect was one to look upon with a mixture of trepidation, confidence, and utter pleasure.

26

Robert

The denizens of the deep caverns were unaccustomed to the bright lights and loud noises the newcomers had brought with them. Hordes of batlike creatures fled before the interlopers, leaving behind a flat, thick flooring of many centuries' accumulated dung. Under limestone walls glistening with slow seepage, alkaline rivulets were now crossed by makeshift plank bridges. In drier corners, under the pale illumination of glow bulbs, the surface beings moved nervously, as if loathe to disturb the stygian quiet.

It was a forbidding place to wake up to. Shadows were stark, acherontic, and surprising. A crag of rock might look innocuous and then, from a slightly different perspective, leap out in familiarity as the silhouette of some monster met a hundred times in nightmares.

It wasn't hard to have bad dreams in a place like this.

Shuffling in robe and slippers, Robert felt positive relief when at last he found the place he'd been looking for, the rebel "operations center." It was a fairly large chamber, lit by more than the usual sparse ration of bulbs. But furniture was negligible. Some ragged card tables and cabinets had been supplemented by benches fashioned from chopped and leveled stalagmites, plus a few partitions knocked together out of raw timber from the forest high above. The effect only made the towering vault seem all the more mighty, and the refugees' works all the more pitiful.

Robert rubbed his eyes. A few chims could be seen clustered around one partition arguing and sticking pins in a large map, speaking softly as they sifted through papers.

182

When one of them raised his voice too loud, echoes reverberated down the surrounding passages making the others look up in alarm. Obviously, the chims were still intimidated by their new quarters.

Robert shuffled into the light. "All right," he said, his larynx still scratchy from lack of use. "What's going on here? Where is she and what is she up to now?"

They stared at him. Robert knew he must look a sight in rumpled pajamas and slippers, his hair uncombed and his arm in a cast to the shoulder.

"Captain Oneagle," one of the chims said. "You really should still be in bed. Your fever—"

"Oh, shove it . . . Micah." Robert had to think to remember the fellow's name. The last few weeks were still a fog in his mind. "My fever broke two days ago. I can read my own chart. So tell me what's happening! Where is everybody? Where's Athaclena?"

They looked at each other. Finally one chimmie took a cluster of colored map pins out of her mouth. "Th' General . . . uh, Mizz Athaclena, is away. She's leading a raid."

"A raid. . . ." Robert blinked. "On the *Gubru*?" He brought a hand to his eyes as the room seemed to waver. "Oh, Ifni."

There was a rush of activity as three chims got in each other's way hauling over a wooden folding chair. Robert sat down heavily. He saw that these chims were all either very young or old. Athaclena must have taken most of the able-bodied with her.

"Tell me about it," he said to them.

A senior-looking chimmie, bespectacled and serious, motioned the others back to work and introduced herself. "I am Dr. Soo," she said. "At the Center I worked on gorilla genetic histories."

Robert nodded. "Dr. Soo, yes. I recall you helped treat my injuries." He remembered her face peering over him through a fog while the infection raged hot through his lymphatic system.

"You were very sick, Captain Oneagle. It wasn't just your badly fractured arm, or those fungal toxins you absorbed during your accident. We are now fairly certain you also inhaled traces of the Gubru coercion gas, back when they dosed the Mendoza Freehold."

Robert blinked. The memory was a blur. He had been on

the mend, up in the Mendoza's mountain ranch, where he
and Fiben had spent a couple of days talking, making plans.
Somehow they would find others and try to get something
started. Maybe make contact with his mother's government
in exile, if it still existed. Reports from Athaclena told of a set
of caves that seemed ideal as a headquarters of sorts. Maybe
these mountains could be a base of operations against the
enemy.

Then, one afternoon, there were suddenly frantic chims
running everywhere! Before Robert could speak, before he
could even stand they had plucked him up and carried him
bodily out of the farmhouse and up into the hills.

There were sonic booms . . . terse images of something
immense in the sky.

"But . . . but I thought the gas was fatal if . . ." His
voice trailed off.

"If there's no antidote. Yes. But your dose was so small."
Dr. Soo shrugged. "As it is, we nearly lost you."

Robert shivered. "What about the little girl?"

"She is with the gorillas." The chim nutritionist smiled.
"She's as safe as anyone can be, these days."

He sighed and sat back a little. "That's good at least."

The chims carrying little April Wu must have got up to
the heights in plenty of time. Apparently Robert barely made
it. The Mendozas had been slower still and were caught in
the stinking cloud that spilled from the belly of the alien ship.

Dr. Soo went on. "The 'rillas don't like the caves, so
most of them are up in the high valleys, foraging in small
groups under loose supervision, away from any buildings.
Structures are still being gassed regularly, you know, whether
they contain humans or not."

Robert nodded. "The Gubru are being thorough."

He looked at the wall-board stuck with multicolored
pins. The map covered the entire region from the mountains
north across the Vale of Sind and west to the sea. There the
islands of the Archipelago made a necklace of civilization.
Only one city lay onshore, Port Helenia on the northern
verge of Aspinal Bay. South and east of the Mulun Mountains
lay the wilds of the main continent, but the most important
feature was depicted along the top edge of the map. Patient,
perhaps unstoppable, the great gray sheets of ice encroached
lower every year. The final bane of Garth.

The map pins, however, dealt with a much closer, nearer-term calamity. It was easy to read the array of pink and red markers. "They've really got a grip on things, haven't they?"

The elderly chim named Micah brought Robert a glass of water. He frowned at the map also. "Yessir. The fighting seems to all be over. The Gubru have been concentrating their energies around the Port and the Archipelago, so far. There's been little activity here in the mountains, except this perpetual harassment by robots dropping coercion gas. But the enemy has established a firm presence every place that was colonized."

"Where do you get your information?"

"Mostly from invader broadcasts and censored commercial stations in Port Helenia. Th' General also sent runners and observers off in all directions. Some of them have reported back, already."

"*Who's* got runners . . . ?"

"Th' Gen- . . . um." Micah looked a bit embarrassed. "Ah, some of the chims find it hard to pronounce Miss Athac- . . . Miss Athaclena's name, sir. So, well . . ." His voice trailed off.

Robert sniffed. *I'm going to have to have a talk with that girl,* he thought.

He lifted his water glass and asked, "Who did she send to Port Helenia? That's going to be a touchy place for a spy to get into."

Dr. Soo answered without much enthusiasm. "Athaclena chose a chim named Fiben Bolger."

Robert coughed, spraying water over his robe. Dr. Soo hurried on. "He *is* a militiaman, captain, and Miss Athaclena figured that spying around in town would require an . . . um . . . unconventional approach."

That only made Robert cough harder. Unconventional. Yes, that described Fiben. If Athaclena had chosen old "Trog" Bolger for that mission, then it spoke well for her judgment. She might not be stumbling in the dark, after all.

Still, she's hardly more than a kid. And an alien at that! Does she actually think she's a general? Commanding what? He looked around the sparsely furnished cavern, the small heaps of scrounged and hand-carried supplies. It was, all told, a pitiful affair.

"That wall map arrangement is pretty crude," Robert observed, picking out one thing in particular.

An elderly chen who hadn't spoken yet rubbed the sparse

hair on his chin. "We could organize much better than this," he agreed. "We've got several mid-size computers. A few chims are working programs on batteries, but we don't have the power to run them at full capacity."

He looked at Robert archly. "Tymbrimi Athaclena insists we drill a geothermal tap first. But I figure if we were to set up a few solar collectors on the surface . . . very well hidden, of course . . ."

He let the thought hang. Robert could tell that one chim, at least, was less than thrilled at being commanded by a mere girl, and one who wasn't even of Earthclan or Terragens citizenship.

"What's your name?"

"Jobert, captain."

Robert shook his head. "Well, Jobert, we can discuss that later. Right now, will someone please tell me about this 'raid'? What is Athaclena up to?"

Micah and Soo looked at each other. The chimmie spoke first.

"They left before dawn. It's already late afternoon outside. We should be getting a runner in any time now."

Jobert grimaced again, his wrinkled, age-darkened face dour with pessimism. "They went out armed with pin-rifles and concussion grenades, hoping to ambush a Gubru patrol.

"Actually," the elderly chim added dryly. "We were expecting news more than an hour ago. I'm afraid they are already very late getting back."

26

Fiben

Fiben awoke in darkness, fetal-curled under a dusty blanket.

Awareness brought back the pain. Just pulling his right arm away from his eyes took a stoic effort of will, and the movement set off a wave of nausea. Unconsciousness beckoned him back seductively.

What made him resist was the filmy, lingering tracery of his dreams. They had driven him to seek consciousness . . . those weird, terrifying images and sensations. The last, vivid scene had been a cratered desert landscape. Lightning struck the stark sands all around him, pelting him with charged, sparking shrapnel whichever way he tried to duck or hide.

He recalled trying to protest, as if there were words that might somehow placate a storm. But speech had been taken from him.

By effort of will, Fiben managed to roll over on the creaking cot. He had to knuckle-rub his eyes before they would open, and then all they made out was the dimness of a shabby little room. A thin line of light traced the overlap of heavy black curtains covering a small window.

His muscles trembled spasmodically. Fiben remembered the last time he had felt anywhere near this lousy, back on Cilmar Island. A band of neo-chimp circus entertainers from Earth had dropped in to do a show. The visiting "strongman" offered to wrestle the college champion, and like an idiot Fiben had accepted.

It had been weeks before he walked again without a limp.

Fiben groaned and sat up. His inner thighs burned like fire. "Oh, mama," he moaned. "I'll never scissors-hold again!"

His skin and body hair were moist. Fiben sniffed the pungent odor of Dalsebo, a strong muscle relaxant. So, at least his captors had taken efforts to spare him the worst aftereffects of stunning. Still, his brain felt like a misbehaving gyroscope when he tried to rise. Fiben grabbed the teetering bedside table for support as he stood up, and held his side while he shuffled over to the solitary window.

He grabbed rough fabric on both sides of the thin line of light and snapped the drapes apart. Immediately Fiben stumbled back, both arms raised to ward off the sudden brightness. Afterimages whirled.

"Ugh," he commented succinctly. It was barely a croak.

What was this place? Some prison of the Gubru? Certainly he wasn't aboard an invader battleship. He doubted the fastidious Galactics would use native wood furnishings, or decorate in Late Antediluvian Shabby.

He lowered his arms, blinking away tears. Through the window he saw an enclosed yard, an unkempt vegetable garden, a couple of climbing trees. It looked like a typical small commune-house, the sort a chim group marriage family might own.

Just visible over the nearby roofs, a line of hilltop eucalyptus trees told him he was still in Port Helenia, not far from Sea Bluff Park.

Perhaps the Gubru were leaving his interrogation to their quislings. Or his captors could be those hostile Probationers. They might have their own plans for him.

Fiben's mouth felt as if dust weavers had been spinning traps in it. He saw a water pitcher on the room's only table. One cup was already poured. He stumbled over and grabbed for it, but missed and knocked it crashing to the floor.

Focus! Fiben told himself. *If you want to get out of this, try to think like a member of a starfaring race!*

It was hard. The subvocalized words were painful just behind his forehead. He could feel his mind try to retreat . . . to abandon Anglic for a simpler, more natural way of thinking.

Fiben resisted an almost overpowering urge to simply grab up the pitcher and drink from it directly. Instead, in spite of his thirst, he concentrated on each step involved in pouring another cup.

His fingers trembled on the pitcher's handle.

Focus!

Fiben recalled an ancient Zen adage. "Before enlightenment, chop wood, pour water. After enlightenment, chop wood, pour water."

Slowing down in spite of his thirst, he turned the simple act of pouring into an exercise. Holding on with two shaking hands, Fiben managed to pour himself about half a cupful, slopping about as much onto the table and floor. No matter. He took up the tumbler and drank in deep, greedy swallows.

The second cup poured easier. His hands were steadier.

That's it. Focus. . . . Choose the hard path, the one using thought. At least chims had it easier than neo-dolphins. The other Earthly client race was a hundred years younger and had to use three languages in order to think at all!

He was concentrating so hard that he didn't notice when the door behind him opened.

"Well, for a boy who's had such a busy night, you sure are chipper this morning."

Fiben whirled. Water splattered the wall as he brought up the cup to throw it, but the sudden movement seemed to send his brain spinning in his head. The cup clattered to the floor and Fiben clutched at his temples, groaning under a wave of vertigo.

Blearily, he saw a chimmie in a blue sarong. She approached carrying a tray. Fiben fought to remain standing, but his legs folded and he sank to his knees.

"Bloody fool," he heard her say. Bile in his mouth was only one reason he couldn't answer.

She set her tray on the table and took hold of his arm. "Only an idiot would try to get up after taking a full stunner jolt at close range!"

Fiben snarled and tried to shake her hands off. Now he remembered! This was the little "pimp" from the Ape's Grape. The one who had stood in the balcony not far from the Gubru and who had him stunned just as he was about to make his escape.

"Lemme 'lone," he said. "I don' need any help from a damn traitor!"

At least that was what he had intended to say, but it came out more as a slurred mumble. "Right. Anything you say," the chimmie answered evenly. She hauled him by one arm back to the bed. In spite of her slight size, she was quite strong.

Fiben groaned as he landed on the lumpy mattress. He kept trying to gather himself together, but rational thought seemed to swell and fade like ocean surf.

"I'm going to give you something. You'll sleep for at least ten hours. Then, maybe, you'll be ready to answer some questions."

Fiben couldn't spare the energy to curse her. All his attention was given over to finding a focus, something to center on. Anglic wasn't good enough anymore. He tried Galactic Seven.

"*Na . . . Ka . . . tcha . . . kresh . . .*" he counted thickly.

"Yes, yes," he heard her say. "By now we're all quite aware how well educated you are."

Fiben opened his eyes as the chimmie leaned over him, a capsule in her hand. With a finger snap she broke it, releasing a cloud of heavy vapor.

He tried to hold his breath against the anesthetic gas, knowing it was useless. At the same time, Fiben couldn't help noticing that she was actually fairly pretty—with a small, childlike jaw and smooth skin. Only her wry, bitter smile ruined the picture.

"My, you *are* an obstinate chen, aren't you? Be a good boy now, breathe in and rest," she commanded.

Unable to hold out any longer, Fiben had to inhale at last. A sweet odor filled his nostrils, like overripe forest fruit. Awareness began dissipating in a floating glow.

It was only then Fiben realized that she, too, had spoken in perfect, unaccented Galactic Seven.

28

Government in Hiding

Megan Oneagle blinked away tears. She wanted to turn away, not to look, but she forced herself to watch the carnage one more time.

The large holo-tank depicted a night scene, a rain-driven beach that shone dimly in shades of gray under faintly visible brooding cliffs. There were no moons, no stars, in fact hardly any light at all. The enhancement cameras had been at their very limits taking these pictures.

On the beach she could barely make out five black shapes that crawled ashore, dashed across the sand, and began climbing the low, crumbling bluffs.

"You can tell they followed procedures precisely," Major Prathachulthorn of the Terragens Marines explained. "First the submarine released the advance divers, who went ahead to scout and set up surveillance. Then, when it seemed the coast was clear, the sabots were released."

Megan watched as little boats bobbed to the surface— black globes rising amid small clouds of bubbles—which then headed quickly for shore. They landed, covers popped off, and more dark figures emerged.

"They carried the finest equipment available. Their training was the best. These were Terragens Marines."

So? Megan shook her head. *Does that mean they did not have mothers?*

She understood what Prathachulthorn was saying, however. If calamity could befall these professionals, who could blame Garth's colonial militia for the disasters of the last few months?

The black shapes moved toward the cliffs, stoop-shouldered under heavy burdens.

For weeks, now, the remnants still under Megan's command had sat with her, deep in their underwater refuge, pondering the collapse of all their well-laid plans for an organized resistance. The agents and saboteurs had been ready, the arms caches and cells organized. Then came the cursed Gubru coercion gas, and all their careful schemes collapsed under those roiling clouds of deadly smoke.

What few humans remained on the mainland were certainly dead by now, or as good as dead. What was frustrating was that nobody, not even the enemy in their broadcasts, seemed to know who or how many had made it to the islands in time for antidote treatment and internment.

Megan avoided thinking about her son. With any luck he was now on Cilmar Island, brooding with his friends in some pub, or complaining to a crowd of sympathetic girls how his mother had kept him out of the war. She could only hope and pray that was the case, and that Uthacalthing's daughter was safe as well.

More of a cause for perplexity was the fate of the Tymbrimi Ambassador himself. Uthacalthing had promised to follow the Planetary Council into hiding, but he had never appeared. There were reports that his ship had tried for deepspace instead, and was destroyed.

So many lives. Lost to what purpose?

Megan watched the display as the sabots began edging back into the water. The main force of men was already climbing the bluffs.

Without humans, of course, any hope of resistance was out of the question. A few of the cleverest chims might strike a blow, here or there, but what could really be expected of them without their patrons?

One purpose of this landing had been to start something going again, to adapt and adjust to new circumstances.

For the third time—even though she knew it was coming—Megan was caught by surprise as lightning suddenly burst upon the beach. In an instant everything was bathed in brilliant colors.

First to explode were the little boats, the sabots.

Next came the men.

"The sub pulled its camera in and dived just in time," Major Prathachulthorn said.

The display went blank. The woman marine lieutenant who had operated the projector turned on the lights. The other members of the Council blinked, adjusting to the light. Several dabbed their eyes.

Major Prathachulthorn's South Asian features were darkly serious as he spoke again. "It's the same thing as during the space battle, and when they somehow knew to gas every secret base we'd set up on land. Somehow they always find out where we are."

"Do you have any idea how they're doing it?" one of the council members asked.

Vaguely, Megan recognized that it was the female Marine officer, Lieutenant Lydia McCue, who answered. The young woman shook her head. "We have all of our technicians working on the problem, of course. But until we have some idea how they're doing it, we don't want to waste any more men trying to sneak ashore."

Megan Oneagle closed her eyes. "I think we are in no condition, now, to discuss matters any further. I declare this meeting adjourned."

When she retired to her tiny room, Megan thought she would cry. Instead, though, she merely sat on the edge of her bed, in complete darkness, allowing her eyes to look in the direction she knew her hands lay.

After a while, she felt she could almost see them, fingers like blobs resting tiredly on her knees. She imagined they were stained—a deep, sanguinary red.

29

Robert

Deep underground there was no way to sense the natural passage of time. Still, when Robert jerked awake in his chair, he knew exactly when it was.

Late. Too damn late. Athaclena was due back hours ago.

If he weren't still little more than an invalid he would have overcome the objections of Micah and Dr. Soo and gone topside himself, looking for the long overdue raiding party. As it was, the two chim scientists had nearly had to use force to stop him.

Traces of Robert's fever still returned now and then. He wiped his forehead and suppressed some momentary shivers. *No*, he thought. *I am in control!*

He stood up and picked his way carefully toward the sounds of muttered argument, where he found a pair of chims working over the pearly light of a salvaged level-seventeen computer. Robert sat on a packing crate behind them and listened for a while. When he made a suggestion they tried it, and it worked. Soon he had almost managed to push aside his worries as he immersed himself in work, helping the chims sketch out military tactics programming for a machine that had never been designed for anything more hostile than chess.

Somebody came by with a pitcher of juice. He drank. Someone handed him a sandwich. He ate.

An indeterminate time later a shout echoed through the underground chamber. Feet thumped hurriedly over low wooden bridges. Robert's eyes had grown accustomed to the bright screen, so it was out of a dark gloom that he saw chims hurrying past, seizing assorted, odd-lot weapons as they rushed up the passage leading to the surface.

He stood and grabbed at the nearest running brown form. "What's happening?"

He might as well have tried to halt a bull. The chim tore free without even glancing his way and vanished up the ragged tunnel. The next one he waved down actually looked at him and halted restlessly. "It's th' expedition," the nervous chen explained. "They've come back. . . . At least I hear some of 'em have."

Robert let the fellow go. He began casting around the chamber for a weapon of his own. If the raiding party had been followed back here . . .

There wasn't anything handy, of course. He realized bitterly that a rifle would hardly do him any good with his right arm immobilized. The chims probably wouldn't let him fight anyway. They'd more likely carry him bodily out of harm's way, deeper into the caves.

For a while there was silence. A few elderly chims waited with him for the sound of gunfire.

Instead, there came voices, gradually growing louder. The shouts sounded more excited than fearful.

Something seemed to stroke him, just above the ears. He hadn't had much practice since the accident, but now Robert's simple empathy sense felt a familiar trace blow into the chamber. He began to hope.

A babbling crowd of figures turned the bend—ragged, filthy neo-chimpanzees carrying slung weapons, some sporting bandages. The instant he saw Athaclena, a knot seemed to let go inside of Robert.

Just as quickly, though, another worry took its place. The Tymbrimi girl had been using the *gheer* transformation, clearly. He felt the rough edges of her exhaustion, and her face was gaunt.

Moreover, Robert could tell that she was still hard at work. Her corona stood puffed out, *sparkling* without light. The chims hardly seemed to notice as stay-at-homes eagerly pumped the jubilant raiders for news. But Robert realized that Athaclena was concentrating hard to *craft* that mood. It was too tenuous, too tentative to sustain itself without her.

"Robert!" Her eyes widened. "Should you be out of bed? Your fever only broke yesterday."

"I'm fine. But—"

"Good. I am happy to see you ambulatory, at last."

Robert watched as two heavily bandaged forms were rushed past on stretchers toward their makeshift hospital. He sensed Athaclena's effort to divert attention away from the bleeding, perhaps dying, soldiers until they were out of sight. Only the presence of the chims made Robert keep his voice low and even. "I want to talk with you, Athaclena."

She met his eyes, and for a brief instant Robert thought he *kenned* a faint form, turning and whirling above the floating tendrils of her corona. It was a harried glyph.

The returning warriors were busy with food and drink, bragging to their eager peers. Only Benjamin, a hand-sewn lieutenant's patch on his arm, stood soberly beside Athaclena. She nodded. "Very well, Robert. Let us go someplace private."

"Let me guess," he said, levelly. "You got your asses kicked."

Chim Benjamin winced, but he did not disagree. He tapped a spot on an outstretched map.

"We hit them here, in Yenching Gap," he said. "It was our fourth raid, so we thought we knew what to expect."

"Your *fourth*." Robert turned to Athaclena. "How long has this been going on?"

She had been picking daintily at a pocket pastry filled with something pungently aromatic. She wrinkled her nose. "We have been practicing for about a week, Robert. But this was the first time we tried to do any real harm."

"And?"

Benjamin seemed immune to Athaclena's mood-tailoring. Perhaps it was intentional, for she would need at least one aide whose judgment was unaffected. Or maybe he was just too bright. He rolled his eyes. "We're the ones who got hurt." He went on to explain. "We split into five groups. Mizz Athaclena insisted. It's what saved us."

"What was your target?"

"A small patrol. Two light hover-tanks and a couple of open landcars."

Robert pondered the site on the map, where one of the few roads entered the first rank of mountains. From what others had told him, the enemy were seldom seen above the Sind. They seemed content to control space, the Archipelago, and the narrow strip of settlement along the coast around Port Helenia.

After all, why should they bother with the back country? They had nearly every human safely locked away. Garth was theirs.

Apparently, the rebels' first three forays had been exercises—a few former militia noncoms among the chims trying to teach raw recruits how to move and fight under the forest shadows. Fourth time out, though, they had felt ready to contact the enemy.

"From the beginning they seemed to know we were there," Benjamin continued. "We followed them as they patrolled, practiced ducking through the trees and keeping them in sight, like before. Then . . ."

"Then you actually attacked the patrol."

Benjamin nodded. "We *suspected* they knew where we were. But we had to be sure. Th' General came up with a plan. . . ."

Robert blinked, then nodded. He still wasn't used to Athaclena's new honorary title. His puzzlement grew as he listened to Benjamin describe this morning's action.

The ambush had been set up so five different parties would each, in turn, get a shot at the patrol with minimum risk.

And without much chance to damage the enemy, either, he noted. The ambuscades were mostly too high or too far away to offer very good shots. With hunting rifles and concussion grenades, what harm could they do?

One small Gubru landcar had been destroyed in the initial fusillade. Another was lightly damaged before withering fire from the tanks forced each squad into retreat. Air cover arrived swiftly from the coast, and the raiders fled barely in time. The aggressive portion of the raid was finished in less than fifteen minutes. The retreat and circuitous covering of tracks took much longer.

"The Gubru weren't fooled, were they?" Robert asked.

Benjamin shook his head. "They always seemed to be able to pick us out. It's a miracle we were able to ding them at all, and a bigger one we got away."

Robert glanced at the "General." He started to voice his disapproval, but then he looked back at the map one more time, pondering the positions the ambushers had taken up. He traced the lines of fire, the avenues of retreat.

"You suspected as much," he said at last to Athaclena.

Her eyes came slightly together and separated again, a

Tymbrimi shrug. "I did not think we should approach too closely, on our first encounter."

Robert nodded. Indeed, if closer, "better" ambush sites had been chosen, few if any of the chims would have made it back alive.

The plan was good.

No, not good. *Inspired*. It hadn't been intended to hurt the enemy but to build confidence. The troops had been dispersed so everyone would get to fire at the patrol with minimum risk. The raiders could return home swaggering, but most important, they would make it home.

Even so, they had been hurt. Robert could sense how exhausted Athaclena was, partly from the effort of maintaining everyone's mood of "victory."

He felt a touch on his knee and took Athaclena's hand in his own. Her long, delicate fingers closed tightly, and he felt her triple-beat pulse.

Their eyes met.

"We turned a possible disaster into a minor success today," Benjamin said. "But so long as the enemy always knows where we are, I don't see how we can ever do more than play tag with them. And even that game'll certainly cost more than we can afford to pay."

30

Fiben

Fiben rubbed the back of his neck and stared irritably across the table. So *this* was the person he had been sent to contact, Dr. Taka's brilliant student, their would-be leader of an urban underground.

"What kind of idiocy was that?" he accused. "You let me

walk into that club blind, ignorant. There were a dozen times I nearly got caught last night. Or even killed!"

"It was two nights ago," Gailet Jones corrected him. She sat in a straight-backed chair and smoothed the blue demisilk of her sarong. "Anyway, I *was* there, at the Ape's Grape, waiting outside to make contact. I saw that you were a stranger, arriving alone, wearing a plaid work shirt, so I approached you with the password."

"Pink?" Fiben blinked at her. "You come up to me and whisper *pink* at me, and that's supposed to be a bloody, reverted *password*?"

Normally he would never use such rough language with a young lady. Right now Gailet Jones looked more like the sort of person he had expected in the first place, a chimmie of obvious education and breeding. But he had seen her under other circumstances, and he wasn't ever likely to forget.

"You call that a password? They told me to look for a *fisherman!*"

Shouting made him wince. Fiben's head still felt as though it were leaking brains in five or six places. His muscles had stopped cramping capriciously some time ago, but he still ached all over and his temper was short.

"A fisherman? In that part of town?" Gailet Jones frowned, her face clouding momentarily. "Listen, everything was chaos when I rang up the Center to leave word with Dr. Taka. I figured her group was used to keeping secrets and would make an ideal core out in the countryside. I only had a few moments to think up a way to make a later contact before the Gubru took over the telephone lines. I figured they were already tapping and recording everything, so it had to be something colloquial, you know, that their language computers would have trouble interpreting."

She stopped suddenly, bringing her hand to her mouth. "Oh no!"

"What?" Fiben edged forward.

She blinked for a moment, then motioned in the air. "I told that fool operator at the Center how their emissary should dress, and where to meet me, then I said I'd pass myself off as a hooker—"

"As a what? I don't get it." Fiben shook his head.

"It's an archaic term. Pre-Contact human slang for one who offers cheap, illicit sex for cash."

Fiben snapped. "Of all the damn fool, Ifni-cursed, loony ideas!"

Gailet Jones answered back hotly. "All right, smartie, what *should* I have done? The militia was falling to pieces. Nobody had even considered what to do if every human on the planet was suddenly removed from the chain of command! I had this wild notion of helping to start a resistance movement from scratch. So I tried to arrange a meeting—"

"Uh huh, posing as someone advertising illicit favors, right outside a place where the Gubru were inciting a sexual *frenzy*."

"How was *I* to know what they were going to do, or that they'd choose that sleepy little club as the place to do it in? I conjectured that social restraints would relax enough to let me pull the pose and so be able to approach strangers. It never occurred to me they'd relax *that* much! My guess was that anyone I came up to by mistake would be so surprised he'd act as you did and I could pull a fade."

"But it didn't work out that way."

"No it did not! Before you appeared, several solitary chens showed up dressed likely enough to make me put on my act. Poor Max had to stun half a dozen of them, and the alley was starting to get full! But it was already too late to change the rendezvous, or the password—"

"Which nobody understood! *Hooker?* You should have realized something like that would get garbled!"

"I knew Dr. Taka would understand. We used to watch and discuss old movies together. We'd study the archaic words they used. I can't understand why she . . ." Her voice trailed off when she saw the expression on Fiben's face. "What? Why are you looking at me like that?"

"I'm sorry. I just realized that you couldn't know." He shook his head. "You see, Dr. Taka died just about the time they got your message, of an allergic reaction to the coercion gas."

Her breath caught. Gailet seemed to sink into herself. "I . . . I feared as much when she didn't show up in town for internment. It's . . . a great loss." She closed her eyes and turned away, obviously feeling more than her words told.

At least she had been spared witnessing the flaming end of the Howletts Center as the soot-covered ambulances came and went, and the glazed, dying face of her mentor as the ecdemic gas took its cruel, statistical toll. Fiben had seen recordings of that fear-palled evening. The images lay in dark layers still, at the back of his mind.

Gailet gathered herself, visibly putting off her mourning for later. She dabbed her eyes and faced Fiben, jaw outthrust defiantly. "I had to come up with something a chim would understand but the Eatees' language computers wouldn't. It won't be the last time we have to improvise. Anyway, what matters is that you are here. Our two groups are in contact now."

"I was almost killed," he pointed out, though this time he felt a bit churlish for mentioning it.

"But you weren't killed. In fact, there may be ways to turn your little misadventure into an advantage. Out on the streets they're still talking about what you did that night, you know."

Was that a faint, tentative note of *respect* in her voice? A peace offering, perhaps?

Suddenly, it was all too much. Much too much for him. Fiben knew it was exactly the wrong thing to do, at exactly the wrong time, but he just couldn't help himself. He broke up.

"A hook . . . ?" He giggled, though every shake seemed to rattle his brain in his skull. "A *hooker*?" He threw back his head and hooted, pounding on the arms of the chair. Fiben slumped. He guffawed, kicking his feet in the air. "Oh, Goodall. That was *all* I needed to be looking for!"

Gailet Jones glared at him as he gasped for breath. He didn't even care, right now, if she called in that big chim, Max, to use the stunner on him again.

It was all just too much.

If the look in her eyes right then counted for anything, Fiben knew this alliance was already off to a rocky start.

31

Galactics

The Suzerain of Beam and Talon stepped aboard its personal barge and accepted the salutes of its Talon Soldier escort. They were carefully chosen troops, feathers perfectly preened, crests neatly dyed with colors noting rank and unit. The admiral's Kwackoo aide hurried forth and took its ceremonial robe. When all had settled onto their perches the pilot took off on gravitics, heading toward the defense works under construction in the low hills east of Port Helenia. The Suzerain of Beam and Talon watched in silence as the new city fence fell behind them and the farms of this small Earthling settlement rushed by underneath.

The seniormost stoop-colonel, military second in command, saluted with a sharp beak-clap. "The conclave went well? Suitably? Satisfactorily?" the stoop-colonel asked.

The Suzerain of Beam and Talon chose to overlook the impudence of the question. It was more useful to have a second who could think than one whose plumage was always perfectly preened. Surrounding itself with a few such creatures was one of the things that had won the Suzerain its candidacy. The admiral gave its inferior a haughty eyeblink of assent. "Our consensus is presently adequate, sufficient, it will do."

The stoop-colonel bowed and returned to its station. Of course it would know that consensus was never perfect at this early stage in a Molt. Anyone could tell that from the Suzerain's ruffled down and haggard eyes.

This most recent Command Conclave had been particularly indecisive, and several aspects had irritated the admiral deeply.

202

For one thing, the Suzerain of Cost and Caution was pressing to release much of their support fleet to go assist other Gubru operations, far from here. And as if that weren't enough, the third leader, the Suzerain of Propriety, still insisted on being carried everywhere on its perch, refusing to set foot on the soil of Garth until all punctilio had been satisfied. The priest was all fluffed and agitated over a number of issues— excessive human deaths from coercion gas, the threatened breakdown of the Garth Reclamation Project, the pitiful size of the Planetary Branch Library, the Uplift status of the benighted, pre-sentient neo-chimpanzees.

On every issue, it seemed, there must be still another realignment, another tense negotiation. Another struggle for consensus.

And yet, there were deeper issues than these ephemera. The Three had also begun to argue over fundamentals, and *there* the process was actually starting to become enjoyable, somehow. The pleasurable aspects of Triumviracy were emerging, especially when they danced and crooned and argued over deeper matters.

Until now it had seemed that the flight to queenhood would be straight and easy for the admiral, for it had been in command from the start. Now it had begun to dawn on the Suzerain of Beam and Talon that all would not be easy. This was not going to be any trivial Molt after all.

Of course the best ones never were. Very diverse factions had been involved in choosing the three leaders of the Expeditionary Force, for the Roost Masters of home had hopes for a new unified policy to emerge from this particular Threesome. In order for that to happen, all of them had to be very good minds, and very different from each other.

Just how good and how different was beginning to become clear. A few of the ideas the others had presented recently were clever, and quite unnerving.

They are right about one thing, the admiral had to admit. *We must not simply conquer, defeat, overrun the wolflings. We must discredit them!*

The Suzerain of Beam and Talon had been concentrating so hard on military matters that it had got in the habit of seeing its mates as impediments, little more.

That was wrong, impertinent, disloyal of me, the admiral thought.

In fact, it was devoutly to be *hoped* that the bureaucrat and the priest were as bright in their own areas as the admiral was in soldiery. If Propriety and Accountancy handled their ends as brilliantly as the invasion had been, then they would be a trio to be remembered!

Some things were foreordained, the Suzerain of Beam and Talon knew. They had been set since the days of the Progenitors, long, long ago. Long before there were heretics and unworthy clans polluting the starlances—horrible, wretched wolflings, and Tymbrimi, and Thennanin, and Soro. . . . It was vital that the clan of Gooksyu-Gubru prevail in this era's troubles! The clan must achieve greatness!

The admiral contemplated the way the eggs of the Earthlings' defeat had been laid so many years before. How the Gubru force had been able to detect and counteract their every move. And how the coercion gas had left all their plans in complete disarray. These had been the Suzerain's own ideas—along with members of its personal staff, of course. They had been years coming to fruition.

The Suzerain of Beam and Talon stretched its arms, feeling tension in the flexors that had, ages before its species' own uplifting, carried his ancestors aloft in warm, dry currents on the Gubru homeworld.

Yes! Let my peers' ideas also be bold, imaginative, brilliant. . . .

Let them be almost, nearly, close to—but not quite—as brilliant as my own.

The Suzerain began preening its feathers as the cruiser leveled off and headed east under a cloud-decked sky.

32

Athaclena

"I am going *crazy* down here. I feel like I'm being kept prisoner!"

Robert paced, accompanied by twin shadows cast by the cave's only two glow bulbs. Their stark light glistened in the sheets of moisture that seeped slowly down the walls of the underground chamber.

Robert's left arm clenched, tendons standing out from fist to elbow to well-muscled shoulder. He punched a nearby cabinet, sending banging echoes down the subterranean passageways. "I warn you, Clennie, I'm not going to be able to wait much longer. When are you going to let me *out* of here?"

Athaclena winced as Robert slammed the cabinet again, giving vent to his frustration. At least twice he had seemed about to use his still-splinted right arm instead of the undamaged left. "Robert," she urged. "You have been making wonderful progress. Soon your cast can come off. Please do not jeopardize that by injuring yourself—"

"You're evading the issue!" he interrupted. "Even wearing a cast I could be out there, helping train the troops and scouting Gubru positions. But you have me trapped down here in these caves, programming minicomps and sticking pins in maps! It's driving me nuts!"

Robert positively radiated his frustration. Athaclena had asked him before to try to damp it down. *To keep a lid on it*, as the metaphor went. For some reason she seemed particularly susceptible to his emotional tides—as stormy and wild as any Tymbrimi adolescent's.

"Robert, you know why we cannot risk sending you out to the surface. The Gubru gasbots have already swept over our surface encampments several times, unleashing their deadly vapors. Had you been above on any of those occasions you would even now be on your way to Cilmar Island, lost to us. And that is at best! I shudder to think of the worst."

Athaclena's ruff bristled at the thought; the silvery tendrils of her corona waved in agitation.

It was mere luck that Robert had been rescued from the Mendoza Freehold just before the persistent Gubru searcher robots swooped down upon the tiny mountain homestead. Camouflage and removal of all electronic items had apparently not been enough to hide the cabin.

Meline Mendoza and the children immediately left for Port Helenia and presumably arrived in time for treatment. Juan Mendoza had been less fortunate. Remaining behind to close down several ecological survey traps, he had been stricken with a delayed allergic reaction to the coercion gas and died within five convulsive minutes, foaming and jerking under the horrified gaze of his helpless chim partners.

"You were not there to see Juan die, Robert, but surely you must have heard reports. Do you want to risk such a death? Are you aware of how close we already came to losing you?"

Their eyes met, brown encountering gold-flecked gray. She could sense Robert's determination, and also his effort to control his stubborn anger. Slowly, Robert's left arm unclenched. He breathed a deep sigh and sank into a canvas-backed chair.

"I'm aware, Clennie. I know how you feel. But you've got to understand, I'm *part* of all this." He leaned forward, his expression no longer wrathful, but still intense. "I agreed to my mother's request, to guide you into the bush instead of joining my militia unit, because Megan said it was important. But now you're no longer my guest in the forest. You're organizing an army! And I feel like a fifth wheel."

Athaclena sighed. "We both know that it will not be much of an army . . . a gesture at best. Something to give the chims hope. Anyway, as a Terragens officer you have the right to take over from me any time you wish."

Robert shook his head. "That's not what I mean. I'm not conceited enough to think I could have done any better. I'm no leader type, and I know it. Most of the chims worship you, and believe in your Tymbrimi mystique.

"Still, I probably *am* the only human with any military training left in these mountains . . . an asset you have to use if we're to have any chance to—"

Robert stopped abruptly, lifting his eyes to look over Athaclena's shoulder. Athaclena turned as a small chimmie in shorts and bandoleer entered the underground room and saluted.

"Excuse me, general, Captain Oneagle, but Lieutenant Benjamin has just gotten in. Um, he reports that things aren't any better over in Spring Valley. There aren't any humans there anymore. But outposts all up and down every canyon are still being buzzed by the damn gasbots at least once a day. There doesn't seem to be any sign of it lettin' up anywhere where our runners have been able to get to."

"How about the chims in Spring Valley?" Athaclena asked. "Is the gas making them sick?" She recalled Dr. Schultz and the effect the coercion gas had had on some of the chims back at the Center.

The courier shook her head. "No, ma'am. Not anymore. It seems to be the same story all over. All the sus-susceptible chims have already been flushed out and gone to Port Helenia. Every person left in the mountains must be immune by now."

Athaclena glanced at Robert and they must have shared the same thought.

Every person but one.

"Damn them!" he cursed. "Won't they ever let up? They have ninety-nine point nine percent of the humans captive. Do they need to keep gassing every hut and hovel, just in order to get every last one?"

"Apparently they are afraid of *Homo sapiens*, Robert." Athaclena smiled. "After all, you are allies of the Tymbrimi. And we do not choose harmless species as partners."

Robert shook his head, glowering. But Athaclena reached out with her aura to touch him, nudging his personality, forcing him to look up and see the humor in her eyes. Against his will, a slow smile spread. At last Robert laughed. "Oh, I guess the damned birds aren't so dumb after all. Better safe than sorry, hmm?"

Athaclena shook her head, her corona forming a glyph of appreciation, a simple one which he might *kenn*. "No, Rob-

ert. They aren't so dumb. But they have missed at least one
human, so their worries aren't over yet."

The little neo-chim messenger glanced from Tymbrimi
to human and sighed. It all sounded scary to her, not funny.
She didn't understand why they smiled.

Probably, it was something subtle and convoluted. Patron-
class humor . . . dry and intellectual. Some chims batted in
that league, strange ones who differed from other neo-
chimpanzees not so much in intelligence as in something
else, something much less definable.

She did not envy those chims. Responsibility was an
awesome thing, more daunting than the prospect of fighting a
powerful enemy, or even dying.

It was the possibility of being *left alone* that terrified
her. She might not understand it, when these two laughed.
But it felt good just to hear it.

The messenger stood a little straighter as Athaclena turned
back to speak to her.

"I will want to hear Lieutenant Benjamin's report personally. Would you please also give my compliments to Dr.
Soo and ask her to join us in the operations chamber?"

"Yesser!" The chimmie saluted and took off at a run.

"Robert?" Athaclena asked. "Your opinion will be welcome."

He looked up, a distant expression on his face. "In a
minute, Clennie. I'll check in at operations. There's just
something I want to think through first."

"All right." Athaclena nodded. "I'll see you soon." She
turned away and followed the messenger down a water-carved
corridor lit at long intervals by dim glow bulbs and wet
reflections on the dripping stalactites.

Robert watched her until she was out of sight. He thought
in the near-total quiet.

*Why are the Gubru persisting in gassing the mountains,
after nearly every human has already been driven out? It
must be a terrific expense, even if their gasbots only swoop
down on places where they detect an Earthling presence?*

*And how are they able to detect buildings, vehicles, even
isolated chims, no matter how well hidden?*

*Right now it doesn't matter that they've been dosing our
surface encampments. The gasbots are simple machines and*

don't know we're training an army in this valley. They just sense "Earthlings!"—then dive in to do their work and leave again.

But what happens when we start operations and attract attention from the Gubru themselves? We can't afford to be detectable then.

There was another very basic reason to find an answer to these questions.

As long as this is going on, I'm trapped down here!

Robert listened to the faint plink of water droplets seeping from the nearest wall. He thought about the enemy.

The trouble on Garth was clearly little more than a skirmish among the greater battles tearing up the Five Galaxies. The Gubru couldn't just gas the entire planet. That would cost far too much for this backwater theater of operations.

So a swarm of cheap, stupid, but efficient seeker robots had been unleashed to home in on anything not natural to Garth . . . anything that had the scent of Earth about it. By now nearly every attack dosed only irritated, resentful chims—immune to the coercion gas—and empty buildings all over the planet.

It was a nuisance, and it was effective. A way had to be found to stop it.

Robert pulled a sheet of paper from a folder at the end of the table. He wrote down the principal ways the gasbots might be using to detect Earthlings on an alien planet.

OPTICAL IMAGING
BODY HEAT INFRARED
SCAN RESONANCE
PSI
REALITY TWIST

Robert regretted having taken so many courses in public administration, and so few on Galactic technologies. He was certain the Great Library's gigayear-old archives contained many methods of detection beyond just these five. For instance, what if the gasbots actually did "sniff out" a Terran odor, tracing anything Earthly by sense of smell?

No. He shook his head. There came a point where one had to cut a list short, putting aside things that were obviously ridiculous. Leaving them as a last resort, at least.

The rebels did have a Library pico-branch he could try,

salvaged from the wreckage of the Howletts Center. The
chances of it having any entries of military use were quite
slim. It was a tiny branch, holding no more information than
all the books written by pre-Contact Mankind, and it was
specialized in the areas of Uplift and genetic engineering.

*Maybe we can apply to the District Central Library on
Tanith for a literature search.* Robert smiled at the ironic
thought. Even a people imprisoned by an invader supposedly had the right to query the Galactic Library whenever
they wished. That was part of the Code of the Progenitors.

Right! He chuckled at the image. *We'll just walk up to
Gubru occupation headquarters and demand that they transmit our appeal to Tanith, . . . a request for information on
the invader's own military technology!*

*They might even do it. After all, with the galaxies in
turmoil the Library must be inundated with queries. They
would get around to our request eventually, maybe sometime
in the next century.*

He looked over his list. At least these were means he
had heard of or knew something about.

Possibility one: There might be a satellite overhead with
sophisticated optical scanning capabilities, inspecting Garth
acre by acre, seeking out regular shapes that would indicate
buildings or vehicles. Such a device could be dispatching the
gasbots to their targets.

Feasible, but why were the same sites raided over and
over again? Wouldn't such a satellite remember? And how
could a satellite know to send robot bombers plunging down
on even isolated groups of chims, traveling under the heavy
forest canopy?

The reverse logic held for infrared direction. The machines couldn't be homing in on the target's body heat. The
Gubru drones still swooped down on empty buildings, for
instance, cold and abandoned for weeks now.

Robert did not have the expertise to eliminate all the
possibilities on his list. Certainly he knew next to nothing
about psi and its weird cousin, reality physics. The weeks
with Athaclena had begun to open doors to him, but he was
far from being more than a rank novice in an area that still
caused many humans and chims to shudder in superstitious
dread.

*Well, as long as I'm stuck here underground I might as
well expand my education.*

He started to get up, intending to join Athaclena and Benjamin. Then he stopped suddenly. Looking at his list of possibilities he realized that there was one more that he had left out.

. . . *A way for the Gubru to penetrate our defenses so easily when they invaded. . . . A way for them to find us again and again, wherever we hide. A way for them to foil our every move.*

He did not want to, but honesty forced him to pick up the stylus one more time.

He wrote a single word.

TREASON

33

Fiben

That afternoon Gailet took Fiben on a tour of Port Helenia—or as much of it as the invader had not placed off limits to the neo-chimp population.

Fishing trawlers still came and went from the docks at the southern end of town. But now they were crewed solely by chim sailors. And less than half the usual number set forth, taking wide detours past the Gubru fortress ship that filled half the outlet of Aspinal Bay.

In the markets they saw some items in plentiful supply. Elsewhere there were sparse shelves, stripped nearly bare by scarcity and hoarding. Colonial money was still good for some things, like beer and fish. But only Galactic pellet-scrip would buy meat or fresh fruit. Irritated shoppers had already begun to learn what that archaic term, "inflation," meant.

Half the population, it seemed, worked for the invader.

There were battlements being built, off to the south of the bay, near the spaceport. Excavations told of more massive structures yet to be.

Placards everywhere in town depicted grinning neo-chimpanzees and promised plenty once again, as soon as enough "proper" money entered circulation. Good work would bring that day closer, they were promised.

"Well? Have you seen enough?" his guide asked.

Fiben smiled. "Not at all. In fact, we've barely scratched the surface."

Gailet shrugged and let him lead the way.

Well, he thought as he looked at the scant market shelves, *the nutritionists keep telling us neo-chimps we eat more meat than is good for us . . . much more than we could get in the wild old days. Maybe this'll do us some good.*

At last their wanderings brought them to the bell tower overlooking Port Helenia College. It was a smaller campus than the University, on Cilmar Island, but Fiben had attended ecological conferences here not so very long ago, so he knew his way around.

As he looked over the school, something struck him as very strange.

It wasn't just the Gubru hover-tank, dug in at the top of the hill, nor the ugly new wall that grazed the northern fringe of the college grounds on its way around town. Rather, it was something about the students and faculty themselves.

Frankly, he was surprised to see them here at all!

They were all chims, of course. Fiben had come to Port Helenia expecting to find ghettos or concentration camps, crowded with the human population of the mainland. But the last mels and fems had been moved out to the islands some days ago. Taking their place had been thousands of chims pouring in from outlying areas, including those susceptible to the coercion gas in spite of the invaders' assurances that it was impossible.

All of these had been given the antidote, paid a small, token reparation, and put to work in town.

But here at the college all seemed peaceful and amazingly close to normal. Fiben and Gailet looked down from the top of the bell tower. Below them, chens and chimmies moved about between classes. They carried books, spoke to one another in low voices, and only occasionally cast furtive glances at the alien cruisers that growled overhead every hour or so.

Fiben shook his head in wonder that they persevered at all.

Sure, humans were notoriously liberal in their Uplift policy, treating their clients as near equals in the face of a Galactic tradition that was far less generous. Elder Galactic clans might glower in disapproval, but chim and dolphin members deliberated next to their patrons on Terragens Councils. The client races had even been entrusted with a few starships of their own.

But a *college* without *men*?

Fiben had wondered why the invader held such a loose rein over the chim population, meddling only in a few crass ways like at the Ape's Grape.

Now he thought he knew why.

"Mimicry! They must think we're playing pretend!" he muttered half aloud.

"What did you say?" Gailet looked at him. They had made a truce in order to get the job done, but clearly she did not savor spending all day as his tour guide.

Fiben pointed at the students. "Tell me what you see down there."

She glowered, then sighed and bent forward to look. "I see Professor Jimmie Sung leaving lecture hall, explaining something to some students." She smiled faintly. "It's probably intermediate Galactic history. . . . I used to TA for him, and I well recall that expression of confusion on the students' faces."

"Good. That's what *you* see. Now look at it through a Gubru's eyes."

Gailet frowned. "What do you mean?"

Fiben gestured again. "Remember, according to Galactic tradition we neo-chimps aren't much over three hundred years old as a sapient client race, barely older than dolphins—only just beginning our hundred-thousand-year period of probation and indenture to Man.

"Remember, also, that many of the Eatee fanatics resent humans terribly. Yet humans had to be granted patron status and all the privileges that go along with it. Why? Because they already had uplifted chims and dolphins before Contact! That's how you get status in the Five Galaxies, by having clients and heading up a clan."

Gailet shook her head. "I don't get what you're driving at. Why are you explaining the obvious?" Clearly, she did not like being lectured by a backwoods chim, one without even a postgraduate degree.

"Think! How did humans win their status? Remember how it happened, back in the twenty-second century? The fanatics were outvoted when it came to accepting neo-chimps and neo-dolphins as sapient." Fiben waved his arm. "It was a diplomatic coup pulled off by the Kanten and Tymbrimi and other moderates before humans even knew what the issues were!"

Gailet's expression was sardonic, and he recalled that her area of expertise was Galactic sociology. "Of course, but—"

"It became a *fait accompli*. But the Gubru and the Soro and the other fanatics didn't have to like it. They still think we're little better than animals. They *have* to believe that, otherwise humans have *earned* a place in Galactic society equal to most, and better than many!"

"I still don't see what you're—"

"*Look* down there." Fiben pointed. "Look with Gubru eyes, and tell me what you see!"

Gailet Jones glared at Fiben narrowly. At last, she sighed. "Oh, if you insist," and she swiveled to gaze down into the courtyard again.

She was silent for a long time.

"I don't like it," she said at last. Fiben could barely hear her. He moved to stand closer.

"Tell me what you see."

She looked away, so he put it into words for her. "What you see are bright, well-trained animals, creatures *mimicking* the behavior of their masters. Isn't that it? Through the eyes of a Galactic, you see clever *imitations* of human professors and human students . . . replicas of better times, reenacted superstitiously by loyal—"

"Stop it!" Gailet shouted, covering her ears. She whirled on Fiben, eyes ablaze. "I hate you!"

Fiben wondered. This was hard on her. Was he simply getting even for the hurt and humiliation he had suffered over the last three days, partly at her hands?

But no. She had to be shown how her people were looked on by the enemy! How else would she ever learn how to fight them?

Oh, he was justified, all right. *Still,* Fiben thought. *It's never pleasant being loathed by a pretty girl.*

Gailet Jones sagged against one of the pillars supporting the roof of the bell tower. "Oh Ifni and Goodall," she cried into her hands. "What if they are right! What if it's true?"

34

Athaclena

The glyph *paraphrenll* hovered above the sleeping girl, a floating cloud of uncertainty that quivered in the darkened chamber.

It was one of the Glyphs of Doom. Better than any living creature could predict its own fate, *paraphrenll* knew what the future held for it—what was unavoidable.

And yet it tried to escape. It could do nothing else. Such was the simple, pure, ineluctable nature of *paraphrenll.*

The glyph wafted upward in the dream smoke of Athaclena's fitful slumber, rising until its nervous fringe barely touched the rocky ceiling. That instant the glyph quailed from the burning reality of the damp stone, dropping quickly back toward where it had been born.

Athaclena's head shook slightly on the pillow, and her breathing quickened. *Paraphrenll* flickered in suppressed panic just above.

The shapeless dream glyph began to resolve itself, its amorphous shimmering starting to assume the symmetrical outlines of a face.

Paraphrenll was an essence—a distillation. Resistance to inevitability was its theme. It writhed and shuddered to hold off the change, and the face vanished for a time.

Here, above the Source, its danger was greatest. *Para-*

phrenll darted away toward the curtained exit, only to be
drawn short suddenly, as if held in leash by taut threads.

The glyph stretched thin, straining for release. Above
the sleeping girl, slender tendrils waved after the desperate
capsule of psychic energy, drawing it back, back.

Athaclena sighed tremulously. Her pale, almost translucent skin throbbed as her body perceived an emergency of
some sort and prepared to make adjustments. But no orders
came. There was no plan. The hormones and enzymes had no
theme to build around.

Tendrils reached out, pulling *paraphrenll*, hauling it in.
They gathered around the struggling symbol, like fingers
caressing clay, fashioning decisiveness out of uncertainty,
form out of raw terror.

At last they dropped away, revealing what *paraphrenll*
had become . . . A *face*, grinning with mirth. Its cat's eyes
glittered. Its smile was not sympathetic.

Athaclena moaned.

A crack appeared. The face divided down the middle,
and the halves separated. Then there were two of them!

Her breath came in rapid strokes.

The two figures split longitudinally, and there were four.
It happened again, eight . . . and again . . . sixteen. Faces
multiplied, laughing soundlessly but uproariously.

"Ah-ah!" Athaclena's eyes opened. They shone with an
opalescent, chemical fear-light. Panting, clutching the blankets, she sat up and stared in the small subterranean chamber, desperate for the sight of real things—her desk, the faint
light of the hall bulb filtering through the entrance curtain.
She could still feel the thing that *paraphrenll* had hatched. It
was dissipating, now that she was awake, but slowly, too
slowly! Its laughter seemed to rock with the beating of her
heart, and Athaclena knew there would be no good in covering
her ears.

What was it humans called their sleep-terror? *Nightmare*.
But Athaclena had heard that they were pale things, dreamed
events and warped scenes taken from daily life, generally
forgotten simply by awakening.

The sights and sensations of the room slowly took on
solidity. But the laughter did not merely vanish, defeated. It
faded into the walls, embedding there, she knew. Waiting to
return.

"*Tutsunacann*," she sighed aloud. Tymbrim-dialect sounded queer and nasal after weeks speaking solely Anglic.

The laughing man glyph, *Tutsunacann*, would not go away. Not until something altered, or some hidden idea became a resolve which, in turn, must become a jest.

And to a Tymbrimi, jokes were not always funny.

Athaclena sat still while rippling motions under her skin settled down—the unasked-for *gheer* activity dissipating gradually. *You are not needed*, she told the enzymes. *There is no emergency. Go and leave me alone.*

Ever since she had been little, the tiny change-nodes had been a part of her life—occasionally inconveniences, often indispensable. Only since coming to Garth had she begun to picture the little fluid organs as tiny, mouselike *creatures*, or busy little gnomes, which hurried about making sudden alterations within her body whenever the need arose.

What a bizarre way of looking at a natural, organic function! Many of the animals of Tymbrim shared the ability. It had evolved in the forests of homeworld long before the starfaring Caltmour had arrived to give her ancestors speech and law.

That was it, of course . . . the reason why she had never likened the nodes to busy little creatures before coming to Garth. Prior to Uplift, her pre-sentient ancestors would have been incapable of making baroque comparisons. And *after* Uplift, they knew the scientific truth.

Ah, but humans . . . the Terran wolflings . . . had come into intelligence without guidance. They were not handed answers, as a child is given knowledge by its parents and teachers. They had emerged ignorant into awareness and spent long millennia groping in darkness.

Needing explanations and having none available, they got into the habit of inventing their own! Athaclena remembered when she had been amused . . . *amused* reading about some of them.

Disease was caused by "vapors," or excess bile, or an enemy's curse. . . . The Sun rode across the sky in a great chariot. . . . The course of history was determined by economics. . . .

And inside the body, there resided *animus*. . . .

Athaclena touched a throbbing knot behind her jaw and started as the small bulge seemed to skitter away, like some small, shy creature. It was a terrifying image, that *meta-*

phor, more frightening than *tutsunacann*, for it invaded her body—her very sense of self!

Athaclena moaned and buried her face in her hands. *Crazy Earthlings! What have they done to me?*

She recalled how her father had bid her to learn more about human ways, to overcome her odd misgivings about the denizens of Sol III. But what had happened? She had found her destiny entwined with theirs, and it was no longer within her power to control it.

"Father," she spoke aloud in Galactic Seven. "I fear."

All she had of him was memory. Even the *nahakieri* glimmer she had felt back at the burning Howletts Center was unavailable, perhaps gone. She could not go down to seek his roots with hers, for *tutsunacann* lurked there, like some subterranean beast, waiting to get her.

More metaphors, she realized. *My thoughts are filling with them, while my own glyphs terrify me!*

Movement in the hall outside made her look up. A narrow trapezoid of light spilled into the room as the curtain was drawn aside. The slightly bowlegged outline of a chim stood silhouetted against the dim glow.

"Excuse me, Mizz Athaclena, ser. I'm sorry to bother you during your rest period, but we thought you'd want to know."

"Ye . . ." Athaclena swallowed, chasing more mice from her throat. She shivered and concentrated on Anglic. "Yes? What is it?"

The chim stepped forward, partly cutting off the light. "It's Captain Oneagle, ser. I'm . . . I'm afraid we can't locate him anywhere."

Athaclena blinked. "Robert?"

The chim nodded. "He's gone, ser. He's just plain disappeared!"

35

Robert

The forest animals stopped and listened, all senses aquiver. A growing rustle and rumble of footfalls made them nervous. Without exception they scuttled for cover and watched from hiding as a tall beast ran past them, leaping from boulder to log to soft forest loam.

They had begun to get used to the smaller two-legged variety, and to the much larger kind that chuffed and shambled along on three limbs as often as two. Those, at least, were hairy and smelled like animals. This one, though, was different. It ran but did not hunt. It was chased, yet it did not try to lose its pursuers. It was warm-blooded, yet when it rested it lay in the open noon sunshine, where only animals stricken with madness normally ventured.

The little native creatures did not connect the running thing with the kind that flew about in tangy-smelling metal and plastic, for that type had always made such noise, and reeked of those things.

This one, though . . . this one ran unclothed.

"Captain, stop!"

Robert hopped one rock farther up the tumbled boulder scree. He leaned against another to catch his breath and looked back down at his pursuer.

"Getting tired, Benjamin?"

The chim officer panted, stooping over with both hands on his knees. Farther downslope the rest of the search party lay strung out, some flat on their backs, barely able to move.

Robert smiled. They must have thought it would be easy

219

to catch him. After all, chims were at home in a forest. And just one of them, even a female, would be strong enough to grab him and keep him immobile for the rest to bundle home.

But Robert had planned this. He had kept to open ground and played the chase to take advantage of his long stride.

"Captain Oneagle . . ." Benjamin tried again, catching his breath. He looked up and took a step forward. "Captain, please, you're not well."

"I feel fine," Robert announced, lying just a little. Actually, his legs shivered with the beginnings of a cramp, his lungs burned, and his right arm itched all over from where he had chipped and peeled his cast away.

And then there were his bare feet. . . .

"Parse it logically, Benjamin," he said. "*Demonstrate* to me that I am ill, and just maybe I'll accompany you back to those smelly caves."

Benjamin blinked up at him. Then he shrugged, obviously willing to clutch at any straw. Robert had proven they could not run him down. Perhaps logic might work.

"Well, ser." Benjamin licked his lips. "First off, there's the fact that you aren't wearing any clothes."

Robert nodded. "Good, go for the direct. I'll even posit, for now, that the simplest, most parsimonious explanation for my nudity is that I've gone bonkers. I reserve the right to offer an alternative theory, though."

The chim shivered as he saw Robert's smile. Robert could not help sympathizing with Benjamin. From the chim's point of view this was a tragedy in progress, and there was nothing he could do to prevent it.

"Continue, please," Robert urged.

"Very well." Benjamin sighed. "Second, you are running away from chims under your own command. A patron afraid of his own loyal clients cannot be in complete control of himself."

Robert nodded. "Clients who would throw this patron into a straitjacket and dope him full of happy juice first chance they got? No good, Ben. If you accept *my* premise, that I have reasons for what I'm doing, then it only follows that I'd try to keep you guys from dragging me back."

"Um . . ." Benjamin took a step closer. Robert casually retreated one boulder higher. "Your reason could be a false one," Benjamin ventured. "A neurosis defends itself by coming up with rationalizations to explain away bizarre behavior. The sick person actually believes—"

"Good point," Robert agreed, cheerfully. "I'll accept, for later discussion, the possibility that my 'reasons' are actually rationalizations by an unbalanced mind. Will you, in exchange, entertain the possibility that they might be valid?"

Benjamin's lip curled back. "You're violating orders being out here!"

Robert sighed. "Orders from an E.T. civilian to a Terragens officer? Chim Benjamin, you surprise me. I agree that Athaclena should organize the ad hoc resistance. She seems to have a flair for it, and most of the chims idolize her. But I choose to operate independently. You know I have the right."

Benjamin's frustration was evident. The chim seemed on the verge of tears. "But you're in danger out here!"

At last. Robert had wondered how long Ben could maintain this game of logic while every fiber must be quivering over the safety of the last free human. Under similar circumstances, Robert doubted many men would have done better.

He was about to say something to that effect when Benjamin's head jerked up suddenly. The chim put a hand to his ear, listening to a small receiver. A look of alarm spread across his face.

The other chims must have heard the same report, for they stumbled to their feet, staring up at Robert in growing panic.

"Captain Oneagle, Central reports acoustic signatures to the northeast. Gasbots!"

"Estimated time of arrival?"

"Four minutes! *Please*, captain, will you come now?"

"Come where?" Robert shrugged. "We can't possibly make the caves in time."

"We can hide you." But from the tone of dread in his voice, Benjamin clearly knew it was useless.

Robert shook his head. "I've got a better idea. But it means we have to cut our little debate short. You must accept that I'm out here for a valid reason, Chim Benjamin. At once!"

The chim stared at him, then nodded tentatively. "I—I don't have any choice."

"Good," Robert said. "Now take off your clothes."

"S-ser?"

"Your clothes! And that sonic receiver of yours! Have everybody in your party strip. Remove everything! As you love your patrons, leave on nothing but skin and hair, then come join me up in those trees at the top of the scree!"

Robert did not wait for the blinking chim to acknowledge the strange command. He turned and took off upslope, favoring the foot most cut up by pebbles and twigs since his early morning foray had begun.

How much time remained? he wondered. Even if he was correct—and Robert knew he was taking a terrible gamble—he would still need to get as much altitude as possible.

He could not help scanning the sky for the expected robot bombers. The preoccupation caused him to stumble and fall to his knees as he reached the crest. He skinned them further crawling the last two meters to the shade under the nearest of the dwarf trees. According to his theory it wouldn't matter much whether or not he concealed himself. Still, Robert sought heavy cover. The Gubru machines might have simple optical scanners to supplement their primary homing mechanism.

He heard shouting below, sounds of chims in fierce argument. Then, from somewhere to the north, there came a faint, whining sound.

Robert backed further into the bushes, though sharp twigs scratched his tender skin. His heart beat faster and his mouth was dry. If he was wrong, or if the chims decided to ignore his command . . .

If he had missed a single bet he would soon be on his way to internment at Port Helenia, or dead. In any event, he would have left Athaclena all alone, the sole patron remaining in the mountains, and spent the remaining minutes or years of his life cursing himself for a bloody fool.

Maybe Mother was right about me. Maybe I am nothing but a useless playboy. We'll soon see.

There was a rattling sound—rocks sliding down the boulder scree. Five brown shapes tumbled into the foliage just as the approaching whine reached its crescendo. Dust rose from the dry soil as the chims turned quickly and stared, wide-eyed. An alien machine had come to the little valley.

From his hiding place Robert cleared his throat. The chims, obviously uncomfortable without their clothes, started in tense surprise. "You guys had better have thrown everything away, including your mikes, or I'm getting out of here now and leaving you behind."

Benjamin snorted. "We're stripped." He nodded down into the valley. "Harry an' Frank wouldn't do it. I told 'em to climb the other slope and stay away from us."

Robert nodded. With his companions he watched the gasbot begin its run. The others had witnessed this phenomenon, but he had not been in much shape to observe during the one opportunity he'd had before. Robert looked on with more than a passing interest.

It measured about fifty meters in length, teardrop-shaped, with scanners spinning slowly at the pointed, trailing end. The gasbot cruised the valley from their right to their left, disturbed foliage rustling beneath its throbbing gravitics.

It seemed to be *sniffing* as it zigzagged up the canyon— and vanished momentarily behind a curve in the bordering hills.

The whine faded, but not for long. Soon the sound returned, and the machine reappeared shortly after. This time a dark, noxious cloud trailed behind, turbulent in its wake. The gasbot passed back down the narrow vale and laid its thickest layer of oily vapor where the chims had left their clothes and equipment.

"Coulda *sworn* those mini-coms couldn't have been detected," one of the naked chims muttered.

"We'll have to go completely without electronics on the outside," another added unhappily, watching as the device passed out of sight again. The valley bottom was already obscured.

Benjamin looked at Robert. They both knew it wasn't over yet.

The high-pitched moan returned as the Gubru mechanism cruised back their way, this time at a higher altitude. Its scanners worked the hills on both sides.

The machine stopped opposite them. The chims froze, as if staring into the eyes of a rather large tiger. The tableau held for a moment. Then the bomber began moving at right angles to its former path.

Away from them.

In moments the opposite hill was swathed in a cloud of black fog. From the other side they could hear coughing and loud imprecations as the chims who had climbed that way cursed this Gubru notion of better living through chemistry.

The robot began to spiral out and higher. Clearly the search pattern would soon bring it above the Earthlings on this side.

"Anybody got anything they didn't declare at customs?" Robert asked, dryly.

Benjamin turned to one of the other neo-chimps. Snapping his fingers, he held out his hand. The younger chim glowered and opened his hand. Metal glittered.

Benjamin seized the little chain and medallion and stood up briefly to throw it. The links sparkled for just a moment, then disappeared into the murky haze downslope.

"That may not have been necessary," Robert said. "We'll have to experiment, lay out different objects at various sites and see which get bombed. . . ." He was talking as much for morale as for content. As much for *his* morale as for theirs. "I suspect it's something simple, quite common, but imported to Garth, so its resonance will be a sure sign of Earthly presence."

Benjamin and Robert shared a long look. No words were needed. *Reason or rationalization.* The next ten seconds would tell whether Robert was right or disastrously wrong.

It might be us it detects, Robert knew. *Ifni. What if they can tune in on human DNA?*

The robot cruised overhead. They covered their ears and blinked as the repulsor fields tickled their nerve endings. Robert felt a wave of déjà vu, as if this were something he and the others had done many times, through countless prior lives. Three of the chims buried their heads in their arms and whimpered.

Did the machine pause? Robert felt suddenly that it *had,* that it was about to . . .

Then it was past them, shaking the tops of trees ten meters away . . . twenty . . . forty. The search spiral widened and the gasbot's whining engine sounds faded slowly with distance. The machine moved on, seeking other targets.

Robert met Benjamin's eyes again and winked.

The chim snorted. Obviously he felt that Robert should not be smug over being right. That was, after all, only a patron's job.

Style counted, too. And Benjamin clearly thought Robert might have chosen a more dignified way to make his point.

*   *   *

Robert would go home by a different route, avoiding any
contact with the still-fresh coercion chemicals. The chims
tarried long enough to gather their things and shake out the
sooty black powder. They bundled up their gear but did not
put the clothes back on.

It wasn't only dislike of the alien stink. For the first time
the items themselves were suspect. Tools and clothing, the
very symbols of sentience, had become betrayers, things not
to be trusted.

They walked home naked.

It took a while, afterward, for life to return to the little
valley. The nervous creatures of Garth had never been harmed
by the new, noxious fog that had lately come at intervals from
a growling sky. But they did not like it any more than they
liked the noisy two-legged beings.

Nervously, timorously, the native animals crept back to
their feeding or hunting grounds.

Such caution was especially strong in the survivors of the
Bururalli terror. Near the northern end of the valley the
creatures stopped their return migration and listened, sniffing the air suspiciously.

Many backed out then. Something else had entered the
area. Until it left, there would be no going home.

A dark form moved down the rocky slope, picking its
way among the boulders where the sooty residue lay thickest.
As twilight gathered it clambered boldly about the rocks,
making no move to conceal itself, for nothing here could
harm it. It paused briefly, casting about as if looking for
something.

A small glint shone in the late afternoon sunshine. The
creature shuffled over to the glittering thing, a small chain
and pendant half hidden in the dusty rocks, and picked
it up.

It sat looking at the lost keepsake for a time, sighing softly
in contemplation. Then it dropped the shiny bauble where it
had lain and moved on.

Only after it had shambled away at last did the creatures
of the forest finish their homeward odyssey, scurrying for
secret niches and hiding places. In minutes the disturbances
were forgotten, dross from a used-up day.

Memory was a useless encumbrance, anyway. The animals had more important things to do than contemplate what had gone on an hour ago. Night was coming, and *that* was serious business. Hunting and being hunted, eating and being eaten, living and dying.

36

Fiben

"We've got to hurt them in ways that they can't trace to us."

Gailet Jones sat cross-legged on the carpet, her back to the embers in the fireplace. She faced the ad hoc resistance committee and held up a single finger.

"The humans on Cilmar and the other islands are completely helpless to reprisals. So, for that matter, are all the urban chims here in town. So we have to begin carefully and concentrate on intelligence gathering before trying to really harm the enemy. If the Gubru come to realize they're facing an organized resistance, there's no telling what they'll do."

Fiben watched from the shadowed end of the room as one of the new cell leaders, a professor from the college, raised his hand. "But how could they threaten the hostages under the Galactic Codes of War? I think I remember reading somewhere that—"

One of the older chimmies interrupted. "Dr. Wald, we can't count on the Galactic Codes. We just don't know the subtleties involved and don't have time to learn them!"

"We could look them up," the elderly chen suggested weakly. "The city Library is open for business."

"Yeah," Gailet sniffed. "With a Gubru Librarian in charge now, I can just imagine asking one of them for a scan-dump on resistance warfare!"

"Well, supposedly . . ."

The discussion had been going on this way for quite a while. Fiben coughed behind his fist. Everyone looked up. It was the first time he had spoken since the long meeting began.

"The point is moot," he said quietly. "Even if we knew the hostages would be safe. Gailet's right for yet another reason."

She darted a look at him, half suspicious and perhaps a little resentful of his support. *She's bright,* he thought. *But we're going to have trouble, she and I.*

He continued. "We have to make our first strikes seem less than they are because right now the invader is relaxed, unsuspecting, and completely contemptuous of us. It's a condition we'll find him in only once. We mustn't squander that until the resistance is coordinated and ready.

"That means we keep things low key until we hear from the general."

He smiled at Gailet and leaned against the wall. She frowned back, but said nothing. They had had their differences over placing the Port Helenia resistance under the command of a young alien. That had not changed.

She needed him though, for now. Fiben's stunt at the Ape's Grape had brought dozens of new recruits out of the woodwork, galvanizing a part of the community that had had its fill of heavy-handed Gubru propaganda.

"All right, then," Gailet said. "Let's start with something simple. Something you can tell your general about." Their eyes met briefly. Fiben just smiled, and held her gaze while other voices rose.

"What if we were to . . ."

"How about if we blow up . . ."

"Maybe a general strike . . ."

Fiben listened to the surge of ideas—ways to sting and fool an ancient, experienced, arrogant, and vastly powerful Galactic race—and felt he knew exactly what Gailet was thinking, what she *had* to be thinking after that unnerving, revealing trip to Port Helenia College.

Are we really sapient beings, without our patrons? Do we dare try even our brightest schemes against powers we can barely perceive?

Fiben nodded in agreement with Gailet Jones. *Yes, indeed. We had better keep it simple.*

37

Galactics

It was all getting pretty expensive, but that was not the only thing bothering the Suzerain of Cost and Caution. All the new antispace fortifications, the perpetual assaults by coercion gas on any and every suspected or detected Earthling site—these were things insisted upon by the Suzerain of Beam and Talon, and this early in the occupation it was hard to refuse the military commander anything it thought needed.

But accounting was not the only job of the Suzerain of Cost and Caution. Its other task was protection of the Gubru race from the repercussions of error.

So many starfaring species had come into existence since the great chain of Uplift was begun by the Progenitors, three billion years ago. Many had flowered, risen to great heights, only to be brought crashing down by some stupid, avoidable mistake.

That was yet another reason for the way authority was divided among the Gubru. There was the aggressive spirit of the Talon Soldier, to dare and seek out opportunities for the Roost. There was the exacting taskmaster of Propriety, to make certain they adhered to the True Path. In addition, though, there must be Caution, the squawk of warning, for-ever warning, that daring can step too far, and propriety too rigid can also make roosts fall.

The Suzerain of Cost and Caution paced its office. Beyond the surrounding gardens lay the small city the humans called Port Helenia. Throughout the building, Gubru and Kwackoo bureaucrats went over details, calculated odds, made plans.

Soon there would be another Command Conclave with

its peers, the other Suzerains. The Suzerain of Cost and Caution knew there would be more demands made.

Talon would ask why most of the battle fleet was being called away. And it would have to be shown that the Gubru Nest Masters had need of the great battleships elsewhere, now that Garth appeared secure.

Propriety would complain again that this world's Planetary Library was woefully inadequate and appeared to have been damaged, somehow, by the fleeing Earthling government. Or perhaps it had been sabotaged by the Tymbrimi trickster Uthacalthing? In any event, there would be urgent insistence that a larger branch be brought in, at horrible expense.

The Suzerain of Cost and Caution fluffed its down. This time it felt filled with confidence. It had let the other two have their way for a time, but things were peaceful now, well in hand.

The other two were younger, less experienced—brilliant, but far too rash. It was time to begin showing them how things were going to be, how they *must* be, if a sane, sound policy was to emerge. This colloquy, the Suzerain of Cost and Caution assured itself, it would prevail!

The Suzerain brushed its beak and looked out onto the peaceful afternoon. These were lovely gardens, with pleasant open lawns and trees imported from dozens of worlds. The former owner of these structures was no longer here, but his taste could be sensed in the surroundings.

How sad it was that there were so few Gubru who understood or even cared about the esthetics of other races! There was a word for this appreciation of otherness. In Anglic it was called *empathy*. Some sophonts carried the business too far, of course. The Thennanin and the Tymbrimi, each in their own way, had made absurdities of themselves, ruining all clarity of their uniqueness. Still, there were factions among the Roost Masters who believed that a small dose of this other-appreciation might prove very useful in the years ahead.

More than useful, caution seemed now to demand it.

The Suzerain had made its plans. The clever schemes of its peers would unite under its leadership. The outlines of a new policy were already becoming clear.

Life was such a serious business, the Suzerain of Cost and Caution contemplated. And yet, every now and then, it actually seemed quite pleasant!

For a time it crooned to itself contentedly.

38

Fiben

"Everything's all set."

The tall chim wiped his hands on his coveralls. Max wore long sleeves to keep the grease out of his fur, but the measure hadn't been entirely successful. He put aside his tool kit, squatted next to Fiben, and used a stick to draw a rude sketch in the sand.

"Here's where th' town-gas hydrogen pipes enter the embassy grounds, an' here's where they pass under the chancery. My partner an' I have put in a splice over beyond those cottonwoods. When Dr. Jones gives the word, we'll pour in fifty kilos of D-17. That ought to do the trick."

Fiben nodded as the other chim brushed away the drawing. "Sounds excellent, Max."

It *was* a good plan, simple and, more important, extremely difficult to trace, whether it succeeded or not. At least that's what they all were counting on.

He wondered what Athaclena would think of this scheme. Like most chims, Fiben's idea of Tymbrimi personality had come mostly out of vid dramas and speeches by the ambassador. From those impressions it seemed Earth's chief allies certainly loved irony.

I hope so, he mused. *She'll need a sense of humor to appreciate what we're about to do to the Tymbrimi Embassy.*

He felt weird sitting out here in the open, not more than a hundred meters from the Embassy grounds, where the rolling hills of Sea Bluff Park overlooked the Sea of Cilmar. In oldtime war movies, men always seemed to set off on missions like this at night, with blackened faces.

But that was in the dark ages, before the days of high tech and infrared spotters. Activity after dark would only draw attention from the invaders. So the saboteurs moved about in daylight, disguising their activities amid the normal routine of park maintenance.

Max pulled a sandwich out of his capacious coveralls and took out large bites while they waited. The big chim was no less impressive here, seated cross-legged, than when they had met, that night at the Ape's Grape. With his broad shoulders and pronounced canines, one might have thought he'd be a revert, a genetic reject. In truth, the Uplift Board cared less about such cosmetic features than the fellow's calm, totally unflappable nature. He had already been granted one fatherhood, and another of his group wives was expecting his second child.

Max had been an employee of Gailet's family ever since she was a little girl and had taken care of her after her return from schooling on Earth. His devotion to her was obvious.

Too few yellow-card chims like Max were members of the urban underground. Gailet's insistence on recruiting almost solely blue and green cards had made Fiben uncomfortable. And yet he had seen her point. With it known that some chims were collaborating with the enemy, it would be best to start creating their network of cells out of those who had the most to lose under the Gubru.

That still didn't make the discrimination smell good to Fiben.

"Feelin' any better?"

"Hmm?" Fiben looked up.

"Your muscles." Max gestured. "Feelin' less sore now?"

Fiben had to grin. Max had apologized all too often, first for doing nothing when the Probationers began harassing him back at the Ape's Grape, and later shooting him with the stunner on Gailet's orders. Of course both actions were understandable in retrospect. Neither he nor Gailet had known what to make of Fiben, at first, and had decided to err on the side of caution.

"Yeah, lots better. Just a twinge now and then. Thanks."

"Mmm, good. Glad." Max nodded, satisfied. Privately, Fiben noted that he had never heard *Gailet* express any regret over what he'd gone through.

Fiben tightened another bolt on the sand-lawn groomer he had been repairing. It was a real breakdown, of course, just in case a Gubru patrol stopped by. But luck had been with them so far. Anyway, most of the invaders seemed to be down at the south side of Aspinal Bay, supervising another of their mysterious construction projects.

He slipped a monocular out of his belt and focused on the Embassy. A low plastic fence topped with glittering wire surrounded the compound, punctuated at intervals by tiny whirling watch buoys. The little spinning disks looked decorative, but Fiben knew better. The protection devices made any direct assault by irregular forces impossible.

Inside the compound there were five buildings. The largest, the chancery, had come equipped with a full suite of modern radio, psi, and quantum wave antennae—an obvious reason why the Gubru moved in after the former tenants cleared out.

Before the invasion, the Embassy staff had been mostly hired humans and chims. The only Tymbrimi actually assigned to this tiny outpost were the ambassador, his assistant/pilot, and his daughter.

The invaders weren't following that example. The place swarmed with avian forms. Only one small building—at the top of the far hill across from Fiben, overlooking the ocean—did not show a full complement of Gubru and Kwackoo constantly coming and going. That pyramidal, windowless structure looked more like a cairn than a house, and none of the aliens approached within two hundred meters of it.

Fiben remembered something the general had told him before he left the mountains.

"If you get an opportunity, Fiben, please inspect the Diplomatic Cache at the Embassy. If, by some chance, the Gubru have left the grounds intact, there might be a message from my father there."

Athaclena's ruff had flared momentarily.

"And if the Gubru have violated the Cache, I must know of that, too. It is information we can use."

It looked unlikely he'd have had a chance to do as she asked, whether the aliens respected the Codes or not. The general would have to settle for a visual report from far away.

"What d'you see?" Max asked. He calmly munched his sandwich as if one started a guerrilla uprising every day.

"Just a minute." Fiben increased magnification and wished he had a better glass. As far as he could tell, the cairn at the top of the hill looked unmolested. A tiny blue light winked from the top of the little structure. Had the Gubru put it there? he wondered.

"I'm not sure," he said. "But I think—"

His belt phone beeped—another bit of normal life that might end once fighting began. The commercial network was still in operation, though certainly monitored by Gubru language computers.

He picked up the phone. "That you, honey? I've been getting hungry. I hope you brought my lunch."

There was a pause. When Gailet Jones spoke there was an edge in her voice. "Yes, *dear*." She stuck to their agreed-upon code, but obviously did not relish it. "Pele's marriage group is on holiday today, so I invited them to join us for a picnic."

Fiben couldn't help digging a little—just for verisimilitude, of course. "That's fine, darling. Maybe you an' I can find time to slip into the woods for some, y'know, ook ook."

Before she could do more than gasp, he signed off. "See you in a little while, sweetie." Putting down the phone, he saw Max looking at him, a wad of food in one cheek. Fiben raised an eyebrow and Max shrugged, as if to say, "None of *my* business."

"I better go see that Dwayne ain't screwed up," Max said. He stood and dusted sand from his coveralls. "Scopes up, Fiben."

"*Filters* up, Max."

The big chim nodded and moved off down the hill, sauntering as if life were completely normal.

Fiben slapped the cover back on the engine and started the groomer. Its motor whistled with the soft whine of hydrogen catalysis. He hopped aboard and took off slowly down the hill.

The park was fairly crowded for a weekday afternoon. That was part of the plan, to get the birds used to chims behaving in unusual ways. Chims had been frequenting the area more and more during the last week.

That had been Athaclena's idea. Fiben wasn't sure he liked it, but oddly enough, it was one Tymbrimi suggestion Gailet had taken up wholeheartedly. An anthropologist's gambit. Fiben sniffed.

He rode over to a copse of willows by a stream not far from the Embassy grounds, near the fence and the small, whirling watchers. He stopped the engine and got off. Walking to the edge of the stream, he took several long strides and leapt up onto the trunk of a tree. Fiben clambered to a convenient branch, where he could look out onto the compound. He took out a bag of peanuts and began to crack them one at a time.

The nearest watcher disk seemed to pause briefly. No doubt it had already scanned him with everything from X-rays to radar. Of course it found him unarmed and harmless. Every day for the last week a different chim had taken his lunch break here at about this time of day.

Fiben recalled the evening at the Ape's Grape. Perhaps Athaclena and Gailet had a point, he thought. If the birds try to condition us, why can't we turn the tables and do it to the birds?

His phone rang again.

"Yeah?"

"Uh, I'm afraid Donal's suffering from a little flatulence. He may not be able to make it to the picnic."

"Aw, too bad," he muttered, and put the phone away. So far, so good. He cracked another peanut. The D-17 had been put into the pipes delivering hydrogen to the Embassy. It would still be several minutes before anything could be expected to happen.

It was a simple idea, even if he had his doubts. The sabotage was supposed to look like an accident, and it had to be timed so that Gailet's unarmed contingent was in position. This raid was meant not so much to do harm as to create a *disturbance*. Both Gailet and Athaclena wanted information on Gubru emergency procedures.

Fiben was to be the general's eyes and ears.

Over on the grounds he saw avians come and go from the chancery and other buildings. The little blue light atop the Diplomatic Cache winked against the bright sea clouds. A Gubru floater hummed overhead and began to settle toward the broad Embassy lawn. Fiben watched with interest, waiting for the excitement to begin.

D-17 was a powerful corrosive when left in contact with town-gas hydrogen for long. It would soon eat through the pipes. Then, when exposed to air, it would have yet another effect.

It would stink to high heaven.

He didn't have long to wait.

Fiben smiled as the first squawks of consternation began

to emanate from the chancery. Within moments the doors and windows burst forth with feathered explosions as aliens boiled out of the building, chirping in panic or disgust. Fiben wasn't sure which and he didn't really care. He was too busy laughing.

This part had been his idea. He broke a peanut and tossed it up to catch in his mouth. This was better than baseball!

Gubru scattered in all directions, leaping from upper balconies even without antigravity gear. Several writhed on broken limbs.

So much the better. Of course this wasn't going to be much of an inconvenience to the enemy, and it could only be done once. The real purpose was to watch how the Gubru dealt with an emergency.

Sirens began to wail. Fiben glanced at his watch. A full two minutes had passed since the first signs of commotion. That meant the alarm was given manually. The vaunted Galactic defense computers weren't omniscient then. They weren't equipped to respond to a bad smell.

The watch buoys rose from the fence together, giving off a threatening whine, whirling faster than before. Fiben brushed peanut shells from his lap and sat up slowly, watching the deadly things warily. If they were programmed to extend the defense perimeter automatically, whatever the emergency, he could be in trouble.

But they merely spun, shining with increased vigilance. It took three more minutes, by Fiben's watch, for a triple sonic boom to announce the arrival of fighter craft, sleek arrows resembling sparrow hawks, which streaked in to pass low over the now empty chancery building. The Gubru on the lawn seemed too nervous to take much cheer in their arrival. They leapt and squawked as sonic booms shook trees and feathers alike.

A Gubru official strutted about the grounds, chirping soothingly, calming its subordinates. Fiben didn't dare lift his monocular with the protector-drones at such high alert, but he peered to try to get a better view of the avian in charge. Several features seemed odd about this Gubru. Its white plumage, for instance, looked more luminous, more lustrous than the others'. It also wore a band of black fabric around its throat.

A few minutes later a utility craft arrived and hovered

until enough chattering avians had stepped aside to give it room to land. From the grounded floater a pair of invaders emerged wearing ornate, crested breathing masks. They bowed to the official, then strode up the steps and into the building.

Obviously the Gubru in charge realized that the stench from the corroded gas pipes posed no threat. All the noise and commotion was doing much more harm to his command of clerks and planners than the bad smell. No doubt he was upset because the work day was ruined.

More minutes passed. Fiben watched a convoy of ground vehicles arrive, sirens wailing, sending the agitated civil servants into a tizzy again. The senior Gubru flapped its arms until the racket finally cut off. Then the aristocrat waved a curt gesture at the supersonic fighters hovering overhead.

The warcraft swiveled about at once and departed as swiftly as they had come. Shock waves again rattled windows and sent the chancery staff shrieking.

"Excitable lot, aren't they?" Fiben observed. No doubt Gubru soldiery were better conditioned for this sort of thing.

Fiben stood up on his branch and looked over toward other areas of the park. Elsewhere the fence was lined with chims, and more streamed in from the city. They kept a respectful distance back from the barrier guardians, but still they came, babbling to each other in excitement.

Here and there among them were Gailet Jones's observers, timing and jotting down every alien response.

"*Almost the first thing the Gubru will read about, when they study Library tapes on your species,*" Athaclena had told him, "*will be the so-called 'monkey reflex' . . . the tendency of you anthropoids to scurry toward commotion, out of curiosity.*

"*Conservative species find it strange, and this tendency of humans and chims will seem particularly bizarre to avian beings, which tend to lack even a semblance of a sense of humor.*"

She had smiled.

"*We will get them used to this type of behavior, until they grow to expect those strange Earthling clients always running toward trouble . . . just to watch.*

"*They will learn not to fear you, but they should . . . speaking as one monkey to another.*"

Fiben had known what she meant, that Tymbrimi were

like humans and chims in this way. Her confidence had filled
him, as well—until he saw her frown suddenly and speak to
herself, quickly and softly, apparently forgetting that he understood Galactic Seven.

*"Monkeys . . . one monkey to another . . . Sumbaturalli!
Must I constantly think in metaphors?"*

It had perplexed Fiben. Fortunately, he did not have to
understand Athaclena, only know that she could ask anything
she wanted of him and he would jump.

After a while more maintenance workers arrived in ground
vehicles, this time including a number of chims wearing
uniforms of the City Gas Department. By the time they
entered the chancery, the Gubru bureaucrats on the lawn
had settled into the shade just outside, chirping irritably at the
still potent stench.

Fiben didn't blame them. The wind had shifted his way.
His nose wrinkled in disgust.

*Well, that's that. We cost them an afternoon's work, and
maybe we learned something. Time to go home and assess the
results.*

He didn't look forward to the meeting with Gailet Jones.
For a pretty and bright chimmie, she had a tendency to get
awfully officious. And she obviously bore some grudge against
him—as if *he* had gunned *her* down with a stunner and
carried *her* off in a sack!

Ah well. Tonight he would be off, back into the mountains with Tycho, carrying a report for the general. Fiben had
been born a city boy, but he had come to prefer the kind of
birds they had out in the country to the sort infesting town of
late.

He turned around, grabbed the tree trunk with both
arms, and started lowering himself. That was when, suddenly,
something that felt like a big flat hand *slammed* hard against
his back, knocking all the breath out of him.

Fiben clawed at the trunk. His head rang and tears filled
his eyes. He managed just barely to keep his grip on the
rough bark as branches whipped and leaves blew away in a
sudden wave of palpable sound. He held on while the entire
tree rocked, as if it were trying to buck him off!

His ears popped as the overpressure wave passed. The
rip of rushing air dropped to a mere roar. The tree swayed in
slowly diminishing arcs. Finally—still gripping the bark
tightly—he gathered the nerve to turn around and look.

A towering column of smoke filled the center of the Embassy lawn where the chancery used to be. Flames licked at shattered walls, and streaks of soot showed where superheated gas had blasted in all directions.

Fiben blinked.

"Hot chicken in a biscuit!" he muttered, not ashamed at all of the first thing to come to mind. There was enough fried bird out there to feed half of Port Helenia. Some of the meat was pretty rare, of course. Some of it still moved.

His mouth was bone dry, but he smacked his lips nonetheless.

"Barbecue sauce," he sighed. "All this, an' not a truckload of barbecue sauce to be seen."

He clambered back onto the branch amid the torn leaves. Fiben checked his watch. It took almost a minute for sirens to begin wailing again. Another for the floater to take off, wavering as it fought the surging convection of superheated air from the fire.

He looked to see what the chims at the perimeter fence had done. Through the spreading cloud of smoke, Fiben saw that the crowd had not fled. If anything, it had grown. Chims boiled out of nearby buildings to watch. There were hoots and shrieks, a sea of excited brown eyes.

He grunted in satisfaction. That was fine, so long as nobody made any threatening moves.

Then he noticed something else. With an electric thrill he saw that the watch disks were down! All along the barrier fence, the guardian buoys had fallen to the ground.

"Bugger all!" he murmured. "The dumb clucks are saving money on smart robotics. The defense mechs were all remotes!"

When the chancery blew up—for whatever ungodly reason it had chosen to do so—it must have taken out the central controller with it! If somebody just had the presence of mind to grab up some of those buoys . . .

He saw Max, a hundred meters to his left, scurry over to one of the toppled disks and prod it with a stick.

Good man, Fiben thought, and then dropped it from his mind. He stood up and leaned against the tree trunk while tossing off his sandals. He flexed his legs, testing the support. *Here goes nothin'*, he sighed.

Fiben took off at full tilt, running along the narrow

branch. At the last moment he rode the bucking tip like a springboard and leaped off into the air.

The fence was set back a way from the stream. One of Fiben's toes brushed the wire at the top as he sailed over. He landed in an awkward rollout on the lawn beyond.

"Oof," he complained. Fortunately, he hadn't banged his still-tender ankle. But his ribs hurt, and as he panted sucked in a lungful of smoke from the spreading fire. Coughing, he pulled a handkerchief from his coveralls and wrapped it over his nose as he ran toward the devastation.

Dead invaders lay strewn across the once pristine lawn. He leapt over a sprawled, Kwackoo corpse—four-legged and soot-covered—and ducked through a roiling finger of smoke. He barely evaded collision with a living Gubru. The creature fled squawking.

The invader bureaucrats were completely disorganized, flapping and running about in total chaos. Their noise was overwhelming.

Slamming sonic booms announced the return of soldiery, overhead. Fiben suppressed a fit of coughing and blessed the smoke. No one overhead would spot him, and the Gubru down here were in no condition to notice much. He hopped over singed avians. The stench from the fire kept even his most atavistic appetites at bay.

In fact, he was afraid he might be sick.

It was touch and go as he ran past the burning chancery. The building was completely in flames. The hair on his right arm curled from the heat.

He burst upon a knot of avians huddling in the shadow of a neighboring structure. They had been gathered in a moaning cluster around one particular corpse, a remnant whose once-bright plumage was now stained and ruined. When Fiben appeared so suddenly the Gubru scattered, chirping in dismay.

Am I lost? There was smoke everywhere. He swiveled about, casting for a sign of the right direction.

There! Fiben spied a tiny blue glow through the black haze. He set off at a run, though his lungs already felt afire. The worst of the noise and heat fell behind him as he dashed through the small copse of trees lining the top of the bluff.

Misjudging the distance, he almost stumbled, sliding to a sudden halt before the Tymbrimi Diplomatic Cache. Panting, he bent over to catch his breath.

In a moment he realized that it was just as well he'd stopped when he had. Suddenly the blue globe at the cairn's peak seemed less friendly. It pulsed at him, throbbing volubly.

So far Fiben had acted in a series of flash decisions. The explosion had been an unexpected opportunity. It had to be taken advantage of.

All right, here I am. Now what? The blue globe might be original Tymbrimi equipment, but it also might have been set there by the invader.

Behind him sirens wailed and floaters began arriving in a continuous, fluttering whine. Smoke swirled about him, whipped by the chaotic comings and goings of great machines. Fiben hoped Gailet's observers on the roofs of the buildings nearby were taking all this down. If he knew his own people, most of them would be staring slack-jawed or capering in excitement. Still, they might learn a lot from this afternoon's serendipity.

He took a step forward toward the cairn. The blue globe pulsed at him. He lifted his left foot.

A beam of bright blue light lanced out and struck the ground where he had been about to step.

Fiben leaped at least a meter into the air. He had hardly landed before the beam shot forth again, missing his right foot by millimeters. Smoke curled up from smoldering twigs, joining the heavier pall from the burning chancery.

Fiben tried to back away quickly, but the damned globe wouldn't let him! A blue bolt sizzled the ground behind him and he had to hop to one side. Then he found himself being herded the other way!

Leap, zap! Hop, curse, zap again!

The beam was too accurate for this to be an accident. The globe wasn't trying to kill him. Nor was it, apparently, interested in letting him go!

Between bolts Fiben frantically tried to think how to get out of this trap . . . this infernal practical joke. . . .

He snapped his fingers, even as he jumped from another smoldering spot. Of course!

The Gubru *hadn't* messed with the Tymbrimi Cache. The blue globe wasn't acting like a tool of the avians. But it was exactly the sort of thing *Uthacalthing* would leave behind!

Fiben cursed as a particularly near miss left one toe slightly singed. Damn bloody Eatees! Even the *good* ones were almost more than anybody could bear! He gritted his teeth and forced himself to take a single step forward.

The blue beam sliced through a small stone near his instep, cutting it precisely in half. Every instinct in Fiben screamed for him to jump again, but he concentrated on leaving the foot in place and taking one more leisurely step.

Normally, one would think that a defensive device like this would be programmed to give warnings at long range and to start frying in earnest when something came nearer. By such logic what he was doing was stupid as hell.

The blue globe throbbed menacingly and cast forth its lightning. Smoke curled from a spot between the tingers and tumb of his left foot.

He lifted the right.

First a warning, then the real thing. That was the way an Earthling defense drone would work. But how would a *Tymbrimi* program his? Fiben wasn't sure he should wager so much on a wild guess. A client-class sophont wasn't supposed to analyze in the middle of fire and smoke, and especially not when he was being shot at!

Call it a hunch, he thought.

His right foot came down and its toes curled around an oak twig. The blue globe seemed to consider his persistence, then the blue bolt lanced out again, this time a meter in front of him. A trail of sizzling humus walked toward him in a slow zigzag, the crackle of burning grass popping louder as it came closer and closer.

Fiben tried to swallow.

It's not designed to kill! he told himself over and over. *Why should it be? The Gubru could have blasted that globe at long range long ago.*

No, its purpose had to be to serve as a gesture, a declaration of rights under the intricate rules of Galactic Protocol, more ancient and ornate than Japanese imperial court ritual.

And it was designed to tweak the beaks of Gubru.

Fiben held his ground. Another chain of sonic booms rattled the trees, and the heat from the conflagration behind him seemed to be intensifying. All the noise pressed hard against his self-control.

The Gubru are mighty warriors, he reminded himself. *But they are excitable. . . .*

The blue beam edged closer. Fiben's nostrils flared. The

only way he could take his gaze away from the deadly sight was by closing his eyes.

If I'm right then this is just another damned Tymbrimi . . .

He opened them. The beam was approaching his right foot from the side. His toes curled from a deep will to leap away. Fiben tasted bile as the searing knife of light tore through a pebble two inches away and proceeded on to . . .

To hit and cross his foot!

Fiben choked and suppressed an urge to howl. Something was wrong! His head spun as he watched the beam cross his foot and then commence leaving a narrow trail of smoky ruin directly under his spread-legged stance.

He stared in disbelief at his foot. He had bet the beam would stop short at the last instant. It hadn't.

Still . . . there his foot was, unharmed.

The beam ignited a dry twig then moved on to climb up his left foot.

There was a faint tickling he knew to be psychosomatic. While touching him, the beam was only a spot of light.

An inch beyond his foot, the burning resumed.

His heart still pounding, Fiben looked up at the blue globe and cursed with a mouth too dry to speak.

"Very funny," he whispered.

There must have been a small psi-caster in the cairn, for Fiben actually felt something like a *smile* spread in the air before him . . . a small, wry, alien smirk, as if the joke had really been a minor thing, after all, not even worth a chuckle.

"Real cute, Uthacalthing," Fiben grimaced as he forced his shaking legs to obey him, carrying him on a wobbling path toward the cairn. "Real cute. I'd hate to see what gives you a belly laugh." It was hard to believe Athaclena came from the same stock as the author of this little bit of whoopee cushion humor.

At the same time, though, Fiben wished he could have been present when the first Gubru approached the Diplomacy Cache to check it out.

The blue globe still pulsed, but it stopped sending forth pencil beams of irritation. Fiben walked close to the cairn and looked it over. He paced the perimeter. Halfway around, where the cliff overlooked the sea only twenty meters away, there was a hatch. Fiben blinked when he saw the array of locks, hasps, bolts, combination slots, and keyholes.

Well, he told himself, it is a cache for diplomatic secrets and such.

But all those locks meant that he had no chance of getting in and finding a message from Uthacalthing. Athaclena had given him a few possible code words to try, if he got the chance, but this was another story altogether!

By now the fire brigade had arrived. Through the smoke Fiben could see chims from the city watch stumbling over stick-figure aliens and stretching out hoses. It wouldn't be long before someone imposed order on this chaos. If his mission here really was futile, he ought to be getting out while the getting was still easy. He could probably take the trail along the bluff, where it overlooked the Sea of Cilmar. That would skirt most of the enemy and bring him out near a bus route.

Fiben bent forward and looked at the hatchway again. Pfeh! There were easily two dozen locks on the armored door! A small ribbon of red silk would be as useful in keeping out an invader. Either the conventions were being respected or they weren't! What the hell good were all these padlocks and things?

Fiben grunted, realizing. It was another Tymbrimi joke, of course. One the Gubru would fail to get, no matter how intelligent they were. There were times when personality counted for more than intelligence.

Maybe that means . . .

On a hunch, Fiben ran around to the other side of the cairn. His eyes were watering from the smoke, and he wiped his nose on his handkerchief as he searched the wall opposite the hatch.

"Stupid bloody guesswork," he grumbled as he clambered among the smooth stones. "It'd take a Tymbrimi to think up a stunt like this . . . or a stupid, lame-brained, half-evolved chim client like m—"

A loose stone slipped slightly under his right hand. Fiben pried at the facing, wishing he had a Tymbrimi's slender, supple fingers. He cursed as he tore a fingernail.

At last the stone came free. He blinked.

He had been right, there *was* a secret hiding place here in back. Only the damn hole was empty!

This time, Fiben couldn't help himself. He shrieked in frustration. It was too much. The covering stone went sailing into the brush, and he stood there on the steep, sloping face of the cairn, cursing in the fine, expressive, indignant tones his ancestors had used before Uplift when inveighing against the parentage and personal habits of baboons.

The red rage only lasted a few moments, but when it cleared Fiben felt better. He was hoarse and raw, and his palms hurt from slapping the hard stone, but at least some of his frustration had been vented.

Clearly it was time to get out of here. Just beyond a thick wisp of drifting smoke, Fiben saw a large floater set down. A ramp descended and a troop of armored Gubru soldiery hurried onto the singed lawn, each accompanied by a pair of tiny, floating globes. *Yep, time to scoot.*

Fiben was about to climb down when he glanced one more time into the little niche in the Tymbrimi cairn. At that moment the diffusing smoke dispersed briefly under the stiffening breeze. Sunlight burst onto the cliffside.

A tiny flash of silvery light caught his eye. He reached into the niche and pulled on a slender thread, thin and delicate as gossamer, that had lined a crack at the back of the little crevice.

At that moment there came an amplified squawk. Fiben swiveled and saw a squad of Gubru Talon Soldiers coming his way. An officer fumbled with the vodor at its throat, dialing among the auto-translation options.

"... *Cathtoo-psh'v'chim'ph* ...
        "... *Kah-koo-kee, k'keee! EeeEeEE! k* ...
          "... *Hisss-s-ss pop *crackle!** ...
          "... *Puna bliv't mannennering* ..."
                "... what you are doing there! Good clients do not play with what they cannot understand!"

Then the officer caught sight of the opened niche—and Fiben's hand stuffing something into a coverall pocket.

"Stop! Show us what ..."

Fiben did not wait for the soldier to finish the command. He scrambled up the cairn. The blue globe throbbed as he passed, and in his mind terror was briefly pushed aside by a powerful, dry laughter as he dove over the top and slid down the other side. Laser bolts sizzled over his head, chipping fragments from the stone structure as he landed on the ground with a thump.

Damn Tymbrimi sense of humor, was his only thought as he scrambled to his feet and dashed in the only possible direction, down the protective shadow of the cairn, straight toward the sheer cliff.

39

Gailet

Max dumped a load of disabled Gubru guard disks onto the rooftop near Gailet Jones. "We yanked out their receivers," he reported. "Still, we'll have to be damn careful with 'em."

Nearby, Professor Oakes clicked his stopwatch. The elderly chen grunted in satisfaction. "Their air cover has been withdrawn, again. Apparently they've decided it was an accident after all."

Reports kept coming in. Gailet paced nervously, occasionally looking out over the roof parapet at the conflagration and confusion in Sea Bluff Park. *We didn't plan anything like this!* she thought. *It could be great luck. We've learned so much.*

Or it could be a disaster. Hard to tell yet.

If only the enemy doesn't trace it to us.

A young chen, no more than twelve years old, put down his binoculars and turned to Gailet. "Semaphore reports all but one of our forward observers has come back in, ma'am. No word from that one, though."

"Who is it?" Gailet asked.

"Uh, it's that militia officer from th' mountains. Fiben Bolger, ma'am."

"I might have guessed!" Gailet sighed.

Max looked up from his pile of alien booty, his face a

grimace of dismay. "I saw him. When the fence failed, he jumped over it and went running toward the fire. Um, I suppose I should've gone along, to keep an eye on him."

"You should have done no such thing, Max. You were exactly right. Of all the foolish stunts!" She sighed. "I might have known he would do something like this. If he gets captured, and gives us away . . ." She stopped. There was no point in worrying the others more than necessary.

Anyway, she thought a little guiltily, *the arrogant chen might only have been killed*.

She bit her lip, though, and went to the parapet to look out in the direction of the afternoon sun.

40

Fiben

Behind Fiben came the familiar *zip zip* of the blue globe firing again. The Gubru squawked less than he might have expected; these were soldiers, after all. Still, they made quite a racket and their attention was diverted. Whether the cache defender was acting to cover his retreat or merely harassing the invaders on general principles, Fiben couldn't speculate. In moments he was too busy even to think about it.

One look over the edge was enough to make him gulp. The cliff wasn't a glassy face, but neither was it the sort of route a picnicker would choose to get down to the shining sands below.

The Gubru were shooting back at the blue globe now, but that couldn't last long. Fiben contemplated the steep dropoff. All told, he would much rather have lived a long, quiet life as country ecologist, donated his sperm samples when required, maybe joined a real fun group family, taken up scrabble.

"*Argh!*" he commented in man dialect, and stepped off over the grassy verge.

It was a four-handed job, for sure. Gripping a knob with the tingers and tumb of his left foot, he swung way out to grab a second handhold and managed to lower himself to another ledge. A short stretch came easily, then it seemed he needed the grasping power of every extremity. Thank Goodall Uplift had left his people with this ability. If he'd had feet like a human's, he surely would have fallen by now!

Fiben was sweating, feeling around for a foothold that *had* to be there, when suddenly the cliff face seemed to lash out, batting away at him. An explosion sent tremors through the rock. Fiben's face ground into the gritty surface as he clutched for dear life, his feet kicking and dangling in midair.

Of all the damn . . . He coughed and spat as a plume of dust floated down from the cliff edge. In peripheral vision he glimpsed bright bits of incandescent stone flying out through the sky, spinning down to hissing graves in the sea below.

The root-grubbing cairn must've blown!

Then something whizzed by his head. He ducked but still caught a flash of blueness and heard, within his head, a chuckling of alien laughter. The hilarity reached a crescendo as something seemed to brush the back of his head, then faded as the blue light zipped off again, dropping to skip away southward, just above the waves.

Fiben wheezed and sought frantically for a foothold. At last he found purchase, and he was able to lower himself to the next fairly safe resting place. He wedged himself into a narrow cleft, out of sight from the clifftop. Only then did he spare the extra energy to curse.

Some day, Uthacalthing. Some day.

Fiben wiped dust from his eyes and looked down.

He had made it about halfway to the beach. If he ever reached the bottom safely it should be an easy walk to the closed amusement park at the northwestern corner of Aspinal Bay. From that point it ought to be simple to disappear into back alleys and side streets.

The next few minutes would tell. The survivors of the Gubru patrol might assume he had been killed in the explosion, blown out to sea along with debris from the cache. Or perhaps they'd figure he would have fled by some other route. After all, only an idiot would try to climb down a bluff like this one without equipment.

Fiben hoped he had it thought out right, because if they came down here looking for him his goose was as surely cooked as those birds in the chancery fire.

Just ahead the sun was settling toward the western horizon. Smoke from this afternoon's conflagration had spread far enough to contribute brilliant umber and crimson hues to the gathering sunset. Out on the water he saw a few boats, here and there. Two cargo barges steamed slowly toward the distant islands—low, brown shapes barely visible on the decks—no doubt carrying food for the hostage human population.

Too bad some of the salts in the seawater on Garth were toxic to dolphins. If the third race of Terragens had been able to establish itself here, it would have been a lot harder for the enemy to isolate the inhabitants of the archipelago so effectively. Besides, 'fins had their own way of thinking. Perhaps they'd have come up with an idea or two Fiben's people had missed.

The southern headlands blocked Fiben's view of the port. But he could see traces of gleaming silver, Gubru warships or tenders involved in the construction of space defenses.

Well, Fiben thought, *nobody's come for me yet. No hurry, then. Catch your breath before trying the rest of the trip.*

This had been the easy part.

Fiben reached into his pocket and pulled out the shimmering thread he had found in the niche. It might easily *be* a spider web, or something similarly insignificant. But it was the only thing he had to show for his little adventure. He didn't know how he would tell Athaclena that his efforts had come only to this. *Well, not only this.* There was also the destruction of the Tymbrimi Diplomatic Cache. That'd be another thing to have to explain.

He took out his monocular and unscrewed the lens cover. Fiben carefully wrapped the thread into the cap and replaced it. He put the magnifier away.

Yeah, it was going to be a real nice sunset. Embers from the fire sparkled, swept into whirling plumes by Gubru ambulances screaming back and forth from the top of the bluffs. Fiben considered reaching into a pocket for the rest of the peanuts while he watched, but right now his thirst was worse than his hunger. Most modern chims ate too much protein, anyway.

Life's rough, he thought, trying to find a comfortable

position in the narrow notch. *But then, it's never been easy for client-class beings, has it?*

There you are, minding your own business in some rain forest, perfectly adequate in your ecological niche, then *bam!* Some authoritarian guy with delusions of godhood is sitting on your chest, forcing the fruit of the Tree of Knowledge down your throat. From then on you're inadequate, because you're being measured against the "higher" standard of your patron; no freedom; you can't even breed as you please, and you've got all those "responsibilities"—Who ever heard of responsibilities back in the jungle?—responsibilities to your patrons, to your descendants. . . .

Rough deal. But in the Five Galaxies there's only one alternative, extermination. Witness the former tenants of Garth.

Fiben licked the sweat salt from his lips and knew that it was nervous reaction that had brought on the momentary wave of bitterness. There was no point to recriminations anyway. If he were a race representative—one of those few chims deputized to speak for all neo-chimpanzees before the Terragens and the great Galactic Institutes—the issues might be worth contemplating. As it was, Fiben realized he was just procrastinating.

I guess they forgot about me, after all, he thought, wondering at his luck.

Sunset reached its peak in a glory of color and texture, casting rich red and orange streamers across Garth's shallow sea.

Hell, after a day like this, what was climbing down a steep cliff in the dark? Anticlimax, that was all.

"Where the devil have you been!" Gailet Jones faced Fiben when he slumped through the door. She approached glowering.

"Aw, teach." He sighed. "Don't scold me. I've had a rough day." He pushed past her and shuffled through the house library, strewn with charts and papers. He stepped right across a large chart laid on the floor, oblivious as two of Gailet's observers shouted indignantly. They ducked aside as he passed straight over them.

"We finished debriefing *hours* ago!" Gailet said as she followed him. "Max managed to steal quite a few of their watch disks . . ."

"I know. I saw," he muttered as he stumbled into the

tiny room he had been assigned. He began undressing right there. "Do you have anything to eat?" he asked.

"Eat?" Gailet sounded incredulous. "We have to get your input to fill in gaps on our Gubru operations chart. That explosion was a windfall, and we weren't prepared with enough observers. Half of the ones we had just stood and stared when the excitement started."

With a "clomp" Fiben's coveralls fell to the floor. He stepped out of them. "Food can wait," he mumbled. "I need a drink."

Gailet Jones blushed and half turned away. "You might have the courtesy not to scratch," she said.

Fiben turned from pouring himself a stiff shot of ping-orange brandy and looked at her curiously. Was this actually the same chimmie who had accosted him with "*pink*" a fortnight or so ago? He slapped his chest and waved away plumes of dust. Gailet looked disgusted.

"I was lookin' forward to a bath, but now I think I'll skip it," he said. "Too sleepy now. Gotta rest. Goin' home, tomorrow."

Gailet blinked. "To the mountains?"

Fiben nodded. "Got to pick up Tycho and head back to report to th' gen'ral." He smiled tiredly. "Don't worry. I'll tell her you're doin' a good job here. Fine job."

The chimmie sniffed disgustedly. "You've spent the afternoon and evening rolling in dirt and getting soused! Some militia officer! And I thought you were supposed to be a scientist!

"Well, next time your precious general wants to communicate with our movement here in town, you make sure she sends somebody *else*, do you hear me?"

She swiveled and slammed the door behind her.

What'd I say? Fiben stared after her. Dimly he knew he could have done better somehow. But he was so tired. His body ached, from his singed toes to his burning lungs. He hardly felt the bed as he collapsed into it.

In his dreams a blueness spun and pulsed. From it there emanated a faint *something* that could be likened to a distant smile.

Amusing, it seemed to say. *Amusing, but not all that much of a laugh.*

More an appetizer for things to come.

In his sleep Fiben moaned softly. Then another image

came to him, of a small neo-chimpanzee, an obvious throw-back, with bony eyeridges and long arms which rested on a keyboard display strapped to its chest. The atavistic chim could not speak, but when it grinned, Fiben shivered.

Then a more restful phase of sleep set in, and at last he went on in relief to other dreams.

41

Galactics

The Suzerain of Propriety could not set foot on unsanctioned ground. Because of this it rode perched upon a gilded staff of reckoning, guided by a convoy of fluttering Kwackoo attendants. Their incessant cooing murmur was more soothing than the grave chirps of their Gubru patrons. Although the Uplift of the Kwackoo had brought them far toward the Gubru way of viewing the world, they nevertheless remained less solemn, less dignified by nature.

The Suzerain of Propriety tried to make allowances for such differences as the clucking swarm of fuzzy, rotund clients carried the antigravity perch from the site where the body had lain. It might be inelegant, but already they could be heard gossiping in low tones over who would be chosen as replacement. Who would become the new Suzerain of Cost and Caution?

It would have to be done soon. Messages had already been sent to the Roost Masters on the homeworld, but if need be a senior bureaucrat would be elevated on the spot. Continuity must be preserved.

Far from being offended, the Suzerain of Propriety found the Kwackoo calming. It needed their simple songs for the distraction they offered. The days and weeks to come would

be stressful. Formal mourning was only one of the many tasks
ahead. Somehow, momentum toward a new policy must be
restored. And, of course, one had to consider the effects this
tragedy would have on the Molt.

The investigators awaited the arrival of the perch amid a
copse of toppled trees near the still smoldering chancery
walls. When the Suzerain nodded for them to begin, they
proceeded into a dance of presentment—part gesticulation
and part audiovisual display—describing what they had determined about the cause of the explosion and fire. As the
investigators chirped their findings in syncopated, a cappella
song, the Suzerain made an effort to concentrate. This was a
delicate matter, after all.

By the codes the Gubru might occupy an enemy embassy, yet they could still be held responsible for any damage
done to it if the fault was theirs.

Yes, yes, it occurred, did occur, the investigators reported. *The building is—has been made—a gutted ruin.*

*No, no, no purposeful activity has been traced, is be-
lieved to have caused these happenings. No sign that this
event path was pre-chosen by our enemies and imposed without our will.*

*Even if the Tymbrimi Ambassador sabotaged his own
buildings, what of it? If we are not the cause, we need not
pay, need not reimburse!*

The Suzerain chirped a brief chastisement. It was not up
to the investigators to determine propriety, only evaluations
of fact. And anyway, matters of expense were the domain of
the officers of the new Suzerain of Cost and Caution, after
they recovered from the catastrophe their bureaucracy had
suffered here.

The investigators danced regretful apologies.

The Suzerain's thoughts kept hovering in numb wonderment about what the consequences would be. This otherwise
minor event had toppled the delicate balance of the Triumvirate just before another Command Conclave, and there would
be repercussions even after a new third Suzerain was appointed.

In the short term, this would help both survivors. Beam
and Talon would be free to pursue what few humans remained at large, whatever the cost. And Propriety could
engage in research without constant carpings about how expensive it all would be.

And then there was the competition for primacy to consider. In recent days it had begun to grow clear just how impressive the old Suzerain of Cost and Caution had been. More and more, against all expectation, it had been the one organizing their debates, drawing their best ideas forth, pushing compromises, leading them toward consensus.

The Suzerain of Propriety was ambitious. The priest had not liked the direction things were heading. Nor was it pleasant seeing its cleverest plans tinkered with, modified, altered to suit a bureaucrat. Especially one with bizarre ideas about empathy with aliens!

No, this was not the worst thing to have happened. Not at all. A new Threesome would be much more acceptable. More workable. And in the new balance the replacement would start at a disadvantage.

Then why, for what reason, for what cause am I afraid? the high priest wondered.

Shivering, the Suzerain of Propriety fluffed its plumage and concentrated, bring its thoughts back to the present, to the investigators' report. They seemed to be implying that the explosion and fire had fallen into that broad category of events that the Earthlings might call *accidents*.

At its erstwhile colleague's urging, the Suzerain had of late been trying to learn Anglic, the wolflings' strange, non-Galactic language. It was a difficult, frustrating effort, and of questionable utility when language computers were facile enough.

Yet the chief bureaucrat had insisted, and surprisingly the priest discovered there were things to be learned from even so beastly a collection of grunts and moans, things such as the hidden meanings underlying that term, *accident*.

The word obviously applied to what the investigators said had happened here, a number of unpredicated factors combined with considerable incompetence in the City Gas Department after the human supervisors had been removed. And yet the way Earthlings defined "accident" was wrong by definition! In Anglic the term actually had no precise meaning! Even the humans had a truism, "There are no accidents."

If so, why have a word for a nonexistent thing?

Accident . . . it served to cover anything from unperceived causality, to true randomness, to a full level seven probability storm! In every case the "results" were "accidental."

How could a species be spacefaring, be classified at the high level of a *patron* of a clan with such a murky, undefined, context-dependent way of looking at the universe? Compared with these Earthlings, even the devil trickster Tymbrimi were transparent and clear as the very ether!

This sort of uncomfortable line of thought was the sort of thing the priest had most hated about the bureaucrat! It was one of the dead Suzerain's most irritating attributes.

It was also one of the things most beloved and valuable. It would be missed.

Such were the confusions when a consensus was broken, when a mating was shattered, half begun.

Firmly, the Suzerain chirped a word-chain of definition. Introspection was taxing, and a decision had to made about what had happened here.

Under some potential futures the Gubru might have to pay damages to the Tymbrimi—and even to the Earthlings— for the destruction that occurred on this plateau. It was unpalatable to consider, and might be prevented altogether when the Gubru grand design was fulfilled.

Events elsewhere in the Five Galaxies would determine that. This planet was a minor, if important, nut to shell with a quick, efficient bill thrust. Anyway, it was the job of the new Suzerain of Cost and Caution to see that expenses were kept down.

To see that the Gubru Alliance—the true inheritors of the Ancient Ones—were not found failing in propriety when the Progenitors returned, that was the priest's own task.

May the winds bring that day, it prayed.

"Judgment deferred, delayed, put off for now," the Suzerain declared aloud. And the investigators at once closed their folders.

The business of the chancery fire being finished, the next stop would be the top of the hill, where there was yet another matter to be evaluated.

The cooing crowd of Kwackoo huddled close and moved as a mass, carrying the Perch of Reckoning with them, a flat ball of puffy clients surging placidly through a feathery crowd of their hopping, excitable patrons.

The Diplomatic Cache still smoked on top from the events of the day before. The Suzerain listened carefully as the investigators reported, sometimes one at a time, occasionally joining together to chirp in unison and then counterpoint. Out of the cacophony the Suzerain gathered a picture of the events that had led to this scene.

A local neo-chimpanzee had been found poking around the cache without first seeking formal passage by the occupying power, a clear violation of wartime protocol. Nobody knew why the silly half-animal had been present. Perhaps it was driven by the "monkey complex"—that irritating, incomprehensible need that drove Earthlings to *seek out* excitement instead of prudently avoiding it.

An armed detachment had come upon the curious neo-chimp while routinely moving to secure the disaster area. The commander had urgently spoken to the furry client-of-humans, insisting that the Earthling creature desist at once and show proper obeisance.

Typical of the upspring of humans, the neo-chimp had been obdurate. Instead of behaving in a civilized manner it had run away. In the process of trying to stop it, some defense device of the cairn was set off. The cairn was damaged in the subsequent shooting.

This time the Suzerain decided that the outcome was most satisfactory. Subclient or no, the chimpanzee was officially an ally of the cursed Tymbrimi. By acting so, it had destroyed the immunity of the cache! The soldiers were within their rights to open fire upon either the chimp or the defender globe without restraint. There had been no violation of propriety, the Suzerain ruled.

The investigators danced a dance of relief. Of course, the more closely ancient procedures were adhered to, the more brilliant would be the plumage of the Gubru when the Progenitors returned.

May the winds hurry the day.

"Open, enter, proceed into the cache," the priest commanded. "Enter and investigate the secrets within!"

Certainly the cache fail-safes would have destroyed most of the contents. Still, there might be some information of value left to be deciphered.

The simpler locks came off quickly, and special devices were brought to remove the massive door. This all took some time. The priest kept occupied holding a service for a company of Talon Soldiers, preaching to reinforce their faith in the ancient values. It was important not to let them lose their keen edge with things so peaceful, so the Suzerain reminded them that in the last two days several small parties of warriors had gone missing in the mountains southeast of this very town. Now would be a useful time for them to remember that their lives belonged to the Nest. The Nest and Honor—nothing else mattered.

At last the final puzzle bolt was solved. For famous tricksters the Tymbrimi did not seem so clever. Their wards were easy enough for Gubru lockpick robots to solve. The door lifted off in the arms of a carrier drone. Holding instruments before them, the investigators cautiously entered the cairn.

Moments later, with a chirp-chain of surprise, a feathered form burst forth holding a black crystalline object in its beak. This one was followed almost immediately by another. The investigators' feet were a blur of dancing excitement as they laid the objects on the ground before the Suzerain's floating perch.

Intact! they danced. Two data-stores were found *intact*, shielded from the self-destruct explosions by a premature rockfall!

Glee spread among the investigators and from there to the soldiers and the civilians waiting beyond. Even the Kwackoo crooned happily, for they, too, could see that this counted as a coup of at least the fourth order. An Earthling client had destroyed the immunity of the cache through obviously irreverent behavior—the mark of flawed Uplift. And the result had been fully sanctioned access to enemy secrets!

The Tymbrimi and humans would be shamed, and the clan of Gooksyu-Gubru would learn much!

The celebration was Gubru-frenetic. But the Suzerain itself danced only for a few seconds. In a race of worriers, it had a role of redoubled concern. There were too many things about the universe that were suspect. Too many things that would be much better dead, lest they by some chance someday threaten the Nest.

The Suzerain tilted its head first one way then another. It looked down at the data cubes, black and shiny on the scorched loam. A strange juxtaposition seemed to overlie the salvaged record crystals, a feeling that *almost*, but not quite, translated into a brooding sense of dread.

It was not a recognizable psi-sense, nor any other form of scientific premonition. If it had been, the Suzerain would have ordered the cubes converted to dust then and there.

And yet . . . It was very strange.

For only a brief moment, it shuddered under the illusion that the faceted crystals were eyes, the shining, space-black eyes of a large and very dangerous snake.

42

Robert

He ran holding in one hand a new wooden bow. A simple, homespun quiver containing twenty new arrows bounced gently against his back as he puffed up the forest trail. His straw hat had been woven from river rushes. His loincloth and the moccasins on his feet were made of native suede.

The young man favored his left leg slightly as he ran. The bandage on that thigh covered only a superficial wound. Even the pain from the burn was a pleasure of sorts, reminding him how much preferable a near miss was over the alternative.

Image of a tall bird, staring unbelievingly at the arrow that had split its breastbone, its laser rifle tumbling to the forest loam, released by death-numbed talons.

The ridge was quiet. Almost the only sound was his steady breathing and the soft rasp of moccasins against the pebbles. Prickles of perspiration dried quickly as the breeze laid tracks of goose bumps up his arms and legs.

The touch of wind freshened as he climbed. The slope of the trail tapered, and Robert at last found himself above the trees, among the towering hill-spines of the ridge crest.

The sudden warmth of the sun was welcome now that he had darkened nearly to the shade of a foon-nut tree. His skin had also toughened, making thorns and nettles less bothersome.

I'm probably starting to look like an oldtime Indian, he thought with some amusement. He leapt over a fallen log and slipped down along a lefthand fork in the trail.

As a child he had made much of his family name. Little Robert Oneagle had never had to take turns as a bad guy when the kids played Confederation Uprising. He *always* got to be a Cherokee or Mohawk warrior, whooping it up in make-believe spacesuit and warpaint, zapping the dictator's soldiers during the Power Satellite War.

When this is all over I've got to find out more about the family gene-history, Robert thought. *I wonder how much of it really is Amerindian stock.*

White, fluffy stratus clouds slid along a pressure ridge to the north, appearing to keep pace with him as he jogged along the ridgetops, across the long hills leading toward home.

Toward home.

The phrase came easily now that he had a job to do out under the trees and open sky. *Now* he could think of those catachtonian caves as home. For they did represent sanctuary in uncertain times.

And Athaclena was there.

He had been away longer than expected. The trip had taken him high into the mountains as far away as Spring Valley, recruiting volunteers, establishing communications, and generally spreading the word.

And of course, he and his fellow partisans had also had a couple of skirmishes with the enemy. Robert knew they had been little things—a small Gubru patrol trapped here and there—and annihilated to the last alien. The Resistance only struck where total victory seemed likely. There could be no survivors to tell the Gubru high command that Earthlings had learned to become invisible.

However minor, the victories had done wonders for morale. Still, while they might make things a bit warm for the Gubru up in the mountains, but what was the use if the enemy stayed out of reach?

Most of his trip had been taken up doing things hardly related to the Resistance. Everywhere Robert had gone he found himself surrounded by chims who whooped and chattered at the sight of him—the sole remaining free human. To his frustration they seemed perfectly happy to make him unofficial judge, arbitrator, and godfather to newborn babies.

Never before had he felt so heavily the burdens that Uplift demanded of the patron race.

Not that he blamed the chims, of course. Robert doubted that in their species' brief history so many chims had ever been cut off from humans for so long.

Wherever he went, it became known that the last human in the mountains would not visit any pre-invasion building or, indeed, even see anyone wearing any clothing or artifact of non-Garth origin. As word spread how the alien gasbots found their targets, chims were soon moving whole communities. Cottage industries sprang up, resurrecting the lost arts of spinning and weaving, of tanning and cobbling.

Actually, the chims in the mountains were doing rather well. Food was plentiful and the young still attended school. Here and there a few responsible types had even begun to reorganize the Garth Ecological Reclamation Project, keeping the most urgent programs going, improvising to replace the lost human experts.

Perhaps they don't really need us, he remembered thinking.

His own kind had come within a hair's breadth of turning Earth-homeworld into an ecological Chelmno, in the years just before humanity awakened into sanity. A horrible calamity was averted by the narrowest of margins. Knowing that, it was humbling to see so many so-called clients behaving more rationally than men had only a century before Contact.

Do we really have any right to play god with these people? Maybe when this blows over we should just go away and let them work out their future for themselves.

A romantic idea. There was a rub, of course.

The Galactics would never let us.

So he let them crowd around him, ask his advice, name their babies after him. Then, when he had done all he could for the time being, he took off down the trail for home. Alone, since by now no chim could keep up with his pace.

The solitude of the last day or so had been welcome. It gave him time to think. He had begun learning a lot about himself these last few weeks and months, ever since that horrible afternoon when his mind had crumpled under pounding fists of agony and Athaclena had come into his mind to rescue him. Oddly, it had not turned out to be the beasts and monsters of his neuroses that mattered most. Those were easily dealt with once he faced them and knew them for what

they were. Anyway, they were probably no worse than any
other person's burdens of unresolved business from the past.

No, what had been more important was coming to grips
with what he was as a man. That was an exploration he had only
just begun, but Robert liked the direction the journey seemed
to be heading.

He jogged around a bend in the mountain trail and came
out of the hill's shadow with the sun on his back. Ahead, to
the south, lay the craggy limestone formations concealing the
Valley of Caves.

Robert stopped as a metallic glint caught his eye. Something sparkled over the prominences beyond the valley, perhaps ten miles away.

Gasbots, he thought. Over in that area Benjamin's techs
had begun laying out samples of everything from electronics
to metals to clothing, in an effort to discover what it was the
Gubru robots homed in on. Robert hoped they had made
some progress while he was away.

And yet, in another sense he hardly cared anymore. The
new longbow felt good in his hand. The chims in the mountains preferred powerful homemade crossbows and arbalests,
requiring less coordination but greater simian strength to
crank. The effect had been the same with all three weapons
. . . dead birds. The use of ancient skills and archaic tools had
turned into a galvanizing theme, resonating with the mythos
of the Wolfling Clan.

There were disturbing consequences as well. Once, after
a successful ambush, he had noticed some of the local mountain chens drifting away from camp. He slipped into the
shadows and followed them to what appeared to be a secret
cook fire, in a side canyon.

Earlier, while they had stripped the vanquished Gubru
of their weapons and carried off the bodies, he had noticed
some of the chims glancing back at him furtively, perhaps
guiltily. That night he watched from a dark hillside as long-
armed silhouettes danced in the firelight under the windblown stars. Something roasted on a spit over the flames, and
the wind carried a sweet, smoky aroma.

Robert had had a feeling there were a few things the
chims did not want seen by their patrons. He faded back into
the shadows and returned to the main camp, leaving them to
their ritual.

The images still flickered in his mind like feral, savage

fantasies. Robert never asked what had been done with the bodies of the dead Galactics, but since then he could not think of the enemy without remembering that aroma.

If only there were a way to get more of them to come into the mountains, he pondered. Only under the trees did it seem possible to hurt the invaders.

The afternoon was aging. Time to finish the long jog home. Robert turned and was about to start down into the valley when he stopped suddenly. He blinked. There was a blur in the air. Something seemed to flutter at the edge of his vision, as if a tricky moth were dancing just within his blind spot. It didn't seem to be possible to look at the thing.

Oh, Robert thought.

He gave up trying to focus on it and looked away, letting the odd *non-thing* chase him instead. Its touch laid open the petals of his mind like a flower unfolding in the sun. The fluttering entity danced timidly and winked at him . . . a simple glyph of affection and mild amusement . . . easy enough for even a thick-thewed, hairy-armed, road-smelly, pinkish-brown *human* to understand.

"Very funny, Clennie." Robert shook his head. But the flower opened still wider and he *kenned* warmth. Without having to be told, he knew which way to go. He turned off the main trail and leapt up a narrow game path.

Halfway to the ridgetop he came upon a brown figure lounging in the shade of a thornbush. The chen looked up from a paperpage book and waved lazily.

"Hi, Robert. You're lookin' a lot better'n when I saw you last."

"Fiben!" Robert grinned. "When did you get back?"

The chim suppressed a tired yawn. "Oh, 'bout an hour ago. The boys down in th' caves sent me right up here to see her nibs. I picked up somethin' for her in town. Sorry. Didn't get anythin' for you, though."

"Did you get into any trouble in Port Helenia?"

"Hmmm, well, some. A little dancin', a little scratchin', a little hootin'."

Robert smiled. Fiben's "accent" was always thickest when he had big news to downplay, the better to draw out the story. If allowed to get away with it, he would surely keep them up all night.

"Uh, Fiben . . ."

"Yeah, yeah. She's up there." The chim gestured toward

the top of the ridge. "And in a right fey mood, if you ask me. But don't ask me, I'm just a chimpanzee. I'll see you later, Robert." He picked up his book again, not exactly the model of a reverent client. Robert grinned.

"Thanks, Fiben. I'll see ya." He hurried up the trail.

Athaclena did not bother to turn around as he approached, for they had already said hello. She stood at the hilltop looking westward, her face to the sun, holding her hands outstretched before her.

Robert at once sensed that another glyph floated over Athaclena now, supported by the waving tendrils of her corona. And it was an impressive thing. Comparing her little greeting, earlier, to this one would be like standing a dirty limerick next to "Xanadu." He could not see it, neither could he even begin to *kenn* its complexity, but it was there, nearly palpable to his heightened empathy sense.

Robert also realized that she held something between her hands . . . like a slender thread of invisible fire—intuited more than seen—that arched across the gap from one hand to the other.

"Athaclena, what is—"

He stopped then, as he came around and saw her face.

Her features had changed. Most of the humaniform contours she had shaped during the weeks of their exile were still in place; but something they had displaced had returned, if only momentarily. There was an alien glitter in her gold-flecked eyes, and it seemed to dance in counterpoint to the throbbing of the half-seen glyph.

Robert's senses had grown. He looked again at the thread in her hands and felt a thrill of recognition.

"Your father . . . ?"

Athaclena's teeth flashed white. *"With-tanna Uthacalthing bellinarri-t'hoo, haoon'nda! . . ."*

She breathed deeply through wide-open nostrils. Her eyes—set as wide apart as possible—seemed to flash.

"Robert, he lives!"

He blinked, his mind overflowing with questions. "That's great! But . . . but where! Do you know anything about my mother? The government? What does he say?"

She did not reply at once. Athaclena held up the thread. Sunlight seemed to run up and down its taut length. Robert might have sworn that he heard sound, *real* sound, emitting from the thrumming fiber.

"*With-tanna Uthacalthing!*" Athaclena seemed to look straight into the sun.

She laughed, no longer quite the sober girl he had known. She chortled, *Tymbrimi* fashion, and Robert was very glad that *he* was not the object of that hilarity. Tymbrimi humor quite often meant that someone else, sometime soon, would definitely not be amused.

He followed her gaze out over the Vale of Sind, where a flight of the ubiquitous Gubru transports moaned faintly as they cruised across the sky. Unable to trace more than the outlines of her glyph, Robert's mind searched for and found something akin to it in the human fashion. In his mind he pictured a metaphor.

Suddenly, Athaclena's smile was something feral, almost *catlike*. And those warships, reflected in her eyes, seemed to take on the aspect of complacent, rather unsuspecting *mice*.

PART THREE

The Garthlings

The evolution of the human race will not be accomplished in the ten thousand years of tame animals, but in the million years of wild animals, because man is and will always be a wild animal.

CHARLES GALTON DARWIN

Natural selection won't matter soon, not anywhere near as much as conscious selection. We will civilize and alter ourselves to suit our ideas of what we can be. Within one more human lifespan, we will have changed ourselves unrecognizably.

GREG BEAR

PART THREE

The Quickening

43

Uthacalthing

Inky stains marred the fen near the place where the yacht had foundered. Dark fluids oozed slowly from cracked, sunken tanks into the waters of the broad, flat estuary. Wherever the slick trails touched, insects, small animals, and the tough salt grass all died.

The little spaceship had bounced and skidded when it crashed, scything a twisted trail of destruction before finally plunging nose first into the marshy river mouth. For days thereafter the wreck lay where it had come to rest, slowly leaking and settling into the mud.

Neither rain nor the tidal swell could wash away the battle scars etched into its scorched flanks. The yacht's skin, once allicient and pretty, was now seared and scored from near-miss after near-miss. Crashing had only been the final insult.

Incongruously large at the stern of a makeshift boat, the Thennanin looked across the intervening flat islets to survey the wreck. He stopped rowing to ponder the harsh reality of his situation.

Clearly, the ruined spaceship would never fly again. Worse, the crash had made a sorrowful mess of this patch of marshlands. His crest puffed up, a rooster's comb ridged with spiky gray fans.

Uthacalthing lifted his own paddle and politely waited for his fellow castaway to finish his stately contemplation. He hoped the Thennanin diplomat was not about to serve up yet another lecture on ecological responsibility and the burdens of patronhood. But, of course, Kault was Kault.

"The spirit of this place is offended," the large being said, his breathing slits rasping heavily. "We sapients have no business taking our petty wars down into nurseries such as these, polluting them with space poisons."

"Death comes to all things, Kault. And evolution thrives on tragedies." He was being ironic, but Kault, of course, took him seriously. The Thennanin's throat slits exhaled heavily.

"I know that, my Tymbrimi colleague. It is why most registered nursery worlds are allowed to go through their natural cycles unimpeded. Ice ages and planetoidal impacts are all part of the natural order. Species are tempered and rise to meet such challenges.

"However, this is a special case. A world damaged as badly as Garth can only take so many disasters before it goes into shock and becomes completely barren. It is only a short time since the Bururalli worked out their madness here, from which this planet has barely begun to recover. Now our battles add more stress . . . such as that filth."

Kault gestured, pointing at the fluids leaking from the broken yacht. His distaste was obvious.

Uthacalthing chose, this time, to keep his silence. Of course every patron-level Galactic race was officially environmentalist. That was the oldest and greatest law. Those spacefaring species who did not at least declare fealty to the Ecological Management Codes were wiped out by the majority, for the protection of future generations of sophonts.

But there were degrees. The Gubru, for instance, were less interested in nursery worlds than in their products, ripe pre-sentient species to be brought into the Gubru Clan's peculiar color of conservative fanaticism. Among the other lines, the Soro took great joy in the manipulation of newly fledged client races. And the Tandu were simply horrible.

Kault's race was sometimes irritating in their sanctimonious pursuit of ecological purity, but at least theirs was a fixation Uthacalthing could understand. It was one thing to burn a forest, or to build a city on a registered world. Those types of damage would heal in a short time. It was quite another thing to release long-lasting poisons into a biosphere, poisons which would be absorbed and accumulate. Uthacalthing's own distaste at the oily slicks was only a little less intense than Kault's. But nothing could be done about it now.

"The Earthlings had a good emergency cleanup team on this planet, Kault. Obviously the invasion has left it inoperative. Perhaps the Gubru will get around to taking care of this mess themselves."

Kault's entire upper body twisted as the Thennanin performed a sneezelike expectoration. A gobbet struck one of the nearby leafy fronds. Uthacalthing had come to know that this was an expression of extreme incredulity.

"The Gubru are slackers and heretics! Uthacalthing, how can you be so naïvely optimistic?" Kault's crest trembled and his leathery lids blinked. Uthacalthing merely looked back at his fellow castaway, his lips a compressed line.

"Ah. Aha," Kault rasped. "I see! You test my sense of humor with a statement of *irony*." The Thennanin made his ridge crest inflate briefly. "Amusing. I get it. Indeed. Let us proceed."

Uthacalthing turned and lifted his oar again. He sighed and crafted *tu'fluk*, the glyph of mourning for a joke not properly appreciated.

Probably, this dour creature was selected as ambassador to an Earthling world because he has what passes for a great sense of humor among Thennanin. The choice might have been a mirror image of the reason Uthacalthing himself had been chosen by the Tymbrimi . . . for his comparatively serious nature, for his restraint and tact.

No, Uthacalthing thought as they rowed, worming by patches of struggling salt grass. *Kault, my friend, you did not get the joke at all. But you will.*

It had been a long trek back to the river mouth. Garth had rotated more than twenty times since he and Kault had to abandon the crippled ship in midair, parachuting into the wilderness. The Thennanin's unfortunate Ynnin clients had panicked and gotten their parasails intertangled, causing them to fall to their deaths. Since then, the two diplomats had been solitary companions.

At least with spring weather they would not freeze. That was some comfort.

It was slow going in their makeshift boat, made from stripped tree branches and parasail cloth. The yacht was only a few hundred meters from where they had sighted it, but it took the better part of four hours to wend through the frequently tortuous channels. Although the terrain was very flat, high grass blocked their view most of the way.

Then, suddenly, there it was, the broken ruin of a once-sleek little ship of space.

"I still do not see why we had to come back to the wreck," Kault rasped. "We got away with sufficient dietary supplements to let us live off the land. When things calm down we can intern ourselves—"

"Wait here," Uthacalthing said, not caring that he interrupted the other. Thennanin weren't fanatical about that sort of punctilio, thank Ifni. He slipped over the side of the boat and into the water. "There is no need that both of us risk approaching any closer. I will continue alone."

Uthacalthing knew his fellow castaway well enough to read Kault's discomfort. Thennanin culture put great store in personal courage—especially since space travel terrified them so.

"I will accompany you, Uthacalthing." He moved to put the oar aside. "There may be dangers."

Uthacalthing stopped him with a raised hand. "Unnecessary, colleague and friend. Your physical form isn't suited for this mire. And you may tip the boat. Just rest. I'll only be a few minutes."

"Very well, then." Kault looked visibly relieved. "I shall await you here."

Uthacalthing stepped through the shallows, feeling for his footing in the tricky mud. He skirted the swirls of leaked ship-fluid and made toward the bank where the broken back of the yacht arched over the bog.

It was hard work. He felt his body try to alter itself to better handle the effort of wading through the muck, but Uthacalthing suppressed the reaction. The glyph *nuturunow* helped him keep adaptations to a minimum. The distance just wasn't worth the price the changes would cost him.

His ruff expanded, partly to support *nuturunow* and partly as his corona felt among the weeds and grass for presences. It was doubtful anything here could harm him. The Bururalli had seen to that. Still, he probed the surrounding area as he waded, and caressed the empathy net of this marshy life-stew.

The little creatures were all around him, all the basic, standard forms: sleek and spindly birds, scaled and horn-mouthed reptiloids, hairy or furry types which scuttled among the reeds. It had long been known that there were three classic ways for oxygen-breathing animals to cover themselves. When skin cells buckled outward it led to feathers. When they buckled inward there was hair. When they thickened, flat and hard, the animal had scales.

All three had developed here, and in a typical pattern. Feathers were ideal for avians, who needed maximum insulation for minimum weight. Fur covered the warm-blooded creatures, who could not afford to lose heat.

Of course, that was the only surface. Within, there was a nearly infinite number of ways to approach the problem of living. Each creature was unique, each world a wonderful experiment in diversity. A planet was *supposed* to be a great nursery, and deserved protection in that role. It was a belief both Uthacalthing and his companion shared.

His people and Kault's were enemies—not as the Gubru were to the humans of Garth, of course, but of a certain style—registered with the Institute for Civilized Warfare. There were many types of conflict, most of them dangerous and quite serious. Still, Uthacalthing liked this Thennanin, in a way. That was preferable. It was usually easier to pull a jest on someone you liked.

His slick leggings shed the greasy water as he slogged up onto the mudbank. Uthacalthing checked for radiation, then stepped lightly toward the shattered yacht.

Kault watched the Tymbrimi disappear around the flank of the broken ship. He sat still, as he had been bid, using the paddle occasionally to stroke against the sluggish current and keep away from the oozing spills. Mucus bubbled from his breathing slits to drive out the stench.

Throughout the Five Galaxies the Thennanin were known as tough fighters and doughty starfarers. But it was only on a living, breathing planet that Kault and his kind could relax. That was why their ships so resembled worlds themselves, solid and durable. A scout craft made by his people would not have been swatted from the sky as this one had, by a mere terawatt laser! The Tymbrimi preferred speed and maneuverability over armor, but disasters such as this one seemed to bear out the Thennanin philosophy.

The crash had left them with few options. Running the Gubru blockade would have been chancy at best, and the other alternative had been hiding out with the surviving human officials. Hardly choices one lingered over.

Perhaps the crash had been the best possible branching

for reality to take, after all. At least here there was the dirt
and water, and they were amid life.

Kault looked up when Uthacalthing reappeared around the
corner of the wreck, carrying a small satchel. As the Tymbrimi
envoy slipped into the water, Uthacalthing's furry ruff was
fully expanded. Kault had learned that it was not as efficient
at dissipating excess heat as the Thennanin crest.

Some groups within his clan took facts like these as
evidence of intrinsic Thennanin superiority, but Kault belonged to a faction that was more charitable in outlook. Each
lifeform had its niche in the evolving Whole, they believed.
Even the wild and unpredictable wolfling humans. Even
heretics.

Uthacalthing's corona fluffed out as he worked his way
back to the boat, but it was not because he was overheated.
He was crafting a special glyph.

Lurrunanu hovered under the bright sunshine. It coa-
lesced in the field of his corona, gathered, strained forward
eagerly, then catapulted over toward Kault, dancing over the
big Thennanin's crest as if in delighted curiosity.

The Galactic appeared oblivious. He noticed nothing,
and he could not be blamed for that. After all, the glyph *was*
nothing. Nothing real.

Kault helped Uthacalthing climb back aboard, grabbing
his belt and pulling him into the rocky boat head first. "I
recovered some extra dietary supplements and a few tools we
might need," Uthacalthing said in Galactic Seven as he rolled
over. Kault steadied him.

The satchel broke open and bottles rolled onto the fabric
bottom. *Lurrunanu* still hovered above the Thennanin, awaiting the right moment. As Kault reached down to help collect
the spilled items, the whirling glyph pounced!

It struck the famed Thennanin obstinacy and rebounded.
Kault's bluff stolidity was too tough to penetrate. Under
Uthacalthing's prodding, *lurrunanu* leapt again, furiously hurl-
ing itself against the leathery creature's crest at just the
moment Kault picked up a bottle that was lighter than the
others and handed it to Uthacalthing. But the alien's obdurate skepticism sent the glyph reeling back once more.

Uthacalthing tried a final time as he fumbled with the
bottle and put it away, but this time *lurrunanu* simply shat-

tered against the Thennanin's impenetrable barrier of assumptions.

"Are you all right?" Kault asked.

"Oh, fine." Uthacalthing's ruff settled down and he exhaled in frustration. Somehow, he would have to find a way to excite Kault's curiosity!

Oh well, he thought. *I never expected it to be easy. There will be time.*

Out there ahead of them lay several hundred kilometers of wildlands, then the Mountains of Mulun, and finally the Valley of the Sind before they could reach Port Helenia. Somewhere in that expanse Uthacalthing's secret partner waited, ready to help execute a long, involved joke on Kault. *Be patient,* Uthacalthing told himself. *The best jests do take time.*

He put the satchel under his makeshift seat and secured it with a length of twine. "Let us be off. I believe we'll find good fishing by the far bank, and those trees will make for good shelter from the midday sun."

Kault rasped assent and picked up his oar. Together they worked their way through the marsh, leaving the derelict yacht behind them to settle slowly into the endurant mud.

44

Galactics

In orbit above the planet the invasion force entered a new phase of operation.

At the beginning, there had been the assault against a brief, surprisingly bitter, but almost pointless resistance. Then came the consolidation and plans for ritual and cleansing. All through this, the major preoccupation of the fleet had been defensive.

The Five Galaxies were in a turmoil. Any of a score of other alliances might have also seen an opportunity in seizing Garth. Or the Terran/Tymbrimi alliance—though hard beset elsewhere—might choose to counterattack here. The tactical computers calculated that the wolflings would be stupid to do so, but Earthlings were so unpredictable, one could never tell.

Too much had been invested in this theater already. The clan of the Gooksyu-Gubru could not afford a loss here.

So the battle fleet had arrayed itself. Ships kept watch over the five local layers of hyperspace, over nearby transfer points, over the cometary time-drop nexi.

News came of Earth's travails, of the desperation of the Tymbrimi, and of the tricksters' difficulties in acquiring allies among the lethargic Moderate clans. As the interval stretched it became clear that no threat would come from those directions.

But some of the other great clans *were* busy. Those who were quick to see advantage. Some were engaged in futile searches for the missing dolphin ship. Others used the confusion as a convenient excuse to carry through on ancient grudges. Millennia-old agreements unraveled like gas clouds before sudden supernovae. Flame licked at the ancient social fabric of the Five Galaxies. From the Gubru Home Perch came new orders. As soon as ground-based defenses were completed, the greater part of the fleet must go on to other duties. The remaining force should be more than adequate to hold Garth against any reasonable threat.

The Roost Masters did accompany the order with compensations. To the Suzerain of Beam and Talon they awarded a citation. To the Suzerain of Propriety they promised an improved Planetary Library for the expedition on Garth.

The new Suzerain of Cost and Caution needed no compensation. The orders were victory in themselves for they manifested caution in their essence. The chief bureaucrat won molt points, badly needed in its competition with its more experienced peers.

The naval units set forth for the nearest transfer point, confident that matters on Garth were well in beak and hand. The ground forces, however, watched the great battleships depart with slightly less certitude. Down on the planet's surface there were portents of a minor resistance movement. The activity—as yet hardly more than a nuisance—had started among the chimpanzee population in the back country. As they were cousins and clients of men, their irritating and unbecoming behavior came as no surprise. The Gubru high command took precautions. Then they turned their attention to other matters.

Certain items of information had come to the attention of the Triumvirate—data taken from an enemy source—information having to do with Planet Garth itself. The hint might turn out to be nothing at all. But if it were true the possibilities were vast!

In any event, these things had to be looked into. Important advantages might be at stake. In this, all three Suzerains agreed completely. It was their first taste of true consensus together.

A platoon of Talon Soldiers kept watch over the expedition making its way into the mountains. Slender avians in battle dress swooped just over the trees, the faint whine of their flight harnesses carrying softly down the narrow canyons. One hover tank cruised ahead on point and another guarded the convoy's rear.

The scientist investigators in their floater barges rode amidst this ample protection. The vehicles headed upland on low cushions of air. Perforce they avoided the rough, spiny ridgetops. There was no hurry, though. The rumor they chased was probably nothing at all, but the Suzerains insisted that it be checked out, just in case.

Their goal came into sight late on the second day. It was a flattened area at the bottom of a narrow valley. A number of buildings had burned to the ground here, not too long ago.

The hover tanks took positions at opposite ends of the scorched area. Then Gubru scientists and their Kwackoo client-assistants emerged from the barges. Standing back from the still stinking ruins, the avians chirped commands to whirring specimen robots, directing the search for clues. Less fastidious than their patrons, the fluffy white Kwackoo dove right into the wreckage, squawking excitedly as they sniffed and probed.

One conclusion was clear immediately. The destruction had been deliberate. The wreckers had wanted to hide something under the smoke and ruin.

Twilight came with subtropical suddenness. Soon the investigators were working uncomfortably under the glare of spotlights. At last the team commander ordered a halt. Full-scale studies would have to wait for morning.

The specialists retired into their barges for the night, chattering about what they had already discovered. There were traces, hints of things exciting and not a little disturbing.

Still, there would be ample time to do the work by day. The technicians closed their barges against the darkness. Six drone watchers rose to hover in silent, mechanical diligence, spinning patiently above the vehicles. Garth turned slowly under the starry night. Faint creakings and rustles told of the busy, serious work of the nocturnal forest creatures—hunting and being hunted. The watcher drones ignored them, rotating unperturbed. The night wore on.

Not long before dawn, new shapes moved through the starlit lanes underneath the trees. The smaller local beasts sought cover and listened as the newcomers crept past, slowly, warily.

The watcher drones noticed these new animals, too, and measured them against their programmed criteria. *Harmless*, came the judgment. Once again, they did nothing.

45

Athaclena

"They're sitting ducks," Benjamin said from his vantage point on the western hillside.

Athaclena glanced up at her chim aide-de-camp. For a moment she struggled with Benjamin's metaphor. Perhaps he was referring to the enemy's avian nature?

"They appear to be complacent, if that is what you mean," she said. "But they have reason. The Gubru rely upon battle robots more extensively than we Tymbrimi—We find them because they are expensive and overly predictable. Nevertheless, those drones can be formidable."

Benjamin nodded seriously. "I'll remember that, ser."

Still, Athaclena sensed that he was unimpressed. He had helped plan this morning's foray, coordinating with representatives of the Port Helenia resistance. Benjamin was blithely certain of its success.

The town chims were to launch a predawn attack in the Vale of Sind just before action was scheduled to begin here. The official aim was to sow confusion among the enemy, and maybe do him some harm he would remember. Athaclena wasn't certain that was really possible. But she had agreed to the venture anyway. She did not want the Gubru finding out too much from the ruins of the Howletts Center.

Not yet.

"They've set up camp under the ruins of the old main building," Benjamin said. "Right where we expected them to plant themselves."

Athaclena looked at the chim's solid-state night binoculars uncomfortably. "You are certain those devices aren't detectable?"

Benjamin nodded without looking up. "Yes'm. We laid instruments like these out on a hillside near a cruising gasbot, and its flightpath didn't even ripple. We've narrowed down the list of materials the enemy's able to sniff. Soon . . ."

Benjamin stiffened. Athaclena felt his sudden tension.

"What is it?"

The chen crouched forward. "I see shapes movin' through the trees. It must be our guys gettin' into position. Now we'll find out if those battle robots are programmed the way you expected."

Distracted as he was, Benjamin did not offer to share the binoculars. *So much for patron-client protocol*, Athaclena thought. Not that it mattered. She preferred to reach out with her own senses.

Down below she detected three different species of biped arranging themselves around the Gubru expedition. If Benjamin had spotted them they certainly had to be well within range of the enemy's sensitive watch drones.

And yet the robots did nothing! Seconds beat past, and the whirling drones did not fire on the shapes approaching under the trees. Nor did they alert their sleeping masters.

She sighed in increased hope. The machines' restraint

was a crucial piece of information. The fact that they spun on silently told her volumes about what was happening not only here on Garth but elsewhere, beyond the flecked star-field that glittered overhead. It told her something about the state of the Five Galaxies as a whole.

There is still law, Athaclena thought. *The Gubru are constrained.*

Like many other fanatic clans, the Gubru Alliance was not pristine in its adherence to the codes of planetary/ecological management. Knowing the avians' dour paranoia, she had figured that they would program their defense robots one way if the rules were still valid, and quite another if they had fallen.

If chaos had completely taken over the Five Galaxies, the Gubru would have programmed their machines to sterilize hundreds of acres rather than allow *any* risk to their feathery frames.

But if the Codes held, then the enemy did not yet dare break them. For those same rules might protect *them*, if the tide of war turned against their faction.

Rule Nine Hundred and Twelve: *Where possible, noncombatants must be spared.* That held for noncombatant *species,* even more than individuals, especially on a catastrophe world such as Garth. Native forms were protected by billion-year-old tradition.

"You are trapped by your own assumptions, you vile things," she murmured in Galactic Seven. Obviously the Gubru had programmed their machines to watch for the trappings of sapiency—factory-produced weapons, clothing, machinery—never imagining that an enemy might assail their camp naked, indistinguishable from the animals of the forest!

She smiled, thinking of Robert. This part had been his idea.

Gray, antelucan translucence was spreading across the sky, gradually driving out the fainter stars. To Athaclena's left their medic, the elderly chimmie Elayne Soo, looked at her all-metal watch. She tapped its lens significantly. Athaclena nodded, giving permission for matters to proceed.

Dr. Soo cupped her mouth and uttered a high trilling sound, the call of a fyuallu bird. Athaclena did not hear the snapping twang of bowstrings as thirty crossbows fired. She tensed though. If the Gubru had invested in really sophisticated drones . . .

"Gotcha!" Benjamin exulted. "Six little tops, all broken to bits! The robots are all down!"

Athaclena breathed again. Robert was down there. Now, perhaps, she could believe that he and the others had a chance. She touched Benjamin's shoulder, and the chim reluctantly handed over the binoculars.

Someone must have noticed when the monitor screens went blank. There was a faint hum, and the upper hatch of one of the hover tanks opened. A helmeted figure peered about the quiet meadow, its beak working in alarm as it saw the wreckage of a nearby watch robot. A sudden movement rustled the branches nearby. The soldier whirled about with its laser drawn as something or someone leaped forth from one of the neighboring trees. Blue lightning blazed at the dark figure.

It missed. The confused Gubru gunner couldn't track a dim shape that neither flew nor fell but *swung* across the narrow clearing at the end of a long vine! Bright bolts went wide two more times, and then the soldier's chance was gone. There was a "crack" as the shadowy figure wrapped its legs around the slender avian and snapped its spine.

Athaclena's triple pulse beat fast as she saw Robert's silhouette stand on the turret of the tank, over the crumpled body of the Talon Soldier. He raised an arm to signal, and suddenly the clearing was filled with running forms.

Chims hurried among the tanks and floaters, carrying earthenware bottles. Behind them shambled larger figures bearing bulky packs. Athaclena heard Benjamin mutter to himself in suppressed resentment. It had been her choice to include gorillas in this operation, and the decision was not popular.

". . . thirty-five . . . thirty-six . . ." Elayne Soo counted off the seconds. As the dawn light spread they could see chims clambering over the alien vehicles. This was gamble number three. Would surprise delay the inevitable reaction long enough?

Their luck ran out after thirty-eight seconds. Sirens shrieked, first from the lead tank and then from the one in the rear.

"Look out!" someone cried below.

The furry raiders scattered for the trees as Talon Soldiers tumbled out of their hover barges, firing searing blasts from their saber rifles. Chims fell screaming, batting at burning fur, or toppled silently into the undergrowth, holed from front to back. Athaclena clamped down on her corona in order not to faint under their agony.

This was her first taste of full-scale war. Right now there seemed to be no joke, only suffering and pointless, hideous death.

Then Talon Soldiers began falling. The avians hopped about seeking targets that had disappeared into the trees and were struck down by missiles as they stood. The fighters adjusted their weapons to seek out energy sources, but there were no lasers out there to home in on, no pulse-projectors, not even chemically powered pellet guns. Meanwhile cross-bow bolts whizzed like stinging gnats. One by one, the Gubru warriors jerked and fell.

First one tank, then the other, began to rise on growling blasts of air. The lead vehicle turned. Its triple barrels then started blasting swaths through the forest.

The tops of towering trees seemed to hang in midair for brief moments as their centers exploded, before plummeting earthward in a haze of smoke and flying wood chips. Taut vines whipped back and forth like agonized snakes, spraying their hard-won liquors in all directions. Chims screamed as they spilled from shattered branches.

Is it worth it? Oh, can anything be worth this?

Athaclena's corona had expanded in the emotion of the moment, and she felt a glyph start to take shape. Angrily she rejected the unformed sense image, an answer to her question. She wanted no laughing Tymbrimi poignancies now. She felt like weeping, human style, but did not know how.

The forest was afroth with fear, and native animals fled the devastation. Some ran right over Athaclena and Benjamin, squeaking in their panicked desperation to get away. The radius of slaughter spread as the deadly vehicles opened up on everything in sight. Explosions and flame were everywhere.

Then, as abruptly as it had started firing, the lead tank stopped! First one, then another barrel glowed reddish white and shut down. Half of the noise abated.

The other fighting machine seemed to be suffering similar problems, but that one tried to continue firing, in spite of its crackling, drooping barrels.

"Duck!" Benjamin cried out as he pulled Athaclena down. The crew on the hillside took cover just in time as the rear tank exploded in a searing, actinic flash. Pieces of metal and shape-plast armor whistled by overhead.

Athaclena blinked away the sharp afterimage. In a momentary confusion brought on by sensory overload, she wondered why Benjamin was so obsessed with Earthly waterfowl.

"The other one's jammed!" Somebody shouted. Sure enough, by the time Athaclena was able to look again it was easy to see smoke rising from the lead tank's apron. The turret emitted grinding noises, and it seemed unable to move. Mixed with the pungent odor of burning vegetation came the sharp smell of corrosion.

"It worked!" Elayne Soo exulted. Then she was over the top and gone, running to tend the wounded.

Benjamin and Robert had proposed using chemicals to disable a Gubru patrol. Athaclena then modified the plan to suit her own purposes. She did not want dead Gubru, as had been their policy so far. This time she wanted live ones.

There they were now, bottled up inside their vehicles, unable to move or act. Their communications antennae were melted, and anyway, by now the attacks in the Sind had surely begun. The Gubru High Command had worries enough closer to home. Help would be some time coming.

Silence held for a moment as debris rained to the forest floor. Dust slowly settled.

Then there was heard a growing chorus of high shrieks—shouts of glee unaltered since before Mankind began meddling with chimpanzee genes. Athaclena heard another sound, as well . . . a rolling, ululating cry of triumph—Robert's "Tarzan" call.

Good, she thought. *It is good to know he lived through all that killing.*

Now if only he follows the plan and stays out of sight from now on!

Chims were emerging from the toppled trees, some hurrying to help Dr. Soo with the injured. Others took up positions around the disabled machines.

Benjamin was looking to the northwest, where a few stars faded before the dawn. Faint, warlike rumblings could be heard coming from that direction. "I wonder how Fiben and the city boys are doin' at their end," he said.

For the first time Athaclena set her corona free. Re-

leased at last, it crafted *kuhunnagarra* . . . the essence of
indeterminacy postponed. "It is beyond our grasp," she told
him. "Here, in this place, is where we act."

With a raised hand she signaled her hillside units forward.

46

Fiben

Smoke rose from the Valley of the Sind. Scattered fires
had broken out in wheat fields and among the orchards,
injecting soot into a morning fast growing pale and dim.

A hundred meters high in the air, perched on the rough
wooden frame of a handmade kite, Fiben used field glasses to
scan the scattered conflagrations. The fighting had not gone
at all well here in the Sind. The operation had been intended as a quick hit-and-run uprising—a way to hurt the
invader. But it had turned into a rout.

And now the cloud deck was dropping, as if overladen
with dark smoke and the sinking of their hopes. Soon he
wouldn't be able to see beyond a kilometer or so.

"*Fiben!*"

Below and to the left, not far from the kite's blocky
shadow, Gailet Jones waved up at him. "Fiben, do you see
anything of C group? Did they get the Gubru guard post?"

He shook his head, exaggeratedly.

"No sign of them!" he called. "But there's dust from
enemy armor!"

"Where? How much? We'll give you more slack so you
can get a better—"

"No way!" he shouted. "I'm comin' down now."

"But we need data—"

He shook his head emphatically. "There are patrols all

over the place! We've got to get out of here!" Fiben motioned
to the chims controlling his tether rope.

Gailet bit her lip and nodded. They started reeling him
in.

As the attack collapsed and their communications unraveled, Gailet had only become more frantic for information.
Frankly, he couldn't blame her. He, too, wanted to know
what was happening. He had friends out there! But right now
it might be better to think of their own skins.

And it all started so well, he thought as his craft slowly
descended. The uprising had begun when chim workers
employed at Gubru construction sites set off explosives carefully emplaced over the last week. At five of the eight target
sites, satisfying fiery plumes had risen to meet the dawn sky.

But then the advantages of technology began to be seen.
It had been mind-numbing, witnessing how quickly the auto-
mated defense systems of the enemy responded, scything
through advancing teams of irregular fighters before their
assaults could barely begin. To his knowledge not a single of
the more important objectives had been taken, let alone
held.

All told, things did not look good at all.

Fiben was forced to luff the kite, spilling air as the crude
glider dropped. The ground rushed up, and he gathered his
legs for the impact. It came with a jarring thud. He heard
one of the wooden spars break as the wing took up most of
the shock.

Well, better a spar than a bone. Fiben grunted as he
undid his harness and wrestled free of the heavy homespun
fabric. A real parasail, with composite struts and duracloth
wings, would have been an awful lot better. But they still
didn't know what it was about some manufactured goods that
the invader was able to home in on. So he had insisted on
homemade—and clumsy—substitutes.

The big, scarred chim named Max stood watch nearby,
a captured Gubru laser rifle in one hand. He offered a hand.
"You okay, Fiben?"

"Yeah, Max, fine. Let's get this thing broken down."

His crew hurried to disassemble the kite and get it
under the cover of the nearby trees. Gubru floaters and
fighters had been whistling overhead ever since the ill-fated
foray had begun before dawn. The kite was almost insignifi-

cant, virtually invisible to radar or infrared. Still, they had surely been pushing their luck using it in daylight like this.

Gailet met them at the edge of the orchard. She had been reluctant to believe in the Gubru secret weapon—the enemy's ability to detect manufactured goods. But she had gone along partway at his insistence. The chimmie wore a half-length brown robe over shorts and a homespun tunic. She clutched a notebook and stylus to her breast.

Getting her to leave behind her portable data screen had taken a major effort of persuasion.

If Fiben had imagined for a moment that he saw relief on her face when he picked himself out of the wreckage, he stood corrected. She was all business now.

"What did you see? How heavy were the enemy reinforcements from Port Helenia? How close did Yossy's team get to the skynet battery?"

Good chens and chimmies have died this morning, but all she seems to care about is her damned data!

The space-defense strongpoint had been one of several targets of opportunity. Until now the few piddling ambushes in the mountains had hardly been enough to raise the enemy's notice. Fiben had insisted that the first raid would have to count big. They would never find the enemy so unprepared again.

And yet Gailet had planned the operation in the Vale of Sind around her observers, not the fighting units. To her, information was more important than any harm they might do to the enemy. And to Fiben's surprise the general had agreed.

He shook his head. "There's a lot of smoke over in that direction, so I guess maybe Yossy accomplished something." Fiben dusted himself off. There was a tear in his homespun overalls. "I saw plenty of enemy reinforcements moving about. It's all up here." He tapped his head.

Gailet grimaced, obviously wishing she could hear it all right now. But the plan had been to be away well before this. It was getting awfully late. "Okay, we'll debrief you later. By now this rendezvous must be compromised."

You gotta be kidding, Fiben thought, sarcastically. He turned. "You guys got that thing buried yet?"

The three chims in the kite team were kicking leaves over a low mound under the bulging roots of a fook sap tree. "All done, Fiben." They began collecting their hunting rifles stacked beneath another tree.

Fiben frowned. "I think we'd better get rid of those. They're Terran-make."

Gailet shook her head emphatically. "And replace them with what? If we're stuck with just our six or ten captured Gubru lasers, what can we accomplish? I'm willing to attack the enemy stark naked if I have to, but not unarmed!" Her brown eyes were hot.

Fiben felt his own anger. "*You're* willing to attack. Why not go after the damn birds with a sharpened pencil then! That's your favorite weapon."

"That's not fair! I'm taking all these notes because—"

She never finished the remark. Max interrupted, shouting, "Take cover!"

The sudden whistle of split air became a rocking boom as something white flashed past nearly at treetop level. Fallen leaves whirled and floated out upon the meadow in its wake. Fiben did not remember diving behind a knotted tree root, but he peered over it in time to see the alien craft rise and come about at the crest of the far hill, then begin its return run.

He felt Gailet nearby. Max was to the left, already high in the branches of another tree. The others had flattened themselves over to the right, closer to the verge of the orchard.

Fiben saw one of them raise his weapon as the scoutcraft approached again.

"*No!*" he shouted, realizing he was already too late.

The edge of the meadow erupted. Gobbets of earth were thrown skyward, as if by angry demons. In the blink of an eye the maelstrom ripped through the nearest trees, propelling fragments of leaves, branches, dirt, flesh, and bone through the air in all directions.

Gailet stared at the chaos, slack-jawed. Fiben threw himself onto her just before the rolling explosion swept past them. He felt the wake of the white fighting craft as it roared past. Surviving trees rattled and shook from the momentum of displaced air. A steady rain of debris fell onto Fiben's back.

"Hmm-mmmph!"

Gailet's face emerged from under his arm. She gasped. "Get friggin' offa me before I *suffocate*, you smelly, flea-crackin', moth-eaten . . ."

Fiben saw the enemy scout plane disappear over the

hill. He got up quickly. "Come on," he said, hauling her to her feet. "We've got to get out of here."

Gailet's colorful curses ceased abruptly as she stood up. She gasped at the sight of what the Gubru weapon had done, staring as one does at what is too horrible to believe.

Bits of wood had been stirred vigorously with the grisly remains of three would-be warriors. The chims' rifles lay scattered among the wreckage.

"If you're plannin' on grabbing one of those weapons, you're on your own, sister."

Gailet blinked, then she shook her head and mouthed one word. *No.* She was convinced.

Then she whirled. "Max!"

She started toward where they had last seen her big, dour servant. But just then there came a rumbling sound.

Fiben stopped her. "Troop transports. We haven't got time. If he's alive and can get away he will. Let's go!"

The drone of giant machines drew closer. She resisted, still. "Oh, for Ifni's sake, think of saving your notes!" he urged.

That struck home. Gailet let him drag her along. She stumbled after him for a few paces, then caught her stride. Together they began to run.

Some girl, Fiben thought as they fled under the cover of the trees. *She might be a pain in the ass, but at least she's got spunk. First time she's ever seen anything like that, and she doesn't even throw up.*

Yeah? Another little voice seemed to say inside him. *And when did you ever see such a mess, either? Space battles are neat, clean, compared to this.*

Fiben admitted to himself that the biggest reason he had not puked was that he'd be damned if he'd ever let himself lose his breakfast in front of this particular chimmie. He'd never give her the satisfaction.

Together they splashed across a muddy stream and sought cover away from there.

47

Athaclena

It was all up to Benjamin now.

Athaclena and Robert watched from cover up on the slopes as their friend approached the grounded Gubru convoy. Two other chims accompanied Benjamin, one holding high a flag of truce. Its device was the same as the symbol for the *Library*—the rayed spiral of Galactic Civilization.

The chim emissaries had doffed homespun and were now decked out in silvery formal robes, cut in a style appropriate for bipeds of their form and status. It took courage to approach this way. Although the vehicles were disabled—there had not been a sign of activity for more than half an hour—the three chims had to be wondering what the enemy would do.

"Ten to one the birds try using a robot first," Robert muttered, his eyes intent on the scene below.

Athaclena shook her head. "No bet, Robert. Notice! The door to the center barge is opening."

From their vantage point they could survey the entire clearing. The wreckage of the Howletts Center buildings loomed darkly over one still smoldering hover tank. Its sister, useless barrels drooping, lay canted on its shattered pressure-skirts.

In between the two wrecked fighting machines, from one of the disabled barges, a floating shape emerged.

"Right," Robert sniffed in disgust. It was, indeed, a robot. It, too, carried a flapping banner, another depiction of the rayed spiral.

"Damn birds won't admit chims are above the level of

groundworms, not unless they're forced to," Robert commented. "They'll try to use a machine to handle the parlay. I only hope Benjamin remembers what he's supposed to do."

Athaclena touched Robert's arm, partly to remind him to keep his voice down. "He knows," she said softly. "And he has Elayne Soo to help him." Nevertheless, they shared a formless feeling of helplessness as they watched. This was patron-level business. Clients should not be asked to face a situation such as this alone.

The floating drone—apparently one of the Gubru's sample collection 'bots, hastily adapted to diplomatic functions—came to a halt four meters from the advancing chims, who had already stopped and planted their banner. The robot emitted a squeal of indignant chatter that Athaclena and Robert could not quite make out. The tone, however, was peremptory.

Two of the chims backed up a step, grinning nervously.

"You can do it, Ben!" Robert growled. Athaclena saw knots stand out in his well-muscled arms. If those bulges had been Tymbrimi change glands, instead . . . She shivered at the comparison and looked back to the scene below.

Down in the valley, Chim Benjamin stood rock still, apparently ignoring the machine. He waited. At last its tirade ran down. There was a moment of silence. Then Benjamin made a simple arm motion—exactly as Athaclena had taught him—contemptuously dismissing the nonliving from involvement in sapient affairs.

The robot squawked again, this time louder, and with a trace of desperation.

The chims simply stood and waited, not even deigning to answer the machine. "What hauteur," Robert sighed. "Good going, Ben. Show 'em you got class."

Minutes passed. The tableau held.

"This convoy of Gubru came into the mountains without psi shields!" Athaclena announced suddenly. She touched her right temple as her corona waved. "That or the shields were wrecked in the attack. Either way, I can tell they are growing nervous."

The invaders still possessed some sensors. They would be detecting movement in the forest, runners drawing nearer. The second assault group would arrive soon, this time bearing modern weapons.

The Resistance had kept its greatest power in reserve for the sake of surprise. Antimatter tended to give off resonances that were detectable from a long way away. Now, though, it was time to show all of their cards. By now the enemy would know that they were not safe, even within their armored craft.

Abruptly, and without ceremony, the robot rose and fled to the center barge. Then, after a brief pause, the lock cycled open again and a new pair of emissaries emerged.

"Kwackoo," Robert announced.

Athaclena suppressed the glyph *syrtunu*. Her human friend did have a propensity for proclaiming the obvious.

The fluffy white quadrupeds, loyal clients of the Gubru, approached the parlay point gobbling to each other excitedly. They loomed large as they arrived in front of the chims. A vodor hung from one thick, feathery throat, but the translator machine remained silent.

The three chims folded their hands before themselves and bowed as one, inclining their heads to an angle of about twenty degrees. They straightened and waited.

The Kwackoo just stood there. It was apparent who was ignoring whom this time.

Through the binoculars Athaclena saw Benjamin speak. She cursed the need to watch all this without any way to listen in.

The chim's words were effective, however. The Kwackoo chirped and blatted in flustered outrage. Through the vodor came words too faint to pick out, but the results were nearly instantaneous. Benjamin did not wait for them to finish. He and his companions picked up their banner, turned about, and marched away.

"Good fellow," Robert said in satisfaction. He knew chims. Right now their shoulder blades must be itching terribly, yet they sauntered coolly.

The lead Kwackoo stopped speaking. It stared, nonplussed. Then it began hopping and giving out sharp cries. Its partner, too, seemed quite agitated. Now those on the hill could hear the amplified voice of the vodor, commanding ". . . come back! . . ." over and over again.

The chims continued walking toward the line of trees until, at last, Athaclena and Robert heard the *word*.

". . . come back . . . PLEASE! . . ."

Human and Tymbrimi looked at each other and shared a smile. *That* was half of what this fight had been about.

Benjamin and his party halted abruptly. They turned

around and sauntered back. With the spiral standard in place once more they stood silently, waiting. At last, quivering from what must have been terrible humiliation, the feathered emissaries bowed.

It was a shallow bow—hardly a bending of two out of four knees—but it served. Indentured clients of the Gubru had recognized as their equals the indentured clients of human beings. "They might have chosen death over this," Athaclena whispered in awe, though she had planned for this very thing. "The Kwackoo are nearly sixty thousand Earth years old. Neo-chimpanzees have been sapient for only three *centuries*, and are the clients of wolflings." She knew Robert would not be offended by her choice of words. "The Kwackoo are far enough along in Uplift that they have the right to choose death over this. They and the Gubru must be stupefied, and have not thought out the implications. They probably can barely believe it is happening."

Robert grinned. "Just wait till they hear the rest of it. They'll wish they'd chosen the easy way out."

The chims answered the bow at the same angle. Then, with that distasteful formality out of the way, one of the giant avioids spoke quickly, its vodor mumbling an Anglic translation.

"The Kwackoo are probably demanding to speak with the leaders of the ambush," Robert commented, and Athaclena agreed.

Benjamin betrayed his nervousness by using his hands as he replied. But that was no real problem. He gestured at the ruins, at the destroyed hover tanks, at the helpless barges and the forest on all sides, where vengeful forces were converging to finish the job.

"He's telling them he *is* the leader."

That was the script, of course. Athaclena had written it, amazed all the while how easily she had adapted from the subtle Tymbrimi art of dissemblement to the more blatant, human technique of outright lying.

Benjamin's hand gestures helped her follow the conversation. Through empathy and her own imagination, she felt she could almost fill in the rest.

We have lost our patrons, Benjamin had rehearsed saying. *You and your masters have taken them from us. We miss them, and long for their return. Still, we know that helpless mourning would not make them proud of us. Only by action may we show how well we have been uplifted.*

*"We are therefore doing as they have taught us—behaving
as sapient creatures of thought and honor.*

*'In honor's name then, and by the Codes of War, I now
demand that you and your masters offer their parole, or face
the consequences of our legal and righteous wrath!"*

"He is doing it," Athaclena whispered half in wonder.

Robert coughed as he tried not to laugh aloud. The
Kwackoo seemed to grow more and more distressed as
Benjamin spoke. When he finished, the feathery quadrupeds
hopped and squawked. They puffed and preened and ob-
jected loudly.

Benjamin, though, would not be bluffed. He referred to
his wrist chronometer then spoke three words.

The Kwackoo suddenly stopped protesting. Orders must
have arrived, for all at once they bowed again, swiveled, and
sped back to the center barge at a gallop.

The sun had risen above the line of hills to the east.
Splashes of morning light blazed through the lanes of shattered trees. It grew warm out on the parlay ground, but the
chims stood and waited. At intervals Benjamin glanced to his
watch and called out the time remaining.

At the edge of the forest Athaclena saw their special
weapons team begin setting up their only antimatter projector. Certainly the Gubru were aware of it, too.

She heard Robert softly counting out the minutes.

Finally—in fact nearly at the very last moment—the
hatches of all three hover craft opened. From each emerged a
procession. The entire complement of Gubru, dressed in the
glistening robes of senior patrons, led the way. They crooned
a high-pitched song, accompanied by the basso of their faithful Kwackoo.

The pageantry was steeped in ancient tradition. It had its
roots in epochs long before life had crawled ashore on the
Earth. It wasn't hard to imagine how nervous Benjamin and
the others must feel as those to be paroled assembled before
them. Robert's own mouth felt dry. "Remember to *bow*
again," he urged in a whisper.

Athaclena smiled, having the advantage of her corona.
"Have no fear, Robert. He will remember." And indeed,
Benjamin folded his hands before him in the deeply respectful fashion of a junior client greeting a senior patron. The
chims bowed low.

Only a flash of white betrayed the fact that Benjamin was grinning from ear to ear.

"Robert," she said, nodding in satisfaction. "Your people have done very well by theirs, in only four hundred years."

"Don't give us the credit," he answered. "It was all there in the raw from the start."

The paroled avians departed toward the Valley of the Sind on foot. No doubt they would be picked up before long. Even if they were not, Athaclena had ordered that word go out. They were to reach home base unmolested. Any chim who touched one feather would be outlawed, his plasm dumped into sewers, his gene-line extinguished. The matter was that serious.

The procession disappeared down the mountain road. Then the hard work began.

Crews of chims hurried to strip the abandoned vehicles in the precious time remaining before retribution arrived. Gorillas chuffed impatiently, grooming and signing to one another as they awaited loads to carry off into the hills.

By then Athaclena had already moved her command post to a spine-covered ridge two miles farther into the mountains. She watched through binoculars as the last salvage was loaded and hauled away, leaving nearly empty hulks under the shadows of the ruined buildings.

Robert had left much earlier, at Athaclena's insistence. He was departing again on another mission tomorrow and needed to get his rest.

Her corona waved, and she *kenned* Benjamin before his softly slapping feet could be heard padding up the trail. When he spoke his voice was somber.

"General, we've had word by semaphore that the attacks in the Sind failed. A few Eatee construction sites were blown up, but the rest of the assault was nearly a total disaster."

Athaclena closed her eyes. She had expected as much. They had too many security problems down below, for one thing. Fiben had suspected the town-side resistance was compromised by traitors.

And yet Athaclena had not disallowed the attacks. They had served a valuable purpose by distracting the Gubru defense forces, keeping their quick-reaction fighters busy far from here. She only hoped that not too many chims had lost their lives drawing the invader's ire.

"The day balances out," she told her aide. Their victories would have to be symbolic, she knew. To try to expel the enemy with forces such as theirs would be futile. With her growing knack at metaphors she likened it to a caterpillar attempting to move a tree.

No, what we win, we will achieve through subtlety.

Benjamin cleared his throat. Athaclena looked down at him. "You still do not believe we should have let them leave alive," she told him.

He nodded. "No, ser, I do not. I think I understand some of what you told me about symbolism and all that . . . and I'm proud you seem to think we handled the parole ceremony all right. But I still believe we should've burned them all."

"Out of revenge?"

Benjamin shrugged. They both knew that was how the majority of the chims felt. They couldn't care less about symbols. The races of Earth tended to look upon all the bowing and fine class distinctions of the Galactics as the mincing foolishness of a mired, decadent civilization.

"You know that's not what I think," Benjamin said. "I'd go along with your logic—about us scoring a real coup here today just by getting them to talk to us—if it weren't for one thing."

"What thing is that?"

"The birds had a chance to snoop around the center. They saw traces of Uplift. And I can't rule out the possibility they caught a glimpse of the gorillas *themselves*, through the trees!" Benjamin shook his head. "I just don't think we should've allowed them to walk out of here after that," he said.

Athaclena put a hand on her aide's shoulder. She did not speak because there did not seem to be anything to say.

How could she explain it to Benjamin?

Syulff-kuonn took form over her head, whirling with satisfaction at the progress of things, things her father had planned.

No, she could not explain to Benjamin that she had insisted on bringing the gorillas along, on making them part of the raid, as a step in a long, involved, and very practical joke.

48

Fiben and Gailet

"Keep your head down!" Fiben growled.

"Will you stop snapping at me?" Gailet answered hotly. She lifted her eyes just to the tops of the surrounding grass stems. "I just want to see if—"

The words cut off as Fiben swept her supporting arms out from under her. She landed with a grunt of expelled air and rolled over spitting dirt. "You pit-scratching, flea-bitten—"

Her eyes remained eloquent even with Fiben's hand clamped firmly over her mouth. "I told you," he whispered. "With their sensors, if you can see them it means they've *got* to see you. Our only chance is to crawl like worms until we can find a way to blend back into the civilian chim population.!"

From not far away came the hum of agricultural machinery. The sound had drawn them here. If they could only get close enough to mingle with the farmers, they might yet escape the invaders' dragnet.

For all Fiben knew, he and Gailet might be the only survivors of the ill-fated uprising in the valley. It was hard to imagine how the mountain guerrillas under Athaclena's command could have done any better. The insurrection seemed all washed up from where he lay.

He drew back his hand from Gailet's mouth. *If looks could kill*, he thought, contemplating the expression in her eyes. With her hair matted and mud-splattered, she was hardly the picture of the serene chimmie intellectual.

"I . . . thought . . . you . . . said . . ." she whispered deliberately, emphasizing calmness, "that the enemy couldn't detect us if we wear only native-made materials."

"That's if they're being lazy and *only* counting on their secret weapon. But don't forget they've also got infrared, radar, seismic sonar, psi—" He stopped suddenly. A low whine approached from his left. If it was the harvester they had heard before, there might be a chance to catch a ride.

"Wait here," he whispered.

Gailet grabbed his wrist. "No! I'm coming with you!" She looked quickly left and right, then lowered her eyes. "Don't . . . don't leave me alone."

Fiben bit his lip. "All right. But stay down low, right behind me."

They moved single file, hugging the ground. Slowly the whine grew louder. Soon Fiben felt a faint tingling up the back of his neck.

Gravitics, he thought. *It's close.*

How close he didn't realize until the machine slipped over the grasstops, coming into view just two meters away.

He had been expecting a large vehicle. But this thing was about the size of a basketball and was covered with silvery and glassy knobs—sensors. It bobbed gently in the afternoon breeze, regarding them.

Aw hell. He sighed, sitting up on his haunches and letting his arms drop in resignation. Not far away he heard faint voices. No doubt this thing's owners.

"It's a battle drone, isn't it?" Gailet asked tiredly.

He nodded. "A sniffer. Cheap model, I think. But good enough to find and hold us."

"What do we do?"

He shrugged. "What *can* we do? We'd better surrender."

Behind his back, however, he sifted through the dark soil. His fingers closed around a smooth stone.

The distant voices were coming this way. *What th' heck,* he thought.

"Listen, Gailet. When I move, duck. Get outta here. Get your notes to Athaclena, if she's still alive."

Then, before she could ask any questions, he let out a shout and hurled the stone with all his might.

Several things happened all at once. Pain erupted in Fiben's right wrist. There was a flash of light, so bright that it dazzled him. Then, during his leap forward, countless stinging pinpricks rained up and down his chest.

As he sailed toward the thing a sudden, strange feeling overcame Fiben, one that said that he had performed this act before—lived this particular moment of violence—not once or twice, but a hundred times, in a hundred prior lives. The wave of familiarity, hooked on the flickering edge of memory, washed over him as he dove through the drone's pulsing gravitic field to wrap himself over the alien machine.

The world bucked and spun as the thing tried to throw him off. Its laser blasted at his shadow and grass fires broke out. Fiben held on for his life as the fields and the sky blended in a sickening blur.

The induced sense of *déjà vu* actually seemed to help! Fiben felt as if he had done this countless times! A small, rational corner of his mind knew that he hadn't, but the memory misfunction said different and gave him a false confidence he badly needed right then as he dared to loosen the grip of his injured right hand and fumbled for the robot's control box.

Ground and sky merged. Fiben tore a fingernail prying at the lid, breaking the lock. He reached in, grabbed wires.

The machine spun and careened, as if sensing his intention. Fiben's legs lost their grip and whipped out. He was whirled around like a rag doll. When his left hand gave way he held on only by a weakening grip on the wires themselves—round and round and round. . . .

At that moment only one thing in the world was not a blur: the lens of the robot's laser, directly in front of him.

Goodbye, he thought, and closed his eyes.

Then something tore loose. He flew away, still holding wires in his right hand. When crunching impact came, it was almost anticlimactic. He cried out and rolled up just short of one of the smoldering fires.

Oh, there was pain, all right. Fiben's ribs felt as if one of the big female gorillas at the Howletts Center had been affectionate with him all night. He had been shot at least twice. Still, he had expected to die. No matter what came after this, it was good just to be alive.

He blinked away dust and soot. Five meters away the wreckage of the alien probe hissed and sputtered inside a ring of blackened, smoking grass. So much for the vaunted quality of Galactic hardware.

What Eatee shyster sold the Gubru that piece of shit? Fiben wondered. *I don't care, even if it was a Jophur made of ten smelly sap rings, I'd kiss him right now, I really would.*

Excited voices. Running feet. Fiben felt a sudden hope.

He had expected Gubru to come after their downed probe. But these were chims! He winced and held his side as he managed to stand. He smiled.

The expression froze on his face when he saw who was approaching.

"Well, well, what do we have here? Mr. Bluecard himself! Looks like you've been running more obstacle courses, college boy. You just don't seem to know when you're beat."

It was a tall chen with carefully shaved facial hair and a mustache, elegantly waxed and curled. Fiben recognized the leader of the Probationer gang at the Ape's Grape. The one calling himself Irongrip.

Of all the chims in all the world, why did it have to be him?

Others arrived. The bright zipsuits bore an added feature, a sash and arm patch, each bearing the same sigil . . . a claw outstretched, three sharp talons glistening in holographic threat.

They gathered around him carrying modified saber rifles, obviously members of the new collaborators' militia he and Gailet had heard rumors of.

"Remember me, college boy?" Irongrip asked, grinning. "Yes, I thought you would. I sure do remember you."

Fiben sighed as he saw Gailet Jones brought forward, held firmly by two other Probationers. "Are you all right?" she asked softly. He could not read the expression in her eyes. Fiben nodded. There seemed to be little to say.

"Come on, my young genetic beauties." Irongrip laughed as he took Fiben hard just above his wounded right wrist. "We've got some people we want you to meet. And this time, there won't be any distractions."

Fiben's gaze was torn away from Gailet's as a jerk on his arm sent him stumbling. He lacked the strength to put up a useless struggle.

As his captors dragged him ahead of Gailet, he had his first chance to look around and saw that they were only a few hundred meters from the edge of Port Helenia! A pair of wide-eyed chims in work dungarees watched from the running boards of a nearby cultivator.

Fiben and Gailet were being taken toward a small gate in the alien wall, the barrier that undulated complacently over the countryside like a net settled firmly over their lives.

49

Galactics

The Suzerain of Propriety displayed its agitation by huffing and dancing a brief series of hops on its Perch of Declamation. The half-formed squirms had actually delayed appearing before its judgment, withholding the news for more than a planetary rotation!

True, the survivors of the mountain ambush were still in shock. Their first thought had been to report to military command. And the military, busy cleaning up the last of the abortive insurrections in the nearby flatlands, had made them wait. What, after all, was a minor scuffle in the hills compared with a nearly effective assault on the deep-space defense battery?

The Suzerain could well understand how such mistakes were made. And yet it was frustrating. The affair in the mountains was actually far more significant than any of the other outbreaks of wild guerrilla warfare.

"You should have extinguished—caused an end—eliminated yourselves!"

The Suzerain chirped and danced out its chastisement before the Gubru scientists. The specialists still looked ruffled and unpreened from their long trek out of the hills. Now they slumped further in dejection.

"In accepting parole you have injured—caused harm—reduced our propriety and honor," the Suzerain finished chiding.

If they had been military the high priest might have demanded reparations from these and their families. But most of their escorts had been killed, and scientists were often less concerned or knowledgeable in matters of propriety than soldiers.

The Suzerain decided to forgive them.

"Nevertheless, your decision is understood—is given sanction. We shall abide by your parole."

The technicians danced in relief. They would not suffer humiliation or worse upon returning to their homes. Their solemn word would not be repudiated.

The parole would be costly however. These scientists had to depart from the Garth system at once and not be replaced for at least a year. Furthermore, an equal number of human beings had to be released from detention!

The Suzerain suddenly had an idea. This brought on a rare flutter of that strange emotion, *amusement*. It would order sixteen humans freed, all right, but the mountain chimpanzees would not be reunited with their dangerous masters. The released humans would be sent to Earth!

That would certainly satisfy the propriety of the parole. The solution would be expensive, true, but not nearly as much as letting such creatures loose again on the main continent of Garth!

It was stunning to contemplate that neo-chimpanzees might have achieved what these reported they had done in the mountains. How could it be? The proto-clients they had observed in town and in the valley hardly seemed capable of such finesse.

Might there, indeed, be humans out there still?

The thought was daunting, and the Suzerain did not see how it would be possible. According to census figures the number unaccounted for was too small to be significant anyway. Statistically, all of those should simply be dead.

Of course the gas bombings would have to be stepped up. The new Suzerain of Cost and Caution would complain, for the program had proved very expensive. But now the Suzerain of Propriety would side with the military completely.

There was a faint stirring. The Suzerain of Propriety felt a twinge inside. Was it an early sign of a change of sexual state? It should not begin yet, when things were still so unsettled, and dominance not yet decided among the three peers. The molting must wait until propriety had been served, until consensus had been reached, so that it would be clear who was strongest!

The Suzerain chirped a prayer to the lost Progenitors, and the others immediately crooned in response.

If only there was some way to be sure which way the battles were going, out in the Galactic swirl! Had the dolphin ship been found yet? Were the fleets of some alliance even now approaching the returned Ancient Ones to call up the end of all things?

Had the time of Change already begun?

If the priest were certain that Galactic Law had indeed broken down irreparably, it would feel free to ignore this unpalatable parole and its implied recognition of neo-chimpanzee sapiency.

There were consolations, of course. Even with humans to guide them, the near-animals would never know the right ways to take advantage of that recognition. That was the way of wolfling-type species. Ignoring the subtleties of the ancient Galactic culture, they barged ahead using the direct approach, and nearly always died.

Consolation, it chirped. *Yes, consolation and victory.*

There was one more matter to take care of—potentially, the most important of all. The priest addressed the leader of the expedition again.

"Your final parole agreement was to avoid—to abjure—to forswear ever visiting that site again."

The scientists danced agreement. One small place on the surface of Garth was forbidden the Gubru until the stars fell, or until the rules were changed.

"And yet, before the attack you found—did discover— did uncover traces of mysterious activity—of gene meddling—of secret Uplift?"

That too had been in their report. The Suzerain questioned them carefully about details. There had only been time for a cursory examination, but the hints were compelling. The implications staggering.

Up in those mountains the chimpanzees were hiding a pre-sentient race! Prior to the invasion, they and their human patrons had been engaging in Uplift of a new client species!

So! The Suzerain danced. The data recovered from the Tymbrimi cairn was no lie! Somehow, by some miracle, this catastrophe world has given birth to a treasure! And now, in spite of Gubru mastery of the surface and the sky, the Earthlings continued to hoard their discovery to themselves!

No wonder the planetary Branch Library had been ransacked of its Uplift files! They had tried to hide the evidence.

But now, the Suzerain rejoiced, *we know of this wonder*.

"You are dismissed—released—set upon your ships for home," it told the bedraggled scientists. Then the Suzerain turned to its Kwackoo aides, gathered below its perch.

"Contact the Suzerain of Beam and Talon," it said with unaccustomed brevity. "Tell my peer that I wish a colloquy at once." One of the fluffy quadrupeds bowed at once, then scurried off to call the commander of the armed forces.

The Suzerain of Propriety stood still upon its perch, disallowed by custom from setting foot upon the surface until the ceremonies of protection had been completed.

Its weight shifted from time to time, and it rested its beak on its chest while standing deep in thought.

PART FOUR

Traitors

Accuse not Nature, she hath done her part;
Do thou but thine.

JOHN MILTON, *Paradise Lost*

50

Government in Hiding

The messenger sat on a couch in the corner of the Council Room, holding a blanket around his shoulders while he sipped from a steaming cup of soup. Now and then the young chen shivered, but mostly he looked exhausted. His damp hair still lay in tangled mats from the icy swim that had brought him on the last leg of his dangerous journey.

It's a wonder he made it here at all, Megan Oneagle thought, watching him. *All the spies and recon teams we sent ashore, carrying the finest equipment—none ever returned. But this little chim makes it to us, sailing a tiny raft made of cut trees, with homespun canvas sails.*

Carrying a message from my son.

Megan wiped her eyes again, remembering the courier's first words to her after swimming the last stretch of underground caves to their deep island redoubt.

"Captain Oneagle sends his felic— his felicitations, ma'am."

He had drawn forth a packet—waterproofed in oli tree sap—and offered it to her, then collapsed into the arms of the medical techs.

A message from Robert, she thought in wonder. *He is alive. He is free. He helps lead an army.* She didn't know whether to exult or shudder at the thought.

It was a thing to be proud of, for sure. Robert might be the sole adult human loose on the surface of Garth, right now. And if his "army" was little more than a ragged band of simian guerrillas, well, at least they had accomplished more

than her own carefully hoarded remnants of the official planetary militia had.

If he had made her proud, Robert had also astonished
her. Might there be more substance to the boy than she had
thought before? Something brought out by adversity, perhaps?

*There may be more of his father in him than I'd wanted
to see.*

Sam Tennace was a starship pilot who stopped at Garth
every five years or so, one of Megan's three spacer husbands.
Each was home for only a few months at a stretch—almost never
at the same time—then off again. Other fems might not have
been able to deal with such an arrangement, but what suited
spacers also met her needs as a politician and career woman.
Of the three, only Sam Tennace had given her a child.

And I never wanted my son to be a hero, she realized.
*As critical as I have been of him, I guess I never really
wanted him to be like Sam at all.*

For one thing, if Robert had not been so resourceful he
might be safe now—interned on the islands with the rest of
the human population, pursuing his playboy hobbies among
his friends—instead of engaged in a desperate, useless struggle against an omnipotent enemy.

Well, she reassured herself. *His letter probably exaggerates.*

To her left, mutterings of amazement grew ever more
pronounced as the government in exile pored over the message, printed on tree bark in homemade ink. "Son of a bitch!"
she heard Colonel Millchamp curse. "So *that's* how they
always knew where we were, what we were up to, before we
even got started!"

Megan moved closer to the table. "Please summarize,
colonel."

Millchamp looked up at her. The portly, red-faced militia officer shook several sheets until someone grabbed his arm
and pried them out of his hand.

"Optical fibers!" he cried.

Megan shook her head. "I beg your pardon?"

"They *doped* them. Every string, telephone cable, communications pipe . . . almost every piece of electronics on the
planet! They're all tuned to resonate back on a probability
band the damn birds can broadcast . . ." Colonel Millchamp's
voice choked on his anger. He swiveled and walked away.

Megan's puzzlement must have shown.

"Perhaps I can explain, madam coordinator," said John Kylie, a tall man with the sallow complexion of a lifetime spacer. Kylie's peacetime profession was captain of an in-system civilian freighter. His merchant vessel had taken part in the mockery of a space battle, one of the few survivors—if that was the right term. Overpowered, battered, finally reduced to peppering Gubru fighting planetoids with its comm laser, the wreck of the *Esperanza* only made it back to Port Helenia because the enemy was leisurely in consolidating the Gimelhai system. Its skipper now served as Megan's naval advisor.

Kylie's expression was stricken. "Madam coordinator, do you remember that excellent deal we made, oh, twenty years ago, for a turnkey electronics and photonics factory? It was a state-of-the-art, midget-scale auto-fac—perfect for a small colony world such as ours."

Megan nodded. "Your uncle was coordinator then. I believe your first merchant command was to finalize negotiations and bring the factory home to Garth."

Kylie nodded. He looked crestfallen. "One of its main products is optical fibers. A few said the bargain we got from the Kwackoo was just too good to be true. But who could have imagined they might have something like this in mind? So far in the future? Just on the off chance that they might someday want to—"

Megan gasped. "The Kwackoo! They're clients of—"

"Of the Gubru." Kylie nodded. "The damn birds must have thought, even then, that something like this might someday happen."

Megan recalled what Uthacalthing had tried to teach her, that the ways of the Galactics are long ways, and patient as the planets in their orbits.

Someone else cleared his throat. It was Major Prathachulthorn, the short, powerfully built Terragens Marines officer. He and his small detachment were the only professional soldiers left after the space battle and the hopeless gesture of defiance at the Port Helenia space-field. Millchamp and Kylie held reserve commissions.

"This is most grave, madam coordinator," Prathachulthorn said. "Optical fibers made at that factory have been incorporated into almost every piece of military and civilian equipment manufactured on the planet. They are integrated into nearly every building. Can we have confidence in your son's findings?"

Megan nearly shrugged, but her politician's instincts stopped her in time. *How the hell would I know?* she thought. *The boy is a stranger to me.* She glanced at the small chen who had nearly died bringing Robert's message to her. She had never imagined Robert could inspire such dedication.

Megan wondered if she was jealous.

A woman Marine spoke next. "The report is co-signed by the Tymbrimi Athaclena," Lieutenant Lydia McCue pointed out. The young officer pursed her lips. "That's a second source of verification," she suggested.

"With all respect, Lydia," Major Prathachulthorn replied. "The tym is barely more than a child."

"She's Ambassador Uthacalthing's daughter!" Kylie snapped. "And chim technicians helped perform the experiments as well."

Prathachulthorn shook his head. "Then we have no truly qualified witnesses."

Several councillors gasped. The sole neo-chimpanzee member, Dr. Suzinn Benirshke, blushed and looked down at the table. But Prathachulthorn didn't even seem to realize he'd said anything insulting. The major wasn't known to be strong on tact. *Also, he's a Marine,* Megan reminded herself. The corps was the elite Terragens fighting service with the smallest number of dolphin and chim members. For that matter, the Marines recruited mostly males, a last bastion of oldtime sexism.

Commander Kylie sifted through the rough-cut pages of Robert Oneagle's report. "Still you must agree, major, the scenario is plausible. It would explain our setbacks, and total failure to establish contact, either with the islands or the mainland."

Major Prathachulthorn nodded after a moment. "Plausible, yes. Nevertheless, we should perform our own investigations before we commit ourselves to acting as if it is true."

"What's the matter, major?" Kylie asked. "You don't like the idea of putting down your phase-burner rifle and picking up bows and arrows?"

Prathachulthorn's reply was surprisingly mild. "Not at all, ser, so long as the enemy is similarly equipped. The problem lies in the fact that he is not."

Silence reigned for long moments. No one seemed to

have anything to say. The pause ended when Colonel Millchamp returned to the table. He slammed the flat of his hand down. "Either way, what's the point in waiting?"

Megan frowned. "What do you mean, colonel?"

Millchamp growled. "I mean what good do our forces do down here?" he demanded. "We're all going slowly stir-crazy. Meanwhile, at this very moment, Earth herself may be fighting for her life!"

"There's no such thing as *this very moment* across inter-stellar space," Commander Kylie commented. "Simultaneity is a myth. The concept is imbedded in Anglic and other Earth tongues, but—"

"Oh, revert the metaphysics!" Millchamp snapped. "What matters is that we can hurt Earth's enemies!" He picked up the tree-bark leaves. "Thanks to the guerrillas, we know where the Gubru have placed many of their major planet-based yards. No matter *what* damned Library-spawned tricks the birds have got up their feathers, they can't prevent us from launching our flicker-swivvers at them!"

"But—"

"We have three hidden away—there weren't any used in the space battle, and the Gubru can't know we have any of 'em. If those missiles are supposed to be good against the Tandu, damn their seven-chambered hearts, they'll surely suffice for Gubru ground targets!"

"And what good will that do?" Lieutenant McCue asked mildly.

"We can bend a few Gubru beaks! Ambassador Uthacal-thing told us that symbols are important in Galactic warfare. Right now they can pretend that we hardly put up a fight at all. But a symbolic strike, one that hurt them, would tell the whole Five Galaxies that we won't be pushed around!"

Megan Oneagle pinched the bridge of her nose. She spoke with eyes closed. "I have always found it odd that my Amerindian ancestors' concept of 'counting coup' should have a place in a hypertechnological galaxy." She looked up. "It may, indeed, come to that, if we can find no other way to be effective.

"But you'll recall that Uthacalthing also advised patience." She shook her head. "Please sit down, Colonel Millchamp. Everybody. I'm determined not to throw our strength away in a gesture, not until I know it's the only thing left to do against the enemy.   •

"Remember, nearly every human on the planet is hostage on the islands, their lives dependent on doses of Gubru antidote. And on the mainland there are the poor chims, for all intents abandoned, alone."

Along the conference the officers sat downcast. *They're frustrated*, Megan thought. *And I can't blame them*.

When war had loomed, when they had begun planning ways to resist an invasion, nobody had ever suggested a contingency like this. Perhaps a people more experienced in the sophistications of the Great Library—in the arcane art of war that the aeons-old Galactics knew—might have been better prepared. But the Gubru's tactics had made a shambles of their modest defense plans.

She had not added her final reason for refusing to sanction a gesture. Humans were notoriously unsophisticated at the game of Galactic punctilio. A blow struck for honor might be bungled, instead giving the enemy excuse for even greater horrors.

Oh, the irony. If Uthacalthing was right, it was a little Earthship, halfway across the Five Galaxies from here, that had *precipitated* the crisis!

Earthlings certainly did have a knack for making trouble for themselves. They'd always had that talent.

Megan looked up as the small chen from the mainland, Robert's messenger, approached the table, still wearing his blanket. His dark brown eyes were troubled.

"Yes, Petri?" she asked.

The chim bowed.

"Ma'am, th' doctor wants me to go to bed now."

She nodded. "That's fine, Petri. I'm sure we'll want to debrief you some more, later . . . ask you some more questions. But right now you should rest."

Petri nodded. "Yes'm. Thank you, ma'am. But there was somethin' else. Somethin' I'd better tell you while I remember."

"Yes? What is it?"

The chen looked uncomfortable. He glanced at the watching humans and back at Megan. "It's personal, ma'am. Somethin' Captain Oneagle asked me to memorize an' tell you."

Megan smiled. "Oh, very well. Will you all excuse me for a moment, please?"

She walked with Petri over to the far end of the room

There she sat down to bring her eyes level with the little chim. "Tell me what Robert said."

Petri nodded. His eyes went unfocused. "Captain Oneagle said to tell you that th' Tymbrimi Athaclena is actually doin' most of the organizing for th' army."

Megan nodded. She had suspected as much. Robert might have found new resources, new depths, but he was not and never would be a born leader.

Petri went on. "Cap'n Oneagle told me to tell you that it was important that th' Tymbrimi Athaclena have honorary patron status to our chims, legally."

Again, Megan nodded. "Smart. We can vote it and send word back."

But the little chim shook his head. "Uh, ma'am. We couldn't wait for that. So, uh, I'm supposed to tell you that Captain Oneagle an' th' Tymbrimi Athaclena have sealed a . . . a *consort* bond . . . I think that's what it's called. I . . ."

His voice trailed off, for Megan had stood up.

Slowly, she turned to the wall and rested her forehead against the cool stone. *That damn fool of a boy!* part of her cursed.

It was the only thing they could do, another part answered.

So, now I'm a mother-in-law, the most ironic voice added.

There would certainly be no grandchildren from *this* union. That was not what interspecies consort marriages were for. But there were other implications.

Behind her, the council debated. Again and again they turned over the options, coming up dry as they had for months now.

Oh, if only Uthacalthing had made it here, Megan thought. *We need his experience, his wry wisdom and humor. We could talk, like we used to. And maybe, he could explain to me these things that make a mother feel so lost.*

She confessed to herself that she missed the Tymbrimi Ambassador. She missed him more than any of her three husbands and more even, God help her, than she missed her own strange son.

51

Uthacalthing

It was fascinating to watch Kault play with a ne' squirrel, one of the native animals of these southern plains. He coaxed the small creature closer by holding out ripe nuts in his great Thennanin hands. He had been at it for over an hour while they waited out the hot noonday sun under the cover of a thick cluster of thorny bramble.

Uthacalthing wondered at the sight. The universe never seemed about to cease surprising him. Even bluff, oblivious, obvious Kault was a perpetual source of amazement.

Quivering nervously, the ne' squirrel gathered its courage. It took two more hops toward the huge Thennanin and stretched out its paws. It plucked up one of the nuts.

Astonishing. How did Kault do it?

Uthacalthing rested in the muggy shade. He did not recognize the vegetation here in the uplands overlooking the estuary where his pinnace had come down, but he felt he was growing familiar with the scents, the rhythms, the gently throbbing pain of daily life that surged and flowed through and all around the deceptively quiet glade.

His corona brought him touches from tiny predators, now waiting out the hot part of the day, but soon to resume stalking even smaller prey. There were no large animals, of course, but Uthacalthing *kenned* a swarm of ground-hugging insectoids grubbing through the detritus nearby, seeking tidbits for their queen.

The tense little ne' squirrel hovered between caution and gluttony as it approached once more to feed from Kault's outstretched hand.

He should not be able to do that. Uthacalthing wondered why the squirrel trusted the Thennanin, so huge, so intimidating and powerful. Life here on Garth was nervous, *paranoid* in the wake of the Bururalli catastrophe—whose deathly pall still hung over these steppes far east and south of the Mountains of Mulun.

Kault could not be soothing the creature as a Tymbrimi might—by glyph-singing to it in gentle tones of empathy. A Thennanin had all the psi sense of a stone.

But Kault spoke to the creature in his own highly inflected dialect of Galactic. Uthacalthing listened.

"Know you—sight-sound-image—an essence of destiny, yours? Little one? Carry you—genes-essence-destiny—the fate of star-treaders, your descendants?"

The ne' squirrel quivered, cheeks full. The native animal seemed mesmerized as Kault's crest puffed up and deflated, as his breathing slits sighed with every moist exhalation. The Thennanin could not commune with the creature, not as Uthacalthing might. And yet, the squirrel somehow appeared to sense Kault's love.

How ironic, Uthacalthing thought. Tymbrimi lived their lives awash in the everflowing music of life, and yet he did not personally identify with this small animal. It was one of hundreds of millions, after all. Why should he care about this particular individual?

Yet *Kault* loved the creature. Without empathy sense, without any direct being-to-being link, he cherished it *entirely in abstract*. He loved what the little thing represented, its potential.

Many humans still claim that one can have empathy without psi, Uthacalthing pondered. To "put one's self into another's shoes," went the ancient metaphor. He had always thought it to be one of their quaint pre-Contact ideas, but now he wasn't so certain. Perhaps Earthlings were sort of midway between Thennanin and Tymbrimi in this matter of how one empathized with others.

Kault's people passionately believed in Uplift, in the potential of diverse life forms eventually to achieve sapiency. The long-lost Progenitors of Galactic culture had commanded this, billions of years ago, and the Thennanin Clan took the injunction very seriously. Their uncompromising fanaticism on this issue went beyond being admirable. At times—as

during the present Galactic turmoil—it made them terribly
dangerous.

But now, ironically, Uthacalthing was counting on that
fanaticism. He hoped to lure it into action of his own design.

The ne' squirrel snatched one last nut from Kault's open
hand and then decided it had enough. With a swish of its
fan-shaped tail it scooted off into the undergrowth. Kault
turned to look at Uthacalthing, his throat slits flapping as he
breathed.

"I have studied genome reports gathered by the Earthling ecologists," the Thennanin Consul said. "This planet had
impressive potential, only a few millennia ago. It should
never have been ceded to the Bururalli. The loss of Garth's
higher life forms was a terrible tragedy."

"The Nahalli were punished for what their clients did,
weren't they?" Uthacalthing asked, though he already knew
the answer.

"Aye. They were reverted to client status and put under
foster care to a responsible elder patron clan. My own, in
fact. It is a most sad case."

"Why is that?"

"Because the Nahalli are actually quite a mature and
elegant people. They simply did not understand the nuances
required in uplifting pure carnivores and so failed horribly
with their Bururalli clients. But the error was not theirs alone.
The Galactic Uplift Institute must take part in the blame."

Uthacalthing suppressed a human-style smile. Instead
his corona spiraled out a faint glyph, invisible to Kault.
"Would good news here on Garth help the Nahalli?" he
asked.

"Certainly." Kault expressed the equivalent of a shrug
with his flapping crest. "We Thennanin were not in any way
associated with the Nahalli when the catastrophe occurred, of
course, but that changed when they were demoted and given
under our guidance. Now, by adoption, my clan shares responsibility for this wounded place. It is why a consul was
sent here, to make certain the Earthlings do not do even
more harm to this sorry world."

"And have they?"

Kault's eyes closed and opened again. "Have they what?"

"Have the Earthlings done a bad job, here?"

Kault's crest flapped again. "No. Our peoples may be at
war, theirs and mine, but I have found no new grievances

here to tally against them. Their ecological management program was exemplary.

"However, I do plan to file a report concerning the activities of the Gubru."

Uthacalthing believed he could interpret bitterness in Kault's voice inflections. They had already seen signs of the collapse of the environmental recovery effort. Two days ago they had passed a reclamation station, now abandoned, its sampling traps and test cages rusting. The gene-storage bins had gone rancid after refrigeration failed.

An agonized note had been left behind, telling of the choice of a neo-chimpanzee ecology aide—who had decided to abandon his post in order to help a sick human colleague. It would be a long journey to the coast for an antidote to the coercion gas.

Uthacalthing wondered if they ever made it. Clearly the facility had been thoroughly dosed. The nearest outpost of civilization was very far from here, even by hover car.

Obviously, the Gubru were content to leave the station unmanned. "If this pattern holds, it must be documented," Kault said. "I am glad you allowed me to persuade you to lead us back toward inhabited regions, so we can collect more data on these crimes."

This time Uthacalthing did smile at Kault's choice of words. "Perhaps we will find something of interest," he agreed.

They resumed their journey when the sun, Gimelhai, had slipped down somewhat from its burning zenith.

The plains southeast of the Mulun range stretched like the undulating wavetops of a gently rolling sea, frozen in place by the solidity of earth. Unlike the Vale of Sind and the open lands on the other side of the mountains, here there were no signs of plant and animal life forms introduced by Earth's ecologists, only native Garth creatures.

And empty niches.

Uthacalthing felt the sparseness of species types as a gaping emptiness in the aura of this land. The metaphor that came to mind was that of a musical instrument missing half its strings.

Yes. Apt. Poetically appropriate. He hoped Athaclena was taking his advice and studying this Earthling way of viewing the world.

Deep, on the level of *nahakieri*, he had dreamt of his

daughter last night. Dream-picted her with her corona reaching, *kenning* the threatening, frightening beauty of a visitation by *tutsunucann*. Trembling, Uthacalthing had awakened against his will, as if instinct had driven him to flee that glyph.

Through anything other than *tutsunucann* he might have learned more of Athaclena, of how she fared and what she did. But *tutsunucann* only shimmered—the essence of dreadful expectation. From that glimmer he knew only that she still lived. Nothing more.

That will have to do, for now.

Kault carried most of their supplies. The big Thennanin walked at an even pace, not too difficult to follow. Uthacalthing suppressed body changes that would have made the trek easier for a short while but cost him in the long run. He settled for a loosening in his gait, a wide flaring of his nostrils—making them flat but broad to let in more air yet keep out the ever-present dust.

Ahead, a series of small, tree-lined hummocks lay by a streambed, just off their path toward the distant ruddy mountains. Uthacalthing checked his compass and wondered if the hills should look familiar. He regretted the loss of his inertial guidance recorder in the crash. If only he could be sure . . .

There. He blinked. Had he imagined a faint blue flash?

"Kault."

The Thennanin lumbered to a stop. "Mmm?" He turned around to face Uthacalthing. "Did you speak, colleague?"

"Kault, I think we should head that way. We can reach those hills in time to make camp and forage before dark."

"Mmm. It is somewhat off our path." Kault puffed for a moment. "Very well. I will defer to you in this." Without delay he bent and began striding toward the three green-topped mounds.

It was about an hour before sunset when they arrived by the watercourse and began setting camp. While Kault erected their camouflaged shelter, Uthacalthing tested pulpy, reddish, oblong fruits plucked from the branches of nearby trees. His portable meter declared them nutritious. They had a sweet, tangy taste.

The seeds inside, though, were hard, obdurate, obviously evolved to withstand stomach acids, to pass through an animal's digestive system and scatter on the ground with its feces. It was a common adaptation for fruit-bearing trees on many worlds.

Probably some large, omnivorous creature had once depended on the fruit as a food source and repaid the favor by spreading the seeds far and wide. If it climbed for its meals it probably had the rudiments of hands. Perhaps it even had Potential. The creatures might have someday become presentient, entered into the cycle of Uplift, and eventually become a race of sophisticated people.

But all that ended with the Bururalli. And not only the large animals died. The tree's fruit now fell too close to the parent. Few embryos could break out of tough seeds that had evolved to be etched away in the stomachs of the missing symbionts. Those saplings that did germinate languished in their parents' shade.

There should have been a forest here instead of a tiny, scrabbling woody patch.

I wonder if this is the place, Uthacalthing thought. There were so few landmarks out on this rolling plain. He looked around, but there were no more tantalizing flashes of blue.

Kault sat in the entrance of their shelter and whistled low, atonal melodies through his breathing slits. Uthacalthing dropped an armload of fruit in front of the Thennanin and wandered down toward the gurgling water. The stream rolled over a bank of semi-clear stones, taking up the reddening hues of twilight.

That was where Uthacalthing found the artifact.

He bent and picked it up. Examined it.

Native chert, chipped and rubbed, flaked along sharp, glassy-edged lines, dull and round on one side where a hand could find a grip. . . .

Uthacalthing's corona waved. *Lurrunanu* took form again, wafting among his silvery tendrils. The glyph rotated slowly as Uthacalthing turned the little stone axe in his hand. He contemplated the primitive tool, and *lurrunanu* regarded Kault, still whistling to himself higher up the hillside.

The glyph tensed and launched itself toward the hulking Thennanin.

Stone tools—among the hallmarks of pre-sentience, Uthacalthing thought. He had asked Athaclena to watch out for signs, for there were rumors . . . tales that told of sightings in the wild back country of Garth . . .

"Uthacalthing!"

He swiveled, shifting to hide the artifact behind his back as he faced the big Thennanin. "Yes, Kault?"

"I . . ." Kault appeared uncertain. *"Metoh kanmi, b'twuil'ph . . . I . . ."* Kault shook his head. His eyes closed and opened again. "I wonder if you have tested these fruits for my needs, as well as yours."

Uthacalthing sighed. *What does it take? Do Thennanin have any curiosity at all?*

He let the crude artifact slip out of his hand, to drop into the river mud where he had found it. "Aye, my colleague. They are nutritious, so long as you remember to take your supplements."

He walked back to join his companion for a fireless supper by the growing sparkle of the galaxies' light.

52

Athaclena

Gorillas dropped over both sharp rims of the narrow canyon, lowering themselves on stripped forest vines. They slipped carefully past smoking crevices where recent explosions had torn the escarpment. Landslides were still a danger. Nevertheless, they hurried.

On their way down they passed through shimmering rainbows. The gorillas' fur glistened under coatings of tiny water droplets.

A terrible growling accompanied their descent, echoing from the cliff faces and covering their labored breathing. It had hidden the noise of battle, smothering the bellow of death that had raged here only minutes before. Briefly, the dinsome waterfall had had competition but not for long.

Where its fremescent torrent had formerly fallen to crash

upon glistening smooth stones, it now splattered and spumed
against torn metal and polymers. Boulders dislodged from the
cliffsides had pounded the new debris at the foot of the falls.
Now the water worked it flatter still.

Athaclena watched from atop the overlooking bluffs. "We
do not want them to know how we managed this," she said to
Benjamin.

"The filament we bunched up under the falls was
pretreated to decay. It'll all wash away within a few hours,
ser. When the enemy gets a relief party in here, they won't
know what ruse we used to trap this bunch."

They watched the gorillas join a party of chim warriors
poking through the wreckage of three Gubru hover tanks.
Finally satisfied that all was clear, the chims slung their
crossbows and began pulling out bits of salvage, directing the
gorillas to lift this boulder or that shattered piece of armor
plate out of the way.

The enemy patrol had come in fast, following the scent
of hidden prey. Their instruments told them that someone
had taken refuge behind the waterfall. And it *was* a perfectly
logical place for such a hideaway—a barrier hard for their
normal detectors to penetrate. Only their special resonance
scanners had flared, betraying the Earthlings who had taken
technology under there.

In order to take those hiding by surprise, the tanks had
flown directly up the canyon, covered overhead by swarming
battle drones of the highest quality, ready for combat.

Only they did not find much of a battle awaiting them.
There were, in fact, no Earthlings at all behind the torrent.
Only bundles of thin, spider-silk fiber.

And a trip wire.

And—planted all through the cliffsides—a few hundred
kilos of homemade nitroglycerin.

Water spray had cleared away the dust, and swirling
eddies had carried off myriad tiny pieces. Still the greater
part of the Gubru strike force lay where it had been when
explosions rocked the overhanging walls, filling the sky with
a rain of dark volcanic stone. Athaclena watched a chim
emerge from the wreckage. He hooted and held up a small,
deadly Gubru missile. Soon a stream of alien munitions found
its way into the packs of the waiting gorillas. The large
pre-sentients began climbing out again through the multi-
hued spray.

Athaclena scanned the narrow streaks of blue sky that could be seen through the forest canopy. In minutes the invader would have its fighters here. The colonial irregulars must be gone by then, or their fate would be the same as the poor chims who rose last week in the Vale of Sind.

A few refugees had made it to the mountains after that debacle. Fiben Bolger was not one of them. No messenger had come with Gailet Jones's promised notes. For lack of information, Athaclena's staff could only guess how long it would take for the Gubru to respond to this latest ambush.

"Pace, Benjamin." Athaclena glanced meaningfully at her timepiece.

Her aide nodded. "I'll go hurry 'em up, ser." He sidled over next to their signaler. The young chimmie began waving flapping flags.

More gorillas and chims appeared at the cliff edge, scrambling up onto the wet, glistening grass. As the chim scavengers climbed out of the water-carved chasm, they grinned at Athaclena and hurried off, guiding their larger cousins toward secret paths through the forest.

Now she no longer needed to coax and persuade. For Athaclena had become an honorary Earthling. Even those who had earlier resented taking orders "from an Eatee" now obeyed her quickly, cheerfully.

It was ironic. In signing the articles that made them consorts, she and Robert had made it so that they now saw less of each other than ever. She no longer needed his authority as the sole free adult human, so he had set forth to raise havoc of his own elsewhere.

I wish I had studied such things better, she pondered. She was unsure just what was legally implied by signing such a document before witnesses. Interspecies "marriages" tended to be more for official convenience than anything else. Partners in a business enterprise might "marry," even though they came from totally different genetic lines. A reptiloid Bi-Gle might enter into consort with a chitinous F'ruthian. One did not expect issue from such joinings. But it was generally expected that the partners appreciate each other's company.

She felt funny about the whole thing. In a special sense, she now had a "husband."

And he was not here.

So it was for Mathicluanna, all those long, lonely years,

Athaclena thought, fingering the locket that hung from a chain around her throat. Uthacalthing's message thread had joined her mother's in there. Perhaps their *laylacllapt'n* spirits wound together in there, close as their bond had been in life.

Perhaps I begin to comprehend something I never understood about them, she wondered.

"Ser? . . . Uh, *ma'am?*"

Athaclena blinked and looked up. Benjamin was motioning to her from the trailhead, where one of the ubiquitous vine clusters came together around a small pool of pinkish water. A chimmie technician squatted by an opening in the crowded vines, adjusting a delicate instrument.

Athaclena approached. "You have word from Robert?"

"Yesser," the chimmie said. "I definitely am detecting one of th' trace chemicals he took along with him."

"Which is it?" she asked tensely.

The chimmie grinned. "Th' one with th' left-handed adenine spiral. It's the one we'd agreed would mean victory."

Athaclena breathed a little easier. So, Robert's party, too, had met with success. His group had gone to attack a small enemy observation post, north of Lorne Pass, and must have engaged the enemy yesterday. Two minor successes in as many days. At this rate they might wear the Gubru down in, say, a million years or so.

"Reply that we, also, have met our goals."

Benjamin smiled as he handed the signaler a vial of clear fluid, which was poured into the pool. Within hours the tagged molecules would be detectable many miles away. Tomorrow, probably, Robert's signaler would report her message.

The method was slow. But she imagined the Gubru would have absolutely no inkling of it—for a while, at least.

"They're finished with the salvage, general. We'd better scoot."

She nodded. "Yes. Scoot we shall, Benjamin."

In a minute they were running together up the verdant trail toward the pass and home.

A little while later, the trees behind them rattled and thunder shook the sky. Clamorous booms pealed, and for a time the waterfall's roar fell away under a raptor's scream of frustrated vengeance.

Too late, she cast contemptuously at the enemy fighters. *This time.*

53

Robert

The enemy had started using better drones. This time the added expense saved them from annihilation.

The battered Gubru patrol retreated through dense jungle, blasting a ruined path on all sides for two hundred meters. Trees blew apart, and sinuous vines whipped like tortured worms. The hover tanks kept this up until they arrived at an area open enough for heavy lifters to land. There the remaining vehicles circled, facing outward, and kept up nearly continuous fire in all directions.

Robert watched as one party of chims ventured too close with their hand catapults and chemical grenades. They were caught in the exploding trees, cut down in a hail of wooden splinters, torn to shreds in the indisciminate scything.

Robert used hand signals to send the withdraw-and-disperse order rippling from squad to squad. No more could be done to this convoy, not with the full force of the Gubru military no doubt already on its way here. His bodyguards cradled their captured saber rifles and darted into the shadows ahead of him and to the flanks.

Robert hated the way the chims kept this web of protection around him, forbidding him to approach a skirmish site until all was safe. There was just no helping it though. They were right, dammit.

Clients were expected to protect their patrons as individuals—and the patron race, in turn, protected the client race as a species.

Athaclena seemed better able to handle this sort of thing. She was from a culture that had come into existence from the start assuming that this was the way things were. *Also*, he admitted, *she doesn't worry about machismo*. One of his problems was that he seldom got to see or touch the enemy. And he so wanted to *touch* the Gubru.

The withdrawal was executed successfully before the sky filled with alien battlecraft. His company of Earthling irregulars split up into small groups, to make their separate ways to dispersed encampments until they received the call to arms again over the forest vine network. Only Robert's squad headed back toward the heights wherein their cave headquarters lay.

That required taking a wide detour, for they were far east in the Mulun range, and the enemy had set up outposts on several mountain peaks, easily supplied by air and defended with space-based weaponry. One of these stood along their most direct path home, so the chim scouts led Robert's group down a jungle crevice, just north of Lorne Pass.

The ropelike transfer vines lay everywhere. They were wonders, certainly, but they made for slow going down here below the heights. Robert had had plenty of time to think. Mostly he wondered what the Gubru were doing coming up here into the mountains at all.

Oh, he was glad they came, for it gave the Resistance a chance to strike at them. Otherwise, the irregulars might as well spit at the enemy, with their vast, overpowering weaponry.

But why were the Gubru bothering at all with the tiny guerrilla movement up in the Mulun when they had a firm grip on the rest of the planet? Was there some symbolic reason—something encrusted in Galactic tradition—that required they reduce every isolated pocket of resistance?

But even that would not explain the large civilian presence at those mountaintop outposts. The Gubru were pouring scientists into the Mulun. They were *looking* for something.

Robert recognized this area. He signaled for a halt.

"Let's stop and look in on the gorillas," he said.

His lieutenant, a bespectacled, middle-aged chimmie named Elsie, frowned and looked at him dubiously. "The enemy's gasbots sometimes dose an area without cause, sir. Just randomly. We chims will only be able to rest easy after you're safe underground again."

Robert was definitely not looking forward to the caverns, especially since Athaclena wouldn't be back from her next mission for several days. He checked his compass and map.

"Come on, the refuge is only a few miles off our path. Anyway, if I know you chims from the Howletts Center, you must be keeping your precious gorillas in a place that's even safer than the caves."

He had her there, and Elsie clearly knew it. She put her fingers to her mouth and trilled a quick whistle, sending the scouts hurrying off in a new direction, to the southwest, darting through the upper parts of the trees.

In spite of the broken terrain, Robert made his way mostly along the ground. He couldn't dash pellmell along narrow branches, not for mile after mile like the chims. Humans just weren't specialized for that sort of thing.

They climbed another side canyon that was hardly more than a split in the side of a mammoth bulwark of stone. Down the narrow defile floated soft wisps of fog, made opalescent by multiple refractions of daylight. There were rainbows, and once, when the sun came out behind and above him, Robert looked down at a bank of drifting moisture and saw his own shadow surrounded by a triply colored halo, like those given saints in ancient iconography.

It was the *glory* . . . an unusually appropriate technical term for a perfect, one-hundred-and-eighty-degree reverse rainbow—much rarer than its more mundane cousins that would arch over any misty landscape, lifting the hearts of the blameless and the sinful alike.

If only I weren't so damn rational, he thought. *If I didn't know exactly what it was, I might have taken it as a sign*.

He sighed. The apparition faded even before he turned to move on.

There were times when Robert actually envied his ancestors, who had lived in dark ignorance before the twenty-first century and seemed to have spent most of their time making up weird, ornate explanations of the world to fill the yawning gap of their ignorance. Back then, one could believe in anything at all.

Simple, deliciously elegant explanations of human behavior—it apparently never mattered whether they were true or not, as long as they were incanted right. "Party lines" and wonderful conspiracy theories abounded. You could even believe in your own sainthood if you wanted. Nobody was there to show you, with clear experimental proof, that there was no easy answer, no magic bullet, no philosopher's stone, only simple, boring sanity.

How narrow the Golden Age looked in retrospect. No more than a century had intervened between the end of the Darkness and contact with Galactic society. For not quite a hundred years, war was unknown to Earth.

And now look at us, Robert thought. *I wonder, does the Universe conspire against us? We finally grow up, make peace with ourselves . . . and emerge to find the stars already owned by crazies and monsters.*

No, he corrected himself. *Not all monsters.* In fact, the majority of Galactic clans were quite decent folk. But moderate majorities were seldom allowed to live in peace by fanatics, either in Earth's past or in the Five Galaxies today.

Perhaps golden ages simply aren't meant to last.

Sound traveled oddly in these closed, rocky confines, amid the crisscross lacing of native vines. One moment it seemed as if he were climbing in a world gone entirely silent, as if the rolling wisps of shining haze were folds of cotton batting that enveloped and smothered all sound. The next instant, he might suddenly pick up a snatch of conversation— just a few words—and know that some strange trick of acoustics had carried back to him a whispered remark between two of his scouts, possibly hundreds of meters away.

He watched them, the chims. They still looked nervous, these irregular soldiers who had until a few months ago been farmers, miners, and backwoods ecological workers. But they were growing more confident day by day. Tougher and more determined.

And more feral, Robert also realized, seeing them flit into and out of view among the untamed trees. There was something fierce and wild in the way they moved, in the way their eyes darted as they leaped from branch to branch. One seldom seemed to need words to know what the other was doing. A grunt, a quick gesture, a grimace, these were often more than enough.

Other than their bows and quivers and handspun weapons pouches, the chims mostly traveled naked. The softening trappings of civilization, the shoes and factory-made fabrics, were all gone. And with them had departed some illusions.

Robert glanced down at himself—bare-shanked, clad in breechcloth, moccasins, and cloth knapsack, bitten, scratched and hardening every day. His nails were dirty. His hair had been getting in the way so he'd cut it off in front and tied it in back. His beard had long ago stopped itching.

Some of the Eatees think that humans need more uplifting—that we are ourselves little more than animals. Robert leaped for a vine and swung over a dark patch of evil-looking thorns, coming to land in an agile crouch upon a fallen log. *It's a fairly common belief among the Galactics. And who am I to say they're wrong?*

There was a scurry of movement up ahead. Rapid hand signals crossed the gaps between the trees. His nearby guards, those directly responsible for his safety, motioned for him to detour along the westward, upwind side of the canyon. After climbing a few score meters higher he learned why. Even in the dampness he caught the musty, oversweet smell of old coercion dust, of corroding metal, and of death.

Soon he reached a point where he could look across the little vale to a narrow scar—already healing under layers of new growth—which ended in a crumpled mass of once-sleek machinery, now seared and ruined.

There were soft chim whispers and hand signals among the scouts. They nervously approached and began picking through the debris while others fingered their weapons and watched the sky. Robert thought he saw jutting white bones amid the wreckage, already picked clean by the ever-hungry jungle. If he had tried to approach any closer, of course, the chims would have physically restrained him, so he waited until Elsie returned with a report.

"They were overloaded," she said, fingering the small, black flight recorder. Emotion obviously made it hard for her to bring forth words. "They were tryin' to carry too many humans to Port Helenia, the day just after th' hostage gas was first used. Some were already sick, and it was their only transport.

"The flitter didn't clear th' peak, up there." She gestured at the fog-shrouded heights to the south. "Must've hit th' rocks a dozen times, to fall this far.

"Shall . . . shall we leave a couple chims, sir? A . . . a burial detail?"

Robert scuffed the ground. "No. Mark it. Map it. I'll ask Athaclena if we should photograph it later, for evidence.

"Meanwhile, let Garth take what she needs from them. I . . ."

He turned away. The chims weren't the only ones finding words hard right now. With a nod he set the party going again. As he clambered higher, Robert's thoughts burned.

There *had* to be a way to hurt the enemy worse than they had so far!

Days ago, on a dark, moonless night, he had watched while twelve selected chims sailed down onto a Gubru encampment, riding the winds on homemade, virtually invisible paper gliders. They had swooped in, dropped their nitro and gas bombs, and slipped away by starlight before the enemy even knew anything was happening.

There had been noise and smoke, uproar and squawking confusion, and no way at all to tell how effective the raid was. Nevertheless, he remembered how he had hated watching from the sidelines. He was a trained pilot, more qualified than any of these mountain chims for a mission like that!

But Athaclena had given firm instructions to which the neo-chimps all adhered. Robert's ass was sacred.

It's my own damn fault, he thought as he scrambled through a dense thicket. By making Athaclena his formal consort, he had given her that added status she had needed to run this small insurrection . . . and some degree of authority over him, as well. No longer could he do as he damn well pleased.

So, she was his *wife* now, in a fashion. *Some marriage*, he thought. While Athaclena kept adjusting her appearance to look more human, that only served to remind him of what she *couldn't* do, frustrating Robert. No doubt that was one reason why interspecies consortions were rare!

I wonder what Megan thinks of the news . . . I wonder if our messenger ever got through.

"Hssst!"

He looked quickly to his right. Elsie stood balanced on a tree branch. She pointed upslope, to where an opening in the fog exposed a view of high clouds skimming like glass-bottomed boats on invisible pressure layers in the deep blue sky. Underneath the clouds could be seen the tree-fringed slope of a mountain. Narrow curls of smoke spiraled upward from shrouded places on its flanks.

"Mount Fossey," Elsie said, concisely. And Robert knew, at once, why the chims felt this might be a safe place . . . safe enough even for their precious gorillas.

Only a few semi-active volcanoes lay along the rim of the Sea of Cilmar. Still, all through the Mulun there were places where the ground occasionally trembled. And at rare intervals lava poured forth. The range was still growing.

Mount Fossey hissed. Vapor condensed in shaggy, serpentine shapes above geothermal vents, where pools of hot water steamed and intermittently burst forth in frothing geysers. The ubiquitous transfer vines came together here from all directions, twisting into great cables as they snaked up the flanks of the semi-dormant volcano. Here they held market in shady, smoky pools, where trace elements that had percolated through narrow trails of hot stone finally entered the forest economy.

"I should've guessed." Robert laughed. Of course the Gubru would be unlikely to detect anything here. A few unclothed anthropoids on these slopes would be nothing amid all this heat, spume, and chemical potpourris. If the invaders ever did come to check, the gorillas and their guardians could just melt into the surrounding jungle and return after the interlopers left.

"Whose idea was this?" he asked as they approached under the shade of a high forest canopy. The smell of sulfur grew stronger.

"Th' gen'ral thought of it," Elsie answered.

Figures. Robert didn't feel resentful. Athaclena was bright, even for a Tymbrimi, and he knew he himself wasn't much above human average, if that. "Why wasn't I told about it?"

Elsie looked uncomfortable. "Um, you never asked, ser. You were busy with your experiments, findin' out about the optical fibers and the enemy's detection trick. And . . ."

Her voice trailed off.

"And?" he insisted.

She shrugged. "And we weren't sure you wouldn't ever get dosed with th' gas, sooner or later. If that happened you'd have to report to town for antidote. You'd be asked questions—and maybe psi-scanned."

Robert closed his eyes. Opened them. Nodded. "Okay. For a moment there I wondered if you trusted me."

"Ser!"

"Never mind." He waved. Athaclena's decision had been proper, logical—once again. He wanted to think about it as little as possible.

"Let's go see the gorillas."

* * *

They sat about in small family groups and were easily distinguished at a distance—much larger, darker, and hairier than their neo-chimpanzee cousins. Their big, peaked faces—as black as obsidian—bore expressions of peaceful concentration as they ate their meals, or groomed each other, or worked at the main task that had been assigned them, weaving cloth for the war.

Shuttles flew across broad wooden looms, carrying home-spun weft over warped strands, snicking and clicking to a rhythm matched by the great apes' rumbling song. The ratcheting and the low, atonal grunting followed Robert as he and his party moved toward the center of the refuge.

Now and then a weaver would stop work, putting her shuttle aside to wave her hands in a flurry of motion, making conversation with a neighbor. Robert knew sign-talk well enough to follow some of the gossip, but the gorillas seemed to speak with a dialect that was quite different from that used by infant chims. It was simple speech, yes, but also elegant in its own way, with a gentle style that was all their own.

Clearly, these were not just big chims but a completely different race, another path taken. A separate route to sentience.

The gorilla groups each seemed to consist of a number of adult females, their young, a few juveniles, and one hulking silver-backed adult male. The patriarch's fur was always gray along his spine and ribs. The top of his head was peaked and imposing. Uplift engineering had altered the neo-gorilla's stance, but the bigger males still had to use at least one knuckle when they walked. Their huge chests and shoulders made them too top-heavy still to move bipedally.

In contrast, the lithe gorilla children moved easily on two legs. Their foreheads were rounded, smooth, without the severe sloping and bony brow ridges that would later give them such deceptively fierce countenances. Robert found it interesting how much alike infants of all three races looked—gorillas, chims, and humans. Only later in life did the dramatic differences of inheritance and destiny become fully apparent.

Neoteny, Robert thought. It was a classic, pre-Contact theory that had proven more valid than not—one proposing that part of the secret of sapiency was to remain as childlike as possible, for as long as possible. For instance, human beings retained the faces, the adaptability, and (when it was not snuffed out) the insatiable curiosity of young anthropoids, even well into adulthood.

Was this trait an accident? One which enabled pre-sentient *Homo habilis* to make the supposedly impossible leap—uplifting himself to starfaring intelligence by his own bootstraps? Or was it a gift from those mysterious beings some thought must have once meddled in human genes, the long-hypothesized missing patrons of humanity?

All that was conjecture, but one thing was clear. Other Earthly mammals largely lost all interest in learning and play after puberty. But humans, dolphins—and now, more and more with each generation, neo-chimpanzees—retained that fascination with the world with which they entered it.

Someday grown gorillas might also share this trait. Already these members of an altered tribe were brighter and remained curious longer than their fallow Earthly kin. Some-day their descendants, too, might live out their life spans forever young.

If the Galactics ever allow it, that is.

Infant gorillas wandered about freely, poking their noses into everything. They were never slapped or chastised, only pushed gently aside when they got in the way, usually with a pat and a chuffed vocalization of affection. As he passed one group, Robert even caught a glimpse of a gray-flanked male mounting one of his females up in the bushes. Three young-sters crawled over the male's broad back, prying at his mas-sive arms. He ignored them, simply closing his eyes and hunkering down—doing his duty by his species.

More infants scurried through breaking foliage to tumble in front of Robert. From their mouths hung strips of some plastic material that they chewed into frayed tatters. Two of the children stared up at him in something like awe. But the last one, less shy than the others, waved its hands in eager, if sloppy signs. Robert smiled and picked the little fellow up.

Higher on the hillside, above the chain of fog-shrouded hot springs, Robert saw other brown shapes moving through the trees. "Younger males," Elsie explained. "And bulls too old to hold a patriarchy. Back before the invasion, the plan-ners at th' Howletts Center were trying to decide whether to intervene in their family system. It's their way, yes, but it's so hard on the poor males—a couple years' pleasure and glory, but at the cost of loneliness most of the rest of their lives." She shook her head. "We hadn't made up our minds before the Gubru came. Now maybe we'll never get the chance."

Robert refrained from commenting. He hated the restrictive treaties, but he still had trouble with what Elsie's colleagues had been doing at the Howletts Center. It had been arrogance to take the decision into their own hands. He could see no happy outcome to it.

As they approached the hot springs, he saw chims moving about seriously on various errands. Here one peered into the mouth of a huge gorilla easily six times her mass, probing with a dental tool. There another patiently taught sign language to a class of ten gorilla children.

"How many chims are here to take care of them?"

"Dr. de Shriver from the Center, about a dozen of the chim techs that used to work with her, plus about twenty guards and volunteers from nearby settlements. It depends on when we sometimes take 'rillas off to help in the war."

"How do they feed them all?" Robert asked as they descended to the banks of one of the springs. Some of the chims from his party had arrived ahead of them and were already lounging by the humid bank, sipping at soup cups. A small nearby cave held a makeshift storage chamber where resident workers in aprons were ladling out more steaming mugs.

"It's a problem." Elsie nodded. "The gorillas have finicky digestions, and it's hard to get them the right balance of foods. Even in th' restored ranges in Africa, a big silver-back needs up to sixty pounds of vegetation, fruit, an' insects a day. Natural gorillas have to move around a lot to get that kind of forage, an' we can't allow that."

Robert lowered himself to the damp stones and released the gorilla infant, who scampered down to the poolside, still chewing his ragged strip of plastic. "It sounds like quite a quandary," he said to Elsie.

"Yeah. Fortunately, Dr. Schultz solved the problem just last year. I'm glad he had that satisfaction before he died."

Robert removed his moccasins. The water looked hot. He dipped a toe and pulled it back quickly. "Ouch! How did he do it?"

"Um, beg your pardon?"

"What was Schultz's solution?"

"Microbiology, ser." She looked up suddenly, her eyes bright. "Ah, here they come with soup for us, too!"

Robert accepted a cup from a chimmie whose apron must have come from cloth woven on the gorillas' looms. She walked with a limp. Robert wondered if she had been wounded in some of the fighting.

"Thank you," he said, appreciating the aroma. He hadn't realized how hungry he was. "Elsie, what d'you mean, microbiology?"

She sipped delicately. "Intestinal bacteria. Symbionts. We all have 'em. Tiny critters that live in our guts, an' in our mouths. They're harmless partners, mostly. Help us digest our food in exchange for a free ride."

"Ah." Of course Robert knew about bio-symbionts; any school kid did.

"Dr. Schultz managed to come up with a suite of bugs that helps the 'rillas eat—and enjoy—a whole lot of native Garth vegetation. They—"

She was interrupted by a high-pitched little cry, unlike anything an ape might produce. "Robert!" shrieked a piping voice.

He looked up. Robert grinned. "April. Little April Wu. How are you, Sunshine?"

The little girl was dressed like Sheena, the jungle girl. She rode on the left shoulder of an adolescent male gorilla whose black eyes were patiently gentle. April tipped forward and waved her hands in a quick series of signs. The gorilla let go of her legs and she climbed up to stand on his shoulder, holding his head for balance. Her guardian chuffed uncomplainingly.

"Catch me, Robert!"

Robert hurried to his feet. Before he could say anything to stop her, she sprang off, a sun-browned windmill that streamed blond hair. He caught her in a tangle of legs. For a moment, until he had a sure grip, his heart beat faster than it had in battle or in climbing mountains.

He had known the little girl was being kept with the gorillas for safety. To his chagrin he realized how busy he had been since recovering from his injuries. Too busy to think of this child, the only other human free in the mountains. "Hi, Pumpkin," he said to her. "How're you doing these days? Are you taking good care of the 'rillas?"

She nodded seriously. "I've *gotta* take good care of th'

'rillas, Robert. We gotta be in charge, 'cause there's just us."

Robert gave her a close hug. At that moment he suddenly felt terribly lonely. He had not realized how badly he missed human company. "Yup. It's just you and me up here," he said softly.

"You an' me an' Tymbimmie Athaclena," she reminded him.

He met her eyes. "Nevertheless, you're doing what Dr. de Shriver asks, aren't you?"

She nodded. "Dr. de Shriver's nice. She says maybe I might get to go see Mommy and Daddy, sometime soon."

Robert winced. He would have to talk to de Shriver about deceiving the youngster. The chim in charge probably could not bear to tell the human child the truth, that she would be in their care for a long time to come. To send her to Port Helenia now would be to give away the secret of the gorillas, something even Athaclena was now determined to prevent.

"Take me down there, Robert." April demanded with a sweet smile. She pointed to a flat rock where the infant gorilla now capered before some of Robert's group. The chims laughed indulgently at the little male's antics. The satisfied, slightly smug tone in their voices was one Robert found understandable. A very young client race would naturally feel this way toward one even younger. The chims were very proprietary and parental toward the gorillas.

Robert, in turn, felt a little like a father with an unpleasant task ahead of him, one who must somehow break it to his children that the puppy would not remain theirs for long.

He carried April across to the other bank and set her down. The water temperature was much more bearable here. No, it was wonderful. He kicked off his moccasins and wriggled his toes in the tingling warmth.

April and the baby gorilla flanked Robert, resting their elbows on his knees. Elsie sat by his side. It was a brief, peaceful scene. If a neo-dolphin were magically to appear in the water, spy-hopping into view with a wide grin, the tableau would have made a good family portrait.

"Hey, what's that you've got in your mouth?" He moved his hand toward the little gorilla, who quickly shied back out of reach. It regarded him with wide, curious eyes.

"What's he chewing on?" Robert asked Elsie.

"It looks like a strip of plastic. But . . . but what's it doing here? There isn't supposed to be anything here that was manufactured on Garth."

"It's *not* Garth-made," someone said. They looked up. It was the chimmie who had served them their soup. She smiled and wiped her hands on her apron before bending over to pick up the gorilla infant. It gave up the material without fuss. "All the little ones chew these strips. They tested safe, and we're absolutely positive nothing about it screams 'Terran!' to Gubru detectors."

Elsie and Robert exchanged a puzzled look. "How can you be so sure? What is the stuff?"

She teased the little ape, waving the strip before its face until it chirped and grabbed it, popping the well-masticated piece back into its mouth.

"Some of their parents brought shredded bits of it back from our first successful ambush, back at the Howletts Center. They said it 'smelled good.' Now the brats chew it all the time."

She grinned down at Elsie and Robert. "It's that superplastic fiber from the Gubru fighting vehicles. You know, that material that stops bullets flat?"

Robert and Elsie stared.

"Hey, Kongie. How about that?" The chimmie cooed at the little gorilla. "You clever little thing, you. Say, if you like chewing armor plating, how about taking on something *really* tasty next? How about a *city*? Maybe something simple, like New York?"

The baby lowered the frayed, wet end long enough to yawn, a wide gaping of sharp, glistening teeth.

The chimmie smiled. "Yum! Y'know, I think little Kongie likes the idea."

54

Fiben

"Hold still now," Fiben told Gailet as he combed his fingers through her fur.

He needn't have said anything. For although Gailet was turned away, presenting her back to him, he knew her face bore a momentary expression of beatific joy as he groomed her. When she looked like that—calm, relaxed, happy with the delight of a simple, tactile pleasure—her normally stern countenance took on a glow, one that utterly transformed her somewhat ordinary features.

It was only for a minute, unfortunately. A tiny, scurrying movement caught Fiben's eye, and he pounced after it on instinct before it could vanish into her fine hair.

"Ow!" she cried when his fingernails bit a corner of skin, as well as a small squirming louse. Her chains rattled as she slapped his foot. "What are you doing!"

"Eating," he muttered as he cracked the wriggling thing between his teeth. Even then, it didn't quite stop struggling.

"You're lying," she said, in an unconvincing tone of voice.

"Shall I show it to you?"

She shuddered. "Never mind. Just go on with what you were doing."

He spat out the dead louse, though for all their captors had been feeding them, he probably could use the protein. In all the thousands of times he had engaged in mutual grooming with other chims—friends, classmates, the Throop Family back on Cilmar Island—he had never before been so clearly reminded of one of the ritual's original purposes,

335

inherited from the jungle of long ago—that of ridding another chim of parasites. He hoped Gailet wouldn't be too squeamish about doing the same for him. After sleeping on straw ticks for more than two weeks, he was starting to itch something awful.

His arms hurt. He had to stretch to reach Gailet, since they were chained to different parts of the stone room and could barely get close enough to do this.

"Well," he said. "I'm almost finished, at least with those places you're willing to uncover. I can't believe the chimmie who said *pink* to me, a couple of months ago, is such a prude about nudity."

Gailet only sniffed, not even deigning to answer. She had seemed glad enough to see him yesterday, when the renegade chims had brought him here from his former place of confinement. So many days of separate carceral isolation had made them as happy to see each other as long-lost siblings.

Now, though, it seemed she was back to finding fault with everything Fiben did. "Just a little more," she urged. "Over to the left."

"Gripe, gripe, gripe," Fiben muttered under his breath. But he complied. Chims needed to touch and be touched, perhaps quite a bit more than their human patrons, who sometimes held hands in public but seldom more. Fiben found it nice to have someone to groom after all this time. Almost as pleasurable as having it done to you was doing it for somebody else.

Back in college he had read that humans once restricted most of their person-to-person touching to their sexual partners. Some dark-age parents had even refrained from hugging their kids! Those primitives hardly ever engaged in anything that could be likened to mutual grooming— completely nonsexual scratching, combing, massaging one another, just for the pleasure of contact, with no sex involved at all.

A brief Library search had verified this slanderous rumor, to his amazement. No historical anecdote had ever brought home to Fiben so well just how much agnosy and craziness poor human mels and fems had endured. It made forgiveness a little easier when he also saw pictures of old-time zoos and circuses and trophies of "the hunt."

Fiben was pulled out of his thoughts by the sound of

keys rattling. The old-style wooden door slid open. Someone knocked and then walked in.

It was the chimmie who brought them their evening meals. Since being moved here, Fiben had not learned her name, but her heart-shaped face was striking, and somehow familiar.

Her bright zipsuit was of the style worn by the band of Probationers that worked for the Gubru. The costume was bound by elastic bands at ankles and wrists, and a holo-projection armband picted outstretched birds' talons a few centimeters into space.

"Someone's comin' to see both of you," the female Probie said lowly, softly. "I thought you'd want to know. Have time to get ready."

Gailet nodded coolly. "Thank you." She hardly glanced at the chimmie. But Fiben, in spite of his situation, watched their jailer's sway as she turned and walked away.

"Damn *traitors!*" Gailet muttered. She strained against her slender chain, rattling it. "Oh, there are times when I wish I were a chen. I'd . . . I'd . . ."

Fiben looked up at the ceiling and sighed.

Gailet strained to turn and look at him. "What! You've maybe got a comment?"

Fiben shrugged. "Sure. If you were a chen, you just might be able to bust out of that skinny little chain. But then, they wouldn't have used something like that if you were a male chim, would they?"

He lifted his own arms as far as they would go, barely enough to bring them into her view. Heavy links rattled. The chafing hurt his bandaged right wrist, so he let his hands drop to the concrete floor.

"I'd guess there were other reasons she wishes she was male," came a voice from the doorway. Fiben looked up and saw the Probationer called Irongrip, the leader of the rene-gades. The chim smiled theatrically as he rolled one end of his waxed mustache, an affectation Fiben was getting quite sick of.

"Sorry. I couldn't help but overhear that last part, folks."

Gailet's upper lip curled in contempt. "So you were listening. So what? All that means is you're an eavesdropper, as *well* as a traitor."

The powerfully built chim grinned. "Shall I go for *voyeur*, also? Why don't I have you two chained together, hm? Ought to make for lots of amusement, you like each other so much."

Gailet snorted. She pointedly moved away from Fiben, shuffling over to the far wall.

Fiben refused to give the fellow the pleasure of a response. He returned Irongrip's gaze evenly.

"Actually," the Probationer went on, in a musing tone, "it's pretty understandable, a chimmie like you, wishing she was a chen. Especially with that white breeding card of yours. Why, a white card's damn near wasted on a girl!

"What I find hard to figure," Irongrip said to Fiben, "is why you two have been doin' what you were doin'—running around playing soldier for the man. It's hard to figure. You with a blue card, her with a white—jeez, you two could do it any time she's pink—with no pills, no asking her guardian, no by-your-leave from the Uplift Board. All th' kids you ever want, whenever you want 'em."

Gailet offered the chim a chilled stare. "You are disgusting."

Irongrip colored. It was especially pronounced with his pale, shaved cheeks. "Why? Because I'm fascinated by what's been deprived me? With what I can't have?"

Fiben growled. "More like with what you can't do."

The blush deepened. Irongrip knew his feelings were betraying him. He bent over to bring his face almost even with Fiben's. "Keep it up, college boy. Who knows what *you'll* be able to do, once we've decided your fate." He grinned.

Fiben wrinkled his nose. "Y'know, the color of a chen's card isn't everything. F'rinstance, even *you'd* probably get more girls if you just used a mouthwash once in a whi—"

He grunted and doubled over as a fist drove into his abdomen. *You pay for your pleasures*, Fiben reminded himself as his stomach convulsed and he fought for breath. Still, from the look on the traitor's face he must have struck paydirt. Irongrip's reaction spoke volumes.

Fiben looked up to see concern written in Gailet Jones's eyes. The expression instantly turned to anger.

"Will you two stop it! You're acting like children . . . like pre-sentient—"

Irongrip whirled and pointed at her. "What do *you* know about it? Hm? Are you some sort of expert? Are you a member of the goddam Uplift Board? Are you even a mother, yet?"

"I'm a student of Galactic Sociology," Gailet said rather stiffly.

Irongrip laughed bittterly. "A title given to reward a clever monkey! You must have really done some beautiful tricks on the jungle gym to get a real-as-life, scale-model, sheepskin doctorate!"

He crouched near her. "Haven't you figured it out yet, little miss? Let me spell it for you. We're *all* goddam presentients! Go ahead. Deny it. Tell me I'm wrong!"

It was Gailet's turn to change color. She glanced at Fiben, and she knew she was remembering that afternoon at the college in Port Helenia, when they had climbed to the top of the bell tower and looked out over a campus empty of humans, filled only with chim students and chim faculty trying to act as if nothing had changed. She had to be remembering how bitter it had been, seeing that scene as a Galactic would.

"I'm a sapient being," she muttered, obviously trying to put conviction into her voice.

"Yeah," Irongrip sneered. "What you *mean* to say, though, is that you're just a little closer than the rest of us . . . closer to what the Uplift Board defines as a target for us neo-chims. Closer to what they think we *ought* to be.

"Tell me, though. What if you took a space trip to Earth, and the captain took a wrong turn onto D-level hyperspace, and you arrived a couple *hundred years* from now? What do you think would happen to your precious white card then?"

Gailet looked away. "*Sic transit gloria mundi.*" Irongrip snapped his fingers. "You'd be a relic then, obsolete, a phase long bypassed in the relentless progress of Uplift." He laughed, reaching out and taking her chin in his hand to make her meet his eyes. "You'd be *Probationer*, honey."

Fiben surged forward but was caught short by his chains. The jolting stop sent pain shooting up from his right wrist, but in his anger Fiben hardly noticed. He was too filled with wrath to be able to speak. Dimly, as he snarled at the other chen, he knew that the same held for Gailet. It was all the more infuriating because it was just one more proof that the bastard was right.

Irongrip met Fiben's gaze for a long moment before letting go of Gailet. "A hundred years *ago*," he went on, "*I* would've been somethin' special. They would've forgiven, ignored, my own little 'quirks and drawbacks.' They'd have given *me* a white card, for my cunning and my strength.

"*Time* is what decides it, my good little chen and chimmie. It's all what generation you're born in."

He stood up straight. "Or is it?" Irongrip smiled. "Maybe it also depends on who your *patrons* are, hm? If the standards change, if the target image of the ideal future *Pans sapiens* changes, well . . ." He spread his hands, letting the implication sink in.

Gailet was the first to find her voice.

"You . . . actually . . . expect . . . th' Gubru . . ."

Irongrip shrugged. "Time's are a changin', my darlings. I may yet have more grandkids than either of you."

Fiben found the key to drive out the incapacitating anger and unlock his own voice. He laughed. He guffawed. "Yeah?" he asked, grinning. "Well, first you'll haveta fix your *other* problem, boyo. How're you going to pass on your genes if you can't even get it up to—"

This time it was Irongrip's unshod foot that lashed out. Fiben was more prepared and rolled aside to take the kick at an angle. But more blows followed in a dull rain.

There were no more words, though, and a quick glance told Fiben that it was Irongrip's turn to be tongue-tied. Low sounds emerged as his mouth opened and closed, flecked with foam. Finally, in frustration, the tall chim gave up kicking at Fiben. He swiveled and stomped out.

The chimmie with the keys watched him go. She stood by the door, looking uncertain what to do.

Fiben grunted as he rolled over onto his back.

"Uh." He winced as he felt his ribs. None seemed to be broken. "At least Simon Legree wasn't able to perform a proper exit line. I half expected him to say: 'I'll be back, just you wait!' or somethin' equally original."

Gailet shook her head. "What do you gain by baiting him?"

He shrugged. "I got my reasons."

Gingerly, he backed against the wall. The chimmie in the billowing zipsuit was watching him, but when their eyes met she quickly blinked and turned to leave, closing the door behind her.

Fiben lifted his head and inhaled deeply, through his nose, several times.

"*Now* what are you doing?" Gailet asked.

He shook his head. "Nothin'. Just passin' the time."

When he looked again, Gailet had turned her back to him again. She seemed to be crying.

Small surprise, Fiben thought. It probably wasn't as much fun for her, being a prisoner, as it had been leading a rebellion. For all the two of them knew, the Resistance was washed up, finished, kaput. And there wasn't any reason to believe things had gone any better in the mountains. Athaclena and Robert and Benjamin might be dead or captured by now. Port Helenia was still ruled by birds and quislings.

"Don't worry," he said, trying to cheer her up. "You know what they say about the truest test of sapiency? You mean you haven't heard of it? Why it's just comin' through when the chimps are down!"

Gailet wiped her eyes and turned her head to look at him. "Oh, shut up," she said.

Okay, so it's an old joke, Fiben admitted to himself. *But it was worth a try.*

Still, she motioned for him to turn around. "Come on. It's your turn. Maybe . . ." She smiled weakly, as if uncertain whether or not to try a joke of her own. "Maybe I can find something to snack on, too."

Fiben grinned. He shuffled about and stretched his chains until his back was as close to her as possible, not minding how it strained his various hurts. He felt her hands working to unknot his tangled, furry thatch and rolled his eyes upward.

"Ah, aahh," he sighed.

A different jailer brought them their noon meal, a thin soup accompanied by two slices of bread. This male Probie possessed none of Irongrip's fluency. In fact, he seemed to have trouble with even the simplest phrases and snarled when Fiben tried to draw him out. His left cheek twitched intermittently in a nervous tic, and Gailet whispered to Fiben that the feral glint in the chim's eyes made her nervous.

Fiben tried to distract her. "Tell me about Earth," he asked. "What's it like?"

Gailet used a bread crust to sop up the last of her soup. "What's to tell? Everybody knows about Earth."

"Yeah. From video and from GoThere cube books, sure. But not from personal experience. You went as a child with your parents, didn't you? That's where you got your doctorate?"

She nodded. "University of Djakarta."

"And then what?"

Her gaze was distant. "Then I applied for a position at the Terragens Center for Galactic Studies, in La Paz."

Fiben knew of the place. Many of Earth's diplomats, emissaries, and agents took training there, learning how the ancient cultures of the Five Galaxies thought and acted. It was crucial if the leaders were to plan a way for the three races of Earth to make their way in a dangerous universe. Much of the fate of the wolfling clan depended on the graduates of the CGS.

"I'm impressed you even applied," he said, meaning it. "Did they . . . I mean, did you pass?"

She nodded. "I . . . it was close. I qualified. Barely. If I'd scored just a little better, they said there'd have been no question."

Obviously, the memory was painful. She seemed undecided, as if tempted to change the subject. Gailet shook her head. "Then I was told that they'd prefer it if I returned to Garth instead. I should take up a teaching position, they said. They made it plain I'd be more useful here."

"They? Who's this 'they' you're talking about?"

Gailet nervously picked at the fur on the back of her arm. She noticed what she was doing and made both hands lay still on her lap. "The Uplift Board," she said quietly.

"But . . . but what do they have to say about assigning teaching positions, or influencing career choices for that matter?"

She looked at him. "They have a *lot* to say, Fiben, if they think neo-chimp or neo-dolphin genetic progress is at stake. They can keep you from becoming a spacer, for instance, out of fear your precious plasm might get irradiated. Or they can prevent you from entering chemistry as a profession, out of fear of unpredicted mutations."

She picked up a piece of straw and twirled it slowly. "Oh, we have a lot more rights than other young client races. I know that, I keep reminding myself."

"But they decided your genes were needed on Garth," Fiben guessed in low voice.

She nodded. "There's a point system. If I'd *really* scored well on the CGS exam it would've been okay. A few chims do get in.

"But I was at the margin. Instead they presented me with that damned white card—like it was some sort of consolation prize, or maybe a wafer for some sacrament—and they sent me back to my native planet, back to poor old Garth.

"It seems my raison d'être is the babies I'll have. Everything else is incidental."

She laughed, somewhat bitterly. "Hell, I've been breaking the law for months now, risking my life and womb in this rebellion. Even if we'd have won—fat chance—I could get a big fat medal from the TAASF, maybe even ticker tape parades, and it wouldn't matter. When all the hooplah died down I'd still be thrown into prison by the Uplift Board!"

"Oh, Goodall," Fiben sighed, sagging back against the cool stones. "But you haven't, I mean you haven't yet—"

"Haven't procreated yet? Good observation. One of the few advantages of being a female with a white card is that I can choose anyone blue or higher for the father, and pick my own timing, so long as I have three or more offspring before I'm thirty. I don't even have to raise them myself." Again came the sharp, bitter laugh. "Hell, half of the chim marriage groups on Garth would shave themselves bald for the right to adopt one of my kids."

She makes her situation sound so awful, Fiben thought. *And yet there must be fewer than twenty other chims on the planet regarded as highly by the Board. To a member of a client race, it's the highest honor.*

Still, maybe he understood after all. She would have come home to Garth knowing one fact. That no matter how brilliant her career, how great her accomplishments, it would only make her ovaries all the more valuable . . . only make more frequent the painful, invasive visits to the Plasm Bank, and only bring on more pressure to carry as many as possible to term in her own womb.

Invitations to join group marriages or pair bonds would be automatic, easy. Too easy. There would be no way to know if a group wanted her for herself. Lone male suitors would seek her for the status fathering her child would bring.

And then there would be the jealousy. He could empathize with that. Chims weren't often very subtle at hiding their feelings, especially envy. Quite a few would be downright mean about it.

"Irongrip was right," Gailet said. "It's got to be different for a chen. A white card would be fun for a male chim, I can see that. But for a chimmie? One with ambition to be something for herself?"

She looked away.

"I . . ." Fiben tried to think of something to say, but for a moment all he could do was sit there feeling thick-headed, stupid. Perhaps, someday, one of his great-to-the-nth grand-children would be smart enough to know the right words, to know how to comfort someone too far gone into bitterness even to want comforting anymore.

That more fully uplifted neo-chim, a few score more generations down the chain of Uplift, might be bright enough. But Fiben knew he wasn't. He was only an ape.

"Um." He coughed. "I remember a time, back on Cilmar Island, it musta been before you returned to Garth. Let's see, was it ten years ago? Ifni! I think I was just a fresh-man. . . ." He sighed. "Anyway, the whole island got all excited, that year, when Igor Patterson came to lecture and perform at the University."

Gailet's head lifted a little. "Igor Patterson? The drummer?"

Fiben nodded. "So you've heard of him?"

She smirked sarcastically. "Who hasn't? He's—" Gailet spread her hands and let them drop, palms up. "He's wonderful."

That summed it up all right. For Igor Patterson was the best.

The thunder dance was only one aspect of the neo-chimpanzee's love affair with rhythm. Percussion was a favor-ite musical form, from the quaint farmlands of Hermes to the sophisticated towers of Earth. Even in the early days—back when chims had been forced to carry keyboard displays on their chests in order to speak at all—even then the new race had loved the beat.

And yet, all of the great drummers on Earth and in the colonies were humans. Everyone until Igor Patterson.

He was the first. The first chim with the fine finger coordination, the delicacy of timing, the sheer chutzpah, to make it alongside the best. Listening to Patterson play "Clash Ceramic Lighting" wasn't only to experience pleasure; for a chim it was to burst with pride. To many, his mere existence meant that chims weren't just approaching what the Uplift Board wanted them to be, but what *they* wanted to be, as well.

"The Carter Foundation sent him on a tour of th' colonies," Fiben went on. "Partly it was as a goodwill trip for all the outlying chim communities. And of course it was also to spread the good luck around a bit."

Gailet snorted at the obviousness of it. Of *course* Patterson had a white card. The chim members of the Uplift Board would have insisted, even if he weren't also as wonderfully charming, intelligent, and handsome a specimen of neo-chimpanzee as anyone could ask to meet.

And Fiben thought he knew what else Gailet was thinking. For a male having a white card wouldn't be much of a problem at all—just one long party. "I'll bet," she said. And Fiben imagined he detected a clear tone of envy.

"Yeah, well, you should've been there, when he showed up to give his concert. I was one of the lucky ones. My seat was way up in back, out of the way, and it happened that I had a real bad cold that night. That was damn fortunate."

"What?" Gailet's eyebrows came together. "What does that have to do with . . . Oh." She frowned at him and her jaw tightened. "Oh. I see."

"I'll bet you do. The air conditioning was set on high, but I'm told the aroma was still overpowering. I had to sit shivering under the blowers. Damn near caught my death—"

"*Will* you get to the point?" Gailet's lips were a thin line.

"Well, as no doubt you've guessed, nearly every green- or blue-card chimmie on the island who happened to be in estrus seemed to have a ticket to the concert. None of 'em used olfa-spray. They came, generally, with the complete okay of their group husbands, wearing flaming pink lipstick, just on the off chance—"

"I get the picture," Gailett said. And for just an instant Fiben wondered if he saw her blink back a faint smile as she pictured the scene. If so, it was only a momentary flicker of her severe frown. "So what happened?"

Fiben stretched, yawning. "What would you expect to happen? A riot, of course."

Her jaw dropped. "Really? At the University?"

"Sure as I'm sitting here."

"But—"

"Oh, the first few minutes went all right. Man, old Igor could play as good as his rep, I'll tell you. The crowd kept getting more and more excited. Even the backup band was feelin' it. Then things kinda got out of hand."

"But—"

"Remember old Professor Olvfing, from the Terragens Traditions Department? You know, the elderly chim who sports a monocle? Used to spend his spare time lobbying to get a chim monogamy bill before the legislature?"

"Yes, I knew him." She nodded, her eyes wide open.

Fiben made a gesture with two hands.

"No! In public? *Professor Olvfing?*"

"With th' dean of th' College of frigging Nutrition, no less."

Gailet let out a sharp sound. She turned aside, hand to her breast. She seemed to suffer a sudden bout of hiccups.

"Of course, Olvfing's pair-bond wife forgave him later. It was that or lose him to a ten-group that said they liked his style."

Gailet slapped her chest, coughing. She turned further away from Fiben, shaking her head vigorously.

"Poor Igor Patterson," Fiben continued. "He had problems of his own, of course. Some of th' guys from the football team had been drafted as bouncers. When it started getting out of hand, they tried using fire extinguishers. That made things slippery, but it didn't slow 'em down much."

Gailet coughed louder. "Fiben . . ."

"It was too bad, really," he mused aloud. "Igor was getting into a great blues riff, really pounding those skins, packin' in a backbeat you couldn't believe. I was groovin' on it . . . until this forty-year-old chimmie, naked and slick as a dolphin, dropped straight onto him from th' rafters."

Gailet doubled over clutching her belly. She held up a hand, pleading for mercy. "Stop, please. . . ." she whimpered, weakly.

"Thank heavens it was the snare drum she fell through. Took her long enough gettin' untangled for poor Igor to escape out the back way, just barely ahead of the mob."

She toppled over sideways. For a moment Fiben felt concern, her face was so flushed and red. She hooted, slapping the floor, and tears streamed from her eyes. Gailet rolled over onto her back, rocking with peals of laughter.

Fiben shrugged. "And all that was just from playin' the first number—Patterson's special version of the bloody national anthem! What a pity. I never did get to hear his variation on 'Inagadda Da Vita.' "

"Now that I think about it, though," he sighed once more, "maybe it's just as well."

*   *   *

Power curfew came at 2000 hours, and no exception was made for prisons. A wind had risen before sunset and soon was rattling the shutters of their small window. It came in off the ocean, carrying a heavy salt smell. In the distance could be heard the faint rumblings of an early summer storm.

They slept curled in their blankets as close to each other as their chains allowed, head to head so they could hear each other breathing in the darkness. They slumbered inhaling the soft tang of stone and the mustiness of straw, and exhaled the soft mutterings of their dreams.

Gailet's hands moved in tiny jerks, as if trying to follow the rhythms of some illusory escape. Her chains tinkled faintly.

Fiben lay motionless, but now and then he blinked, his eyes occasionally opening and closing without the light of consciousness in them. Sometimes a breath caught and held for a long moment before releasing, at last.

They did not notice the low humming sound that penetrated from the hallway outside, nor the light which speared into their cell through cracks in the wooden door. Feet shuffled and claws clicked on flagstones.

When keys rattled in the lock, Fiben jerked, rolled to one side, and sat up. He knuckled his eyes as the hinges creaked. Gailet lifted her head. She used her hand to block the sharp glare of two lamps, held high on poles.

Fiben sneezed, smelling lavender and feathers. When he and Gailet were hauled to their feet by several of the zipsuited chims, he recognized the gruff voice of their head captor, Irongrip.

"You two better behave yourselves. You've got important visitors."

Fiben blinked, trying to adjust to the light. At last he made out a small crowd of feathered quadrupeds, large balls of white fluff bedecked in ribbons and sashes. Two of them held staffs from which the bright lanterns hung. The rest twittered around what looked like a short pole ending in a narrow platform. On that perch stood a most singular-looking bird.

It, too, was arrayed in bright ribbons. The large, bipedal Gubru shifted its weight from one leg to another, nervously. It might have been the way the light struck the alien's plumage, but the coloration seemed richer, more luminous than the normal off-white shade. It reminded Fiben of something, as if he had seen this invader or one like it before, somewhere.

What the hell is the thing doing, moving around at night? Fiben wondered. *I thought they hated to do that.*

"Pay proper respect to honored elders, members of the high clan Gooksyu-Gubru!" Irongrip said, sharply, nudging Fiben.

"I'll show th' damn thing my respect." Fiben made a rude sound in his throat and gathered phlegm.

"No!" Gailet cried. She grabbed his arm and whispered urgently. "Fiben, don't! Please. Do this for me. Act *exactly* as I do!"

Her brown eyes were pleading. Fiben swallowed. "Aw hell, Gailet." She turned back toward the Gubru and folded her arms across her chest. Fiben imitated her, even as she bowed low.

The Galactic peered at them, first with one large, unblinking eye, then another. It shuffled to one end of the perch, forcing its holders to adjust their balance. Finally, it began chirping in a series of sharp, clipped squawks.

From the quadrupeds there emerged a strange, swooping accompaniment, rising and falling, sounding something like "*Zoooon.*"

One of the Kwackoo servitors ambled forward. A bright, metallic disk hung from a chain around its neck. The vodor gave forth a low, jerky Anglic translation.

> "*It has been judged . . . judged in honor*
> *judged in propriety . . .*
> *That you two have not transgressed . . .*
> *have not broken . . .*
> *The rules of conduct . . . the rules of war.*
> *Zooooon.*

> "*We judge that it is right . . . proper . . .*
> *meet to allow for infant status . . .*
> *To charitably credit . . . believe . . .*
> *that your struggles were on your patrons' behalf.*
> *Zoooooon.*

> "*It comes to our attention . . . awareness . . .*
> *knowledge that your status is*

As leaders of your gene-flux . . . race-flow . . .
  species in this place and time.
            Zooooooon.

"*We therefore offer . . . present . . .*
  deign to honor you
With an invitation . . . a blessing . . .
  a chance to earn the boon of representation.
            Zooooooon.

"*It is an honor . . . beneficence . . .*
  glory to be chosen
To seek out . . . penetrate . . .
  create the future of your race.
            Zoon!"

There it finished as abruptly as it had begun.

"Bow again!" Gailet urged in a whisper. He bent over
with arms crossed, as she demonstrated. When Fiben looked
up again, the small crowd of alien avians had swiveled and
moved toward the doorway. The perch was lowered, but still
the tall Gubru had to duck down, feathered arms splayed
apart for balance, in order to pass through. Irongrip followed
behind. The Probationer's parting glare at them was one of
pure loathing.

Fiben's head rang. He had given up trying to follow the
bird's queer, formal dialect of Galactic Three after the first
phrase. Even the Anglic translation had been well nigh impossible to understand.

The sharp lighting faded as the procession moved away
down the hallway in a babble of clucking gabble. In the
remaining dimness, Fiben and Gailet turned and looked at
each other.

"Now who th' hell was *that?*" he asked.

Gailet frowned. "It was a Suzerain. One of their three
leaders. If I'm not wrong—and I could easily be—it was the
Suzerain of Propriety."

"That tells me a whole lot. Just what on Ifni's roulette
wheel is a Suzerain of Propriety?"

Gailet waved away his question. Her forehead was knotted in deep concentration. "Why did it come to *us*, instead
of having us brought to *it?*" she wondered aloud, though
obviously she wasn't soliciting his opinion. "And why meet us

at night? Did you notice it didn't even stay to hear if we accepted its offer? It probably felt compelled, by propriety, to make it in person. But its aides can get our answer later."

"Answer to what? *What* offer? Gailet, I couldn't even follow—"

But she made a nervous waving motion with both hands. "Not now. I've got to think, Fiben. Give me a few minutes." She walked back to the wall and sat down on the straw facing the blank stone. Fiben had a suspicion it would be considerably longer than she'd estimated before she was done.

You sure can choose 'em, he thought. *You deserve what you get when you fall in love with a genius. . . .*

He blinked. Shook his head. *Say what?*

But movement in the hall distracted him from pursuing his own unexpected thought. A solitary chim entered, carrying an armload of straw and folded bolts of dark brown cloth. The load hid the short neochimp's face. Only when she lowered it to the ground did Fiben see that it was the chimmie who had stared at him earlier, the one who seemed so strangely familiar.

"I brought you some fresh straw, and some more blankets. These nights are still pretty cool."

He nodded. "Thank you."

She did not meet his eyes. She turned and walked back toward the door, moving with a lithe grace that was obvious, even under the billowing zipsuit. "Wait!" he said suddenly.

She stopped, still facing the door. Fiben walked toward her as far as the heavy chains would allow. "What's your name?" he asked softly, not wanting to disturb Gailet in her corner.

Her shoulders were hunched. She still faced away from him. "I'm . . ." Her voice was very low. "S-some people call me Sylvie. . . ."

Even in swirling quickly through the doorway she moved like a dancer. There was a rattle of keys, and hurried footsteps could be heard receding down the hall outside.

Fiben stared at the blank door. "Well, I'll be a monkey's grandson."

He turned around and walked back to the wall where Gailet sat, muttering to herself, and leaned over to drape a blanket upon her shoulders. Then he returned to his own corner to collapse into a heap of sweet-smelling straw.

55

Uthacalthing

Scummy algae foamed in the shallows where a few small, stilt-legged native birds picked desultorily for insects. Bushy plants lay in clumps, outlining the surrounding steppes.

Footprints led from the banks of the small lake up into the nearby scrub-covered hillside. Just glancing at the muddy tracks, Uthacalthing could tell that the walker had stepped with a pigeon-toed gait. It seemed to use a three-legged stance.

He looked up quickly as a flash of blue caught the corner of his eye—the same glimmer that had led him to this place. He tried to focus on the faint twinkle, but it was gone before he could track it.

He knelt to examine the impressions in the mud. A smile spread as he measured them with his hands. Such beautiful outlines! The third foot was off center from the other two and its print was much smaller than the others, almost as if some bipedal creature had crossed from lake to brush leaning on a blunt-headed staff.

Uthacalthing picked up a fallen branch, but he hesitated before brushing away the outlines.

Shall I leave them? he wondered. *Is it really necessary to hide them?*

He shook his head.

No. As the humans say, do not change game plans in midstream.

The footprints disappeared as he swept the branch back and forth. Just as he was finishing, he heard heavy footsteps and the sound of breaking shrubs behind him. He turned as

351

Kault rounded a bend in the narrow game trail to the small prairie lake. The glyph, *lurrunanu*, hovered and darted over the Thennanin's big, crested head like some frustrated parasitic insect, buzzing about in search of a soft spot that never seemed to be there.

Uthacalthing's corona ached like an overused muscle. He let *lurrunanu* bounce against Kault's bluff stolidity for a minute longer before admitting defeat. He drew the defeated glyph back in and dropped the branch to the ground.

The Thennanin wasn't looking at the terrain anyway. His concentration was on a small instrument resting in his broad palm. "I am growing suspicious, my friend," Kault said as he drew even with the Tymbrimi.

Uthacalthing felt blood rush in the arteries at the back of his neck. *At last?* he wondered.

"Suspicious of what, my colleague?"

Kault folded an instrument and put it away in one of his many vest pouches. "There are signs . . ." His crest flapped. "I have been listening to the uncoded transmissions of the Gubru, and something odd seems to be going on."

Uthacalthing sighed. No, Kault's one-track mind was concentrating on a completely different subject. There was no use trying to draw him away from it with subtle clues.

"What are the invaders up to now?" he asked.

"Well, first of all, I am picking up much less excited military traffic. Suddenly they appear to be engaged in fewer of those small-scale fights up in the mountains than they were days and weeks ago. You'll recall we were both wondering why they were expending so much effort to suppress what had to be a rather tiny partisan resistance."

Actually, Uthacalthing had been pretty certain he knew the reason for the frantic flurry of activity on the part of the Gubru. From what the two of them had been able to piece together, it seemed the invaders were very anxious to *find* something up in the Mountains of Mulun. They had thrown soldiers and scientists into the rough range with apparent reckless energy, and appeared to have paid a heavy cost for the effort.

"Can you think of a reason why the fighting has ebbed?" he asked Kault.

"I am uncertain from what I can decipher. One possibility is that the Gubru have found and captured the thing they were so desperately looking for—"

Doubtful, Uthacalthing thought with conviction. *It is hard to cage a ghost.*

"Or they may have given up searching for it—"

More likely, Uthacalthing agreed. It was inevitable that, sooner or later, the avians should realize they had been made fools of, and cease chasing wild gooses.

"Or, perhaps," Kault concluded, "the Gubru have simply finished suppressing all opposition and liquidated whoever was opposing them."

Uthacalthing prayed the last answer was not the correct one. It was among the risks he had taken, of course, in arranging to tease the enemy into such a frenzy. He could only hope that his daughter and Megan Oneagle's son had not paid the ultimate price to further his own convoluted hoax on the malign birds.

"Hmm," he commented. "Did you say there was something else puzzling you?"

"This," Kault went on. "That after five twelves of planetary days, during which they have done nothing at all for the benefit of this world, suddenly the Gubru are making announcements, offering amnesty and employment to former members of the Ecological Recovery Service."

"Yes? Well, maybe it just means they've completed their consolidation and can now spare a little attention to their responsibilties."

Kault snorted. "Perhaps. But the Gubru are accountants. Credit counters. Humorless, selfish worriers. They are fanatically prim about those aspects of Galactic tradition that interest them, yet they hardly seem to care at all about preserving planets as nursery worlds, only about the near-term status of their clan."

Although Uthacalthing agreed with that assessment, he considered Kault less than an impartial observer. And the Thennanin was hardly the one to accuse others of being humorless.

Anyway, one thing was obvious. So long as Kault was distracted like this, thinking about the Gubru, it would be useless to try to draw his attention to subtle clues and footprints in the ground.

He could sense movement in the prairie all around him. The little carnivores and their prey were all seeking cover, settling into small niches and burrows to wait out midday, when the fierce heat of summer would beat down and it would cost too much energy either to give chase or to flee. In that respect, tall Galactics were no exception. "Come," Uthacalthing said. "The sun is high. We must find a shady place to rest. I see some trees over on the other side of the water."

Kault followed without comment. He appeared to be indifferent about minor deviations in their path, so long as the distant mountains grew perceptibly closer each day. The white-topped peaks were now more than just a faint line against the horizon. It might take weeks to reach them, and indeterminably longer to find a way through unknown passes to the Sind. But Thennanin were patient when it suited their purposes.

There were no blue glimmerings as Uthacalthing found them shelter under a too-tight cluster of stunted trees, though he kept his eye "peeled" anyway. Still, with his corona he thought he *kenned* a touch of feral joy from some mind hiding out there on the steppe, something large, clever, and familiar.

"I am, indeed, considered to be something of an expert on Terrans," Kault said a little later as they made conversation under the gnarled branches. Small insects buzzed near the Thennanin's breathing slits, only to be blown away every time they approached. "That, plus my ecological expertise, won me my assignment to this planet."

"Don't forget your sense of humor," Uthacalthing added, with a smile.

"Yes," Kault's crest puffed in the Thennanin equivalent of a nod. "At home I was thought quite the devil. Just the sort to deal with wolflings and Tymbrimi pixies." He finished with a rapid, low set of raspy breaths. It was obviously a conscious affectation, for Thennanin did not have a laughter reflex as such. *No matter,* Uthacalthing thought. *As Thennanin humor goes, it was pretty good.*

"Have you had much first-hand experience with Earthlings?"

"Oh, yes," Kault said. "I have been to Earth. I have had the delight of walking her rain forests and seeing the strange, diverse lifeforms there. I have met neo-dolphins and whales. While my people believe humans themselves should never have been declared fully uplifted—they would profit much from a few more millennia of polishing under proper guidance—

I can admit that their world is beautiful and their clients promising."

One reason the Thennanin were in this current war was in hopes of picking up all three Earthling species for their clan by forced adoption—"for the Terrans' own good," of course. Though, to be fair, it was also clear that there were disagreements over this among the Thennanin themselves. Kault's party, for instance, preferred a ten-thousand-year campaign of *persuasion*, to try to win the Earthlings over to adoption voluntarily, with "love."

Obviously, Kault's party did not dominate the present government.

"And of course, I met a few Earthlings in the course of a term working for the Galactic Institute of Migration, during an expedition to negotiate with the Fah'fah'n*fah."

Uthacalthing's corona erupted in a whirl of silvery tendrils, an open show of surprise. He knew his stunned expression was readable even to Kault, and did not care. "You . . . you have been to meet the hydrogen breathers?" He did not even know the trick of pronouncing the hyper-alien name, not part of any sanctioned Galactic tongue.

Kault had surprised him once again!

"The Fah'fah'n*fah." Again Kault's breathing slits pulsed in mimicry of laughter. This time, it sounded much more realistic. "The negotiations were held in the Poul-Kren subquadrant, not far from what the Earthlings call the Orion sector."

"That's very close to Terra's Canaan colonies."

"Yes. That is one reason why they were invited to take part. Even though these infrequent meetings between the civilizations of oxygen breathers and hydrogen breathers are among the most critical and delicate in any era, it was thought appropriate to bring a few Terrans along, to show them some of the subtleties of high-level diplomacy."

It must have been his state of confused surprise, but at that moment Uthacalthing thought he actually caught a *kenning* from Kault . . . a trace of something deep and troubling to the Thennanin. *He is not telling me all of it*, Uthacalthing realized. *There were other reasons Earthlings were involved*.

For billions of years, uneasy peace had been maintained between two parallel, completely separate cultures. It was almost as if the Five Galaxies were actually Ten, for there were at least as many stable worlds with hydrogen atmospheres as planets like Garth and Earth and Tymbrim. The two strands of life, each supporting vast numbers of species and lifeforms, had almost nothing in common. The Fah'fah'n*fah wanted nothing of rock, and their worlds were too vast and cold and heavy for the Galactics ever to covet.

Also, they seemed even to operate on different levels or rates of *time*. The hydrogen breathers preferred the slow routes, through D-Level hyperspace and even normal space between the stars—the realm where relativity ruled—leaving the quicker lanes among the stars to the fast-living heirs of the fabled Progenitors.

Sometimes there were conflicts. Entire systems and clans died. There were no rules to such wars.

Sometimes there was trade, metals for gases, or machinery in exchange for strange things not found even in the records of the Great Library.

There were periods when whole spiral arms would be abandoned by one civilization or the other. The Galactic Institute of Migration organized these huge movements for the oxygen breathers, every hundred million years or so. The official reason was to allow great tracts of stars to "go fallow" for an era, to give their planets time to develop new presentient life. Still, the other purpose was widely known . . . to put space between hydrogen and oxygen life where it seemed impossible to ignore each other any longer.

And now Kault was telling him that there had been a recent negotiation right in the Poul-Kren sector? And humans had been there?

Why have I never heard of this before? he wondered.

He wanted to follow this thread, but had no opportunity. Kault was obviously unwilling to pursue it, and returned to the earlier topic of conversation.

"I still believe there is something anomalous about the Gubru transmissions, Uthacalthing. From their broadcasts it is clear that they are combing both Port Helenia and the islands, seeking out the Earthlings' ecology and uplift experts."

Uthacalthing decided that his curiosity could wait—a hard decision for a Tymbrimi. "Well, as I suggested earlier, perhaps the Gubru have decided to do their duty by Garth, at last."

Kault gurgled in a tone Uthacalthing knew denoted doubt. "Even if that were so, they would require ecologists, but why Uplift specialists? I intuit that something curious is still going on," Kault concluded. "The Gubru have been extremely agitated for several megaseconds."

Even without their small receiver, or any news over the airwaves at all, Uthacalthing would still have known that much. It was implicit in the intermittent blue light he had been following since weeks ago. The flickering glow meant that the Tymbrimi Diplomatic Cache had to have been breached. The bait he had left inside the cairn, along with numerous other hints and clues, could only lead a sapient being to one conclusion.

It was apparent his jest on the Gubru had proved very expensive for them.

Still, all good things come to an end. By now even the Gubru must have figured out that it was all just a Tymbrimi trick. The avians weren't exactly stupid. They had to discover sooner or later that there really weren't any such things as "Garthlings."

The sages say that it can be a mistake to push a joke too far. Am I making that error trying to pull the same jest on Kault?

Ah, but in this case the procedure was so totally different! Fooling Kault was turning into a much slower, more difficult, more *personal* task.

Anyway, what else have I to do, to pass the time?

"Do tell me more about your suspicions," Uthacalthing said aloud to his companion. "I am very, very interested."

56

Galactics

Against all expectation, the new Suzerain of Cost and Caution was actually scoring points. Its plumage had barely even begun to show the royal hues of candidacy, and it had started out far, far behind its peers in the competition. Nevertheless, when it danced the other Suzerains were forced to watch closely and pay heed to its well-parsed arguments.

"This effort was misguided, costly, unwise," it chirped and whirled in delicate rhythm. "We have spent treasure, time, and honor

   seeking,

     chasing,

       hunting

a chimera!"

The new chief bureaucrat did have a few advantages. It had been trained by its predecessor—the impressive deceased Suzerain of Cost and Caution. Also, to this conclave it had brought an equally impressive, indicting array of facts. Data cubes lay scattered across the floor. The presentation by the head civil servant had, in fact, been quite devastating.

"There is no way, no possibility, no *chance* that this world could have hidden upon it a pre-sentient survivor of the Bururalli! It was a hoax, a ruse, a fiendish wolfling-and-Tymbrimi plot to get us to

   waste,

     squander,

       throw away

our wealth!"

To the Suzerain of Propriety this was most humiliating. In fact, it was not much short of catastrophic.

During the hiatus, while a new bureaucratic candidate was being chosen, the priest and the admiral had reigned supreme, with no one to hold them in check. They had well known that it was not wise to act so, without the voice of a third peer to restrain them, but what being always acted wisely when opportunity beckoned seductively?

The admiral had gone on personal search and destroy missions in pursuit of the mountain partisans, seeking gloss to add to its personal honor. For its part, the priest had ordered expensive new works built and had rushed the delivery of a new planetary Branch Library.

It had been a lovely interregnum of two-way consensus. The Suzerain of Beam and Talon approved every purchase, and the Suzerain of Propriety blessed every foray of the Talon Soldiers. Expedition after expedition was sent into the mountains as closely guarded scientists eagerly sought out a prize beyond price.

Mistakes were made. The wolflings proved diabolical in their ambushes and animal elusiveness. And yet, there would never have been any carping about cost had they actually found what they were looking for. It all would have been worth it, if only . . .

But we were tricked, fooled, made fools of, the priest thought bitterly. The treasure had been a lie. And now the new Suzerain of Cost and Caution was rubbing it in for all it was worth. The bureaucrat danced a brilliant dance of chastisement of excess. Already it had dominated several points of consensus—for instance, that there would be no more useless chases into the mountains, not until a cheaper way was found to eliminate the resistance fighters.

The plumage of the Suzerain of Beam and Talon drooped miserably. The priest knew how much this must gall the admiral. But they were both held hypnotized by the righteous correctness of the Dance of Chastisement. Two could not outvote one when that one was so clearly in the right.

Now the bureaucrat had launched into a new cadence, leading into a new dance. It proposed that the new construction projects be abandoned. They had nothing to do with defending the Gubru hold upon this world. They had been begun on the assumption that these "Garthling" creatures would be found. Now it was simply pointless to continue building a hyperspace shunt and a ceremonial mound!

The dance was powerful, convincing, backed up with charts and statistics and tables of figures. The Suzerain of Propriety realized that something would have to be done and done soon, or this upstart would end the day in the foremost position. It was unthinkable that such a sudden reverse of order should happen just as their bodies were starting to give them twinges preliminary to Molt!

Even leaving out the question of molt order, there was also the message from the Roost Masters to consider. The queens and princes back home were desperate in their queries. Had the Three on Garth come up with a bold new policy yet? Calculations showed that it would be important to have something original and imaginative soon, or else the initiative would pass forever to some other clan.

It was intimidating to have the fate of the race riding in one's slipstream.

And for all of its obvious finesse and fine preening, one thing was readily apparent about the new chief bureaucrat. The new Suzerain of Cost and Caution lacked the depth, the clarity of vision of its dead predecessor. The Suzerain of Propriety knew that no grand policy was going to come out of picayune, short sighted credit-pinching.

Something had to be done, and done now! The priest took up a posture of presentiment, spreading its brightly feathered arms in display. Politely, perhaps even indulgently, the bureaucrat cut short its own dance and lowered its beak, yielding time.

The Suzerain of Propriety started slowly, shuffling in small steps upon its perch. Purposely, the priest adopted a cadence used earlier by its adversary.

"Although there may be no Garthlings, there remains a chance, opportunity, opening, for us to use the ceremonial site we have
    planned,
        built,
            dedicated
at such cost.

"There is a plan, scheme, concept, which may still yet win
    glory,
        honor,

propriety
for our clan.

"At the center, focus, essence of this plan, we shall
examine,
> inspect,
> > investigate
the clients of wolflings."

Across the chamber the Suzerain of Beam and Talon
looked up. A hopeful light appeared in the dejected admiral's
eye, and the priest knew that it could win a temporary
victory, or at least a delay.

Much, much would depend in the days ahead upon
finding out whether this bold new idea would work.

57

Athaclena

"You see?" he called down to her. "It moved during the
night!"

Athaclena had to shade her eyes as she looked at her
human friend—perched on a tree branch more than thirty
feet above the forest floor. He pulled on a leafy green cable
that stretched down to him at a forty-five-degree angle from
its even higher anchor.

"Are you certain that is the same vine you snipped last
night?" she called.

"It sure is! I climbed up and poured a liter of chromium-
rich water—the very stuff this particular vine specializes in—
into the crotch of that branch, way up there above me. Now
you can see this vine has reanchored itself to that exact spot!"

Athaclena nodded. She felt a fringe of truth around his
words. "I see it, Robert. And now I believe it."

She had to smile. Sometimes Robert acted so much like a young Tymbrimi male—so quick, impulsive, puckish. It was a little disconcerting, in a way. Aliens were supposed to behave in strange and inscrutable ways, not just like . . . well, *boys*.

But Robert is not an alien, she reminded herself. *He is my consort*. And anyway, she had been living among Terrans for so long, she wondered if she had started to think like one.

When—if—I ever get home, will I disconcert all around me, frightening and amazing them with metaphors? With bizarre wolfling attitudes? Does that prospect attract me?

A lull had settled over the war. The Gubru had stopped sending vulnerable expeditions into the mountains. Their outposts were quiescent. Even the ceaseless droning of gasbots had been absent from the high valleys for more than a week, to the great relief of the chim farmers and villagers.

With some time on their hands, she and Robert had decided to have themselves just one day off while they had a chance, to try to get to know each other better. After all, who knew when the fighting would resume? Would there ever be another opportunity?

They both needed distraction anyway. There had still been no reply from Robert's mother, and the fate of Ambassador Uthacalthing remained unclear, in spite of the glimpse she had been given of her father's design. All she could do was try to perform her part as well as possible, and hope he was still alive and able to do his.

"All right," she called up to Robert. "I accept it. The vines can be trained, after a fashion. Now come down! Your perch looks precarious."

But Robert only smiled. "I'll come down, in my own way. You know me, Clennie. I can't resist an opportunity like this."

Athaclena tensed. There it was again, that whimsy at the edges of his emotional aura. It wasn't unlike *syulff-kuonn*, the coronal *kenning* surrounding a young Tymbrimi who was savoring an anticipated jest.

Robert gave the vine a hearty tug. He inhaled, expanding his ribcage to a degree no Tymbrimi could have equaled, then thumped his chest hollowly, rapidly, and gave out a long, ululating yodel. It echoed down the forest corridors.

Athaclena sighed. *Oh, yes. He must pay respects to their wolfling deity, Tarzan.*

With the vine clutched in both hands, Robert vaulted from the branch. He sailed, legs outstretched together, in a smooth arc down and across the forest meadow, barely clearing the low shrubs. He whooped aloud.

Of course it was just the sort of thing humans would have invented during those dark centuries between the advent of intelligence and their discovery of science. None of the Library-raised Galactic races, not even the Tymbrimi, would ever have thought up such a mode of transportation.

The pendulum swing carried Robert upward again, toward a thick mass of leaves and branchlets halfway up the side of a forest giant. Robert's warbling cry cut off suddenly as he crashed through the foliage with a splintering sound and disappeared.

The silence was punctuated only by a faint, steady rain of minor debris. Athaclena hesitated, then called out. "Robert?"

There was neither reply nor movement up there in that high thicket. "Robert! Are you all right? Answer me!" The Anglic words felt thick in her mouth.

She tried to locate him with her corona, the little strands above her ears strained forward. He was in there, all right . . . and in some degree of pain, she could tell.

She ran across the meadow, leaping over low obstacles as the *gheer* transformation set in—her nostrils automatically widening to accept more air as her heart rate tripled. By the time she reached the tree, her finger- and toenails had already begun to harden. She kicked off her soft shoes and began climbing at once, quickly finding holds in the rough bark as she shimmied up the giant bole to the first branch.

The ubiquitous vines clustered here, snaking at an angle toward the leafy morass that had swallowed Robert. She tested one of the ropy cables, then used it to shimmy up to the next level.

Athaclena knew she should pace herself. For all of her Tymbrimi speed and adaptability, her musculature wasn't as strong as a human's, and coronal-radiation didn't dissipate heat as well as Terran sweat glands. Still, she could not taper off from full, emergency speed.

It felt dim and close within the leafy blind where Robert had crashed. Athaclena blinked and sniffed as she entered the darkness. The odors reminded her that this was a wild world, and she was no wolfling to be at home in a ferine jungle. Athaclena had to retract her tendrils so they wouldn't get

tangled in the thicket. That was why she was taken by surprise when something reached out from the shadows to grab
her tightly.

Hormones rushed. She gasped and coiled around to
strike out at her assailant. Just in time she recognized
Robert's aura, his human male odor very near, and his strong
arms holding her close. Athaclena experienced a momentary
wave of dizziness as the *gheer* reaction braked hard.

It was in that stunned state, while still immobilized by
change-rigor, that her surprise was redoubled. For that was
when Robert began touching her *mouth* with his. At first his
actions seemed meaningless, insane. But then, as her corona
unwound, she started picking up feelings again. . . . and all
at once she remembered scenes from human video dramas—
scenes involving mating and sexual play.

The storm of emotions that swept over Athaclena was so
powerfully contradictory that she remained frozen for a while
longer. Also, part of it might have been the relaxed power in
his arms. Only when Robert finally let go of her did Athaclena
back away from him quickly, wedging herself against the bole
of the giant tree, gasping.

"*An . . . An-thwillathbielna! Naha. . . .* You . . . you
blenchuq! How dare you . . . *Cleth-tnub.* . . ." She ran out
of breath and had to stop her polyglot cursing, panting slowly.
It didn't seem to be penetrating Robert's mild expression of
good cheer anyway.

"Uh, I didn't catch all that, Athaclena. My GalSeven is
still pretty bad, though I've been working on it. Tell me,
what's a . . . a *blenchuq*?"

Athaclena made a gesture, a twist of the head that was
the Tymbrimi equivalent to an irritated shrug. "Never mind
that! Tell me at once. Are you badly hurt? And if not, why
did you do what you just did?

"Third, tell me why I should not punish you for tricking
and assaulting me like that!"

Robert's eyes widened. "Oh, don't take it all so seriously,
Clennie. I appreciate the way you came charging to my
rescue. I was still a bit dazed, I guess, and got carried away
being happy to see you."

Athaclena's nostrils flared. Her tendrils waved, preparing she knew not what caustic glyph. Robert clearly sensed
this. He held up a hand. "All right, all right. In order—I'm
not badly hurt, only a bit scraped. Actually, it was fun."

He erased his smile on seeing her expression. "'Uh, as for question number two—I greeted you that way because it's a common human courtship ritual that I was strongly motivated to perform with you, even though I admit you might not have understood it.'"

Now Athaclena frowned. Her tendrils curled in confusion.

"And finally," Robert sighed. "I can't think of a single reason why you shouldn't punish me for my presumption. It's your privilege, as it'd be the right of any human female to break my arm for handling her without permission. I don't doubt you could do it, too.

"All I can say in my defense is that a broken arm is sometimes an occupational hazard to a young human mel. Half the time a courtship can hardly get started unless a fellow pulls something impulsive. If he's read the signs right, the fem likes it and doesn't give him a black eye. If he's wrong, he pays."

Athaclena watched Robert's expression turn thoughtful. "You know," he went on. "I'd never quite parsed it out that way before. It's true, though. Maybe humans *are* crazy *cleth th-tnubs*, at that."

Athaclena blinked. The tension had begun to leak away, dripping from the tips of her corona as her body returned to normal. The change nodes under her skin pulsed, reabsorbing the *gheer* flux.

Like little mice, she remembered, but she shuddered a little less this time.

In fact, she found herself smiling. Robert's strange confession had put matters—almost laughably—on a logical plane. "Amazing," she said. "As usual, there are parallels in Tymbrimi methodology. Our own males must take chances as well."

She paused then, frowning. "But stylistically this technique of yours is so crude! The error rate must be tremendous, since you are without coronae to sense what the female is feeling. Beyond your crude empathy sense, you have only hints and coquetry and body cues to go on. I'm surprised you manage to reproduce at all without killing each other off well beforehand!"

Robert's face darkened slightly, and she knew he was blushing. "Oh, I exaggerated a bit, I suppose."

Athaclena couldn't help but smile once more, not only a subtlety of the mouth, but an actual, full widening of the separation between her eyes.

"That much, Robert, I had already guessed."

The human's features reddened even more. He looked down at his hands and there was silence. Athaclena felt a stirring within her own deepself, and she *kenned* the simple sense-glyph *kiniwullun* . . . the parable-boy caught doing what boys inevitably do. Sitting there, his open aura of abashed sincerity seemed to cover over his fix-eyed, big-nosed alienness and make him more familiar to her than most of her peers had been back in school.

At last Athaclena slipped down from the dusty corner where she had wedged herself in self-defense.

"All right, Robert," she sighed. "I will let you explain to me why you were 'strongly motivated' to attempt this classical human mating ritual with a member of another species—me. I suppose it is because we have signed an agreement to be consorts? Did you feel honor bound to consummate it, in order to satisfy human tradition?"

He shrugged, looking away. "No, I can't use that as an excuse. I know interspecies marriages are for business. It's just, well—I think it was just because you're pretty and bright, and I'm lonely, and . . . and maybe I'm just a bit in love with you."

Her heart beat faster. This time it was not the *gheer* chemicals responsible. Her tendrils lifted of their own accord, but no glyph emerged. Instead, she found they were *reaching* toward him along subtle, strong lines, like the fields of a dipole.

"I think, I think I understand, Robert. I want you to know that I . . ."

It was hard to think of what to say. She wasn't sure herself just what she was thinking at that moment. Athaclena shook her head. "Robert?" she said softly. "Will you do me a favor?"

"Anything, Clennie. Anything in the world." His eyes were wide open.

"Good. Then, taking care not to get carried away, perhaps you might go on to explain and demonstrate what you were doing, when you touched me just then . . . the various physical aspects involved. Only this time, more slowly please?"

The next day they strolled slowly on their way back to the caves.

She and Robert dawdled, stopping to contemplate how

the sunlight came down in little glades, or standing by small pools of colored liquid, wondering aloud which trace chemical was stockpiled here or there by the ubiquitous trade vines, and not really caring about the answer. Sometimes they just held hands while they listened to the quiet sounds of Garth Planet's forest life.

At intervals they sat and experimented, gently, with the sensations brought on by touching.

Athaclena was surprised to find that most of the needed nerve pathways were already in place. No deep auto-suggestion was required—just a subtle shifting of a few capillaries and pressure receptors—in order to make the experiment feasible. Apparently, the Tymbrimi might have once engaged in a courtship ritual such as kissing. At least they had the capability.

When she resumed her old form she just might keep some of these adaptations to her lips, throat, and ears. The breeze felt good on them as she and Robert walked. It was like a rather nice empathy glyph tingling at the tips of her corona. And kissing, that warm pressure, stirred intense, if primitive feelings in her.

Of course none of it would have been possible if humans and Tymbrimi weren't already so very similar. Many charming, stupid theories had circulated among unsophisticated people of both races to explain the coincidence—for instance, proposing that they might once have had a common ancestor.

The idea was ridiculous, of course. Still, she knew that her case was not the first. Close association over several centuries had led to quite a few cases of cross-species dalliance, some even openly avowed. Her discoveries must have been made many times before.

She just hadn't been aware, having considered such tales rather seamy while growing up. Athaclena realized her friends back on Tymbrim must have thought her pretty much of a prude. And here she was, behaving in a way that would have shocked most of them!

She still wasn't sure she wanted anyone back home—assuming she ever made it there again—to think her consortion with Robert was anything but businesslike. Uthacalthing would probably laugh.

No matter, she told herself firmly. *I must live for today.* The experiment helped to pass the time. It did have its pleasant aspects. And Robert was an enthusiastic teacher.

Of course she was going to have to set limits. She was

willing to adjust the distribution of fatty tissues in her breasts, for instance, and it was fun to play with the sensations made possible by new nerve endings. But where it came to fundamentals she would have to be adamant. She wasn't about to go changing any really basic mechanisms . . . not for any human being!

On the return trip they stopped to inspect a few rebel outposts and talk with small bands of chim fighters. Morale was high. The veterans of three months' hard battles asked when their leaders would find a way to lure more Gubru up into the mountains within reach. Athaclena and Robert laughed and promised to do what they could about the lack of target practice.

Still, they found themselves hard pressed for ideas. After all, how does one invite back a guest whose beak one has repeatedly bloodied? Perhaps it was time to try taking the war to the enemy, instead.

The problem was lack of good intelligence about matters down in the Sind and Port Helenia. A few survivors of the urban uprising had wandered in and reported that their organization was a shambles. Nobody had seen either Gailet Jones or Fiben Bolger since that ill-fated day. Contact with a few individuals in town was restored, but on a patchy, piecemeal basis.

They had considered sending in new spies. There seemed to be an opportunity offered by the Gubru public announcements, offering lucrative employment to ecological and uplift experts. But by now the avians must certainly have tuned their interrogation apparatus and developed a fair chim lie detector. In any event, Robert and Athaclena decided against taking the risk. For now, at least.

They were walking homeward up a narrow, seldom-visited valley, when they encountered a slope with a southern exposure, covered with a low-lying expanse of peculiar vegetation. They stood quietly for a time, looking over the green field of flat, inverted bowls.

"I never did cook you a meal of baked plate ivy root," Robert commented at last, dryly.

Athaclena sniffed, appreciating his irony. The place where the accident had occurred was far from here. And yet, this bumpy hillside brought back vivid memories of that horrible afternoon when their "adventures" all began.

"Are the plants sick? Is there something wrong with them?" She gestured at the field of plates, overlapping closely like the scales of some slumbering dragon. The upper layers did not look glassy smooth and fat, like those she recalled. The topmost caps in this colony seemed much less thick and sturdy.

"Hm." Robert bent to examine the nearest. "Summer's on its way out, soon. All this heat is already drying the uppermost plates. By mid-autumn, when the east winds come blowing down the Mulun range, the caps will be as thin and light as wafers. Did I ever tell you they were seed pod carriers? The wind will catch them, and they'll blow away into the sky like a cloud of butterflies."

"Oh, yes. I remember you did mention it." Athaclena nodded thoughtfully. "But did not you also say that—"

She was interrupted by a sharp call.

"General! Captain Oneagle!"

A group of chims hurried into view, puffing along the narrow forest trail. Two were members of their escort squad, but the third was Benjamin! He looked exhausted. Obviously he had run all the way from the caves to meet them.

Athaclena felt Robert grow tense with sudden worry. But with the advantage of her corona, she already knew that Ben was not bringing dire news. There was no emergency, no enemy attack.

And yet, her chim aide clearly was confused and distraught. "What is it, Benjamin?" she asked.

He mopped his brow with a homespun handkerchief. Then he reached into another pocket and drew out a small black cube. "Sers, our courier, young Petri, has finally returned."

Robert stepped forward. "Did he reach the refuge?"

Benjamin nodded. "He got there, all right, and he's brought a message from th' Council. This is it here." He held out the cube.

"A message from Megan?" Robert sounded breathless as he looked down at the recording.

"Yesser. Petri says she's well, and sends her best."

"But—but that's great!" Robert whooped. "We're in contact again! We aren't alone anymore!"

"Yesser. That's true enough. In fact . . ." Athaclena watched Benjamin struggle to find the right words. "In fact, Petri brought more than a message. There are five people waiting for you, back at the caves."

Both Robert and Athaclena blinked. "Five humans?"

Benjamin nodded, but with a look that implied he wasn't exactly sure that term was the most applicable. "Terragens Marines, ser."

"Oh," Robert said. Athaclena merely maintained her silence, *kenning* more closely than she was listening.

Benjamin nodded. "Professionals, ser. Five humans. I swear, it's incredible how it feels after all this time without—I mean, with only th' two of you until now. It's made the chims pretty hyper right at the moment. I think it might be best if you both came on back as quick as possible."

Robert and Athaclena spoke almost at once.

"Of course."

"Yes, let's go at once."

Almost imperceptibly, the closeness between Athaclena and Robert altered. They had been holding hands when Benjamin ran up. Now they did not renew that grasp. It seemed inappropriate as they marched along the narrow trail. A new unknown factor had slipped in between them. They did not have to look at each other to know what the other was thinking.

For better or for worse, things had changed.

58

Robert

Major Prathachulthorn pored over the readouts that lay like blown leaves spread across the plotting table. The chaos was only apparent, Robert realized as he watched the small, dark man work, for Prathachulthorn never needed to search for anything. Whatever it was he wanted, somehow he found it with barely a flick of his shadowed eyes and a quick grasp of his callused hands.

At intervals the Marine officer glanced over to a holo-tank and muttered subvocally into his throat microphone. Data whirled in the tank, shifting and turning in subtle rearrangements at his command.

Robert waited, standing at ease in front of the table of rough-cut logs. It was the fourth time Prathachulthorn had summoned him to answer tersely phrased questions. Each time Robert grew more awed by the man's obvious precision and skill.

Clearly, Major Prathachulthorn was a professional. In only a day he and his small staff had started to bring order to the partisans' makeshift tactical programs, rearranging data, sifting out patterns and insights the amateur insurgents had never even imagined.

Prathachulthorn was everything their movement had needed. He was exactly what they had been praying for.

No question about it. Robert hated the man's guts. Now he was trying to figure out exactly why.

I mean, besides the fact that he's making me stand here in silence until he's good and ready. Robert recognized that for a simple way of reinforcing the message of who was boss. Knowing that helped him take it with good grace, mostly.

The major looked every inch the compleat Terragens commando, even though his sole military adornment was an insignia of rank at his left shoulder. Not even in full dress uniform would Robert ever look as much a soldier as Prathachulthorn did right now, draped in ill-fitting cloth woven by gorillas under a sulfrous volcano.

The Earthman spent some time drumming his fingers on the table. The repetitious thumping reminded Robert of the headache he'd been trying to fight off with biofeedback for an hour or more. For some reason the technique wasn't working this time. He felt closed in, claustrophobic, short of breath. And seemed to be getting worse.

At last Prathachulthorn looked up. To Robert's surprise the man's first remark could be taken as something distantly akin to a compliment.

"Well, Captain Oneagle," Prathachulthorn said. "I confess to having feared things would be much, much worse than I find them here.'

"I'm relieved to hear it, sir."

Prathachulthorn's eyes narrowed, as if he suspected an ever-so-thin veneer of sarcasm in Robert's voice. "To be precise," he went on, "I feared I would discover that you had lied in your report to the Council in Exile, and that I would have to shoot you."

Robert suppressed an impulse to swallow and managed to maintain an impassive expression. "I'm glad that did not turn out to be necessary, sir."

"So am I. I'm sure your mother would have been irritated, for one thing. As it is, and bearing in mind that yours was a strictly amateur enterprise, I'm willing to credit you with a good effort here."

Major Prathachulthorn shook his head. "No, that's unfairly restrained. Let me put it this way. There is much I'd have done otherwise, had I been here. But in light of how poorly the official forces have fared, you and your chims have performed very well indeed."

Robert felt a hollowness in his chest begin to relax. "I'm sure the chims will be glad to hear it, sir. I'd like to point out, though, that I was not sole leader here. The Tymbrimi Athaclena carried a good part of that burden."

Major Prathachulthorn's expression turned sour. Robert wasn't sure if it was because Athaclena was a Galactic, or because Robert, as a militia officer, should have retained all authority himself.

"Ah, yes. The 'General.'" His indulgent smile was patronizing, at the very least. He nodded. "I will mention her assistance in my report. Ambassador Uthacalthing's daughter is clearly a resourceful young alien. I hope she is willing to continue helping us, in some capacity."

"The chims worship her, sir," Robert pointed out.

Major Prathachulthorn nodded. As he looked over toward the wall, his voice took on a thoughtful tone. "The Tymbrimi mystique, I know. Sometimes I wonder if the media knows what the hell it's doing, creating such ideas. Allies or no allies, our people have got to understand that Earthclan will always be fundamentally alone. We'll never be able to fully trust anything Galactic."

Then, as if he felt he might have said too much, Prathachulthorn shook his head and changed the subject. "Now about future operations against the enemy—"

"We've been thinking about that, sir. Their mysterious

surge of activity in the mountains seems to have ended, though for how long we don't know. Still, there are some ideas we've been batting around. Things we might use against them when and if they come back."

"Good." Prathachulthorn nodded. "But you must understand that in the future we'll have to coordinate all actions in the Mulun with other planetary forces. Irregulars are simply incapable of hurting the enemy where his real assets are. That was demonstrated when the city chim insurrectionists were wiped out trying to attack the space batteries near Port Helenia."

Robert saw Prathachulthorn's point. "Yessir. Although since then we have captured some munitions which could be useful."

"A few missiles, yes. They might be handy, if we can figure out how to use them. And especially if we have the right information about where to point them.

"We have altogether too little data," the major went on. "I want to gather more and report back to the Council. After that, our task will be to prepare to support any action they choose to undertake."

Robert finally asked the question that he had put off since returning to find Prathachulthorn and his small group of human officers here, turning the cave refuge upside down, poking into everything, taking over. "What will be done with our organization, sir? Athaclena and I, we've given a number of chims working officer status. But except for me nobody here has a real colonial commission."

Prathachulthorn pursed his lips. "Well, you're the simplest case, captain. Clearly you deserve a rest. You can escort Ambassador Uthacalthing's daughter back to the Refuge with our next report, along with my recommendation for a promotion and a medal. I know the Coordinator would like that. You can fill them in on how you made your fine discovery about the Gubru resonance tracking technique."

From his tone of voice, the major made it quite clear what he would think of Robert if he took up the offer. "On the other hand, I'd be pleased to have you join my staff, with a brevet marine status of first lieutenant in addition to your colonial commission. We could use your experience."

"Thank you, sir. I think I'll remain here, if it's all right with you."

"Fine. Then we'll assign someone else to escort—"

"I'm sure Athaclena will want to stay as well," Robert hurriedly added.

"Hmm. Well, yes. I am certain she could be helpful for a while. Tell you what, captain. I'll put the matter to the Council in my next letter. But we must be sure of one thing. Her status is no longer military. The chims are to cease referring to her as a command officer. Is that clear?"

"Yessir, quite clear." Robert only wondered how one enforced that sort of order on civilian neo-chimpanzees, who tended to call anybody and anything whatever they pleased.

"Good. Now, as for those formerly under your command . . . I do happen to have brought with me a few blank colonial commissions which we can assign to chims who have shown notable initiative. I have no doubt you'll recommend names."

Robert nodded. "I will, sir."

He recalled that one other member of their "army" besides himself had already been in the militia. The thought of Fiben—certainly dead for a long time, now—made him suddenly even more depressed. *These caves! They're driving me nuts. It's getting harder and harder to bear the time I must spend down here.*

Major Prathachulthorn was a disciplined soldier and had spent months in the Council's underground refuge. But Robert had no such firmness of character. *I've got to get out!*

"Sir," he said quickly. "I'd like to ask your permission to leave base camp for a few days, to run an errand down near Lorne Pass . . . at the ruins of the Howletts Center."

Prathachulthorn frowned. "The place where those gorillas were illegally gene-meddled?"

"The place where we won our first victory," he reminded the commando, "and where we made the Gubru accept parole."

"Hmph," the major grunted. "What do you expect to find there?"

Robert suppressed an impulse to shrug. In his suddenly worsening claustrophobia, in his need for any excuse to get away, he pulled forth an idea that had until then only been a glimmer at the back of his mind.

"A possible weapon, sir. It's a concept for something that might help a lot, if it worked."

That piqued Prathachulthorn's interest. "What is this weapon?"

"I'd rather not be specific right now, sir. Not until I've

had a chance to verify a few things. I'll only be gone three or four days at the most. I promise."

"Hmm. Well." Prathachulthorn's lips pursed. "It will take that long just to put these data systems into shape. You'll only get underfoot till that's done. Afterwards, though, I'll be needing you. We've got to prepare a report to the Council."

"Yessir, I'll hurry back."

"Very well, then. Take Lieutenant McCue with you. I want one of my own men to see the countryside. Show McCue how you accomplished your little coup, introduce her to the leaders of the more important chim partisan bands in that area, then return without delay. Dismissed."

Robert came to attention. *I think I know now why I hate him,* Robert realized as he saluted, performed an about-face, and walked out through the hanging blanket that served as a door to the subterranean office.

Ever since he had returned to the caves to find Prathachulthorn and his aides moving around like owners, patronizing the chims and judging everything they had all done together, Robert had been unable to stop feeling like a *child* who had, until that moment, been allowed to play a wonderful dramatic role, a really fun *game*. But now the child had to bear paternal pats on the head—strokes that burned, even if intended in praise.

It was an embarrassing analogy, and yet he knew that in a sense it was true after all.

Robert blew a silent sigh and hurried away from the office and dark armory he had shared with Athaclena, but which now had been completely taken over by grownups.

Only when he was finally back under the tall forest canopy did Robert feel he could breathe freely again. The trees' familiar scents seemed to cleanse his lungs of the dank cave odors. The scouts who flitted ahead of him and alongside were those he knew, quick, loyal, feral-looking with their crossbows and sooty faces. *My chims,* he thought, feeling a little guilty that it came to him in those words. But the feeling of proprietorship was there anyway. It was like the "old days"— before yesterday—when he had felt important and needed.

The illusion broke apart, though, the next time Lieutenant McCue spoke.

"These mountain forests are very beautiful," she said. "I wish I'd taken the time to come up here before the war broke

out." The Earthling officer stopped by the side of the trail to
touch a blue-veined flower, but it folded away from her fingers
and retreated backward into the thicket. "I've read about these
things, but this is my first chance to see them for myself."

Robert grunted noncommittally. He would be polite and
answer any direct question, but he wasn't interested in conversation, especially with Major Prathachulthorn's second in
command.

Lydia McCue was an athletic young woman, with dark,
well-cut features. Her movements, lithe like a commando's—or
an assassin's—were by that same nature also quite graceful.
Dressed in homespun kilt and blouse, she might have been
taken for a peasant dancer, if it weren't for the self-winding
arbalest she cradled in the crook of one arm like a child. In
hip pouches were enough darts to pincushion half the Gubru
within a hundred kilometers. The knives sheathed at her
wrists and ankles were for more than show.

She seemed to have very little trouble keeping up with
his rapid pace through the criss-cross jungle mesh of vines.
That was just as well, for he wasn't about to slow down. At
the back of his mind Robert knew he was being unfair. She
was probably a nice enough person in her own way, for a
professional soldier. But for some reason everything likable
about her seemed to irritate him all the more.

Robert wished Athaclena had consented to come along.
But she had insisted on remaining in her glade near the
caves, experimenting with tame vines and crafting strange,
ornate glyphs that were far too subtle to be *kenned* by his
own weak powers. Robert had felt hurt and stormed off,
almost outracing his escorts for the first few kilometers.

"So much life." The Earth woman kept pace beside him
and inhaled the rich odors. "This is a peaceful place."

You're wrong on both counts, Robert thought, with a
trace of contempt for her dull, human insensitivity to the
truth about Garth, a truth he could feel all around him.
Through Athaclena's tutoring he now could reach out—albeit
tentatively, awkwardly—and trace the life-waves that fluxed
through the quiet forest.

"This is an unhappy land," he replied simply. He did
not elaborate, even when she gave him a puzzled look. His
primitive empathy sense withdrew from her confusion.

For a while they moved in silence. The morning aged.
Once the scouts whistled, and they took cover under thick

branches as great cruisers lumbered overhead. When the way was clear Robert took to the trail again without a word.

At last, Lydia McCue spoke again. "This place we're heading for," she asked, "this Howletts Center. Would you please tell me about it?"

It was a simple request. He could not refuse, since Prathachulthorn had sent her along to be shown things. But Robert avoided her black eyes as he spoke. He tried to be matter-of-fact, but emotion kept creeping into his voice. Under her low prompting Robert told Lydia McCue about the sad, misguided, but brilliant work of the renegade scientists. His mother had known nothing of the Howletts Center, of course. It was only by accident that he himself had learned of it a year or so before the invasion, and he had decided to keep silent.

Of course the daring experiment was over now. It would take more than a miracle to save the neo-gorillas from sterilization, now that the secret was known to people like Major Prathachulthorn.

Prathachulthorn might hate Galactic Civilization with a passion that bordered on fanaticism, but he knew how essential it was that Terrans not break their solemn pacts with the great Institutes. Right now, Earth's only hope lay in the ancient codes of the Progenitors. To keep the protection of those codes, weak clans had to be like Caesar's wife, above reproach.

Lydia McCue listened attentively. She had high cheekbones and eyes that were sultry in their darkness. It pained Robert to look at them, though. Those eyes seemed somehow to be set too close together, too immobile. He kept his attention on the crooked path ahead of him.

And yet, with a soft voice the young Marine officer drew him out. Robert found himself talking about Fiben Bolger, about their narrow escape together from the gas-bombing of the Mendoza Freehold, and of his friend's first journey down into the Sind.

And the second, from which he never returned.

They crested a ridge topped with eerie spine-stones and came to an opening overlooking a narrow vale, just west of Lorne Pass. He gestured to the tumbled outlines of several burned structures. "The Howletts Center," he said, flatly.

"This is where you forced the Gubru to acknowledge chim combatants, isn't it? And made them give parole?" Lydia McCue asked. Robert realized he was hearing *respect* in her voice, and turned briefly to stare at her. She returned his look with a smile. Robert felt his face grow warm.

He swung back quickly, pointing to the hillside nearest the center and rapidly describing how the trap had been laid and sprung, skipping only his own trapeze leap to take out the Gubru sentry. His part had been unimportant, anyway. The chims were the crucial ones that morning. He wanted the Earthling soldiers to know that.

He was finishing his story when Elsie approached. The chimmie saluted him, something that had never seemed necessary before the Marines arrived.

"I don't know about actually goin' down there, ser," she said, earnestly. "The enemy's already shown an interest in those ruins. They may have come back."

Robert shook his head. "When Benjamin paroled the enemy survivors, one condition they accepted was to stay out of this valley, and not even keep its approaches under surveillance, from then on. Has there been any sign of them breaking their word?"

Elsie shook her head. "No, but—" Her lips pressed together, as if she felt she ought to forbear comment on the wisdom of trusting the pledges of Eatees.

Robert smiled. "Well, then. Come on. If we hurry we can be in and back out by nightfall."

Elsie shrugged. She made a quick set of hand gestures. Several chims darted out of the spine-stones and down into the forest. After a moment there came an all-clear whistle. The rest of the party crossed the gap at a brisk run.

"They are very good," Lydia McCue told him softly after they were back under the trees again.

Robert nodded, recognizing that she had not qualified her remark by adding, "for amateurs," as Prathachulthorn would have done. He was grateful for that, and wished she wasn't being so nice.

Soon they were picking their way toward tumbled ruins, carefully searching for signs that anyone else had been there since the battle, months ago. There did not seem to be any, but that did not diminish the intense vigilance of the chims.

Robert tried to *kenn*, to use the Net to probe for intruders, but his own jumbled feelings kept getting in the way. He wished Athaclena were here.

The wreckage of the Howletts Center was even more complete than had been apparent from the hillside. The fire-blackened buildings had collapsed further under wild jungle vegetation now growing rampant over former lawns. The Gubru vehicles, long ago stripped of anything useful, lay in tangles of thick grass as tall as his waist.

No, clearly nobody's been here, he thought. Robert kicked through the wreckage. Nothing remained of interest. *Why did I insist on coming?* he wondered. He knew his hunch—whether it panned out or not—had actually been little more than an excuse to escape from the caves—to get away from Prathachulthorn.

To get away from uncomfortable glimpses of himself.

Perhaps one reason he had chosen to come to this place was because it was here that he had had his own brief moment of hand-to-hand contact with the enemy.

Or maybe he had hoped to recreate the feelings of only a few days ago, traveling unfettered and unjudged. He had hoped to come here with different female company than the woman who now followed him, eyes darting left and right, putting everything under professional scrutiny.

Robert turned away from his brooding thoughts and walked toward the ruined alien hover tanks. He sank to one knee, brushing aside the tall, rank grass.

Gubru machinery, the exposed guts of the armored vehicles, gears, impellers, gravitics . . .

A fine yellow patina overlay many of the parts. In some places the shining plastimesh had discolored, thinned, and even broken through. Robert pulled on a small chunk which came off, crumbling, in his hands.

Well I'll be a blue-nosed gopher. I was right. My hunch was right.

"What is it?" Lieutenant McCue asked over his shoulder.

He shook his head. "I'm not sure, yet. But something seems to be eating through a lot of these parts."

"May I see?"

Robert handed her the piece of corroded ceramet.

"This is why you wanted to come here? You suspected this?"

He saw no point in telling her all the complex reasons, the personal ones. "That was a large part of it. I thought, maybe, there might be a weapon in it. They burned all the records and facilities when they evacuated the center. But they couldn't eradicate all the microbes developed in Dr. Schultz's lab."

He didn't add that he had a vial of gorilla saliva in his pack. If he had not found the Gubru armor in this state, on arriving here, he had planned to perform his own experiments.

"Hm." Lydia McCue crumbled the material in her hand. She got down and crawled under the machine to examine which parts had been affected. Finally she emerged and sat next to Robert.

"It could prove useful. But there would still be the problem of a delivery system. We don't dare venture out of the mountains to spray the little bugs over Gubru equipment in Port Helenia.

"Also, bio-sabotage weapons are very short term in their effectiveness. They have to be used all at once and by surprise, since countermeasures are usually swift and effective. After a few weeks, the bugs would be neutralized—chemically, with coatings, or by cloning another beastie to eat ours.

"Still," she turned another piece over and looked up to smile at Robert. "This is great. What you did here before, and now this . . . These are the right ways to fight guerrilla war! I like it. We'll find a way to use it."

Her smile was so open and friendly that Robert couldn't help responding. And in that shared moment he felt a stirring that he had been trying to suppress all day.

Damn, she's attractive, he realized, miserably. His body was sending him signals more powerful than it ever had in the company of Athaclena. And he barely knew this woman! He didn't love her. He wasn't bound up with her, as he was with his Tymbrimi consort.

And yet his mouth was dry and his heart beat faster as she looked at him, this narrow-eyed, thin-nosed, tall-browed, female human. . . .

"We'd better be heading home," he said quickly. "Go ahead and take some samples, lieutenant. We'll test them back at base."

He ignored her long look as he stood up and signaled to Elsie. Soon, with specimens stowed away in their packs, they were climbing once more toward the spine-stones. The watchful guards showed obvious relief as they shouldered their rifles and leaped back into the trees.

Robert followed his escort with little attention to the path. He was trying not to think of the other member of his own race walking beside him, so he frowned and kept himself banked in behind a brumous cloud of his own thoughts.

59

Fiben

Fiben and Gailet sat near each other under the unblinking regard of masked Gubru technicians, who focused their instruments on the two chims with dispassionate, clinical precision. Multi-lensed globes and flat-plate phrased arrays floated on all sides, peering down at them. The testing chamber was a jungle of glistening tubes and shiny-faced machinery, all antiseptic and sterile.

Still, the place reeked of alien bird. Fiben's nose wrinkled, and once again he disciplined himself to avoid thinking unfriendly thoughts about the Gubru. Certainly several of the imposing machines must be psi detectors. And while it was doubtful they could actually "read his mind," the Galactics certainly would be able to trace his surface attitudes.

Fiben reached for something else to think about. He leaned to his left and spoke to Gailet.

"Um, I talked to Sylvie before they came for us this morning. She told me she hasn't been back to the Ape's Grape since that night I first came to Port Helenia."

Gailet turned to look at Fiben. Her expression was tense, disapproving.

"So? Games like that striptease of hers may be obsolete now, but I'm sure the Gubru are finding other ways to use her unique talents."

"She's refused to do anything like that since then, Gailet. Honestly. I can't see why you're so hostile toward her."

"And *I* find it hard to understand how you can be so friendly with one of our jailers!" Gailet snapped. "She's a probationer and a collaborator!"

381

Fiben shook his head. "Actually, Sylvie's not really a probie at all, nor even a gray or yellow. She has a green repro-card. She joined them because—"

"I don't give a damn what her reasons were! Oh, I can imagine what sort of sob story she's told you, you big dope, while she batted her eyelashes and softened you up for—"

From one of the nearby machines came a low, atonal voice. "*Young neo-chimpanzee sophonts . . . be still. Be still, young clients . . .*" it soothed.

Gailet swiveled to face forward, her jaw set.

Fiben blinked. *I wish I understood her better,* he thought. Half the time he had no idea what would set Gailet off.

It was Gailet's moodiness that had started him talking with Sylvie in the first place, simply for company. He wanted to explain that to Gailet, but decided it would do no good. Better to wait. She would come out of this funk. She always did.

Only an hour ago they had been laughing, jostling each other while they fumbled with a complicated mechanical puzzle. For a few minutes they had been able to forget the staring mechanical and alien eyes while they worked as a team, sorting and resorting the pieces and arranging them together. When they stood back at last and looked on the completed tower they had made, they both knew that they had surprised the note-takers. In that moment of satisfaction, Gailet's hand had slipped, innocently and affectionately, into his.

Imprisonment was like that. Part of the time, Fiben actually felt as if he were profiting from the experience. It was the first time in his life, for instance, that he'd ever really had time to just sit and think. Their captors now let them have books, and he was catching up on quite a few volumes he'd always wanted to read. Conversations with Gailet had opened up the arcane world of alienology. He, in turn, had spoken to her of the great work being done here on Garth, delicately nudging a ruined ecosystem back toward health.

But then, all too common, had been the long, darker intervals, when the hours dragged on and on. A pall hung over them at such times. The walls seemed to close in, and conversation always came back to the War, to memories of their failed insurrection, to lost friends and gloomy speculations over the fate of Earth itself.

At such times, Fiben thought he might trade all hope of

a long life for just an hour to run free under trees and clean sky.

So even this new routine of testing by the Gubru had come as a relief for both of them. At least it was a distraction.

Without warning, the machines suddenly pulled away, opening an avenue in front of their bench. *"We are finished, finished. . . . You have done well, done well, you have . . . Now follow the globe, follow it, toward transportation."*

As Fiben and Gailet stood up, a brown, octahedral projection took form in front of them. Without looking at each other they followed the hologram past the silent, brooding avian technicians, out of the testing chamber, and down a long hallway.

Service robots swept past them with the soft whisper of well-tuned machinery. Once a Kwackoo technician darted out of an office door, favored them with a startled look, then ducked back inside. At last Fiben and Gailet passed through a hissing portal and emerged into bright sunshine. Fiben had to shade his eyes. The day was fair, but with a bite that seemed to say that brief summer was now well on its way out. The chims he could see in the streets, beyond the Gubru compound, were wearing light sweaters and sneakers, another sure sign that autumn was near.

None of the chims looked their way. The distance was too great for Fiben to tell anything of their mood, or to hope that somebody might recognize him or Gailet.

"We won't be riding the same car back," whispered Gailet. And she motioned down a long parapet toward the landing ramp below. Sure enough, the tan military van that had brought them had been replaced by a large, roofless hover barge. An ornate pedestal stood in the open deck behind the pilot's station. Kwackoo servitors adjusted a sunshade to keep the fierce light of Gimelhai off their master's beak and crest.

The large Gubru was recognizable. Its thick, faintly luminous plumage looked shaggier than the last time they had seen it, in the furtive darkness of their suburban prison. The effect was to make it seem even more different than the run-of-the-mill Gubru functionaries they had seen. In some places the allochroous feathers had begun to appear frayed, tattered. The avian aristocrat wore a striped collar. It paced impatiently atop its perch.

"Well, well," Fiben muttered. "If it ain't our old friend, the Somethin' of Good Housekeeping."

Gailet snorted in something just short of a small laugh. "It's called the Suzerain of Propriety," she reminded him. "The striped torc means it's the leader of the priestly caste. Now just you remember to behave yourself. Try not to scratch too much, and watch what I do."

"I'll imitate yer very steps precisely, mistress."

Gailet ignored his sarcasm and followed the brown guidance hologram down the long ramp toward the brightly colored barge. Fiben kept pace just a little behind her.

The guide projection vanished as they reached the landing. A Kwackoo, with its feathery ruff tinted a garish shade of pink, offered them both a very shallow bow. "You are honored—honored . . . that our patron—noble patron does deign to show you—you half-formed ones . . . the favor of your destiny."

The Kwackoo spoke without the assistance of a vodor. That in itself was no small miracle, given the creature's highly specialized speech organs. In fact, it spoke the Anglic words fairly clearly, if with a breathless quality which made the alien sound nervous, expectant.

It wasn't likely the Suzerain of Propriety was the easiest boss in the Universe to work for. Fiben imitated Gailet's bow and kept silent as she replied. "We are honored by the attention that your master, the high patron of a great clan, condescends to offer us," she said in slow, carefully enunciated Galactic Seven. "Nevertheless, we retain, in our own patrons' names, the right to disapprove its actions."

Even Fiben gasped. The assembled Kwackoo cooed in anger, fluffing up threateningly.

Three high, chirped notes cut their outrage off abruptly. The lead Kwackoo swiveled quickly and bowed to the Suzerain, who had scuttled to the end of its perch closest to the two chims. The Gubru's beak gaped as it bent to regard Gailet, first with one eye, then the other. Fiben found himself sweating rivulets.

Finally, the alien straightened and squawked a pronouncement in its own highly clipped, inflected version of Galactic Three. Only Fiben saw the tremor of relief that passed down Gailet's tense spine. He could not follow the Suzerain's stilted prose, but a vodor nearby commenced translating promptly.

"Well said—said well . . . spoken well for captured,

client-class soldiers of foe-clan Terra. . . . Come, then—come and see . . . come and see and hear a bargain you will certainly not disapprove—not even in your patrons' names."

Gailet and Fiben glanced at each other. Then, as one, they bowed.

The late morning air was clear, and the faint ozone smell probably did not foretell rain. Such ancient cues were useless in the presence of high technology anyway.

The barge cruised south past the closed pleasure piers of Port Helenia and out across the bay. It was Fiben's first chance to see how the harbor had changed since the aliens had arrived.

The fishing fleet had been crippled for one thing. Only one in four trawlers did not lie beached or in dry dock. The main commercial port was almost dead as well. A clump of dispirited-looking seafaring vessels listed at their moorings, clearly untouched for months. Fiben watched one of the still working fishing trawlers heave into view around the point of the bay, probably returning early with a fortuitous catch—or with a mechanical failure the chim crew felt unable to deal with at sea. The tub-bottomed boat rose and fell as it rode the standing swell where sea met bay. The crew had to struggle since the passage was narrower than it had been in days of peace. Half of the strait was now blocked by a towering, curving cliff face—a great fortress of alien cerametal.

The Gubru battleship seemed to shimmer in a faint haze. Water droplets condensed at the fringes of its ward-screens, rainbows sparkled, and a mist fell over the struggling trawler as it forced its way past the northern tongue of land at last. Fiben could not make out the faces of the chim crew as the Suzerain's barge swept overhead, but he saw several long-armed forms slump in relief as the boat reached calm waters at last.

From Point Borealis the upper arm of the bayshore swept several kilometers north and east toward Port Helenia itself. Except for a small navigation beacon, those rough heights were unoccupied. The branches of ridgetop pines riffled gently in the sea breezes.

Southward, however, across the narrow strait, things were quite different. Beyond the grounded battleship, the terrain had been transformed. Forest growth had been removed, the contours of the bluffs altered. Dust rose from a site just out of view beyond the headland. A swarm of hovers and heavy lifters could be seen buzzing to and fro in that direction.

Much farther to the south, toward the spaceport, new domes had been erected as part of the Gubru defensive network—the facilities the urban guerrillas had only mildly inconvenienced in their abortive insurrection. But the barge did not seem to be heading that way. Rather they turned toward the new construction on the narrow, hilly slopes between Aspinal Bay and the Sea of Cilmar.

Fiben knew it was hopeless asking their hosts what was going on. The Kwackoo technicians and servitors were polite, but it was a severe sort of courtesy, probably on orders. And they were not forthcoming with much information.

Gailet joined him at the railing and took his elbow. "Look," she whispered in a hushed voice.

Together they stared as the barge rose over the bluffs.

A hilltop had been shorn flat near the ocean shoreline. Buildings Fiben recognized as proton power plants lay clustered around its base, feeding cables upward, along its flanks. At the top, a hemispherical structure lay face upward, glimmering and open like a marble bowl in the sunshine.

"What is it? A force field projector? Some kind of weapon?"

Fiben nodded, shook his head, and finally shrugged. "Beats me. It doesn't look military. But whatever it does sure must take a lot of juice. Look at all those power plants. Goodall!"

A shadow slipped over them—not with the fluffy, ragged coolness of a cloud passing before the sun, but with the sudden, sharp chill of something solid and huge rumbling over their heads. Fiben shivered, only partly from the drop in temperature. He and Gailet couldn't help crouching as they looked up at the giant lifter-carrier that cruised only a hundred meters higher. Their avian hosts, on the other hand, appeared unruffled. The Suzerain stood on its perch, placidly ignoring the thrumming fields that made the chims tremble.

They don't like surprise, Fiben thought. *But they are pretty tough when they know what's happening*.

Their transport began a long, slow, lazy circuit around the perimeter of the construction site. Fiben was pondering the white, upturned bowl below when the Kwackoo with the pink ruff approached and inclined its head ever so slightly.

"The Great One deigns—does offer favor . . . and will

suggest commonality—complementarity . . . of goals and aims."

Across the barge, the Suzerain of Propriety could be seen perched regally on its pedestal. Fiben wished he could read expressions on a Gubru face. *What's the old bird got in mind?* he wondered. Fiben wasn't entirely sure he really wanted to know.

Gailet returned the shallow bow of the Kwackoo. "Please tell your honored patron we will humbly attend his offer."

The Suzerain's Galactic Three was stilted and formal, embellished with mincing, courtly dance steps. The vodor translation did not help Fiben much. He found himself watching Gailet, rather than the alien, as he tried to follow what the hell they were talking about.

". . . *allowable revision to Ritual of Choice of Uplift Advisor . . . modification made during time of stress, by foremost client representatives . . . if performed truly in best interests of their patron race . . .*" Gailet seemed visibly shaken, looking up at the Gubru. Her lips pressed together in a tight line, and her intertwined fingers were white with tension. When the Suzerain stopped chirping, the vodor continued on for a moment, then silence closed in around them, leaving only the whistle of passing air and the faint droning of the hover's engines.

Gailet swallowed. She bowed and seemed to have difficulty finding her voice.

You can do it, Fiben urged silently. Speechlock could strike any chim, especially under pressure like this, but he knew he dared not do anything to help her.

Gailet coughed, swallowed again, and managed to bring forth words.

"Hon-honored elder, we . . . we cannot speak for our patrons, or even for all the chims on Garth. What you ask is . . . is . . ."

The Suzerain spoke again, as if her reply had been complete. Or perhaps it simply was not considered impolite for a patron-class being to interrupt a client.

"You have no need—need not . . . to answer now," the vodor pronounced as the Gubru chirped and bobbed on its perch. "Study—learn—consider . . . the materials you will be given. This opportunity will be to your advantage."

The chirping ceased again, followed by the buzzing vodor.

The Suzerian seemed to dismiss them then, simply by closing its eyes.

As if at some signal invisible to Fiben, the pilot of the hover barge banked away from the frenzied activity atop the ravaged hilltop and sent the craft streaking back across the bay, northward, toward Port Helenia. Soon the battleship in the harbor—gigantic and imperturbable—fell behind them in its wreath of mist and rainbows.

Fiben and Gailet followed a Kwackoo to seats at the back of the barge. "What was all that about?" Fiben whispered to her. "What was the damn thing sayin' about some sort of ceremony? What does it want us to do?"

"Sh!" Gailet motioned for him to be silent. "I'll explain later, Fiben. Right now, please, let me think."

Gailet settled into a corner, wrapping her arms around her knees. Absently, she scratched the fur on her left leg. Her eyes were unfocused, and when Fiben made a gesture, as if to offer to groom her, she did not even respond. She only looked off toward the horizon, as if her mind were very far away.

Back in their cell they found that many changes had been made. "I guess we passed all those tests," Fiben said, staring at their transformed quarters.

The chains had been taken away soon after the Suzerain's first visit, that dark night weeks ago. After that occasion the straw on the floor had been replaced by mattresses, and they had been allowed books.

Now, though, that was made to seem Spartan, indeed. Plush carpeting had been laid down, and an expensive holo-tapestry covered most of one wall. There were such amenities as beds and chairs and a desk, and even a music deck.

"Bribes," Fiben muttered as he sorted through some of the record cubes. "Hot damn, we've got something they want. Maybe the Resistance *isn't* over. Maybe Athaclena and Robert are stinging them, and they want us to—"

"This hasn't got anything to do with your general, Fiben," Gailet said in a very low voice, barely above a whisper. "Or not much, at least. It's a whole lot bigger than that." Her expression was tense. All the way back, she had been silent and nervous. At times Fiben imagined he could hear wheels turning in her head.

Gailet motioned for him to follow her to the new holo-wall. At the moment it was set to depict a three-dimensional scene of abstract shapes and patterns—a seemingly endless vista of glossy cubes, spheres, and pyramids stretching into the infinite distance. She sat cross-legged and twiddled with the controls. "This is an expensive unit," she said, a little louder than necessary. "Let's have some fun and find out what it can do."

As Fiben sat down beside her, the Euclidean shapes blurred and vanished. The controller clicked under Gailet's hand, and a new scene suddenly leaped into place. The wall now seemed to open onto a vast, sandy beach. Clouds filled the sky out to a lowering, gray horizon, pregnant with storms. Breakers rolled less than twenty meters away, so realistic that Fiben's nostrils flared as he tried to catch the salt scent.

Gailet concentrated on the controls. "This may be the ticket," he heard her mumble. The almost perfect beachscape flickered, and in its place there suddenly loomed a wall of leafy green—a jungle scene, so near and real that Fiben almost felt he could leap through and escape into its green mists, as if this were one of those mythical "teleportation devices" one read of in romantic fiction, and not just a high-quality holo-tapestry.

He contemplated the scene Gailet had chosen. Fiben could tell at once that it wasn't a jungle of Garth. The creeper-entwined rain forest was a vibrant, lively, noisy scene, filled with color and variety. Birds cawed and howler monkeys shrieked.

Earth, then, he thought, and wondered if the Galaxy would ever let him fulfill his dream of someday seeing the homeworld. *Not bloody likely, the way things are*.

His attention drew back as Gailet spoke. "Just let me adjust this here, to make it more realistic." The sound level rose. Jungle noise burst forth to surround them. *What is she trying to do?* he wondered.

Suddenly he noticed something. As Gailet twiddled with the volume level, her left hand moved in a crude but eloquent gesture. Fiben blinked. It was a sign in baby talk, the hand language all infant chims used until the age of four, when speech finally became useful.

Grownups listening, she said.

Jungle sounds seemed to fill the room, reverberating

from the other walls. "There," she said in a low voice. "Now they can't listen in on us. We can talk frankly."

"But—" Fiben started to object, then he saw the gesture again. *Grownups listening. . . .*

Once more his respect for Gailet's cleverness grew. *Of course* she knew this simple method would not stop snoopers from picking up their every word. But the Gubru and their agents might imagine the chims foolish enough to think it would! If the two of them acted as if they *believed* they were safe from eavesdropping . . .

Such a tangled web we weave, Fiben thought. This was real spy stuff. Fun, in a way.

It was also, he knew, dangerous as hell.

"The Suzerain of Propriety has a problem," Gailet told him aloud. Her hands lay still on her lap.

"It *told* you that? But if the Gubru are in trouble, why—"

"I didn't say the *Gubru*—although I think that's true, as well. I was talking about the Suzerain of Propriety itself. It's having troubles with its peers. The priest seriously overcommitted itself in a certain matter, some time back, and now it seems there's hell to pay over it."

Fiben just sat there, amazed that the lofty alien lord had deigned to tell an earthworm of a Terran client such things. He wasn't comfortable with the idea. Such confidences were likely to be unhealthy. "What were these overcommitments?" he asked.

"Well, for one thing," Gailet went on, scratching her kneecap, "some months ago it insisted that many parties of Talon Soldiers and scientists be sent up into the mountains."

"What for?"

Gailet's face took on an expression of severe control. "They were sent searching for . . . for Garthlings."

"For *what?*" Fiben blinked. He started to laugh. Then he cut short when he saw the warning flicker in her eyes. The hand scratching her knee curled and turned in a motion that signified caution.

"For Garthlings," she repeated.

Of all the superstitious nonsense, Fiben thought. *Ignorant, yellow-card chims use Garthling fables to frighten their children.* It was rich to think of the sophisticated Gubru falling for such tall tales.

Gailet did not seem to find the idea amusing, though.

"You can imagine why the Suzerain would be excited, Fiben, once it had reason to believe Garthlings might exist. Imagine what a fantastic coup it would be for any clan who claimed adoption rights on a pre-sentient race that had survived the Bururalli Holocaust. Immediate takeover of Earth's tenancy rights here would be the very least of the consequences."

Fiben saw her point. "But . . . but what in the world made it think in the first place, that—"

"It seems our Tymbrimi Ambassador, Uthacalthing, was largely responsible for the Suzerain's fixation, Fiben. You remember that day of the chancery explosion, when you tried to break into the Tymbrimi Diplomatic Cache?"

Fiben opened his mouth. He closed it again. He tried to think. What kind of game was Gailet playing now?

The Suzerain of Propriety obviously knew that he, Fiben, was the chim who had been sighted ducking through the smoke and stench of fried Gubru clerical workers on the day of the explosion at the one-time Tymbrimi Embassy. It knew Fiben was the one who had played a frustrated game of tag with the cache guardian, and who later escaped over a cliff face under the very beaks of a squad of Talon Soldiers.

Did it know because Gailet had told it? If so, had she also told the Suzerain about the secret message Fiben had found in the back of the cache and delivered to Athaclena?

He could not ask her these things. The warning look in her eyes kept him silent. *I hope she knows what she's doing,* he prayed fervently. Fiben felt clammy under his arms. He brushed a bead of sweat from his eyebrow. "Go on," he said in a dry voice.

"Your visit invalidated diplomatic immunity and gave the Gubru the excuse they were looking for, to break into the cache. Then the Gubru had what they thought was a real stroke of luck. The cache autodestruct partially failed. There was evidence inside, Fiben, evidence pertaining to private investigations into the Garthling question by the Tymbrimi Ambassador."

"By *Uthacalthing*? But . . ." And then it hit Fiben. He stared at Gailet, goggle-eyed. Then he doubled over, coughing as he fought not to laugh out loud. Hilarity was like a head of steam in his chest, a force in its own right, barely contained. A sudden, brief spell of speechlock was actually a blessing, as it kept Gailet from having to shush him. He coughed some more and slapped his chest. "Excuse me," he said in a small voice.

"The Gubru now believe that the evidence was contrived, a clever ruse," she went on.

No kidding, Fiben thought silently.

"In addition to faked data, Uthacalthing also arranged to have the Planetary Library stripped of its Uplift files, making it seem to the Suzerain as if something was being hidden. It cost the Gubru a lot to find out that Uthacalthing had tricked them. A research-class Planetary Library was shipped in, for instance. And they lost quite a few scientists and soldiers up in the mountains before they figured it out."

"*Lost* them?" Fiben sat forward. "Lost how?"

"Chim irregulars," Gailet answered tersely. And again there was that warning look. *Come on, Gailet,* he thought. *I'm not an idiot.* Fiben knew better than to refer in any way to Robert or Athaclena. He shied away from even thinking about them.

Still, he couldn't quite suppress a smile. So that was why the Kwackoo had been so polite! If chims were waging intelligent war, *and* by the official rules at that, then *all* chims had to be treated with some minimal degree of respect.

"The mountain chims survived that first day! They must've stung the invaders, and kept stingin' 'em!" He knew he was free to vent a bit of exultation. It would only be keeping in character.

Gailet's smile was thin. This news must have given rise to mixed feelings. After all, her own part of the insurrection had gone very much worse.

So, Fiben thought, *Uthacalthing's elaborate ruse persuaded the Gubru that there was something on the planet at least as important as the colony's value as hostage. Garthlings! Imagine that. They went up into the mountains chasing a myth. And somehow the general found a way to hurt them as soon as they came within reach.*

Oh, I'm sorry for all those things I thought about her old man. What a great jape, Uthacalthing!

But now the invaders are wise to it. I wonder if . . .

Fiben glanced up and saw that Gailet was watching him intently, as if gauging his very thoughts. At last Fiben understood one of the reasons why she could not be completely open and frank with him.

We have to make a decision, he realized. *Should we try to lie to the Gubru?*

He and Gailet might make the attempt, try to prop up Uthacalthing's practical joke for just a while longer. They might succeed in convincing the Suzerain just one more time to go off hunting mythical-Garthlings. It would be worth the effort if it drew even one more party of Gubru within reach of the mountain fighters.

But did either he or Gailet have anywhere near enough sophistication to pull off such a ruse? What would it take? He could just picture it. *Oh yes, massa, there is Garthlin's after all, yes boss. You can believe brer chim, yassa.*

Or, alternatively, they could try reverse psychology. *D-o-o-on't throw me in dat briar patch . . . !*

Neither approach at all resembled the way Uthacalthing had done it, of course. The tricky Tymbrimi had played a game of subtle, colubrine misdirection. Fiben did not even toy with the idea of trying to operate on so sophisticated a plane.

And anyway, if he and Gailet were caught trying to lie to the Gubru, it could very well disqualify the two of them from whatever special status the Suzerain of Propriety seemed to be offering this afternoon. Fiben had no idea what the creature wanted of them, but it just might mean a chance to find out what the invaders were building out there by the Sea of Cilmar. That could be vital information.

No, it just wasn't worth the risk, Fiben decided.

Now he faced another problem, how to communicate these thoughts to Gailet.

"Even the most sophisticated sophont race can make mistakes," he said slowly, enunciating carefully. "Especially when they are on a strange world." Pretending to look for a flea, he shaped the baby talk sign for *Game finished now?*

Obviously Gailet agreed. She nodded firmly. "The mistake is over now. They're sure Garthlings are a myth. The Gubru are convinced it was just a Tymbrimi trap. Anyway, I get an impression the other Suzerains—the ones that share command with the high priest—won't allow any more pointless forays into the mountains, where they can be potshotted by guerrillas."

Fiben's head jerked up. His heart pounded for a few, quick moments. Then it came to him what Gailet had meant . . . how the last word she had spoken was intended to be spelled. Homonyms were one of many awkward drawbacks modern Anglic had inherited from old-style English, Chinese, and Japanese. While Galactic languages had been carefully designed to maximize information content and eliminate ambiguity, wolfling tongues had evolved rough and wild, with lots of idiosyncrasies, such as words with identical sounds but different meanings.

Fiben found his fists had clenched. He forced himself to relax. *Guerrillas, not gorillas. She doesn't know about the clandestine Uplift project in the mountains*, Fiben reassured himself. *She has no idea how ironic her remark sounded.*

One more reason, though, to end Uthacalthing's "joke" once and for all. The Tymbrimi could not have been any more aware of the Howletts Center than his daughter. Had he known about the secret work there, Uthacalthing would certainly have chosen a different ruse, not one meant to send the Gubru into those very same mountains.

The Gubru must not go back into the Mulun, Fiben realized. *It's only luck they haven't already discovered the 'rillas.*

"Stupid birds," he muttered, playing to Gailet's line. "Imagine them falling for a dumb, wolfling folk tale. After Garthlings, what'll they go after next? Peter Pan?"

Superficially, Gailet's expression was reproving. "You must try to be more respectful, Fiben." Underneath, though, he felt a strong current of approval. They might not have the same reasons, but they were in agreement this far. Uthacalthing's joke was over.

"What they're going after next, Fiben, is us."

He blinked. "Us?"

She nodded. "I'm guessing the war isn't going very well for the Gubru. Certainly they haven't found the dolphin ship that everyone's chasing, over on the other side of the Galaxy. And taking Garth hostage doesn't seem to have budged Earth or the Tymbrimi. I'd bet it only stiffened the resistance, and gained Terra some sympathy among former neutrals."

Fiben frowned. It had been so long since he had thought about the larger scope—about the turmoil raging all across the Five Galaxies—about the *Streaker*—about the siege of Terra. Just how much did Gailet *know*, and how much was mere speculation?

In the nearby weather wall, a big black bird with a huge, gaily colored bill was depicted landing in a rustle very close to the carpet where Fiben and Gailet sat. It stepped forward and seemed to regard Fiben, first with one eye, then the other. The Toucan reminded him of the Suzerain of Propriety. Fiben shivered.

"Anyway," Gailet went on, "the enterprise here on Garth seems to be a drain on their resources that the Gubru can't afford too well, especially if peace does return to Galactic society, and the Institute for Civilized Warfare makes them give the planet back in only a few decades or so. I figure they're looking real hard for some way to make a profit out of all this."

Fiben had an inspiration. "All that construction by South Point is part of that, right? It's part of the Suzerain's plan to save his hash."

Gailet's lips pursed. "Colorfully put. Have you figured out what it is they're building?"

The multicolored bird on the branch cawed sharply and seemed to be laughing at Fiben. But when he glanced sharply that way it had already returned to the serious business of picking through the imaginary detritus on the forest floor. Fiben looked back at Gailet. "You tell me," he said.

"I'm not sure I can remember well enough to translate what the Suzerain said. I was pretty nervous, you'll remember." Her eyes closed for a moment. "Would—would a *hyperspace shunt* mean anything to you?"

The bird in the wall took off in an explosion of feathers and leaves as Fiben leaped to his feet, backing more than a meter away. He stared down at Gailet in disbelief.

"A *what*? But that's . . . that's crazy! Build a shunt on the surface of a *planet*? It's just not—"

Then he stopped, remembering the great marble bowl, the mammoth power plants. Fiben's lips quivered and his hands came together, pulling on opposite thumbs. In this way, Fiben reminded himself that he was officially almost the equal of a man—that he should be able to think like one when facing such incredible improbability. "What . . ." He whispered, licked his lips, and concentrated on the words. "What's it *for*?"

"I'm not so clear on that," Gailet said. He could barely hear her over the squawking from the make-believe forest. Her finger traced a hand sign on the carpet, one which stood for confusion. "I think it was originally intended for some ceremony, if they were ever able to find and claim Garthlings.

Now, the Suzerain needs something to salvage out of their investment, probably another use for the shunt.

"If I understood the Gubru leader, Fiben, it wants to use the shunt for us."

Fiben sat down again. For a long moment they did not look at each other. There were only the amplified jungle sounds, the colors of a luminescent fog flowing in between the leaves of a holographic rain forest, and the inaudible murmur of their own uncertain fear. The facsimile of a bright bird watched them for a little while longer from a replicant branch high overhead. When the ghostly fog turned to insubstantial rain, however, it finally spread fictitious wings and flew away.

60

Uthacalthing

The Thennanin was obdurate. There did not seem to be any way to get through to him.

Kault seemed almost a stereotype, a caricature of his race—bluff, open, honorable to a fault, and so trusting that it threatened to drive Uthacalthing into fits of frustration. The glyph, *teev'nus*, was incapable of expressing Uthacalthing's bafflement. Over the last few days, something stronger had begun taking shape in the tendrils of his corona—something pungent and reminiscent of human metaphor.

Uthacalthing realized he was starting to get "pissed off."

Just what would it take to raise Kault's suspicions? Uthacalthing wondered if he should pretend to talk in his sleep, muttering dire hints and confessions. Would that raise an inkling under the Thennanin's thick skull? Or maybe he should abandon all subtlety and *write out* the entire scenario, leaving the unfolded pages in the open for Kault to find!

Individuals can vary widely within a species, Uthacalthing knew. And Kault was an anomaly, even for a Thennanin. It would probably never occur to the fellow to spy on his Tymbrimi companion. Uthacalthing found it hard to understand how Kault could have made it this far in the diplomatic corps of *any* race.

Fortunately, the darker aspects of the Thennanin nature were not also exaggerated in him. Members of Kault's faction, it seemed, weren't quite as smugly sanctimonious or utterly convinced of their own righteousness as those currently in charge of clan policy. More the pity, then, that one side effect of Uthacalthing's planned jest, if it ever succeeded, would be to weaken that moderate wing even more.

Regrettable. But it would take a miracle to ever bring Kault's group into power anyway, Uthacalthing reminded himself.

Anyway, the way things were heading, he was going to be spared the moral quandary of worrying about the consequences of his practical joke. At the moment it was getting exactly nowhere. So far this had been a most frustrating journey. The only compensation was that this was not, after all, a Gubru detention camp.

They were in the low, rolling countryside leading inexorably upward toward the southern slopes of the Mountains of Mulun. The variety-starved ecosystem of the plains was giving way gradually to somewhat less monotonous scenery—scrub trees and eroded terraces whose reddish and tan sedimentary layers glittered with the morning light, winking as if in secret knowledge of long departed days.

As the wanderers' trek brought them ever closer to the mountains, Uthacalthing kept adjusting their path, guided by a certain blue twinkle on the horizon—a glimmer so faint that his eyes could barely make it out at times. He knew for a fact that Kault's visual apparatus could not detect the spark at all. It had been planned that way.

Faithfully following the intermittent glow, Uthacalthing had led the way and kept a careful watch for the telltale clues. Every time he spotted one, Uthacalthing went through the motions, dutifully rubbing out traces in the dirt, surreptitiously throwing away stone tools, making furtive notes and hiding them quickly when his fellow refugee appeared around the bend.

By now anyone else would be positively *seething* with curiosity. But not Kault. No, not Kault.

Just this morning it had been the Thennanin's turn to lead. Their route took them along the edge of a mud flat, still damp from the recent onset of autumn rains. There, crossing their path in plain sight, had been a trail of footprints no more than a few hours old, obviously laid by something shuffling on two legs and a knuckle. But Kault just strode on past, sniffing the air with those great breathing slits of his, commenting in his booming voice on how fresh the day felt!

Uthacalthing consoled himself that this part of his scheme had always been a long shot anyway. Maybe his plan just wasn't meant to come about.

Perhaps I am simply not clever enough. Perhaps both Kault's race and my own assigned their dullest types to duty on this back-of-the-arm planet.

Even among humans, there were those who certainly would have been able to come up with something better. One of those legendary agents of the Terragens Council, for instance.

Of course there were no agents or other, more imaginative Tymbrimi here on Garth when the crisis hit. He had been forced to come up with the best plan he could.

Uthacalthing wondered about the other half of his jest. It was clear the Gubru had fallen for his ruse. But how deeply? How much trouble and expense had it cost them? More importantly from the point of view of a Galactic diplomat, how badly had they been embarrassed?

If the Gubru had proved as dense and slow as Kault . . .

But no, the Gubru are reliable, Uthacalthing reassured himself. *The Gubru, at least, are quite proficient at deceit and hypocrisy.* It made them easier enemies than the Thennanin.

He shaded his eyes, contemplating how the morning had aged. The air was getting warm. There was a swishing sound, the crackle of breaking foliage. Kault strode into view a few meters back, grumbling a low marching tune and using a long stick to brush shrubs out of his path. Uthacalthing wondered. *If our peoples are officially at war, why is it so hard for Kault to notice that I am obviously hiding something from him?*

"Hmmmph," the big Thennanian grunted as he approached. "Colleague, why have we stopped?"

The words were in Anglic. Recently they had made a

game of using a different language every day, for practice. Uthacalthing gestured skyward. "It is almost midday, Kault. Gimelhai is getting fierce. We had better find a place to get out of the sun."

Kault's leathery ridge crest puffed. "Get out of the sun? But we are not *in* . . . oh. Aha. Ha. Ha. A wolfling figure of speech. Very droll. Yes, Uthacalthing. When Gimelhai reaches zenith, it might indeed feel somewhat as if we were roasting in its outer shell. Let us find shelter."

A small stand of brushy trees stood atop a hillock, not far away. This time Kault led, swinging his homemade staff to clear a path through the tall, grassy growth.

By now they were well practiced at the routine. Kault did the heavy work of delving a comfortable niche, down to where the soil was cool. Uthacalthing's nimble hands tied the Thennanin's cape into place as a sunshade. They rested against their packs and waited out the hot middle part of the day.

While Uthacalthing dozed, Kault spent the time entering data in his lap datawell. He picked up twigs, berries, bits of dirt, rubbed them between his large, powerful fingers, and held the dust up to his scent-slits before examining it with his small collection of instruments salvaged from the crashed yacht.

The Thennanin's diligence was all the more frustrating to Uthacalthing, since Kault's serious investigations of the local ecosystem had somehow missed every single clue Uthacalthing had thrown his way. *Perhaps it is* because *they were thrown at him*. Uthacalthing pondered. The Thennanin were a systematic folk. Possibly, Kault's worldview prevented him from seeing that which did not fit into the pattern that his careful studies revealed.

An interesting thought. Uthacalthing's corona fashioned a glyph of appreciated surprise as, all at once, he saw that the Thennanin approach might not be as cumbersome as he had thought. He had assumed that it was stupidity that made Kault impervious to his fabricated clues, but . . .

But after all, the clues really are lies. My confederate out in the bush lays out hints for me to "find" and "hide." When Kault ignores them, could it be because his obstinate worldview is actually superior? In reality, he has proven almost impossible to fool!

True or not, it was an interesting idea. *Syrtunu* riffled and tried to lift off, but Uthacalthing's corona lay limp, too lazy to abet the glyph.

Instead, his thoughts drifted to Athaclena.

He knew his daughter still lived. To try to learn more would invite detection by the enemy's psi devices. Still, there was something in those traces—trembling undertones down in the *nahakieri* levels of feeling—which told Uthacalthing that he would have much new to learn about Athaclena, should they ever meet again in this world.

"In the end, there is a limit to the guidance of parents," a soft voice seemed to say to him as he drifted in half-slumber. *"Beyond that, a child's destiny is her own."*

And what of the strangers who enter her life? Uthacalthing asked the glimmering figure of his long-dead wife, whose shape seemed to hover before him, beyond his closed eyelids.

"Husband, what of them? They, too, will shape her. And she them. But our own time ebbs."

Her face was so clear. . . . This was a dream such as humans were known to have, but which was rarer among Tymbrimi. It was visual, and meaning was conveyed in words rather than glyphs. A flux of emotion made his fingertips tremble.

Mathicluanna's eyes separated, and her smile reminded him of that day in the capital when their coronae had first touched . . . stopping him, stunned and still in the middle of a crowded street. Half-blinded by a glyph without any name, he had hunted the trace of her down alleyways, across bridges, and past dark cafes, seeking with growing desperation until, at last, he found her waiting for him on a bench not twelve sistaars from where he had first sensed her.

"You see?" she asked in the dream voice of that long ago girl. *"We are shaped. We change. But what we once were, that, too, remains always."*

Uthacalthing stirred. His wife's image rippled, then vanished in wavelets of rolling light. *Syullf-tha* was the glyph that hovered in the space where she had been . . . standing for the joy of a puzzle not yet solved.

He sighed and sat up, rubbing his eyes.

For some reason Uthacalthing thought that the bright daylight might disperse the glyph. But *syullf-tha* was more than a mere dream by now. Without any volition on his part, it rose and moved slowly away from Uthacalthing toward his companion, the big Thennanin.

Kault sat with his back to Uthacalthing, still absorbed in his studies, completely unaware as *syullf-tha* transformed

. . . changed subtly into *syulff-kuonn*. It settled slowly over Kault's ridge crest, descended, settled in, and disappeared. Uthacalthing stared, amazed, as Kault grunted and looked up. The Thennanin's breath-slits wheezed as he put down his instruments and turned to face Uthacalthing.

"There is something very strange here, colleague. Something I am at a loss to explain."

Uthacalthing moistened his lips before answering. "Do tell me what concerns you, esteemed ambassador."

Kault's voice was a low rumble. "There appears to be a creature . . . one that has been foraging in these berry patches not long ago. I have seen traces of its eating for some days now, Uthacalthing. It is large . . . very large for a creature of Garth."

Uthacalthing was still getting used to the idea that *syulff-kuonn* had penetrated where so many subtler and more powerful glyphs had failed. "Indeed? Is this of significance?"

Kault paused, as if uncertain whether to say more. The Thennanin finally sighed. "My friend, it is most odd. But I must tell you that there should be no animal, since the Bururalli Holocaust, able to reach so high into these bushes. And its manner of foraging is quite extraordinary."

"Extraordinary in what way?"

Kault's crest inflated in short puffs, indicating confusion. "I ask that you do not laugh at me, colleague."

"Laugh at you? Never!" Uthacalthing lied.

"Then I shall tell you. By now I am convinced that this creature has *hands*, Uthacalthing. I am sure of it."

"Hm," Uthacalthing commented noncommittally.

The Thennanin's voice dropped even lower. "There is a mystery here, colleague. There is something very odd going on here on Garth."

Uthacalthing suppressed his corona. He extinguished all facial expression. Now he understood why it had been *syulff-kuonn*—the glyph of anticipation of a practical joke fulfilled— that penetrated where none had succeeded before.

The joke was on me!

Uthacalthing looked beyond the fringe of their sunshade, where the bright afternoon had begun to color from an overcast spilling over the mountains.

Out there in the bush his confederate had been laying "clues" for weeks, ever since the Tymbrimi yacht came down where Uthacalthing had intended it to, at the edge of the marshlands far southeast of the mountains. Little Jo-Jo—the throwback chim who could not even speak except with his hands—moved just ahead of Uthacalthing, naked as an animal, laying tantalizing footprints, chipping stone tools to leave in their path, maintaining tenuous contact with Uthacalthing through the blue Warder Globe.

It had all been part of a convoluted plan to lead the Thennanin inexorably to the conclusion that pre-sentient life existed on Garth. but Kault had seen none of the clues! None of the specially contrived hints!

No, what Kault had finally noticed was Jo-Jo *himself* . . . the traces the little chim left as he foraged and lived off the land!

Uthacalthing realized that *syulff-kuonn* was exactly right. The joke on himself was rich, indeed.

He thought he could almost hear Mathicluanna's voice once again. "*You never know* . . ." she seemed to say.

"Amazing," he told the Thennanin. "That is simply amazing."

61

Athaclena

Every now and then she worried that she was getting too used to the changes. The rearranged nerve endings, the redistributed fatty tissues, the funny protrusion of her now-so-humanoid nose—these were things now so accustomed that she sometimes wondered if she would ever be able to return to standard Tymbrimi morphology.

The thought frightened Athaclena.

Until now there had been good reasons for maintaining these humaniform alterations. While she was leading an army of half-uplifted wolfling clients, looking more like a human female had been more than good politics. It had been a sort of bond between her and the chims and gorillas.

And with Robert, she remembered.

Athaclena wondered. Would the two of them ever again experiment, as they once had, with the half-forbidden sweetness of interspecies dalliance? Right now it seemed so very unlikely. Their consortship was reduced to a pair of signatures on a piece of tree bark, a useful bit of politics. Nothing else was the same as before.

She looked down. In the murky water before her, Athaclena saw her own reflection. "Neither fish nor fowl," she whispered in Anglic, not remembering where she had read or heard the phrase, but knowing its metaphorical meaning. Any young Tymbrimi male who saw her in her present form would surely break down laughing. And as for Robert, well, less than a month ago she had felt very close to him. His growing attraction toward her—the raw, wolfling hunger of it—had flattered and pleased her in a daring sort of way.

Now, though, he is among his own kind again. And I am alone.

Athaclena shook her head and resolved to drive out such thoughts. She picked up a flask and scattered her reflection by pouring a quarter liter of pale liquid into the pool. Plumes of mud stirred near the bank, obscuring the fine web of tendrils that laced through the pond from overhanging vines.

This was the last of a chain of small basins, a few kilometers from the caves. As Athaclena worked she concentrated and kept careful notes, for she knew she was no trained scientist and would have to make up for that with meticulousness. Still, her simple experiments had already begun to bear promising results. If her assistants returned from the next valley in time with the data she had sent for, she might have something of importance to show Major Prathachulthorn.

I may look like a freak, but I am still Tymbrimi! I shall prove my usefulness, even if the Earthmen do not think of me as a warrior.

So intense was her concentration, so quiet the still forest, that sudden words were like thunderclaps.

"So this is where you are, Clennie! I've been looking all over for you."

Athaclena spun about, almost spilling a vial of umber-colored fluid. The vines all around her suddenly felt like a net

woven just to catch her. Her pulse pounded for the fraction
of a second it took to recognize *Robert*, looking down at her
from the arching root of a giant near-oak.

He wore moccasins, a soft leather jerkin, and hose. The
bow and quiver across his back made him look like the hero
of one of those old-time wolfling romances Athaclena's mother
used to read to her when she was a child. It took longer to
regain her composure than she would have preferred.

"Robert. You startled me."

He blushed. "Sorry. Didn't mean to."

That wasn't strictly true, she knew. Robert's psi shield
was better than before, and he obviously was proud of being
able to approach undetected. A simple but clear version of
kiniwullun flickered like a pixie over Robert's head. If she
squinted, she might almost imagine a young Tymbrimi male
standing there. . . .

Athaclena shuddered. She had already decided she could
not afford this. "Come and sit down, Robert. Tell me what
you have been doing."

Holding onto a nearby vine, he swung lightly onto the
leaf-strewn loam and stepped over to where her experiment
case lay open beside the dark pool. Robert slipped off his bow
and quiver and sat down, cross-legged.

"I've been looking around for some way to be useful."
He shrugged. "Prathachulthorn's finished pumping me for
information. Now he wants me to serve as sort of a glorified
chim morale officer." His voice rose a quarter octave as he
mimicked the Terragens Marine's South Asian accent. "We
must keep the little fellows' chins up, Oneagle. Make them
feel they're important to the Resistance!"

Athaclena nodded, understanding Robert's unspoken
meaning. In spite of the partisans' past successes, Prathachulthorn obviously considered the chims superfluous—at
best useful in diversions or as grunt soldiery. Liaison to
childlike clients would seem an appropriate cubbyhole to
assign the undertrained, presumably spoiled young son of the
Planetary Coordinator.

"I thought Prathachulthorn liked your idea of using di-
gestion bacteria against the Gubru," Athaclena said.

Robert sniffed. He picked up a twig and twirled it deftly
from finger to finger. "Oh, he admitted it was intriguing that
the gorillas' gut critters dissolved Gubru armor. He agreed to
assign Benjamin and some of the chim techs to my project."

Athaclena tried to trace the murky pattern of his feelings. "Did not Lieutenant McCue help you persuade him?"

Robert looked away at the mention of the young Earthling woman. His shield went up at the same time, confirming some of Athaclena's suspicions.

"Lydia helped, yeah. But Prathachulthorn says it'd be next to impossible to deliver enough bacteria to important Gubru installations before they detect it and neutralize it. I still get the impression Prathachulthorn thinks it a side issue, maybe slightly useful to his main plan."

"Do you have any idea what he has in mind?"

"He smiles and says he's going to bloody the birds' beaks. There's been intelligence of some major facility the Gubru are building, south of Port Helenia, and that may make a good target. But he won't go into any more detail than that. After all, strategy and tactics are for professionals, don't y'know."

"Anyway, I didn't come here to talk about Prathachulthorn. I brought something to show you." Robert shrugged out of his pack and reached inside to pull out an object wrapped in cloth. He unfolded the coverings. "Look familiar at all?"

At first sight it appeared to be a pile of wrinkled rags with knotted strings hanging off the edges. On closer examination, the thing on Robert's lap reminded Athaclena of a shriveled fungus of some sort. Robert grabbed the largest knot, where most of the thin fibers came together in a clump, and extended the strings until the filmy fabric unfolded entirely in the gentle breeze.

"It . . . it looks familiar, Robert. I would say it was a small parachute, but it is obviously natural . . . as if it came from some sort of plant." She shook her head.

"Pretty close. Try to think back a few months, Clennie, to a certain rather traumatic day . . . one I don't think either of us will ever forget."

His words were opaque, but flickerings of empathy drew her memories forth. "This?" Athaclena fingered the soft, almost translucent material. "This is from the *plate ivy?*"

"That's right." Robert nodded. "In springtime the upper layers are glossy, rubbery, and so stiff you can flip them and ride them as sleds—"

"If you are coordinated," Athaclena teased.

"Um, yeah. But by the time autumn rolls around, the upper plates have withered back until they're like this." He waved the floppy, parachute-like plate by its fibrous shrouds, catching the wind. "In a few more weeks they'll be even lighter."

Athaclena shook her head. "I recall you explained the reason. It is for propagation, is it not?"

"Correct. This little spore pod here"—he opened his hand to show a small capsule where the lines met—"gets carried aloft by the parachute into the late autumn winds. The sky fills with the things, making air travel hazardous for some time. They cause a real mess down in the city.

"Fortunately, I guess, the ancient creatures that used to pollinate the plate ivy went extinct during the Bururalli fiasco, and nearly all of the pods are sterile. If they weren't, I guess half the Sind would be covered with plate ivy by now. Whatever used to eat it is long dead as well."

"Fascinating." Athaclena followed a tremor in Robert's aura. "You have plans for these things, do you not?"

He folded the spore carrier away again. "Yeah. An idea at least. Though I don't imagine Prathachulthorn will listen to me. He's got me too well categorized, thanks to my mother."

Of course Megan Oneagle was partly responsible for the Earthling officer's assessment and dismissal of her son. *How can a mother so misunderstand her own child?* Athaclena wondered. Humans might have come a long way since their dark centuries, but she still pitied the *k'chu-non*, the poor wolflings. They still had much to learn about themselves.

"Prathachulthorn might not listen to you directly, Robert. But Lieutenant McCue has his respect. She will certainly hear you out and convey your idea to the major."

Robert shook his head. "I don't know."

"Why not?" Athaclena asked. "This young Earthwoman likes you, I can tell. In fact, I was quite certain I detected in her aura—"

"You shouldn't *do* that, Clennie," Robert snapped. "You shouldn't nose around in people's feelings that way. "It's . . . it's none of your business."

She looked down. "Perhaps you are right. But you are my friend and consort, Robert. When you are tense and frustrated, it is bad for both of us, no?"

"I guess so." He did not meet her gaze.

"Are you sexually attracted to this Lydia McCue, then?" Athaclena asked. "Do you feel affection for her?"

"I don't see why you have to ask—"

"Because I cannot *kenn* you, Robert!" Athaclena interrupted, partly out of irritation. "You are no longer open to me. If you are having such feelings you should share them with me! Perhaps I can help you."

Now he looked at her, his face flushed. "*Help* me?"

"Of course. You are my consort and friend. If you desire this woman of your own species, should I not be your collaborator? Should I not help you achieve happiness?"

Robert only blinked. But in his tight shield Athaclena now found cracks. She felt her tendrils wafting over her ears, tracing the edges of those loose places, forming a delicate new glyph. "Were you feeling guilty over these feelings, Robert? Did you think they were somehow being *disloyal* to me?" Athaclena laughed. "But interspecies consorts may have lovers and spouses of their own race. You knew that!

"So what would you have of me, Robert? I certainly cannot give you children! If I could, can you imagine what mongrels they would be?"

This time Robert smiled. He looked away. In the space between them her glyph took stronger form.

"And as for recreational sex, you know that I am not equipped to leave you anything but frustrated, you overendowed/underendowed, wrong-shaped ape-man! Why should I *not* take joy in it, if you find one with whom you might share such things?"

"It's . . . it's not as easy as that, Clennie. I . . ."

She held up a hand and smiled, at once beseeching him to be quiet and to let go. "I am here, Robert," she said, softly.

The young man's confusion was like an uncertain quantum potential, hesitating between two states. His eyes darted as he glanced upward and tried to focus on the *nonthing* she had made. Then he remembered what he had learned and looked away again, allowing *kenning* to open him to the glyph, her gift.

La'thsthoon hovered and danced, beckoning to him. Robert exhaled. His eyes opened in surprise as his own aura unlocked without his conscious will. Uncurling like a flower. Something—a twin to *la'thsthoon*—emerged, resonating, amplifying against Athaclena's corona.

Two wisps of nothing, one human, one Tymbrimi, touched, darted apart playfully, and came together again.

"Do not fear that you will lose what you have with me, Robert," Athaclena whispered. "After all, will any human lover be able to do *this* with you?"

At that, he smiled. They shared laughter. Overhead, mirrored *la'thsthoon* manifested intimacy performed in pairs.

Only later, after Robert had departed again, did Athaclena loosen the deep shield she had locked around her own innermost feelings. Only when he was gone did she let herself acknowledge her envy.

He goes to her now.

What Athaclena had done was right, by any standard she knew. She had done the proper thing.

And yet, it was so unfair!

I am a freak. I was one before I ever came to this planet. Now I am not even anything recognizable any longer.

Robert might have an Earthly lover, but in that area Athaclena was all alone. She could seek no such solace with one of her own kind.

To touch me, to hold me, to mingle his tendrils and his body with mine, to make me feel aflame . . .

With some surprise, Athaclena noticed that this was the first time she had ever felt this thing . . . this longing to be with a man of her own race—not a friend, or classmate, but a *lover*—perhaps a mate.

Mathicluanna and Uthacalthing had told her it would happen someday—that every girl has her own pace. Now, however, the feeling was only bitter. It enhanced her loneliness. A part of her blamed Robert for the limitations of his species. If only he could have changed *his* body, as well. If only he could have met her halfway!

But she was the Tymbrimi, one of the "masters of adaptability." How far that malleability had gone was made evident when Athaclena felt wetness on her cheeks. Miserably, she wiped away salty tears, the first in her life.

That was how her assistants found her hours later, when they returned from the errands she had sent them on—sitting by the edge of a small, muddy pool, while autumn winds blew through the treetops and sent gravid clouds hurrying eastward toward the gray mountains.

62

Galactics

The Suzerain of Cost and Caution was worried. All signs pointed to a molting, and the direction things appeared to be going was not to its liking.

Across the pavilion, the Suzerain of Beam and Talon paced in front of its aides, looking more erect and stately than ever. Beneath the shaggy outer feathers there was a faint reddish sheen to the military commander's underplumage. Not a single Gubru present could help but notice even a trace of that color. Soon, perhaps within only a twelve-day, the process would have progressed beyond the point of no return.

The occupation force would have a new queen.

The Suzerain of Cost and Caution contemplated the unfairness of it all as it preened its own feathers. They, too, were starting to dry out, but there were still no discernible signs of a final color.

First it had been elevated to the status of candidate and chief bureaucrat after the death of its predecessor. It had dreamed of such a destiny, but not to be plunged into the midst of an already mature Triumvirate! Its peers were already well on the way toward sexuality by that time. It had been forced to try to catch up.

At first that had seemed to matter little. To the surprise of all, it had won many points from the start. Discovering the foolishness the other two had been up to during the interregnum had enabled the Suzerain of Cost and Caution to make great leaps forward.

Then a new equilibrium was reached. The admiral and

the priest had proven brilliant and imaginative in the defense of their political positions.

But the molting was supposed to be decided by correctness of policy! The prize was supposed to go to the leader whose wisdom had proven most sage. It was the way!

And yet, the bureaucrat knew that these matters were as often decided by happenstance, or by quirks of metabolism.

Or by alliance of two against the third, it reminded itself. The Suzerain of Cost and Caution wondered if it had been wise to support the military against Propriety, these last few weeks, giving the admiral by now an almost unassailable advantage.

But there had been no choice! The priest *had* to be opposed, for the Suzerain of Propriety appeared to have lost all control!

First had come that nonsense about "Garthlings." If the bureaucrat's predecessor had lived, perhaps the extravagance might have been kept down. As it was, however, vast amounts had been squandered . . . bringing in a new Planetary Branch Library, sending expeditions into the dangerous mountains, building a hyperspace shunt for a Ceremony of Adoption— before there was any confirmation that anything existed to adopt!

Then there was the matter of ecological management. The Suzerain of Propriety insisted that it was essential to restore the Earthlings' program on Garth to at least a minimal level. But the Suzerain of Beam and Talon had adamantly refused to allow any humans to leave the islands. So, at great cost, help was sent for off-planet. A shipload of Linten gardeners, neutrals in the present crisis, were on the way. And the Great Egg only knew how they were to pay for them!

Now that the hyperspace shunt was nearing completion, both the Suzerain of Propriety and the Suzerain of Beam and Talon were ready to admit that the rumors of "Garthlings" were just a Tymbrimi trick. But would they allow construction to be stopped?

No. Each, it seemed, had its reasons for wanting completion. If the bureaucrat had agreed it would have made a consensus, a step toward the policy so much desired by the Roost Masters. But how could it agree with such nonsense!

The Suzerain of Cost and Caution chirped in frustration. The Suzerain of Propriety was late for yet another colloquy.

Its passion for rectitude did not extend, it seemed, to courtesy to its peers.

By this point, theoretically, the initial competitiveness among the candidates should have begun transforming into respect, and then affection, and finally true mating. But here they were, on the verge of a Molt, still dancing a dance of mutual loathing.

The Suzerain of Cost and Caution was not happy about how things were turning out, but at least there would be one satisfaction if things went on in the direction they seemed headed—when Propriety was brought down from its haughty perch at last.

One of the chief bureaucrats' aides approached, and the Suzerain took its proffered message slab. After picting its contents, it stood in thought.

Outside there was a commotion . . . no doubt the third peer arriving at last. But for a moment the Suzerain of Cost and Caution still considered the message it had received from its spies.

Soon, yes soon. Very soon we will penetrate secret plans, plans which may not be good policy. Then perhaps we shall see a change, a change in sexuality . . . soon.

63

Fiben

His head ached.

Back when he had been a student at the University he had also been forced to study hour after hour, days at a stretch, cramming for tests. Fiben had never thought of himself as a scholar, and sometimes examinations used to make him sick in anticipation.

But at least back then there were also extracurricular activities, trips home, *breathing spells,* when a chen could cut loose and have some fun!

And back at the University Fiben had liked some of his professors. Right at this moment, though, he had had just about as much as he could take of Gailet Jones.

"So you think Galactic Sociology's stuffy and tedious?" Gailet accused him after he threw down the books in disgust and stalked off to pace in the farthest corner of the room. "Well, I'm sorry Planetary Ecology isn't the subject, instead," she said. "Then, maybe, you'd be the teacher and I'd be the student."

Fiben snorted. "Thanks for allowing for the possibility. I was beginning to think you already knew everything."

"That's not fair!" Gailet put aside the heavy book on her lap. "You know the ceremony's only weeks away. At that point you and I may be called upon to act as spokesmen for our entire race! Shouldn't we try to be as prepared as possible beforehand?"

"And you're so certain you know what knowledge will be relevant? What's to say that Planetary Ecology *won't* be crucial then, hm?"

Gailet shrugged. "It might very well be."

"Or mechanics, or space piloting, or . . . or beer-swilling, or *sexual aptitude,* for Goodall's sake!"

"In that case, our race will be fortunate you were selected as one of its representatives, won't it?" Gailet snapped back. There was a long, tense silence as they glared at each other. Finally, Gailet lifted a hand. "Fiben. I'm sorry. I know this is frustrating for you. But I didn't ask to be put in this position either, you know."

No. But that doesn't matter, he thought. *You were designed for it. Neo-chimpdom couldn't hope for a chimmie better suited to be rational, collected, and oh, so cool when the time comes.*

"As for Galactic Sociology, Fiben, you know there are several reasons why it's the essential topic."

There it was again, that *look* in Gailet's eyes. Fiben knew it meant that there were levels and levels in her words.

Superficially, she meant that the two chim representatives would have to know the right protocols, and pass certain stringent tests, during the Rituals of Acceptance, or the officials of the Institute of Uplift would declare the ceremonies null and void.

The Suzerain of Propriety had made it abundantly clear that the outcome would be most unpleasant if that happened.

But there was another reason Gailet wanted him to know as much as possible. *Sometime soon we pass the point of no return . . . when we can no longer change our minds about cooperating with the Suzerain. Gailet and I cannot discuss it openly, not with the Gubru probably listening in all the time. We'll have to act in consensus, and to her that means I've got to be educated.*

Or was it simply that Gailet did not want to bear the burden of their decision all by herself, when the time came?

Certainly Fiben knew a lot more about Galactic civilization than before his capture. Perhaps more than he had ever wanted to know. The intricacies of a three-billion-year-old culture made up of a thousand diverse, bickering patron-client clan lines, held together loosely by a network of ancient institutes and traditions, made Fiben's head swim. Half the time he would come away cynically disgusted—convinced that the Galactics were little more than powerful spoiled brats, combining the worst qualities of the old nation-states of Earth before Mankind's maturity.

But then something would crystallize, and Gailet would make clear to him some tradition or principle that displayed uncanny subtlety and hard-won *wisdom*, developed over hundreds of millions of years.

It was getting to the point where he didn't even know what to think anymore. "I gotta get some air," he told her. "I'm going for a walk." He stepped over to the coatrack and grabbed his parka. "See you in an hour or so."

He rapped on the door. It slid open. He stepped through and closed it behind him without looking back.

"Need an escort, Fiben?"

The chimmie, Sylvie, picked up a datawell and scribbled an entry. She wore a simple, ankle-length dress with long sleeves. To look at her now, it was hard to imagine her up on the dance mound at the Ape's Grape, driving crowds of chens to the verge of mob violence. Her smile was hesitant, almost timid. And it occurred to Fiben that there was something unaccountably nervous about her tonight.

"What if I said no?" he asked. Before Sylvie could look alarmed he grinned. "Just kidding. Sure, Sylvie. Give me

Rover Twelve. He's a friendly old globe, and he doesn't spook the natives too much."

"Watch robot RVG-12. Logged as escort to Fiben Bolger for release outside," she said into the datawell. A door opened down the hallway behind her, and out floated a remote vigilance globe, a simple version of a battle robot, whose sole mission was to accompany a prisoner and see that he did not escape.

"Have a nice walk, Fiben."

He winked at Sylvie and affected an airy burr. "Now, lass, what other kind is there, for a prisoner?"

The last one, Fiben answered himself. *The one leading to the gallows*. But he waved gaily. "C'mon, Rover." The front door hissed as it slid back to let him emerge into a blustery autumn afternoon.

Much had changed since their capture. The conditions of their imprisonment grew gentler as he and Gailet seemed to become more important to the Suzerain of Propriety's inscrutable plan. *I still hate this place*, Fiben thought as he descended concrete steps and made his way through an unkempt garden toward the outer gate. Sophisticated surveillance robots rotated slowly at the corners of the high wall. Near the portal, Fiben came upon the chim guards.

Irongrip was not present, fortunately, but the other Probationers on duty were hardly friendlier. For although the Gubru still paid their wages, it seemed their masters had recently deserted their cause. There had been no overturning of the Uplift program on Garth, no sudden reversal of the eugenics pyramid. *The Suzerain tried to find fault in the way neo-chimps are being uplifted*, Fiben knew. *But it must've failed. Otherwise, why would it be grooming a blue card and a white card, like me and Gailet, for their ceremony?*

In fact, the use of Probationers as auxiliaries had sort of backfired on the invaders. The chim population resented it.

No words passed between Fiben and the zipsuited guards. The ritual was well understood. He ignored them, and they dawdled just as long as they dared without giving him an excuse to complain. Once, when the claviger delayed too long with the keys, Fiben had simply turned around and marched back inside. He did not even have to say a word to Sylvie. Next watch, those guards were gone. Fiben never saw them again.

This time, just on impulse, Fiben broke tradition and spoke. "Nice weather, ain't it?"

The taller of the two Probationers looked up in surprise. Something about the zipsuited chen suddenly struck Fiben as eerily familiar, although he was certain he had never met him before. "What, are you kidding?" The guard glanced up at rumbling cumulonimbus clouds. A cold front was moving in, and rain could not be far off.

"Yeah," Fiben grinned. "I'm kidding. Actually, it's too sunny for my tastes."

The guard gave Fiben a sour look and stepped aside. The gate squeaked open, and Fiben slipped out onto a back street lined by ivy-decked walls. Neither he nor Gailet had ever seen any of their neighbors. Presumably local chims kept a low profile around Irongrip's crew and the watchful alien robots.

He whistled as he walked toward the bay, trying to ignore the hovering watch globe following just a meter above and behind him. The first time he had been allowed out this way, Fiben avoided the populated areas of Port Helenia, sticking to back alleys and the now almost abandoned industrial zone. Nowadays he still kept away from the main shopping and business areas, where crowds would gather and stare, but he no longer felt he had to avoid people completely.

Early on he had seen other chims accompanied by watch globes. At first he thought they were prisoners like himself. Chens and chimmies in work clothes stepped aside and gave the guarded chims wide berth, as they did him.

Then he noticed the differences. Those other escorted chims wore fine clothes and walked with a haughty bearing. Their watch globes' eye facets and weaponry faced *outward*, rather than upon the ones they guarded. *Quislings*, Fiben realized. He was pleased to see the faces many chim citizens cast at these high-level collaborators when their backs were turned—looks of sullen, ill-concealed disdain.

After that, in his quarters, he had stenciled the proud letters P-R-I-S-O-N-E-R on the back of his parka. From then on, the stares that followed him were less cold. They were curious, perhaps even respectful.

The globe was not programmed to let him speak to people. Once, when a chimmie dropped a folded piece of paper in his path, Fiben tested the machine's tolerance by bending over to pick it up . . .

He awoke sometime later in the globe's grasp, on his

way back to prison. It was several days before he was allowed out again.

No matter. It had been worth it. Word of the episode spread. Now, chens and chimmies nodded as he passed store-fronts and long ration lines. Some even signed little messages of encouragement in hand talk.

They haven't twisted us, Fiben thought proudly. A few traitors hardly mattered. What counted was the behavior of a people, as a whole. Fiben remembered reading how, during the most horrible of Earth's old, pre-Contact world wars, the citizens of the little nation of Denmark resisted every effort of the Nazi conquerors to dehumanize them. Instead they be-haved with startling unity and decency. It was a story well worth emulating.

We'll hold out, he replied in sign language. *Terra re-members, and will come for us.*

He clung to the hope, no matter how hard it became. As he learned the subtleties of Galactic law from Gailet, he came to realize that even if peace broke out all across the spiral arms, it might not be enough to eject the invaders. There were tricks a clan as ancient as the Gubru knew, ways to invalidate a weaker clan's lease on a planet like Garth. It was apparent one faction of the avian enemy wanted to end Earth's tenancy here and take it over for themselves.

Fiben knew that the Suzerain of Propriety had searched in vain for evidence the Earthlings were mishandling the ecological recovery on Garth. Now, after the way the occupa-tion forces had bollixed decades of hard work, they dared not raise that issue.

The Suzerain had also spent months hunting for elusive "Garthlings." If the mysterious pre-sentients had proven real, a claim on them would have justified every dime spent here. Finally, they saw through Uthacalthing's practical joke, but that did not end their efforts.

All along, ever since the invasion, the Gubru had tried to find fault with the way neo-chimpanzees were being up-lifted. And just because they seemed to have accepted the status of advanced chims like Gailet, that did not mean they had given up completely.

There was this business of the damned Ceremony of Acceptance—whose implications still escaped Fiben no mat-ter how hard Gailet tried to make them clear to him.

He hardly noticed the chims on the streets as his feet

kicked windblown leaves and snatches of Gailet's explanations came back to him.

"... *client species pass through phases, each marked by ceremonies sanctioned by the Galactic Uplift Institute.... These ceremonies are expensive, and can be blocked by political maneuvering.... For the Gubru to offer to pay for and support a ceremony for the clients of wolfling humans is more than unprecedented.... And the Suzerain also offers to commit all its folk to a new policy ending hostilities with Earth....*

"... *Of course, there is a catch....*"

Oh, Fiben could well imagine there would be a catch!

He shook his head, as if to drive all the words out of it. There was something unnatural about Gailet. Uplift was all very well and good, and she might be a peerless example of neo-chimpdom, but it just wasn't natural to think and talk so much without giving the brain some off-time to air out!

He came at last to a place by the docks where fishing boats lay tied up against the coming storm. Seabirds chirped and dove, trying to catch a last meal in the time remaining before the water became too choppy. One of them ventured too close to Fiben and was rewarded with a warning shock from "Rover," the watch robot. The bird—no more a biological cousin to the avian invaders than Fiben was—squawked in anger and took off toward the west.

Fiben took a seat on the end of the pier. From his pocket he removed half a sandwich he had put there earlier in the day. He munched quietly, watching the clouds and the water. For the moment, at least, he was able to stop thinking, stop worrying. And no words echoed in his head.

Right then all it would have taken to make him happy would have been a banana and a beer, and freedom.

An hour or so later, "Rover" began buzzing insistently. The watch robot maneuvered to a position interposing itself between him and the water, bobbing insistently.

With a sign Fiben got up and dusted himself off. He walked back along the dock and soon was headed past drifts of leaves toward his urban prison. Very few chims were still about on the windy streets.

The guard with the oddly familiar face frowned at him when Fiben arrived at the gate, but there was no delay passing him through. *It's always been easier gettin' into jail than gettin' out*, Fiben thought.

Sylvie was still on duty at her desk. "Did you have a nice walk, Fiben?"

"Hm. You ought to come along sometime. We could stop at the Park and I'd show you my Cheetah imitation." He gave her an amiable wink.

"I've already seen it, remember? Pretty unimpressive, as I recall." But Sylvie's tone did not match her banter. She seemed tense. "Go on in, Fiben. I'll put Rover away."

"Yeah, well." The door hissed open. "Good night, Sylvie."

Gailet was seated on a plush throw rug in front of the weather wall—now tuned to show a scene of steamy savannah heat. She looked up from the book on her lap and took off her reading glasses. "Hello. Feeling better?"

"Yeah." He nodded. "Sorry about earlier. I guess I just had a bad case of cabin fever. I'll knuckle down and get back to work now."

"No need. We're done for today." She patted the rug. "Why don't you come over and give me back a scratch? Then I'll reciprocate."

Fiben did not have to be asked twice. One thing he had to grant Gailet, she was a truly fine grooming partner. He shrugged out of his parka and came over to sit behind her. She laid one hand idly on his knee while he began combing his fingers through her hair. Soon her eyes were closed. Her breath came in soft, low sighs.

It was frustrating trying to define the relationship he had with Gailet. They were not lovers. For most chimmies, that was only possible or practical during certain parts of their bodily cycles, anyway. And Gailet had made it clear that hers was a very private sense of sexuality, more like a human female's. Fiben understood this and had put no pressure on her.

Trouble was, he just could not get her out of his mind.

He reminded himself not to confuse his sex drive with other things. *I may be obsessed with her, but I'm not crazy.* Lovemaking with this chimmie would require a level of bonding he wasn't sure he was ready to think about.

As he worked his way through the fur at the back of Gailet's neck he encountered knots of tension. "Say, you're really tight! What's the matter? Have th' damn Gu—"

The fingers on his knee dug in sharply, though Gailet

did not move otherwise. Fiben thought quickly and changed what he had been about to say.

". . . g-guards been making moves on you? Have those Probationers been getting fresh?"

"And what if they had? What would you do about it, march out there and defend my honor?" She laughed. But he felt her relief, expressed through her body. Something was going on. He had never seen Gailet so worked up.

As he scratched her back, his fingers encountered an object embedded in the fur . . . something round, thin, disk-like. "I think there's a knot of hair, back there," Gailet said quickly as he started to pull it free. "Be careful, Fiben."

"Uh, okay." He bent over. "Um, you're right. It's a knot all right. I'm gonna have to work this out with my teeth."

Her back trembled and her aroma was sweaty as he brought his face close. *Just as I thought. A message capsule!* As his eye came even with it, a tiny holographic projector came alight. The beam entered his iris and automatically adjusted to focus on his retina.

There were just a few, simple lines of text. What he read, however, made him blink in surprise. It was a document written in his own name!

STATEMENT OF WHY I AM DOING THIS: RECORDED BY LUTENANT FIBEN BOLGER, NEOCHIMPANZEE.

ALTHOUGH IVE BEEN WELL TREATED SINCE BEING CAPTURED, AND I APPRECIATE THE KIND ATTENTION IVE BEEN GIVEN, IM AFRAID I JUST HAVE GOT TO GET OUT OF HERE. THERES STILL A WAR GOING ON, AND ITS MY DUTY TO ESCAPE IF I CAN.

IN TRYING TO ESCAPE I DONT MEAN ANY INSULT TO THE SUZERAIN OF PROPRIETY OR THE CLAN OF THE GUBRU. ITS JUST THAT IM LOYAL TO THE HUMANS AND MY CLAN. THAT MAKES THIS SOMETHING I JUST HAVE TO DO.

Below the text was an area that *pulsed* redly, as if expectantly. Fiben blinked. He pulled back a little and the message disappeared.

Of course he knew about records such as this. All he had to do was look at the red spot, and earnestly will it, and the disk would record his assent, along with his retinal pattern.

The document would be at least as binding as a signature on some piece of paper.

Escape! The very thought made Fiben's heart race faster. *But . . . how?*

He had not failed to notice that the record mentioned only *his* name. If Gailet had intended to go with him, she surely would have included herself.

And even if it were possible, would it be the *right* thing to do? He had apparently been chosen by the Suzerain of Propriety to be Gailet's partner in an enterprise as complex and potentially hazardous as any in the history of their race. How could Fiben desert her at a time like this?

He brought his eye close and read the message again, thinking furiously.

When did Gailet ever have a chance to write this? Was she in contact with elements of the Resistance somehow?

Also, something about the text struck Fiben as *wrong*. It wasn't just the misspellings and less than erudite grammar. Just at a glance, Fiben could think of several improvements the statement badly needed if it was to do any good at all.

Of course. Someone other than Gailet must have written it, and she was just passing it on for him to read!

"Sylvie came in a while ago," Gailet said. "We groomed each other. She had trouble with the same knot."

Sylvie! So. No wonder the chimmie had been so nervous, earlier.

Fiben considered carefully, trying to reassemble a puzzle. Sylvie must have planted the disk on Gailet. . . . No, she must have worn it *herself*, let Gailet read it, and then transferred it to Gailet's fur with her permission.

"Maybe I was wrong about Sylvie," Gailet continued. "She strikes me as a rather nice chimmie after all. I'm not sure how dependable she is, but my guess is she's pretty solid, down deep."

What was Gailet telling him now? That this wasn't her idea at all but Sylvie's? Gailet would have had to consider the other chimmie's proposition without being able to speak aloud at all. She would not even be able to give Fiben any advice. Not out in the open, at least.

"It's a tough knot," Fiben said, leaving a patch of wet fur as he sat back. "I'll try again in a minute."

"That's all right. Take your time. I'm sure you'll work it out."

He combed through another area, near her right shoulder, but Fiben's thoughts were far from there.

Come on, think, he chided himself.

But it was all so damn murky! The Suzerain's fancy test equipment must have been on the fritz when the technicians selected him as an "advanced" neo-chimp. At that moment Fiben felt far from being anyone's sterling example of a sapient being.

Okay, he concentrated. *So I'm being offered a chance to escape. First off, is it valid?*

For one thing, Sylvie could be a plant. Her offer could be a trap.

But that didn't make any sense! For one thing, Fiben had never given his parole, never agreed not to run away, if he ever got the chance. In fact, as a Terragens officer it was his duty to do so, especially if he could do it *politely,* satisfying Galactic punctilio.

Actually, accepting the offer might be considered the *correct* answer. If this were yet another Gubru test, his proper response might be to say yes. It could *satisfy* the inscrutable ETs . . . show them he understood a client's duties.

Then again, the offer might be for real. Fiben remembered Sylvie's agitation earlier. She had been very friendly toward him the last few weeks, in ways a chen would hate to think were just playacting.

Okay. But if it's for real, how does she plan to pull it off?

There was only one way to find out, and that was by asking her. Certainly, any escape would have to involve fooling the surveillance system. Perhaps there was a way to do that, but Sylvie would only be able to use it one time. Once he and Gailet started asking open questions aloud, the decision would already have to be made.

So what I'm really deciding is whether to tell Sylvie, "Okay, let's hear your plan." If I say yes, I had better be ready to go.

Yeah, but go where?

There was only one answer, of course. Up to the mountains, to report to Athaclena and Robert all he had learned. That meant getting out of Port Helenia, as well as this jail.

"The Soro tell a story," Gailet said in a low voice. Her eyes were closed, and she seemed almost relaxed as he rubbed her shoulder. "They tell about a certain Paha warrior, back when the Paha were still being uplifted. Would you like to hear it?"

Puzzled Fiben nodded. "Sure, tell me about it, Gailet."

"Okay. Well, you've surely heard of the Paha. They're tough fighters, loyal to their Soro patrons. Back then they were coming along nicely in the tests given by the Uplift Institute. So one day the Soro decide to give 'em some responsibility. Sent a group of them to guard an emissary to the Seven Spin Clans."

"Seven Spin . . . Uh, they're a machine civilization, right?"

"Yes. But they aren't outlaws. They're one of the few machine cultures who've joined Galactic society as honorary members. They keep mostly out of the way by sticking to high-density spiral arm areas, useless to both oxygen and hydrogen breathers."

What's she getting at? Fiben wondered.

"Anyway, the Soro Ambassador is dickering with the high muckity mucks of the Seven Spinners when this Paha scout detects something out at the edge of the local system and goes to investigate.

"Well, as luck would have it, he comes upon the scene to find one of the Seven Spinners' cargo vessels under attack by rogue machines."

"Berserkers? Planet busters?"

Gailet shuddered. "You read too much science fiction, Fiben. No, just outlaw robots looking for loot. Anyway, when our Paha scout gets no answer to his calls for instructions, he decides to take some initiative. He dives right in, guns blazing."

"Let me guess, he saved the cargo ship."

She nodded. "Sent the rogues flying. The Seven Spinners were grateful, too. The reward turned a questionable business deal into a profit for the Soro."

"So he was a hero."

Gailet shook her head. "No. He went home in disgrace, for acting on his own without guidance."

"Crazy Eatees," Fiben muttered.

"No, Fiben." She touched his knee. "It's an important point. Encouraging initiative in a new client race is fine, but during sensitive Galactic-level negotiations? Do you trust a bright child with a fusion power plant?"

Fiben understood what Gailet was driving at. The two of

them were being offered a deal that sounded very sweet for Earth—on the surface, at least. The Suzerain of Propriety was offering to finance a major Ceremony of Acceptance for neo-chimps. The Gubru would end their policy of obstructing humanity's patron status and cease all hostilities against Terra. All the Suzerain seemed to want in exchange was for Fiben and Gailet to tell the Five Galaxies, by hyperspacial shunt, what great guys the Gubru were.

It sounded like a face-saving gesture for the Suzerain of Propriety, and a major coup for Earthkind.

But, Fiben wondered, did he and Gailet have the *right* to make such a decision? Might there be ramifications beyond what they could figure out for themselves? Potentially deadly ramifications?

The Suzerain of Propriety had told them that there were reasons why they weren't allowed to consult with human leaders, out on the island detention camps. Its rivalry with the other Suzerains was reaching a critical phase, and they might not approve of how much it was planning on giving away. The Suzerain of Propriety needed surprise in order to outmaneuver them and present a *fait accompli*.

Something struck Fiben as odd about that logic. But then, aliens were alien by definition. He couldn't imagine any Terran-based society operating in such a way.

So was Gailet telling him that they should pull out of the ceremony? Fine! As far as Fiben was concerned, she could decide. After all, they only had to say *no* . . . respectfully, of course.

Gailet said. "The story doesn't end there."

"There's more?"

"Oh, yes. A few years later the Seven Spin Clans came forward with evidence that the Paha warrior really had made every effort to call back for instructions before beginning his intervention, but subspace conditions had prevented any message from getting through."

"So?"

"So that made all the difference to the Soro! In one case he was taking responsibility he didn't merit. In the other he was only doing the best he could!

"The scout was exonerated, posthumously, and his heirs were granted advanced Uplift rights."

There was a long silence. Neither of them spoke as Fiben thought carefully. Suddenly it was all clear to him.

It's the effort that counts. That's what she means. It'd be unforgivable to cooperate with the Suzerain without at least trying to consult with our patrons. I might fail, probably will fail, but I must try.

"Let's take a look at that knot again." He bent over, brought his eye close to the message capsule. Again the lines of text appeared, along with the pulsing red spot. Fiben looked right at the expectant blob and thought hard.

I agree to this.

The patch changed color at once, signifying his assent. *Now what?* Fiben wondered as he sat back.

His answer came a moment later, when the door opened quietly. Sylvie entered, wearing the same ankle-length dress as before. She sat down in front of them.

"Surveillance is off. I'm feeding the cameras a tape loop. It ought to work for at least an hour before their computer gets suspicious."

Fiben plucked the disk out of Gailet's fur and she held out her hand for it. "Give me a minute," Gailet whispered, and hurried over to her personal datawell to drop the capsule inside. "No offense, Sylvie, but the wording needs improvement. Fiben can initial my changes."

"I'm not offended. I knew you'd have to fix it up. I just wanted it to be clear enough for you two to understand what I was offering."

It was all happening so fast. And yet Fiben felt the adrenaline already starting to sing in his veins. "So I'm going?"

"*We're* going," Sylvie corrected. "You and me. I've got supplies stashed, disguises, and a route out of town."

"Are you with the underground, then?"

She shook her head. "I'd like to join, of course, but this is strictly my own show. I . . . I'm doing this for a price."

"What is it you want?"

Sylvie shook her head, indicating she would wait for Gailet to return. "If you two agree to take the chance, I'll go back outside and call in the night guard. I picked him out carefully and worked hard to get Irongrip to assign him duty tonight."

"What's so special about that guy?"

"Maybe you noticed, that Probationer looks a lot like you, Fiben, and he's got a similar build. Close enough to fool the spy-comps in the dark for a while, I'd guess."

So that was why that chen at the gate had looked so familiar! Fiben speculated concisely. "Drug him. Leave him with Gailet while I sneak out in his clothes, using his pass."

"There's a lot more to it, believe me." Sylvie looked nervous, exhausted. "But you get the general idea. He and I both go off shift in twenty minutes. So it's got to be before then."

Gailet returned. She handed the pellet to Fiben. He held it up to one eye and read the revised text carefully, not because he planned to criticize Gailet's work, but so he would be able to recite it word for word if he ever did make it back to Athaclena and Robert.

Gailet had entirely rewritten the message.

STATEMENT OF INTENT: RECORDED BY FIBEN BOLGER, A-CHIM-AB-HUMAN, CLIENT CITIZEN OF THE TERRAGENS FEDERATION AND RESERVE LIEUTENANT, GARTH COLONIAL DEFENSE FORCE.

I ACKNOWLEDGE THE COURTESY I HAVE BEEN SHOWN DURING MY IMPRISONMENT, AND AM COGNIZANT OF THE KIND ATTENTION GIVEN ME BY THE EXALTED AND RESPECTED SUZERAINS OF THE GREAT CLAN OF THE GUBRU. NEVERTHELESS, I FIND THAT MY DUTY AS A COMBATANT IN THE PRESENT WAR BETWEEN MY LINE AND THAT OF THE GUBRU COMPELS ME TO RESPECTFULLY REFUSE FURTHER CONFINEMENT, HOWEVER COURTEOUS.

IN ATTEMPTING TO ESCAPE, I IN NO WAY SPURN THE HONOR GRANTED ME BY THE EXALTED SUZERAIN, IN CONSIDERING ME FOR THE STATUS OF RACE-REPRESENTATIVE. BY CONTINUING HONORABLE RESISTANCE TO THE GUBRU OCCUPATION OF GARTH, I HOPE THAT I AM BEHAVING AS SUCH A CLIENT-SOPHONT SHOULD, IN PROPER OBEDIENCE TO THE WILL OF MY PATRONS.

I ACT NOW IN THE TRADITIONS OF GALACTIC SOCIETY, AS BEST I HAVE BEEN GIVEN TO UNDERSTAND THEM.

Yeah. Fiben had learned enough under Gailet's tutelage to see how much better this version was. He registered his assent again, and once more the recording spot changed color. Fiben handed the disk back to Gailet.

What matters is that we try, he told himself, knowing how forlorn this venture certainly was.

"Now." Gailet turned to Sylvie. "What is this fee you spoke of? What is it you want?"

Sylvie bit her lip. She faced Gailet, but pointed at Fiben. "Him," she said quickly. "I want you to share him with me."

"*What?*" Fiben started to get up, but Gailet shushed him with a quick gesture. "Explain," she asked Sylvie.

Sylvie shrugged. "I wasn't sure what kind of marriage arrangement the two of you had."

"We don't have any!" Fiben said, hotly. "And what business—"

"Shut up, Fiben," Gailet told him evenly. "That's right, Sylvie. We have no agreement, group or monogamous. So what's this all about? What is it you want from him?"

"Isn't it obvious?" Sylvie glanced over at Fiben. "Whatever his Uplift rating was before, he's now effectively a white card. Look at his amazing war record, and the way he foiled the Eatees against all odds, not once but twice, in Port Helenia. Any of those'd be enough to advance him from blue status.

"And now the Suzerain's invited him to be a race-representative. That kind of attention sticks. It'll hold *whoever* wins the war, you know that, Dr. Jones."

Sylvie summarized. "He's a white card. I'm a green. I also happen to like his style. It's that simple."

Me? A Goodall-damned whitie? Fiben burst out laughing at the absurdity of it. It was just dawning on him what Sylvie was driving at.

"Whoever wins," Sylvie went on, quietly ignoring him. "Whether it's Earth or the Gubru, I want my child to ride the crest of Uplift and be protected by the Board. My child is going to have a destiny. I'll have grandchildren, and a piece of tomorrow."

Sylvie obviously felt passionately about this. But Fiben was in no mood to be sympathetic. *Of all the metaphysical claptrap!* he thought. And she wasn't even telling this to *him*. Sylvie was talking to *Gailet*, appealing to her! "Hey, don't I have anything to say about this?" he protested.

"Of course not, silly," Gailet replied, shaking her head. "You're a chen. A male chim will screw a goat, or a leaf, if nothing better is available."

An exaggeration, but a stereotype based on enough truth to make Fiben blush. "But—"

"Sylvie's attractive and approaching pink. What do you

expect you'll do once you get free, if all of us have agreed in advance that your duty *and* pleasure coincide?" Gailet shifted. "No, this is not your decision. Now for the last time be quiet, Fiben."

Gailet turned back to ask Sylvie a new question, but at that moment Fiben could not even hear the words. The roaring in his ears drowned out every other sound. All he could think of at that moment was the drummer, poor Igor Patterson. *No. Oh, Goodall, protect me!*

". . . males work that way."

"Yes, of course. But I figure you have a bond with him, whether it's formal or not. Theory is fine, but anyone can tell he's got an honor-streak a mile thick. He might prove obstinate unless he knew it was all right with you."

Is this how females think of us chens, down deep? Fiben pondered. He remembered secondary school "health" classes, when the young male chims would be taken off to attend lectures about procreative rights and see films about VD. Like the other boy-chims, he used to wonder what the chimmies were learning at those times. *Do the schools teach them this cold-blooded type of logic? Or do they learn it the hard way? From us?*

"I do not own him." Gailet shrugged. "If you are right, nobody will ever have that sort of claim on him . . . nobody but the Uplift Board, poor fellow." She frowned. "All I demand of you is that you get him to the mountains safely. He doesn't touch you till then, understood? You get your fee when he's safe with the guerrillas."

A male human would not put up with this, Fiben pondered bitterly. But then, male humans weren't unfinished, client-level creatures who would "screw a goat, or a leaf, if nothing better was available," were they?

Sylvie nodded in agreement. She extended her hand. Gailet took it. They shared a long look, then separated.

Sylvie stood up. "I'll knock before I come in. It'll be about ten minutes." When she looked at Fiben her expression was *satisfied*, as if she had done very well in a business arrangement. "Be ready to leave by then," she said, and turned to go.

When she had left, Fiben finally found his voice. "You assume too much with all your glib theories, Gailet. What the hell makes you so sure—"

"I'm not sure of anything!" she snapped back. And the

confused, hurt look on her face stunned Fiben more than anything else that had happened that evening.

Gailet passed a hand in front of her eyes. "I'm sorry, Fiben. Just do as you think best. Only please don't get offended. None of us can really afford pride right now. Anyway, Sylvie's not asking all that much, on the scale of things, is she?"

Fiben read the suppressed tension in Gailet's eyes, and his outrage leaked away. It was replaced by concern for her. "Are . . . are you sure you'll be okay?"

She shrugged. "I guess so. The Suzerain'll probably find me another partner. I'll do my best to delay things as long as I can."

Fiben bit his lip. "We'll get word back to you from the humans, I promise."

Her expression told him that she held out little hope. But she smiled. "You do that, Fiben." She reached up and touched the side of his face gently. "You know," she whispered. "I really will miss you."

The moment passed. She withdrew her hand and her expression was serious once more. "Now you'd better gather whatever you want to take with you. Meanwhile, there are a few things I suggest you ought to tell your general. You'll try to remember, Fiben?"

"Yeah, sure." But for one instant he mourned, wondering if he would ever again see the gentleness that had shone so briefly in her eyes. All business once more, she followed him around the room as he gathered food and clothing. She was still talking a few minutes later when there came a knock on the door.

64

Gailet

In the darkness, after they had left, she sat on her mattress with a blanket over her head, hugging her knees and rocking slowly to the tempo of her loneliness.

Her darkness was not entirely solitary. Far better if it had been, in fact. Gailet sensed the sleeping chen near her, wrapped in Fiben's bedclothes, softly exhaling faint fumes from the drug that had rendered him unconscious. The Probie guard would not awaken for many hours yet. Gailet figured this quiet time probably would not last as long as his slumber.

No, she was not quite alone. But Gailet Jones had never felt quite so cut off, so isolated.

Poor Fiben, she thought. *Maybe Sylvie's right about him. Certainly he is one of the best chens I'll ever meet. And yet . . .* She shook her head. *And yet, he only saw part of the way through this plot. And I could not even tell him the rest. Not without revealing what I knew to hidden listeners.*

She wasn't sure whether Sylvie was sincere or not. Gailet never had been much good at judging people. *But I'll bet gametes to zygotes Sylvie never fooled the Gubru surveillance.*

Gailet sniffed at the very idea—that one little chimmie could have bollixed the Eatees' monitors in such a way that they would not have instantly noticed it. *No, this was all far too easy. It was arranged.*

By whom? Why?

Did it really matter?

We never had any choice, of course. Fiben had to accept the offer.

Gailet wondered if she would ever see him again. If this

429

were just another sapiency test ordered by the Suzerain of Propriety, then Fiben might very well be back tomorrow, credited with one more "appropriate response" . . . appropriate for an especially advanced neo-chimpanzee, at the vanguard of his client-level race.

She shuddered. Until tonight she had never considered the implications, but Sylvie had made it all too clear. Even if they were brought together again, it would never be the same for her and Fiben. If her white card had been a barrier between them before, his would almost certainly be a yawning chasm.

Anyway, Gailet had begun to suspect that this wasn't just another test, arranged by the Suzerain of Propriety. And if not, then some faction of the Gubru had to be responsible for tonight's escapade. Perhaps one of the *other* Suzerains, or . . .

Gailet shook her head again. She did not know enough even to guess. There wasn't sufficient data. Or maybe she was just too blind/stupid to see the pattern.

A play was unfolding all around them, and at every stage it seemed there was no choice which way to turn. Fiben *had* to go tonight, whether the offer of escape was a trap or not. She *had* to stay and wrestle with vagaries beyond her grasp. That was her written fate.

This sensation of being manipulated, with no real power over her own destiny, was a familiar one to Gailet, even if Fiben was only beginning to get used to it. For Gailet it had been a lifelong companion.

Some of the old-time religions of Earth had included the concept of predetermination—a belief that all events were foreordained since the very first act of creation, and that so-called free will was nothing more than an illusion.

Soon after Contact, two centuries ago, human philosophers had asked the first Galactics they met what they thought of this and many other ideas. Quite often the alien sages had responded patronizingly. *"These are questions that can only be posed in an illogical wolfling language,"* had been a typical response. *"There are no paradoxes,"* they had assured.

And no mysteries left to be solved . . . or at least none that could ever be approached by the likes of Earthlings.

Predestination was not all that hard for the Galactics to understand actually. Most thought the wolfling clan predestined for a sad, brief story.

And yet, Gailet found herself suddenly recalling a time, back when she was living on Earth, when she had met a certain neo-dolphin—an elderly, retired poet—who told her stories about occasions when he had swum in the slipstreams of great whales, listening for hours on end to their moaning songs of ancient cetacean gods. She had been flattered and fascinated when the aged 'fin composed a poem especially for her.

> *Where does a ball alight,*
> *Falling through the bright midair?*
> *Hit it with your snout!*

Gailet figured the haiku had to be even more pungent in Trinary, the hybrid language neo-dolphins generally used for their poetry. She did not know Trinary, of course, but even in Anglic the little allegory had stuck with her.

Thinking about it, Gailet gradually came to realize that she was smiling.

Hit it with your snout, indeed!

The sleeping form next to her snored softly. Gailet tapped her tongue against her front teeth and pretended to be listening to the rhythm of drums.

She was still sitting there, thinking, some hours later when the door slid open with a loud bang and light spilled in from the hall. Several four-legged avian forms marched in. Kwackoo. At the head of the procession Gailet recognized the pastel-tinted down of the Servitor of the Suzerain of Propriety. She stood up, but her shallow bow received no answer.

The Kwackoo stared at her. Then it motioned down at the form under the blankets. "Your companion does not rise. This is unseemly."

Obviously, with no Gubru around, the Servitor did not feel obligated to be courteous. Gailet looked up at the ceiling. "Perhaps he is indisposed."

"Does he require medical assistance?"

"I imagine he'll recover without it."

The Kwackoo's three-toed feet shuffled in irritation. "I shall be frank. We wish to inspect your companion, to ascertain his identity."

She raised an eyebrow, even though she knew the gesture was wasted on this creature. "And who do you think he might be? Grandpa Bonzo? Don't you Kwackoo keep track of your prisoners?"

The avian's agitation increased. "This confinement area was placed under the authority of neo-chimpanzee auxiliaries. If there was a failure, it is due to their animal incompetence. Their unsapient negligence."

Gailet laughed. "Bullshit."

The Kwackoo stopped its dance of irritation and listened to its portable translator. When it only stared at her, Gailet shook her head. "You can't palm this off on us, Kwackoo. You and I both know putting chim Probationers in charge here was just a sham. If there's been a security breach, it was inside your own camp."

The Servitor's beak opened a few degrees. Its tongue flicked, a gesture Gailet by now knew signified pure hatred. The alien gestured, and two globuform robots whined forward. Gently but firmly they used gravitic fields to pick up the sleeping neo-chimp without even disturbing the blankets, and backed away with him toward the door. Since the Kwackoo had not bothered to look under the covers, obviously it already knew what it would find there.

"There will be an investigation," it promised. Then it swiveled to depart. In minutes, Gailet knew, they would be reading Fiben's "goodbye note," which had been left attached to the snoring guard. Gailet tried to help Fiben with one more delay.

"Fine," she said. "In the meantime, I have a request. . . . No, make that a demand, that I wish to make."

The Servitor had been stepping toward the door, ahead of its entourage of fluttering Kwackoo. At Gailet's words, however, it stopped, causing a mini traffic jam. There was a babble of angry cooing as its followers brushed against each other and flicked their tongues at Gailet. The pink-crested leader turned back and faced her.

"You are not able to make demands."

"I make this one in the name of Galactic tradition," Gailet insisted. "Do not force me to send my petition directly to its eminence, the Suzerain of Propriety."

There was a long pause, during which the Kwackoo seemed to contemplate the risks involved. At last it asked. "What is your foolish demand?"

Now though, Gailet remained silent, waiting.

Finally, with obvious ill grace, the Servitor bowed, a

bending so minuscule as to be barely detectable. Gailet returned the gesture, to the same degree.

"I want to go to the Library," she said in perfect GalSeven. "In fact, under my rights as a Galactic citizen, I insist on it."

65

Fiben

Exiting in the drugged guard's clothes had turned out to be absurdly simple, once Sylvie taught him a simple code phrase to speak to the robots hovering over the gate. The sole chim on duty had been mumbling around a sandwich and waved the two of them through with barely a glance.

"Where are you taking me?" Fiben asked once the dark, vine-covered wall of the prison was behind them.

"To the docks," Sylvie answered over her shoulder. She maintained a quick pace down the damp, leaf-blown sidewalks, leading him past blocks of dark, empty, human-style dwellings. Then, further on, they passed through a chim neighborhood, consisting mostly of large, rambling, group-marriage houses, brightly painted, with doorlike windows and sturdy trellises for kids to climb. Now and then, as they hurried by, Fiben caught glimpses of silhouettes cast against tightly drawn curtains.

"Why the docks?"

"Because that's where the boats are!" Sylvie replied tersely. Her eyes darted to and fro. She twisted the chronometer ring on her left hand and kept looking back over her shoulder, as if worried they might be followed.

That she seemed nervous was natural. Still, Fiben had reached his limit. He grabbed her arm and made her stop.

"Listen, Sylvie. I appreciate everything you've done so far. But now don't you think it's time for you to let me in on the plan?"

She sighed. "Yeah, I suppose so." Her anxious grin reminded him of that night at the Ape's Grape. What he had imagined then to be animal lust that evening must have been something like this instead, fear suppressed under a well-laid veneer of bravado.

"Except for the gates in the fence, the only way out of the city is by boat. My plan is for us to sneak aboard one of the fishing vessels. The night fishers generally put to sea at"—she glanced at her finger watch—"oh, in about an hour."

Fiben nodded. "Then what?"

"Then we slip overboard as the boat passes out of Aspinal Bay. We'll swim to North Point Park. From there it'll be a hard march north, along the beach, but we should be able to make hilly country by daybreak."

Fiben nodded. It sounded like a good plan. He liked the fact that there were several points along the way where they could change their minds if problems or opportunities presented themselves. For instance, they might try for the *south* point of the bay, instead. Certainly the enemy would not expect two fugitives to head straight toward their new hypershunt installation! There would be a lot of construction equipment parked there. The idea of stealing one of the Gubru's own ships appealed to Fiben. If he ever pulled something like *that* off, maybe he'd actually merit a white card after all!

He shook aside that thought quickly, for it made him think of Gailet. Damn it, he missed her already.

"Sounds pretty well thought out, Sylvie."

She smiled guardedly. "Thanks, Fiben. Uh, can we go now?"

He gestured for her to lead on. Soon they were winding their way past shuttered shops and food stands. The clouds overhead were low and ominous, and the night smelled of the coming storm. A southwesterly wind blew in stiff but erratic gusts, pushing leaves and bits of paper around their ankles as they walked.

When it started to drizzle, Sylvie raised the hood of her parka, but Fiben left his own down. He did not mind wet hair half as much as having his sight and hearing obstructed now.

Off toward the sea he saw a flickering in the sky, accompanied by distant, gray growling. *Hell,* Fiben thought. *What am I thinking!* He grabbed his companion's arm again. "'Nobody's going to go to sea in this kind of weather, Sylvie."

"The captain of this boat will, Fiben." She shook her head. "I really shouldn't tell you this, but he's . . . he's a smuggler. Was even before the war. His craft has foul weather integrity and can partially submerge."

Fiben blinked. "What's he smuggling, nowadays?"

Sylvie looked left and right. "Chims, some of the times. To and from Cilmar Island."

"Cilmar! Would he take *us* there?"

Sylvie frowned. "I promised Gailet I'd get you to the mountains, Fiben. And anyway, I'm not sure I'd trust this captain that far."

But Fiben's head was awhirl. Half the humans on the *planet* were interned on Cilmar Island! Why settle for Robert and Athaclena, who were, after all, barely more than children, when he might be able to bring Gailet's questions before the experts at the University!

"Let's play it by ear," he said noncommittally. But he was already determined to evaluate this smuggler captain for himself. Perhaps under the cover of this storm it might turn out to be possible! Fiben thought about it as they resumed their journey.

Soon they were near the docks—in fact, not far from the spot where Fiben had spent part of the afternoon watching the gulls. The rain now fell in sudden, unpredictable sheets. Each time it blew away again the air was left startlingly clear, enhancing every odor—from decaying fish to the beery stink of a fisherman's tavern across the way, where a few lights still shone and low, sad music leaked into the night.

Fiben's nostrils flared. He sniffed, trying to trace something that seemed to fade in and out with the fickle rain. Likewise, Fiben's senses fed his imagination, laying out possibilities for his consideration.

His companion led him around a corner and Fiben saw three piers. Several dark, bulky shadows lay moored next to each. One of those, no doubt, was the smugglers' boat. Fiben stopped Sylvie, again with a hand on her arm.

"We'd better hurry," she urged.

"Wouldn't do to be too early," he replied. "It's going to be cramped and smelly in that boat. Come on back here.

There's something we may not have a chance to do for some time."

She gave him a puzzled expression as he drew her back around the corner, into the shadows. When he put his arms around her, she stiffened, then relaxed and tilted her face up.

Fiben kissed her. Sylvie answered in kind.

When he started using his lips to nibble from her left ear across the line of her jaw and down her neck, Sylvie sighed. "Oh, Fiben. If only we had time. If only you knew how much . . ."

"Shh," he told her as he let go. With a flourish he took off his parka and laid it on the ground. "What . . . ?" she began. But he drew her down to sit on the jacket. He settled down behind her.

Her tension eased a bit when he began combing his fingers through her hair, grooming her.

"Whoosh," Sylvie said. "For a moment I thought—"

"Who me? You should know me better than that, darlin'. I'm the kind who likes to build up slowly. None of this rush-rush stuff. We can take our time."

She turned her head to smile up at him. "I'm glad. I won't be pink for a week, anyway. Though, I mean, we don't really have to wait *that* long. It's just—"

Her words cut short suddenly as Fiben's left arm tightened hard around her throat. In a flash he reached into her parka and clicked open her pocket knife. Sylvie's eyes bulged as he pressed the sharp blade close against her carotid artery.

"One word," he whispered directly into her left ear. "One sound and you feed the gulls tonight. Do you understand?"

She nodded, jerkily. He could feel her pulse pound, the vibration carrying up the knife blade. Fiben's own heart was not beating much slower. "Mouth your words," he told her hoarsely. "I'll lip read. Now tell me, where are tracers planted?"

Sylvie blinked. Aloud, she said, "What—" That was all. Her voice stopped as he instantly increased pressure.

"Try again," he whispered.

This time she formed the words silently.

"What . . . are . . . you talking about, Fiben?"

His own voice was a barely audible murmur in her ear. "They're waiting for us out there, aren't they, darlin'? And I don't mean fairy tale chim smugglers. I'm talking *Gubru*, sweets. You're leading me right into their fine feathered clutches."

Sylvie stiffened. "Fiben . . . I . . . no! No, Fiben."

"I smell bird!" he hissed. "They're out there, all right. And as soon as I picked up that scent it all suddenly made perfect sense!"

Sylvie remained silent. Her eyes were eloquent enough by themselves.

"Oh, Gailet must think I'm a prize sap. Now that I think on it, of *course* the escape must've been arranged! In fact, the date must've been set for some time. You all probably didn't count on this storm tying up the fishing fleet. That tale about a smuggler captain was a resourceful ad lib to push back my suspicions. Did you think of it yourself, Sylvie?"

"Fiben—"

"Shut up. Oh, it was appealing, all right, to imagine some chims were smart enough to be pulling runs to Cilmar and back, right under the enemy's beak! Vanity almost won, Sylvie. But I was once a scout pilot, remember? I started thinking about how hard that'd be to pull off, even in weather like this!"

He sniffed the air, and there it was again, that distinct musty odor.

Now that he thought about it, he realized that none of the tests he and Gailet had been put through, during the last several weeks, had dealt with the sense of smell. *Of course not. Galactics think it's mostly a relic for animals*.

Moisture fell onto his hand, even though it was not raining just then. Sylvie's tears dripped. She shook her head.

"You . . . won't . . . be harmed, Fiben. The Suz— Suzerain just wants to ask you some questions. Then you'll be let go! It . . . It promised!"

So this was just another test, after all. Fiben felt like laughing at himself for ever believing escape was possible. *I guess I'll see Gailet again sooner than I thought*.

He was beginning to feel ashamed of the way he had terrorized Sylvie. After all, this had all been just a "game" anyway. Simply one more examination. It wouldn't do to take anything too seriously under such conditions. She was only doing her job.

He started to relax, easing his grip on her throat, when suddenly part of what Sylvie had said struck Fiben.

"The Suzerain said it'd let me *go*?" he whispered. "You mean it'll send me back to jail, don't you?"

She shook her head vigorously. "N-no!" she mouthed.

"It'll drop us off in the mountains. I meant that part of my deal with you and Gailet! The Suzerain promised, if you answer its questions—"

"Wait a minute," Fiben snapped. "You aren't talking about the Suzerain of Propriety, are you?"

She shook her head.

Fiben felt suddenly lightheaded. "Which . . . *Which* Suzerain is waiting for us out there?"

Sylvie sniffed. "The Suzerain of Cost and . . . of Cost and Caution," she whispered.

He closed his eyes in the dreadful realization of what this meant. This was no "game" or test, after all. *Oh, Goodall,* he thought. Now he had to think to save his own neck!

If it had been the Suzerain of Beam and Talon, Fiben would have been ready to throw in the towel right then and there. For then all of the resources of the Gubru military machine would have been arrayed against him. As it was, the chances were slim enough. But Fiben was starting to get ideas.

Accountants. Insurance agents. Bureaucrats. Those made up the army of the Suzerain of Cost and Caution. *Maybe,* Fiben thought. *Just maybe.*

Before doing anything, though, he had to deal with Sylvie. He couldn't just tie her up and leave her. And he simply wasn't a bloody-minded killer. That led to only one option. He had to win her cooperation, and quickly.

He might tell her of his certainty that the Suzerain of Cost and Caution wasn't quite the stickler for truth the Suzerain of Propriety was. When it was its word against hers, why should the bird keep any promise to release them?

In fact, tonight's raid on its peer might even be illegal, by the invaders' standards, in which case it would be stupid to let two chims who knew about it run around free. Knowing the Gubru, Fiben figured the Suzerain of Cost and Caution would probably let them go, all right—straight out an airlock into deep space.

Would she believe me, though, if I told her?

He couldn't chance that. Fiben thought he knew another way to get Sylvie's undivided attention. "I want you to listen to me carefully," he told her. "I am not going out to meet your Suzerain. I am not going out there for one simple reason. If I walk out there, *knowing what I now know,* you and I can kiss my white card goodbye."

Her eyes locked onto his. A tremor ran down her spine.

"You see, darlin'. I have to behave like a superlative example to chimpdom in order to qualify for that encomium. And what kind of superchimp goes and walks right into somethin' he *already knows* is a trap? Hmm?

"No, Sylvie. We'll probably still get caught anyway. But we've gotta be caught tryin' our very best to escape or it just won't count! Do you see what I mean?"

She blinked a few times, and finally nodded.

"Hey," he whispered amiably. "Cheer up! You should be *glad* I saw through this stunt. It just means our kid'll be all the more clever a little bastard. He'll probably find a way to blow up his kindergarten."

Sylvie blinked. Hesitantly, she smiled. "Yeah," she said quietly. "I guess that's right."

Fiben let his knife hand drop away and released Sylvie's throat. He stood up. This was the moment of truth. All she probably had to do was let out a shout and the followers of the Suzerain of Cost and Caution would be on them in moments.

Instead, though, she pulled off her ring watch and handed it to Fiben. *The tracer.*

He nodded and offered her his hand to help her rise. She stumbled at first, still trembling from reaction. But he kept his arm around her as he led her back one block and a little south.

Now, if only this idea works, he thought.

The dovecote was where he remembered it, behind an ill-kempt group house in the neighborhood bordering the harbor. Everyone was asleep apparently. But Fiben nevertheless kept quiet as possible as he cut a few wires and crept into the coop.

It was dank and smelled uncomfortably of bird. The pigeons' soft cooing reminded Fiben of Kwackoo.

"Come on, kids," he whispered to them. "You're gonna help me fool your cousins, tonight."

He had recalled this place from one of his walks. The proximity was more than convenient, it was probably essential. He and Sylvie dared not leave the harbor area until they had disposed of the tracer.

The pigeons edged away from him. While Sylvie kept watch, Fiben cornered and seized a fat, strong-looking bird.

With a piece of string he bound the ring watch to its foot. "Nice night for a long flight, don't ya think?" he whispered, and threw the pigeon into the air. He repeated the process with his own watch, for good measure.

He left the door open. If the birds returned early, the Gubru might follow the tracer signal here. But their typically noisy arrival would send the whole flock flapping off again, starting another wild goose chase.

Fiben congratulated himself on his cleverness as he and Sylvie ran eastward, away from the harbor. Soon they were in a dilapidated industrial area. Fiben knew where he was. He had been here before, leading the placid horse, Tycho, on his first foray into town after the invasion. Sometime before they reached the wall, he signaled for a stop. He had to catch his breath, though Sylvie seemed hardly winded at all.

Well, she's a dancer, of course, he thought.

"Okay, now we strip," he told her.

To her credit, Sylvie did not even bat an eye. The logic was inescapable. Her watch might not have been the only tracer planted on their person. She hurried through the disrobing and was finished before him. When everything lay in a pile, Fiben spared her a brief, appreciative whistle. Sylvie blushed. "Now what?" she asked.

"Now we go for the fence," he answered.

"The fence? But Fiben—"

"C'mon. I've wanted to look at the thing close up for some time anyway."

It was only a few hundred yards farther before they reached the broad strip of ground the aliens had leveled all the way around Port Helenia. Sylvie shivered as they approached the tall barrier, which glistened damply under the light of bright watch globes placed at wide intervals along its length.

"Fiben," Sylvie said as he stepped out onto the strip. "We can't go out there."

"Why not?" he asked. Still, he stopped and turned to look back at her. "Do you know anyone who has?"

She shook her head. "Why *would* anybody? It's obviously crazy! Those *watch globes* . . ."

"Yeah," Fiben said contemplatively. "I was just wondering how many of 'em it took to line a fence around the whole city. Ten thousand? Twenty? Thirty?"

He was remembering the guardian drones that had lined

the much smaller and much more sensitive perimeter around
the former Tymbrimi Embassy, that day when the chancery
building exploded and Fiben had had his lesson in ET humor. Those devices had turned out to be pretty unimpressive
compared with "Rover," or the typical battle robot the Gubru
Talon Soldiers took into battle.

I wonder about these, he thought, and took another step
forward.

"Fiben!" Sylvie sounded close to panic. "Let's try the
gate. We can tell the guards . . . we can tell them we were
robbed. We were hicks from the farms, visiting town, and
somebody stole our clothes and ID cards. If we act dumb
enough, maybe they'll just let us through!"

Yeah, sure. Fiben stepped closer still. Now he stood no
more than half a dozen meters from the barrier. He saw that it
comprised a series of narrow slats connected by wire at the
top and bottom. He had chosen a point between two of the
glowing globes, as far from each as possible. Still, as he
approached he felt a powerful sensation that they were *watching*
him.

The certainty filled Fiben with resignation. By now, of
course, Gubru soldiery were on their way here. They would
arrive any minute now. His best course was to turn around.
To run. Now!

He glanced back at Sylvie. She stood where he had left
her. It was easy to tell that she would rather be almost
anywhere else in the world than here. He wasn't at all sure
why she had remained.

Fiben grabbed his left wrist with his right hand. His
pulse was fast and thready and his mouth felt dry as sand.
Trembling, he made an effort of will and took another step
toward the fence.

An almost palpable dread seemed to close in all around
him, as he had felt when he heard poor Simon Levin's death
wail, during that useless, futile battle out in space. He felt a
dark foreboding of imminent doom. Mortality pressed in—a
sense of the futility of life.

Fiben turned around, slowly, to look at Sylvie.

He grinned.

"Cheap chickenshit birds!" he grunted. "They aren't watch
globes at all! They're stupid *psi radiators!*"

Sylvie blinked. Her mouth opened. Closed. "Are you
sure?" she asked unbelievingly.

"Come on out and see," he urged. "Right there you'll suddenly be sure you're being watched. Then you'll think every Talon Soldier in space is coming after you!"

Sylvie swallowed. She clenched her fists and moved out onto the empty strip. Step by step, Fiben watched her. He had to give Sylvie credit. A lesser chimmie would have cut and run, screaming, long before she reached his position.

Beads of perspiration popped out on her brow, joining the intermittent raindrops.

Part of him, distant from the adrenaline roar, appreciated her naked form. It helped to distract his mind. *So, she really has nursed.* The faint stretch marks of childbearing and lactation were often faked by some chimmies, in order to make themselves look more attractive, but in this case it was clear that Sylvie had borne a child. *I wonder what her story is.*

When she stood next to him, eyes closed tightly, she whispered. "What . . . what's happening to me right now?"

Fiben listened to his own feelings. He thought of Gailet and her long mourning for her friend and protector, the giant chim Max. He thought of the chims he had seen blown apart by the enemy's overpowering weaponry.

He remembered Simon.

"You feel like your best friend in all the world just died," he told her gently, and took her hand. Her answering grip was hard, but across her face there swept a look of relief.

"Psi emitters. That's . . . that's all?" She opened her eyes. "Why . . . why those cheap, chickenshit birds!"

Fiben guffawed. Sylvie slowly smiled. With her free hand she covered her mouth.

They laughed, standing there in the rain in the midst of a riverbed of sorrow. They laughed, and when their tears finally slowed they walked together the rest of the way to the fence, still holding hands.

"Now when I say push, push!"

"I'm ready, Fiben." Sylvie crouched beneath him, feet set, shoulder braced against one of the tall slats, arms gripping the part of the wall next to it.

Standing over her, Fiben took a similar stance and planted his feet in the mud. He took several deep breaths.

"Okay, *push!*"

Together they heaved. The slats were already a few

centimeters apart. As he and Sylvie strained, he could feel the space begin to widen. *Evolution is never wasted*, Fiben thought as he heaved with all his might.

A million years ago humans were going through all the pangs of self-uplift, evolving what the Galactics said could only be given—sapiency—the ability to think and to covet the stars.

Meanwhile, though, Fiben's ancestors had not been idle. *We were getting strong!* Fiben concentrated on that thought while sweat popped out on his brow and the plastisheath slats groaned. He grunted and could feel Sylvie's own desperate struggle as her back quivered against his leg.

"Ah!" Sylvie lost her footing in the mud and her legs flew out, throwing her backward hard. Recoil spun Fiben about, and the springy slats bounced back, tossing him on top of her.

For a minute or two they just lay there, breathing in shuddering gasps. Finally though, Sylvie spoke.

"Please, honey . . . not tonight. I gotta headache."

Fiben laughed. He rolled off of her and onto his back, coughing. They needed humor. It was their best defense against the constant hammering of the psi globes. Panic was incipient, ever creeping on the verge of their minds. Laughter kept it at bay.

They helped each other up and inspected what they had accomplished. The gap was noticeably larger, perhaps ten centimeters, now. But it was still far from wide enough. And Fiben knew they were running out of time. They would need at least three hours to have any hope of reaching the foothills before daybreak.

At least if they made it through they would have the storm on their side. Another sheet of rain swept across them as he and Sylvie settled in again, bracing themselves. The lightning had drawn closer over the last half hour. Thunder rolled, shaking trees and rattling shutters.

It's a mixed blessing, Fiben thought. For while it no doubt hampered Gubru scanners, the rain also made it hard to get a good grip on the slippery fence material. The mud was a curse.

"You ready?" he asked.

"Sure, if you can manage to keep that thing of yours out of my face," Sylvie said, looking up at him. "It's distracting, you know."

"It's what you told Gailet you wanted to share, honey. Besides, you've seen it all before, back at the Thunder Mound."

"Yes." She smiled. "But it didn't look quite the same."

"Oh, shut up and push," Fiben growled. Together they heaved again, putting all their strength into the effort.

Give! Give way! He heard Sylvie gasp, and his own muscles threatened to cramp as the fence material creaked, budged ever so slightly, and creaked again.

This time it was Fiben who slipped, letting the springy material bounce back. Once more they collapsed together in the mud, panting.

The rain was steady now, Fiben wiped a rivulet out of his eyes and looked at the gap again. *Maybe twelve centimeters. Ifni! That's not anywhere near enough.*

He could feel the captivating power of the psi globes broadcasting their gloom into his skull. The message was sapping his strength, he knew, pushing him and Sylvie toward resignation. He felt terribly heavy as he slowly stood up and leaned against the obdurate fence.

Hell, we tried. We'll get credit for that much. Almost made it, too. If only . . .

"No!" he shouted suddenly. "*No!* I won't let you!" He hurled himself at the gap, tried to pry his body through, wriggled and writhed against the recalcitrant opening. Lightning struck, somewhere in the dark realm just beyond, illuminating an open countryside of fields and forests and, beyond them, the beckoning foothills of the Mulun range.

Thunder pealed, setting the fence rocking. The slats squeezed Fiben between them, and he howled in agony. When they let go he fell, half-numbed with pain, to the ground near Sylvie. But he was on his feet again in an instant. Another electric ladder lit the glowering clouds. He screamed back at the sky. He beat the ground. Mud and pebbles flew up as he threw handful into the air. More thunder drove the stones back, pelting them into his face.

There was no longer any such thing as speech. No words. The part of him that knew such things reeled in shock, and in reaction other older, sturdier portions took control.

Now there was only the storm. The wind and rain. The lightning and thunder. He beat his breast, lips curled back, baring his teeth to the stinging rain. The storm *sang* to Fiben, reverberating in the ground and the throbbing air. He answered with a howl.

This music was no prissy, human thing. It was not poetical, like the whale dream phantoms of the dolphins. No, *this* was music he could feel clear down to his bones. It rocked him. It rolled him. It lifted Fiben like a rag doll and tossed him down into the mud. He came back up, spitting and hooting.

He could feel Sylvie's gaze upon him. She was slapping the ground, watching him, wide-eyed, excited. That only made him beat his breast harder and shriek louder. He knew he was not drooping now! Throwing pebbles into the air he cried defiance to the storm, calling out for the lightning to come and *get* him!

Obligingly, it came. Brilliance filled space, charging it, sending his hair bristling outward, sparking. The soundless bellow blew him backward, like a giant's hand come down to slap him straight against the wall.

Fiben screamed as he struck the slats. Before he blacked out, he distinctly smelled the aroma of burning fur.

66

Gailet

In the darkness, with the sound of rain pelting against the roof tiles, she suddenly opened her eyes. Alone, she stood up with the blanket wrapped around her and went to the window.

Outside, a storm blew across Port Helenia, announcing the full arrival of autumn. The caliginous clouds rumbled angrily, threateningly.

There was no view to the east, but Gailet let her cheek rest against the cool glass and faced that way anyway.

The room was comfortably warm. Nevertheless, she closed her eyes and shivered against a sudden chill.

67

Fiben

*Eyes . . . eyes . . . eyes were everywhere. They whirled
and danced, glowing in the darkness, taunting him.*

*An elephant appeared—crashing through the jungle, trum-
peting with red irises aflame. He tried to flee but it caught
him, picked him up in its trunk, and carried him off bouncing, jouncing him, cracking his ribs.*

*He wanted to tell the beast to go ahead and eat him
already, or trample him . . . only to get it over with! After a
while, though, he grew used to it. The pain dulled to a
throbbing ache, and the journey settled into a steady
rhythm. . . .*

The first thing he realized, on awakening, was that the
rain was somehow missing his face.

He lay on his back, on what felt like grass. All around
him the sounds of the storm rolled on, scarcely diminished.
He could feel the wet showers on his legs and torso. And yet,
none of the raindrops fell onto his nose or mouth.

Fiben opened his eyes to look and see why . . . and,
incidentally, to find out how he happened to be alive.

A silhouette blocked out the dim underglow of the clouds.
A lightning stroke, not far away, briefly illuminated a face
above his own. Sylvie looked down in concern, holding his
head in her lap.

Fiben tried to speak. "Where . . ." but the word came
out as a croak. Most of his voice seemed to be gone. Fiben
dimly recalled an episode of screaming, howling at the sky. . . .
That had to be why his throat hurt so.

446

"We're outside," Sylvie said, just loud enough to be heard over the rain. Fiben blinked. *Outside?*

Wincing, he lifted his head just enough to look around.

Against the stormy backdrop it was hard to see anything at all. But he was able to make out the dim shapes of trees and low, rolling hills. He turned to his left. The outline of Port Helenia was unmistakable, especially the curving trail of tiny lights that followed the course of the Gubru fence.

"But . . . but how did we get here?"

"I carried you," she said matter-of-factly. "You weren't in much shape for walking after you tore down that wall."

"Tore down . . . ?"

She nodded. There appeared to be a shining light in Sylvie's eyes. "I thought I'd seen thunder dances before, Fiben Bolger. But that was one to beat all others on record. I swear it. If I live to ninety, and have a hundred respectful grandchildren, I don't imagine I'll ever be able to tell it so I'll be believed."

Dimly, it sort of came back to him now. He recalled the anger, the outrage over having come so close, and yet so far from freedom. It shamed him to remember giving in that way to frustration, to the animal within him.

Some white card. Fiben snorted, knowing how stupid the Suzerain of Propriety had to be to have chosen a chim like him for such a role.

"I must've lost my grip for a while."

Sylvie touched his left shoulder. He winced and looked down to see a nasty burn there. Oddly, it did not seem to hurt as badly as a score of lesser aches and bruises.

"You taunted the storm, Fiben," she said in a hushed voice. "You *dared* it to come down after you. And when it came . . . you made it do your bidding."

Fiben closed his eyes. *Oh, Goodall. Of all the silly, superstitious nonsense.*

And yet, there was a part of him, deep down, that felt warmly satisfied. It was as if that portion actually believed that there had been cause and effect, that he had done exactly what Sylvie described!

Fiben shuddered. "Help me sit up, okay?"

There was a disorienting moment or two as the horizon tilted and vision swam. At last, though, when she had him seated so the world no longer wavered all around him, he gestured for her to help him stand.

"You should rest, Fiben."

"When we reach the Mulun," he told her. "Dawn can't be far off. And the storm won't last forever. Come on, I'll lean on you."

She took his good arm over her shoulder, bracing him. Somehow, they managed to get him onto his feet.

"Y'know," he said. "You're a strong lil' chimmie. Hmph. Carried me all the way up here, did you?"

She nodded, looking up at him with that same light. Fiben smiled. "Okay," he said. "Pretty damn okay."

Together they started out, limping toward the glowering dark hummocks to the east.

PART FIVE

Avengers

In ancient days, when Poseidon still reigned and the ships of man were as weak as tinder, bad luck struck a certain Thracian freighter, who foundered and broke apart under an early winter storm. All hands were lost under those savage waves, save one—the boat's mascot—a monkey.

As the fates would have it, a dolphin appeared just as the monkey was gasping its last breath. Knowing of the great love between man and dolphin, the monkey cried out, "Save me! For the sake of my poor children in Athens!"

Quick as a streak, the dolphin offered its broad back. "Thou art very strange, small, and ugly for a man," the dolphin said as the monkey took a desperate grip.

"As men go, I might be quite handsome," replied the monkey, who coughed, holding on tightly as the dolphin turned towards land. "You say you are a man of Athens?" the wary sea creature asked.

"Indeed, who would claim it were he not?" the monkey proclaimed.

"Then you know Piraeus?" the suspicious dolphin inquired further.

The monkey thought quickly. "Oh, yes!" he cried. "Piraeus is my dear friend. I only spoke with him last week!"

With that the dolphin bucked angrily and flung the monkey into the sea to drown. The moral of the story, one might suppose, is that one should always get one's story straight, when pretending to be what one is not.

M. N. PLANO

68

Galactics

The image in the holographic display flickered. That was not surprising, since it came from many parsecs away, refracted through the folded space of the Pourmin transfer point. The muddy picture wavered and occasionally lost definition.

Still, to the Suzerain of Propriety the message was coming in all too clearly.

A diverse collection of beings stood depicted before the Suzerain's pedestal. It recognized most of the races by sight. There was a Pila, for instance—short, furry, and stubby-armed. And there was a tall, gangling Z'Tang who stood beside a spiderlike Serentin. A Bi-Gle glowered lazily, coiled next to a being the Suzerain did not immediately recognize, and which might have been a client or a decorative pet.

Also, to the Suzerain's dismay, the delegation included a Synthian and a human.

A human!

And there was no way to complain. It was only appropriate to include a Terran among the official observers—if a qualified human were available—since this world was registered to the wolflings. But the Suzerain had felt certain that there *were* none employed by the Uplift Institute in this sector!

Perhaps this was one more sign that the political situation in the Five Galaxies had worsened. Word had come from the homeworld Roost Masters telling of serious setbacks out between the spiral arms. Battles had gone badly. Allies had proven unreliable. Tandu and Soro fleets dominated once

451

profitable trade routes and now monopolized the siege of Earth.

These were trying times for the great and powerful clan of the Gooksyu-Gubru. All now depended on certain important neutralist patron-lines. Should something happen to draw one or two of them into an alliance, triumph might yet be attained for the righteous.

On the other side of the wing, it would be disastrous to see any of the neutrals turn against the Great Clan!

To influence such matters had been a major reason, back when the Suzerain of Propriety originated the idea of invading Garth in the first place. Superficially this expedition had been intended to seize hostages for use in prying secrets out of the High Command of Earth. But psychological profiles had always made success in that seem unlikely. Wolflings were obstinate creatures.

No, what had won the Roost Masters over to the priest's proposal was the possibility that this would bring honor to the cause of the clan—to score a coup and win new alliances from wavering parties. And at first all seemed to go so well! The first Suzerain of Cost and Caution—

The priest chirped a deep note of mourning. It had not before realized what wisdom they had lost, how the old bureaucrat had tempered the rash brilliance of the younger two with deep and reliable sense.

What a consensus, unity, policy we might have had.

Now, though, in addition to the constant struggles among the still disunited Triumvirate, there was this latest bad news. A *Terran* would be among the official observers from the Uplift Institute. The implications were unpleasant to consider.

And that was not to be the worst of it! As the Suzerain watched in dismay, the Earthling stepped forward as spokesman! Its statement was in clear Galactic Seven.

"Greetings to the Triumvirate of the Forces of Gooksyu-Gubru, now in contested occupation of the limited-leasehold world known as Garth. I greet you in the name of Cough'Quinn*3, Grand High Examiner of the Uplift Institute. This message is being sent ahead of our vessel by the quickest available means, so that you may prepare for our arrival. Conditions in hyperspace and at transfer points indicate that causality will almost certainly allow us to attend the proposed ceremonies, and administer appropriate sapiency tests at the time and place requested by you.

"You are further informed that Galactic Uplift Institute has gone to great lengths to accommodate your unusual request—first in exercising such haste and second in acting on the basis of so little information.

"Ceremonies of Uplift are joyous occasions, especially in times of turmoil such as these. They celebrate the continuity and perpetual renewal of Galactic culture, in the name of the most revered Progenitors. Client species are the hope, the future of our civilization, and on such occasions as this we demonstrate our responsibility, our honor, and our love.

"We approach this event, then, filled with curiosity as to what wonder the clan of Gooksyu-Gubru plans to unveil before the Five Galaxies."

The scene vanished, leaving the Suzerain to contemplate this news.

It was too late, of course, to recall the invitations and cancel the ceremony. Even the other Suzerains recognized this. The shunt must be completed, and they must prepare to receive honored guests. To do otherwise might damage the Gubru cause irrevocably.

The Suzerain danced a dance of anger and frustration. It muttered short, sharp imprecations.

Curse the devil-trickster Tymbrimi! In retrospect, the very idea of "Garthlings"—native pre-sentients that survived the Holocaust of the Bururalli—was absurd. And yet the trail of false evidence had been so startlingly plausible, so striking in its implied opportunity!

The Suzerain of Propriety had begun this expedition in a lead position. Its place in the eventual Molt had seemed assured after the untimely demise of the first Suzerain of Cost and Caution.

But all that changed when no Garthlings were found—when it became clear just how thoroughly Propriety had been tricked. Failure to find evidence of human misuse of Garth or their clients meant that the Suzerain still had not yet set foot upon the soil of this planet. That, in turn, had retarded the development of completion hormones. All of these factors were setbacks, throwing the Molt into serious doubt.

Then, insurrection among the neo-chimpanzees helped bring the military to the fore. Now the Suzerain of Beam and Talon was rapidly growing preeminent, unstoppable.

The coming Molt filled the Suzerain of Propriety with foreboding. Such events were supposed to be triumphant, transcendent, even for the losers. Moltings were times of renewal and sexual fulfillment for the race. They were also supposed to represent *crystallization of policy*—consensus on correct action.

This time, however, there was little or no consensus. Something was very wrong, indeed, about this molting.

The only thing all three Suzerains were in agreement about was that the hyperspace shunt must be used for some sort of Uplift ceremony. To do otherwise would be suicidal at this point. But beyond that they parted company. Their incessant arguing had begun affecting the entire expedition. The more religious Talon Soldiers had taken to bickering with their comrades. Bureaucrats who were retired soldiers sided with their former comrades over logistical expenditures, or turned sullen when their chief overruled them. Even among the priesthood there were frequent arguments where there should already be unanimity.

The priest had just recently discovered what factionalism could do. The divisiveness had gone all the way to the point of betrayal! Why else had one of its two race-leader chimpanzees been stolen?

Now the Suzerain of Cost and Caution was insisting on a role in choosing the new male. No doubt the bureaucrat was responsible for the "escape" of the Fiben Bolger chimp in the first place! Such a promising creature it had been! By now it no doubt had been converted to vapor and ashes.

There would be no way to pin this on either of the rival Suzerains, of course.

A Kwackoo servitor approached and knelt, proffering a data cube in its beak. Given assent, it popped the record into a player unit.

The room dimmed and the Suzerain of Propriety watched a camera's-eye view of driving rain and darkness. It shivered involuntarily, disliking the ugly, dank dinginess of a wolfling town.

The view panned over a muddy patch in a dark alley . . . a broken shack made of wire and wood, where Terran birds had been kept as pets . . . a pile of soggy clothing beside a padlocked factory . . . footprints leading to a churned up field of mud beside a bent and battered fence . . . more footprints leading off into the dim wilderness. . . .

The implications were apparent to the Suzerain before the investigators' report reached its conclusion.

The male neo-chimpanzee had perceived the trap set for it! It appeared to have made good its escape!

The Suzerain danced upon its perch, a series of mincing steps of ancient lineage.

> *"The harm, damage, setback*
> *to our program is severe.*
> *But it is not, may not be*
> *irreparable!"*

At a gesture its Kwackoo followers hurried forward. The Suzerain's first command was straightforward.

> *"We must increase, improve, enhance*
> *our commitment, our incentives.*
> *Inform the female that we agree,*
> *accept, acquiesce to her request.*
>
> *"She may go to the Library."*

The servitor bowed, and the other Kwackoo crooned. "*Zoooon!*"

69

Government in Exile

The holo-tank cleared as the interstellar message ran to its end. When the lights came on, the Council members looked at each other in puzzlement. "What . . . what does it mean?" Colonel Maiven asked.

"I'm not sure," said Commander Kylie. "But it's clear the Gubru are up to something."

Refuge Administrator Mu Chen drummed her fingers on the table. "They appeared to be officials from the Uplift Institute. It seems to mean the invaders are planning some sort of Uplift ceremony, and have invited witnesses."

That much is obvious, Megan thought. "Do you think this has anything to do with that mysterious construction south of Port Helenia?" she asked. The site had been a topic of much discussion lately.

Colonel Maiven nodded. "I had been reluctant to admit the possibility before, but now I'd have to say so."

The chim member spoke. "Why would they want to hold an Uplift ceremony for the Kwackoo here on Garth? It doesn't make sense. Would that improve their claim on our leasehold?"

"I doubt it," Megan said. "Maybe . . . maybe it isn't for the Kwackoo at all."

"But then for who?"

Megan shrugged. Kylie commented. "The Uplift Institute officials appear to be in the dark as well."

There was a long silence. Then Kylie broke it again.

"How significant do you think it is that the spokesman was human?"

Megan smiled. "Obviously it was meant as a dig at the Gubru. That man might have been no more than a junior clerk trainee at the local Uplift Institute branch. Putting him out in front of Pila and Z'Tang and Serentini means Earth isn't finished yet. And certain powers want to point that out to the Gubru."

"Hm. Pila. They're tough customers, and members of the Soro clan. Having a human spokesman might be an insult to the Gubru, but it's no guarantee Earth is okay."

Megan understood what Kylie meant. If the Soro now dominated Earthspace, there were rough times ahead.

Again, another long silence. Then Colonel Maiven spoke.

"They mentioned a hyperspace shunt. Those are expensive. The Gubru must set great store by this ceremony thing."

Indeed, Megan thought, knowing that a motion had been put before the Council. And this time she realized that it would be hard to justify holding to Uthacalthing's advice.

"You are suggesting a target, colonel?"

"I sure am, madam coordinator." Maiven sat up and met her eyes. "I think this is the opportunity we've been waiting for."

There were nods of agreement up and down the table.

*They are voting out of boredom, and frustration, and sheer
cabin fever,* Megan knew. *And yet, is this not a golden
chance, to be seized or lost forever?*

"We cannot attack once the emissaries from the Uplift
Institute have arrived," she emphasized, and saw that everybody understood how important that was. "However, I agree
that there may be a window of opportunity during which a
strike could be made."

Consensus was obvious. In a corner of her mind, Megan
felt there really ought to be more discussion. But she, too,
was near filled to bursting with impatience.

"We shall cut new orders to Major Prathachulthorn then.
He shall receive carte blanche, subject only to the condition
that any attack be completed by November first. Is it agreed?"

A simple raising of hands. Commander Kylie hesitated,
then joined in to make it unanimous.

We are committed, Megan thought. And she wondered if
Hell reserved a special place for mothers who send their own
sons into battle.

70

Robert

*She didn't have to go away, did she? I mean she herself
said it was all right.*

Robert rubbed his stubbled chin. He thought about taking a shower and shaving. Major Prathachulthorn would be
calling a meeting sometime after it reached full light, and the
commander liked to see his officers well groomed.

What I really should be doing is sleeping, Robert knew.
They had just finished a whole series of night exercises. It
would be wise to catch up on his rest.

And yet, after a couple of hours of fitful slumber he had found himself too nervous, too full of restless energy to stay in bed any longer. He had risen and gone to his small desk, setting up the datawell so its light would not disturb the chamber's other occupant. For some time he read through Major Prathachulthorn's detailed order of battle.

It was ingenious, professional. The various options appeared to offer a number of efficient ways to use limited forces to strike the enemy, and strike him hard. All that remained was choosing the right target. There were several choices available, any of which ought to do.

Still, something about the entire edifice struck Robert as *wrong*. The document did not increase his confidence, as he had hoped it would. In the space over his head Robert almost imagined something taking form—something faintly akin to the dark clouds that had shrouded the mountains in storms so recently—a symbolic manifestation of his unease.

Across the little chamber a form moved under the blankets. One slender arm lay exposed, and a smooth length of calf and thigh.

Robert concentrated and erased the nonthing that he had been forming with his simple aura-power. It had begun affecting Lydia's dreams, and it wouldn't be fair to inflict his own turmoil upon her. For all of their recent physical intimacy, they were still in many ways strangers.

Robert reminded himself that there were some positive aspects to the last few days. The battle plan, for instance, showed that Prathachulthorn was at last taking some of his ideas seriously. And spending time with Lydia had brought more than physical pleasure. Robert had not realized how much he missed the simple touch of his own kind. Humans might be able to withstand isolation better than chims—who could fall into deep depression if they lacked a grooming partner for very long. But mel and fem humans, too, had their apelike needs.

Still, Robert's thoughts kept drifting. Even during his most passionate moments with Lydia, he kept thinking of somebody else.

Did she really have to leave? Logically there was no reason to have to go to Mount Fossey. The gorillas were already well cared for.

Of course, the gorillas might have been just an excuse. An excuse to escape the disapproving aura of Major Prathachulthorn. An excuse to avoid the sparking discharges from human passion.

Athaclena might be correct that there was nothing wrong with Robert seeking his own kind. But logic was not everything. She had feelings, too. Young and alone, she could be hurt even by what she knew to be right.

"Damn!" Robert muttered. Prathachulthorn's words and graphs were a blur. "Damn, I miss her."

There was a commotion outside, beyond the flap of cloth that sectioned off this chamber from the rest of the caves. Robert looked at his watch. It was still only four a.m. He stood up and gathered his trousers. Any unplanned excitement at this hour was likely to be bad news. Just because the enemy had been quiet for a month did not mean it had to stay that way. Perhaps the Gubru had gotten wind of their plans and were striking preemptively!

There was the slap of unshod feet upon stone. "Capt'n Oneagle?" a voice said from just beyond the cloth. Robert strode over and pulled it aside. A winded chim messenger breathed heavily. "What's happening?" Robert asked.

"Um, sir, you'd better come quick."

"All right. Let me get my weapons."

The chim shook her head. "It's not fighting, sir. It's . . . it's some chims just arrivin' from Port Helenia."

Robert frowned. New recruits from town had been arriving in small groups all along. What was all the excitement about this time? He heard Lydia stir as the talking disturbed her sleep. "Fine," he told the chimmie. "We'll interview them a little later—"

She interrupted. "Sir! It's Fiben! Fiben Bolger, sir. He's come back."

Robert blinked. "What?"

There was movement behind him. "Rob?" a feminine voice spoke. "What is—"

Robert whooped. His shout reverberated in the closed spaces. He hugged and kissed the surprised chimmie, then caught up Lydia and tossed her lightly into the air.

"What . . . ?" she started to ask, then stopped, for she found herself addressing only the empty space where he had been.

Actually, there was little need to hurry. Fiben and his escorts were still some distance away. By the time their horses could be seen, puffing up the trail from the north, Lydia had dressed and joined Robert up on the escarpment. There dawn's gray light was just driving out the last wan stars.

"Everybody's up," Lydia commented. "They even roused the major. Chims are dashing all over the place, jabbering in excitement. This must be some chen we're waiting for."

"Fiben?" Robert laughed. He blew into his hands. "Yeah, you might say old Fiben's unusual."

"I gathered as much." She shaded her eyes against the glow to the east and watched the mounted party pass a switchback climbing the narrow trail. "Is he the one in the bandages?"

"Hm?" Robert squinted. Lydia's eyesight had been bio-organically enhanced during her Marine training. He was envious. "It wouldn't surprise me. Fiben's always getting banged up, one way or another. Claims he hates it. Says it's all due to innate clumsiness and a universe that has it in for him, but I've always suspected it was an affinity for trouble. Never known a chim who went to such lengths just to get a story to tell."

In a minute he could make out the features of his friend. He shouted and raised his hand. Fiben grinned and waved back, although his left arm was immobilized in a sling. Next to him, on a pale mare, rode a chimmie Robert did not recognize.

A messenger arrived from the cave entrance and saluted. "Sers, the major requests that you an' Lieutenant Bolger come down just as soon's he's here."

Robert nodded. "Please tell Major Prathachulthorn we'll be right there."

As the horses climbed the last switchback, Lydia slipped her hand into his, and Robert felt a sudden wave of both gladness and guilt. He squeezed back and tried not to let his ambivalence show.

Fiben's alive! he thought. *I must get word to Athaclena. I'm sure she'll be thrilled.*

Major Prathachulthorn had a nervous habit of tugging at one ear or the other. While listening to reports from his subordinates, he would shift in his chair, occasionally leaning over to mumble into his datawell, retrieving some quick dollop of information. At such times he might seem distracted, but if the speaker stopped talking, or even slowed down, the major would snap his fingers, impatiently. Apparently, Prathachulthorn had a quick mind and was able to juggle several tasks at once. However, these behaviors were very hard on some of the chims, often making them nervous and tongue-tied. That, in turn, did not improve the major's opinion of the irregulars that had only recently been under Robert's and Athaclena's command.

In Fiben's case, though, this was no problem. As long as he was kept supplied with orange juice, he kept on with his story. Even Prathachulthorn, who usually interrupted reports with frequent questions, probing mercilessly for details, sat silently through the tale of the disastrous valley insurrection, Fiben's subsequent capture, the interviews and tests by the followers of the Suzerain of Propriety, and the theories of Dr. Gailet Jones.

Now and then Robert glanced at the chimmie Fiben had brought with him from Port Helenia. Sylvie sat to one side, between the chims Benjamin and Elsie, her posture erect and her expression composed. Occasionally, when asked to verify or elaborate on something, she answered in a quiet voice. Otherwise, her gaze remained on Fiben constantly.

Fiben carefully described the political situation among the Gubru, as he understood it. When he came to the evening of the escape, he told of the trap that had been laid by the "Suzerain of Cost and Caution," and concluded simply by saying, "So we decided, Sylvie and I, that we'd better exit Port Helenia by a different route than by sea." He shrugged. "We got out through a gap in the fence and finally made it to a rebel outpost. So here we are."

Right! Robert thought sardonically. Of course Fiben had left out any mention of his injuries and exactly *how* he escaped. He would no doubt fill in the details in his written report to the major, but anyone else would have to bribe them out of him.

Robert saw Fiben glance his way and wink. *I'd bet this is at least a five-beer tale*, Robert thought.

Prathachulthorn leaned forward. "You say that you actually saw this hyperspace shunt? You know exactly where it is located?"

"I was trained as a scout, major. I know where it is. I'll include a map, and a sketch of the facility, in my written report."

Prathachulthorn nodded. "If I had not already had other reports of this thing I'd never have credited this story. As it is though, I am forced to believe you. You say this facility is expensive, even by Gubru standards?"

"Yessir. That's what Gailet and I came to believe. Think about it. Humans have only been able to throw one Uplift ceremony for each of their clients in all the years since Contact, and both had to be held on Tymbrim. That's why other clients like the Kwackoo can get away with snubbing us.

"Part of the reason has been political obstruction by antagonistic clans like the Gubru and the Soro, who've been able to drag out Terran applications for status. But another reason is because we're so frightfully poor, by Galactic standards."

Fiben had been learning things, obviously. Robert realized part of it must have been picked up from this Gailet Jones person. With his heightened empathy sense, he picked up faint tremors from his friend whenever her name came up.

Robert glanced at Sylvie. *Hmm. Life seems to have grown complicated for Fiben.*

That reminded Robert of his own situation, of course. *Fiben isn't the only one*, he thought. All his life he had wanted to learn to be more sensitive, to better understand others and his own feelings. Now he had his wish, and he hated it.

"By Darwin, Goodall, and Greenpeace!" Prathachulthorn pounded the table. "Mr. Bolger, you bring your news at a most opportune time!" He turned to address Lydia and Robert. "Do you know what this means, gentlemen?"

"Um," Robert began.

"A target, sir," Lydia answered succinctly.

"A target is right! This fits perfectly with that message we just received from the Council. If we can smash this shunt—preferably before the dignitaries from the Uplift Institute arrive—then we could rap the Gubru right where it pains them most, in their wallets!"

"But—" Robert started to object.

"You heard what our spy just told us." Prathachulthorn said. "The Gubru are *hurting* out there in space! They're overextended, their leaders here on Garth are at each others' throats, and this could be the last straw! Why, we might even be able to time it so their entire Triumvirate is at the same place at the same time!"

Robert shook his head. "Don't you think we ought to give it some thought, sir? I mean, what about the offer that the Suzerain of Probity—"

"Propriety," Fiben corrected.

"Propriety. Yes. What about the offer it made to Fiben and Dr. Jones?"

Prathachulthorn shook his head. "An obvious trap, Oneagle. Be serious now."

"I *am* being serious, sir. I'm no more an expert on these matters than Fiben, and certainly less of one than Dr. Jones. And certainly I concede it *may* be a trap. But on the surface, at least, it sounds like a terrific deal for Earth! A deal I don't think we can pass up without at least reporting this back to the Council."

"There isn't time." Prathachulthorn said, shaking his head. "My orders are to operate at my own discretion and, if appropriate, to act before the Galactic dignitaries arrive."

Robert felt a growing desperation. "Then at least let's consult with Athaclena. She's the daughter of a diplomat. She might be able to see some ramifications we don't."

Prathachulthorn's frown spoke volumes. "If there's time, of course I'll be happy to solicit the young Tymbrimi's opinion." But it was clear that even mentioning the idea had brought Robert down a peg in the man's eyes.

Prathachulthorn slapped the table. "Right now I think we had better have a staff meeting of commissioned officers and discuss potential tactics against this hypershunt installation." He turned and nodded to the chims. "That will be all for now, Fiben. Thank you very much for your courageous and timely action. That goes the same to you too, miss." He nodded at Sylvie. "I look forward to seeing your written reports."

Elsie and Benjamin stood up and held the door. As mere brevet officers they were excluded from Prathachulthorn's inner staff. Fiben rose and moved more slowly, aided by Sylvie.

Robert hurriedly spoke in a low voice to Prathachulthorn. "Sir, I'm sure it only slipped your mind, but Fiben holds a full commission in the colonial defense forces. If he's excluded it might not go down well, um, politically."

Prathachulthorn blinked. His expression barely flickered,

though Robert knew he had once again failed to score points. "Yes, of course," the major said evenly. "Please tell Lieutenant Bolger he is welcome to stay, if he's not too tired."

With that he turned back to his datawell and started calling up files. Robert could feel Lydia's eyes on him. *She may despair of my ever learning tact,* he thought as he hurried to the door and caught Fiben's arm just as he was leaving.

His friend grinned at him. "I guess it's grownup time again, here," Fiben said, sotto voce, glancing in Prathachulthorn's direction.

"It's worse even than that, old chim. I just got you tapped as an honorary adult."

If looks could maim, Robert mused on seeing Fiben's sour expression. *And you thought it was Miller time, didn't you?* They had argued before about the possible historical origins of that expression.

Fiben squeezed Sylvie's shoulder and hobbled back into the room. She watched him for a moment, then turned and followed Elsie down the hall.

Benjamin, however, lingered for a moment. He had caught Robert's gesture bidding him to stay. Robert slipped a small disk into the chim's palm. He dared not say anything aloud, but with his left hand he made a simple sign.

"*Auntie,*" he said in hand talk.

Benjamin nodded quickly and walked away.

Prathachulthorn and Lydia were already deep into the arcana of battle planning as Robert returned to the table. The major turned to Robert, "I'm afraid there just won't be time to use enhanced bacteriological effects, as ingenious as your idea was on its own merits. . . ."

The words washed past unnoted. Robert sat down, thinking only that he had just committed his first felony. By secretly recording the meeting—including Fiben's lengthy report—he had violated procedure. By giving the pellet to Benjamin he had broken protocol.

And by ordering the chim to deliver the recording to an alien he had, by some lights, just committed treason.

71

Max

A large neo-chimpanzee shambled into the vast underground chamber, hands cuffed together, drawn along at the end of a stout chain. He remained aloof from his guards, chims wearing the invader's livery, who pulled at the other end of his leash, but occasionally he did glare defiantly at the alien technicians watching from catwalks overhead.

His face had not been unblemished to start with, but now fresh patterns of pink scar tissue lay livid and open, exposed by patches of missing fur. The wounds were healing, but they would never be pretty.

"C'mon, Reb," one of the chim guards said as he pushed the prisoner forward. "Bird wants to ask you some questions."

Max ignored the Probie as best he could as he was led over to a raised area near the center of the huge chamber. There several Kwackoo waited, standing upon an elevated instrument platform.

Max kept his eyes level on the apparent leader, and his bow was shallow—just low enough to force the avian to give one in return.

Next to the Kwackoo stood three more of the quislings. Two were well-dressed chims who had made tidy profits providing construction equipment and workers to the Gubru—it was rumored that some of the deals had been at the expense of their missing human business partners. Other stories implied approval and direct connivance by men interned on Cilmar and the other islands. Max didn't know which version he wanted to believe. The third chim on the platform was the

465

commander of the Probie auxiliary force, the tall, haughty chen called Irongrip.

Max also knew the proper protocol for greeting traitors. He grinned, exposing his large canines to view, and spat at their feet. With a shout the Probies yanked at his chain, sending him stumbling. They lifted their truncheons. But a quick chirp from the lead Kwackoo stopped them in mid-blow. They stepped back, bowing.

"You are sure—certain that this one—this individual is the one we have been looking for?" the feathered officer asked Irongrip. The chim nodded.

"This one was found wounded near the site where Gailet Jones and Fiben Bolger were captured. He was seen in their company before the uprising, and was known to be one of her family's retainers for many years before that. I have prepared an analysis showing how his contact with these individuals makes him appropriate for close attention."

The Kwackoo nodded. "You have been most resourceful," he told Irongrip. "You shall be rewarded—compensated with high status. Although one of the candidates of the Suzerain of Propriety has escaped our net somehow. *We* are now in a good position to choose—select his replacement. You will be informed."

Max had lived under Gubru rule long enough to recognize that these were *bureaucrats*, followers of the Suzerain of Cost and Caution. Though what they wanted from him, what use he could be to them in their internal struggles, he had no idea.

Why had he been brought here? Deep in the bowels of the handmade mountain, across the bay from Port Helenia, there sat an intimidating honeycomb of machinery and humming power supplies. During the long ride down the autolift, Max had felt his hair stand out with static electricity as the Gubru and their clients tested titanic devices.

The Kwackoo functionary turned to regard him with one eye. "You will serve two functions," it told Max. "Two purposes now. You will give us information—data about your former employer, information of use to us. And you will help—assist us in an experiment."

Again, Max grinned. "I won't do neither, an' I don't even care if it *is* disrespectful. You can go put on a clown suit an' ride a tricycle, for all I'll tell you."

The Kwackoo blinked once, twice, as it listened to a

computer translation for verification. It chirped an exchange with its associates, then turned back to face him.

"You misunderstand—mistake our meaning. There will be no questions. You need not speak. Your cooperation is not necessary."

The complacent assuredness of the statement sounded dire. Max shivered under a sudden premonition.

Back when he had first been captured, the enemy had tried to get information out of him. He had steeled himself to resist with all his might, but it really rocked him when all they seemed to be interested in were "Garthlings." That's what they asked him about again and again. *"Where are the pre-sentients?"* they had inquired.

Garthlings?

It had been easy to mislead them, to lie in spite of all the drugs and psi machines, because the enemy's basic *assumptions* had been so cockeyed dumb. Imagine Galactics falling for a bunch of children's tales! He had had a field day, and learned many tricks to fool the questioners.

For instance, he struggled hard *not* to "admit" that Garthlings existed. For a while that seemed to convince them all the more that the trail was hot.

At last, they gave up and left him alone. Perhaps they finally figured out how they'd been duped. Anyway, after that he was assigned to a work detail at one of the construction sites, and Max thought they'd forgotten about him.

Apparently not, he now knew. Anyway, the Kwackoo's words disturbed him.

"What do you mean, you won't be asking questions?"

This time it was the Probationer leader who replied. Irongrip stroked his mustache with relish. "It means you're going to have everything you know *squeezed* out of you. All this machinery"—he waved around him—"will be focused on just little ol' you. Your answers will come out. But you won't."

Max inhaled sharply and felt his heart beat faster. What kept him steady was one firm resolve; he wasn't going to give these traitors the satisfaction of finding him tongue-tied! He concentrated to form words.

"That . . . that's against th' . . . the Rules of War."

Irongrip shrugged. He left it to the Kwackoo bureaucrat to explain.

"The Rules protect—provide for species and worlds far

more than individuals. And anyway, none of those you see here are followers of priests!"

So, Max realized. *I'm in the hold of fanatics.* Mentally he said farewell to the chens and chimmies and kids of his group family, especially his senior group wife, whom he now knew he would never see again. Also mentally, he bent over and kissed his own posterior goodbye.

"Y'made two mistakes," he told his captors. "Th' first was lettin' it slip that Gailet is alive, an' that Fiben's made a fool of you again. Knowin' that makes up for anythin' you can do to me."

Irongrip growled. "Enjoy your brief pleasure. You're still going to be a big help in bringing your ex-employer down a few pegs."

"Maybe." Max nodded. "But your second mistake was leaving me attached to this—"

He had been letting his arms go slack. Now he brought them back with a savage jerk and pulled the chain with all his might. It yanked two of the Probie guards off their feet before the links flew out of their hands.

Max planted his feet and snapped the heavy chain like a whip. His escorts dove for cover, but not all of them made it in time. One of the chim contractors had his skull laid open by a glancing blow. Another stumbled in his desperation to get away and knocked down all three Kwackoo like bowling pins.

Max shouted with joy. He whirled his makeshift weapon until everyone was either toppled or out of reach, then he worked the arc sideways, changing the axis of rotation. When he let go, the chain flew upwards at an angle and wrapped itself around the guardrail of the catwalk overhead.

Shimmying up the heavy links was the easy part. They were too stunned to react in time to stop him. But at the top he had to waste precious seconds unwrapping the chain. Since it was attached to his handcuffs, he'd have to take it along.

Along where? he wondered as he got the links gathered. Max spun about when he glimpsed white feathers over to his right. So he ran the other way and scurried up a flight of stairs to reach the next level.

Of course escape was an absurd notion. He had only two short-term objectives: doing as much harm as possible, and then ending his own life before he could be forced against his will to betray Gailet.

The former goal he accomplished as he ran, flailing the tip of the chain against every knob, tube, or delicate-looking instrument within reach. Some bits of equipment were tougher than they looked, but others smashed and tinkled nicely. Trays of tools went over the edge, toppling onto those below.

He kept a watch out, though, for other options. If no ready implement or weapon presented itself before the time came, he ought to try to get high enough for a good leap over the railing to do the trick.

A Gubru technician and two Kwackoo aides appeared around a corner, immersed in technical discussions in their own chirping dialect. When they looked up Max hollered and swung his chain. One Kwackoo gained a new apterium as feathers flew. During the backstroke Max yelled, "Boo!" at the staring Gubru, who erupted in a squawk of dismay, leaving a cloud of down in its wake.

"With respect," Max added, addressing the departing avian's backside. One never knew if cameras were recording an event. Gailet had told him it was okay to kill birds, just so long as he was polite about it.

Alarms and sirens were going off on all sides. Max pushed a Kwackoo over, vaulted another, and swept up a new flight of steps. One level up he found a target just too tempting to pass by. A large cart carrying about a ton of delicate photonics parts lay abandoned very near the edge of a loading platform. There was no guardrail to the lifter shaft. Max ignored all the shouts and noise that approached from every side and put his shoulder to the back end. *Move!* he grunted, and the wheeled wagon started forward.

"Hey! He's over this way!" he heard some chim cry out. Max strained harder, wishing his wounds had not weakened him so. The cart started rolling.

"You! Reb! Stop that!"

There were footsteps, too late, he knew, to prevent inertia from doing its work. The wagon and its load toppled over the edge. *Now to follow it,* Max thought.

But as the command went to his legs they spasmed suddenly. He recognized the agonizing effects of a neural stunning. Recoil spun him about in time to see the gun held by the chim called Irongrip.

Max's hands clenched spastically, as if the Probie's throat were within reach. Desperately, he willed himself to fall backward, into the shaft.

Success! Max felt victory as he plummeted past the landing. The tingling numbness would not last long. *Now we're even, Fiben,* he thought.

But it wasn't the end after all. Max distantly felt his nerve-numbed arms half yanked out of their sockets as he came up suddenly short. The cuffs around his wrists had torn bleeding rents, and the taut chain led upward past the end of the landing. Through the metal mesh of the platform, Max could see Irongrip straining, holding on with all his might. Slowly, the Probie looked down at him, and smiled.

Max sighed in resignation and closed his eyes.

When he came to his senses Max snorted and pulled away involuntarily from an odious smell. He blinked and blearily made out a mustachioed neo-chimp holding a broken snap-capsule in his hand. From it still emitted noxious fumes.

"Ah, awake again, I see."

Max felt miserable. Of course he ached all over from the stunning and could barely move. But also his arms and wrists seemed to be burning. They were tied behind him, but he could guess they were probably broken.

"Wh . . . where am I?" he asked.

"You're at the focus of a hyperspace shunt," Irongrip told him matter-of-factly.

Max spat. "You're a Goodall-damned liar."

"Have it your way." Irongrip shrugged. "I just figured you deserved an explanation. You see, this machine is a special kind of shunt, what's called an *amplifier*. It's s'pozed to take images out of a brain and make 'em clear for all to see. During the ceremony it'll be under Institute control, but their representatives haven't arrived yet. So today we're going to overload it just a bit as a test.

"Normally the subject's supposed to be cooperative, and the process is benign. Today though, well, it just isn't going to matter that much."

A sharp, chirping complaint came from behind Irongrip. Through a narrow hatch could be seen the technicians of the Suzerain of Cost and Caution. "Time!" the lead Kwackoo snapped. "Quickly! Make haste!"

"What's your hurry?" Max asked. "Afraid some of the other Gubru factions may have heard the commotion and be on their way?"

Irongrip looked up from closing the hatch. He shrugged.

"All that means is we've got time to ask just one question. But it'll serve. Just tell us all about Gailet."

"Never!"

"You won't be able to help it." Irongrip laughed. "Ever tried *not* to think about something? You won't be able to avoid thoughts about her. And once it's got somethin' to get a grip on, the machine will rip the rest out of you."

"You . . . you . . ." Max strugggled for words, but this time they were gone. He writhed, trying to move out of the focus of the massive coiled tubes aimed at him from all sides. But his strength was gone. There was nothing he could do.

Except not think of Gailet Jones. But by trying *not* to, of course, he *was* thinking about her! Max moaned, even as the machines began giving out a low hum in superficial accompaniment. All at once he felt as if the gravitic fields of a hundred starships were playing up and down his skin.

And in his mind a thousand images whirled. More and more of them pictured his former employer and friend.

"No!" Max struggled for an idea. He mustn't try *not* to think of something. What he had to do was find something *else* to contemplate. He had to find something *new* to focus his attention on during the remaining seconds before he was torn apart.

Of course! He let the enemy be his guide. For weeks they had questioned him, asking only about Garthlings, Garthlings, nothing but Garthlings. It had become something of a chant. For him it now became a mantra.

"Where are the pre-sentients?" they had insisted. Max concentrated, and in spite of the pain it just had to make him laugh. "Of . . . all th' stupid . . . dumb . . . idiotic . . ."

Contempt for the Galactics filled him. They wanted a projection out of him? Well let them amplify *this!*

Outside, in the mountains and forests, he knew it would be about dawn. He pictured those forests, and the closest thing he could imagine to "Garthlings," and laughed at the image he had made.

His last moments were spent guffawing over the idiocy of life.

72

Athaclena

The autumn storms had returned again, only this time as a great cyclonic front, rolling down the Valley of the Sind. In the mountains the accelerated winds surged to savage gusts that sloughed the outer leaves from trees and sent them flying in tight eddies. The debris gave shape and substance to whirling devil outlines in the gray sky.

As if in counterpoint, the volcano had begun to grumble as well. Its rumbling complaint was lower, slower in building than the wind, but its tremors made the forest creatures even more nervous as they huddled in their dens or tightly grasped the swaying tree trunks.

Sentience was no certain protection against the gloom. Within their tents, under the mountain's shrouded flanks, the chims clung to each other and listened to the moaning zephyrs. Now and then one would give in to the tension and disappear screaming into the forest, only to return an hour or so later, disheveled and embarrassed, dragging a trail of torn foliage behind him.

The gorillas also were susceptible, but they showed it in other ways. At night they stared up at the billowing clouds with a quiet, focused concentration, sniffling, as if searching for something expectantly. Athaclena could not quite decide what it reminded her of, that evening, but later, in her own tent under the dense forest canopy, she could easily hear their low, atonal singing as they answered the storm.

It was a lullaby that eased her into sleep, but not without a price.

Expectancy . . . such a song *would*, of course, beckon back that which had never completely gone away.

Athaclena's head tossed back and forth on her pillow. Her tendrils waved—seeking, repelled, probing, compelled. Gradually, as if in no particular hurry, the familiar essence gathered.

"*Tutsunucann* . . ." she breathed, unable to awaken or avoid the inevitable. It formed overhead, fashioned out of that which was not.

"*Tutsunucann, s'ah brannitsun. A'twillith't* . . ."

A Tymbrimi knew better than to ask for mercy, especially from Ifni's universe. But Athaclena had changed into something that was both more and less than mere Tymbrimi. *Tutsunucann* had allies now. It was joined by visual images, *metaphors*. Its aura of threat was amplified, made almost palpable, filled out by the added substance of human-style nightmare. ". . . *s'ah brannitsun, . . .*" she sighed, pleading antephialticly in her sleep.

Night winds blew the flaps of her tent, and her dreaming mind fashioned the wings of huge birds. Malevolent, they flew just over the tree tops, their gleaming eyes searching, searching. . . .

A faint volcanic trembling shook the ground beneath her bedroll, and Athaclena shivered in syncopation, imagining burrowing creatures—the *dead*—the unavenged, wasted Potential of this world—ruined and destroyed by the Bururalli so long ago. They squirmed just underneath the disturbed ground, seeking. . . .

"*S'ah brannitsun, tutsunucann!*"

The brush of her own waving tendrils felt like the webs and feet of tiny spiders. *Gheer* flux sent tiny gnomes wriggling under her skin, busy fashioning unwilled changes.

Athaclena moaned as the glyph of terrible expectant laughter hovered nearer and regarded her, bent over her, reached down—

"General? Mizz Athaclena. Excuse me, ma'am, are you awake? I'm sorry to disturb you, ser, but—"

The chim stopped. He had pulled aside the tent flap to enter, but now he rocked back in dismay as Athaclena sat up suddenly, eyes wide apart, catlike irises dilated, her lips curled back in a rictus of somnolent fear.

She did not appear to be aware of him. He blinked, staring at the pulsations that coursed slowly, like soliton waves, down her throat and shoulders. Above her agitated tendrils he briefly glimpsed something terrible.

He almost fled right then. It took a powerful effort of courage to swallow instead, to bear down, and to choke forth words.

"M-Ma'am, p-please. It's me . . . S-Sammy . . ."

Slowly, as if drawn back by the sheerest force of will, the light of awareness returned to those gold-flecked eyes. They closed, reopened. With a tremulous sigh, Athaclena shuddered. Then she collapsed forward.

Sammy stood there, holding her while she sobbed. At that moment, stunned and frightened and astonished, all he could think of was how light and frail she felt in his arms.

" . . . *That was when Gailet became convinced that any trick, if th' Ceremony was a trick at all, had to be a subtle one.*

"*You see, the Suzerain of Propriety seems to have done a complete about-face regarding chim Uplift. It had started out convinced it would find evidence of mismanagement, and perhaps even cause to take neo-chimps away from humans. But now the Suzerain seemed to be earnest in searchin' out . . . in searchin' out appropriate race representatives . . .*"

The voice of Fiben Bolger came from a small playback unit resting on the rough-hewn logs of Athaclena's table. She listened to the recording Robert had sent. The chim's report back at the caves had had its amusing moments. Fiben's irrepressible good nature and dry wit had helped lift Athaclena's limp spirits. Now, though, while relating Dr. Gailet Jones's ideas about Gubru intentions, his voice had dropped, and he sounded reticent, almost embarrassed.

Athaclena could feel Fiben's discomfort through the vibrations in the air. Sometimes one did not need another's presence in order to sense their essence.

She smiled at the irony. *He is starting to know who and what he is, and it frightens him.* Athaclena sympathized. A sane being wished for peace and serenity, not to be the mortar in which the ingredients of destiny are finely ground.

In her hand she held the locket containing her mother's legacy thread, and her father's. For the moment, at least, *tutsunucann* was held at bay. But Athaclena knew somehow that the glyph had returned for good. There would be no sleep now, no rest until *tutsunucann* changed into something else. Such a glyph was one of the largest known manifestations of quantum mechanics—a probability amplitude that hummed and throbbed in a cloud of uncertainty, pregnant with a thousand million possibilities. Once the wave function collapsed, all that remained would be fate.

"*. . . delicate political maneuverings on so many levels—among the local leaders of th' invasion force, among factions back on the Gubru homeworld, between the Gubru and their enemies and possible allies, between the Gubru and Earth, and among th' various Galactic Institutes . . .*"

She stroked the locket. Sometimes one does not need another's presence in order to sense their essence.

There was too much complexity here. What did Robert think he would accomplish by sending her this taping? Was she supposed to delve into some vast storehouse of sage Galactic wisdom—or perform some incantation—and somehow come up with a policy to guide them through this? Through *this*?

She sighed. *Oh father, how I must be a disappointment to you.*

The locket seemed to vibrate under her trembling fingers. For some time it seemed that another trance was settling in, drawing her downward into despair.

"*. . . By Darwin, Goodall, and Greenpeace!*"

It was the voice of Major Prathachulthorn that jarred her out of it. She listened for a while longer.

"*. . . a target! . . .*"

Athaclena shuddered. So. Things were, indeed, quite dire. All was explained now. Particularly the sudden, gravid insistence of an impatient glyph. When the pellet ran out she turned to her aides, Elayne Soo, Sammy, and Dr. de Shriver. The chims watched her patiently.

"I will seek altitude now," she told them.

"But—but the storm, ma'am. We aren't sure it's passed. And then there's the volcano. We've been talking about an evacuation."

Athaclena stood up. "I do not expect to be long. Please send nobody along to guard or look out for me, they will only disturb me and make more difficult what I must do."

She stopped at the flap of the tent then, feeling the wind push at the fabric as if searching for some gap at which to pry. *Be patient. I am coming.* When she spoke to the chims again, it was in a low voice. "Please have horses ready for when I return."

The flap dropped after her. The chims looked at each other, then silently went about preparing for the day.

Mount Fossey steamed in places where the vapor could not be entirely attributed to rising dew. Moist droplets still fell from leaves that shivered in the wind—now waning but still returning now and then in sudden, violent gusts.

Athaclena climbed doggedly up a narrow game trail. She could tell that her wishes were being respected. The chims remained behind, leaving her undisturbed.

The day was beginning with low clouds cutting through the peaks like the vanguards of some aerial invasion. Between them she could see patches of dark blue sky. A human's eyesight might even have picked out a few stubborn stars.

Athaclena climbed for height, but even more for solitude. In the upper reaches the animal life of the forest was even sparser. She sought emptiness.

At one point the trail was clogged with debris from the storm, sheets of some clothlike material that she soon recognized. *Plate ivy parachutes.*

They reminded her. Down in the camp the chim techs had been striving to meet a strict timetable, developing variations on gorilla gut bacteria in time to meet nature's deadline. Now, though, it looked as if Major Prathachulthorn's schedule would not allow Robert's plan to be used.

Such foolishness, Athaclena thought. *How did humans last even this long, I wonder?*

Perhaps they had to be lucky. She had read of their twentieth century, when it seemed more than Ifni's chance that helped them squeeze past near certain doom . . . doom not only for themselves but for all future sapient races that might be born of their rich, fecund world. The tale of that narrow escape was perhaps one reason why so many races feared or hated the *k'chu'non*, the wolflings. It was uncanny, and unexplained to this day.

The Earthlings had a saying, "There, but for the love of God, go I." The sick, raped paucity of Garth was mild compared to what they might easily have done to Terra.

How many of us would have done better under such circumstances? That was the question that underlay all the smug, superior posturings, and all of the contempt pouring from the great clans. For they had never been tested by the ages of ignorance Mankind suffered. What might it have felt like, to have no patrons, no Library, no ancient wisdom, only the bright flame of mind, unchanneled and undirected, free to challenge the Universe or to consume the world? The question was one few clans dared ask themselves.

She brushed aside the little parachutes. Athaclena edged past the snagged cluster of early spore carriers and continued her ascent, pondering the vagaries of destiny.

At last she came to a stony slope where the southern outlook gave a view of more mountains and, in the far distance, just the faintest possible colored trace of a sloping steppe. She breathed deeply and took out the locket her father had given her.

Growing daylight did not keep away the thing that had begun to form amid her waving tendrils. This time Athaclena did not even try to stop it. She ignored it—always the best thing to do when an observer does not yet want to collapse probability into reality.

Her fingers worked the clasp, the locket opened, and she flipped back the lid.

Your marriage was true, she thought of her parents. For where two threads had formerly lain, now there was only one larger one, shimmering upon the velvety lining.

An end curled around one of her fingers. The locket tumbled to the rocky ground and lay there forgotten as she plucked the other end out of the air. Stretched out, the tendril *hummed*, at first quietly. But she held it tautly in front of her, allowing the wind to stroke it, and she began to hear harmonics.

Perhaps she should have eaten, should have built her strength for this thing she was about to attempt. It was something few of her race did even once in their lifetimes. On occasions Tymbrimi had *died*. . . .

"*A t'ith'tuanoo, Uthacalthing*," she breathed. And she added her mother's name. "*A t'ith'tuanine, Mathicluanna!*"

The throbbing increased. It seemed to carry up her arms, to resonate against her heartbeat. Her own tendrils responded to the notes and Athaclena began to sway. "*A t'ith'tuanoo, Uthacalthing* . . ."

"It's a beauty, all right. Maybe a few more weeks' work would make it more potent, but this batch will do, an' it'll be ready in time for when the ivy sheds."

Dr. de Shriver put the culture back into its incubator. Their makeshift laboratory on the flanks of the mountain had been sheltered from the winds. The storm had not interfered with the experiments. Now, the fruit of their labors seemed nearly ripe.

Her assistant grumbled, though. "What's th' use? The Gubru'd just come up with countermeasures. And anyway, the major says the attack is gonna take place before the stuff's ready to be used."

De Shriver took off her glasses. "The point is that we keep working until Miss Athaclena tells us otherwise. I'm a civilian. So're you. Fiben and Robert may have to obey the chain of command when they don't like it, but you and I can choose . . ."

Her voice trailed off when she saw that Sammy wasn't listening any longer. He stared over her shoulder. She whirled to see what he was looking at.

If Athaclena had appeared strange, eerie this morning, after her terrifying nightmare, now her features made Dr. de Shriver gasp. The disheveled alien girl blinked with eyes narrow and close together in fatigue. She clutched the tent pole as they hurried forward, but when the chims tried to move her to a cot she shook her head.

"No," she said simply. "Take me to Robert. Take me to Robert now."

The gorillas were singing again, their low music without melody. Sammy ran out to fetch Benjamin while de Shriver settled Athaclena into a chair. Not knowing what to do, she spent a few moments brushing leaves and dirt from the young Tymbrimi's ruff. The tendrils of her corona seemed to give off a heavy, fragrant heat that she could feel with her fingers.

And above them, the thing that *tutsunucann* had become made the air seem to ripple even before the eyes of the befuddled chim.

Athaclena sat there, listening to the gorillas' song, and feeling for the first time as if she understood it.

All, all would play their role, she now knew. The chims would not be very happy about what was to come. But that was their problem. Everybody had problems.

"Take me to Robert," she breathed again.

73

Uthacalthing

He trembled, standing there with his back to the rising sun, feeling as if he had been sucked as dry as a husk.

Never before had a metaphor felt more appropriate. Uthacalthing blinked, slowly returning to the world . . . to the dry steppe facing the looming Mountains of Mulun. All at once it seemed that he was old, and the years lay heavier than ever before.

Deep down, on the *nahakieri* level, he felt a numbness. After all of this, there was no way to tell if Athaclena had even survived the experience of drawing so much into herself.

She must have felt great need, he thought. For the first time his daughter had attempted something neither of her parents could ever have prepared her for. Nor was this something one picked up in school.

"You have returned," Kault said, matter-of-factly. The Thennanin, Uthacalthing's companion for so many months, leaned on a stout staff and watched him from a few meters away. They stood in the midst of a sea of brown savannah grass, their long shadows gradually shortening with the rising sun.

"Did you receive a message of some sort?" Kault asked. He had the curiosity shared by many total nonpsychics about matters that must seem, to him, quite unnatural.

"I—" Uthacalthing moistened his lips. But how could he explain that he had not really *received* anything at all? No, what happened was that his daughter had taken him up on an offer he had made, in leaving both his own thread and his

479

dead wife's in her hands. She had called in the debt that parents owe a child for bringing her, unasked, into a strange world.

One should never make an offer without knowing full well what will happen if it is accepted.

Indeed, she drained me dry. He felt as if there was nothing left. And after all that, there was still no guarantee she had even survived the experience. Or that it had left her still sane.

Shall I lie down and die, then? Uthacalthing shivered.

No, I think. Not quite yet.

"I did experience a communion, of sorts," he told Kault.

"Will the Gubru be able to detect this thing you have done?"

Uthacalthing could not even craft a *palanq* shrug. "I do not think so. Maybe." His tendrils lay flat, like human hair. "I don't know."

The Thennanin sighed, his breathing slits flapping. "I wish you would be honest with me, colleague. It pains me to be forced to believe that you are hiding things from me."

How Uthacalthing had tried and tried to get Kault to utter those words! And now he could not really bring himself to care. "What do you mean?" he asked.

The Thennanin blew in exasperation. "I mean that I have begun to suspect that you know more than you are telling me about this fascinating creature I have seen traces of. I warn you, Uthacalthing, I am building a device that will solve this riddle for me. You would be well served to be direct with me before I discover the truth all by myself!"

Uthacalthing nodded. "I understand your warning. Now, though, perhaps we had better be walking again. If the Gubru did detect what just happened, and come to investigate, we should try to be far from here before they arrive."

He owed Athaclena that much, still. Not to be captured before she could make use of what she had taken.

"Very well, then," Kault said. "We shall speak of this later."

Without any great interest, more out of habit than for any other reason, Uthacalthing led his companion toward the mountains—in a direction selected—again by habit—by a faint blue twinkling only his eyes could see.

74

Gailet

The new Planetary Branch Library was a beauty. Its beige highlights glistened on a site recently cleared atop Sea Bluff Park, a kilometer south of the Tymbrimi Embassy.

The architecture did not blend as well as the old branch had, into the neo-Fullerite motif of Port Helenia. But it was quite stunning nevertheless—a windowless cube whose pastel shades contrasted well with the nearby chalky, cretaceous outcrops.

Gailet stepped out into a cloud of dry dust as the aircar settled onto the landing apron. She followed her Kwackoo escort up a paved walkway toward the entrance of the towering edifice.

Most of Port Helenia had turned out to watch, a few weeks ago, as a huge freighter the size of a Gubru battleship cruised lazily out of a chalybeous sky and lowered the structure into place. For a large part of the afternoon the sun had been eclipsed while technicians from the Library Institute set the sanctuary of knowledge firmly into place in its new home.

Gailet wondered if the new Library would ever really benefit the citizens of Port Helenia. There were landing pads on all sides, but no provision had been made for groundcar or bicycle or foot access to these bluffs from the town nearby. As she passed through the ornate columned portal, Gailet realized that she was probably the first chim ever to enter the building.

Inside, the vaulted ceiling cast a soft light that seemed to come from everywhere at once. A great ruddy cube dominated the center of the hall, and Gailet knew at once that this was, indeed, an expensive setup. The main data store was many times larger than the old one, a few miles from here. It might even be bigger than Earth's Main Library, where she had done research at La Paz.

But the vastness was mostly empty compared to the constant, round-the-clock bustle she was used to. There were Gubru, of course, and Kwackoo. They stood at study stations scattered about the broad hall. Here and there avians clustered in small groups. Gailet could see their beaks move in sharp jerks, and their feet were constantly in motion as they argued. But no sound at all escaped the muffled privacy zones.

In ribbons and hoods and feather dyes she saw the colors of Propriety, of Accountancy, and of Soldiery. For the most part, each faction kept apart in its own area. There was bristling and some ruffling of down when the follower of one Suzerain passed too close to another.

In one place, however, a multi-hued gaggle of fluttering Gubru displayed that some communication remained among the factions. There was much head ducking and preening and gesturing toward floating holographic displays, all apparently as much ritualistic as based on fact and reason.

As Gailet hurried by, several of the hopping, chattering birds turned to stare at her. Pointing talons and beak gestures made Gailet guess that they knew exactly who she was, and what she was supposed to represent.

She did not hesitate or linger. Gailet's cheeks felt warm.

"Is there any way I can be of service to you, miss?"

At first Gailet thought that what stood at the dais, directly beneath the rayed spiral of the Five Galaxies, was a decorative plant of some sort. When it addressed her, she jumped slightly.

The "plant" spoke perfect Anglic! Gailet took in the rounded, bulbous foliage, lined with silvery bits which tinkled gently as it moved. The brown trunk led down to knobby rootlets that were mobile, allowing the creature to move in a slow, awkward shuffle.

A Kanten, she realized. *Of course, the Institutes provided a Librarian.*

The vege-sentient Kanten were old friends of Earth. Individual Kanten had advised the Terragens Council since the early days after Contact, helping the wolfling humans weave their way through the complex, tricky jungle of Galactic politics and win their original status as patrons of an independent clan. Nevertheless, Gailet restrained her initial surge of hope. She reminded herself that those who entered the service of the great Galactic Institutes were supposed to forsake all prior loyalties, even to their own lines, in favor of a holier mission. Impartiality was the best she could hope for, here.

"Um, yes," she said, remembering to bow. "I want to look up information on Uplift Ceremonies."

The little bell-like things—probably the being's sensory apparatus—made a chiming that almost sounded *amused*.

"That is a very broad topic, miss."

She had expected that response and was ready with an answer. Still, it was unnerving talking with an intelligent being without anything even faintly resembling a face. "I'll start with a simple overview then, if you please."

"Very well, miss. Station twenty-two is formatted for use by humans and neo-chimpanzees. Please go there and make yourself comfortable. Just follow the blue line."

She turned and saw a shimmering hologram take form next to her. The blue trail seemed to hang in space, leading around the dais and on toward a far corner of the chamber. "Thank you," she said quietly.

As she followed the guide trail she imagined she heard sleigh bells behind her.

Station twenty-two was like a friendly, familiar song. A chair and desk and beanbag sat next to a standard holo-console. There were even well-known versions of datawells and styluses, all neatly arranged on a rack. She sat at the desk gratefully. Gailet had been afraid she would have to stand stiltwise, craning her neck to use a Gubru study station.

As it was, she felt nervous. Gailet hopped slightly as the display came alight with a slight "pop." Anglic text filled the central space. PLEASE ASK FOR ADJUSTMENTS ORALLY. REQUESTED REMEDIAL SURVEY WILL BE-GIN AT YOUR SIGNAL.

"Remedial survey . . ." Gailet muttered. But yet, it would be best to begin at the simplest level. Not only would it guarantee that she had not forgotten some vital fundamental, but it would tell her what the Galactics themselves considered most basic.

"Proceed," she said.

The side displays came alight with pictures, displaying images of faces, the faces of other beings on worlds far away in both space and time.

"When nature brings forth a new pre-sentient race, all Galactic society rejoices. For it is then that the adventure of Uplift is about to begin. . . ."

Soon the old patterns reasserted themselves. Gailet swam easily into the flow of information, drinking from the font of knowledge. Her datawell filled with notes and cross-references. Soon she lost all sense of the passage of time.

Food appeared on the desktop without Gailet ever becoming aware of how it arrived. A nearby enclosure took care of her other needs, when nature's call grew too insistent to ignore.

During some periods of Galactic history, Uplift Ceremonies have been almost purely ceremonial. Patron species have been responsible for declaring their clients suitable, and their word was simply accepted that their charges were ready. There have been other epochs, however, in which the role of the Uplift Institute has been much stronger, such as during the Sumubulum Meritocracy, when the entire process was under direct Institution supervision in all cases.

The present era falls somewhere in between these extremes, featuring patron responsibility but with medium to extensive Institute involvement. The latter participation has increased since a rash of Uplift failures forty to sixty thousand GYUs ago* resulted in several severe and embarrassing ecological holocausts (Ref: Gl'kahesh, Bururalli, Sstienn, Muhurn8.) Today the patron of a client cannot vouch alone for its client's development. It must allow close observation by the client's Stage Consort, and by the Uplift Institute.

Uplift Ceremonies are now more than perfunctory celebrations. They serve two other major purposes. First, they allow representatives from the client race to be tested—under rigorous and stressful circumstances—to satisfy the Institute that the race is ready to assume the rights and duties appropriate to the next Stage. Also, the ceremony allows the client race an opportunity to choose a new consort for the subsequent Stage, to watch over it and, if necessary, to intercede on its behalf.

The criteria used in testing depend upon the level of

---

*GYU = Galactic year unit (approximately fourteen Earth months)

development the client race has reached. Among other impor-
tant factors are phagocity type (e.g., carnivore, herbivore,
autophagic, or ergogenic), modality of movement (e.g., bipedal
or quadrupedal walker, amphibious, roller, or sessile), men-
tal technique (e.g., associative, extrapolative, intuitive, holo-
graphic, or nulutative) . . .

Slowly she worked her way through the "remedial" stuff.
It was fairly heavy plodding. This Library branch would need
some new translation routines if the chim-on-the-street in
Port Helenia was going to be able to use the vast storehouse
of knowledge. Assuming Joe and Jane Chim ever got the
opportunity.

Nevertheless, it was a wonderful edifice—far, far greater
than the miserable little branch they'd had before. And unlike back at La Paz, there was not the perpetual hustle and
bustle of hundreds, thousands of frantic users, waving priority slips and arguing over access timeslots. Gailet felt as if she
could just sink into this place for months, years, drinking and
drinking knowledge until it leaked out through her very
pores.

For instance, here was a reference to how special arrangements were made to allow Uplift among machine cultures. And there was one brief, tantalizing paragraph about a
race of *hydrogen breathers* which had seceded from that
mysterious parallel civilization and actually applied for membership in Galactic society. She ached to follow that and
many other fascinating leads, but Gailet knew she simply did
not have the time. She had to concentrate on the rules
regarding bipedal, warm-blooded, omnivorous Stage Two
clients with mixed mental faculties, and even that made for a
daunting reading list.

Narrow it down, she thought. So she tried to focus on
ceremonies which take place under contention or in time of
war. Even under those constraints she found it hard slogging.
Everything was all so complicated! It made her despair over
the shared ignorance of her people and clan.

. . . whether an agreement of co-participation is or is not
made in advance, it can and shall be verified by the Institutes
in a manner taking into account methods of adjudication
considered traditional by the two or more parties involved . . .

Gailet did not recall falling asleep on the beanbag. But
for some time it was a raft, floating upon a dim sea which
rocked to the rhythm of her breathing. After a while, mists

seemed to close in, coalescing into a black and white dream-scape of vaguely threatening shapes. She saw contorted images of the dead, her parents, and poor Max.

"Mm-mm, no," she muttered. At one point she jerked sharply. "No!"

She started to rise, began to emerge from slumber. Her eyes fluttered, fragments of dreams clinging in shreds to the lids. A *Gubru* seemed to hover overhead, holding a mysterious device, like those which had probed and peered at her and Fiben. But the image wavered and fell apart as the avian pressed a button on the machine. She slumped back, the Gubru image rejoining the many others in her disturbed sleep.

The dream state passed and her breathing settled into the slow cycle of deep somnolence.

She only awoke sometime later, when she dimly sensed a hand stroke her leg. Then it seized her ankle and pulled hard.

Gailet's breath caught as she sat up quickly, before she could even bring her eyes to focus. Her heart raced. Then vision cleared and she saw that a rather large chim squatted beside her. His hand still rested on her leg, and his grin was instantly recognizable. The waxed handlebar mustache was only the most superficial of many attributes she had come to detest.

So suddenly drawn out of sleep, she had to take a moment to find speech again. "Wh . . . what are *you* doing here?" she asked acerbically, yanking her leg away from his grasp.

Irongrip looked amused. "Now, is that the way to say hello to someone as important as I am to you?"

"You do serve your purpose well," she admitted. "'As a bad example!" Gailet rubbed her eyes and sat up. "You didn't answer my question. Why are you bothering me? Your incompetent Probies aren't in charge of guarding anybody anymore."

The chen's expression soured only slightly. Obviously he was relishing something. "Oh, I just figured I ought to come on down to th' Library and do some studying, just like you."

"*You*, studying? Here?" She laughed. "I had to get special permission from the Suzerain. *You're* not even supposed—"

"Now those were the exact words I was about to use," he interrupted.

Gailet blinked. "What?"

"I mean, I was gonna tell you that the Suzerain told me to come down here and study with you. After all, partners ought to get to know each other well, especially before they step forward together as race-representatives."

Gailet's breath drew in audibly. "You . . . ?" Her head whirled. "I don't believe you!"

Irongrip shrugged. "You needn't sound so surprised. My genetic scores are in the high nineties almost across the board . . . except in two or three little categories that shouldn't ever have counted in the first place."

That Gailet could believe easily enough. Irongrip was obviously clever and resourceful, and his aberrant strength could only be considered an asset by the Uplift Board. But sometimes the price was just too great to pay. "All that means is that your loathsome qualities must be even worse than I had imagined."

The chen rocked back and laughed. "Oh, by human standards, I suppose you're right," he agreed. "By those criteria, most Probationers *shouldn't* be allowed anywhere near chimmies and children! Still standards change. And now I have the opportunity to set a new style."

Gailet felt a chill. It was just sinking in what Irongrip was driving at.

"You're a liar!"

"Admitted, *mea culpa.*" He pretended to beat his breast. "But I'm not lying about being in the testing party, along with a few of my fellow donner boys. There've been some changes, you see, since your little mama's boy and teacher's pet ran off into the jungle with our Sylvie."

Gailet wanted to spit. "Fiben's ten times the chen you are, you, you atavistic mistake! The Suzerain of Propriety would never choose *you* as his replacement!"

Irongrip grinned and raised a finger. "Aha. *There's* where we misunderstand each other. You see we've been talking about different birds, you and I."

"Different . . ." Gailet gasped. Her hand covered the open collar of her shirt. "Oh Goodall!"

"You get it," he said, nodding. "Smart, aristophrenic little monkey you are."

Gailet slumped. What surprised her most was the depth of her mourning. At that moment she felt as if her heart had been torn out.

We were pawns all along, she thought. *Oh, poor Fiben!*

This explained why Fiben had not been brought back the evening he took off with Sylvie. Or the next day, or the next. Gailet had been so *sure* that the "escape" would turn out to have been just another propriety and intelligence test.

But clearly it wasn't. It had to have been arranged by one or both of the other Gubru commanders, perhaps as a way to weaken the Suzerain of Propriety. And what better way to do that than by robbing it of one of its most carefully chosen chim "race-representatives." The theft couldn't even be pinned on anybody, for no body would ever be found.

Of course the Gubru would have to go ahead with the ceremony. It was too late to recall the invitations. But each of the three Suzerains might prefer to see different outcomes.

Fiben . . .

"So, professor? Where do we start? You can start teaching me how to act like a proper white card now."

She closed her eyes and shook her head. "Go away," she said. "Just please go away."

There were more words, more sarcastic comments. But she blocked them out behind a numbing curtain of pain. Tears, at least, she managed to withhold until she sensed that he was gone. Then she burrowed into the soft bag as if it was her mother's arms, and wept.

75

Galactics

The other two danced around the pedestal, puffing and cooing. Together they chanted in perfect harmony.

> *"Come down, come down,*
> *—down, come down!*
> *Come down off your perch.*

> *"Join us, join us,*
> *—us, join us!*
> *Join us in consensus!"*

The Suzerain of Propriety shivered, fighting the changes. They were completely united in opposition now. The Suzerain of Cost and Caution had given up hope of achieving the prized position—and was supporting the Suzerain of Beam and Talon in its bid for dominance. Caution's objective was now second place—the male Molt-status.

Two out of three had agreed then. But in order to achieve their objectives, both sexual and in policy, they had to bring the Suzerain of Propriety down off its perch. They had to force it to step onto the soil of Garth.

The Suzerain of Propriety fought them, squawking well-timed counterpoint to disrupt their rhythm and inserting pronouncements of logic to foil their arguments.

A proper Molt was not supposed to go this way. This was coercion, not true consensus. This was rape.

For this the Roost Masters had not invested so much hope in the Triumvirate. They needed policy. Wisdom. The other two seemed to have forgotten this. They wanted to take the easy way out with the Uplift Ceremony. They wanted to make a terrible gamble in defiance of the Codes.

If only the first Suzerain of Cost and Caution had lived! The priest mourned. Sometimes one only knew the value of another after that one was gone, gone.

> *"Come, down come down,*
> *Down off your perch."*

Against their united voice it was only a matter of time, of course. Their unison pierced through the wall of honor and resolve the priest had built around itself and penetrated down to the realm of hormone and instinct. The Molt hung suspended, held back by the recalcitrance of one member, but it would not be forestalled forever.

> *"Come down and join us.*
> *Join us in consensus!"*

The Suzerain of Propriety shuddered and held on. How much longer it could do so, it did not know.

76

The Caves

"Clennie!" Robert shouted joyfully. When he saw the mounted figures come around a bend in the trail he nearly dropped his end of the missile he and a chim were carrying out of the caves.

"Hey! Watchit with that thing, you . . . captain." One of Prathachulthorn's Marine corporals corrected himself at the last second. In recent weeks they had begun treating Robert with more respect—he'd been earning it—but on occasion the noncoms still showed their fundamental contempt for anyone non-Corps.

Another chim worker hurried up and easily lifted the nose cone out of Robert's grasp, looking disgusted that a human should even *try* lifting things.

Robert ignored both insults. He ran to the trailhead just as the band of travelers arrived and caught the halter of Athaclena's horse. His other hand reached out for her.

"Clennie, I'm glad you . . ." His voice faltered for an instant. Even as she squeezed his hand he blinked and tried to cover up his discomfiture. ". . . um, I'm glad you could come."

Athaclena's smile was unlike any he remembered her ever wearing before, and there was sadness in her aura that he had never *kenned*.

"Of course I came, Robert." She smiled. "Could you ever doubt I would?"

He helped her dismount. Underneath her superficial air of control he could feel her tremble. *Love, you have gone through changes.* As if she sensed his thought, she reached

490

up and touched the side of his face. "There are a few ideas shared by both Galactic society and yours, Robert. In both, sages have spoken of life as being something like a wheel."

"A wheel?"

"Yes." Her eyes glittered. "It turns. It moves forward. And yet it remains the same."

With a sense of relief he felt *her* again. Underneath the changes she was still Athaclena. "I missed you," he said.

"And I, you." She smiled. "Now tell me about this major and his plans."

Robert paced the floor of the tiny storage chamber, stacked to the overhead stalactites with supplies. "I can argue with him. I can try persuasion. Hell, he doesn't even mind if I yell at him, so long as it's in private, and so long as after all the debate is over I still leap two meters when he says 'Jump.' " Robert shook his head. "But I can't actively obstruct him, Clennie. Don't ask me to break my oath."

Robert obviously felt caught between conflicting loyalties. Athaclena could sense his tension.

His arm still in a sling, Fiben Bolger watched them argue, but he kept his silence for the time being.

Athaclena shook her head. "Robert, I explained to you that what Major Prathachulthorn has planned is likely to prove disastrous."

"Then tell *him!*"

Of course she had tried, over dinner that very evening. Prathachulthorn had listened courteously to her careful explanation of the possible consequences of attacking the Gubru ceremonial site. His expression had been indulgent. But when she had finished, he only asked one question. Would the assault be considered one against the Earthlings' legitimate enemy, or against the Uplift Institute itself.

"After the delegation from the Institute arrives, the site becomes their property," she had said. "An attack then would be catastrophic for humanity."

"But *before* then?" he had asked archly.

Athaclena had shaken her head irritably. "Until then the Gubru still own the site. But it's not a military site! It was built for what might be called holy purposes. The propriety of the act, without handling it just right . . ."

It had gone on for some time, until it became clear that all argument would be useless. Prathachulthorn promised to

take her opinions into account, ending the matter. They all
knew what the Marine officer thought of taking advice from
"E.T. children."

"We'll send a message to Megan," Robert suggested.

"I believe you have already done that," Athaclena
answered.

He scowled, confirming her guess. Of course it violated
all protocol to go over Prathachulthorn's head. At minimum it
would seem like a spoiled boy crying to mama. It might even
be a court-martial offense.

That he had done so proved that it wasn't out of fear for
himself that Robert was reticent about directly opposing his
commander, but out of loyalty to his sworn oath.

Indeed, he was right. Athaclena respected his honor.

But I am not ruled by the same duty, she thought.
Fiben, who had been silent so far, met her gaze. He rolled
his eyes expressively. About Robert they were in complete
agreement.

"I already suggested to th' major that knocking out the
ceremonial site might actually be doin' the enemy a favor.
After all, they built it to use it on Garthlings. Whatever their
scheme with us chims, it's probably a last ditch effort to make
up some of their losses. But what if th' site is insured? We
blow it up, they blame us and collect?"

"Major Prathachulthorn mentioned your idea about that."
Athaclena said to Fiben. "I find it acute, but I'm afraid he did
not credit it as very likely."

"Y'mean he thought it was a cuckoo pile of apeshi—"

He stopped as they heard footsteps on the cool stone
outside. "Knock knock!" A feminine voice said from beyond
the curtain. "May I come in?"

"Please do, Lieutenant McCue," Athaclena said. "We
were nearly finished anyway." The dusky-skinned human
woman entered and sat on one of the crates next to Robert.
He gave her a faint smile but soon was staring down at his
hands again. The muscles in his arms rippled and tensed as
his fists clenched and unclenched.

Athaclena felt a twinge when McCue placed her hand on
Robert's knee and spoke to him. "His nibs wants another
battle-planning conference before we all turn in." She turned
to look at Athaclena and smiled. Her head inclined. "You're
welcome to attend should you wish. You're our respected
guest, Athaclena."

Athaclena recalled when she had been the mistress of these caverns and had commanded an army. *I must not let that influence me*, she reminded herself. All that mattered now was to see that these creatures harmed themselves as little as possible in the coming days.

And, if at all possible, she was dedicated to furthering a certain jest. One that she, herself, still barely understood, but had recently come to appreciate.

"No, thank you, lieutenant. I think that I shall go say hello to a few of my chim friends and then retire. It was a long several days' ride."

Robert glanced back at her as he left with his human lover. Over his head a metaphorical cloud seemed to hover, flickering with lightning strokes. *I did not know you could do that with glyphs*, Athaclena wondered. Every day, it seemed, one learned something new.

Fiben's loose, unhinged grin was a boost as he followed the humans. Did she catch a sense of something from him? A conspiratorial wink?

When they were gone, Athaclena started rummaging through her kit. *I am not bound by their duty*, she reminded herself. *Or by their laws*.

The caves could get quite dark, especially when one extinguished the solitary glow bulb that illuminated an entire stretch of the hallway. Down here eyesight was not an advantage, but a Tymbrimi corona gave quite an edge.

Athaclena crafted a small squadron of simple but special glyphs. The first one had the sole purpose of darting ahead of her and to the sides, scouting out a path through the blackness. Since cold, hard matter was searing to that which was not, it was easy to tell where the walls and obstacles lay. The little wisp of nothing avoided them adroitly.

Another glyph spun overhead, reaching forth to make certain that no one was aware of an intruder in these lower levels. There were no chims sleeping in this stretch of hallway, which had been set aside for human officers.

Lydia and Robert were out on patrol. That left only one aura beside hers in this part of the cave. Athaclena stepped toward it carefully.

The third glyph silently gathered strength, awaiting its turn.

Slowly, silently, she padded over the packed dung of a

thousand generations of flying insectivore creatures who had dwelt here until being ousted by Earthlings and their noise. She breathed evenly, counting in the silent human fashion to help maintain the discipline of her thoughts.

Keeping three watchful glyphs up at once was something she'd not have attempted only a few days ago. Now it seemed easy, natural, as if she had done it hundreds of times.

She had ripped this and so many other skills away from Uthacalthing, using a technique seldom spoken of among the Tymbrimi, and even less often tried.

Turning jungle fighter, trysting with a human, and now this. Oh, my classmates would be amazed.

She wondered if her father retained any of the craft she had so rudely taken from him.

Father, you and mother arranged this long ago. You prepared me without my even knowing it. Did you already know, even then, that it would be necessary someday?

Sadly, she suspected she had taken away more than Uthacalthing could afford to spare. *And yet, it is not enough.* There were huge gaps. In her heart she felt certain that this thing encompassing worlds and species could not reach its conclusion without her father himself.

The scout glyph hovered before a hanging strip of cloth. Athaclena approached, unable to see the covering, even after she touched it with her fingertips. The scout unraveled and melted back into the waving tendrils of her corona.

She brushed the cloth aside with deliberate slowness and crept into the small side chamber. The watch glyph sensed no sign that anyone was aware within. She only *kenned* the steady rhythms of human slumber.

Major Prathachulthorn did not snore, of course. And his sleep was light, vigilant. She stroked the edges of his ever-present psi-shield, which guarded his thoughts, dreams, and military knowledge.

Their soldiers are good, and getting better, she thought. Over the years Tymbrimi advisors had worked hard to teach their wolfling allies to be fierce Galactic warriors. And the Tymbrimi, in truth, often came away having learned some fascinating bits of trickery themselves, ideas that could never have been imagined by a race brought up under Galactic culture.

But of all Earth's services, the Terragens Marines used no alien advisors. They were anachronisms, the *true* wolflings.

The glyph *z'schutan* cautiously approached the slumbering human. It settled down, and Athaclena saw it metaphorically as a globe of liquid metal. It *touched* Prathachulthorn's psi-shield and slid in golden rivulets over it, swiftly coating it under a fine sheen.

Athaclena breathed a little easier. Her hand slipped into her pocket and withdrew a glassy ampule. She stepped closer and carefully knelt next to the cot. As she brought the vial of anesthetic gas near the sleeping man's face, her fingers tensed.

"I wouldn't," he said, casually.

Athaclena gasped. Before she could move his hands darted out, catching her wrists! In the dim light all she could see were the whites of his eyes. Although he was awake his psi-shield remained undisturbed, still radiating waves of slumber. She realized that it had been a phantasm all along, a carefully fabricated trap!

"You Eatees just have to *keep* on underrating us, don't you? Even you smarty-pants Tymbrimi never seem to get it."

Gheer hormones surged. Athaclena heaved and pulled to get free, but it was like trying to escape a metal vice. Her clawed nails scratched, but he nimbly kept her fingers out of reach of his callused hands. When she tried to roll aside and kick he deftly applied slight pressure to her arms, using them as levers to keep her on her knees. The force made her groan aloud. The gas pellet tumbled from her limp hand.

"You see," Prathachulthorn said in an amiable voice, "there are some of us who think it's a mistake to compromise at all. What can we accomplish by trying to turn ourselves into good Galactic citizens?" he sneered. "Even if it worked, we'd only become horrors, awful things totally divorced from what it means to be human. Anyway, that option isn't even open. They won't let us become citizens. The deck is stacked. The dice are loaded. We both know that, don't we?"

Athaclena's breath came in ragged gasps. Long after it was clearly useless, the *gheer* flux kept her jerking and fighting againt the human's incredible strength. Agility and quickness were to no avail against his reflexes and training.

"We have our secrets, you know," Prathachulthorn confided. "Things we do not tell our Tymbrimi friends, or even most of our own people. Would you like to know what they are? Would you?"

Athaclena could not find the breath to answer. Prathachulthorn's eyes held something feral, almost animally fierce.

"Well, if I told you some of them it would be your death sentence," he said. "And I'm not ready to decide that quite yet. So I'll tell you one fact some of your people already know."

In an instant he had transferred both of her wrists to one hand. The other sought and found her throat.

"You see, we Marines are also taught how to disable, and even kill, members of an allied Eatee race. Would you like to know how long it will take me to render you unconscious, miss? Tell you what. Why don't you start counting?"

Athaclena heaved and bucked, but it was useless. A painful pressure closed in around her throat. Air started getting thick. Distantly, she heard Prathachulthorn mutter to himself.

"This universe is a goddam awful place."

She would never have imagined it could get blacker, but an even deeper darkness started closing in. Athaclena wondered if she would ever awaken again. *I'm sorry, father*. She expected those to be her last thoughts.

Continued consciousness came as something of a surprise then. The pressure on her throat, still painful, eased ever so slightly. She sucked a narrow stream of air and tried to figure out what was happening. Prathachulthorn's arms were quivering. She could tell he was bearing down hard, but somehow the force wasn't arriving!

Her overheated corona was no help. It was in total ignorance and amazement—when Prathachulthorn's grip loosened—that she dropped limply to the floor.

The *human* was breathing hard, now. There were grunts of exertion, and then a crash as the cot toppled over. A water pitcher shattered and there was a sound like that a datawell would make, getting smashed.

Athaclena felt something under her hand. *The ampule*, she realized. But what had happened to Prathachulthorn?

Fighting enzyme exhaustion, she crawled in a random direction until her hand came down upon the broken datawell. By accident her fingers brushed the power switch, and the rugged machine's screen spilled forth a dim luminescence.

In that glow, Athaclena saw a stark tableau . . . the human mel straining—his powerful muscles bulged and sinewy—against two long brown arms that held him from behind.

Prathachulthorn bucked and hissed. He threw his weight

left and right. But every effort to get free was to no avail. Athaclena saw a pair of brown eyes over the man's shoulder. She hesitated for only a moment, then hurried forward with the ampule.

Now Prathachulthorn had no psi-shield. His hatred was open for all to *kenn* if they had the power. He heaved desperately as she brought forward the little cylinder and broke it under his nose.

"He's holdin' his breath," the neo-chimpanzee muttered as the cloud of blue vapor hovered around the man's nostrils, then slowly fell groundward.

"That is all right," Athaclena answered. From her pocket she drew forth ten more.

When he saw them, Prathachulthorn let out a faint sigh. He redoubled his efforts to get away, but all it served was to bring closer the moment when he would finally have to breathe. The man was stubborn. It took five minutes, and even then Athaclena suspected he had fainted of anoxia before he ever felt the drug.

"Some guy," Fiben said when he finally let go. "Goodall, they make them Marines strong." He shuddered and collapsed next to the unconscious man.

Athaclena sat limply across from him.

"Thank you, Fiben," she said quietly.

He shrugged. "Hell, what's treason an' assault on a patron? All in a day's work."

She indicated his sling, where his left arm had rested ever since the evening of his escape from Port Helenia. "Oh, this?" Fiben grinned. "Well, I guess I have been milking the sympathy a bit. Please don't tell anybody, okay?"

Then, in a more serious mood, he looked down at Prathachulthorn. "I may not be any expert. But I'll bet I didn't win any points with th' old Uplift Board, tonight."

He glanced up at Athaclena, then smiled faintly. In spite of everything she had been through, she found she could not help but find everything suddenly *hilarious*.

She found herself laughing—quietly, but with her father's rich tones. Somehow, that did not surprise her at all.

The job wasn't over. Wearily, Athaclena had to follow as Fiben carried the unconscious human through the dim tunnels. As they tiptoed past Prathachulthorn's dozing corporal, Athaclena reached out with her tender, almost limp tendrils

and soothed the Marine's slumber. He mumbled and rolled
over on his cot. Especially wary now, Athaclena made doubly
sure the man's psi-shield was no ruse, that he actually slept
soundly.

Fiben puffed, his lips curled back in a grimace as she led
him over a tumbled slope of debris from an ancient landslide
and into a side passage that was almost certainly unknown to
the Marines. At least it wasn't on the cave map she had
accessed earlier today from the rebel database.

Fiben's aura was pungent each time he stubbed his toes
in the dim, twisting climb. No doubt he wanted to mutter
imprecations over Prathachulthorn's dense weight. But he
kept his comments within until they emerged at last into the
humid, silent night.

"Sports an' mutations!" he sighed as he laid his burden
down. "At least Prathachulthorn isn't one of th' tall ones. I
couldn't've managed with his hands and feet dragging in the
dust all the way."

He sniffed the air. There was no moon, but a fog spilled
over the nearby cliffs like a vaporous flood, and it gave off a
faint lambience. Fiben glanced back at Athaclena. "So? Now
what, chief? There's gonna be a hornet's nest here in a few
hours, especially after Robert and that Lieutenant McCue get
back. Do you want I should go get Tycho and haul away this
bad example to Earthling clients for you? It'll mean desert-
ing, but what the hell, I guess I was never a very good
soldier."

Athaclena shook her head. She sought with her corona
and found the traces she was looking for. "No, Fiben. I could
not ask that of you. Besides, you have another task. You
escaped from Port Helenia in order to warn us of the Gubru
offer. Now you must return there and face your destiny."

Fiben frowned. "Are you sure? You don't need me?"

Athaclena brought her hands over her mouth. She trilled
the soft call of a night bird. From the darkness downslope
there came a faint reply. She turned back to Fiben. "Of
course I do. We all need you. But where you can do the most
good is down there, near the sea. I also sense that you want
to go back."

Fiben pulled at his thumbs. "Gotta be crazy, I guess."

She smiled. "No. It is only one more indicator that the
Suzerain of Propriety knew its business in choosing you . . .

even though it might prefer that you showed a little more respect to your patrons."

Fiben tensed. Then he seemed to sense some of her irony. He smiled. There was the soft clattering of horses' hooves on the trail below. "All right," he said as he bent over to pick up the limp form of Major Prathachulthorn. "Come on, papa. This time I'll be as gentle as I would with my own maiden aunt." He smacked his lips against the Marine's shadowed cheek and looked up at Athaclena.

"Better, ma'am?"

Something she had borrowed from her father made her tired tendrils fizz. "Yes, Fiben." She laughed. "That's much better."

Lydia and Robert had their suspicions when they returned by the dawn's light to find their legal commander missing. The remaining Terragens Marines glared at Athaclena in open distrust. A small band of chims had gone through Prathachulthorn's room, cleaning away all signs of struggle before any humans got there, but they couldn't hide the fact that Prathachulthorn had gone without a note or any trace.

Robert even ordered Athaclena restricted to her chamber, with a Marine at the door, while they investigated. His relief over a likely delay in the planned attack was momentarily suppressed under an outraged sense of duty. In comparison, Lieutenant McCue was an eddy of calm. Outwardly, she seemed unconcerned, as if the major had merely stepped out. Only Athaclena could sense the Earth woman's underlying confusion and conflict.

In any event, there was nothing they could do about it. Search parties were sent out. They caught up with a party of Athaclena's chims returning on horseback to the gorilla refuge. But by that time Prathachulthorn was no longer with them. He was high in the trees, being passed from one forest giant to another, by now conscious and fuming, but helpless and trussed up like a mummy.

It was a case of humans paying the penalty for their "liberalism." They had brought up their clients to be individualists and citizens, so it was possible for chims to rationalize imprisoning one man for the good of all. In his own way Prathachulthorn had helped to bring this about, with his patronizing, deprecating attitudes. Nevertheless, Athaclena was certain the Marine would be delicately, carefully treated.

That evening, Robert chaired a new council of war. Athaclena's vague status of house arrest was modified so she could attend. Fiben and the chim brevet lieutenants were present, as well as the Marine noncommissioned officers.

Neither Lydia nor Robert brought up going ahead with Prathachulthorn's plan. It was tacitly assumed that the major wouldn't want it put under way without him.

"Maybe he went off on a personal scouting trip, or a snap inspection of some outpost. He might return tonight or tomorrow," Elayne Soo suggested in complete innocence.

"Maybe. We'd best assume the worst, though," Robert said. He avoided looking at Athaclena. "Just in case, we'd better send word to the refuge. I suppose it'll take ten days or so to get new orders from the Council, and for them to send a replacement."

He obviously assumed that Megan Oneagle would never leave him in charge.

"Well, I want to go back to Port Helenia," Fiben said simply. "I'm in a position to get close to the center of things. And anyway, Gailet needs me."

"What makes you think the Gubru will take you back, after running away?" Lydia McCue asked. "Why won't they simply shoot you?"

Fiben shrugged. "If I meet up with the wrong Gubru, that's what they'll probably do."

There was a long silence. When Robert asked for other suggestions, the humans and remaining chims remained silent. At least when Prathachulthorn had been here, dominating the discourse and the mood, there had been his overbearing confidence to override their doubts. Now their situation came home to them again. They were a tiny army with only limited options. And the enemy was about to set into motion things and events they could not even understand, let alone prevent.

Athaclena waited until the atmosphere was thick with gloom. Then she said four words. "We need my father."

To her surprise, both Robert and Lydia nodded. Even when orders finally arrived from the Council-in-Exile, those instructions would likely be as confused and contradictory as ever. It was obvious that they could use good advice, especially with matters of Galactic diplomacy at stake.

At least the McCue woman does not share Prathachulthorn's xenophobia, Athaclena thought. She found herself forced to admit that she approved of what she *kenned* of the Earthling female's aura.

"Robert told me you were sure your father was alive." Lydia said. "That's fine. But where is he? How can we find him?"

Athaclena leaned forward. She kept her corona still. "I know where he is."

"You do?" Robert blinked. "But . . ." His voice trailed off as he reached out to touch her with his inner sense, for the first time since yesterday. Athaclena recalled how she felt then, seeing him holding Lydia's hand. She momentarily resisted his efforts. Then, feeling foolish, she let go.

Robert sat back heavily and exhaled. He blinked several times. "Oh." That was all he said.

Now Lydia looked back and forth, from Robert to Athaclena and back again. Briefly, she shone with something faintly like envy.

I, too, have him in a way that you cannot, Athaclena mused. But mostly, she shared the moment with Robert.

". . . *N'tah'hoo*, Uthacalthing," he said in GalSeven. "We had better do something, and fast."

77

Fiben and Sylvie

She awaited him as he led Tycho up the trail emerging out of the Valley of Caves. She sat patiently next to an overhanging fip pine, just beyond a switchback, and only spoke when he drew even. "Thought you'd just sneak out without saying goodbye, did you?" Sylvie asked. She wore a long skirt and kept her arms wrapped around her knees.

He tied the horse's tether to a tree limb and sat down

next to her. "Nah," Fiben said. "I knew I wouldn't be so lucky."

She glanced at him sidelong and saw that he was grinning. Sylvie sniffed and looked back into the canyon, where the early mists were slowly evaporating into a morning that promised to be clear and cloudless. "I figured you'd be heading back."

"I have to, Sylvie. It's—"

She cut him off. "I know. Responsibility. You have to get back to Gailet. She needs you, Fiben."

He nodded. Fiben didn't have to be reminded that he still had a duty to Sylvie as well. "Um. Dr. Soo came by, while I was packing. I . . ."

"You filled the bottle she gave you. I know." Sylvie bowed her head. "Thank you. I consider myself well paid."

Fiben looked down. He felt awkward, talking around the edges of the topic like this. "When will you—"

"Tonight, I guess. I'm ready. Can't you tell?"

Sylvie's parka and long skirt certainly hid any outward signs. Still, she was right. Her scent was undisguised. "I sincerely hope you get what you want, Sylvie."

She nodded again. They sat there awkwardly. Fiben tried to think of something to say. But he felt thick headed, stupid. Whatever he tried, he knew, would surely turn out all wrong.

Suddenly there was a small rustle of motion down below, where the switchbacks diverged into paths leading in several directions. A tall human form emerged around a rocky bend, jogging tirelessly. Robert Oneagle ran toward a junction in the narrow trails, carrying only his bow and a light backpack.

He glanced upward, and on spotting the two chims he slowed. Robert grinned in response as Fiben waved, but on reaching the fork he turned southward, along a little-used track. Soon he had disappeared into the wild forest.

"What's he doing?" Sylvie asked.

"Looked like he was running."

She slapped his shoulder. "I could see that. Where is he *going?*"

"He's gonna try to make it through the passes before it snows."

"Through the *passes?* But—"

"Since Major Prathachulthorn disappeared, and since

time is so short, Lieutenant McCue and th' other Marines agreed they'd go along with the alternative plan Robert and Athaclena have cooked up."

"But he's running south," Sylvie said. Robert had taken the little-used trail that led deeper into the Mulun range.

Fiben nodded. "He's going looking for somebody. He's the only one who can do the job." It was obvious to Sylvie from his tone that that was all he would say about the matter.

They sat there for a little while longer in silence. At least Robert's brief passage had brought a welcome break in the tension. *This is silly*, Fiben thought. He liked Sylvie, a lot. They had never had much chance to talk, and this might be their last opportunity.

"You never . . . you never did tell me about your first baby," he said in a rush, wondering, as the words came out, if it was any of his business to ask.

Of course it was obvious that Sylvie had given birth before, and nursed. Stretch marks were signs of attractiveness in a race a quarter of whose females never bred at all. *But there is pain there as well*, he knew.

"It was five years ago. I was very young." Her voice was level, controlled. "His name was—we called him Sichi. He was tested by the Board, as usual, but he was found . . . 'anomalous.'"

"Anomalous?"

"Yes, that was the word they used. They classified him superior in some respects . . . 'odd' in others. There were no obvious defects, but some 'strange' qualities, they said. A couple of the officials were concerned. The Uplift Board decided they'd have to send him to Earth for further evaluation.

"They were very nice about it." She sniffed. "They offered me the choice of coming along."

Fiben blinked. "You didn't go, though."

She glanced at him. "I know what you're thinking. I'm terrible. That's why I never told you before. You'd have refused our deal. You think I'm an unfit mother."

"No, I—"

"At the time it seemed different, though. My mother was ill. We didn't have a clan-family, and I didn't feel I could just leave her in the care of strangers, an' probably never see her again.

"I was only a yellow card at the time. I knew my child

would get a good home on Earth or . . . Either he'd find
favored treatment and be raised in a high-caste neo-chimp
home or he'd meet a fate I didn't want to know. I was so
worried we would go all that way and they would only take
him away anyway. I guess I also dreaded the shame if he was
declared a Probationer."

She stared down at her hands. "I couldn't decide, so I
tried to get advice. There was this counselor in Port Helenia,
a human with the local Uplift Board. He told me what he
thought th' odds were. He said he was sure I'd given birth to
a Probie.

"I stayed behind when they took Sichi away. Six . . . six
months later my mother died."

She looked up at Fiben. "And then, three years after
that, word came back from Earth. The news was that my
baby was now a happy, well-adjusted little blue card, growing
up in a loving blue-card family. And oh, yeah, I was to be
promoted to green."

Her hands clenched. "Oh, how I hated that damned
card! They took me off compulsory yearly contracept injec-
tions, so I didn't have to ask permission anymore if I wanted
to conceive again. Trusted me to control my own fertility,
like an adult." She snorted. "Like an adult? A chimmie who
abandons her own child? They ignore *that*, and promote me
because he passes some damn tests!"

So, Fiben thought. This was the reason for her bitterness, and for her early collaboration with the Gubru. Much
was explained.

"You joined Irongrip's band out of resentment against
the system? Because you hoped things might be different
under the Galactics?"

"Something like that, maybe. Or maybe I was just angry." Sylvie shrugged. "Anyway, after a while I realized
something."

"What was it?"

"I realized that, however bad the system was under
humans, it could only be far worse under the Galactics. The
humans are arrogant all right. But at least a lot of them feel
guilty over their arrogance. They try to temper it. Their
horrible history taught them to be wary of hub . . . hub . . ."

"Hubris."

"Yeah. They know what a trap it can be, acting like gods
and coming to believe it's true.

"But the Galactics are *used* to this meddlesome business! It never occurs to them to have any doubts. They're so damned *smug* . . . I hate them."

Fiben thought about it. He had learned much during the last few months, and he figured Sylvie might be stating her case a little too strongly. Right now she sounded a lot like Major Prathachulthorn. But Fiben knew there were quite a few Galactic patron races who had reputations for kindness and decency.

Still, it was not his place to judge her bitterness.

Now he understood her nearly single-minded determination to have a child who would be at least a green card from the very start. There had to be no question. She wanted to keep her next baby, and to be sure of grandchildren.

Sitting there next to her, Fiben was uncomfortably certain of Sylvie's present condition. Unlike human females, chimmies had set cycles of receptivity, and it took some effort to hide them. It was one reason for some of the social and family differences between the two cousin species.

He felt guilty to be aroused by her condition. A soft, poignant feeling lay over the moment, and he was determined not to spoil it by being insensitive. Fiben wished he could console her somehow. And yet, he did not know what to offer her.

He moistened his lips. "Uh. Look, Sylvie."

She turned. "Yes, Fiben?"

"Um, I really do hope you get . . . I mean I hope I left enough . . ." His face felt warm.

She smiled. "Dr. Soo says there probably was. If not, there's more where that came from."

He shook his head. "Your confidence is appreciated. But I wouldn't bet I'll ever be back again." He looked away, toward the west.

She took his hand. "Well, I'm not too proud to take extra insurance if it's offered. Another donation will be accepted, if you feel up to it."

He blinked, feeling the tempo of his pulse rise. "Uh, you mean right now?"

She nodded. "When else?"

"I was hoping you'd say that." He grinned and reached for her. But she held up a hand to stop him.

"Just a minute," she said. "What kind of girl do you think

I am? Candlelight and champagne may be in short supply up
here, but a fem generally appreciates at least a little foreplay."

"Fine by me," Fiben said. He turned around to present
his back for grooming. "Do me, then I'll do you."

But she shook her head. "Not that kind of foreplay,
Fiben. I had in mind something much more stimulating."

She reached behind the tree and brought forth a cylin-
drical object made of carved wood, one end covered by
a tautly stretched skin. Fiben's eyes widened. "A *drum?*"

She sat with the little handmade instrument between
her knees. "It's your own damn fault, Fiben Bolger. You
showed me something special, and from now on I'll never be
satisfied with anything less."

Her deft fingers rattled off a quick rhythm.

"Dance," she said. "Please."

Fiben sighed. Obviously she wasn't kidding. This choreo-
maniac chimmie was crazy, of course, whatever the Uplift
Board said. It seemed to be the type he fell for.

There are some ways we'll never be like humans, he
thought as he picked up a branch and shook it tentatively. He
dropped it and tried another. Already he felt flushed and full
of energy.

Sylvie tapped the drum, starting with a rapid, exhilarating tempo that made his breath sharpen. The shine in her
eyes seemed to warm his blood.

That is as it should be. We are our own selves, he knew.

Fiben took the branch in a two-handed grip and brought
it down on a nearby log, sending leaves and brush exploding
in all directions. "Ook . . ." he said.

His second blow was harder though, and as the beat
picked up his next cry came with more enthusiasm.

The morning fog had evaporated. No thunder rolled.
The uncooperative universe had not even provided a single
cloud in the sky. Still, Fiben figured he could probably
manage this time without the lightning.

78

Galactics

In Gubru Military Enacampment Sixteen, the chaos at the top had begun affecting those lower down in the ranks. There were squabbles over allotments and supplies, and over the behavior of common soldiers, whose contempt for the support staff reached new and dangerous levels.

At afternoon prayer time, many of the Talon Soldiers put on the traditional ribbons of mourning for the Lost Progenitors and joined the priestly chaplain to croon in low unison. The less devout majority, who generally kept a respectful silence during such services, now seemed to make it a special occasion for gambling and loud commotion. Sentries preened and purposely sent loose feathers drifting in strong breezes so they would pass distractingly among the faithful.

Discordant noises could be heard during work, during maintenance, during training exercises.

The stoop-colonel in charge of the eastern encampments happened to be on an inspection tour and witnessed this disharmony in person. It wasted no time on indecision. At once the stoop-colonel ordered all personnel of Encampment Sixteen assembled. Then the officer gathered the camp's chief administrator and the chaplain by its side upon a platform and addressed those gathered below.

"Let it not be said, bandied, rumored,
  That Gubru soldiers have lost their vision!
Are we orphans? Lost? Abandoned?
  Or members of a great clan!

What were we, are we, shall we be?
       Warriors, builders, but most of all—
Proper carriers of tradition!"

For some time the stoop-colonel spoke to them so—joined
in persuasive song by the camp's administrator and its spiritual
advisor—until, at last, the shamed soldiers and staff began to
coo together in a rising chorus of harmony.

They made the effort, invested the time, one small united
regiment of military, bureaucrats, and priests, and struggled
as one to overcome their doubts.

For a brief while then, there did indeed take shape a
consensus.

79

Gailet

*. . . Even among those rare and tragic cases, wolfling
species, there have existed crude versions of these techniques.
While primitive, their methods also involved rituals of "combat-
of-honor," and by such means kept aggressiveness and warfare under some degree of restraint.*

*Take, for example, the most recent clan of wolflings—the
"humans" of Sol III. Before their discovery by Galactic culture, their primitive "tribes" often used ritual to hold in
check the cycles of ever-increasing violence normally to be
expected from such an unguided species. (No doubt these
traditions derived from warped memories of their long lost
patron race.)*

*Among the simple but effective methods used by pre-
Contact humans (see citations) were the method of counting
coup for honor among the "american indians," trial by champion*

among the "medieval europeans," and deterrence by mutual assured destruction, *among the "continental tribal states."*

Of course, these techniques lacked the subtlety, the delicate balance and homeostasis, of the modern rules of behavior laid out by the Institute for Civilized Warfare . . .

"That's it. Break time. I'm puttin' a T on it. Enough."

Gailet blinked, her eyes unfocusing as the rude voice drew her back out of her reading trance. The library unit sensed this and froze the text in front of her.

She looked to her left. Sprawled in the beanbag, her new "partner" threw his datawell aside and yawned, stretching his lanky, powerful frame. "Time for a drink," he said lazily.

"You haven't even made it through the first edited summary," Gailet said.

He grinned. "Aw, I don't know why we've got to study this shit. The Eatees'll be surprised if we remember to bow and recite our own species-name. They don't expect neo-chimps to be geniuses, y'know."

"Apparently not. And your comprehension scores will certainly reinforce the impression."

That made him frown momentarily. He forced a grin again. "You, on the other hand, are tryin' so hard—I'm sure the Eatees will find it terribly cute."

Touché, Gailet thought. It hadn't taken the two of them very long to learn how to cut each other where it hurt.

Maybe this is yet another test. They are seeing how far my patience can be stretched before it snaps.

Maybe . . . but not very likely. She had not seen the Suzerain of Propriety for more than a week. Instead, she had been dealing with a committee of three pastel-tinged Gubru, one from each faction. And it was the blue-tinted Talon Soldier who strutted foremost at these meetings.

Yesterday they had all gone down to the ceremonial site for a "rehearsal." Although she was still undecided whether to cooperate in the final event, Gailet had come to realize that it might already be too late to change her mind.

The seaside hill had been sculpted and landscaped so that the giant power plants were no longer visible. The terraced slopes led elegantly upward, one after another, marred only by bits of debris brought in by the steady autumnal winds. Already, bright banners flapped in the easterlies, marking the stations where the neo-chimp representatives would be asked to recite, or answer questions, or submit to intense scrutiny.

There at the site, with the Gubru standing close by, Irongrip had been to all outward appearances a model student. And perhaps it had been more than a wish to curry favor that had made him so uncharacteristically studious. After all, these were facts that had direct bearing upon his ambitions. That afternoon, his quick intelligence had shone.

Now though, with them alone together under the vast vault of the New Library, other aspects of his nature came to the fore. "So how 'bout it?" Irongrip said, as he leaned over her chair and gave her a cyprian leer. "Want to step outside for some air? We could slip into the eucalyptus grove and—"

"There are two chances of that," she snapped. "Fat and slim."

He laughed. "Put it off until the ceremony, then, if you like it public. Then it'll be you an' me, babe, with the whole Five Galaxies watchin'." He grinned and flexed his powerful hands. His knuckles cracked.

Gailet turned away and closed her eyes. She had to concentrate to keep her lower lip from trembling. *Rescue me,* she wished against all hope or reason.

Logic chided her for even thinking it. After all, her white knight was only an ape, and almost certainly dead.

Still, she couldn't help crying inside. *Fiben, I need you. Fiben, come back.*

80

Robert

His blood sang.

After months in the mountains—living as his ancestors had, on wits and his own sweat, his toughened skin growing used to the sun and the scratchy rub of native fibers—Robert still had not yet realized the changes in himself, not until he puffed up the last few meters of the narrow, rocky trail and crossed in ten long strides from one watershed to another.

The top of Rwanda Pass. . . . I've climbed a thousand meters in two hours, and my heart is scarcely beating fast.

He did not really feel any need to rest, however Robert made himself slow down to a walk. Anyway, the view was worth lingering over.

He stood atop the very spine of the Mulun range. Behind him, to the north, the mountains stretched eastward in a thickening band, and westward toward the sea, where they continued in an archipelago of fat, towering islands.

It had taken him a day and a half of running to get here from the caves, and now he saw ahead of him the panorama he would have yet to cross to reach his destination.

I'm not even sure how to find what I'm looking for! Athaclena's instructions had been as vague as her own impressions of where to send him.

More mountains stretched ahead of him, dropping away sharply toward a dun-colored steppe partially obscured by haze. Before he reached those plains there would be still more rise and fall over narrow trails that had only felt a few score feet even during peacetime. Robert was probably the first to come this way since the outbreak of war.

The hardest part was over, though. He didn't enjoy down-hill running, but Robert knew how to take the jolting, fall-stepping so as to avoid damaging his knees. And there would be water lower down.

He shook his leather canteen and took a sparing swallow. Only a few deciliters remained, but he was sure they'd do.

He shaded his eyes and looked beyond the nearest purple peaks to the high slopes where he would have to make his camp tonight. There would be streams all right, but no lush rain forests like on the wet northern side of the Mulun. And he would have to think about hunting for food soon, before he sallied forth onto the dry savannah.

Apache braves could run from Taos to the Pacific in a few days and not eat anything but a handful of parched corn along the way.

He wasn't an Apache brave, of course. He did have a few grams of vitamin concentrate with him, but for the sake of speed he had chosen to travel light. For now, quickness counted more than his grumbling stomach.

He skirted aside where a recent landslide had broken the path. Then he set a slightly faster pace as the trail dropped into a set of tight switchbacks.

That night Robert slept in a moss-filled notch just above a trickling spring, wrapped in a thin silk blanket. His dreams were slow and as quiet as he imagined space might be, if one ever got away from the constant humming of machines.

Mostly, it was the stillness in the empathy net, after months living in the riot of the rain forest, that lent a soft loneliness to his slumber. One might *kenn* far in an empty land such as this—even with senses as crude as his.

And for the first time there was not the harsh—meta-phorically almost *metallic*—hint of alien minds to be felt off in the northwest. He was shielded from the Gubru, and from the humans and chims for that matter. Solitude was a strange sensation.

The strangeness did not evaporate by the dawn's light. He filled his canteen from the spring and drank deeply to take the edge off his hunger. Then the run began anew.

On this steeper slope the descent was wearing, but the miles did go by quickly. Before the sun was more than halfway toward the zenith the high steppe had opened up around him. He ran across rolling foothills now—kilometers falling behind him like thoughts barely contemplated and then forgotten. And as he ran, Robert probed the countryside. Soon he felt certain that the expanse held odd entities, somewhere out there beyond or among the tall grasses.

If only *kenning* were more of a localizing sense! Perhaps it was this very imprecision that had kept humans from ever developing their own crude abilities.

Instead, we concentrated on other things.

There was a game that was often played both on Earth and among interested Galactics. It consisted of trying to reconstruct the fabled "lost patrons of humanity," the half-mythical starfarers who supposedly began the Uplift of human beings perhaps fifty thousand years ago and then departed in mystery, leaving the job "only half done."

Of course there were a few bold heretics—even among the Galactics—who held that the old Earthling theories were actually true, that it was somehow possible for a race to Uplift itself . . . to *evolve* starfaring intelligence and pull itself up by its bootstraps out of darkness and into knowledge and maturity.

But even on Earth most now thought the idea quaint. Patrons uplifted clients, who later took their own turn uplifting newer pre-sentients. It was the way and had been ever since the days of the Progenitors, so long ago.

There was a real dearth of clues. Whoever the patrons of Man might have been, they had hidden their traces well, and for good reason. A patron race who abandoned a client was generally branded as an outlaw.

Still, the guessing game went on.

Certain patron clans were ruled out because they would never have chosen an omnivorous species to raise. Others were unsuited to living on Earth even for short visits—because of gravity or atmosphere or a host of other reasons.

Most agreed that it couldn't have been a clan which believed in specialization either. Some uplifted their clients with very specific goals in mind. The Uplift Institute demanded that any new sapient race be able to pilot starships, exercise judgment and logic and be capable of patron status itself someday. But beyond that the Institute put few constraints on the types of niches into which client species might be made to fit. Some were destined to become skilled craftsmen, some philosophers, and some mighty warrior castes.

But humanity's mysterious patrons had to have been

generalists. For Man, the animal, was very much a flexible beast.

Yes, and for all of the vaunted flexibility of the Tymbrimi, there were some things not even those masters of adaptation could even think of doing.

Such as this, Robert thought.

A covey of native birds exploded into the air in a flurry of beating wings as Robert ran across their feeding grounds. Small, skittering things felt the rumble of his approach and took cover.

A herd of animals, long-legged and fleet like small deer, darted away, easily outdistancing him. They happened to flee southward, the direction he was going anyway, so he followed them. Soon Robert was approaching where they had stopped to feed again.

Once more they bolted, opened a wide berth behind them, then settled down again to browse.

The sun was getting high. It was a time of the day when all the plains animals, both the hunters and the hunted, tended to seek shelter from the heat. Where there were no trees, they scraped the soil in narrow runnels to find cooler layers and lay down in what shade there was to wait out the blazing sun.

But on this day one creature did not stop. It kept coming. The pseudo-deer blinked in consternation as Robert approached again. Once more, they arose and took flight, leaving him behind. This time they put a little more distance in back of them. They stood atop a small hill, panting and staring unbelievingly.

The thing on two legs just kept coming!

An uneasy stir riffled through the herd. A premonition that this just might be serious.

Still panting, they fled once more.

Perspiration shone like oil on Robert's olive skin. It glistened in the sunlight, quivering in droplets that sometimes shook loose with the constant drumming of his footsteps.

Mostly, though, the sweat spread out and coated his skin and evaporated in the rushing wind of his own passage. A dry, southeasterly breeze helped it change state into vapor, sucking up latent heat in the process. He maintained a steady, even pace, not even trying to match the sprints of the deerlike creatures. At intervals he walked and took sparing swigs from his water bag, then he resumed the chase.

His bow lay strapped across his back. But for some reason Robert did not even think of using it. Under the noonday sun he ran on and on. *Mad dogs and Englishmen,* he thought.

And Apache . . . and Bantu . . . and so many others. . . .

Humans were accustomed to thinking that it was their brains which distinguished them so from the other members of Earth's animal kingdom. And it was true that weapons and fire and speech had made them the lords of their homeworld long before they ever learned about ecology, or the duty of senior species to care for those less able to understand. During those dark millennia, intelligent but ignorant men and women had used fires to drive entire herds of mammoths and sloths and so many other species over cliffs, killing hundreds for the meat contained in one or two. They shot down millions of birds so the feathers might adorn their ladies. They chopped down forests to grow opium.

Yes, intelligence in the hands of ignorant children was a dangerous weapon. But Robert knew a secret.

We did not really need all these brains in order to rule our world.

He approached the herd again, and while hunger drove him, he also contemplated the beauty of the native creatures. No doubt they were growing rapidly in stature with each passing generation. Already they were far larger than their ancestors had been back when the Bururalli slew all the great ungulates which used to roam these plains. Someday they might fill some of those empty niches. Even now they were already far swifter than a man.

Speed was one thing. But *endurance* was quite another matter. As they turned to flee him again, Robert saw that the herd members had begun to look a little panicky. The pseudo-deer now wore flecks of foam around their mouths. Their tongues hung out, and their rib cages heaved in rapid tempo.

The sun beat down. Perspiration beaded and covered him in a thin sheen. This evaporated, leaving him cool. Robert paced himself.

Tools and fire and speech gave us the surplus. They gave us what we needed to begin culture. But were they all we had?

A song had begun to play in the network of fine sinuses behind his eyes, in the gentle squish of fluid that damped his brain against the hard, driving accelerations of every footstep. The throbbing of his heartbeat carried him along like a faithful bass rhythm. The tendons of his legs were like taut, humming bows . . . like violin strings.

He could smell them now, his hunger accentuating the atavistic thrill. He identified with his intended prey. In an odd way Robert knew a fulfillment he had never experienced before. He was *alive*.

He barely noticed as he began overtaking deer who had collapsed to the ground. Mothers and their fawns blinked in dull surprise as he ran past them without a glance. Robert had spotted his target, and he projected a simple glyph to tell the others to relax, to slip aside, while he chased a big male buck at the head of the herd.

You are the one, he thought. *You have lived well, passed on your genes. Your species does not need you anymore, not as much as I do.*

Perhaps his ancestors actually used empathy-sense quite a bit more than modern man. For now he saw a real function for it. He could *kenn* the growing dread of the buck as, one by one, its overheated companions dropped aside. The buck put in a desperate burst of speed and leaped far ahead. But then it had to rest, panting miserably to try to cool off, its sides heaving as it watched Robert come on.

Foaming, it turned to flee again.

Now it was just the two of them.

Gimelhai blazed. Robert bore on.

A little while later he brought his left hand to his belt as he ran, and loosened the sheath of his knife. Even that tool he chose with some reluctance. What decided him to use it, instead of his bare hands, was empathy with his prey, and a sense of mercy.

It was some hours later, his stomach no longer growling urgently, that Robert felt his first glimmerings of a clue. He had begun making his way southwestward, in the direction Athaclena had hoped would lead him to his goal. As the day aged, Robert shaded his eyes against the late afternoon glare. Then he closed them and reached forth with other senses.

Yes, something was close enough to *kenn*. If he thought of it metaphorically, it came as a very familiar flavor.

He headed forth at a jog, following traces that came and went, sometimes cool and sentient and sometimes as wild as the buck who had shared its life with Robert so recently.

When the traces grew quite strong, Robert found himself near a vast thicket of ugly thorn bush. Soon it would be sunset, and there was no way he would be able to chase down the thing emanating those vibrations, not in this dense, hurtful undergrowth. Anyway, he did not want to "hunt" this creature. He wanted to talk to it.

He was sure the being was aware of him now. Robert halted. He closed his eyes again and cast forth a simple glyph. It darted left, right, then plunged into the vegetation. There came a rustle.

He opened his eyes. Two dark, glittering pools blinked back at him. "All right," he said, softly. "Please come on out now. We had better talk."

There was another moment's hesitation. Then there shambled forth a long-armed chim, hairier than most, with thick brows and a heavy jaw. He was dirty, and totally naked.

There were a few stains that Robert was sure came from caked blood, and it had not come from the chim's own minor scratches. *Well, we are cousins, after all. And vegetarians don't live long on a steppe.*

When he sensed that the comate chim was reluctant to make eye contact, Robert did not insist. "Hello, Jo-Jo," he said softly, and with sincere gentleness. "I've come a long way to bring a message to your employer."

81

Athaclena

The cage consisted of thick wooden slats bound by wire. It hung from a tree branch in a sheltered vale, under the leeward shoulder of a simmering volcano. Still the guy cables holding it in place trembled under occasional gusts of wind, and the cage itself swayed.

Its occupant—naked, unshaven, and looking very much the wolfling—stared down at Athaclena with an expression that would have burned even without the loathing he radiated. To Athaclena it felt as if the little glade were saturated with the prisoner's hatred. She planned to keep her visit as short as possible.

"I thought you would want to know. The Gubru Triumvirate has declared a protocol truce under the Rules of War," she told Major Prathachulthorn. "The ceremonial site is now sacrosanct, and no armed force on Garth can act except in self-defense for the duration."

Prathachulthorn spat through the bars. "So? If we'd attacked when I planned, we'd have made it before this."

"I find it doubtful. Even the best plans are seldom executed perfectly. And if we were forced to abort the mission at the last minute, every secret we had would have been revealed for nothing."

"That's your opinion," Prathachulthorn snorted.

Athaclena shook her head. "But that is not the only or even the most important reason." She had grown tired of fruitlessly explaining the nuances of Galactic punctilio to the Marine officer, but somehow she found the will to try one more time. "I told you before, major. Wars are known to feature cycles of what you humans sometimes call 'tit-for-tat' where one side punishes the other side for its last insult, and then that other side retaliates in turn. Left unconstrained, this can escalate forever! Since the days of the Progenitors, there have been developed rules which help keep such exchanges from growing out of all proportion."

Prathachulthorn cursed. "Damn it, you admitted that our raid would've been legal if done in time!"

She nodded. "Legal, perhaps. But it also would have served the enemy well. Because it would have been the *last* action before the truce!"

"What difference does that make?"

Patiently, she tried to explain. "The Gubru have declared a truce while still in an overpowering position of strength, major. That is considered honorable. You might say they 'win points' for that.

"But their gain is multiplied if they do so immediately after taking *damage*. If they show restraint by not retaliating, the Gubru are then performing an act of forbearance. They gather credit—"

"Ha!" Prathachulthorn laughed. "Fat lot of good it'd do them, with their ceremonial site in ruins!"

Athaclena inclined her head. She really did not have time for this. If she spent too long here, Lieutenant McCue might suspect that this was where her missing commander was being hidden. The Marines had already swooped down on several possible hiding places.

"The upshot might have been to force *Earth* to finance a new site as a replacement," she said.

Prathachulthorn stared at her. "But—but we're at *war!*"

She nodded, misunderstanding him. "Exactly. One cannot allow war without rules, and powerful neutral forces to enforce them. The alternative would be barbarism."

The man's sour look was her only answer.

"Besides, to destroy the site would have implied that humans do not want to see their clients tested and judged for promotion! But now it is the *Gubru* who must pay honor-gild for this truce. Your clan has gained a segment of status by being the aggrieved party, unavenged. This sliver of propriety could turn out to be crucial in the days ahead."

Prathachulthorn frowned. For a moment he seemed to concentrate, as if a thread of her logic hung almost within reach. She felt his attention shimmer as he tried . . . but then it faded. He grimaced and spat again. "What a load of crap. Show me dead birds. That's currency I can count. Pile them up to the level of this cage, little Miss Ambassador's Daughter, and maybe, just *maybe* I'll let you live when I finally break out of here."

Athaclena shivered. She knew how futile it was to try to hold a man such as this prisoner. He should have been kept drugged. He should have been killed. But she could not bring herself to do either, or to further prejudice the fate of the chims in her cabal by involving them in such crimes.

"Good day, major," she said. And turned to go.

He did not shout as she left. In a way, the parsimonious use he made of his threats made those few seem all the more menacing and believable.

She took a hidden trail from the secret glade over a shoulder of the mountain, past warm springs that hissed and steamed uncertainly. At the ridge crest Athaclena had to draw in her tendrils to keep them from being battered in the autumn wind. Few clouds could be seen in the sky, but the air was hazy with dust blowing in from faraway deserts.

Hanging from a nearby branch she encountered one of the parachutelike kite and spore pod combinations blown up here from some field of plate ivy. The autumn dispersal was fully under way now. Fortunately, it had begun in earnest more than two days ago, before the Gubru announced their truce. That fact might turn out to be very important indeed.

The day felt odd, more so than any time since that night of terrible dreams, shortly before she climbed this mountain to wrestle with her parents' fierce legacy.

Perhaps the Gubru are warming up their hyperwave shunt, again.

She had since learned that her fit of dreams on that fateful night had coincided with the invaders' first test of their huge new facility. Their experiments had let surges of unallocated probability loose in all directions, and those who were psychically sensitive reported bizarre mixtures of deathly dread and hilarity.

That sort of mistake did not sound like the normally meticulous Gubru, and it seemed to be validation of Fiben Bolger's report, that the enemy had serious leadership problems.

Was that why *tutsunucann* collapsed so suddenly and violently that evening? Was all that loose energy responsible for the terrific power of her *s'ustru'thoon* rapport with Uthacalthing?

Could that and the subsequent tests of those great engines explain why the gorillas had begun behaving so very strangely?

All Athaclena knew for certain was that she felt nervous and afraid. *Soon*, she thought. *It will all approach climax very soon.*

She had descended halfway down the trail leading back to her tent when a pair of breathless chims emerged from the forest, hurrying uphill toward her. "Miss . . . miss . . ." one of them breathed. The other held his side, panting audibly.

Her initial reading of their panic triggered a brief hormone rush, which only subsided slightly when she traced their fear and *kenned* that it did not come from an enemy attack. Something *else* had them terrified half out of their wits.

"Miss Ath-Athaclena," the first chim gasped. "You gotta come quick!"

"What is it, Petri? What's happening?"

He swallowed. "It's the 'rillas. We can't control 'em anymore!"

So, she thought. For more than a week the gorillas' low, atonal music had been driving their chim guardians to nervous fits. "What are they doing now?"

"They're leaving!" the second messenger wailed plaintively.

She blinked. "What did you say?"

Petri's brown eyes were filled with bewilderment. "They're leaving. They just got up and left! They're headin' for the *Sind*, an' there doesn't seem t'be anythin' we can do to stop 'em!"

82

Uthacalthing

Their progress toward the mountains had slackened considerably recently. More and more of Kault's time seemed to be spent laboring over his makeshift instruments . . . and in arguing with his Tymbrimi companion.

How quickly things change, Uthacalthing thought. He had labored long and hard to bring Kault to this fever pitch of suspicion and excitement. And now he found himself recalling with fondness their earlier peaceful comradeship—the long, lazy days of gossip and reminiscences and common exile—however frustrating they had seemed at the time.

Of course that had been when Uthacalthing was whole, when he had been able to look upon the world through Tymbrimi eyes, and the softening veil of whimsy.

Now? Uthacalthing knew that he had been considered dour and serious by others of his race. Now, though, they would surely think him crippled. Perhaps better off dead.

Too much was taken from me, he thought, while Kault

muttered to himself in the corner of their shelter. Outside, heavy gusts blew through the veldt grasses. Moonlight brushed long hillcrests that resembled sluggish ocean waves, locked amid a rolling storm.

Did she actually have to tear away so much? he wondered, without really being able to feel or care very much.

Of course Athaclena had hardly known what she was doing, that night when she decided in her need to call in the pledge her parents had made. *S'ustru'thoon* was not something one trained for. A recourse so drastic and used so seldom could not be well described by science. And by its very nature, *s'ustru'thoon* was something one could do but once in one's lifetime.

Anyway, now that he looked back upon it, Uthacalthing remembered something he hadn't noticed at the time.

That evening had been one of great tension. Hours beforehand he had felt disturbing waves of energy, as if ghostly half-glyphs of immense power were throbbing against the mountains. Perhaps that explained why his daughter's call had carried such strength. She had been tapping some outside source!

And he remembered something else. In the *s'ustru'thoon* storm Athaclena triggered, not *everything* torn from him had gone to her!

Strange that he had not thought of it until now. But Uthacalthing now seemed vaguely to recall some of his essences flying *past* her. But where they had actually been bound he could not even imagine. Perhaps to the source of those energies he had felt earlier. Perhaps . . .

Uthacalthing was too tired to come up with rational theories. *Who knows? Maybe they were drawn in by Garth lings.* It was a poor joke. Not even worth a tiny smile. And yet, the irony was encouraging. It showed that he had not lost absolutely everything.

"I am certain of it now, Uthacalthing." Kault's voice was low and confident as the Thennanin turned to face him. He put aside the instrument he had constructed out of odd items salvaged from the wrecked pinnace.

"Certain of what, colleague?"

"Certain that our separate suspicions are focusing in on a probable fact! See here. The data you showed me—your private spools regarding these 'Garthling' creatures—allowed me to tune my detector until I am now sure that I have found the resonance I was seeking."

"You are?" Uthacalthing didn't know what to make of this. He had never expected Kault to find actual *confirmation* of mythical beasts.

"I know what concerns you, my friend," Kault said, raising one massive, leather-plated hand. "You fear that my experiments will draw down upon us the attention of the Gubru. But rest assured. I am using a very narrow band and am reflecting my beam off the nearer moon. It is very unlikely they would ever be able to localize the source of my puny little probe."

"But . . ." Uthacalthing shook his head. "What are you looking for?"

Kault's breathing slits puffed. "A certain type of cerebral resonance. It is quite technical," he said. "It has to do with something I read in your tapes about these Garthling creatures. What little data you had seemed to indicate that these pre-sentient beings might have brains not too dissimilar to those of Earthlings, or Tymbrimi."

Uthacalthing was amazed by the way Kault used his faked data with such celerity and enthusiasm. His former self would have been delighted. "So?" he asked.

"So . . . let me see if I can explain with an example. Take humans—"

Please, Uthacalthing inserted, without much enthusiasm, more out of habit.

"—Earthlings represent one of many paths which can be taken to arrive eventually at intelligence. Theirs involved the use of *two* brains that later became one."

Uthacalthing blinked. His own mind was working so slowly. "You . . . you are speaking of the fact that their brains have two partially independent hemispheres?"

"Aye. And while these halves are similar and redundant in some ways, in others they divide the labor. The split is even more pronounced among their neo-dolphin clients.

"Before the Gubru arrived, I was studying data on neo-chimpanzees, which are similar to their patrons in many respects. One of the things the humans had to do, early in their Uplift program, was find ways to unite the functions of the two halves of pre-sentient chimpanzee brains comfortably into one consciousness. Until that was done neo-chimpanzees would suffer from a condition called 'bicamerality.' . . ."

Kault droned on, gradually letting his jargon grow more and more technical, eventually leaving Uthacalthing far behind. The arcana of cerebral function seemed to fill their shelter, as if in thick smoke. Uthacalthing felt almost tempted to craft a glyph to commemorate his own boredom, but he lacked the energy even to stir his tendrils.

". . . so the resonance appears to indicate that there are, indeed, bicameral minds within the range of my instrument!"

Ah, yes, Uthacalthing thought. Back in Port Helenia, at a time when he had still been a clever crafter of complex schemes, he had suspected that Kault might turn out to be resourceful. That was one reason why Uthacalthing chose for a confederate an atavistic chim. Kault was probably picking up traces from poor Jo-Jo, whose throwback brain was in many ways similar to fallow, non-uplifted chimpanzees of centuries ago. Jo-Jo no doubt retained some of this "bicamerality" characteristic Kault spoke of.

Finally Kault concluded. "I am therefore quite convinced, from your evidence and my own, that we cannot delay any longer. We must somehow get to and use a facility for sending interstellar messages!"

"How do you expect to do that?" Uthacalthing asked in mild curiosity.

Kault's breathing slits pulsed in obvious, rare excitement. "Perhaps we can sneak or bluff or fight our way to the Planetary Branch Library, claim sanctuary, and then invoke every priority under the fifty suns of Thennan. Perhaps there is another way. I do not care if it means stealing a Gubru starship. Somehow we must get word to my clan!"

Was this the same creature who had been so anxious to flee Port Helenia before the invaders arrived? Kault seemed as changed outwardly as Uthacalthing felt inwardly. The Thennanin's enthusiasm was a hot flame, while Uthacalthing had to stoke his own carefully.

"You wish to establish a claim on the pre-sentients before the Gubru manage it?" he asked.

"Aye, and why not? To save them from such horrible patrons I would lay down my life! But there may be need for much haste. If what we have overheard on our receiver is true, emissaries from the Institutes may already be on their way to Garth. I believe the Gubru are planning something big. Perhaps they have made the same discovery. We must act quickly if we are not to be too late!"

Uthacalthing nodded. "One more question then, distinguished colleague." He paused. "Why should I help you?"

Kault's breath sighed like a punctured balloon, and his ridge crest collapsed rapidly. He looked at Uthacalthing with an expression as emotion-laden as any the Tymbrimi had ever seen upon the face of a dour Thennanin.

"It would greatly benefit the pre-sentients," he hissed. "Their destiny would be far happier."

"Perhaps. Arguable. Is that it, though? Are you relying on my altruism alone?"

"Errr. Hrm." Outwardly Kault seemed offended that anything more should be asked. Still, could he really be surprised? He was, after all, a diplomat, and understood that the best and firmest deals are based on open self-interest. "It would . . . It would greatly help my own political party if I delivered such a treasure. We would probably win government," he suggested.

"A slight improvement over the intolerable is not enough to get excited about." Uthacalthing shook his head. "You still haven't explained to me why I should not stake a claim for my own clan. I was investigating these rumors before you. We Tymbrimi would make excellent patrons for these creatures."

"*You!* You . . . *K'ph mimpher'rrengi?*" The phrase stood for something vaguely equivalent to "juvenile delinquents." It was almost enough to make Uthacalthing smile again. Kault shifted uncomfortably. He made a visible effort to retain diplomatic composure.

"You Tymbrimi have not the strength, the power to back up such a claim," he muttered.

At last, Uthacalthing thought. *Truth.*

In times like this, under circumstances as muddy as these, it would take more than mere priority of application to settle an adoption claim on a pre-sentient race. Many other factors would officially be considered by the Uplift Institute. And the humans had a saying that was especially appropriate. "Possession is nine points of the law." It certainly applied here.

"So we are back to question number one." Uthacalthing nodded. "If neither we Tymbrimi nor the Terrans can have the Garthlings, why should we help *you* get them?"

Kault rocked from one side to the other, as if he were trying to work his way off a hot seat. His misery was blatantly obvious, as was his desperation. Finally, he blurted forth, "I

can almost certainly guarantee a cessation of all hostilities by
my clan against yours."

"Not enough," Uthacalthing came back quickly.

"What more could you ask of me!" Kault exploded.

"An actual alliance. A promise of Thennanin aid against
those now laying siege upon Tymbrim."

"But—"

"And the guarantee must be firm. In advance. To take
effect *whether or not* these pre-sentients of yours actually
turn out to exist."

Kault stammered. "You cannot expect—"

"Oh, but I can. Why should *I* believe in these 'Garthling'
creatures? To me they have only been intriguing rumors. I
never told you I believed in them. And yet you want me to
risk my life to get you to message facilities! Why should I do
that without a guarantee of benefit for my people?"

"This . . . this is unheard of!"

"Nevertheless, it is my price. Take it or leave it."

For a moment Uthacalthing felt a thrilled suspicion he
was about to witness the unexpected. It seemed as if Kault
might lose control . . . might actually burst forth into violence. At the sight of those massive fists, clenching and
unclenching rapidly, Uthacalthing actually felt his blood stir
with change enzymes. A surge of nervous fear made him feel
more alive than he had in days.

"It . . . it shall be as you demand," Kault growled at last.

"Good." Uthacalthing sighed as he relaxed. He drew
forth his datawell. "Let us work out together how to parse
this for a contract."

It took more than an hour to get the wording right. After
it was finished, and when they had both signified their affir-
mation on each copy, Uthacalthing gave Kault one record
pellet and kept the second for himself.

Amazing, he thought at that point. He had planned and
schemed to bring about this day. This was the second half of
his grand jest, fulfilled at last. To have fooled the Gubru was
wonderful. This was simply unbelievable.

And yet, right now Uthacalthing found himself feeling
numb rather than triumphant. He did not look forward to the
climb ahead, a furious race into the steep towers of the
Mulun range, followed by a desperate attempt that would, no
doubt, result only in the two of them dying side by side.

"You know of course, Uthacalthing, that my people will

not carry out this bargain if I turn out to be mistaken. If there are no Garthlings after all, the Thennanin will repudiate me. They will pay diplomatic gild to buy out this contract, and I will be ruined."

Uthacalthing did not look at Kault. This was another reason for his sense of depressed detachment, certainly. *A great jokester is not supposed to feel guilt,* he told himself. *Perhaps I have spent too much time around humans.*

The silence stretched on for a while longer, each of them brooding in his own thoughts.

Of course Kault would be repudiated. Of course the Thennanin were not about to be drawn into an alliance, or even peace with the Earth-Tymbrimi entente. All Uthacalthing had ever hoped to accomplish was to sow confusion among his enemies. If Kault should by some miracle manage to get his message off and truly draw Thennanin armadas to this backwater system, then two great foes of his people would be drawn into a battle that would drain them . . . a battle over nothing. Over a nonexistent species. Over the ghosts of creatures murdered fifty thousand years ago.

Such a great jest! I should be happy. Thrilled.

Sadly, he knew that he could not even blame *s'ustru'thoon* for his inability to take pleasure out of this. It was not Athaclena's fault that the feeling clung to him . . . the feeling that he had just betrayed a friend.

Ah, well, Uthacalthing consoled himself. *It is all probably moot, anyway. To get Kault the kind of message facilities he needs now will take seven more miracles, each greater than the last.*

It seemed fitting that they would probably die together in the attempt, uselessly.

In his sadness, Uthacalthing found the energy to lift his tendrils slightly. They fashioned a simple glyph of regret as he raised his head to face Kault.

He was about to speak when something very surprising suddenly happened. Uthacalthing felt a *presence* wing past in the night. He started. But no sooner had it been there than it was gone.

Did I imagine it? Am I falling apart?

Then it was back! He gasped in surprise, *kenning* as it circled the tent in an ever-tightening spiral, brushing at last against the fringes of his indrawn aura. He looked up, trying

to spot something that whirled just beyond the fringe of their
shelter.

What am I doing? Trying to see a glyph?

He closed his eyes and let the un-thing approach.
Uthacalthing opened a *kenning.*

"*Puyr'iturumbul!*" he cried.

Kault swiveled. "What is it, my friend? What . . . ?"

But Uthacalthing had risen. As if drawn up by a string he
stepped out into the cool night.

The breeze brought odors to his nostrils as he sniffed,
using all his senses to seek in the acherontic darkness. "Where
are you?" Uthacalthing called. "Who is there?"

Two figures stepped forward into a dim pool of moonlight. *So it is true!* Uthacalthing thought. A *human* had
sought him out with an empathy sending, one so skillful it
might have come from a young Tymbrimi.

And that was not the end to surprises. He blinked at the
tall, bronzed, bearded warrior—who looked like nothing but
one of the heroes of those pre-Contact Earthling barbarian
epics—and let out another cry of amazement as he suddenly
recognized Robert Oneagle, the playboy son of the Planetary
Coordinator!

"Good evening, sir," Robert said as he stopped a few
meters away and bowed.

Standing a little behind Robert, the neo-chimpanzee,
Jo-Jo, wrung his hands nervously. This, certainly, was not
according to the original plan. He did not meet Uthacalthing's
eyes.

"*V'hooman'ph? Idatess!*" Kault exclaimed in Galactic Six.
"Uthacalthing, what is a human doing here?"

Robert bowed again. Enunciating carefully, he made
formal greetings to both of them, including their full species-
names. Then he went on in Galactic Seven.

"I have come a long way, honored gentlebeings, in order
to invite you all to a party."

83

Fiben

"Easy, Tycho. Easy!"

The normally placid animal bucked and pulled at its reins. Fiben, who had never been much of a horseman, was forced to dismount hurriedly and grab the animal's halter.

"There now. Relax," he soothed. "It's just another transport going by. We've heard 'em all day. It'll be gone soon."

As he promised, the shrieking whine faded as the flying machine passed quickly overhead and disappeared beyond the nearby trees, traveling in the direction of Port Helenia.

A lot had changed since Fiben had first come this way, mere weeks after the invasion. Then he had walked in sunshine down a busy highway, surrounded by spring's verdant colors. Now he felt blustery winds at his back as he passed through a valley showing all the early signs of a bitter winter. Half the trees had already dropped their leaves, leaving them in drifts across meadows and lanes. Orchards were bare of fruit, and the back roads devoid of traffic.

Surface traffic, that is. Overhead the swarm of transports seemed incessant. Gravitics teased his peripheral nerves as Gubru machines zoomed past. The first few times, his hackles had risen from more than just the pulsing fields. He had expected to be challenged, to be stopped, perhaps to be shot on sight.

But in fact the Galactics had ignored him altogether, apparently not deigning to distinguish one lonely chim from others who had been sent out to help with the harvest, or the specialists who had begun staffing a few of the ecological management stations once again.

529

Fiben had spoken with a few of the latter, many of them old acquaintances. They told of how they had given their parole in exchange for freedom and low-level support to resume their work. There wasn't much to be done, of course, with winter coming on. But at least there was a program again, and the Gubru seemed quite satisfied to leave them alone to do their work.

The invaders were, indeed, preoccupied elsewhere. The real focus of Galactic activity seemed to be over to the southwest, toward the spaceport.

And the ceremonial site, Fiben reminded himself. He didn't really know what he was going to do in the unlikely event he actually made it through to town. What would happen if he just marched right up to the shabby house that had been his former prison? Would the Suzerain of Propriety take him back?

Would Gailet?

Would she even be there?

He passed a few chims dressed in muffled cloaks, who desultorily picked through the stubble in a recently harvested field. They did not greet him, nor did he expect them to. Gleaning was a job generally given the poorest sort of Probationer. Still, he felt their gaze as he walked Tycho toward Port Helenia. After the animal had calmed a bit, Fiben clambered back onto the saddle and rode.

He had considered trying to reenter Port Helenia the way he left it, over the wall, at night. After all, if it had worked once, why not a second time? Anyway, he had no wish to meet up with the followers of the Suzerain of Cost and Caution.

It was tempting. Somehow, though, he figured that once was lucky. Twice would be simple stupidity.

Anyway, the choice was made for him when he rounded a bend and found himself staring at a Gubru guard post. Two battle robots of sophisticated design whirled and focused upon him.

"Easy does it, guys." Fiben said it more for his own benefit than theirs. If they were programmed to shoot on sight, he never would have seen them in the first place.

In front of the blockhouse there sat a squat armored hover craft, propped up on blocks. Two pairs of three-toed feet stuck out from underneath, and it did not take much knowledge of Galactic Three to tell that the chirped mutterings were expressing frustration. When the robots' warning whistled forth there came a sharp bang under the hover, followed by an indignant squawk.

Soon a pair of hooked beaks poked out of the shadows. Yellow eyes watched him unblinkingly. One of the disheveled Gubru rubbed its dented head frill.

Fiben pressed his lips together to fight back a smile. He dismounted and approached until he was even with the bunker, puzzled when neither the aliens nor the machines spoke to him.

He stopped before the two Gubru and bowed low.

They looked at each other and twittered irritably to each other. From one there came something that sounded like a resigned moan. The two Talon Soldiers emerged from under the disabled machine and stood up. Each of them returned a very slight but noticeable nod.

Silence stretched.

One of the Gubru whistled another faint sigh and brushed dust from its feathers. The other simply glared at Fiben.

Now what? he tried to think, but what was he supposed to *do?* Fiben's toes itched.

He bowed again. Then, with a dry mouth, he backed away and took the horse's tether. With affected nonchalance he started walking toward the dark fence surrounding Port Helenia, now visible just a kilometer ahead.

Tycho nickered, swished his tail, and cut loose an aromatic crepidation.

Tycho, pu-lease! Fiben thought. When a bend in the road at last cut off all view of the Gubru, Fiben sank to the ground. He just sat and shook for a few moments.

"Well," he said at last. "I guess there really is a truce after all."

After that, the guard post at the town gate was almost anticlimactic. Fiben actually enjoyed making the Talon Soldiers acknowledge his bow. He remembered some of what Gailet had taught him about Galactic protocol. Grudging acknowledgment from the client-class Kwackoo had been vital to achieve. To get it from the Gubru was delicious.

It also clearly meant that the Suzerain of Propriety was holding out. It had not yet given in.

Fiben left a trail of startled chims behind him as he rode Tycho at a gallop through the back streets of Port Helenia. One or two of them shouted at him, but at that moment he had no thought except to hurry toward the site of his former imprisonment.

When he arrived, however, he found the iron gate open and untended. The watch globes had vanished from the stone wall. He left Tycho to graze in the unkempt garden and beat aside a couple of limp plate ivy parachutes that festooned the open doorway.

"Gailet!" he shouted.

The Probationer guards were gone too. Dustballs and scraps of paper blew in through the open door and rolled down the hall. When he came to the room he had shared with Gailet, Fiben stopped and stared.

It was a mess.

Most of the furnishings were still there, but the expensive sound system and holo-wall had been torn out, no doubt taken by the departing Probies. On the other hand, Fiben saw his personal datawell sitting right where he had left it that night.

Gailet's was gone.

He checked the closet. Most of their clothes still hung there. Clearly she hadn't packed. He took down the shiny ceremonial robe he had been given by the Suzerain's staff. The silky material was almost glass-smooth under his fingers.

Gailet's robe was missing.

"Oh, Goodall," Fiben moaned. He spun about and dashed down the hall. It took only a second to leap into the saddle, but Tycho barely looked up from his feeding. Fiben had to kick and yell until the beast began to comprehend some of the urgency of the situation. With a yellow sunflower still hanging from his mouth, the horse turned and clomped through the gate and back onto the street. Once there, Tycho brought his head down and gamely gathered momentum.

They made quite a sight, galloping down the silent, almost empty streets, the robe and the flower flapping like banners in the wind. But few witnessed the wild ride until they finally approached the crowded wharves.

It seemed as if nearly every chim in town was there. They swarmed along the waterfront, a churning mass of brown, callipose bodies dressed in autumn parkas, their heads bobbing like the waters of the bay just beyond. More chims leaned precariously over the rooftops, and some even hung from drainage spouts.

It was a good thing Fiben wasn't on foot. Tycho was really quite helpful as he snorted and nudged startled chims aside with his nose. From his perch on the horse's back, Fiben soon was able to spy what some of the commotion was about.

About half a kilometer out into the bay, a dozen fishing vessels could be seen operating under neo-chimpanzee crews. A cluster of them jostled and bumped near a sleek white craft that glistened in cliquant contrast to the battered trawlers.

The Gubru vessel was dead in the water. Two of the avian crew members stood atop its cockpit, twittering and waving their arms, offering instructions which the chim seamen politely ignored as they tied hausers to the crippled craft and began gradually towing it toward the shore.

So what? Big deal, Fiben thought. So a Gubru patrol boat suffered a breakdown. For this all the chims in town had spilled out into the streets? The citizens of Port Helenia really must be hard up for entertainment.

Then he realized that only a few of the townfolk were actually watching the minor rescue in the harbor. The vast majority stared southward, out across the bay.

Oh. Fiben's breath escaped in a sigh, and he, too, was momentarily struck speechless.

New, shining towers stood atop the far mesa where the colonial spaceport lay. The lambent monoliths looked nothing like Gubru transports, or their hulking, globular battleships. Instead, these resembled glimmering steeples—spires which towered high and confident, manifesting a faith and tradition more ancient than life on Earth.

Tiny winklings of light lifted from the tall starships—*carrying Galactic dignitaries*, Fiben guessed—and cruised westward, drawing nearer along the arc of the bay. At last the aircraft joined a spiral of traffic descending over South Point. That was where everyone in Port Helenia seemed to sense that something special was going on.

Unconsciously Fiben guided Tycho through the crowd until he arrived at the edge of the main wharf. There a chain of chims wearing oval badges held back the crowd. *So there are proctors again*, Fiben realized. *The Probationers proved unreliable, so the Gubru had to reinstate civil authority*.

A chen wearing the brassard of a proctor corporal grabbed Tycho's halter and started to speak. "Hey, bub! You can't . . ." Then he blinked. "Ifni! Is that you, Fiben?"

Fiben recognized Barnaby Fulton, one of the chims who had been involved in Gailet's early urban undergound. He smiled, though his thoughts were far across the choppy waters. "Hello, Barnaby. Haven't seen you since the valley uprising. Glad to see you still scratchin'."

Now that attention had been drawn his way, chens and chimmies started nudging each other and whispering in hushed voices. He heard his own name repeated. The susurration of the crowd ebbed as a circle of silence spread around him. Two or three of the staring chims reached out to touch Tycho's heavy flanks, or Fiben's leg, as if to verify that they were real.

Barnaby made a visible effort to match Fiben's insouciance. "Whenever it itches, Fiben. Uh, one rumor had it you were s'pozed to be over there." He gestured toward the monumental activity taking place across the harbor. "Another said you'd busted out an' taken to the hills. A third . . ."

"What did the third say?"

Barnaby swallowed. "Some said your number'd come up."

"Hmph," Fiben commented softly. "I guess all of them were right."

He saw that the trawlers had dragged the crippled Gubru patrol boat nearly to the dock. A number of other chim-crewed vessels cruised farther out, but none of them crossed a line of buoys that could be seen stretching all the way across the bay.

Barnaby looked left and right, then spoke in a low voice. "Uh, Fiben, there are quite a few chims in town who . . . well, who've been reorganizing. I had to give parole when I got my brassard back, but I can get word to Professor Oakes that you're in town. I'm sure he'd want to get together a meetin' tonight. . . ."

Fiben shook his head. "No time. I've got to get over there." He motioned to where the bright aircraft were alighting on the far headlands.

Barnaby's lips drew back. "I dunno, Fiben. Those watch buoys. They've kept everybody back."

"Have they actually burned anybody?"

"Well, no. Not that I've seen. But—"

Barnaby stopped as Fiben shook the reins and nudged with his heels. "Thanks, Barnaby. That's all I needed to know," he said.

The proctors stood aside as Tycho stepped along the wharf. Farther out the little rescue flotilla had just come to dock and were even now tying up the prim white Gubru warcraft. The chim sailors did a lot of bowing and moved in uncomfortable crouched postures under the glare of the irritated Talon Soldiers and their fearsome battle drones.

In contrast, Fiben steered his steed just outside of the range that would have required him to acknowledge the aliens. His posture was erect, and he ignored them completely as he rode past the patrol boat to the far end of the pier, where the smallest of the fishing boats had just come to rest.

He swung his feet over the saddle and hopped down. "Are you good to animals?" he asked the startled sailor, who looked up from securing his craft. When he nodded, Fiben handed the dumbfounded chim Tycho's reins. "Then we'll swap."

He leaped aboard the little craft and stepped behind the cockpit. "Send a bill for the difference to the Suzerain for Propriety. You got that? The Gubru Suzerain of Propriety."

The wide-eyed chen seemed to notice that his jaw was hanging open. He closed it with an audible clack.

Fiben switched the ignition on and felt satisfied with the engine's throaty roar. "Cast off," he said. Then he smiled. "And thanks. Take good care of Tycho!"

The sailor blinked. He seemed about to decide to get angry when some of the chims who had followed Fiben caught up. One whispered in the boatman's ear. The fisherman then grinned. He hurried to untie the boat's tether and threw the rope back onto the foredeck. When Fiben awkwardly hit the pier backing up, the chim only winced slightly. "G-good luck," he managed to say.

"Yeah. Luck, Fiben," Barnaby shouted.

Fiben waved and shifted the impellers into forward. He swung about in a wide arc, passing almost under the duraplast sides of the Gubru patrol craft. Up close it did not look quite so glistening white. In fact, the armored hull looked pitted and corroded. High, indignant chirps from the other side of the vessel indicated the frustration of the Talon Soldier crew.

Fiben spared them not a thought as he turned about and
got his borrowed boat headed southward, toward the line of
buoys that split the bay and kept the chims of Port Helenia
away from the high, patron-level doings on the opposite
shore.

Foamed and choppy from the wind, the water was
cinerescent with the usual garbage the easterlies always brought
in, this time of year—everything from leaves to almost transparent plate ivy parachutes to the feathers of molting birds.
Fiben had to slow to avoid clots of debris as well as battered
boats of all description crowded with chim sightseers.

He approached the barrier line at low speed and felt
thousands of eyes watching him as he passed the last shipload, containing the most daring and curious of the Port
Helenians.

Goodall, do I really know what I'm doing? he wondered.
He had been acting almost on automatic so far. But now it
came to him that he really was out of his depth here. What
did he hope to accomplish by charging off this way? What was
he going to do? Crash the ceremony? He looked at the towering starships across the bay, glistening in power and splendor.

As if he had any business sticking his half-uplifted nose
into the affairs of beings from great and ancient clans! All he'd
accomplish would be to embarrass himself, and probably his
whole race for that matter.

"Gotta think about this," he muttered. Fiben brought
the boat's engine down to idle as the line of buoys neared. He
thought about how many people were watching him right
now.

My people, he recalled. *I . . . I was supposed to represent them.*

*Yes, but I ducked out, obviously the Suzerain realized its
mistake and made other arrangements. Or the other Suzerain's won, and I'd simply be dead meat if I showed up!*

He wondered what they would think if they knew that,
only days ago, he had manhandled and helped kidnap one of his
own patrons, and his legal commander at that. Some race-
representative!

*Gailet doesn't need the likes of me. She's better off
without me.*

Fiben twisted the wheel, causing the boat to come about

just short of one of the white buoys. He watched it go by as he turned.

It, too, looked less than new on close examination—somewhat corroded, in fact. But then, from his own lowly state, who was *he* to judge?

Fiben blinked at that thought. Now that was laying it on *too* thick!

He stared at the buoy, and slowly his lips curled back. *Why . . . why you devious sons of bitches. . . .*

Fiben cut the impellers and let the engine drop back to idle. He closed his eyes and pressed his hands against his temples, trying to concentrate.

I was girding myself against another fear *barrier . . . like the one at the city fence, that night. But this one is more subtle! It plays on my sense of my own unworthiness. It trades on my humility.*

He opened his eyes and looked back at the buoy. Finally, he grinned.

"*What* humility?" Fiben asked aloud. He laughed and turned the wheel as he set the craft in motion again. This time when he headed for the barrier he did not hesitate, or listen to the doubts that the machines tried to cram into his head.

"After all," he muttered, "what can they do to shake the confidence of a fellow who's got delusions of adequacy?" The enemy had made a serious mistake here, Fiben knew as he left the buoys behind him and, with them, their artificially induced doubts. The resolution that flowed back into him now was fortified by its very *contrast* to the earlier depths. He approached the opposite headland wearing a fierce scowl of determination.

Something flapped against his knee. Fiben glanced down and saw the silvery ceremonial robe—the one he had found in the closet back at the old prison. He had crammed it under his belt, apparently, just before leaping atop Tycho and riding, pell-mell, for the harbor. No wonder people had been staring at him, back at the docks!

Fiben laughed. Holding onto the wheel with one hand, he wriggled into the silky garment as he headed toward a silent stretch of beach. The bluffs cut off any view of what was going on over on the sea side of the narrow peninsula. But the drone of still-descending aircraft was—he hoped—a sign that he might not be too late.

He ran the boat aground on a shelf of sparkling white sand, now made unattractive under a tidal wash of flotsam. Fiben was about to leap into the knee-high surf when he glanced back and noticed that something seemed to be going on back in Port Helenia. Faint cries of excitement carried over the water. The churning mass of brown forms at the dockside was now surging to the right.

He plucked up the pair of binoculars that hung by the capstan and focused them on the wharf area.

Chims ran about, many of them pointing excitedly eastward, toward the main entrance to town. Some were still running in that direction. But now more and more seemed to be heading the other way . . . apparently not so much in fear as in *confusion*. Some of the more excitable chims capered about. A few even fell into the water and had to be rescued by the more level-headed.

Whatever was happening did not seem to be causing panic so much as acute, near total bewilderment.

Fiben did not have time to hang around and piece together this added puzzle. By now he thought he understood his own modest powers of concentration.

Focus on just one problem at a time, he told himself. *Get to Gailet. Tell her you're sorry you ever left her. Tell her you'll never ever do it again.*

That was easy enough even for him to understand.

Fiben found a narrow trail leading up from the beach. It was crumbling and dangerous, especially in the gusting winds. Still, he hurried. And his pace was held down only by the amount of oxygen his limited lungs and heart could pump.

84

Uthacalthing

The four of them made a strange-looking group, hurrying northward under overcast skies. Perhaps some little native animals looked up and stared at them, blinking in momentary astonishment before they ducked back into their burrows and swore off the eating of overripe seeds ever again.

To Uthacalthing, though, the forced march was something of a humiliation. Each of the others, it seemed, had advantages over him.

Kault puffed and huffed and obviously did not like the rugged ground. But once the hulking Thennanin got moving he kept up a momentum that seemed unstoppable.

As for Jo-Jo, well, the little chim seemed by now to be a creature *of* this environment. He was under strict orders from Uthacalthing never to knuckle-walk within sight of Kault—no sense in taking a chance with arousing the Thennanin's suspicions—but when the terrain got too rugged he sometimes just scrambled over an obstacle rather than going around it. And over the long flat stretches, Jo-Jo simply rode Robert's back.

Robert had insisted on carrying the chim, whatever the official gulf in status between them. The human lad was impatient enough as it was. Clearly, he would rather have run all the way.

The change in Robert Oneagle was astonishing, and far more than physical. Last night, when Kault asked him to explain part of his story for the third time, Robert clearly and unself-consciously manifested a simple version of *teev'nus* over his head. Uthacalthing could *kenn* how the human deftly

539

used the glyph to contain his frustration, so that none of it
would spill over into outward discourtesy to the Thennanin.

Uthacalthing could see that there was much Robert was
not telling. But what he said was enough.

*I knew that Megan underestimated her son. But of this I
had no expectation.*

Clearly, he had underrated his own daughter as well.

Clearly. Uthacalthing tried not to resent his flesh and
blood for her power, the power to rob him of more than he
had thought he could ever lose.

He struggled to keep up with the others, but Uthacalthing's
change nodes already throbbed tiredly. It wasn't just that
Tymbrimi were more talented at adaptability than endurance. It was also a fault in his *will*. The others had purpose,
even enthusiasm.

He had only duty to keep him going.

Kault stopped at the top of a rise, where the looming
mountains towered near and imposing. Already they were
entering a forest of scrub trees that gained stature as they
ascended. Uthacalthing looked up at the steep slopes ahead,
already misted in what might be snow clouds, and hoped
they would not have to climb much farther.

Kault's massive hand closed around his as the Thennanin
helped him up the final few meters. He waited patiently as
Uthacalthing rested, breathing heavily through wide-open
nostrils.

"I still can scarcely believe what I have been told," Kault
said. "Something about the Earthling's story does not ring
true, my colleague."

"*T'funatu . . .*" Uthacalthing switched to Anglic, which
seemed to take less air. "What—what do you find hard to
believe, Kault? Do you think Robert is lying?"

Kault waved his hands in front of himself. His ridgecrest
inflated indignantly. "Certainly not! I only believe that the
young fellow is naive."

"Naive? In what way?" Uthacalthing could look up now
without his vision splitting into two separate images in his
cortex. Robert and Jo-Jo weren't in sight. They must have
gone on ahead.

"I mean that the Gubru are obviously up to much more
than they claim. The deal they are offering—peace with
Earth in exchange for tenancy on some Garthian islands and
minor genetic purchase rights from neo-chimpanzee stock—

such a deal seems barely worth the cost of an interstellar ceremony. It is my suspicion that they are after something else on the sly, my friend."

"What do you think they want?"

Kault swung his almost neckless head left and right, as if looking to make sure no one else was within listening range. His voice dropped in both volume and timbre.

"I suspect that they intend to perform a snap-adoption."

"Adoption? Oh . . . you mean—"

"Garthlings," Kault finished for him. "This is why it is so fortunate your Earthling allies brought us this news. We can only hope that they will be able to provide transport, as they promised, or we will never be in time to prevent a terrible tragedy!"

Uthacalthing mourned all that he had lost. For Kault had raised a perplexing question, one well worth a well-crafted glyph of delicate wryness.

He had been successful, of course, beyond his wildest expectations. According to Robert, the Gubru had swallowed the "Garthling" myth "hook, line, and sinker." At least for long enough to cause them harm and embarrassment.

Kault, too, had come to believe in the ghostly fable. But what was one to make of Kault's claim that his own instruments *verified* the story?

Incredible.

And now, the Gubru seemed to be behaving as if they, too, had more to go on than the fabricated clues he had left. They, too, acted as if there were confirmation!

The old Uthacalthing would have crafted *syulff-kuonn* to commemorate such amazing turns. At this moment, though, all he felt was confused, and very tired.

A shout caused them both to turn. Uthacalthing squinted, wishing right then that he could trade some of his unwanted empathy sense for better eyesight.

Atop the next ridge he made out the form of Robert Oneagle. Seated atop the young human's shoulders, Jo-Jo waved at them. And something else was there, too. A blue glimmering that seemed to spin next to the two Earth creatures and radiate all of the good will of a perfect prankster.

It was the beacon, the light that had led Uthacalthing ever onward, since the crash months before.

"What are they saying?" Kault asked. "I cannot quite make out the words."

Neither could Uthacalthing. But he knew what the Terrans were saying. "I believe they are telling us that we don't have very much farther to go," he said with some relief. "They are saying that they have found our transport."

The Thennanin's breathing slits puffed in satisfaction. "Good. Now if only we can trust the Gubru to follow custom and proper truce behavior when we appear and offer correct diplomatic treatment to accredited envoys."

Uthacalthing nodded. But as they began marching uphill together again, he knew that that was only one of their worries.

85

Athaclena

She tried to suppress her feelings. To the others, this was serious, even tragic.

But there was just no way to keep it in; her delight would not be contained. Subtle, ornate glyphs spun off from her waving tendrils and diffracted away through the trees, filling the glades with her hilarity. Athaclena's eyes were at their widest divergence, and she covered her mouth with her hand so the dour chims would not see her human-style smile as well.

The portable holo unit had been set up on a ridgetop overlooking the Sind to the northwest in order to improve reception. It showed the scene being broadcast just then from Port Helenia. Under the truce, censorship had been lifted. And even without humans the capital had plenty of chim "newshounds" on the spot with mobile cameras to show all the debris in stunning detail.

"I can't stand it," Benjamin moaned. Elayne Soo muttered helplessly as she watched. "That tears it."

The chimmie spoke volumes, indeed. For the holo-tank displayed what was left of the fancy wall the invaders had thrown around Port Helenia . . . now literally ripped down and torn to shreds. Stunned chim citizens milled about a scene that looked as if a cyclone had hit it. They stared around in amazement, picking through the shattered remnants. A few of those who were more exuberant than thoughtful threw pieces of fence material into the air jubilantly. Some even made chest-thumping motions in honor of the unstoppable wave that had crested there only minutes before, then surged onward into the town itself.

On most of the stations the voice-over was computer generated, but on Channel Two a chim announcer was able to speak over his excitement.

"At—at first we all thought it was a nightmare come true. You know . . . like an archetype out of an old TwenCen flatmovie. Nothing would stop them! They crashed through the Gubru barrier as if it was made of tish-tissue paper. I don't know about anybody else, but at any moment I expected the biggest of them to go around grabbing our prettiest chimmies and drag them screaming all the way to the top of the Terragens Tower. . . ."

Athaclena clapped her hand tigher over her mouth in order to keep from laughing out loud. She fought for self-control, and she was not alone, for one of the chims—Fiben's friend, Sylvie—let out a high chirp of laughter. Most of the others frowned at her in disapproval. After all, this was serious! But Athaclena met the chimmie's eyes and recognized the light in them.

"But it—it appears that these creatures aren't complete kongs, after all. They—after their demolishment of the fence, they don't seem to have done much more damage in their s-sudden invasion of Port Helenia. Mostly, right now, they're just milling around, opening doors, eating fruit, going wherever they want to. After all, where does a four-hundred-pound gor . . . oh, never mind."

This time, another chim joined Sylvie. Athaclena's vision blurred and she shook her head. The announcer went on.

"They seem completely unaffected by the Gubru's psi-drones, which apparently aren't tuned to their brain patterns. . . ."

Actually, Athaclena and the mountain fighters had known for more than two days where the gorillas were headed. After their first frantic attempts to divert the powerful pre-sentients, they gave up the effort as useless. The gorillas politely pushed aside or stepped over anybody who got in their way. There had simply been no stopping them.

Not even April Wu. The little blond girl had apparently made up her mind to go and find her parents, and short of risking injury to her, there was no way anybody would be able to pry her off the shoulders of one of the giant, silver-backed males.

Anyway, April had told the chims quite matter-of-factly, *somebody* had to go along and supervise the 'rillas, or they might get into trouble!

Athaclena remembered little April's words as she looked at the mess the pre-sentients had made of the Gubru wall. *I'd hate to see the trouble they could cause if they* weren't *supervised!*

Anyway, with the secret out, there was no reason the human child should not be reunited with her family. Nothing she said could hurt anybody now.

So much for the last secrecy of the Howletts Center Project. Now Athaclena might as well just toss away all the evidence she had so dutifully gathered, that first, fateful evening so many months ago. Soon the entire Five Galaxies would know about these creatures. And by some measures that was, indeed, a tragedy. And yet . . .

Athaclena remembered that day in early spring, when she had been so shocked and indignant to come upon the illegal Uplift experiment hidden in the forest. Now she could scarcely believe she had actually been like that. *Was I really such a serious, officious little prig?*

Now, *syulff-kuonn* was only the simplest, most *serious* of the glyphs she sparked off, casually, tirelessly, in joy over a simply marvelous joke. Even the chims could not help being affected by her profligate aura. Two more laughed when one of the channels showed an alien staff car, manned by squawking irate Kwackoo, in the process of being peeled back by gorillas who seemed passionately interested in how it would taste. Then another chim chuckled. The laughter spread.

Yes, she thought. *It is a wonderful jest.* To a Tymbrimi, the best jokes were those that caught the joker, as well as everybody else. And this fit the bill beautifully. It was, in truth, a religious experience. For her people believed in a Universe that was more than mere clockwork physics, more than even Ifni's capricious flux of chance and luck.

It was when something like this happened—the Tymbrimi sages said—that one really knew that God, Himself, was still in charge.

Was I, then, also an agnostic before? How silly of me. Thank you then, Lord, and thank you too, father, for this miracle.

The scene shifted to the dock area, where milling chims danced in the streets and stroked the fur of their giant, patient cousins. In spite of the likely tragic consequences of all this, Athaclena and her warriors could not help but smile at the delight the brown-furred relations obviously took in each other. For now, at least, their pride was shared by all the chims of Port Helenia.

Even Lieutenant Lydia McCue and her wary corporal could not help but laugh when a gorilla baby danced past the cameras, wearing necklace made of broken Gubru psi-globes. They caught a glimpse of little April, riding in triumph through the streets, and the sight of a human child seemed to galvanize the crowds.

By now the glade was saturated with her glyphs. Athaclena turned and walked away, leaving the others to resonate in the wry joy. She moved up a forest trail until she came to a place with a clear view of the mountains to the west. There she stood, reaching and *kenning* with her tendrils.

It was there that a chim messenger found her. He hurried up and saluted before handing her a slip of paper. Athaclena thanked him and opened it, though she thought she already knew what it would say.

"*W'ith'tanna, Uthacalthing,*" she said, softly. Her father was back in touch with the world again. For all of the events of the past few months, there was a solid, practical part of her, still, who was relieved to have this confirmation by radio.

She had had faith that Robert would succeed, of course. That was why she had not gone to Port Helenia with Fiben, or after that with the gorillas. What could she accomplish there, with her poor expertise, that her father could not do a thousand times better? If anyone could help turn their slim hopes into more and still greater miracles, it would be Uthacalthing.

No, her job was to remain here. For even in the event of miracles, the Infinite expected mortals to provide their own insurance.

She shaded her eyes. Although she had no hope of personally sighting a little aircraft against the bright clouds, she kept looking for a tiny dot that would be carrying all her love and all her prayers.

86

Galactics

Gay pavilions dotted the manicured hillside, occasionally billowing and flapping in the gusting breeze. Quick robots hurried to pluck up any debris brought in by the wind. Others fetched and carried refreshments to the gathered dignitaries.

Galactics of many shapes and colors milled in small groups that merged and separated in an elegant pavane of diplomacy. Courteous bows and flattenings and tentacle wavings conveyed complex nuances of status and protocol. A knowledgeable observer might tell a great deal from such subtleties— and there were many knowledgeable observers present on this day.

Informal exchanges abounded as well. Here a squat, bearlike Pila conversed in clipped, ultrasonic tones with a gangling Linten gardener. A little upslope, three Jophur ring-priests keened in harmonious complaint to an official from the War Institute over some alleged violation out among the starlanes.

It was often said that much more practical diplomacy was accomplished at these Uplift Ceremonies than at formal negotiation conferences. More than one new alliance might be made today, and more than one broken.

Only a few of the Galactic visitors spared more than passing attention to those being honored here today—a caravan of small, brown forms which had taken the entire morning to labor halfway up the mound, circling it four times along the way.

By now nearly a third of the neo-chimpanzee candidates had failed one test or another. Those rejected were already trooping back down the sloping path, in downcast ones and twos.

The remaining forty or so continued their ascent, symbolically reiterating the process of Uplift that had brought their race to this stage in its history, but ignored, for the most part, by the bright crowds on the slopes.

Not all of the observers were inattentive, of course. Near the pinnacle, the Commissioners from the Galactic Uplift Institute paid close attention to the results relayed up by each test station. And nearby, from beneath their own pavilion, a party of the neo-chimpanzees' human patrons watched, glumly.

Looking somewhat lost and helpless, they had been brought out from Cilmar Island only this morning—a few mayors, professors, and a member of the local Uplift Board. The delegation had put forward a procedural protest over the irregular way the ceremony had come about. But when pressed, none of the humans actually claimed a right to cancel it altogether. The possible consequences were potentially just too drastic.

Besides, what if this were the real thing? Earth had been agitating to be allowed to hold just such a ceremony for neo-chimpanzees for two hundred years.

The human observers definitely looked unhappy. For they had no idea what to do, and few of the grand Galactic envoys present even deigned to acknowledge them amid the flurry of informal diplomacy.

On the opposite side of the Evaluators' pavilion sat the elegant Sponsors' Tent. Many Gubru and Kwackoo stood just outside, nervously hopping from time to time, watching every detail with unblinking, critical eyes.

Until moments ago, the Gubru Triumvirate had been visible also, two of them strutting about with their Molt colorings already starting to show and the third still obstinately perched upon its pedestal.

Then one of them received a message, and all three disappeared into the tent for an urgent parlay. That had been some time ago. They still had not emerged.

The Suzerain of Cost and Caution fluttered and spat as it let the message drop to the floor.

"I protest! I protest this interference! This interference and intolerable betrayal!"

The Suzerain of Propriety stared down from its perch, totally at a loss. The Suzerain of Cost and Caution had proved to be a crafty opponent, but never had it been purposely obtuse. Obviously something had happened to upset it terribly.

Crouching Kwackoo servitors hurriedly plucked up the message pellet it had dropped, duplicated the capsule, and brought copies to the other two Gubru lords. When the Suzerain of Propriety viewed the data, it could scarcely believe what it saw.

It was a *solitary neo-chimpanzee*, climbing the lower slopes of the towering Ceremonial Mound, passing rapidly through the automatic first-stage screens and gradually beginning to close the wide gap separating it from the official party, higher on the hillside.

The neo-chimp moved with an erect determination, a clearness of purpose that could be read in its very posture. Those of its con-specifics who had already failed—and who were spiraling slowly down the long trail again—first stared, then grinned and reached out to touch the newcomer's robe as he passed. They offered words of encouragement.

"This was not, cannot have been rehearsed!" the Suzerain of Beam and Talon hissed. The military commander cried out, "It is an interloper, and I shall have it burned down!"

"You should not, must not, *shall* not!" the Suzerain of Propriety squawked back in anger. "There has not yet been a coalescence! No complete molting! You do not yet have a queen's wisdom!

"Ceremonies are run, governed, ruled by traditions of honor! *All* members of a client race may approach and be tried, tested, evaluated!"

The third Gubru lord snapped its beak open and shut in agitation. Finally, the Suzerain of Cost and Caution fluffed its ragged feathers and agreed. "We would be charged reparations. The Institute officials might leave, depart, lay sanctions. . . . The cost . . ." It turned away in a downy huff. "Let it proceed, then. For now. Alone, solitary, in isolation it can do no harm."

But the Suzerain of Propriety was not so sure. Once, it had set great store in this particular client. When it seemed to have been stolen, the Suzerain of Propriety suffered a serious setback.

Now, however, it realized the truth. The neo-chimp male had *not* been stolen and eliminated by its rivals, the other Suzerains. Instead, the chimp had *actually* escaped!

And now it was back, alone. How? And what did it hope to accomplish? Without guidance, without the aid of a group, how far did it think it could go?

At first, on seeing the creature, the Suzerain of Propriety had felt joyful amazement—an unusual sensation for a Gubru. Now its emotion was something even more uncomfortable . . . a worry that this was only the *beginning* of surprise.

87

Fiben

So far it had been a piece of cake. Fiben wondered what all the fuss was about.

He had feared they would ask him to solve calculus problems in his head—or recite like Demosthenes, with marbles in his mouth. But at first there had only been a series of force-screen barriers that peeled back for him automatically. And after that there were only more of those funny-looking instruments he had seen the Gubru techs use weeks, months ago—now wielded by even funnier-looking aliens.

So far so good. He made it around the first circuit in what had to be record speed.

Oh, a few times they asked him some questions. What was his earliest memory? Did he enjoy his profession? Was he satisfied with the physical form of this generation of neo-chimpanzee, or might it be improved somehow? Would a prehensile tail be a convenient aid in tool use, for instance?

Gailet would have been proud of the way he remained polite, even then. Or at least he hoped she'd be proud of him.

Of course the Galactic officials had his entire record—genetic, scholastic, military—and were able to access it the moment he passed a group of startled Talon Soldiers on the bayside bluffs and strode through the outer barriers to meet his first test.

When a tall, treelike Kanten asked him about the note he had left, that night when he "escaped" from imprisonment, it was clear that the Institute was capable of subpoenaing the invaders' records as well. He answered truthfully that Gailet had worded the document but that he had understood its purpose and concurred.

The Kanten's foliage tinkled in the chiming of tiny, silvery bells. The semi-vegetable Galactic sounded pleased and amused as it shuffled aside to let him pass.

The intermittent wind helped keep Fiben cool as long as he was on the eastward slopes, but the westward side faced the afternoon sun and was sheltered from the breeze. The effort of maintaining his rapid pace made him feel as if he were wearing a thick coat, even though a chim's sparse covering of body hair was technically not fur at all.

The parklike hill was neatly landscaped, and the trail paved with a soft, resilient surface. Nevertheless, through his toes he sensed a faint trembling, as if the entire artificial mountain were throbbing in harmonies far, far below the level of hearing. Fiben, who had seen the massive power plants before they were buried, knew that it was not his imagination.

At the next station a Pring technician with huge, glowing eyes and bulging lips looked him up and down and noted something in a datawell before allowing him to proceed. Now some of the dignitaries dotting the slopes seemed to have begun to notice him. A few drifted nearer and accessed his test results in curiosity. Fiben bowed courteously to those nearby and tried not to think about all the different kinds of eyes that were watching him like some sort of specimen.

Once their ancestors had to go through something like this, he consoled himself.

Twice Fiben passed a few spirals below the party of official candidates, a gradually dwindling band of brownish creatures in short, silvery robes. The first time he hurried by, none of the chims noticed him. On the second occasion, though, he had to stand under the scrutiny of instruments held by a being whose species he could not even identify. That time he was able to make out a few figures among those up above. And some of the chims noticed him as well. One nudged a companion and pointed. But then they all disappeared around the corner again.

He had not seen Gailet, but then, she would likely be at the head of the party, wouldn't she? "Come on," Fiben muttered impatiently, concerned over the time this creature was taking. Then he considered that the machines focused on him might read either his words or his mood, and he concentrated on preserving discipline. He smiled sweetly and bowed as the alien technician indicated a passing score with a few terse, computer-mediated words.

Fiben hurried on. He grew more and more irritated with the long distances between the stations and wondered if there wasn't any dignified way he could *run*, in order to cut down on the gap even faster.

Instead though, things only started going slower as the tests grew more serious, calling for deeper learning and more complex thought. Soon he met more chims on their way back down. Apparently these were now forbidden to talk to him, but a few rolled their eyes meaningfully, and their bodies were damp with perspiration.

He recognized several of these dropouts. Two were professors at the college in Port Helenia. Others were scientists with the Garth Ecological Recovery Program. Fiben began to grow worried. All of these chims were blue-card types—among the brightest! If they were failing, something had to be very wrong here. Certainly this ceremony wasn't perfunctory, as that celebration for the Tytlal, which Athaclena had told him about.

Perhaps the rules *were* stacked against Earthlings!

That was when he approached a station manned by a tall Gubru. It did not help that the avian wore the colors of the

Uplift Institute and was supposedly sworn to impartiality.
Fiben had seen too many of that clan wearing Institute livery
today to satisfy him.

The birdlike creature used a vodor and asked him a
simple question of protocol, then let him proceed.

A thought suddenly occurred to Fiben as he quickly left
that test site. What if the Suzerain of Propriety had been
completely defeated by its peers? Whatever its real agenda,
that Suzerain had, at least, been sincere about wanting to run
a real ceremony. A promise made had to be kept. But what of
the others? The admiral and the bureaucrat? Certainly they
would have different priorities.

Could the whole thing be rigged so that neo-chimps
could not win, no matter how ready they were for advancement? Was that possible?

Could such a result be of real benefit to the Gubru in
some way?

Filled with such troubling thoughts, Fiben barely passed
a test that involved juggling several complex motor functions
while having to solve an intricate three-dimensional puzzle.
As he left that station, with the waters of Aspinal Bay falling
under late afternoon shadows to his left, he almost failed to
notice a new commotion far below. At the last moment he
turned to see where a growing sound was coming from.

"What in Ifni's incontinence?" He blinked and stared.

He was not alone in that. By now half of the Galactic
dignitaries seemed to be drifting down that way, attracted by
a brown tide that was just then spilling up to the foot of the
Ceremonial Mound.

Fiben tried to see what was happening, but patches of
sunlight, reflected by still-bright water, made it hard to make
out anything in the shadows just below. What he could tell
was that the bay appeared to be covered with *boats*, and
many were now emptying their passengers onto the isolated
beach where he had landed, hours before.

So, more of the city chims had come out to get a better
look after all. He hoped none of them misbehaved, but he
doubted any harm would be done. The Galactics surely knew
that monkey curiosity was a basic chimp trait, and this was
only acting true to form. Probably the chims'd be given a
lower portion of the slope from which to watch, as was their
right by Galactic Law.

He couldn't afford to waste any more time dawdling,

though. Fiben turned to hurry onward. And although he passed the next test on Galactic History, he also knew that his score had not helped his cumulative total much.

Now he was glad when he arrived on the westward slope. As the sun sank lower, this was the side on which the wind did not bite quite as fiercely. Fiben shivered as he plodded on, slowly gaining on the diminishing crowd above him.

"Slow *down*, Gailet," he muttered. "Can't you drag your feet or somethin'? You don't haveta answer every damn question the very second it's asked. Can't you tell I'm comin'?"

A dismal part of him wondered if she already knew, and maybe didn't care.

88

Gailet

She found it increasingly hard to feel that it mattered. And the cause of her depression was more than just the fatigue of a long, hard day, or the burden of all these bewildered chims relying upon her to lead them ever onward and upward through a maze of ever more demanding trials.

Nor was it the constant presence of the tall chen named Irongrip. It certainly was frustrating to see him breeze through tests that other, better chims failed. And as the other Sponsors' Choice, he was usually right behind her, wearing an infuriating, smug grin. Still, Gailet could grit her teeth and ignore him most of the time.

Nor, even, did the examinations themselves bother her much. Hell, they were the best part of the day! Who was the ancient human sage who had said that the purest pleasure, and the greatest force in the ascent of Mankind, had been the skilled worker's joy in her craft? While Gailet was concentrating she could block out nearly everything, the world, the Five Galaxies, all but the challenge to show her skill. Underneath all the crises and murky questions of honor and duty, there was always a clean sense of satisfaction whenever she finished a task and *knew* she had done well even before the Institute examiners told her so.

No, the tests weren't what disturbed her. What bothered Gailet most was the growing suspicion that she had made the wrong choice after all.

I should have refused to participate, she thought. *I should have simply said no*.

Oh, the logic was the same as before. By protocol and all of the rules, the Gubru had put her in a position where she simply had no choice, for her own good and the good of her race and clan.

And yet, she also knew she was being *used*. It made her feel defiled.

During that last week of study at the Library she had found herself repeatedly dozing off under the screens, bright with arcane data. Her dreams were always disturbed, featuring birds holding threatening instruments. Images of Max and Fiben and so many others lingered, thickening her thoughts every time she jerked awake again.

Then the Day arrived. She had donned her robe almost with a sense of relief that now, at least, it was all finally approaching an end. But *what* end?

A slight chimmie emerged from the most recent test booth, mopped her forehead with the sleeve of her silvery tunic, and walked tiredly over to join Gailet. Michaela Noddings was only an elementary school teacher, and a green card, but she had proven more adaptable and enduring than quite a few blues, who were now walking the lonely spiral back down again. Gailet felt deep relief on seeing her new friend still among the candidates. She reached out to take the other chimmie's hand.

"I almost flunked that one, Gailet," Michaela said. Her fingers trembled in Gailet's grasp.

"Now, don't you dare flake out on me, Michaela," Gailet said soothingly. She brushed her companion's sweaty locks. "You're my strength. I couldn't go on if you weren't here."

In Michaela's brown eyes was a soft gratitude, mixed with irony. "You're a liar, Gailet. That's sweet of you to say, but you don't need any of us, let alone little me. Whatever I can pass, you take at a breeze."

Of course that wasn't strictly true. Gailet had figured out that the examinations offered by the Uplift Institute were *scaled* somehow, in order to measure not only how intelligent the subject was but also how hard he or she was trying. Sure, Gailet had advantages over most of the other chims, in training and perhaps in IQ, but at each stage her own trials got harder, too.

Another chim—a Probationer known as Weasel—emerged from the booth and sauntered over to where Irongrip waited with a third member of their band. Weasel did not seem to be much put out. In fact, all three of the surviving Probationers looked relaxed, confident. Irongrip noticed Gailet's glance and winked at her. She turned away quickly.

One last chim came out then and shook his head. "That's it," he said.

"Then Professor Simmins . . . ?"

When he shrugged, Gailet sighed. This just did not make sense. Something was wrong when fine, erudite chims were failing, and yet the tests did not cull out Irongrip's bunch from the very start.

Of course, the Uplift Institute might judge "advancement" differently than the human-led Earthclan did. Irongrip and Weasel and Steelbar were *intelligent*, after all. The Galactics might not view the Probationers' various character flaws as all that terrible, loathsome as they were to Terrans.

But no, that wasn't the reason at all, Gailet realized, as she and Michaela stepped past the remaining twenty or so to lead the way upward again. Gailet knew that something else had to be behind this. The Probies were just too cocky. Somehow they knew that a fix was in.

It was shocking. The Galactic Institutes were supposed to be above reproach. But there it was. She wondered what, if anything, could be done about it.

As they approached the next station—this one manned by a plump, leathery Soro inspector and six robots—Gailet looked around and noticed something for the first time, that nearly all of the brightly dressed Galactic observers—the aliens unaffiliated with the Institute who had come to watch and engage in informal diplomacy—nearly all of them had drifted away. A few could still be seen, moving swiftly

downslope and to the east, as if drawn by something interesting happening off that way.

Of course they won't bother telling us what's going on,
she thought bitterly.

"Okay, Gailet," Michaela sighed. "You first again. Show
'em we can talk real good."

So, even a prim schoolteacher will use grunt dialect as
an affectation, a bond. Gailet sighed. "Yeah. Me go do that
thing."

Irongrip grinned at her, but Gailet ignored him as she
stepped up to bow to the Soro and submit to the attentions
of the robots.

89

Galactics

The Suzerain of Beam and Talon strutted back and forth
under the flapping fabric of the Uplift Institute pavilion. The
Gubru admiral's voice throbbed with a vibrato of outrage.

"Intolerable! Unbelievable! Impermissible! This invasion
must be stopped, held back, put into abeyance!"

The smooth routine of a normal Uplift Ceremony had
been shattered. Officials and examiners of the Institute—
Galactics of many shapes and sizes—now rushed about under
the great canopy, hurriedly consulting portable Libraries,
seeking precedents for an event none of them had ever
witnessed or imagined before. An unexpected disturbance
had triggered chaos everywhere, and especially in the corner
where the Suzerain danced its outrage before a spiderlike
being.

The Grand Examiner, an arachnoid Serentini, stood relaxed in a circle of datatanks, listening attentively to the Gubru officer's complaint.

"Let it be ruled a violation, an infraction, a capital offense! My soldiers shall enforce propriety severely!" The Suzerain fluffed its down to display the pinkish tint already visible under the outer feathers—as if the Serentini would be impressed to see that the admiral was nearly female, almost a queen.

But the sight failed to impress the Grand Examiner. Serentini were *all* female, after all. So what was the big deal?

The Grand Examiner kept her amusement hidden, however. "The new arrivals fit all of the criteria for being allowed to participate in this ceremony," she replied patiently in Galactic Three. "They have caused consternation, of course, and will be much discussed long after this day is done. Still, they are only one of many features of this ceremony which are, well, unconventional."

The Gubru's beak opened, then shut. "What do you mean by that?"

"I mean that this is the most irregular Uplift Ceremony in megayears. I have several times considered canceling it altogether."

"You dare not! We should appeal, seek redress, seek compensation . . ."

"Oh, you would love that, wouldn't you?" The Grand Examiner sighed. "Everyone knows the Gubru are overextended now. But a judgment against one of the Institutes could cover some of your costs, no?"

This time, the Gubru was silent. The Grand Examiner used two feelers to scratch a crease in her carapace. "Several of my associates believe that that was your plan all along. There are so many irregularities in this ceremony you've arranged. But on close examination each one seems to stop *just* short of illegality. You have been clever at finding precedents and loopholes.

"For instance, there is the matter of human approval of a ceremony for their own clients. It is unclear these hostage officials of yours understood what they were agreeing to when they signed the documents you showed me."

"They were—had been—offered Library access."

"A skill for which wolflings are not renowned. There is suspicion of coercion."

"We have a message of acceptance from Earth! From their homeworld! From their nest-mothers!"

"Aye," the Serentini agreed. "They accepted your offer of peace and a free ceremony. What poor wolfling race in their dire circumstances could turn down such a proposal? But semantic analysis shows that they thought they were only agreeing to *discuss* the matter further! They obviously did not understand that you had purchased liberation of their *old* applications, some made more than fifty paktaars ago! This allowed the waiting period to be waived."

"Their misunderstandings are not our concern," clipped the Suzerain of Beam and Talon.

"Indeed. And does the Suzerain of Propriety hold with this view?"

This time there was only silence. Finally, the Grand Examiner lifted both forelegs and crossed them in a formal bow. "Your protest is acknowledged. The ceremony shall continue, under the ancient rules set down by the Progenitors."

The Gubru commander had no choice. It bowed in return. Then it swiveled and flounced outside, angrily pushing aside a crowd of its guards and aides, leaving them cackling, disturbed, in its wake.

The Examiner turned to a robot assistant. "What were we discussing before the Suzerain arrived?"

"An approaching craft whose occupants claim diplomatic protection and observer status," the thing replied in Galactic One.

"Ah, yes. Those."

"They are growing quite perturbed, as Gubru interceptors now seem about to cut them off, and may do them harm."

The Examiner hesitated only a moment. "Please inform the approaching envoys that we will be only too happy to grant their request. They should come directly to the Mount, under the protection of the Uplift Institute."

The robot hurried off to pass on the order. Other aides then approached, waving readouts and picting preliminary reports on still more anomalies. One after another of the holo-screens lit up to show the crowd that had arrived at the base of the hill, tumbling out of rusty boats and surging up the unguarded slopes.

"This event grows ever more interesting," the Grand Examiner sighed reflectively. "I wonder, what will happen next?"

90

Gailet

It was after sunset and Gimelhai had already sunk below a western horizon turbid with dark clouds by the time the worn-down survivors finally passed through the last examination screen to collapse in exhaustion upon a grassy knoll. Six chens and six chimmies lay quietly close to each other for warmth. They were too tired to engage in the grooming all felt they needed.

"Momma, why didn't they choose dogs to uplift, instead? Or pigs?" One of them moaned.

"Baboons," another voice suggested, and there was a murmur of agreement. Such creatures deserved this kind of treatment.

"Anybody but us," a third voice summarized, succinctly.

Ex exaltavit humilis, Gailet thought silently. *They have lifted up the humble of origins*. The motto of the Terragens Uplift Board had its origins in the Christian Bible. To Gailet it had always carried the unfortunate implication that someone, somewhere, was going to get crucified.

Her eyes closed and she felt a light sleep close in immediately. *Just a catnap*, she thought. But it did not last long. Gailet felt a sudden return of that dream—the one in which a Gubru stood over her, peering down the barrel of a malevolent machine. She shivered and opened her eyes again.

The last shreds of twilight were fading. Bitterly clear, the stars twinkled as if through something more refracting than mere atmosphere.

She and the others stood up quickly as a brightly lit floater car approached and settled down in front of them. Out

stepped three figures, a tall, downy-white Gubru, a spiderlike
Galactic, and a pudgy human mel whose official gown hung
on him like a potato sack. As she and the other chims bowed,
Gailet recognized Cordwainer Appelbe, the head of Garth's
local Uplift Board.

The man looked bewildered. Certainly he must be over-
awed to be taking part in all this. Still, Gailet also wondered
whether Appelbe was drugged.

"Um, I want to congratulate you all," he said, stepping
just ahead of the other two. "You should know how proud we
are of all of you. I've been told that, while there are certain
test scores that are still in dispute, the overall judgment of
the Uplift Institute is that *Pan argonostes*—the neo-chimpanzees of Earthclan—are, or, well, actually have been ready
for stage three for quite some time."

The arachnoid official stepped forward then. "That is
true. In fact, I can promise that the Institute will favorably
consider any future applications by Earthclan for further
examinations."

Thank you, Gailet thought as she and the others bowed
again. *But please, don't bother picking me for the next one.*

Now the Grand Examiner launched into a lengthy speech
about the rights and duties of client races. She spoke of the
long-departed Progenitors, who began Galactic civilization so
long ago, and the procedures they set down for all succeeding
generations of intelligent life to follow.

The Examiner used Galactic Seven, which most of the
chims could at least follow. Gailet tried to pay attention, but
within her troubled thoughts kept turning to what was certainly to come after this.

She was sure she felt underfoot an increase in the faint
trembling which had accompanied them all the way up the
mountain. It filled the air with a low, barely audible rumbling. Gailet swayed as a wave of *unreality* seemed to pass
through her. She looked up and saw that several of the
evening stars appeared to flare suddenly brighter. Others fled
laterally as an oval distortion inserted itself directly overhead.
A *blackness* began to gather there.

The Examiner's aeolian speech droned on. Cordwainer
Appelbe listened raptly, a bemused expression on his face.
But the white-plumed Gubru grew visibly impatient with
each passing moment. Gailet could well understand why.
Now that the hyperspace shunt was warmed up and ready,

every passing minute was costing the invaders. When she realized this, Gailet felt warmer toward the droning Serentini official. She nudged Michaela when her friend seemed about to doze off, and put on an attentive expression.

Several times the Gubru opened its beak as if about to commit the ungraceful act of interrupting the Examiner. Finally, when the spiderlike being stopped briefly for a breath, the avian cut in sharply. Gailet, who had been studying hard for months, easily understood the clipped words in Galactic Three.

"—*delaying, dawdling, stalling! Your motives are in doubt, incredible, suspect! I insist that you proceed, move along, get on with it!*"

But the Examiner scarcely missed a beat, continuing in Galactic Seven.

"In passing the formidable gauntlet you faced today, more rigorous than any testing I have heretofore witnessed, you have demonstrated your worthiness as junior citizens of our civilization, and bring credit to your clan.

"What you receive today, you have earned—the right to reaffirm your love of your patrons, and to choose a stage consort. The latter decision is an important one. As consort you must select a known, oxygen-breathing, starfaring race, one that is not a member of your own clan. This race will defend your interests and impartially intercede in disputes between you and your patrons. If you wish, you may select the Tymbrimi, of the Clan of the Krallnith, who have been your consort-advisors up until now. Or you may make a change.

"Or, you may choose yet another option—to end your participation in Galactic civilization, and ask that the meddling of Uplift be reversed. Even this drastic step was prescribed by the Progenitors, as insurance of the fundamental rights of living things."

Could we? Could we really do that? Gailet felt numb at the very idea. Even though she knew that it was almost never allowed in practice, the option was there!

She shuddered and refocused her attention as the Grand Examiner lifted two arms in a benediction. "In the name of the Institute of Uplift, and before all of Galactic civilization, I therefore pronounce you, the representatives of your race, qualified and capable of choosing and bearing witness. Go forth, and do all living things proud."

The Serentini stepped back. And at last it was the turn of the ceremony sponsor. Normally, this would have been a human, or perhaps a Tymbrimi, but not this time. The Gubru emissary did a little dance of impatience. Quickly, it barked into a vodor, and words in Galactic Seven boomed forth.

"Ten of you shall accompany the final representatives to the shunt and offer witness. The selected pair shall carry the burden of choice and honor. These two I shall name now.

"Doctor Gailet Jones, female, citizen of Garth, Terragens Federation, Clan of Earth."

Gailet did not want to move, but Michaela, her friend, betrayed her by planting a hand in the small of her back and gently urging her forward. She stepped a few paces toward the dignitaries and bowed. The vodor boomed again.

"Irongrip Hansen, male, citizen of Garth, Terragens Federation, Clan of Earth."

Most of the chims behind her gasped in shock and dismay. But Gailet only closed her eyes as her worst fears were confirmed. Up until now she had clung to a hope that the Suzerain of Propriety might still be a force among the Gubru. That it might yet compel the Triumvirate to play fair. But now . . .

She felt *him* step up next to her and knew the chen she hated most was wearing that grin.

Enough! I've stood for this long enough! Surely the Grand Examiner suspects something. If I tell her . . .

But she did not move. Her mouth did not open to speak.

Suddenly, and with brutal clarity, Gailet realized the real reason why she had gone along with this farce for so long!

They've fooled with my mind!

It all made sense. She recalled the dreams . . . nightmares of helplessness under the subtle, adamant coercion of machines held in ruthless talons.

The Uplift Institute wouldn't be equipped to test for that.

Of course they wouldn't! Uplift Ceremonies were invariably joyous occasions, celebrated by patron and client alike. Who ever heard of a race-representative having to be conditioned or forced to participate?

It must've been done after Fiben was taken away. The Suzerain of Propriety couldn't have agreed to such a thing. If the Grand Examiner only knew, we could squeeze a planet's worth of reparation gild from the Gubru!

Gailet opened her mouth. "I . . ." She tried to make words come. The Grand Examiner looked at her.

Perspiration condensed on Gailet's brow. All she had to do was make the accusation. Even *hint* at it!

But her brain was frozen. It felt as if she had forgotten *how* to make words!

Speechlock. Of course. The Gubru had learned how easy it was to impose on a neo-chimpanzee. A human, perhaps, might have been able to break the hold, but Gailet recognized how futile it was in her case.

She could not read arthropoid expressions, but it seemed somehow as if the Serentini looked disappointed. The Examiner stepped back. "Proceed to the hyperspace shunt," she said.

No! Gailet wanted to cry. But all that escaped was a faint sigh as she felt her right hand lift of its own accord and meet Irongrip's left. He held on and she could not let go.

That was when she felt an image begin to form in her mind—an avian face with a yellow beak and cold, unblinking eyes. No effort could rid her of the picture. Gailet knew with terrible certainty that she was about to carry that image with her to the top of the ceremonial mound, and once there she and Irongrip would send it upward, into the oval of warped space overhead, for all to see, here and on a thousand other worlds.

The part of her mind that still belonged to her—the logical entity, now cut off and isolated—saw the cold covinous logic of the plan.

Oh, humans were sure to claim that the choice made today had been rigged. And probably more than half of the clans in the Five Galaxies would believe it. But that wouldn't change anything. The choice would still stand! The alternative would be to discredit the entire system. Stellar civilization was under such pressure, right now, that it could not stand much further strain.

In fact, quite a few clans might decide that there had already been quite enough trouble over one little tribe of wolflings. Whatever the rights and wrongs, there would be substantial sentiment for ending the problem, once and for all.

It came to Gailet all in a rush. The Gubru did not merely want to become chims' new stage consort "protectors." They meant to bring about the extinction of *humanity*. Once that was accomplished, her own people would be up for adoption, and she had little doubt how *that* would go!

Gailet's heart pounded. She struggled not to turn in the direction Irongrip was guiding her, but to no avail. She prayed that she would have a stroke.

Let me die!

Her life hardly mattered. They certainly planned to have her "disappear" immediately after the ceremony anyway, to dispose of the evidence. *Oh, Goodall and Ifni, strike me down now!* She wanted to scream.

At that moment, words came. *The* words . . . but it was not her voice that spoke them.

"Stop! An injustice is being done, and I demand a hearing!"

Gailet had not thought her heart could beat any quicker, but now tachycardia made her feel faint. *Oh God, let it be . . .*

She heard Irongrip curse and let go of her hand. That alone brought her joy. There was the sound of squawking Gubru anger, and high "eeps" of chim surprise. Someone— Michaela, she realized—took her arm and turned her around.

It was full night now. Scattered clouds were underlit by the bright beacons of the mound, and by the turbulent, lambent tunnel of energy now taking form above the artificial mountain. Into the stark light of the floater car's headlamps a solitary neo-chimpanzee in a dust-coated formal robe approached from the last test station. He wiped sweat from his brow and strode purposefully toward the three surprised officials.

Fiben, Gailet thought. Dazed, she found that old habits were the first to reassert themselves. *Oh, Fiben, don't swagger! Try to remember your protocol. . . .*

When she realized what she was doing, Gailet suddenly giggled in a brief wave of hysteria. It shook her partially free of her immobility, and she managed to lift her hand to cover her mouth. "Oh, Fiben," she sighed.

Irongrip growled, but the new arrival only ignored the Probationer. Fiben caught her eye and winked. It struck Gailet how the gesture that had once so infuriated her now made her knees feel weak with joy.

He stepped before the three officials and bowed low. Then, with hands clasped respectfully, Fiben awaited permission to speak.

"—dishonorable, incorrigible, impermissible interruptions—" the Gubru's vodor boomed. "We demand immediate removal and sanction, punishment—"

The noise suddenly cut off as the Grand Examiner used one of her forward arms to reach up and switch the vodor off. She stepped daintily forward and addressed Fiben.

"Young one, I congratulate you on making your way up to this place all alone. Your ascent provided much of the excitement and unconventionality that is making this one of the most memorable of all ceremonies on record. By virtue of your test scores and other accomplishments, you have earned a place on this pinnacle." The Serentini crossed two arms and lowered her forebody. "Now," she said as she rose again, "can we assume that you have a complaint to voice? One important enough to explain such abruptness of tone?"

Gailet tensed. The Grand Examiner might be sympathetic, but there was a veiled threat implied in those words. Fiben had better make this good. One mistake and he could make matters even worse than before.

Fiben bowed again. "I—I respectfully request an explanation of . . . of how the race-representatives were chosen."

Not too bad. Still, Gailet struggled against her conditioning. If only she could step forward and help!

For some time the dim slopes beyond the circle of lights had begun to fill with the Galactic dignitaries—those who had departed earlier to watch unknown events downslope. Now they were all hushed, watching a humble client from one of the newest of all species demand answers from a lord of the Institute.

The Grand Examiner's voice was patient when she answered. "It is traditional for the ceremony sponsors to select a pair from among those who pass all trials. While it is true that the sponsors are, on this occasion, declared enemies of your clan, their enmity will officially end upon completion of the rites. Peace will exist between the clan of Terrans and that of Gooksyu-Gubru. Do you object to this, young one?"

"No." Fiben shook his head. "Not to that. I just want to know this: Do we absolutely *have to accept* the sponsors' choice as our representatives?"

The Gubru emissary immediately squawked indignantly. The chims looked at one another in surprise. Irongrip muttered, "When this is over, I'm gonna take that little frat boy an' . . ."

The Examiner waved for silence. Its many-faceted eyes

focused upon Fiben. "Young one, what would you do, were it up to you? Would you have us put it to a vote of your peers?"

Fiben bowed. "I would, your honor."

This time the Gubru's shriek was positively painful to the ear. Gailet tried once again to step forward, but Irongrip held her arm tightly. She was forced to stand there, listening to the Probationer's muttered curses.

The Serentini official spoke at last. "Although I am sympathetic, I cannot see how I can allow your request. Without precedent—"

"But there *is* precedent!"

It was a new, deep voice, coming from the dim slope behind the officials. From the crowd of Galactic visitors four figures now emerged into the light, and if Gailet had felt surprise before, now she could only stare in disbelief.

Uthacalthing!

The slender Tymbrimi was accompanied by a bearded human mel whose ill-fitting formal robe had probably been borrowed from some bipedal but not quite humanoid Galactic and was thrown over what seemed to be *animal skins*. Beside the young man walked a neo-chimp who had obvious trouble standing completely erect and who bore many of the stigmata of atavism. The chim hung back when they approached the clearing, as if he knew he did not belong on this ground.

It was the fourth being—a towering figure whose bright, inflated crest ballooned upward in dignity—who bowed casually and addressed the Grand Examiner.

"I see you, Cough*Quinn'3 of the Uplift Institute."

The Serentini bowed back. "I see you, honored Ambassador Kault of the Thennanin, and you, Uthacalthing of the Tymbrimi, and your companions. It is pleasant to witness your safe arrival."

The big Thennanin spread his arms apart. "I thank your honor for allowing me to use your transmitting facilities to contact my clan, after so long an enforced isolation."

"This is neutral ground," the Uplift official said. "I also know that there are serious matters regarding this planet which you wish to press with the Institute, once this ceremony is at an end.

"But for now, I must insist we maintain pertinence. Will you please explain the remark you made on your arrival?"

Kault gestured toward Uthacalthing. "This respected envoy represents the race which has served as stage consort and protector to the neo-chimpanzees ever since their wolfling patrons encountered Galactic society. I shall let him tell you."

All at once Gailet noticed how *tired* Uthacalthing looked. The tym's usually expressive tendrils lay flat, and his eyes were set close together. It was with obvious effort that he stepped forward and offered a small, black cube. "Here are the references," he began.

A robot came forward and plucked the data out of his hand. From that instant the Institute's staff would be inspecting the citations. The Examiner herself listened attentively to Uthacalthing.

"The references will show that, very early in Galactic history, Uplift Ceremonies evolved out of the Progenitors' desire to protect themselves from *moral fault*. They who began the process we now know as Uplift frequently consulted with their client races, as humans do with theirs, today. And the clients' representatives were never imposed upon them."

Uthacalthing gestured toward the assembled chims.

"Strictly speaking, the ceremonial sponsors are making a *suggestion*, when they make their selection. The clients, having passed all the tests appropriate to their stage, are legally permitted to ignore the choice. In the purest sense, this plateau is their territory. We are here as their guests."

Gailet saw that the Galactic observers were agitated. Many consulted their own datawells, accessing the precedents Uthacalthing had provided. Polylingual chatter spread around the periphery. A new floater arrived, carrying several Gubru and a portable communications unit. Obviously, the invaders were doing furious research of their own.

All this time the power of the hyperspace shunt could be felt building just upslope. The low rumbling was now omnipresent, making Gailet's tendons quiver in imposed rhythm.

The Grand Examiner turned to the nominal human official, Cordwainer Appelbe. "In the name of your clan, do you support this request for a departure from normal procedure?"

Appelbe bit his lower lip. He looked at Uthacalthing, then at Fiben, then back at the Tymbrimi Ambassador. Then, for the first time, the man actually smiled. "Hell, yes! I sure do!" he said in Anglic. Then he blushed and switched to carefully phrased Galactic Seven. "In the name of my clan, I support Ambassador Uthacalthing's request."

The Examiner turned away to hear a report from her staff. When she came back the entire hillside was hushed. Suspense held them all riveted until she bowed to Fiben.

"Precedent is, indeed, interpretable in favor of your request. Shall I ask your comrades to indicate their choice by hand? Or by secret ballot?"

"Right!" came an Anglic whisper. The young human who had accompanied Uthacalthing grinned and gave Fiben a thumbs-up sign. Fortunately, none of the Galactics were looking that way to witness the impertinence.

Fiben forced a serious expression and bowed again. "Oh, a hand vote will do nicely, your honor. Thank you."

Gailet was more bemused than anything as the election was held. She tried hard to decline her own nomination, but the same captation, the same implacable force that had kept her from speaking earlier made her unable to withdraw her name. She was chosen unanimously.

The contest for male representative was straightforward as well. Fiben faced Irongrip, looking calmly up into the tall Probationer's fierce eyes. Gailet found that the best she could make herself do was abstain, causing several of the others to look at her in surprise.

Nevertheless, she almost sobbed with relief when the poll came in nine to three . . . in favor of Fiben Bolger. When he finally approached, Gailet sagged into his arms and sobbed.

"There. There," he said. And it wasn't so much the cliché as the sound of his voice that comforted her. "I told you I'd come back, didn't I?"

She sniffed and rubbed away tears as she nodded. One cliché deserved another. She touched his cheek, and her voice was only slightly sardonic as she said, "My hero."

The other chims—all except the outnumbered Probies—gathered around, pressing close in a jubilant mass. For the first time it began to look as if the ceremony just might turn into a celebration after all.

They formed ranks, two by two, behind Fiben and Gailet, and started forth along the final path toward the pinnacle where, quite soon, there would be a physical link from this world to spaces far, far away.

That was when a shrill whistle echoed over the small plateau. A new hover car landed in front of the chims, blocking their path. "Oh, no," Fiben groaned. For he instantly recognized the barge carrying the three Suzerains of the Gubru invasion force.

The Suzerain of Propriety looked dejected. It drooped on its perch, unable to lift its head even to look down at them. The other two rulers, however, hopped nimbly onto the ground and tersely addressed the Examiner.

"We, as well, wish to present, offer, bring forward . . . a precedent!"

91

Fiben

How easily is defeat snatched from the jaws of victory?

Fiben wondered about that as he stripped out of his formal robe and allowed two of the chims to rub oil into his shoulders. He stretched and tried to hope that he would remember enough from his old wrestling days to make a difference.

I'm too old for this, he thought. *And it's been a long, hard day.*

The Gubru hadn't been kidding when they gleefully announced that they had found an out. Gailet tried to explain it to him while he got ready. As usual, it all seemed to have to do with an *abstraction*.

"As I see it, Fiben, the Galactics don't reject the idea of evolution itself, just evolution of *intelligence*. They believe in something like what we used to call "Darwinism" for creatures all the way up to pre-sentients. What's more, it's assumed that nature is wise in the way she forces every species to demonstrate its fitness in the wild."

Fiben sighed. "Please get to the point, Gailet. Just tell

me why I have to go face to face against that momzer. Isn't trial-by-combat pretty silly, even by Eatee standards?"

She shook her head. For a little while she had seemed to suffer from speechlock. But that had disappeared as her mind slipped into the familiar pedantic mode.

"No, it isn't. Not if you look at it carefully. You see, one of the risks a patron race runs in uplifting a new client species all the way to starfaring intelligence is that by meddling too much it may deprive the client of its essence, of the very *fitness* that made it a candidate for Uplift in the first place."

"You mean—"

"I mean that the Gubru can accuse humans of doing this to chims, and the only way to disprove it is by showing that we can still be passionate, and tough, and physically strong."

"But I thought all those tests—"

Gailet shook her head. "They showed that everyone on this plateau meets the criteria for Stage Three. Even" —Gailet grimaced as she seemed to have to fight for the words— "even those Probies are superior, at least in most of the ways Institute regulations test for. They're only deficient by our own, quaint, Earth standards."

"Such as decency and body odor. Yeah. But I still don't get—"

"Fiben, the Institute really doesn't *care* who actually steps into the shunt, not once we've passed all its tests. If the Gubru want our male race-representative to prove he's better by one more criterion—that of 'fitness'—well it's precedented all right. In fact, it's been done more often than voting."

Across the small clearing, Irongrip flexed and grinned back at Fiben, backed up by his two confederates. Weasel and Steelbar joked with the powerful Probationer chief, laughing confidently over this sudden swerve in their favor.

Now it was Fiben's turn to shake his head and mutter lowly. "Goodall, what a way to run a galaxy. Maybe Pratha-chulthorn was right after all."

"What was that, Fiben?"

"Nothin'," he said as he saw the referee, a Pila Institute official, approach the center of the ring. Fiben turned to meet Gailet's eyes. "Just tell me you'll marry me if I win."

"But—" She blinked, then nodded. Gailet seemed about to say something else, but that *look* came over her again, as if she simply could not find the phrases. She shivered, and in a strange, distant voice she managed to choke out five words.

"Kill—him—for—me, Fiben."

It was not feral bloodlust, that look in her eyes, but something much deeper. Desperation.

Fiben nodded. He suffered no illusions over what Irongrip intended for him.

The referee called them forward. There would be no weapons. There would be no rules. Underground the rumbling had turned into a hard, angry growl, and the zone of nonspace overhead flickered at the edges, as if with deadly lightning.

It began with a slow circling as Fiben and his opponent faced each other warily, sidestepping a complete circuit of the arena. Nine of the other chims stood on the upslope side, alongside Uthacalthing and Kault and Robert Oneagle. Opposite them, the Gubru and Irongrip's two compatriots watched. The various Galactic observers and officials of the Uplift Institute took up the intervening arcs.

Weasel and Steelbar made fist signs to their leader and bared their teeth. "Go get 'im, Fiben," one of the other chims urged. All of the ornate ritual, all of the arcane and ancient tradition and science had come to this, then. This was the way Mother Nature finally got to cast the tie-breaking vote.

"Be-gin!" The Pila referee's sudden shout struck Fiben's ears as an ultrasonic squeal an instant before the vodor boomed.

Irongrip was quick. He charged straight ahead, and Fiben almost decided too late that the maneuver was a feint. He started to dodge to the left, and at barely the last moment changed directions, striking out with his trailing foot.

The blow did not finish in the satisfying crunch he'd hoped for, but Irongrip did cry out and reel away, holding his ribs. Unfortunately, Fiben was thrown off balance and could not follow up his brief opportunity. In seconds it was gone as Irongrip moved forward again, more warily this time, with murder written in his eyes.

Some days it just doesn't pay to get out of bed, Fiben thought as they resumed circling.

Actually, today had begun when he awoke in the notch of a tree, a few miles outside the walls of Port Helenia, where plate ivy parachutes festooned the stripped branches of a winter-barren orchard. . . .

Irongrip jabbed, then punched out with a hard right.

Fiben ducked under his opponent's arm and riposted with a backhand blow. It was blocked, and the bones of their forearms made a loud *crack* as they met.

. . . The Talon Soldiers had shown grudging courtesy, so he rode Tycho hard until he arrived at the old prison. . . .

A fist whistled past Fiben's ear like a cannonball. Fiben stepped inside the outstretched arm and swiveled to plant his elbow into his enemy's exposed stomach.

. . . Staring at the abandoned room, he had known that there was very little time left. Tycho had galloped through the deserted streets, a flower dangling from his mouth. . . .

The jab wasn't hard enough. Worse, he was too slow to duck aside as Irongrip's arm folded fast to come around to cross his throat.

. . . and the docks had been filled with chims—they lined the wharves, the buildings, the streets, staring. . . .

A crushing constriction threatened to cut off his breath. Fiben crouched, dropping his right foot backward between his opponent's legs. He tensed in one direction until Irongrip counterbalanced, then Fiben whirled and threw his weight the other way while he kicked out. Irongrip's right leg slipped out from under him, and his own straining overbalance threw Fiben up and over. The Probationer's incredible grasp held for an astonishing instant, tearing loose only along with shreds of Fiben's flesh.

. . . He traded his horse for a boat, and headed across the bay, toward the barrier buoys. . . .

Blood streamed from Fiben's torn throat. The gash had missed his jugular vein by half an inch. He backed away when he saw how quickly Irongrip found his feet again. It was downright intimidating how fast the chen could move.

. . . He fought a mental battle with the buoys, earning— through reason—the right to pass through. . . .

Irongrip bared his teeth, spread his long arms, and let out a blood-curdling shriek. The sight and sound seemed to pierce Fiben like a memory of battles fought long, long before chims ever flew starships, when *intimidation* had been half of any victory.

"You can do it, Fiben!" Robert Oneagle cried, countering Irongrip's threat magic. "Come on, guy! Do it for Simon."

Shit, Fiben thought. *Typical human trick, guilt-tripping me!*

Still, he managed to wipe away the momentary wave of

doubt and grinned back at his enemy. "Sure, you can scream, but can you do this?"

Fiben thumbed his nose. Then he had to dive aside quickly as Irongrip charged. This time both of them landed clear blows that sounded like beaten drums. Both chims staggered to opposite ends of the arena before managing to turn around again, panting hard and baring their teeth.

. . . The beach had been littered, and the trail up the bluffs was long and hard. But that turned out to be only the beginning. The surprised Institute officials had already started disassembling their machines when he suddenly appeared, forcing them to remain and test just one more. They assumed it would not take long to send him home again. . . .

The next time they came together, Fiben endured several hard blows to the side of his face in order to step inside and throw his opponent to the ground. It wasn't the most elegant example of jiu-jitsu. Forcing it, he felt a sudden tearing sensation in his leg.

For an instant, Irongrip was rolling, helpless. But when Fiben tried to pounce his leg nearly collapsed.

The Probationer was on his feet again in an instant. Fiben tried not to show a limp, but something must have betrayed him, for this time Irongrip charged his right side, and when Fiben tried to backpedal, the left leg gave way.

. . . grueling tests, hostile stares, the tension of wondering if he would ever make it in time. . . .

As he fell backward, he kicked out, but all that earned him was a grip that seized his ankle like a roller-press. Fiben scrambled for leverage, but his fingers clawed in the loose soil. He tried to slip aside as his opponent hauled him back and then fell upon him.

. . . And he had gone through all of that just to arrive here? Yeah. All in all, it had been one hell of a day. . . .

There are certain tricks a wrestler can try against a stronger opponent in a much heavier weight class. Some of these came back to Fiben as he struggled to get free. Had he been a little less close to utter exhaustion, one or two of them might even have worked.

As it was, he managed to reach a point of quasi-equilibrium. He attained a small advantage of leverage which just counterbalanced Irongrip's horrendous strength. Their bodies strained and tugged as hands clutched, probing for the smallest opening. Their faces were pressed near the ground and close enough together to smell each other's hot breath.

The crowd had been silent for some time. No more shouts of encouragement came, from one side or the other. As he and his enemy rocked gradually back and forth in a deadly serious battle of deceptive slowness, Fiben found himself with a clear view of the downward slope of the Ceremonial Mound. With a small corner of his awareness, he realized that the crowd was gone now. Where there had been a dense gathering of multiformed Galactics, now there was only an empty stretch of trampled grass.

The remnants could be seen hurrying downhill and eastward, shouting and gesticulating excitedly in a variety of tongues. Fiben caught a glimpse of the arachnoid Serentini, the Grand Examiner, standing amid a cluster of her aides, paying no attention any longer to the two chims' fight. Even the Pila referee had turned away to face some growing tumult downslope.

This, after talking as if the fate of everything in the Universe depended upon a battle to the death between two chims? That same detached part of Fiben felt insulted.

Curiosity betrayed him, even here and now. He wondered. *What in th' world are they up to?*

Lifting his eyes even an inch in an attempt to see was enough to do it. He missed by milliseconds an opening Irongrip created as the Probationer shifted his weight slightly. Then, as Fiben followed through too late, Irongrip took advantage in a sudden slip and hold. He began applying pressure.

"Fiben!" It was Gailet's voice, thick with emotion. So he knew that at least *somebody* was still paying attention, if only to watch his final humiliation and end.

Fiben fought hard. He used tricks dragged up out of the well of memory. But the best of them required strength he no longer had. Slowly he was forced back.

Irongrip grinned as he managed to lay his forearm against Fiben's windpipe. Suddenly breath came in hard, high whistles. Air was very dear, and his struggles took on new desperation.

Irongrip held on just as urgently. His bared canines reflected bitter highlights as he panted in an open-mouthed grin over Fiben.

Then the glints faded as something occulted the lights, casting a dark shadow over both of them. Irongrip blinked, and all at once seemed to notice that something bulky had appeared next to Fiben's head. A hairy black *foot*. The attached brown leg was short, as stout as a tree trunk, and led upwards to a mountain of fur. . . .

For Fiben the world, which had started to spin and go dim, came slowly back into focus as the pressure on his airpipe eased somewhat. He sucked air through the constricted passage and tried to look to see why he was still alive.

The first thing he saw was a pair of mild brown eyes, which stared back in friendly openness from a jet black face set at the top of a hill of muscle.

The mountain also had a smile. With an arm the length of a small chimpanzee, the creature reached out and touched Fiben, curiously. Irongrip shuddered and rocked back in amazement, or maybe fear. When the creature's hand closed on Irongrip's arm, it only squeezed hard enough to test the chim's strength.

Obviously, there was no comparison. The big male gorilla chuffed, satisfied. It actually seemed to laugh.

Then, using one knuckle to help it walk, it turned and rejoined the dark band that was even then trooping past the amazed rank of chims. Gailet stared in disbelief, and Uthacalthing's wide eyes blinked rapidly at the sight.

Robert Oneagle seemed to be talking to himself, and the Gubru gabbled and squawked.

But it was Kault who was the focus of the gorillas' attention for a long moment. Four females and three males clustered around the big Thennanin, reaching up to touch him. He responded by speaking to them, slowly, joyfully.

Fiben refused to make the same mistake twice. What *gorillas* were doing here, here atop the Ceremonial Mound the Gubru invaders had built, was beyond his ability to guess, and he wasn't even about to try. His concentration returned just a split instant sooner than his opponent's. When Irongrip looked back down, the Probie's eyes betrayed instantaneous dismay as he recognized the looming shape of Fiben's fist.

The small plateau was a cacophony, a mad scene devoid of any vestige of order. The boundaries of the combat arena did not seem to matter anymore as Fiben and his enemy rolled about under the legs of chims and gorillas and Gubru and whatever else could walk or bounce or slither about. Hardly anybody seemed to be paying them any attention, and Fiben did not really care. All that mattered to him was that he had a promise that he had to keep.

He pummeled Irongrip, not allowing him to regain balance until the chen roared and in desperation threw Fiben off like an old cloak. As he landed in a painful jolt, Fiben caught a glimpse of motion behind him and turned his head to see the Probationer called Weasel lifting his leg, preparing to strike down with his foot. But the blow missed as the Probie was grabbed up by an affectionate gorilla, who lifted him into a crushing embrace.

Irongrip's other comrade was held back by Robert Oneagle—or, rather, held *up*. The male chim might have vastly greater strength than most humans, but it did him no good suspended in midair. Robert raised Steelbar high overhead, like Hercules subduing Anteus. The young man nodded to Fiben.

"Watch out, old son."

Fiben rolled aside as Irongrip hit the ground where he had lain, sending dust plumes flying. Without delay Fiben leaped onto his opponent's back and slipped into a half-Nelson hold.

The world spun as he seemed to ride a bucking bronco. Fiben tasted blood, and the dust seemed to fill his lungs with clogging, searing pain. His tired arms throbbed and threatened to cramp. But when he heard his enemy's labored breathing he knew he could stand it for a little while longer.

Down, down Irongrip's head went. Fiben got his feet around the chim and kicked the other's legs out from under him.

The Probationer's solar plexus landed on Fiben's heel. And while a flash of pain probably meant several of Fiben's toes were broken, there was also no mistaking the whistling squeak as Irongrip's diaphragm momentarily spasmed, stopping all flow of air.

Somewhere he found the energy. In a whirl he had his foe turned over. Gripping in a tight scissors lock, he brought his forearm around and applied the same illegal-but-who-cares strangulation hold that had earlier been used on him.

Bone ground against gristle. The ground beneath them seemed to throb and the sky rumbled and growled. Alien feet shuffled on all sides, and there was the incessant squawking and chatter of a dozen jabbering tongues. Still, Fiben listened only for the breath that did not flow through his enemy's throat . . . and felt only for the throbbing pulse he so desperately had to silence. . . .

That was when something seemed to explode inside his skull.

It was as if something had broken open within him, spilling what seemed a brilliant light *outward* from his cortex. Dazzled, Fiben first thought a Probationer or a Gubru must have struck him a blow to the head from behind. But the luminance was not the sort coming from a concussion. It hurt, but not in that way.

Fiben concentrated on first priorities—holding tightly to his steadily weakening opponent. But he could not ignore this strange occurrence. His mind sought something to compare it to, but there was no correct metaphor. The soundless outburst felt somehow simultaneously alien and eerily familiar.

All at once Fiben remembered a blue light which danced in hilarity as it fired infuriating bolts at his feet. He remembered a "stink bomb" that had sent a pompous, furry little diplomat scurrying off in abandoned dignity. He remembered stories told at night by the general. The connections made him suspect . . .

All around the plateau, Galactics had ceased their multi-tongued babble and stared upslope. Fiben would have to lift his head a bit to see what so captivated them. Before he did so, however, he made certain of his foe. When Irongrip managed to drag in a few thin, desperate breaths, Fiben restored just enough pressure to keep the big chen balanced on the edge of consciousness. That accomplished, he raised his eyes.

"Uthacalthing," Fiben whispered, realizing the source of his mental confusion.

The Tymbrimi stood a little uphill from the others. His arms opened wide and the capelike folds of his formal robe flapped in the cyclone winds circling the gaping hyperspace shunt. His eyes were set far apart.

Uthacalthing's corona tendrils waved, and over his head *something* whirled.

A chim moaned and pressed her palms against her temples. Somewhere a Pring's tooth-mashies clattered. To many of those present, the glyph was barely detectable. But for the first time in his life, Fiben actually *kenned*. And what he *kenned* named itself *tutsunucann*.

The glyph was a monster—titanic with long-pent energy. The essence of delayed indeterminacy, it danced and whirled. And then, without warning, it blew apart. Fiben felt it sweep around and through him—nothing more or less than distilled, unadulterated *joy*.

Uthacalthing poured the emotion forth as if a dam had burst. *"N'ha s'urustuannu, k'hammin't Athaclena w'thtanna!"* he cried. "Daughter, do you send these to me, and so return what I had lent you? Oh, what interest compounded and multiplied! What a fine jest to pull upon your proud parent!"

His intensity affected those standing nearby. Chims blinked and stared. Robert Oneagle wiped away tears.

Uthacalthing turned and pointed up the trail leading toward the Site of Choosing. There, at the pinnacle of the Ceremony Mound, everyone could see that the shunt was connected at last. The deeply buried engines had done their job, and now a *tunnel* gaped overhead, one whose edges glistened but whose interior contained a color emptier than blackness.

It seemed to *suck away* light, making it difficult even to recognize that the opening was there. And yet Fiben knew that this was a link in real time, from this place to countless others where witnesses had gathered to observe and commemorate the evening's events.

I hope the Five Galaxies are enjoying the show. When Irongrip showed signs of reviving, Fiben gave the Probie a whack to the side of the head and looked up again.

Halfway up the narrow trail leading to the pinnacle there stood three ill-matched figures. The first was a small neo-chimpanzee whose arms seemed too long and whose ill-formed legs were bowed and short. Jo-Jo held onto one hand of Kault, the huge Thennanin, ambassador. Kault's other massive paw was grasped by a tiny human girl, whose blond hair flapped like a bright banner in the whirling breeze.

Together, the unlikely trio watched the pinnacle itself, where an unusual band had gathered.

A dozen gorillas, males and females, stood in a circle directly under the half-invisible hole in space. They rocked back and forth, staring up into the yawning emptiness overhead, and crooned a low, atonal melody.

"I believe . . ." said the awed Serentini Grand Examiner of the Uplift Institute. ". . . I believe this has happened before . . . once or twice . . . but not in more than a thousand aeons."

Another voice muttered, this time in gruff, emotion-drenched Anglic. "It's no fair. This was s'pozed t'be *our* time!" Fiben saw tears streaming down the cheeks of several of the chims. Some held each other and sobbed.

Gailet's eyes welled also, but Fiben could tell that she saw what the others did not. Hers were tears of relief, of joy.

From all sides there were heard other expressions of amazement.

"—But what sort of creatures, entities, beings can they *be*?" One of the Gubru Suzerains asked.

". . . pre-sentients," another voice answered in Galactic Three.

". . . They passed through all the test stations, so they *had* to be ready for a stage ceremony of some sort," mumbled Cordwainer Appelbe. "But how in the world did goril—"

Robert Oneagle interrupted his fellow human with an upraised hand. "Don't use the old name anymore. Those, my friend, are *Garthlings*."

Ionization filled the air with the smell of lightning. Uthacalthing chanted his pleasure at the symmetry of this magnificent surprise, this great jest, and in his Tymbrimi voice it was a rich, unearthly sound. Caught up in the moment, Fiben did not even notice climbing to his feet, standing to get a better view.

Along with everyone else he saw the coalescence that took place above the giant apes, humming and swaying on the hilltop. Over the gorillas' heads a milkiness swirled and began to thicken with the promise of *shapes*.

"In the memory of no living race has this happened," the Grand Examiner said in awe. "Client races have had countless Uplift Ceremonies, over the last billion years. They have graduated levels and chosen Uplift consorts to assist them. A few have even used the occasion to request an end of Uplift . . . to return to what they had been before. . . ."

The filminess assumed an oval outline. And within, dark forms grew more distinct, as if emerging slowly from a deep fog.

". . . But only in the ancient sagas has it been told of a

new species coming forth *of its own will*, surprising all Galactic society, and demanding the right to select its own patrons."

Fiben heard a moan and looked down to see Irongrip beginning to rise, trembling, to his elbows. A cruor of blood-tinted dust covered the battered chen from face to foot.

Got to hand it to him. He's got stamina. But then, Fiben did not imagine he himself looked a whole lot better.

He raised his foot. It would be so easy. . . . He glanced aside and saw Gailet watching him.

Irongrip rolled over onto his back. He looked up at Fiben in blank resignation.

Aw, hell. Instead he reached down and offered his hand to his former foe. *I don't know what we were fighting over. Somebody else got the brass ring, anyway*.

A moan of surprise rippled through the crowd. From the Gubru came grating wails of dismay. Fiben finished hauling Irongrip to his feet, got him stable, then looked up to see what the gorillas had wrought to cause such consternation.

It was the face of a *Thennanin*. Giant, clear as anything, the image hovering in the focus of the hyperspace shunt looked enough like Kault to be his brother.

Such a sober, serious, earnest expression, Fiben thought. So typically Thennanin.

A few of the assembled Galactics chattered in amazement, but most acted as if they had been frozen in place. All except Uthacalthing, whose delighted astonishment still sparked in all directions like a Roman candle.

"Z'wurtin's'tatta. . . . I worked for this, and never knew!"

The titanic image of the Thennanin drifted backward in the milky oval. All could see the thick, slitted neck, and then the creature's powerful torso. But when its arms came into view, it became clear that two figures stood on either side of it, holding its hands.

"Duly noted," the Grand Examiner said to her aides. "The unnamed Stage One client species tentatively called Garthlings have selected, as their patrons, the Thennanin. And as their consorts and protectors, they have jointly chosen the neo-chimpanzees and humans of Earth."

Robert Oneagle shouted. Cordwainer Appelbe fell to his knees in shock. The sound of renewed Gubru screeching was quite deafening.

Fiben felt a hand slip into his. Gailet looked up at him, the poignancy in her eyes now mixed with pride.

"Oh, well," he sighed. "They wouldn't have let us keep 'em, anyway. At least, this way, we get visitation rights. And I hear the Thennanin aren't too bad as Eatees go."

She shook her head. "You knew something about these creatures and didn't tell me?"

He shrugged. "It was supposed to be a secret. You were busy. I didn't want to bother you with unimportant details. I forgot. *Mea culpa*. Don't hit, please."

Briefly, her eyes seemed to flash. Then she, too, sighed and looked back up the hill. "It won't take them long to realize these aren't really Garthlings, but creatures of Earth."

"What'll happen then?"

It was her turn to shrug. "Nothing, I guess. Wherever they come from, they're obviously ready for Uplift. Humans signed a treaty—unfair as it was—forbidding Earthclan to raise 'em, so I guess this'll stand. *Fait accompli*. At least we can play a role. Help see the job's done right."

Already, the rumbling beneath their feet had begun to diminish. Nearby, the cacophony of Gubru squawking rose in strident tones to replace it. But the Grand Examiner appeared unmoved. Already she was busy with her assistants, ordering records gathered, detailing followup tests to be made, and dictating urgent messages to Institute headquarters.

"And we must help Kault inform his clan," she added. "They will no doubt be surprised at this news."

Fiben saw the Suzerain of Beam and Talon stalk off to a nearby Gubru flyer and depart at top speed. The boom of displaced air ruffled the feathers of the avians who remained behind.

It happened then that Fiben's gaze met that of the Suzerain of Propriety, staring down from its lonely perch. The alien stood more erect now. It ignored the babbling of its fellows and watched Fiben with a steady, unblinking yellow eye.

Fiben bowed. After a moment, the alien politely inclined its head in return.

Above the pinnacle and the crooning gorillas—now officially the youngest citizens of the Civilization of the Five Galaxies—the opalescent oval shrank back into the narrowing funnel. It diminished, but not before those present were treated to yet one more sight none had ever seen before . . . one they were not likely ever to see again.

Up there in the sky, the image of the Thennanin and those of the chim and human all looked at each other. Then the Thennanin's head rocked back and he actually *laughed*.

Richly, deeply, sharing hilarity with its diminutive partners, the leathery figure chortled. It roared.

Among the stunned onlookers, only Uthacalthing and Robert Oneagle felt like joining in as the ghostly creature above did what Thennanin were never known to do. The image kept right on laughing even as it faded back, back, to be swallowed up at last by the closing hole in space and covered by the returning stars.

PART SIX

Citizens

I am a kind of farthing dip,
Unfriendly to the nose and eyes;
A blue-behinded ape, I skip
Upon the trees of Paradise.

ROBERT LOUIS STEVENSON, "A PORTRAIT"

92

Galactics

"They exist. They have substance! They are!"

The assembled Gubru officials and officers bobbed their downy heads and cried out in unison.

"*Zooon!*"

"This prize was denied us, honor was set aside, opportunity abandoned, all in the name of penny-pinching, miserly bean-counting! Now the cost will be greater, multiplied, exponentiated!"

The Suzerain of Cost and Caution stood miserably in the corner, listening amid a small crowd of loyal assistants while it was berated from all sides. It shivered each time the conclave turned and shouted its refrain.

The Suzerain of Propriety stood tall upon its perch. It stepped back and forth, fluffing up to best display the new color that had begun to show under its molting plumage. The assembled Gubru and Kwackoo reacted to that shade with chirps of passionate devotion.

"And now a derelict, recalcitrant, stubborn one forestalls our Molt and consensus, out of which we might at least regain something. Gain honor and allies. Gain peace!"

The Suzerain spoke of their missing colleague, the military commander, who dared not, it seemed, come and face Propriety's new color, its new supremacy.

A four-legged Kwackoo hurriedly approached, bowed, and delivered a message to its leader's perch. Almost as an afterthought, a copy made its way to the Suzerain of Cost and Caution as well.

The news from the Pourmin transfer point was not

surprising—echoes had been heard of great starships bearing
down upon Garth in mighty numbers. After that debacle of
an Uplift Ceremony, the new arrivals were only to be expected.

"Well?" The Suzerain of Propriety queried the several
military officers who were present. "Does Beam and Talon
plan a defense of this world, against all advice, all wisdom,
and all honor?"

The officers, of course, did not know. They had deserted
their warrior leader as the confusing, unhappy Molt-coalescence
suddenly reversed direction.

The Suzerain of Propriety danced a dance of impatience.
"You do me no good, do the clan no good, standing about in
righteousness. Go back, seek out, return to your posts. Do
your duties as he commands, but keep me informed of what
he plans and does!"

Use of the male pronoun was deliberate. Though Molt
was not yet complete, anyone could tell without dropping
feathers which way the wind was blowing.

The officers bowed and rushed as one out of the pavilion.

93

Robert

Debris littered the now quiescent Ceremonial Mound.
Stiff easterly winds riffled the lawnlike slopes, tugging at
stringy rubbish blown in earlier from the distant mountains.
Here and there, city chims poked through trash on the lower
terraces, looking for souvenirs.

Higher up only a few pavilions still stood. Around these
several dozen large black forms lazily groomed each other's
fur and gossiped with their hands, as if they had never had

anything more momentous on their minds than who would mate with whom and what they would be fed next meal.

To Robert it seemed as if the gorillas were quite well satisfied with life. *I envy them,* he thought. In his case even a great victory did not bring an end to worry. Things were still quite dangerous on Garth. Perhaps even more so than two nights ago, when fate and coincidence intervened to surprise them all.

Life was troubling sometimes. All the time.

Robert returned his attention to his datawell and the letter the Uplift Institute officials had relayed to him only an hour before.

 . . . . Of course it's very hard for an old women—especially one who, like me, has grown so used to having her own way—but I know I must acknowledge how mistaken I was about my own son. I have wronged you, and for that I am sorry.

In my own defense I can only say that outward appearances *can* be misleading, and you were outwardly such an aggravating boy. I suppose I should have had the sense to see underneath, to the strength you have shown during these months of crisis. But that just never occurred to me. Perhaps I was afraid of examining my own feelings too closely.

In any event, we'll have much time to talk about this after peace comes. Let's let it go now by saying that I am very proud of you. Your country and your clan owe you much, as does your grateful mother.

With affection,

Megan

How odd, Robert thought, that after so many years despairing of ever winning her approval, now he had it, and didn't know how to deal with it. Ironically, he felt sympathy for his mother; it was obviously so very difficult for her to say these things at all. He made allowances for the cool tone of the words themselves.

All Garth saw Megan Oneagle as a gracious lady and fair administrator. Only her wandering husbands and Robert himself knew the other side, the one so utterly terrified by permanent obligation and issues of private loyalty. This was the first time in all his life that Robert recalled her apologizing for something really important, something involving family and intense emotions.

Blurring of vision made him close his eyes. Robert blamed the symptoms on the fringing fields of a lifting starship, whose keening engines could be heard all the way from the spaceport. He wiped his cheeks and watched the great liner—silvery and almost angelic in its serene beauty—rise and pass overhead on its leisurely way out to space and beyond.

"One more batch of fleeing rats," he murmured.

Uthacalthing did not bother turning to look. He lay back on his elbows watching the gray waters. "The Galactic visitors have already had more entertainment than they bargained for, Robert. That Uplift Ceremony was plenty. To most of them, the prospect of a space battle and siege are much less enticing."

"One of each has been quite enough for me," Fiben Bolger added without opening his eyes. He lay a little downslope, his head on Gailet Jones's lap. For the moment, she also had little to say, but concentrated on removing a few tangles from his fur, careful of his still livid black and blue bruises. Meanwhile, Jo-Jo groomed one of Fiben's legs.

Well, he's earned it, Robert thought. Although the Uplift Ceremony had been preempted by the gorillas, the test scores handed down by the Institute still held. If humanity managed to get out of its present troubles and could afford the expense of a new ceremony, two rustic colonials from Garth would lead the next procession ahead of all the sophisticated chims of Terra. Though Fiben himself seemed uninterested in the honor, Robert was proud of his friend.

A female chim wearing a simple frock approached up the trail. She bowed languidly in a brief nod to Uthacalthing and Robert. "Who wants the latest news?" Michaela Noddings asked.

"Not me!" Fiben grumped. "Tell th' Universe t'go f—"

"Fiben," Gailet chided gently. She looked up at Michaela. "I want to hear it."

The chimmie sat and began working on Fiben's other shoulder. Mollified, he closed his eyes again.

"Kault has heard from his people," Michaela said. "The Thennanin are on their way here."

"Already." Robert whistled. "They aren't wasting any time, are they?"

Michaela shook her head. "Kault's folk have already contacted the Terragens Council to negotiate purchase of the fallow gorilla genetic base and to hire Earth experts as consultants."

"I hope the Council holds out for a good price."

"Beggars can't be choosers," Gailet suggested. "According to some of the departing Galactic observers, Earth is in pretty desperate straits, as are the Tymbrimi. If this deal means we lose the Thennanin as enemies, and maybe win them as allies instead, it could be vital."

At the price of losing gorillas—our cousins—as clients of our own. Robert mulled. On the night of the ceremony he had only seen the hilarious irony of it all, sharing that Tymbrimi way of viewing things with Uthacalthing. Now, though, it was harder not to count the cost in serious terms.

They were never really ours in the first place, he reminded himself. *At least we'll have a say in how they're raised. And Uthacalthing says some Thennanin aren't as bad as many.*

"What about the Gubru?" he asked. "They agreed to make peace with Earth in exchange for acceptance of the ceremony."

"Well, it wasn't exactly the sort of ceremony they had in mind, was it?" Gailet answered. "What do you think, Ambassador Uthacalthing?"

The Tymbrimi's tendrils waved lazily. All of yesterday and this morning he had been crafting little glyphs of puzzle-like intricacy, far beyond Robert's limited ability to *kenn*, as if he were delighting in the rediscovery of something he had lost.

"They will act in what they see to be their own self-interest, of course," Uthacalthing said. "The question is whether they will have the sense to *know* what is good for them."

"What do you mean?"

"I mean that the Gubru apparently began this expedition with confused goals. Their Triumvirate reflected conflicting factions back home. The initial intent of their expedition here was to use the hostage population of Garth to pry secrets out of the Terragens Council. But then they learned that Earth is as ignorant as everybody else about what that infamous dolphin-ship of yours discovered."

"Has there been any new word about the *Streaker*?" Robert interrupted.

Spiraling off a *palanq* glyph, Uthacalthing sighed. "The dolphins seem to have miraculously escaped a trap set for them by a dozen of the most fanatic patron lines—an astonishing feat by itself—and now the *Streaker* seems to be loose on the starlanes. The humiliated fanatics lost tremendous face, and so tensions have reached an even higher level than before. It is one more reason why the Gubru Roost Masters grow increasingly frightened."

"So when the invaders found they couldn't use hostages to coerce secrets out of Earth, the Suzerains searched for other ways to make some profit out of this expensive expedition," Gailet surmised.

"Correct. But when the first Suzerain of Cost and Caution was killed it threw their leadership process out of balance. Instead of negotiating toward a consensus of policy, the three Suzerains engaged in unbridled competition for the top position in their Molt. I'm not sure that even now I understand all of the schemes that might have been involved. But the final one—the one they settled on at last—will cost them very dearly. Blatantly interfering with the proper outcome of an Uplift Ceremony is a grave matter."

Robert saw Gailet wince in revulsion as she obviously recollected how she had been used. Without opening his eyes, Fiben reached out and took her hand. "Where does that leave us now?" Robert asked Uthacalthing.

"Both common sense and honor would demand the Gubru keep their bargain with Earth. It's the only way out of a terrible bind."

"But you don't expect them to see it that way."

"Would I remain confined here, on neutral ground, if I did? You and I, Robert, would be with Athaclena right now, dining on *khoogra* and other delicacies I'd cached away, and we would speak for hours of, oh, so many things. But that will not happen until the Gubru decide between logic and self-immolation."

Robert felt a chill. "How bad could it get?" he asked in a low voice. The chims, too, listened quietly.

Uthacalthing looked around. He inhaled the sweet, chill air as if it were of fine vintage. "This is a lovely world," he sighed. "And yet it has suffered horror. Sometimes, so-called civilization seems bent on destroying those very things which it is sworn to protect."

94

Galactics

"After them!" cried the Suzerain of Beam and Talon.
"Chase them! Pursue them!"

Talon Soldiers and their battle drones swooped down
upon a small column of neo-chimpanzees, taking them by
surprise. The hairy Earthlings turned to fight, firing their
ill-sorted weapons upward at the stooping Gubru. Two small
fireballs did erupt, emitting sprays of singed feathers, but for
the most part resistance was useless. Soon, the Suzerain was
stepping delicately among the blasted remains of trees and
mammals. It cursed as its officers reported only chim bodies.

There had been stories of others, humans and Tymbrimi
and, yes, thrice-cursed Thennanin. Had not one of them
suddenly appeared out of the wilderness? They had to all be
in league together! It had to be a plot!

Now there were constant messages, entreaties, demands
that the admiral return to Port Helenia. That it join with the
other commanders for a conclave, a meeting, a new struggle
for consensus.

Consensus! the Suzerain of Beam and Talon spat on the
trunk of a shattered tree. Already it could feel the ebbing of
hormones, the leaching away of color that had *almost* been its
own!

Consensus? The admiral would show them consensus! It
was determined to win back its position of leadership. And
the only way to do that, after that catastrophe of an Uplift
Ceremony, was to demonstrate the efficacy of the military
option. When the Thennanin came to claim their "Garthling"

prizes, they would be met with force! Let them engage in Uplift of their new clients from deepspace!

Of course, to keep them at bay—in order to return this world for the Roost Masters—there must be complete surety that there would be no attacks from behind, from the surface. The ground opposition had to be eliminated!

The Suzerain of Beam and Talon refused even to consider the possibility that anger and revenge might also have colored its decisions. To have admitted that would be to begin to fall under the sway of Propriety. Already, several good officers had deserted down that path, only to be ordered back to their posts by the sanctimonious high priest. That was particularly galling.

The admiral was determined to win their loyalty back in its own right, with victory!

"The new detectors work, are effective, are efficient!" It danced in satisfaction. "They let us hunt the Earthlings without needing to scent special materials. We trace them by their very blood!"

The Suzerain's assistants shared its satisfaction. At this rate, the irregulars should soon all be dead.

A pall fell over the celebration when it was reported that one of the troop carriers that had brought them here had broken down. Another casualty of the plague of corrosion that had struck Gubru equipment all over the mountains and the Vale of Sind. The Suzerain had ordered an urgent investigation.

"No matter! We shall all ride the remaining carriers. Nothing, nobody, no event shall stop our hunt!"

The soldiers chanted.

"*Zooon!*"

95

Athaclena

She watched as the hirsute human read the message for the fourth time, and could not help wondering whether she was doing the right thing. Rank-haired, bearded, and naked, Major Prathachulthorn looked the very essence of a wild, carnivorous wolfling . . . a creature far too dangerous to trust.

He looked down at the message, and for a moment all she could read were the waves of tension that coursed up his shoulders and down his arms to those powerful, tightly flexed hands.

"It appears that I am under orders to forgive you, and to follow your policies, miss." The last word ended in a hiss. "Does this mean that I'll be set free if I promise to be good? How can I be sure this order is for real?"

Athaclena knew she had little choice. In the days ahead she would not be able to spare the chimpower to continue guarding Prathachulthorn. Those she could rely upon to ignore the human's command-voice were very few, and he had already nearly escaped on four separate occasions. The alternative was to finish him off here and now. And for that she simply had not the will.

"I have no doubt you would kill me the instant you discovered the message wasn't genuine," Athaclena replied.

His teeth seemed to flash. "You have my word on that," he assured her.

"And on what else?"

He closed and then reopened his eyes. "According to these orders from the Government in Exile, I have no choice

but to act as if I was never kidnapped, to pretend there was
no mutiny, and to conform my strategy to your advice. All
right. I agree to this, as long as you remember that I'm going
to appeal to my commanders on Earth, first chance I get.
And they will take this to the TAASF. And once Coordinator
Oneagle is overruled, I will find you, my young Tymbrimi. I
will come to you."

The bald, open hatred in his mind simultaneously made
her shiver and also reassured her. The man held nothing
back. *Truth* burned beneath his words. She nodded to
Benjamin.

"Let him go."

Looking unhappy, and avoiding eye contact with the
dark-haired human, the chims lowered the cage and cut open
the door. Prathachulthorn emerged rubbing his arms. Then,
quite suddenly, he whirled and leaped in a high kick landing
in a stance one blow away from her. He laughed as Athaclena
and the chims backed away.

"Where is my command?" he asked tersely.

"I do not know, precisely," Athaclena answered, as she
tried to abort a *gheer* flux. "We've scattered into small parties
and even had to abandon the caves when it was clear they
were compromised."

"What about this place?" Prathachulthorn motioned to
the steaming slopes of Mount Fossey.

"We expect the enemy to stage an assault here at any
moment," she replied honestly.

"Well," he said. "I didn't believe half of what you told
me, yesterday, about that 'Uplift Ceremony' and its consequences. But I'll give you this; you and your dad do seem to
have stirred up the Gubru good."

He sniffed the air, as if already he were trying to pick up
a spoor. "I assume you have a tactical situation map and a
datawell for me?"

Benjamin brought one of the portable computer units
forward, but Prathachulthorn held up a hand. "Not now.
First, let's get out of here. I want to get away from this
place."

Athaclena nodded. She could well understand how the
man felt.

He laughed when she declined his mock-chivalrous bow
and insisted that he go first. "As you wish," he chuckled.

Soon they were swinging through the trees and running under the thick forest canopy. Not much later, they heard what sounded like thunder back where the refuge had been, even though there were no clouds in the sky.

96

Sylvie

The night was lit by fiery beacons which burst forth actinically and cast stark shadows as they drifted slowly groundward. Their impact on the senses was sudden, dazzling, overwhelming even the noise of battle and the screams of the dying.

It was the defenders who sent the blazing torches into the sky, for their assailants needed no light to guide them. Streaking in by radar and infrared, they attacked with deadly accuracy until momentarily blinded by the brilliance of the flares.

Chims fled the evening's fireless camp in all directions, naked, carrying only food and a few weapons on their backs. Mostly, they were refugees from mountain hamlets burned down in the recent surge of fighting. A few trained irregulars remained behind in a desperate rearguard action to cover the civilians' retreat.

They used what means they had to confuse the airborne enemy's deadly, precise detectors. The flares were sophisticated, automatically adjusting their fulminations to best interfere with active and passive sensors. They slowed the avians down, but only for a little while. And they were in short supply.

Besides, the enemy had something new, some secret system that was letting them track chims even under the heaviest growth, even naked, without the simplest trappings of civilization.

All the pursued could do was split up into smaller and smaller groups. The prospect facing those who made it away from here was to live completely as animals, alone or at most in pairs, wild-eyed and cowering under skies that had once been theirs to roam at will.

Sylvie was helping an older chimmie and two children climb over a vine-covered tree trunk when suddenly upraised hackles told her of gravitics drawing near. She quickly signed for the others to take cover, but something—perhaps it was the unsteady rhythm of those motors—made her stay behind, peering over the rim of a fallen log. In the blackness she barely caught the flash of a dim, whitish shape, plummeting through the starlit forest to crash noisily among the branches and then disappear into the jungle gloom.

Sylvie stared down the dark channel the plunging vessel had cut. She listened, chewing on her fingernails, as debris rained down in its wake.

"Donna!" she whispered. The elderly chimmie lifted her head from under a pile of leaves. "Can you make it with the children the rest of the way to the rendezvous?" Sylvie asked. "All you have to do is head downhill to a stream, then follow that stream to a small waterfall and cave. Can you do that?"

Donna paused for a long moment, concentrating, and at last nodded. "Good," Sylvie, said. "When you see Petri, tell him I saw an enemy scout come down, and I'm goin' to go and look it over."

Fear had widened the older chimmie's eyes so that the whites shone around her irises. She blinked a couple of times, then held out her arms for the children. By the time they were gathered under her protection, Sylvie had already cautiously entered the tunnel of broken trees.

Why am I doing this? Sylvie wondered as she stepped over broken branches still oozing pungent sap. Tiny skittering motions told of native creatures seeking cover after the ruination of their homes. The smell of ozone put Sylvie's hair on end. And then, as she drew nearer, there came another familiar odor, one of overripe bird.

Everything looked eerie in the dimness. There were absolutely no colors, only shades of stygian gray. When the off-white bulk of the crashed aircraft loomed in front of her,

Sylvie saw that it lay canted at a forty degree slope, its front end quite crumpled from the impact.

She heard a faint crackling as some piece of electronics shorted again and again. Other than that, there came no sound from within. The main hatch had been torn half off its hinges.

Touching the still warm hull for guidance, she approached cautiously. Her fingers traced the outlines of one of the gravitic impellers, and flakes of corrosion came off. *Lousy maintenance*, she thought, partly in order to keep her mind busy. *I wonder if that's why it crashed.* Her mouth was dry and her heart felt in her throat as she reached the opening and bent to peer around the corner.

Two Gubru still lay strapped at their stations, their sharp-beaked heads lolling from slender, broken necks.

Sylvie tried to swallow. She made herself lift one foot and step gingerly onto the sloping deck. Her pulse threatened to stop when the plates groaned and one of the Talon Soldiers moved.

But it was only the broken vessel, creaking and settling slightly. "Goodall," Sylvie moaned as she brought her hand down from her breast. It was hard to concentrate with all of her instincts screaming just to get the hell out of here.

As she had for many days, Sylvie tried to imagine what Gailet Jones would do under circumstances like this. She knew she would never be the chimmie Gailet was. That just wasn't in the cards. But if she tried *hard* . . .

"Weapons," she whispered to herself, and forced her trembling hands to pull the soldiers' sidearms from their holsters. Seconds seemed like hours, but soon two racked saber rifles joined the pistols in a pile outside the hatch. Sylvie was about to lower herself to the ground when she hissed and slapped her forehead. "Idiot! Athaclena needs intelligence more than popguns!"

She returned to the cockpit and peered about, wondering if she would recognize something significant even if it lay right in front of her.

Come on. You're a Terragens citizen with most of a college education. And you spent months working for the Gubru.

Concentrating, she recognized the flight controls, and—from symbols obviously pertaining to missiles—the weapons console. Another display, still lit by the craft's draining bat-

teries, showed a relief territory map, with multiple sigils and
designations written in Galactic Three.

Could this be what they're using to find us? she wondered.

A dial, just below the display, used words she knew in
the enemy's language. "Band Selector," the label said. Ex-
perimentally, she touched it.

A window opened in the lower left corner of the display.
More arcane writing spilled forth, much too complex for her.
But above the text there now whirled a complex design that
an adult of any civilized society would recognize as a chemical
diagram.

Sylvie was no chemist, but she had had a basic education, and something about the molecule depicted there looked
oddly familiar to her. She concentrated and tried to sound
out the indentifier, the word just below the diagram. The
GalThree syllabary came back to her.

"Hee . . . Heem . . . Hee Moog . . ."

Sylvie felt her skin suddenly course with goose bumps.
She traced the line of her lips with her tongue and then
whispered a single word.

"Hemoglobin."

97

Galactics

"Biological warfare!" The Suzerain of Beam and Talon
hopped about the bridge of the cruising battleship on which
it held court and pointed at the Kwackoo technician who had
brought the news. "This corrosion, this decay, this blight on
armor and machinery, it was created by *design?*"

The technician bowed. "Yes. There are several agents—
bacteria, prions, molds. When we saw the pattern counter-

measures were instituted at once. It will take time to treat all affected surfaces with organisms engineered against theirs, but success will eventually reduce this to a mere nuisance."

Eventually, the admiral thought bitterly. "How were these agents delivered?"

The Kwackoo pulled from its pouch a filmy clump of clothlike material, bound by slender strands. "When these things began blowing in from the mountains, we consulted Library records and questioned the locals. Irritating infestations occur regularly on this continental coast with the onset of winter, so we ignored them.

"However, it now appears the mountain insurgents have found a way to infect these airborne spore carriers with biological entities destructive to our equipment. By the time we were aware, the dispersal was nearly universal. The plot was most ingenious."

The military commander paced. "How bad, how severe, how catastrophic is the damage?"

Again, a deep bow. "One third of our planet-side transport is affected. Two of the spaceport defense batteries will be out of commission for ten planetary days."

"Ten days!"

"As you know, we are no longer receiving spares from the homeworld."

The admiral did not need to be reminded. Already most routes to Gimelhai had been interdicted by the approaching alien armadas, now patiently clearing mines away from the fringes of Garth system.

And if that weren't enough, the two other Suzerains were now united in opposing the military. There was nothing they could do to prevent the coming battles if the admiral's party chose to fight, but they could withhold both religious and bureaucratic support. The effects of that were already showing.

The pressures had built until a steady, throbbing pain seemed to pulse within the admiral's head. "They will pay!" the Suzerain shrieked. *Curse* the limitations of priests and egg counters!

The Suzerain of Beam and Talon recalled with fond longing the grand fleets it had led into this system. But long ago most of those ships had been pulled away by the Roost Masters to meet other desperate needs, and probably quite a

few of them were already smoking ruins or vapor, out on the
contentious Galactic marches.

In order to avoid such thoughts the admiral contemplated instead the noose now tightening around the shrinking
mountain strongholds of the insurgents. Soon that worry, at
least, would be over forever.

And then, well, let the Uplift Institute enforce the neu-
trality of its sacred Ceremonial Mound in the midst of a
pitched planet-space battle! Under such circumstances, missiles were known to fall astray—such as into civilian towns, or
even neutral ground.

Too bad! There would be commiseration, of course. Such
a pity. But those were the fortunes of war!

98

Uthacalthing

No longer did he have to hold secret the yearnings in his
heart, or keep contained his deep-stored reservoir of feelings.
It did not matter if alien detectors pinpointed his psychic
emanations, for they surely would know where to find him,
when the time came.

At dawn, while the east grew gray with the cloud-shrouded
sun, Uthacalthing walked along the dew-covered slopes and
reached out with everything he had.

The miracle of some days back had burst the chrysalis of
his soul. Where he thought only winter would forever reign,
now bright shoots burst forth. To both humans and Tymbrimi,
love was considered the greatest power. But there was, indeed, something to be said for *irony*, as well.

I live, and kenn the world as beautiful.

He poured all of his craft into a glyph which floated,

delicate and light, above his wafting tendrils. To be brought to this place, so near where his schemes began . . . and to witness how all his jests had been turned around upon himself, giving him all he had wanted, but in such amazing ways . . .

Dawn brought color to the world. It was a winter land-and seascape of barren orchards and tarp-covered ships. The waters of the bay wore lines of wind-flecked foam. And yet, the sun gave warmth.

He thought of the Universe, so strange, often bizarre, and so filled with danger and tragedy.

But also surprise.

Surprise . . . the blessing that tells one that this is real—he spread his arms to encompass it all—*that even the most imaginative of us could not have made all of this up within his own mind*.

He did not set the glyph free. It cast loose as if of its own accord and rose unaffected by the morning winds, to drift wherever chance might take it.

Later came long consultations with the Grand Examiner, with Kault and Cordwainer Appelbe. They all sought his advice. He tried not to disappoint them.

Around noon Robert Oneagle drew him aside and brought up again the idea of escape. The young human wanted to break out of their confinement on the Ceremonial Mound and head off with Fiben to cause the Gubru grief. They all knew of the fighting in the mountains, and Robert wanted to help Athaclena in any way possible.

Uthacalthing sympathized. "But you underestimate yourself in thinking you could ever do this, my son," he told the young man.

Robert blinked. "What do you mean?"

"I mean that the Gubru military are now well aware of how dangerous you and Fiben are. And perhaps through some small efforts of my own they include me on their list. Why do you think they maintain such patrols, when they must have other pressing needs?"

He motioned at the craft which cruised just beyond the perimeter of Institute territory. No doubt even the coolant lines leading to the power stations were watched by expensive drones of deadly sophistication. Robert had suggested

using handmade gliders, but the enemy was surely wise even
to that wolfling trick by now. They had had expensive lessons.

"In this way we help Athaclena," Uthacalthing said. "By
thumbing our noses at the enemy, by smiling as if we have
thought of something special which they have not. By frightening creatures who deserve what they get for having no
sense of humor."

Robert made no outward gesture to show that he understood. But to Uthacalthing's delight he recognized the glyph
the young man formed, a simple version of *kiniwullun*. He
laughed. Obviously, it was one Robert had learned—and
earned—from Athaclena.

"Yes, my strange adopted son. We must keep the Gubru
painfully aware that boys will do what boys do."

It was later, though, toward sunset, that Uthacalthing
stood up suddenly in his dark tent and walked outside. He
stared again to the east, tendrils waving, seeking.

Somewhere, out there, he knew his daughter was thinking furiously. Something, some news perhaps, had come to
her. And now she was concentrating as if her life depended
on it.

Then the brief, fey moment of linkage passed. Uthacalthing
turned, but he did not go back to his own shelter. Instead, he
wandered a little north and pulled aside the flap of Robert's
tent. The human looked up from his reading, the light of the
datawell casting a wild expression onto his face.

"I believe there actually is one way by which we could
get off of this mountain," he told the human. "At least for a
little while."

"Go on," Robert said.

Uthacalthing smiled. "Did I not once say to you—or was
it your mother—that all things begin and end at the Library?"

99

Galactics

Matters were dire. Consensus was falling apart irreparably, and the Suzerain of Propriety did not know how to heal the breach.

The Suzerain of Cost and Caution had nearly withdrawn into itself. The bureaucracy operated on inertia, without guidance.

And their vital third, their strength and virility, the Suzerain of Beam and Talon, would not answer their entreaties for a conclave. It seemed, in fact, bound and determined upon a course that might bring on not only their own destruction but possibly vast devastation to this frail world as well. If that occurred, the blow to the already tottering honor of this expedition, this branch of the clan of Gooksyu-Gubru, would be more than one could stand.

And yet, what could the Suzerain of Propriety do? The Roost Masters, distracted with problems closer to home, offered no useful advice. They had counted on the expedition Triumvirate to meld, to molt, and to reach a consensus of wisdom. But the Molt had gone wrong, desperately wrong. And there was no wisdom to offer them.

The Suzerain of Propriety felt a sadness, a hopelessness, that went beyond that of a leader riding a ship headed for shoals—it was more that of a priest doomed to oversee sacrilege.

The loss was intense and personal, and quite ancient at the heart of the race. True, the feathers sprouting under its white down were now red. But there were names for Gubru queens who achieved their femaleness without the joyous consent and aid of two others, two who share with her the pleasure, the honor, the glory.

Her greatest ambition had come true, and it was a barren prospect, a lonely and bitter one.

The Suzerain of Propriety tucked her beak under her arm, and in the way of her own people, softly wept.

100

Athaclena

"Vampire plants," was how Lydia McCue summed it up. She stood watch with two of her Terragens Marines, their skins glistening under painted layers of monolayer camouflage. The stuff supposedly protected them from infrared detection and, one could hope, the enemy's new resonance detector as well.

Vampire plants? Athaclena thought. *Indeed. It is a good metaphor.*

She poured about a liter of a bright red fluid into the dark waters of a forest pool, where hundreds of small vines came together in one of the ubiquitous nutrient trading stations.

Elsewhere, far away, other groups were performing similar rituals in little glades. It reminded Athaclena of wolfling fairy tales, of magical rites in enchanted forests and mystical incantations. She would have to remember to tell her father of the analogy, if she ever got the chance.

"Indeed," she said to Lieutenant McCue. "My chims drained themselves nearly white to donate enough blood for our purposes. There are certainly more subtle ways to do this, but none possible in the time available."

Lydia answered with a grunt and a nod. The Earth woman was still in conflict with herself. Logically, she probably agreed that the results would have been catastrophic had Major Prathachulthorn been left in charge, weeks ago. Subsequent events had proven Athaclena and Robert right.

But Lieutenant McCue could not disassociate herself so easily from her oath. Until recently the two women had begun to become friends, talking for hours and sharing their different longings for Robert Oneagle. But now that the truth about the mutiny and kidnapping of Major Prathachulthorn was out, a gulf lay between them.

The red liquid swirled among the tiny rootlets. Clearly, the semi-mobile vines were already reacting, drawing in the new substances.

There had been no time for subtlety, only a brute force approach to the idea that had struck her suddenly, soon after hearing Sylvie's report. *Hemoglobin. The Gubru had detectors that can trace resonance against the primary constituent of Earthling blood. At such sensitivity, the devices must be frightfully expensive!*

A way had to be found to counteract the new weapon or she might be left the only sapient being in the mountains. The one possible approach had been drastic, and symbolic of the demands a nation made of its people. Her own unit of guerrillas now tottered around, so depleted by her demands for raw blood that some of the chims had changed her nickname. Instead of 'the general' they had taken to referring to Athaclena as 'the countess,' and then grimacing with outthrust canines.

Fortunately, there were still a few chim technicians—mostly those who had helped Robert devise little microbes to plague enemy machinery—who could help her with this slapdash experiment.

Bind hemoglobin molecules to trace substances sought by certain vines. Hope the new combination still meets their approval. And pray the vines transfer it along fast enough.

A chim messenger arrived and whispered to Lieutenant McCue. She, in turn, approached Athaclena.

"The major is nearly ready," the dark human woman told her. Casually, she added, "And our scouts say they detect aircraft heading this way."

Athaclena nodded.

"We are finished here. Let us depart. The next few hours will tell."

101

Galactics

"There! We note a concentration, gathering, accumulation of the impudent enemy. The wolflings flee in a predictable direction. And now we may strike, pounce, swoop to conquer!"

Their special detectors made plain the quarry's converging trails through the forest. The Suzerain of Beam and Talon spoke a command, and an elite brigade of Gubru soldiery stooped upon the little valley where their fleeing prey was trapped, at bay.

"Captives, hostages, new prisoners to question . . . these I want!"

102

Major Prathachulthorn

The bait was invisible. Their lure consisted of little more than a barely traceable flow of complex molecules, coursing through the intricate, lacy network of jungle vegetation. In fact, Major Prathachulthorn had no way of knowing for certain that it was there at all. He felt awkward laying enfilade and ambush on the slopes overlooking a series of small ponds in an otherwise unoccupied forest vale.

And yet, there was something symmetrical, almost poetic about the situation. If this trick by some chance actually worked, there would be the joy of battle on this morn.

And if it did not, then he intended to have the satisfaction of throttling a certain slender alien neck, whatever the effects on his career and his life.

"Feng!" he snapped at one of his Marines. "Don't scratch." The Marine corporal quickly checked to make sure he had not rubbed off any of the monolayer coating that gave his skin a sickly greenish cast. The new material had been mixed quickly, in hopes of blocking the hemoglobin resonance the enemy were using to track Terrans under the forest canopy. Of course, their intelligence on that matter might be completely wrong. Prathachulthorn had only the word of *chims*, and that damned Tym—

"Major!" someone whispered. It was a neo-chimpanzee trooper, looking even more uncomfortable in green-tinted fur. He motioned quickly from midway up a tall tree. Prathachulthorn acknowledged and sent a hand gesture rippling in both directions.

Well, he thought, *some of these local chims are turning into pretty fair irregulars, I'll admit.*

A series of sonic booms rocked the foliage on all sides, followed by the shriek of approaching aircraft. They swept up the narrow valley at treetop level, following the hilly terrain with computer-piloted precision. At just the right moment, Talon Soldiers and their accompanying drones spilled out of long troop carriers to fall serenely toward a certain jungle grove.

The trees there were unique in only one way, in their hunger for a certain trace chemical brought to them by far-reaching, far-trading vines. Only now those vines had delivered something else as well. Something drawn from Earthly veins.

"Wait," Prathachulthorn whispered. "Wait for the big boys."

Sure enough, soon they all felt the effects of approaching gravitics, and on a major scale. Over the horizon appeared a Gubru battleship, cruising serenely several hundred meters above.

Here was a target well worth anything they had to sacrifice. Up until now, though, the problem had been how to know in advance where one would come. Flicker-swivvers were wonderful weapons, but not very portable. One had to set them up well in advance. And surprise was essential.

"Wait," he murmured as the great vessel drew nearer. "Don't spook 'em."

Down below, the Talon Soldiers were already chirping in dismay, for no enemy awaited them, not even any chim civilians to capture and send above for questioning. At any moment, one of the troopers would surely guess the truth. Still, Major Prathachulthorn urged, "Wait just a minute more, until—"

One of the chim gunners must have lost patience. Suddenly, lightning lanced upward from the heights on the opposite side of the valley. In an instant, three more streaks converged. Prathachulthorn ducked and covered his head.

Brilliance seemed to penetrate from *behind,* through his skull. Waves of *déjà vu* alternated with surges of nausea, and for a moment it felt as if a tide of anomalous gravity were trying to lift him from the forest loam. Then the concussion wave hit.

It was some time before anyone was able to look up

again. When they did, they had to blink through clouds of
drifting dust and grit, past toppled trees and scattered vines.
A seared, flattened area told where the Gubru battle cruiser
had hovered, only moments ago. A rain of red-hot debris still
fell, setting off fires wherever the incandescent pieces landed.

Prathachulthorn grinned. He fired off a flare into the
air—the signal to advance.

Several of the enemy's grounded aircraft had been broken by the overpressure wave. Three, however, lifted off and
made for the sites where the missiles had been fired, screaming for vengeance. But their pilots did not realize they were
facing Terragens Marines now. It was amazing what a captured saber rifle could do in the right hands. Soon three more
burning patches smoldered on the valley floor.

Down below grim-faced chims moved forward, and combat soon became much more personal, a bloody struggle
fought with lasers and pellet guns, with crossbows and arbalests.

When it came down to hand-to-hand, Prathachulthorn
knew that they had won.

I cannot leave all of the close-in stuff to these locals, he
thought. That was how he came to join the chase through the
forest, while the Gubru rear guard furiously tried to cover
the survivors' escape. And for as long as they lived thereafter, the chims who saw it talked about what they saw:
a pale green figure in loin cloth and beard, swinging through
the trees, meeting fully armed Talon Soldiers with knife and
garrote. There seemed to be no stopping him, and indeed,
nothing living withstood him.

It was a damaged battle drone, brought back into partial
operation by self-repair circuitry—perhaps making a logical
connection between the final collapse of the Gubru forces and
this fearsome creature who seemed to take such joy in battle.
Or maybe it was nothing more than a final burst of mechanical and electrical reflex.

He went as he would have wanted to, wearing a bitter
grin, with his hands around a feathered throat, throttling one
more hateful thing that did not belong in the world he
thought ought to be.

103

Athaclena

So, she thought as the excited chim messenger gasped forth the joyous news of total victory. On any scale, this was the insurgents' greatest coup.

In a sense, Garth *herself became our greatest ally. Her injured but still subtly powerful web of life.*

The Gubru had been lured by fragments of chim and human hemoglobin, carried to one site by the ubiquitous transfer vines. Frankly, Athaclena was surprised their makeshift plan had worked. Its success proved just how foolish had been the enemy's overdependence on sophisticated hardware.

Now we must decide what to do next.

Lieutenant McCue looked up from the battle report the winded chim messenger had brought and met Athaclena's eyes. The two women shared a moment's silent communion. "I'd better get going," Lydia said at last. "There'll be reconsolidation to organize, captured equipment to disburse . . . and I am now in command."

Athaclena nodded. She could not bring herself to mourn Major Prathachulthorn. But she acknowledged the man for what he had been. A warrior.

"Where do you think they will strike next?" she asked.

"I couldn't begin to guess, now that their main method of tracking us has been blown. They act as if they haven't much time." Lydia frowned pensively. "Is it certain the Thennanin fleet is on its way here?" Lydia asked.

"The Uplift Institute officials speak about it openly on the airwaves. The Thennanin come to claim their new clients. And as part of their arrangement with my father and with

Earth, they are bound to help expel the Gubru from this system."

Athaclena was still quite in awe over the extent to which her father's scheme had worked. When the crisis began, nearly one Garth year ago, it had been clear that neither Earth nor Tymbrim would be able to help this faraway colony. And most of the "moderate" Galactics were so slow and judicious that there was little hope of persuading one of those clans to intervene. Uthacalthing had hoped to fool the Thennanin into doing the job instead—pitting Earth's enemies against each other.

The plan had worked beyond Uthacalthing's expectations because of one factor her father had not know of. *The gorillas*. Had their mass migration to the Ceremonial Mound been triggered by the *s'ustru'thoon* exchange, as she had earlier thought? Or was the Institute's Grand Examiner correct to declare that fate itself arranged for this new client race to be at the right time and place to choose? Somehow, Athaclena felt sure there was more to it than anyone knew, or perhaps ever would know.

"So the Thennanin are coming to chase out the Gubru." Lydia seemed uncertain what to make of the situation. "Then we've won, haven't we? I mean, the Gubru can't hold them off indefinitely. Even if it were possible militarily, they'd lose so much face across the Five Galaxies that even the moderates would finally get upset and mobilize."

The Earth woman's perceptiveness was impressive. Athaclena nodded. "Their situation would seem to call for negotiation. But that assumes logic. The Gubru military, I'm afraid, is behaving irrationally."

Lydia shivered. "Such an enemy is often far more dangerous than a rational opponent. He doesn't act out of intelligent self-interest."

"My father's last call indicated that the Gubru are badly divided," Athaclena said. The broadcasts from Institute Territory were now the guerrillas' best source of information. Robert and Fiben and Uthacalthing had all taken turns, contributing powerfully to the mountain fighters' morale and surely adding to the invader's severe irritation.

"We'll have to act under the assumption the gloves are off then." The woman Marine sighed. "If Galactic opinion doesn't matter to them, they may even turn to using space

weaponry down here on the planet. We'd better disperse as
widely as possible."

"Hmm, yes." Athaclena nodded. "But if they use burn-
ers or hell bombs, all is lost anyway. From such weapons we
cannot hide.

"I cannot command your troops, lieutenant, but I would
rather die in a bold gesture—one which might help stop this
madness once and for all—than end my life burying my head
in the sand, like one of your Earthly oysters."

Despite the seriousness of the proposition, Lydia McCue
smiled. And a touch of appreciative irony danced along the
edges of her simple aura. "Ostriches," the Earth woman
corrected gently. "It's big birds called ostriches that bury
their heads.

"Now why don't you tell me what you have in mind."

104

Galactics

Buoult of the Thennanin inflated his ridgecrest to its
maximum height and preened his shining elbow spikes before
stepping out upon the bridge of the great warship, *Athanasfire*.
There, beside the grand display, where the disposition of the
fleet lay spread out in sparkling colors, the human delegation awaited him. Their leader, an elderly female whose pale
hair tendrils still gleamed in places with the color of a yellow
sun, bowed at a prim, correct angle. Buoult replied with a
precise waistbend of his own. He gestured toward the display.

"Admiral Alvarez, I assume you can perceive for yourself
that the last of the enemy's mines have been cleared. I am
ready to transmit to the Galactic Institute for Civilized War-

fare our declaration that the Gubru interdiction of this system has been lifted by *force majeur*."

"That is good to hear," the woman said. Her human-style smile—a suggestive baring of teeth—was one of their easier gestures to interpret. One as experienced with Galactic affairs as the legendary Helene Alvarez surely knew the effect the wolfling expression often had on others. She must have made a conscious decision to use it.

Well, such subtle intimidations played an acceptable role in the complex game of bluff and negotiation. Buoult was honest enough to admit that he did it too. It was why he had inflated his towering crest before entering.

"It will be good to see Garth again," Alvarez added. "I only hope we aren't the proximate cause of yet another holocaust on that unfortunate world."

"Indeed, we shall endeavor to avoid that at all costs. And if the worst happens—if this band of Gubru are completely out of control—then their entire nasty clan shall pay for it."

"I care little about penalties and compensation. There are people and an entire frail ecosphere at risk here."

Buoult withheld comment. *I must be more careful,* he thought. *It is not meet for others to remind Thennanin— defenders of all Potential—of the duty to protect such places as Garth.*

It was especially galling to be chided righteously by wolflings.

And from now on they will be at our elbows, carping and criticizing, and we will have to listen, for they will be stage consorts to one of our clients. It is only one price we must pay for this treasure Kault found for us.

The humans were pressing negotiations hard, as was to be expected from a clan as desperate for allies as they. Already Thennanin forces had withdrawn from all areas of conflict with Earth and Tymbrim. But the Terragens were demanding much more than that in exchange for help managing and uplifting the new client race called "Gorilla."

In effect, they were demanding that the great clan of the Thennanin ally itself with forlorn and despised wolflings and bad-boy prankster Tymbrimi! This at a time when the horrible Soro–Tandu alliance appeared to be unstoppable out on the starlanes. Why, to do so might conceivably risk annihilation for the Thennanin themselves!

If it were up to Buoult, who had had enough of Earthlings to last him a lifetime, the choice would be to tell them to go to Ifni's Hell and seek their allies there.

But it was not up to Buoult. There had long been a strong minority streak of sympathy for Earthclan, back home. Kault's coup, allowing the Great Clan to achieve another treasured laurel of patronhood, could win that faction government soon. Under such circumstances, Buoult figured it wise to keep his own opinions to himself.

One of his undercommanders approached and saluted. "We have determined the positions taken up by the Gubru defense flotilla," he reported. "They are clustered quite close to the planet. Their dispersement is unusual. Our battle computers are finding it very hard to crack."

Hmm, yes, Buoult thought on examining the close-in display. *A brilliant arrangement of limited forces. Even original, perhaps. How unlike the Gubru.*

"No matter," he huffed. "Even if there is no subtle way, they will nonetheless see that we came with more than adequate firepower to do the job by brute force if necessary. They will concede. They must concede."

"Of course they must," the human admiral agreed. But she did not sound convinced. In fact, she seemed worried.

"We are ready to approach to fail-safe envelopment," the officer of the deck reported.

Buoult nodded quickly. "Good. Proceed. From there we can contact the enemy and announce our intentions."

Tension built as the armada advanced closer to the system's modest yellow sun. Although the Thennanin claimed proudly to possess no psychic powers, Buoult seemed to *feel* the gaze of the Earthling woman upon him, and he wondered how it was possible that he found her so intimidating.

She is only a wolfling, he reminded himself.

"Shall we resume our discussions, commander?" Admiral Alvarez asked at last.

He had no choice but to comply, of course. It would be best if much was decided before they arrived and the siege manifesto was read aloud.

Still, Buoult planned to sign no agreements until he had a chance to confer with Kault. That Thennanin had a reputation for vulgarity and, well, *frivolity*, that had won him exile to this backwater world. But now he appeared to have achieved unprecedented miracles. His political power back home would be great.

Buoult wanted to tap Kault's expertise, his apparent knack at dealing with these infuriating creatures.

His aides and the human delegation filed out of the bridge toward the meeting room. But before Buoult left he glanced one more time back at the situation tank and the deadly-looking Gubru battle array. Air noisily escaped his breathing slits.

What are the avians planning? he wondered. *What shall I do if these Gubru prove to be insane?*

105

Robert

In some parts of Port Helenia, there were more guard drones than ever, protecting their masters' domains rigorously, lashing out at anyone who passed too near.

Elsewhere, however, it was almost as if a revolution had already taken place. The invader's posters lay tattered in the gutters. Above one busy street corner Robert glimpsed a new mural that had recently been erected in place of Gubru propaganda. Painted in the style called Focalist Realism, it depicted a family of gorillas staring with dawning but hopeful sentience out upon a glowing horizon. Protectively standing beside them, showing the way to that wonderful future, was a pair of idealized, high-browed neo-chimpanzees.

Oh, yes, there had also been a human and a Thennanin in the picture, vague and in the background. Robert thought it really nice of the artist to have remembered to include them.

The heavily guarded shuttle he was in passed through the intersection too quickly to see much detail, but he thought the rendering of the female chim hadn't quite done Gailet justice. *Fiben*, on the other hand, ought to be flattered.

Soon the "free" parts of town were behind them, and they passed westward into areas patrolled with strict military discipline. When they landed their Talon Soldier guards hurried outside and stood watch as Robert and Uthacalthing left the shuttle to climb the ramp leading to the shining new Branch Library.

"This is an expensive setup, isn't it?" he asked the Tymbrimi Ambassador. "Do we get to keep it if the Thennanin manage to kick the birds out?"

Uthacalthing shrugged. "Probably. And maybe the Ceremonial Mound as well. Your clan is due reparations, certainly."

"But you have your doubts."

Uthacalthing stood in the vast entranceway surveying the vaulted chamber and the towering cubic data store within. "It is just that I think it would be unwise to count your chickens before they have met the rooster."

Robert understood Uthacalthing's point. Even defeat for the Gubru might come at unthinkable cost.

"It's counting one's *eggs* before they're *laid*," he told the Tymbrimi, who was always anxious to improve his grasp of Anglic metaphors. This time, however, Uthacalthing didn't thank Robert. His wide-spread eyes seemed to flash as he looked back, sidelong. "Think about it," he said.

Soon Uthacalthing was deep in conversation with the Kanten Chief Librarian. At a loss to follow their rapid, inflected Galactic, Robert started a circuit of the new Library, taking its measure and looking at its current users.

Except for a few members of the Grand Examiner's team, all of the occupants were avians. The Gubru present were divided by a gulf he could *kenn*, as well as see. Nearly two thirds of them clustered over to the left. They cooed and cast disapproving glances at the smaller group, which consisted almost entirely of soldiers. The military did not give off happy vibrations, but they hid it well, strutting about their tasks with crisp efficiency, returning their peers' disapproval with arrogant disdain.

Robert made no effort to avoid being seen. The wave of stares he attracted was pleasing. They obviously knew who he was. If just passing near caused an interruption in their work, so much the better.

Approaching one cluster of Gubru—by their ribbons obviously members of the priestly Caste of Propriety—he bowed to an angle he hoped was correct and grinned as the entire offended gaggle was forced to form up and reply in kind.

Finally Robert came upon a data station formatted in a way he understood. Uthacalthing was still immersed in conversation with the Librarian, so Robert decided to see what he could find out on his own.

He made very little progress. The enemy had obviously set up safeguards to prevent the unauthorized from accessing information about near-space, or the presumably converging battle fleets of the Thennanin. Still, Robert kept on trying. Time passed as he explored the current data net, finding out where the invaders had set up their blocks.

So intense was his concentration that it took a while before he grew aware that something had changed in the Library. Automatic sound dampers had kept the growing hubbub from intruding on his concentration, but when he looked up at last Robert saw that the Gubru were in an uproar. They waved their downy arms and formed tight clusters around holo-tanks. Most of the soldiers had simply vanished from sight.

What on Garth has gotten into them? he wondered.

Robert didn't imagine the Gubru would welcome him peering over their shoulders. He felt frustrated. Whatever was happening, it sure had them perturbed!

Hey! Robert thought. *Maybe it's on the local news.*

Quickly he used his own screen to access a public video station. Until recently censorship had been severe, but during the last few days, as soldiers were called away to combat duty, the networks had fallen under the control of the Caste of Cost and Caution. Those glum, apathetic bureaucrats now hardly enforced even modest discipline.

The tank flickered, then cleared to show an excited chim reporter.

". . . and so, at latest reports, it seems the surprise offensive from the Mulun hasn't yet engaged the occupation forces. The Gubru seem unable to agree on how to answer the manifesto of the approaching forces. . . ."

Robert wondered, had the Thennanin made their pronouncement of intent already? That had not been expected

for a couple of days at least. Then one word caught in his
mind.

From the *Mulun?*

". . . We'll now rebroadcast the statement read just five minutes ago by the joint commanders of the army right now marching
on Port Helenia."

The view in the holo-tank shifted. The chim announcer
was replaced by a recently recorded image showing three
figures standing against a forest background. Robert blinked.
He knew these faces, two of them intimately. One was a chen
named Benjamin. The other two were women he loved.

". . . and so we challenge our oppressors. In combat we have
behaved well, under the dicta of the Galactic Institute for Civilized Warfare. This cannot be said of our enemies. They have
used criminal means and have allowed harm to noncombatant
fallow species native to a fragile world.

"Worst of all, they have *cheated.*"

Robert gaped. The image panned back to show platoons
of chims—bearing a motley assortment of weapons—trooping
forth from the forest out into the open, accompanied by a few
fierce-eyed humans. The one speaking into the camera was
Lydia McCue, Robert's human lover. But Athaclena stood
next to her, and in his alien consort's eyes he saw and knew
who had written the words.

And he knew, without any doubt, whose idea this was.

"We demand, therefore, that they send forth their best soldiers, armed as we are armed, to meet our champions out in the
open, in the Valley of the Sind. . . ."

"Uthacalthing," he said, hoarsely. Then again, louder.
"Uthacalthing!"

The noise suppressors had been developed by a hundred
million generations of librarians. But in all that time there
had been only a few wolfling races. For just an instant the
vast chamber echoed before dampers shut down the impolite
vibrations and imposed hushed quiet once again.

There was nothing, however, to be done about running
in the halls.

106

Gailet

"Recombinant Rats!" Fiben cried upon hearing the beginnings of the declaration. They watched a portable holo set up on the slopes of the Ceremonial Mound.

Gailet gestured for silence. "Be quiet, Fiben. Let me hear the rest of it."

But the meaning of the message had been obvious from the first few sentences. Columns of irregulars, wearing makeshift uniforms of homespun cloth, marched steadily across open, winter-barren fields. Two squads of *horse cavalry* skirted the ragged army's perimeter, like escapees from some pre-Contact flatmovie. The marching chims grinned nervously and watched the skies, fondling their captured or mountain-made weapons. But there was no mistaking their attitude of grim resolve.

As the cameras panned back, Fiben did a quick count. "That's everybody," he said in awe. "I mean, allowing for recent casualties, it's everybody who's had any training or would be any good at all in a fight. It's all or nothing." He shook his head. "Clip my blue card if I can figure what she hopes to accomplish."

Gailet glanced up at him. "Some blue card," she sniffed. "And I'd have to say she knows *exactly* what she's doing, Fiben."

"But the city rebels were *slaughtered* out on the Sind."

She shook her head. "That was then. We didn't know the score. We hadn't achieved any respect or status. Anyway, there weren't any witnesses.

"But the mountain forces have won victories. They've been acknowledged. And now the Five Galaxies are watching."

Gailet frowned. "Oh, Athaclena knows what she's doing. I just didn't know things were this desperate."

They sat quietly for a moment longer, watching the insurgents advance slowly across orchards and winter-barren fields. Then Fiben let out another exclamation. "What?" Gailet asked. She looked where he pointed in the tank, and it was her turn to hiss in surprise.

There, carrying a saber rifle along with the other chim soldiers, strode someone they both knew. Sylvie did not seem uncomfortable with her weapon. In fact, she appeared an island of almost zenlike calm in the sea of nervous neo-chimpanzees.

Who would've figured it? Gailet thought. *Who would've thought that about her?*

They watched together. There was little else they could do.

107

Galactics

"This must be handled with delicacy, care, rectitude!" the Suzerain of Propriety proclaimed. "If necessary, we must meet them one on one."

"But the expense!" wailed the Suzerain of Cost and Caution. "The losses to be expected!"

Gently, the high priest bent over from her perch and crooned to her junior.

"Consensus, consensus. . . . Share with me a vision of harmony and wisdom. Our clan has lost much here, and stands in dire jeopardy of losing far more. But we have not yet forfeited the one thing that will maintain us even at night, even in darkness—our nobility. Our honor."

Together, they began to sway. A melody rose, one with a single lyric.

"*Zoooon. . . .*"

Now if only their strong third were here! Coalescence seemed so near. A message had been sent to the Suzerain of Beam and Talon urging that he return to them, join them, become one with them at last.

How, she wondered. *How could he resist knowing, concluding, realizing at last that it is his fate to be my male? Can an individual be so obstinate?*

The three of us can yet be happy!

But a messenger arrived with news that brought despair. The battle cruiser in the bay had lifted off and was heading inland with its escorts. The Suzerain of Beam and Talon had decided to act. No consensus would restrain him.

The high priest mourned.

We could have been happy.

108

Athaclena

"Well, this may be our answer," Lydia commented resignedly.

Athaclena looked up from the awkward, unfamiliar task of controlling a horse. Mostly, she let her beast simply follow the others. Fortunately, it was a gentle creature who responded well to her coronal singing.

She peered in the direction pointed out by Lydia McCue, where scattered clouds and haze partially obscured the western horizon. Already many of the chims were gesturing that way. Then Athaclena also saw the glint of flying craft. And she *kenned* the approaching forces. Confusion . . . determination . . . fanaticism . . . regret . . . loathing . . . a turmoil of alien-tinged feelings bombarded her from the ships. But one thing was clear above all.

The Gubru were coming with vast and overwhelming strength.

The distant dots took shape. "I believe you are right, Lydia," Athaclena told her friend. "It seems we have our answer."

The woman Marine swallowed. "Shall I order a dispersal? Maybe a few of us can get away." She sounded doubtful.

Athaclena shook her head. A sad glyph formed. "No. We must play this out. Call all units together. Have the cavalry bring everyone to yonder hilltop."

"Any particular reason we should make things easy for them?"

Above Athaclena's waving tendrils the glyph refused to become one of despair. "Yes," she answered. "There is a reason. The best reason in all the world."

109

Galactics

The stoop-colonel of Talon Soldiers watched the ragged army of insurgents on a holo-screen and listened as its high commander screamed in delight.

"They shall burn, shall smoke, shall curl into cinders under our fire!"

The stoop-colonel felt miserable. This was intemperate language, bereft of proper consideration of consequences.

The stoop-colonel knew, deep within, that even the most brilliant military plans would eventually come to nothing if they did not take into account such matters as cost, caution, and propriety. Balance was the essence of consensus, the foundation of survival.

And yet the Earthlings' challenge had been honorable! It might be ignored. Or even met with a decent excess of force. But what the leader of the military now planned was unpleasant, his methods extreme.

The stoop-colonel noted that it had already come to think of the Suzerain of Beam and Talon as "he." The Suzerain of Beam and Talon was a brilliant leader who had inspired his followers, but now, as a prince, he seemed blind to the truth.

To even think of the commander in this critical way caused the stoop-colonel physical pain. The conflict was deep and visceral.

The doors to the main lift opened and out onto the command dais stepped a trio of white-plumed messengers—a priest, a bureaucrat, and one of the officers who had deserted to the other Suzerains. They strode toward the admiral and proffered a box crafted of richly inlaid wood. Shivering, the Suzerain of Beam and Talon ordered it opened.

Within lay a single, luxuriant feather, colored iridescent red along its entire length except at the very tip.

"Lies! Deceptions! An obvious hoax!" the admiral cried, and knocked the box and its contents out of the startled messengers' arms.

The stoop-colonel stared as the feather drifted in eddies from the air circulators before fluttering down to the deck. It felt like sacrilege to leave it lying there, and yet the stoop-colonel dared not move to pick it up.

How could the commander ignore *this*? How could he refuse to accept the rich, blue shades spreading now at the roots of his own down? "The Molt can reverse again," the Suzerain of Beam and Talon cried out. "It can happen if we win victory at arms!"

Only now what he proposed would not be victory, it would be slaughter.

"The Earthlings are gathering, clustering, coming together upon a single hillmount," one of the aides reported. "They offer, display, present us with a single, simple target!"

The stoop-colonel sighed. It did not take a priest to tell

what this meant. The Earthlings, realizing that there would
be no fair fight, had come together to make their demise
simple. Since their lives were already forfeit, there was only
one possible reason.

*They do it in order to protect the frail ecosystem of this
world. The purpose of their lease-grant was, after all, to save
Garth.* In their very helplessness the stoop-colonel saw and
tasted bitter defeat. They had forced the Gubru to choose
flatly between power and honor.

The crimson feather had the stoop-colonel captivated, its
colors doing things to its very blood. "I shall prepare my
Talon Soldiers to go down and meet the Terrans," the stoop-
colonel suggested, hopefully. "We shall drop down, advance,
attack in equal numbers, lightly armed, without robots."

"No! You must not, will not, shall not! I have carefully
assigned roles for all my forces. I need, require them all
when we deal with the Thennanin! There shall be no wasteful
squandering.

"Now, heed me! At this moment, this instant, the Earthlings below shall feel, bear, sustain my righteous vengeance!"
the Suzerain of Beam and Talon cried out. "I command that the
locks be removed from the weapons of mass destruction. We
shall sear this valley, and the next, and the next, until all life
in these mountains—"

The order was never finished. The stoop-colonel of Talon
Soldiers blinked once, then dropped its saber pistol to the
deck. The clatter was followed by a double thump as first the
head and then the body of the former military commander
tumbled as well.

The stoop-colonel shuddered. Lying there, the body
clearly showed those iridescent shades of royalty. The admiral's blood mixed with the blue princely plumage and spread
across the deck to join, at last, with the single crimson feather
of his queen.

The stoop-colonel told its stunned subordinates, "Inform, tell, transmit to the Suzerain of Propriety that I have
placed myself under arrest, pending the outcome, result,
determination of my fate.

"Refer to Their Majesties what it is that must be done."

For a long, uncertain time—completely on inertia—the
task force continued toward the hilltop where the Earthlings
had gathered, waiting. Nobody spoke. On the command dais
there was hardly any movement at all.

*   *   *

When the report arrived it was like confirmation of what they had known for some time. A pall of mourning had already settled over the Gubru administration compound. Now the former Suzerain of Propriety and the former Suzerain of Cost and Caution crooned together a sad dirge of loss.

Such great hopes, such fine prospects they had had on setting out for this place, this planet, this forlorn speck in empty space. The Roost Masters had so carefully planned the right oven, the correct crucible, and just the right ingredients— three of the best, three fine products of genetic manipulation, their very finest.

We were sent to bring home a consensus, the new queen thought. *And that consensus has come*.

It is ashes. We were wrong to think this was the time to strive for greatness.

Oh, many factors had brought this about. If only the first candidate of Cost and Caution had not died. . . . If only they had not been fooled *twice* by the trickster Tymbrimi and his "Garthlings." . . . If only the Earthlings had not proven so wolfishly clever at capitalizing on every weakness—this last maneuver for instance, forcing Gubru soldiery to choose between dishonor and regicide. . . .

But there are no accidents, she knew. *They could not have taken advantage if we had not shown flaws*.

That was the consensus they would report to the Roost Masters. That there were weaknesses, failures, mistakes which this doomed expedition had tested and brought to light.

It would be valuable information.

Let that console me for my sterile, infertile eggs, she thought, as she comforted her sole remaining partner and lover.

To the messengers she gave one brief command.

"Convey to the stoop-colonel our pardon, our amnesty, our forgiveness. And have the task force recalled to base."

Soon the deadly cruisers had turned about and were headed homeward, leaving the mountains and the valley to those who seemed to want them so badly.

110

Athaclena

The chims stared in amazement as Death seemed to change its mind. Lydia McCue blinked up at the retreating cruisers and shook her head. "You knew," she said as she turned to look at Athaclena. Again she accused. "You knew!"

Athaclena smiled. Her tendrils traced faint, sad imprints in the air.

"Let us just say that I thought there was a possibility," she said at last. "Had I been wrong, this would still have been the honorable thing to do.

"I am very glad, however, to find out that I was right."

PART SEVEN

Wolflings

*Not a whit, we defy augury; there's a special providence
in the fall of a sparrow. If it be now, 'tis not to come;
if it be not to come, it will be now;
if it be not now, yet it will come;
the readiness is all.*

Hamlet, Act V, scene ii

111

Fiben

"Goodall, how I hate ceremonies!"

The remark brought a jab in his ribs. "Quit fidgeting, Fiben. The whole world is watching!"

He sighed and made an effort to sit up straight. Fiben could not help remembering Simon Levin and the last time they had stood parade together, just a short distance from here. *Some things never change*, he thought. Now it was Gailet nagging him to try to look dignified.

Why did everyone who loved him also incessantly try to correct his posture? He muttered. "If they wanted clients who looked elegant, they'd have uplif—"

The words cut short in an "oof!" of exhaled breath. Gailet's elbows were sure a lot sharper than Simon's had been. Fiben's nostrils flared and he chuffed irritably, but he kept quiet. So prim in her well-cut new uniform, *she* might be glad to be here, but had anyone asked *him* if he wanted a damn medal? No, of course not. Nobody ever asked him.

At last the triple-cursed Thennanin admiral finished his droning, boring homily on virtue and tradition, garnering scattered applause. Even Gailet seemed relieved as the hulking Galactic returned to his seat. Alas, so many others also seemed to want to make speeches.

The mayor of Port Helenia, back from internment on the islands, praised the doughty urban insurrectionists and proposed that his chim deputy ought to take over City Hall more often. That got him hearty applause . . . and probably a few more chim votes, come next election, Fiben thought cynically.

Cough*Quinn'3, the Uplift Institute Examiner, summa-

rized the agreement recently signed by Kault on behalf of the
Thennanin, and for Earthclan by the legendary Admiral
Alvarez, under which the fallow species formerly called goril-
las would henceforth enter upon the long adventure of sapiency.
The new Galactic citizens—already widely known as "The
Client Race That Chose"—would be given leasehold on the
Mountains of Mulun for fifty thousand years. Now they were,
in truth, "Garthlings."

In return for technical assistance from Earth, and fallow
gorilla genetic stock, the mighty clan of the Thennanin would
also undertake to defend the Terran leasehold of Garth, plus
five other human and Tymbrimi colony worlds. They would
not interfere directly in conflicts now raging with the Soro
and Tandu and other fanatic clans, but easing pressure on
those fronts would allow desperately needed help to go to the
homeworlds.

And the Thennanin themselves were no longer enemies
of the trickster–wolfling alliance. That fact alone was worth
the power of great armadas.

We've done what we can, and more, Fiben thought.
Until this point, it had seemed that the great majority of
Galactic "moderates" would simply sit aside and let the fanatics have their way. Now there was some hope that the apparent "inevitable tide of history" that was said to doom all
wolfling clans would not be seen as quite so unstoppable.
Sympathy for the underdogs had grown as a result of events
here on Garth.

Whether there actually were more allies to be won,
more magic tricks to be pulled, Fiben couldn't predict. But
he was pretty sure the final outcome would be decided thousands of parsecs away from here. Perhaps on old mother
Earth herself.

When Megan Oneagle began speaking Fiben realized it
was finally time to get through the morning's worst unpleas-
antness.

". . . will turn out to be a total loss if we do not learn
from months such as those we have just passed through. After
all, what is the use of hard times if they do not make us
wiser? For what did our honored dead give up their lives?"

The Planetary Coordinator coughed for a brief moment
and rustled her old-fashioned paper notes.

"We shall propose modification of the probation system,
which causes resentments the enemy were able to exploit.

We'll endeaver to use the new Library facilities for the benefit of all. And we certainly shall service and maintain the
equipment on the Ceremonial Mound, against the day when
peace returns and it can be used for its proper purpose, the
celebration of status the race of *Pan argonostes* so richly
deserves.

"And most important of all, we shall use Gubru reparations to finance resumption of our major job here on Garth,
reversing the decline of this planet's frail ecosphere, using
hard-won knowledge to halt the downward spiral and return
this, our adopted home, to its proper task—the task of breeding wonderful species diversity, the wellspring of all sentience.

"More of these plans will be presented for public discussion over the coming weeks." Megan looked up from her
notes and smiled. "But today we also have an added chore,
the pleasurable chore of honoring those who have made us
proud. Those who made it possible for us to stand here in
freedom today. It is our chance to show them how grateful
we are, and how very much they are loved."

You love me? Fiben asked silently. *Then let me outta
here!*

"Indeed," the Coordinator went on. "For some of our
chim citizens, recognition of their achievements will not finish with their lives or even with their places in history books,
but shall continue in the veneration with which we hold their
descendants, the future of their race."

From his left, Sylvie leaned forward far enough to look
across Fiben to Gailet on his right. The two shared a glance
and a grin.

Fiben sighed. At least he had persuaded Cordwainer
Appelbe to keep that damned upgrade to white card secret!
Fat lot of good it would do, of course. Green- and blue-status
chimmies from all over Port Helenia were after him already.
And Gailet and Sylvie were hardly any help at all. Why the hell
had he married them, anyway, if not for protection! Fiben
sniffed at the thought. Protection, indeed! He suspected the
two of them were interviewing and evaluating *candidates*.

Whether or not two species came from the same clan, or
even the same planet, there would always be some basics that
were different between them. Look at how much pre-Contact
humans had varied for simply cultural reasons. Of course
matters of love and reproduction among chims had to be
based on their own sexual heritage, from long before Uplift.

Still, there was enough human conditioning in Fiben to make him blush when he thought of what these two were going to put him through, now that they were close friends. *How did I let myself get into such a situation?*

Sylvie caught his eye and smiled sweetly. He felt Gailet's hand slip into his.

Well, he admitted with a sigh. *I guess it wasn't all that hard.*

They were reading names now, calling people up to accept their medals. But for a while Fiben felt just the three of them, sitting there together, as if the rest of the world were only an illusion. Actually, under his outward cynicism, he felt pretty good.

Robert Oneagle rose and stepped to the dais to accept his medal, looking much more comfortable in his uniform than Fiben felt. Fiben watched his human pal. *I've got to ask him who his tailor is.*

Robert had kept his beard, and the hard body won in rugged mountain living. He was no stripling any longer. In fact, he looked every inch a storybook hero.

Such nonsense. Fiben sniffed in disgust. *Gotta get that boy pissed drunk real soon. Beat him arm-wrestling. Save him from believing ever'thing the press writes.*

Robert's mother, on the other hand, seemed to have aged appreciably during the war. Over the last week Fiben had seen her repeatedly blink up at her tall, bronzed son, walking by with the grace of a jungle cat. She seemed proud but bewildered at the same time, as if the fairies had taken away her own child and left a changeling in its place.

It's called growing up, Megan.

Robert saluted and turned to head back toward his seat. As he passed in front of Fiben, his left hand made a quick motion, sign talk spelling out a single word.

Beer!

Fiben started laughing but choked it back as both Sylvie and Gailet turned to look at him sharply. No matter. It was good to know Robert felt as he did. Talon Soldiers were almost preferable to this ceremonial nonsense.

Robert returned to his seat next to Lieutenant Lydia McCue, whose own new decoration shone on the breast of her glistening dress tunic. The woman Marine sat erect and attentive to the proceedings, but Fiben could see what was invisible to the dignitaries and the crowd, that the toe of her boot had already lifted the cuff of Robert's trouser leg.

Poor Robert fought for composure. Peace, it seemed, offered its own travails. In its way, war was simpler.

Out in the crowd Fiben caught sight of a small cluster of humanoids, slender bipedal beings whose foxlike appearance was belied by fringes of gently waving tendrils just above their ears. Among the gathered Tymbrimi he easily picked out Uthacalthing and Athaclena. Both had declined every honor, every award. The people of Garth would have to wait until the two departed before erecting any memorials. That restraint, in a sense, would be their reward.

The ambassador's daughter had erased many of the facial and bodily modifications which had made her look so nearly human. She chatted in a low voice with a young male Tym who Fiben supposed could be called handsome, in an Eatee sort of way.

One would think the two young people—Robert and his alien consort—had readjusted completely to returning to their own folk. In fact, Fiben suspected each was now far more at ease with the opposite sex than they had been before the war. And yet . . .

He had seen them come together once, briefly, during one of the endless series of diplomatic receptions and conferences. Their heads had drawn quite near, and although no words were exchanged, Fiben was certain he saw or sensed *something* whirl lightly in the narrow space between them.

Whatever mates or lovers they would have in the future, it was clear that there was something Athaclena and Robert would always share, however much distance the Universe put between them.

Sylvie returned to her seat upon receiving her own commendation. Her dress could not quite hide the rounding of her figure. Another change Fiben would have to get used to pretty soon. He figured the Port Helenia Fire Department would probably have to hire more staff when that little kid started taking chemistry in school.

Gailet embraced Sylvie and then approached the podium herself. This time the cheers and applause were so sustained that Megan Oneagle had to motion for order.

But when Gailet spoke, it was not the rousing victory paean the crowd obviously expected. Her message, it seemed, was much more serious.

"Life is not fair," she said. The murmuring audience went silent as Gailet looked out across the assembly and seemed to meet their eyes as individuals. "Anyone who says it is, or even that it *ought* to be, is a fool or worse. Life can be *cruel*. Ifni's tricks can be capricious games of chance and probability. Or cold equations will cut you down if you make one mistake in space, or even step off the sidewalk at the wrong moment and try too quickly to match momentum with a bus.

"This is not the best of all possible worlds. For if it were, would there be illogic? Tyranny? Injustice? Even evolution, the wellspring of diversity and the heart of nature, is so very often a callous process, depending on death to bring about new life.

"No, life is not just. The Universe is not fair.

"And yet"—Gailet shook her head—"and yet, if it is not fair, at least it can be *beautiful*. Look around you now. There is a sermon greater than anything *I* can tell you. Look at this lovely, sad world that is our home. *Behold* Garth!"

The gathering took place upon the heights just south of the new Branch Library, in a meadow with an open view in all directions. To the west, all could see the Sea of Cilmar, its gray-blue surface colored with streaks of floating plant life and dotted with the spumelike trails of underwater creatures. Above lay the blue sky, scrubbed clean by the last storm of winter. Islands gleamed in the morning sunlight, like distant magical kingdoms.

On the north side of the meadow lay the beige tower of the Branch Library, its rayed spiral sigil embossed in sparkling stone. Freshly planted trees from two score worlds swayed gently in the breezes stroking over and around the great monolith, as timeless as its store of ancient knowledge.

To the east and south, beyond the busy waters of Aspinal Bay, lay the Valley of the Sind, already beginning to sprout with early green shoots, filling the air with the aromas of spring. And in the distance the mountains brooded, like sleeping titans ready to shrug off their brumal coats of snow.

"Our own petty lives, our species, even our clan, feel terribly important to us, but what are they next to this? This nursery of creation? *This* was what was worth fighting for. Protecting this"—she waved at the sea, the sky, the valley, and the mountains—"was our success.

"We Earthlings know better than most how unfair life

can be. Perhaps not since the Progenitors themselves has a clan understood so well. Our beloved human patrons nearly destroyed our more beloved Earth before they learned wisdom. Chims and dolphins and gorillas are only the beginnings of what would have been lost had they not grown up in time."

Her voice dropped, went hushed. "As the true Garthlings were lost, fifty thousand years ago, before they ever got the chance to blink in amazement at a night sky and wonder, for the first time, what that light was that glimmered in their minds."

Gailet shook her head. "No. The war to protect Potential has gone on for many aeons. It did not finish here. It may, indeed, never end."

When Gailet turned away there was at first only a long, stunned silence. The applause that followed was scattered and uncomfortable. But when she returned to Sylvie's and Fiben's embrace, Gailet smiled faintly.

"That's tellin' 'em," he said to her.

Then, inevitably, it was Fiben's turn. Megan Oneagle read a list of accomplishments that had obviously been gone over by some publicity department hack in order to hide how dirty and smelly and founded on simple dumb *luck* it all had been. Read aloud this way, it all sounded unfamiliar. Fiben hardly remembered doing half the stuff attributed to him.

It hadn't occurred to him to wonder why he'd been selected to go last. Probably, he assumed, it had been out of pure spite. *Following an act like Gailet will be pure murder*, he realized.

Megan called him forward. The hated shoes almost made him trip as he made his way to the dais. He saluted the Planetary Coordinator and tried to stand straight as she pinned on some garish medal and an insignia making him a reserve colonel in the Garth Defense Forces. The cheers of the crowd, especially the chims, made his ears feel hot, and it only got worse when, per Gailet's instructions, he grinned and waved for the cameras.

Okay, so maybe I can stand this, in small doses.

When Megan offered him the podium Fiben stepped forward. He had a speech of sorts, scrawled out on sheets in his pocket. But after listening to Gailet he decided he had better merely tell them all thank you and then sit down again.

Struggling to adjust the podium downward, he began. "There's just one thing I want to say, and that's—YOWP!"

He jerked as sudden electricity coursed through his left foot. Fiben hopped, grabbing the offended member, but then another shock hit his right foot! He let out a shriek. Fiben glanced down just in time to see a small blue brightness emerge slightly from beneath the podium and reach out now for *both* ankles. He leaped, hooting loudly, two meters into the air—alighting atop the wooden lectern.

Panting, it took him a moment to separate the panicked roaring in his ears from the hysterical cheering of the crowd. He blinked, rubbed his eyes, and stared.

Chims were standing on their folding chairs and waving their arms. They were jumping up and down, howling. Confusion reigned in the ranks of the polished militia honor guard. Even the humans were laughing and clapping uproariously.

Fiben glanced, dumbfounded, back at Gailet and Sylvie, and the pride in their eyes explained what it all meant.

They thought that was my prepared speech! he realized.

In retrospect he saw how perfect it was, indeed. It broke the tension and seemed an ideal commentary on how it felt to be at peace again.

Only I didn't write it, damnit!

He saw a worried look on the face of his lordship the mayor of Port Helenia. *No! Next they'll have me running for office! Who did this to me?*

Fiben searched the crowd and noticed immediately that one person was reacting differently, completely unsurprised. He stood out from the rest of the crowd partly due to his widely separated eyes and waving tendrils, but also because of his all too human expression of barely contained mirth.

And there was something else, some nonthing that Fiben somehow *sensed* was there, floating above the laughing Tymbrimi's wafting coronae.

Fiben sighed. And if looks alone could maim, Earth's greatest friends and allies would have to send a replacement ambassador to the posting on Garth right away.

When Athaclena winked at Fiben, it just confirmed his suspicions.

"Very funny," Fiben muttered caustically under his breath, even as he forced out another grin and waved again to the cheering crowds.

"T'rifically funny, Uthacalthing."

Postscript and Acknowledgments

First we feared the other creatures who shared the Earth with us. Then, as our power grew, we thought of them as our property, to dispose of however we wished. The most recent fallacy (a rather nice one, in comparison) has been to play up the idea that the animals are virtuous in their naturalness, and it is only humanity who is a foul, evil, murderous, rapacious canker on the lip of creation. This view says that the Earth and all her creatures would be much better off without us.

Only lately have we begun embarking upon a fourth way of looking at the world and our place in it. A new view of life.

If we evolved, one must ask, are we then not like other mammals in many ways? Ways we can learn from? And where we differ, should that not also teach us?

Murder, rape, the most tragic forms of mental illnesses—all of these we are now finding among the animals as well as ourselves. Brainpower only exaggerates the horror of these dysfunctions in us. It is not the root cause. The cause is the darkness in which we have lived. It is ignorance.

We do not have to see ourselves as monsters in order to teach an ethic of environmentalism. It is now well known that our very survival depends upon maintaining complex ecological networks and genetic diversity. If we wipe out Nature, we ourselves will die.

But there is one more reason to protect other species. One seldom if ever mentioned. Perhaps we *are* the first to talk and think and build and aspire, but we may not be the last. Others may follow us in this adventure.

Some day we may be judged by just how well we served, when alone we were Earth's caretakers.

The author gratefully acknowledges his debt to those who looked over this work in manuscript form, helping with everything from aspects of natural simian behavior to correcting bad grammar outside quotation marks.

I want to thank Anita Everson, Nancy Grace, Kristie McCue, Louise Root, Nora Brackenbury, and Mark Grygier for their valued insights. Professor John Lewis and Ruth Lewis also offered observations, as did Frank Catalano, Richard Spahl, Gregory Benford, and Daniel Brin. Thanks also to Steve Hardesty, Sharon Sosna, Kim Bard, Rick Sturm, Don Coleman, Sarah Bartter, and Bob Goold.

To Lou Aronica, Alex Berman, and Richard Curtis, my gratitude for their patience.

And to our hairy cousins, I offer my apologies. Here, have a banana and a beer.

David Brin
November 1986

THE EXTRAORDINARY WORLDS OF
DAVID BRIN
SUNDIVER

The first novel in the Uplift universe. Circling the sun, in
the caverns of Mercury, Expedition Sundiver prepares for
the most momentous journey in human history. A journey
into the broiling inferno of the sun . . . to find our final
destiny in the cosmic order of life.

STARTIDE RISING

The remarkable winner of the Nebula, Hugo and Locus
Awards. The Terran exploration vessel *Streaker* has crashed
on the uncharted water-world Kithrup, bearing one of
the most important discoveries in galactic history. There,
a handful of *Streaker's* human and dolphin crew battles
armed rebellion and a hostile planet to safeguard her
secret—the fate of the Progenitors, the fabled First Race
who seeded wisdom throughout the stars.

THE POSTMAN

The towering winner of the John W. Campbell Memorial
and Locus Awards. A timeless novel as urgently compelling
as *War Day* or *Alas, Babylon*, this is the dramatically
moving saga of the world after a nuclear holocaust and a
man who rekindled the spirit of America through the
power of a dream.

HEART OF
THE COMET

The #1 science fiction bestseller, written with Gregory
Benford. An odyssey of discovery from a shattered society
through the solar system with a handful of men and
women who ride a cold, hurtling ball of ice to the shaky
promise of a distant, unknowable future.

THE PRACTICE EFFECT

A delightful change-of-pace adventure. Physicist Dennis Nuel finds himself on a world very similar to our own—with one extremely perplexing difference. To his astonishment, he is hailed as a wizard and finds himself fighting beside a beautiful woman with strange powers against a mysterious warlord as he struggles to solve the riddle of this baffling land.

THE RIVER OF TIME

David Brin's first story collection, bringing together eleven of his finest shorter works. Included are "The Crystal Spheres," winner of the Hugo Award for Best Short Story, and for new pieces published here for the first time, each with an afterword by the author.

Buy all of David Brin's books, on sale wherever Bantam Spectra Books are sold, or use the handy coupon below for ordering:

☐ HEART OF THE COMET (25839-7 • $4.50 • $5.50 in Canada)
☐ THE POSTMAN (25704-8 • $3.95 • $4.95 in Canada)
☐ THE PRACTICE EFFECT (25593-2 • $3.50 • $3.95 in Canada)
☐ THE RIVER OF TIME (26281-5 • $3.50 • $4.50 in Canada)
☐ STARTIDE RISING (25603-3 • $3.95 • $4.50 in Canada)
☐ SUNDIVER (25594-0 • $3.50 • $3.95 in Canada)